A WIFE FOR THE SURGEON SHEIKH

MEREDITH WEBBER

THE ITALIAN SURGEON'S SECRET BABY

SUE MACKAY

MILLS & BOON

First Published in Great Britain 2019
by Mills & Boon, an imprint of HarperCollins*Publishers*
1 London Bridge Street, London, SE1 9GF

ISBN: 978-0-263-26965-9

This book is produced from independently certified FSC™ paper
to ensure responsible forest management.
For more information visit www.harpercollins.co.uk/green.

Mere
Queensland, Australia, but takes regular trips west into the Outback, fossicking for gold or opal. These eaks in the beautiful and sometimes cruel red earth ountry provide her with an escape from the writing esk and a chance for her mind to roam free—not to nention getting some much needed exercise. They lso supply the kernels of so many stories that it's rd for her to stop writing!

e **MacKay** lives with her husband in New aland's beautiful Marlborough Sounds, with the ter on her doorstep and the birds and the trees at back door. It is the perfect setting to indulge her sions of entertaining friends by cooking them nptuous meals, drinking fabulous wine, going hill walks or kayaking around the bay—and, of urse, writing stories.

Also by Meredith Webber

Healed by Her Army Doc
New Year Wedding for the Crown Prince

The Halliday Family miniseries

A Forever Family for the Army Doc
Engaged to the Doctor Sheikh
A Miracle for the Baby Doctor
From Bachelor to Daddy

Also by Sue MacKay

Resisting Her Army Doc Rival
Pregnant with the Boss's Baby
Falling for Her Fake Fiancé
Her New Year Baby Surprise
Baby Miracle in the ER
Surprise Twins for the Surgeon
ER Doc's Forever Gift

Discover more at millsandboon.co.uk.

A WIFE FOR THE SURGEON SHEIKH

MEREDITH WEBBER

MILLS & BOON

CHAPTER ONE

LAUREN SUPPOSED SHE had known there'd be an executive director of finance and logistics—after all, someone would have to look after the money side of the hospital—but in the nearly two years she'd worked here she'd never heard of Mr Marshall, to whose office she had been summoned at the end of her shift.

Was there something wrong with her superannuation? No, she was sure chief executives had more important things to do than worry about very minor employees' superannuation.

So, what could he possibly want?

Unanswerable questions kept worry at bay as the elevator rose to the rarefied air of the sixth floor, but walking down the corridor in search of Room 279 she found panic building…

A beautifully dressed secretary—or perhaps a personal assistant—looked her up and down, and offered a disdainful eyebrow lift at the sight of her dishevelled end-of-shift clothes, which were probably bloodstained somewhere an apron didn't cover, before ushering her through a door into the inner sanctum.

'Sister Macpherson,' the woman announced, and Lauren stepped forward, wondering which of the two men was Mr Marshall. Surely not the one in the grey silk suit that hung on him with such precision he could have been a model in a very expensive tailor's shop.

A very good-looking model, from what she could see, as he stood with the light behind him. Although his shoulders were probably wider than the norm so the suit had, undoubtedly, been tailor-made.

But Silk Suit remained by the window, studying her, she was sure, from beneath heavy eyelids.

Hawk's eyes…

Hooded…

Scanning for prey?

She felt a shiver of apprehension, and a slight stirring of something she couldn't quite place, and definitely didn't want to think about…

'I'm Ted Marshall,' the other man said, interrupting her fantasy and stepping forward. He held out his hand towards Lauren and positively radiated goodwill. 'Please, come in and sit down. Sheikh Madani has something he wishes to discuss with you, and as he's come a long way to see our new children's wing, the very least I can do is offer him the hospitality of my room.'

Twit!

But the name he'd mentioned—it couldn't be… It was impossible.

Though of course it had to be, and as a feeling of inevitability all but swamped her, Lauren told herself she was *not* afraid.

Well, not much…

Practically falling over himself to please Silk Suit, Ted Marshall waved the other visitor forward, though Lauren hadn't sat down, flight-or-fight instinct telling her she'd be better off on her feet.

'Sheikh Madani, this is Sister Macpherson. Now, I'll leave the two of you to discuss your business.'

Leave her here with Madani?

No way!

She knew the name Madani only too well. Knew it and hated it with a passion. Hadn't it been a Madani who had stolen her sister?

'You can't do that!' she said to the departing Mr Marshall. 'You can't get me up here and leave me in a room with a total stranger because he praised your new hospital! That's irresponsible and unethical and probably illegal!'

She knew her cheeks were probably scarlet and her hair was probably standing on end, and forget being afraid—terror had prompted her outburst. Not for herself, but for Nim.

Silk Suit watched from the window, his eyes, lids lifted now, focussed in her direction.

And if that was a smirk twitching at his lips, she'd kill him.

Or get Joe to kill him.

'You need fear no danger from me,' the man said, his voice as smooth as the sleek clothes he wore, the accompanying smile as friendly as a shark's

'There, you see,' Ted Marshall said, edging closer to the door. 'The sheikh has business with the hospital then mentioned wanting to see you. Apparently, there's a family matter he wishes to discuss with you, and I'm sure it would be to your advantage to listen to him.'

And on that note he scuttled out of the door.

Lauren remained where she was, paralysed by the knowledge that this man might well have been behind the murder of her sister and parents.

And if not him, surely one of his relations…

But there was no way she could reveal the panic in her heart or the clutch of icy fingers gripping her stomach.

She took a deep breath, and aimed for being cool.

'You have business with me?'

Cool *and* polite.

'I think you know I do.'

His deep, treacly voice rasped against her skin and sent shivers down her spine, but Lily had been taken in by a treacly voice and silk suits—by money, and jewellery, and private planes that swept her from one holiday playground to the next.

Beautiful, vibrant, fun-loving Lily…

And look how that had ended.

'Oh?' Lauren managed, dragging herself out of the past, and ignoring the catch in her own breathing as he moved closer.

'The boy! You have the boy!'

It wasn't a question, but how much did he actually know?

Not where she lived or he'd have come to the house—possibly even kidnapped Nim—though that would have happened over Joe's dead body.

'What boy?' she asked, stalling.

He waved away her pretence, eyes like obsidian boring into hers.

'He needs to be taken home.' His voice was glacial now. 'He needs to know the country he will one day rule.'

'And just who are you to be making these demands?'

The man drew himself up to an impressive height and seemed to summon a sense of power from the ether.

'I am Abdul-Malik Madani, I am called Malik, and my name means Protector of the King.'

Refusing to be intimidated, Lauren straightened, and although five feet five wasn't a very impressive height, she made the most of it with a tilt of her chin and a glare in her eyes.

'Well, if Nim's father was the former heir, then you didn't do too good a job of it!'

She heard his reaction—a quick snatch of breath—and saw it in the stricken look on his face, the sudden bowing of his head to hide his emotion.

She watched his chest expand as he breathed deeply, and knew the depth of his pain when he spoke again, voice strained with grief.

'You are right,' he said. 'I could not save my brother, but it is his son that I must protect now—protect at all costs, even with my life.'

That was a bit melodramatic, but hadn't all her admittedly brief contact with the Madanis been overly melodramatic?

She closed her eyes, remembering, shuddering, aware of this man's presence in every cell of her being, trying to focus on what he was saying.

He was either a consummate actor or genuine, but did she really want to find out which?

She moved towards the door, intending to keep walking until she was well away from this man. Somewhere quiet where she *could* think quietly and halt the panic.

But in two strides he had overtaken her so he now stood directly in front of her—less than a foot away—towering over her with some kind of inner presence that made her feel more queasy than afraid.

Strange, unsettled butterflies rioted in her stomach, zapping their disquiet along her nerves. Up close, the man's face was beautiful—not in a pretty-boy way but with hard carved features: a thin straight nose separating those deep-set eyes; high ridges of cheekbones; and lips full enough for his mouth to scream sensual but not too full—not fleshy, just there, unsmiling…

'The child's name is Nimr!'

The words were like a slap.

So much for her thinking she'd scored a point on him earlier.

'We call him Nim,' she retorted. 'Easier than trying to roll that unfamiliar "r" at the end. But, yes, it's spelled Nimr on official documents.'

'And yet you asked what boy?'

Sarcasm iced the words and Lauren felt them cut into her skin—saying Nim's name had brought back the fear. Just because this man said he'd give his life for Nim, what proof was that?

For all Lauren knew, he could have been behind his brother's death.

As soon as she thought it, she knew she shouldn't have gone there—memories threatened to swamp her again and right now she needed to be strong.

As for his assumption that Nim would want to be King of the godforsaken country this man was talking about—well, that was for the future, *and* for Nim himself to decide!

'Nim was left in my care and that's where he stays,' Lauren said, not adding Lily's almost hysterical warning of deadly danger. Of people—Tariq's family members even—trying to track her down to kill her and her son. And Lauren, for her sins, had dismissed it all, sure Lily had been exaggerating—blaming her state on a hormone-fuelled fantasy.

That was until the accident, and then when Nim had been taken…

Don't go there, she told her frantic thoughts.

'And now I need to leave,' she said, taking a side step, hoping to get behind him to the door—

Which proved hopeless.

She tried a glare, one that usually sent overexcited adolescents straight back to their beds, but felt it bounce off him.

'Perhaps we should begin again, discuss this in more congenial surroundings. As Mr Marshall said, I had some business with the hospital, and thought you might feel more at ease meeting me here with other people's knowledge of the meeting. But there are other places...'

He touched her, oh, so lightly on the shoulder as he spoke, and fire spread through her body, confirming the danger she'd felt in this man from the beginning.

Was this how Lily had felt when she'd first met Tariq?

'There's nothing to discuss,' she told him, forcing her voice to stay firm. 'Nim is my child, properly adopted. He stays here!'

'With security lights all around your house, and alarms hard-wired back to the police station, and a guard to follow him wherever he goes?'

Panic swelled in Lauren.

He *did* know where she lived! And *how* they lived! The only thing he didn't know was her constant fear...

But there was no way this man was going to get her child!

'He's not a guard, he's a nanny,' she snapped. 'Most working mothers have them!'

'Six-two male? SAS-trained? Do most Australian working mothers have such a nanny?'

She stepped back, aware of giving ground, but she couldn't yell at him successfully when she was so close. Something about the man flustered her and she was pretty sure it wasn't fear...

She took another deep breath.

'I lost my entire family in that accident—everyone but Nim—and no one can tell me how or why it happened, or, worse, who the target was. I don't know whether it was my sister and our parents, or your brother.'

'There was a doubt about the intended victim?' he demanded, his voice sharp with tension as he broke into her explanation.

Closing her eyes briefly to regain a little composure, Lauren explained.

'My father had many business interests in the west, from mining to pastoral holdings and beyond. The police thought…'

She couldn't go on, remembering the horror of those days when grief had been overwhelming her and policemen had been constantly asking questions—

'Tell me.'

His voice was gentle now, not a plea exactly but with enough emotion in it that she understood he needed to know.

'It was only when Nim was snatched they turned their attention to your brother.'

'Someone took the child?'

His eyes blazed with anger now, but the memories were pressing down on her and she had to get the story told before she broke down from the remembered terror.

'A police family liaison officer was staying with me. The detectives were there one morning with so many questions, their voices unsettled Nim. He was only tiny. So I took him out for a walk in his pram, and someone hit me on the head and ran off with him.'

She tried to quell the memories of her pain and fear. She had thought that not only had she lost her parents and Lily but the baby as well—the baby she'd promised Lily she'd protect.

Had he read it in her eyes that he steered her back into a chair.

'Sit, take deep breaths! They found the child?'

He asked the question in the same calm voice he'd used to make her sit.

She nodded.

'At the airport, dressed all in pink, travelling on a passport as Lucy someone, two parents travelling with her. It was luck, nothing more, that they found Nim—another twenty minutes and they'd have boarded, the plane doors would have shut.'

'And the couple?

Lauren looked up at the man hovering impatiently in front of her.

'They admitted to being paid to kidnap the child and take him to the United States, where he could be sold to adoptive parents in some quasi-criminal deal. But they denied all knowledge of the accident. Further police investigations couldn't prove they'd been involved.'

She read confusion in his eyes and understood it, for those few months of her life still seemed unreal to her.

But this man needed answers, so she picked up where she'd left off earlier.

'So, yes, I have security to protect my child, but none of it intrudes on his having a normal childhood. That is one thing I work very hard to ensure.'

Lauren paused, needing to catch her breath, needing to see his face—his expression—as she finalised this business.

'So, really, there's nothing else to discuss. I'm guessing you spent a considerable amount of money to track me down, but Nim is mine now—a little Australian boy with a future here, not in his father's country. So I'll be getting home to my son.'

'Son? You *have* adopted him?'

She'd been expecting more objections to her leaving, not this shocked disbelief.

'Lily left him with me that night, telling me to take great care of him—telling me again of threats. To do that when she was…' Lauren made a huge effort to pull herself together '…gone, he had to be legally mine, so of course I've adopted him.'

She looked directly into his eyes this time—into darkness that held no light or shadows, and about as much humanity and understanding as a statue's blank gaze.

Malik was only too aware he'd made a mess of this. First the fawning executive, setting up the meeting with this woman as if he was conferring a great honour on her.

And then underestimating the stubborn female who'd had the guts to adopt his nephew. There might not be much of her, and most of what he could see was tired and grubby, but despite the dark shadows beneath her large grey eyes, and the fear, which had been an almost palpable thing in the room, she'd stood up to him.

Though with what she'd been through he could understand that fear…

Coming here, he'd thought she'd be willing to hand the boy over to him—perhaps with due recompense—but every word he'd heard held the cadences of her love for Nimr.

Had he been judging her by her sister, that he'd thought this way? One look at her had dispelled any physical resemblance, and he doubted Lily would have stood up to him the way Lauren had, or taken the extreme measures he now knew of, to keep his nephew safe.

No, Lily had been beautiful, captivating, and could charm birds from a tree, but how much more attractive was the courage and quiet determination of this sister?

Something he hadn't felt for a long time stirred inside him, something he'd have to think about later, because his business was far from finished.

As far as she was concerned, Nimr was her child and she'd probably have killed him if he'd mentioned recompense.

He looked down at her, close now as she tried once more to get out the door, and he was almost sure he detected a tremble in her body, and definitely saw fear behind the defiance in her eyes.

He touched her gently on the shoulder—felt the tremors running through her and the coldness of her skin and knew he hadn't imagined the fear, knew he'd caused it, and that wounded him.

'I'm sorry. This has come as a surprise for you, but I have had top private investigators looking for Nimr for two years now and to suddenly have him so close—well, I wasn't sure what to do. I thought meeting you publicly through the hospital might be easier for you, but all I've done is barge into your life and upset you.'

She'd stepped away from his hand.

'I have to go,' she said, slipping behind him as he moved forward, escaping this time, though not for long.

He caught up with her by the time they'd reached the elevator.

'We need to talk!' he said, probably too loudly from the stares he got as they entered the already packed space.

She was pressed against him so he couldn't see her face, but the shake of her head, dark curls moving beneath his chin—brushing his skin—gave him his answer.

Soft dark curls from what he could see, giving off a hint of something he recognised but couldn't name.

Rosewater?

Back home, it was used in many local dishes—but in hair?

He breathed in the scent again as the elevator reached the ground floor—whatever it was that had stirred inside him earlier stirring again—and they led the exodus out into the corridor.

Expecting her to make a dash for some bolthole he'd never find in the big hospital, he caught her arm.

She spun towards him.

'I'll call Security,' she warned, but his mind was still on rosewater.

'Is it rosewater I can smell?'

The words were out before he considered how inappropriate they were.

'Rosewater?' she demanded, outrage warming her cheeks to a rosy pink. Grey eyes spitting fire, all fear gone. She probably had some kind of emergency call button somewhere on her person—

'I could smell rosewater,' he said, aware of how lame it sounded. 'The women use it in cooking at home.'

'The women, huh?' she said, but a lot of her tension was gone, and he kind of thought her soft pink lips might be trying hard not to smile.

Pleased they'd seemed to reach some kind of armistice, he raised both hands in surrender.

'I will *not* get into an argument with you about women's rights! I'm a believer in them myself. In fact, that's one of the reasons I'm so anxious to take Nimr home. My country needs to be dragged into the twenty-first century, and as his regent I could at least begin the task.'

She studied him for a moment, not bothering to hide the suspicion that had flared in her wide eyes.

'And you can't do that without him there—a boy of

four? Surely, if you're related and next in line after him, you can get started without his presence.'

Malik sighed. He'd had a long journey, spent far too long convincing the finance man to arrange his meeting with this woman, thinking it was better to do it with an authority figure to introduce them—as it would have been at home. And now she was demanding answers to questions that could take hours to explain.

'I've got to get home,' she said, halting any further conversation. 'Joc goes to swimming training and I have to be there for Nim.'

'Nimr,' Malik corrected automatically, giving the 'r' on the end of his nephew's name the slight roll it required.

'Whatever!' his companion snapped. 'But we'll never get through any conversation if you're going to correct his name every time I say it! And you know nothing about Australian kids if you imagine he could get through childhood with a rolled "r" on the end of his name without incessant teasing, so here he's Nim!'

And she stalked away, her anger back, and clearly seen in the straight shoulders and swift strides that somehow drew his attention to strong, shapely legs and a trim figure.

Kept his attention for an instant too long...

He sighed again.

He had more important matters at hand than a woman with grey eyes and a trim figure. Although Tariq had always been the practised negotiator—when he'd bothered—he, Malik, had stepped in often enough to be a competent one. But he'd blown it this time. He could understand her fighting him if she'd grown fond of the boy—that would be understandable—but part of her resistance had definitely been fear.

At least he knew where she lived.

In fear?

* * *

Rattled by the encounter, Lauren made her way out of the hospital by the nearest exit, finding herself in the wrong car park, so by the time she'd found her small vehicle she was shaking with the tension the stranger's appearance had generated.

Tension and fear—and something else, something she really didn't want to acknowledge.

She unlocked the door and slumped gratefully into the driving seat, opening windows and starting the air-conditioning as the vehicle, after standing in the summer sun all day, was like an inferno. Even the steering wheel was too hot to touch, so the idea of resting her forearms on it and having a wee cry had to be denied.

Not that she'd let that man make her cry! She'd shed enough tears four years ago—enough to last a lifetime. Although admittedly there'd been more, when Nim had been a baby and, teething or not well, impossible to settle, she'd felt totally alone.

Then Aunt Jane had sold her parents' house for her, found the duplex for them on the other side of the country, set up the security, and made it safe enough for her to finally give Nim a home.

It was time to get home to her son. She couldn't let Joe down. Without Joe she'd be lost, she *and* Nim.

And no matter what that man said, Nim was hers and hers he was going to stay. He could grow up as an ordinary Australian boy and need never know much at all about that strange place thousands of miles away where his birth mother had lost her bearings.

Oh, *Lily.*

With a huff of impatience at the sudden sense of loss inside her, she drove out of the parking area and headed for home, her mind back on practical matters.

Did she have to stop at the shops for fruit for Nim's lunchbox tomorrow or had Joe called in on his way back from kindy?

He probably had and she couldn't think of anything else they needed.

Except perhaps a magic carpet to whisk Sheikh whoever he was back to where he'd come from. But magic carpets were fairly rare in Abbotsfield, for all it was a thriving regional city.

Regional city?

How *had* the man found her here, thousands of miles from where she'd grown up in Perth? All the police reports on the so-called accident had put the family's place of residence as Perth. And after that she'd disappeared. The family's assets had been frozen so she'd borrowed enough from Aunt Jane to buy the campervan, and she and tiny baby Nim had lived like gypsies, moving constantly, she doing anything to keep him safe.

Lauren's mind was lost in the past and, driving on autopilot, it was only as she was using the remote to open the outer gate that she saw the sleek black luxury vehicle parked outside.

The fear she'd felt earlier turned to terror and she dropped the remote as if it would burn her fingers. She parked behind the ominous car, only too aware of who would be inside it.

Or inside her house?

Dear heaven, surely not!

She shot from her car, and strode towards the limo, hauling open the driver's door so suddenly a slim man in a blue suit and matching cap almost fell out, his cap coming askew on his head.

'Who are you and what are you doing here?" she demanded, hoping Joe was inside with one finger poised above the alarm.

'He's my driver. He owns the hire car.'

Sheikh whatever was emerging from the back seat on the passenger side. 'I had no time to waste finding my way around your city, small though it might be.'

'Oh, and I suppose *your* city is ginormous!' Lauren shot at him, and immediately regretted it as this wasn't the argument she should be having.

Especially as the wretched man had the nerve to smile.

Well, she supposed it was a smile—he'd definitely moved his lips and revealed a dazzling array of perfectly aligned white teeth, but it was a crocodile that came to mind rather than rapprochement.

'Would you feel easier discussing the situation here?" he continued, as smooth as custard.

'There is no situation to discuss,' she said, hoping she sounded a lot more determined than she felt. Seeing the man who might just be a murderer standing outside her home had brought back all her fear, yet in some offbeat section of her brain she was simply seeing the man.

Bizarre, to say the least.

It wasn't as if she didn't see dozens of men every day, but this was definitely not that kind of seeing.

He'd taken off his suit jacket and rolled up his sleeves a little to reveal smooth olive skin that gleamed in the sunlight, while his shirt clung to a body she guessed had been shaped through exercise—not too much, just enough to give definition to hard pecs and wide shoulders beneath the snowy-white material.

She wouldn't look at his neck, rising from the now tieless shirt—well, only to see it as a strong column…

Ye gods! What was the matter with her? She was standing in the street mooning over a man who was undoubtedly her enemy?

'I don't want you in my house,' she finally said, meaning, I don't want you anywhere near me, not now, not ever, but especially not now when I'm so damned confused I can't think straight.

Fortunately, Joe appeared in the doorway at that moment, preceded by Ghost, Joe's pale German shepherd, and with Nim no doubt right behind, probably peering through Joe's legs, for all he was supposed to stay inside when people came.

'The gentleman's just leaving,' Lauren said, speaking to Joe but with her eyes on the Sheikh.

'We need to talk,' he said to her. 'It's imperative. I will not invade the sanctity of your home—' was there a 'not right now' hovering behind the words? '—but I shall call for you at seven.'

'Get into a car with a stranger? I think not! If we do need to talk, then we can talk at your hotel. Where are you staying?'

'The Regal.'

Lauren nodded.

'I'll meet you there at eight,' she said, hoping she'd spoken loftily enough for him to assume she dined at The Regal regularly, and at the same time wondering desperately what she might have in her wardrobe that she could wear to such a place. And whether Joe would be back from training, or, if not, there was always Aunt Jane who'd stand in…

The Sheikh nodded graciously, before pointing a finger at the gathering in the doorway.

'Security's a little lax. I could have shot the dog, then the nanny, and grabbed the boy.'

'You wouldn't!' Lauren whispered, then slid limply to

the ground, a black cloud closing over her as the events of the afternoon finally caught up with her.

Joe darted forward but Malik was there first, lifting Lauren into his arms and marching towards the front door, telling the dog to sit in such a firm voice it dropped to his haunches.

'Get a cool, wet cloth,' he said to the so-called nanny. 'It's just a faint. I can feel her coming round already, so I'd better put her down because if she realises it's me holding her she's likely to hit me.'

'You can put her on the couch,' a small boy said, his eyes wide with unshed tears as he saw his mother in such a helpless state.

'She'll be better soon,' Malik assured the boy who was, without doubt, Nimr, for he was the dead spit of Tariq at that age.

Tariq, the brother Malik had worshipped all his young life and followed around like a puppy.

'Here!'

The nanny had returned, and the hoarseness in his voice made Malik turn to look at him—to see a face distorted by the scars of operations that had somehow put it back together.

'I am Malik,' he said, holding out his hand.

'That's Joe,' Nimr said, looking up from where he was wiping his mother's face with the damp hand towel. 'Joe looks after us.'

'I noticed that,' Malik told the boy, although his eyes were on the mother now—Lauren—dark lashes fluttering against her cheeks as she slowly became aware of her surroundings. Something that wasn't entirely guilt fluttered inside him, moved by her paleness—her vulnerability…

Her eyes opened, deep grey pools of fear and confusion—

and *he* had caused the fear, first by arriving as he had and then with his foolish words about their protection.

Although that part was deadly serious. If there really was a threat against his nephew, he'd be better off back in Madan.

He should take the boy home, no matter what.

She sat up so suddenly he was knocked from where he crouched by the couch, landing awkwardly on his butt.

At least it gave Nimr a laugh.

'You're in my house!'

Outrage vied with disbelief as Lauren took in this man's presence. He was so close she could hardly not notice that his eyes were not the black she'd thought them but a surprising warm toffee colour, and right now were looking intently at her.

'You have to go,' she said, unable to tell if her hyper-awareness of him—the unsettled feeling in her chest—was to do with the shock she'd had or the man himself.

Whatever it was, she wanted it gone too.

He hesitated, aware of the nanny standing behind him, ready to break him in two if he so much as touched the recovering woman.

He moved back a little, and said gently, 'I'm sorry, but we do have to talk, and I think the sooner the better.'

Lauren forced her fuzzy brain to sort out the words, and one thing became perfectly clear. This man was not leaving until he'd said what he'd come to say.

And considering that, wouldn't it be better to listen to him here and now—well, not right now as she had to get Nim's dinner, her own dinner, too, given that lunch had been a snatched apple and cup of coffee and her stomach was making her aware that she was famished.

She heaved herself upright on the sofa, Nim slipping up to sit beside her and take her hand.

'I'm all right,' she assured him. 'I just forgot to have my lunch and that's what made me faint like that.'

Lying to her son? She knew full well it was the man's suggestion that it would have been easy to abduct Nim that had made her mind shut down.

Which left her with the man—the Madani man!

He was standing back—against a window once again—and, much as she hated having him in her house, she knew she wouldn't be rid of him until she'd listened to what he'd come to say.

'I have to give Nim his dinner and I usually eat with him so you might as well stay and eat with us. That way we can talk when Nim's gone to bed. I'll just have a quick wash—Nim, you need to wash your hands for dinner so you come with me.'

'You get off to training,' she added to Joe, who was standing, watching them all. 'I'm fine now and I'll have an early night.'

She was leaving the room when she remembered the big black car parked outside her yard, and added to Malik, 'You'd better get your driver and bring him in for dinner too.'

'The driver?'

He sounded so incredulous, Lauren almost laughed.

'Drivers do eat, you know,' she said. 'And there's plenty so it's hardly fair to leave him sitting out there.'

Well, she hoped there was plenty…

'Please go out and invite him in.'

Wondering if this was a quirk of democracy in this country or because the woman didn't want to be alone with him,

Malik went, returning with the driver, who'd protested he was quite okay and happy to wait without food.

But already aware that he was dealing with a stubborn woman, Malik had insisted.

He found the woman in question bent double over a large chest freezer, pulling out various plastic-wrapped containers and muttering to herself.

'We're having shepherd's pie,' Nimr announced. 'It's my turn to choose and it's my favourite.'

Malik looked at the boy he knew yet didn't know and felt pain stab into his heart.

'Oh, yes?' he said. 'Do you make it out of shepherds?'

The boy laughed.

'No, silly! Mum makes it with meat, and puts potato on the top, and it's yummy and you don't have to cut it up so it's easy to eat.'

Malik smiled at the boy, feeling a weird kind of pleasure that the child had offered him this small confidence.

'Ha, knew I had one!'

The triumphant cry from the freezer had them moving into the kitchen where their pink-cheeked hostess, apparently fully recovered from her faint, had emerged from the freezer in triumph.

Seeing the two men, the driver trying to hide behind the door, her cheeks went a deeper pink.

'Sorry,' she said. 'I tend to cook a lot on my days off, and I always make different sizes of each dish for when Joe's here—'

'And when Joe and Aunt Jane both come,' Nim finished for her, turning to the visitors to hold up four fingers. 'That's four, you see, and tonight it's four too.'

Perhaps embarrassed by her son's delight in the visitors, his mother had stripped layers of plastic from the frozen dish and set it going in the microwave. And with her back resolutely turned to the two men, she was peeling carrots and cutting chunks of broccoli off a large green head.

Wishing it was my head, no doubt, Malik thought, as she slashed the knife down.

Her shoulders rose as he watched and he knew she was taking a deep breath.

After which, she turned towards her visitors and said quietly, 'It will be half an hour. Would you like to wait in the living room? Perhaps you'd like a glass of cold water?'

'Thank you,' Malik said, then aware of the driver lurking behind him, remembered his manners.

'This is my driver, Peter—'

'Cross,' their hostess finished for him, stepping forward and, to Malik's surprise, giving the man a hug.

'Oh, sorry, Peter, I hadn't realised it was you I made fall out of the car. How's Susie?'

The man held up crossed fingers.

'So far, so good, Lauren. You know how it goes.'

'I do indeed,' Lauren told him. 'Now, a glass of water, each of you?'

'That'd be lovely,' Peter said, and well aware that he'd lost what little conversational control he might have had, Malik agreed, following the other man back into the living room.

It was Nimr who brought the water, two tall glasses balanced on a round tray.

Malik took his, thanked the boy, and wondered what on earth one said to start a conversation with a four-year-old.

Not that he needed to worry, for the boy sat down on the sofa next to the driver and, easily adopting the role of host, turned to Malik to explain.

'Susie's my best friend at kindy. She's been sick. She wears cute hats because she's got no hair. No one minds she's got no hair anyway, and when she first had no hair we all shaved our heads, even the girls, to show it was okay, but she wears the hats because she likes them.'

Malik turned to Peter, who was smiling at the boy.

'Leukaemia?' he asked quietly.

A nod in reply, and, although knowing many of the childhood variants of leukaemia had a high rate of recovery, Malik didn't want to probe too deeply.

Particularly as the earlier conversation and the man's crossed fingers now made sense. Susie must be in remission at the moment, and Malik knew only too well the tightrope parents walked at such times.

'And we have rabbits at kindy too,' Nimr announced. 'Sometimes in the holidays some of the kids get to take them home but Mum says we can't because she has to work and Joe can't be expected to look after a rabbit *and* me.'

Malik hid a smile. The boy was obviously repeating his mother's words, but his aggrieved tone left his listeners in no doubt about his opinion of this edict.

'Do you have rabbits?' he asked.

Malik shook his head.

'No rabbits, but we do have many interesting animals where I live, and many dogs that are tall and run very fast and are called saluki hounds.'

Nimr seemed to ponder this information for a moment, then said knowledgably, 'Hound is another name for a dog. I like dogs, but—'

Malik was pretty sure he was about to hear Mum's opinion of keeping a dog when they were called into the kitchen for dinner. Considering it was little over an hour since she'd fainted in the gateway, Sister Lauren Macpherson had done a sterling job.

The small wooden table had a blue bowl of flowers in the middle of it and four places neatly set, with water glasses in front of each place.

Nimr had gone in front of them and lifted a tall, plastic jug of water from the refrigerator.

'See how strong I am,' he said, holding it a little higher.

'But not quite strong enough to pour,' his mother said, as she saved the tilting jug and filled the water glasses.

'Maybe when I'm five,' Nimr said, climbing onto what must be his accustomed chair.

He was a confident young man, Malik realised, and polite as well. His work as a paediatrician had brought him into contact with countless children, and he'd learned to appreciate the ones with good manners and the quiet confidence he sensed in the boy.

And something very likeable.

He tried to think back to when he and Tariq had been children, but suspected that Tariq had probably not been likeable even then.

Lovable, yes!

He, Malik, had adored him, as had their mother, but he'd been a tease, daring his brother to do things that they'd known were wrong, laughing when Malik had refused.

Was it that challenge to try everything—good or bad—that had led him to drugs, or simply the jet-setting lifestyle he'd led from his late teens, money giving him the freedom their restricted upbringing had denied them?

CHAPTER TWO

THE MEAL WAS simple but delicious, and, perhaps sensing an atmosphere he didn't understand, it was his driver who kept the conversation going, with considerable help from the boy, who was happy to join in on any subject.

Although, Malik realised rather sadly, the man was steering the conversation so the boy could join in, no doubt because he had a child of the same age.

He was wondering how he'd react to children of his own—certainly he'd never experienced a meal like this as a child of Nimr's age. He'd still have been eating with the women and listening to their high-pitched chatter and gossip—

'Now, I think Sheikh Madani wishes to talk with your mother, young Nim, and Joe's still at training, so how about I do your bath and bedtime story?'

Peter Cross's words had broken into Malik's memories, and Nimr was already excusing himself from the table, only too willing to have someone different supervising his bedtime routine.

'Thanks, Peter,' his hostess said, confirming Malik's suspicions that the man was a close family friend.

Through their children or through the hospital?

He didn't ask as Lauren was speaking again.

'I'll just rinse off these dishes and stack the dishwasher and be with you shortly.'

'I can rinse dishes,' Malik said, stacking dirty plates together, before standing up and carrying them to the sink.

He read the surprise on her face, and couldn't help adding, 'Don't judge me by my brother,' before setting to work on his task, rinsing the plates and passing them to Lauren—he had to get used to calling her that in his mind—to stack into place.

She was silent as she worked, but as she shut the door of the machine and set it to wash, she said quietly, 'I didn't know him well—your brother, I mean. He'd barely arrived in Australia when the—the accident happened.'

Which made him wonder if he'd spoken too harshly.

He sought to make amends.

'I've often wondered if I knew him at all,' he told her, 'although as children we were inseparable.'

'It's because Nim doesn't have a brother—or even a sister—that I like him to go to kindy where he can play with other children, and he's so looking forward to going to school next year.'

'Aren't we all,' a deep, slightly fractured voice said, and Malik turned to see Joe in the doorway, back from wherever he had been.

'Peter tells me you're wanted in the bedroom for a goodnight kiss,' he said to Lauren, who, to Malik's considerable surprise, said quietly, 'Perhaps you'd like to say goodnight, too.'

'Joe and I have things to discuss about the new boys' club we want to set up in the community centre, so we'll talk in the kitchen,' Peter said as they met in the short passage. 'Would you like us to bring coffee in to you and the Sheikh?'

* * *

Lauren shook her head.

This was all getting far too matey, in her opinion, but she was thankful the two men would be there.

'Do they worry about you, that they are staying close?' her guest asked, as they walked towards the boy's bedroom.

'I doubt that, but they know it would be wrong of them to leave me here with a stranger.'

'You have loyal friends,' he said with a smile, and that was a mistake. Not the smile, which was warm and slightly teasing, but the way it made her feel.

Tingles from a smile?

For pity's sake, this was the man who had quite possibly killed her entire family—except for Nim.

Yet she'd been conscious of that inner—what, tension?—from the moment she'd first seen him and wondered if that's how Tariq had made Lily feel…

Stupid! That's what it was.

Especially as the man wanted to take her child…

She opened the door into the bedroom, but the excitement of the visitors had meant she'd left it too late to get her goodnight kiss.

But she could leave one, and she leant over the child she loved with all her heart and kissed him gently on his cheek.

She turned to the man who stood watching in the doorway.

'He'll be sorry to have missed you,' she said quietly, but knew he hadn't heard her. He was watching the sleeping boy and the sadness she read in his eyes was almost more than she could stand.

She slipped past him, heading for the living room, aware he was following her, horribly aware of *him*.

She took the armchair and waved the man towards the

not-very-comfortable sofa, which had been cheap and had very quickly taken to the shape of her and Nim's posteriors so no one else's quite seemed to fit it.

And she wouldn't think about his posterior either…

'So talk!' she said, determined to find out exactly what he wanted. Why he'd come. She knew he'd come for Nim, but she wanted to know why.

'Do you know much about Madan?'

The question, when it finally came, surprised her, as he'd seemed more like a man who'd cut to the chase and she knew the chase, in this case, was Nim.

'I know the usual stuff from the internet. It's a small country, with enough oil beneath its sands to make it wealthy. Incredibly wealthy, if the way Tariq threw money around was any indication. I know my sister hated it, preferring to spend her time jet-setting around the world to glitzy hotels and ultra-trendy resorts—to wherever there was a party going on. Although, to be fair, that all stopped once she became pregnant.'

She watched the man as she spoke, and saw his face darken, but when he spoke she could hear regret, and also love, in his voice.

'My brother was not a wise man.'

Lauren waited. He was here for a reason, so it was his story to tell.

He began slowly. 'My father, in his declining years, was also not wise. His mind weakened and he began to listen to those around him—to listen to advice that would benefit the speaker but not the country. He had governed well but strictly, refusing to allow the new-found wealth of the country to change it.'

A pause, before he added rather bitterly, 'In any way!'

'And his advisors?' Lauren asked when the man had sat in brooding silence for a few moments.

'Advised stupidity. Advised progress, but far too quickly for the land or the people to handle. We are the keepers of our land, our settlement built around a large oasis so for many, many centuries we have been an important place on the trading routes that cross from Asia to Europe.'

'Like the Silk Road—I've read so much about that, it's such an ancient highway.'

Malik nodded.

'Traders followed the routes, but they required new supplies of food, and somctimes shelter, always new animals—camels and sheep—to replace those they lost along the way. So really our people are farmers and shopkeepers—that has been their role for generation after generation.'

'And it's changed how?'

He didn't need to look at the woman to see her interest. It charged her voice, and something deep inside him whispered a small hope.

Maybe this sister would be different…

'In the beginning, the oil men who held the leases built a hotel for their senior staff and guests, and an air terminal and runways for their planes. Then my father and his friends took this as progress—as the way to go. They built a bigger hotel and an airline company. And more hotels and shopping malls, all the things they thought a desert city might need to attract the tourist dollars, but—'

'You feel money would be better spent on other things? On things that benefit your own people, not the tourists.'

He nodded.

'Hospitals and schools, a university and training colleges. With health and education our people can go anywhere, do anything. They can become the doctors and the architects and engineers of the new Madan. They can build a city for them and their families, a city *they* would want to live in.'

'And a shopping mall doesn't cut it?' she said with a smile. But she'd heard the real passion in his voice, and understood his desire to give his people the skills to live in this new world—*their* new world.

Would Tariq have felt the same?

But something told her that this man had a deep integrity his brother had lacked, and admiration for him joined the whatever else it was that had been going on inside her…

'So, where does Nim come into this?'

He didn't answer immediately—this man whose name meant Protector of the King.

Did he see it as his duty to protect Nim or did he want him for reasons of his own?

'The country will, one day, be under Nimr's rule, so he needs to grow up there, to learn the history and know the people. But until he comes of age, which is twenty-two in Madan, the head of state will be his regent.'

'Which is you?'

He shook his head.

'Not necessarily. As the closest relative, yes, it should be my position, but you must understand that until my father died less than a year ago, I had assumed Nimr had been killed in the accident.'

'But surely someone—your father—would have received a report? The investigation from the police, the coroner's office, along with the inquest results, all took for ever, I know, but he'd have seen the final reports, surely?'

He nodded.

'There were many reports,' he said, 'but none that I had seen until after my father's death and I was going through his papers. It was then I realised the child had survived, and began my search for him.'

'And *found* us!'

'Just so!' Malik said, then those observant eyes studied her for a few moments, before he added, 'I would never harm either you or Nimr, you must believe that. I did not kill my brother and your family, but I have sworn to find out who did, and I shall.'

He paused, but she'd heard both the commitment and determination in his voice.

'But that is for the future,' he continued, while she wondered why she believed him—she who had trusted so few people in the last four years.

Think about it later, she told herself, turning her attention back to his words—his explanations.

'I cannot afford the time to make it a priority. Right now, my country needs strong rule—a plan for the future and immediate direction. As Nimr's regent—if the child is *seen* to be in my care—I can appoint people who will provide that. I'll have to do a certain level of official business, but I am a doctor, not a politician, and once I have the right people in place, I can return to my job at the hospital, such as it is.'

'So you want to take my son?' Lauren said, her voice shaking with the tension she was feeling. The man had made a valid argument, and he was as closely related to Nim as she was. Except—

'Except you can't!' she said. 'I've adopted him and he's legally mine. I'm quite sure there must be someone—yourself, no doubt—who's the next in line after him. Take the reins yourself or use someone you trust. Let Nim grow up an ordinary Aussie boy.'

'Surrounded by security and with you living in fear of what might happen to him?' Malik snapped. 'Do you not understand I would protect him with my life? Do you not believe that? But I cannot do it while he is here.'

She *did* understand him—the passion in his voice as he'd spoken of his country had been very real, but…

'You're just being stubborn,' she told him. 'Can't you see that if someone else becomes ruler, Nim will no longer matter? He will no longer need protection of any kind because your successors or those of whoever you get to rule the land will follow on. People will forget he ever existed.'

'Nimr, the son of Tariq, will never be forgotten, not in my heart, and not in the hearts of my people.'

'But your people don't know of his existence!' Lauren argued. 'He was born here—he was only two weeks old when his parents were killed. Even before that, Lily had determined to divorce Tariq, to settle down here in Australia.'

'And you could see that happening?' the aggravating man demanded. 'The beautiful butterfly settling anywhere?'

There was no way that Lauren was going to admit she shared his doubts about her sister—or *her* doubts about Lily leaving Tariq?

'That's beside the point,' she said. 'I cannot believe that there is no way you can help your country without dragging a four-year-old boy along behind you.'

'He would *not* be *behind* me, he would be King. I would be nothing more than his regent—a caretaker for the country until he comes of age.'

It was all far too complicated, but the idea of Nim being some kind of figurehead to be paraded at will was just too much for her to take in.

'Well, I'm sorry. I understand you mean well, and that you want what is best for your country, but I have to think about my son, and his welfare, and his future.'

'And you think that's here? Surrounded by security all his life, and not very effective security at that?'

Her earlier moment of absolute terror flashed before

her eyes and she had to hold back a gasp. But she couldn't show more weakness, not to this man…

'Joe opened that door for *me*, and it would have been obvious to him that I knew you—or at least knew who you were. If you'd approached on your own it would have been a different story.'

It sounded weak even to her own ears.

'And he'll be there with Nimr when he plays in the park with his friends from school? How long will a boy put up with that kind of shadow? How long before he gets embarrassed about it, and finds ways of avoiding Joe's protection?'

He was giving voice to the thoughts that kept Lauren awake most nights and she hid the dread they brought.

'I'm not stupid!' she snapped. 'Lily's stories about people conspiring to get rid of her and Tariq, which I'd thought gross exaggerations, were proven to be true. And I've always known I could only go so far to protect Nim. But after four years I'd begun to hope that anyone who actually knew of his existence would have forgotten about him.'

Those conversations—well, them and the accident and abduction—were the reasons Lauren had fled. With help from the police liaison officer, she'd officially changed her name and disappeared, moving constantly for the first two years—in touch with the police in different places who had twice alerted her that someone from Madan was looking for them—never entirely sure they were safe.

And now Lily's words were coming true. Now this man was here, wanting to take her child—*Lily's* child.

'I'm sorry,' she said. 'I'm sure you mean well, but I have to think of Nim, so no more talk. He's not going—*we're* not going—anywhere.'

Except to move as soon as possible to another town, maybe a city… Would a city be easier to lose themselves in? Even with half the money from the sale of her parents' mansion put away for Nim, she still had more than enough to take them anywhere in the world.

But the thought of moving again made her feel ill. Aunt Jane and Joe were settled in the other half of the duplex, They'd done more than enough for her and Nim already, and weren't even true family, for all Aunt Jane had been her mother's best friend, and Joe had worshipped Lily since they were children—

'*What* did you say?'

She shook her head to clear it, realising it was tiredness that had led her mind to stray away from this man—from danger.

He was watching her, his face devoid of expression, but his eyes were focussed.

Seeking her reaction?

'I said I would prefer not to go through official channels, but by the law of *my* country Nimr became *my* child on the death of his father. I have every right in law to claim him.'

Lauren ran her tongue over suddenly dry lips, tried to think, but shock and anger, and possibly exhaustion, had closed her brain.

Malik saw what little colour she'd had in her cheeks fade, and the tip of her tongue slide across her pale lips.

And found himself wanting nothing more than to take care of her—this small, fiercely protective woman. Not only to keep her safe but to lift the burden of fear from her slim shoulders.

To hold her, tell her it would all work out.

To hold her?

Get your mind back on the job.

But guilt at how he'd hurt her with his words made

him reach out and touch one small, cold hand, where it lay in her lap.

'I'm sorry, I shouldn't have threatened you like that—you look exhausted, and all this has been a shock to you. No one should make decisions when they're tired, but there's a way out of this for all of us. Don't answer now, we will talk again in the morning. I shall phone your Mr Marshall and explain you won't be in to work.'

But she'd obviously stopped listening earlier in his conversation.

'A way out for all of us?' she asked, looking at him with a thousand questions in her lovely eyes.

'Of course,' he told her, and felt a small spurt of unexpected excitement even thinking about his solution.

'We shall get married,' he announced. 'That way Nim is both of ours and will be doubly protected.'

Her eyes had widened and although he hadn't thought she could get any paler, she was now sheet-white.

But she stood up, and for a moment he thought she might physically attack him, but in the end she glared at him and said, 'You must be mad!' before turning towards the kitchen.

'Peter, your customer is ready to leave,' she called, before disappearing down the passage, presumably into her bedroom.

As his driver appeared, with Joe looming behind him, Malik realised there was no point in arguing, but the idea, which had come to him out of nowhere, was brilliant.

All he had to do was convince Lauren.

Her name rolled a little on his tongue and, inside his head, he tried it out a few times.

He said goodnight to Joe, and followed Peter out to the car, but his mind, for once, was not on Nimr, but on the woman he'd decided to marry…

CHAPTER THREE

SHEER EXHAUSTION BLOCKED Lauren's mind so no matter how hard she tried to think about Malik's ridiculous proposal, her brain refused to work.

She went into Nim's room and sat on the edge of his bed, a place where peace and contentment usually washed over her. But not tonight. Tonight all she saw was a little boy she'd sworn to protect, a little boy she loved with all her heart.

Brushing his cheek with one last goodnight kiss, she took herself to bed. Bed was a good place to think!

It was no good. The man's arrival, her fainting when she never fainted, the fact that he knew where they lived—the jumble of thoughts was too much to untangle, and that was without the marriage bit.

Contrary to all her expectations, her mind shut down on it all and she slept, well and deeply, until Nim bounced into her bed at seven the next morning.

He was full of the joys another day might bring; so happy and loving as he snuggled down with her, she thought her heart might stop.

She put her arms around him and drew him closer, breathing in the little-boy smell of him, remembering the man—Malik—talking about rosewater, the scent of her shampoo...

'What's with you two this morning?'

Joe's call from the front of the house reminded her it was a workday, and already she was well behind schedule. Nim was gone, off to greet Joe, but Lauren made it out of bed, then stood uncertainly beside it.

Was Malik going ahead and arranging time off for her this morning?

No, she was sure she hadn't agreed to that! But what had she agreed to?

Definitely not to his ridiculous idea that they marry.

Go to work, that's what she'd do, and once there she'd have no time to think of anything but her patients…

She had a quick shower to freshen up, put on a clean uniform, and by the time she could smell bacon sizzling in the pan, she was ready for the day ahead.

A *normal* day ahead!

Until Joe looked her up and down, glanced towards the calendar on the fridge and said, 'I thought you were working the late shift today.'

Of course she was! Two to ten, and Joe would know because he missed his training on late-shift evenings.

'Forgot,' she mumbled as she sat down to her bacon and eggs, a treat Joe cooked for them about once a week.

'Can we have this every day, Mum?' Nim asked, and she shook her head.

'You know it's a Joe special,' she reminded Nim, 'and anyway, cereal will make you strong.'

But Nim had already forgotten the argument. He was peering out the kitchen door, and through the living room where a window revealed a long black limousine pulling up outside.

'It looks like Susie's dad's car,' he said. 'Do you think he might drive me to school in it?'

Rendered speechless by the thought of who might be in

the hire car, Lauren was saved answering by a long peal of the doorbell.

'I'll go,' Joe said, and the words brought Lauren back to panic mode.

'Check who's out there before you open the door,' she reminded him, totally unnecessarily, but at least she'd managed to speak.

'And, Nim, run along to your bedroom and get dressed or you'll be late for kindy.'

Once she had Joe and Nim out of the house, perhaps she'd be able to think clearly.

She smiled to herself.

She was ready for work—a ready-made excuse not to talk to the man. *Hello and goodbye, sorry I can't stop…*

She guessed it was only putting off the inevitable, but it would give her time to think.

Then he was there, taller than she remembered, and so darned good-looking in a casual polo shirt and pale chinos that she hoped she wasn't gaping at him.

'I was told you are not on duty until later,' he said by way of greeting. 'I contacted Mr Marshall to explain we had more business to discuss, and ask if it was possible for you to have some time off, and he explained.'

Lauren closed her eyes and swore to herself. Mr Marshall was no doubt toadying up to someone he thought might have money to give away. He'd found where she was working the previous day so had probably had no trouble checking her roster.

But a uniform was a bit like armour. It made you a stronger person. Or so she told herself when she realised he'd foiled her planned escape and she'd *have* to talk to him.

Joe was ushering the visitor into the living room,

offering coffee, although he and Nim should be leaving for kindy.

Lauren followed, trying to convince herself the uniform as armour idea hadn't worked the previous evening because it had been rumpled and grubby…

She sat down and wondered what to do next. If Joe hadn't offered coffee, she could have done that and escaped into the kitchen, but apparently her visitor refused coffee for Joe was in Nim's bedroom, putting on his shoes, from the sound of things, urging him to hurry or they'd be late.

'Would you want to bring Joe?'

The question was so bamboozling, it forced Lauren into speech.

'Would I want to bring Joe where?' she asked.

'To Madan, of course.'

He didn't actually add 'you idiot', but Lauren heard it hovering at the end of the words.

'You're not making sense,' she said.

And he smiled.

Uniforms weren't good armour against smiles. For some unfathomable reason, that smile had melted something inside her—something hard and unrelenting that had taken her four years to build.

'When we marry,' he was saying now, as if everything had been settled in some glitch in time, and they were moving on to the next stage of their lives.

'When we *marry*?' she echoed, but heard a traitorous tremor in her voice and sat up straighter, shoring up the defences that smile had fractured. 'I haven't agreed to marry you!'

That was better—her voice was stronger.

Another smile, but this one she was ready for, steeled herself against it…

'Oh, but you will, when you've had time to take it in, and realise it's the best solution for all of us.'

He paused, and she felt his scrutiny.

'You're still tired, and you do need time, but I have to leave and want to make all the arrangements before I go. You will need passports, of course, for you and Nimr. But back to where we started, do you want to bring Joe with you?'

Lauren shook her head.

It was useless arguing with the man, he simply did not listen, and to keep repeating that she hadn't agreed to marry him was pointless.

'Go away,' she said. 'You're right, I'm not on duty until late. I could meet you for an early lunch at twelve. We could talk then.'

Somewhere neutral, not here in her home—the home that had once been a safe haven for her and Nim but now felt more like a battleground.

He was talking again, suggesting The Regal once more, telling her he'd send Peter to collect her.

'And drive me home from work late in the evening?' she snapped. 'I will make my own arrangements, thank you. I will see you at twelve.'

And she stood up so he would know his visit was over.

Except that Nim came bounding out to greet the visitor, who touched the boy's head so gently Lauren felt her defences begin to crumble again.

She kissed her little boy goodbye, and wondered if she'd been fooling herself in thinking she could keep him safe. Then they were all gone, Nim having won a lift in the limo. Lauren slumped down on the sofa, stretched out on her back, and looked up at the ceiling, which was as blank as her mind…

* * *

Malik felt strangely satisfied as they drove away from the small duplex, the man called Joe silent beside him, Nim in the front seat, chattering away to Peter about cars he'd ridden in.

He'd learned more of Joe from Peter on his way back to the hotel. A decorated soldier, badly wounded, a left-leg amputee, although Malik hadn't picked up on that just from seeing the man move.

A family friend more than a relation, Peter had thought, Joe lived in the flat next door with his mother, training for some games for wounded service people, Peter had heard.

So Lauren had chosen her 'nanny' well, although he, Malik, sensed from her reaction to his appearance at the hospital that she had been starting to believe they were safe.

And that in itself was enough to strengthen his determination to take Nimr home to Madan. Whoever had killed his brother had waited until he was out of the country, where such an assassination would barely raise a ripple in Madan itself.

The knowledge that Tariq had died had saddened his people, but most were unaware of the violence of his death, and certainly not aware of the Australian police's suspicions that it had been murder.

But the fact remained that *someone* had killed Tariq, and that person could still go after Nimr, especially as now, a year after his father's death—the end of the mourning period—that the succession had to be formalised.

They'd pulled up outside the school, and the small boy, so like his father, reached over the seat to shake his hand and say goodbye. Joe nodded a farewell, and they were gone, Joe accompanying the boy right inside the building.

But Malik barely saw them go, his mind caught up in where his thoughts had led. What if whoever had killed Tariq was inside the palace itself?

Wasn't that the most likely answer?

And in that case, taking the boy there could be playing into that person or persons' hands. The palace with its labyrinthine corridors and upward of a hundred staff, who would know which person might wish, or be paid, to harm the boy?

'Back to their home,' he said to Peter, knowing that he needed to get things settled right away. He had his mother's legacy, the huge house she'd built when his father had married his second wife. They'd go there. He'd staff it with people loyal only to him. Loyalty was part of his culture—his people had only survived because they trusted one another and would fight to the death against anyone who threatened one of their own.

He probably wouldn't tell Lauren that part in the argument he intended to put to her.

Back at her residence, he considered asking Peter to accompany him inside so Lauren wouldn't feel threatened, but the place was small, and even from the kitchen he was fairly certain his words would be overheard.

He could do this—*would* do this, *had* to do this!

He knew she was checking him through the spyhole before opening the door, knew she hadn't expected him to return, for she'd changed into white shorts and a red tank top. With her slim, tanned legs and small bare feet, she looked little more than a child herself, and for a moment he hesitated.

Should he rethink his plan?

Then he remembered the small boy, offering his hand to be shaken, saying goodbye, and knew his way was best.

She led him wordlessly back into the living room and subsided into a chair.

He followed her, took the damnably uncomfortable sofa, and drew a deep breath.

'I know you would like more time to think through my offer, but I realised, as we drove Nimr to his kindergarten, that I may have put you both in more danger just by being here.'

He paused, aware of the tension he'd caused with his words but needing to get them said.

'If I could find you, so could others, and while they may have taken longer, I may also have unwittingly led them to you. You will need a passport, of course.'

'I have a passport—and Nim is on it. At one time I thought we might go to New Zealand, but I hardly see—'

'New Zealand would never have been far enough away from someone who wished harm to Nimr. In Madan I can keep you both safe.'

Even as he said the words, he knew it was somehow important to him that this woman stay as safe as the child…

Lauren stared at him—the bit about New Zealand not being far enough kept echoing in her head. It had always been in her mind as a last resort.

New Zealand had always *seemed* safe…

And if it wasn't?

'But why the marriage?' she asked. 'Could we not just go with you and live there? I could get work and Nim could go to school, like normal people.'

He shook his head.

'You would be living in my home—not the palace—and that would be unseemly for an unmarried woman. It need be marriage in name only, but only if we are married, and Nimr my son, can I keep you both safe.'

She ignored the shiver the word 'married' had given

her, told herself she should feel relieved about the 'in name only' part of the conversation, but once again her brain was flooded with too much information and too many questions for her to think straight.

She must have been looking as lost as she felt because he said gently, 'I am sorry. This has been too great a shock for you to take in all at once. I have lived in torment that I could not save my beloved brother.'

He sighed before continuing, 'We, well, I, had thought he and Lily had split up, she returning to her family in Australia. Tariq had settled down, his wild lifestyle seemingly over. He was taking an interest in affairs of state and readying himself to take over from our father.'

Another pause, and Lauren could almost feel the anguish in Malik's soul.

'Then one day he was gone—out of the country, flying first to the United Kingdom, then the US. I was angry that he hadn't spoken to me or told me what he was doing. But for six months he'd been the perfect heir, the model Madani, and I had no suspicion he would end up in Australia. And no idea he was heading this way for the birth of his son.'

'You hadn't known Lily was pregnant?'

'No one did, not at home, I'm sure of that. And I suppose that hurts more than anything—that my brother, whom I loved for all we were so different, hadn't felt able to confide in me. Hadn't told me such joyous news…'

The pain in his voice pierced deep into Lauren's heart because she knew he'd carried it with him every day for four long years.

She wanted to say something—but what?

I'm sorry?

Too late—he was speaking again.

'Since he was killed, I've realised Tariq must have

known he had an enemy and had sent Lily away for safety. When Nimr was born, he contacted our father to tell him the wonderful news, and two weeks later he was dead.'

'They were all dead—except for Nim,' Lauren reminded him, and he nodded, looking directly at her, his eyes burning with a fierce intensity.

'I have vowed to avenge them, Lauren, all of them. I will not kill their murderers, but I will find and punish them, I promise you.'

Lauren closed her eyes and tried to still her heart rate, to control whatever it was that fizzed along her nerves, for Malik hadn't finished his dramatic tale.

'My father was an old man even then, but he would not have betrayed Tariq's trust. He would, though, not have been able to hide his delight and someone close to him guessed…'

'But why?'

It was the question she'd asked herself a thousand times four years ago, and, so far, had no answer.

'To be the leader of Madan is a powerful position in our land and neighbouring states. There is wealth, but many people have wealth now. It is the power of the position that some men crave.'

'The men who are building hotels instead of schools and hospitals?' Lauren asked, remembering their earlier conversation.

'Those, and others like them,' Malik told her. 'I know I am asking something almost impossible of you, but believe me when I say I would give my life for Nimr, and I ask that you trust me to take care of both of you.'

He paused, then added, 'I know I cannot prove my words and that I am asking you to put your faith in a stranger, but I swear, on my brother's name, that I will prove myself worthy of it.'

Lauren closed her eyes.

'I need to think,' she said, trying to put the pieces of the puzzle together. 'To start with, you said we won't be living in the palace, and I assume that means you think someone in the palace, close to your father, is the—enemy?'

It was totally ridiculous. Like a spy story, but even that didn't make sense. Not that anything much had made sense these last four years.

'But surely the people in the palace aren't prisoners? They can come and go? I'm sure no high-up person came to Australia to kill your brother—they would have sent someone. Can they not send someone to your home?'

She saw broad shoulders lift with a sigh, and looking at his face, saw the shadows beneath his eyes.

Perhaps he'd had less sleep than she had.

Perhaps he was genuinely very worried about all this…

'My home is staffed by my people who, as I have told you, would give their lives for me, or mine. Tariq was foolish to think distance would protect his family. It was far easier for whoever wanted him dead to have him killed in a foreign country. To kill him at home, there would have been a furore—accusations flying, suspicion everywhere, our police battling against age-old traditions of secrecy and conspiracy.'

'Which is why you feel it is safer for us to be there rather than here?'

Lauren hoped the shiver that ran down her spine wasn't echoed in her words.

'I believe it with all my heart,' he said, and although there were probably a hundred reasons why she *not* believe this man, she could sense the depth of passion in his words, and understood he'd loved his playboy brother as deeply as she'd loved her wayward sister…

And she'd heard the pain in his voice when he'd spoken

of the wrongs being done in his country, and to its people, by those who put tourism and the money it might bring in above improving the health and education of the population. His commitment to a better future had shone through his words—he was doing this for Madan.

The words were powerful, but an even more powerful thought occurred to her. She got up and walked to the window, her mind tracking back through the conversation—his father dead, a year of mourning, now a succession to be settled…

There it was!

She'd had warnings the last two times someone had come from Madan, but not this time.

There had been no warning of this man's presence in the country, which could only mean the police no longer believed Nim was in danger. Yet with the succession in doubt, surely this was when he'd be in the most danger?

She clutched her stomach where fear ran rampant, and breathed deeply.

She had to think.

She returned to her chair, hoping her inner turmoil wasn't showing on her face.

'We'll go with you,' she said, and where she'd expected to feel dread she was surprised to find the words, once out, made her feel lighter, as if the burden she'd carried for four years had suddenly been lifted from her shoulders.

All the running, the phone calls to and from police, the checks in places as far apart as Coolgardie and Coober Pedy. And behind it all the sense of guilt that she'd never, for a minute, taken Lily's words of plots and murder seriously—never believed her own sister that such things could happen.

All of it over…

Don't be stupid, she warned herself. *You will still have to be wary and suspicious, careful whom you trust...*

But Malik had moved to stand in front of her. He bent and took her hand.

'I swear by all that is holy you will not regret that decision.'

His hand was warm, the palm firm, and he drew her to her feet so that she stood before him, close enough to smell his maleness, to feel the warmth of his body.

Then, to her astonishment, he kissed her lightly on the forehead, squeezed her fingers, and said, 'How long will it take you to pack?'

CHAPTER FOUR

DARNED MAN!

He'd walked out of her life again—well, out of her home—before she'd had time to register what he was saying, let alone throw up objections like having to give notice at work.

On the other hand, his being gone meant she could sit quietly and try to get her head around all that had happened in the last twenty-four hours. Except her mind refused to cooperate. It kept telling her it didn't know where to start thinking about it.

For a while, she just sat in her corner of the sofa and tried to relax. Only now her brain had found something it *could* think about—practicalities.

She'd have to get rid of the furniture before she could rent the flat—or should she rent it furnished?

No, there were things from her parents' home she didn't want to part with. Should she store them? Or leave the flat empty? She needed to talk to Aunt Jane—maybe Joe would like to live in the flat. *Aunt Jane*?

What on earth was she going to tell her?

And if she was leaving as soon as the man, Malik, seemed to think possible…

She clasped her head in her hands, ran her fingers through her hair, trying to stop the panic rattling in her mind.

She needed to take one thing at a time.

She had to go to work this afternoon—did she have something in the freezer for dinner, or should she shop?

This was easier—there was plenty in the freezer, including Nim's other favourite, bolognaise sauce, and she had pasta in the cupboard, but she could make jelly and custard for afters as a treat for Nim.

Nim, who was about to be thrust into a whole new world, far from his friends and all that was familiar to him.

Why was she thinking of jelly and custard when she had Nim's immediate future to consider?

She had a book somewhere—a book Lily had sent when she'd first landed in Madan, which was quite by accident, of course, she'd simply got her flight bookings muddled...

And Nim had looked at the book quite often, though probably not for a year. He knew his father had come from the place in the pictures. They could look at it together—really look from Lauren's point of view—to get some idea of what lay ahead of her, as well as Nim.

She knew from her previous foray on the internet that Madan was an extremely traditional country, still holding onto the past as far as the separation between men and women's roles. Men were heads of the households—the decision-makers—well, she could have guessed that, having met with the strong will of Malik Madani!

No doubt that was what Lily had found difficult, although from the little she'd seen of Tariq and Lily together, Lily had had him wound around her little finger.

Well, she, Lauren, could handle that, and was happy to go about her own business. But the kind of essential part of what lay ahead of her—the marriage deal—was a bit harder to think about.

Although it wouldn't be a real marriage, so maybe she didn't need to think about that part. Malik was an attractive man, and her body was aware of that attraction, but it need go no further—could go no further. It could definitely not become love. She already had one hostage to love in Nim and, given the past, that was more than enough.

It would be a marriage in name only.

And having come full circle in her head, she groaned, stood up and headed for the bathroom. She should have another shower—to clear her head?—then get dressed and go to work. It didn't matter that she'd be early, she could tell whoever needed to be told that she was leaving, then find something to do. Young Eve Lassik rarely had visitors, she could spend some time with her…

But even that plan, feeble though it was, was doomed, for she arrived on the ward to be greeted by Andy, who was duty sister for the day shift.

'Thank heavens you're here,' he said. 'I've just had word from on high that some potential benefactor has arrived and has to be shown around our wards. He's particularly keen to see the new kids' cancer centre and as it's practically your second home, there's no one better to show it to him.'

Should she have felt a premonition of disaster, or a feeling of strange apprehension?

Probably, but she didn't, going blithely to the door of the new unit to meet the representative of the powers-that-be and his or her visitor.

How could she ever have compared Malik to a tailor's dummy? The man walking towards the entrance to the centre seemed to zing with life, his face animated as he spoke to Ross Carstairs, Head of Paediatrics, hands moving with precision through the air as he explained some detail of his conversation.

Was this how Lily had felt when she'd seen Tariq unexpectedly?

Lauren closed her eyes on the thought!

'Ah, Lauren,' Ross greeted her. 'I'm delighted you're here. Andy thought you weren't on until later, but there's no one better to show Sheikh Madani around the new centre than you.'

Ross turned back to his guest.

'I can leave you in Lauren's capable hands. Lauren, this is Sheikh Madani. Malik, this is Lauren Macpherson, the angel of the cancer centre.'

Lauren muttered something she hoped Ross would take as a welcome to the visitor, while the wretched man looked down at her and smiled—in delight.

Lauren could see the laughter in his eyes as he said, '"The Angel of the Cancer Centre", huh? That's some position!'

Lauren turned away from the distraction caused by laughing eyes.

'This way, please,' she said, brisk and efficient. 'The new centre has only recently opened. It means we can treat more children with cancer closer to their homes, which means less stress on their families. Before it opened, we could do some treatments, but mainly provided follow-up services when the children returned from the city hospital.'

'And Susie, was she treated here?'

The question pulled Lauren out of her 'showing the centre' spiel, and she looked directly at the visitor, saw the smile still lingering in his eyes, felt something flutter inside her, and all but growled at him.

'Are you following me?' she demanded.

And he smiled again.

'*You're* the one not supposed to be here, and I made this appointment yesterday with your friend Mr Marshall. Well, he arranged it.'

It was hopeless trying to argue with the man, Lauren realised, and she should forget about those smiling eyes…

'Yes, Susie was treated here. She was one of our first patients.'

They'd been walking through the bright lobby, with native birds and animals painted on the walls.

'This is the reception area, as you can see,' Lauren said, in perfect tour-guide mode. 'There are paediatric specialists' rooms at the back on this floor. Most of the city's paediatricians now work out of here.'

She led the way to the elevator.

'The first floor is Day Surgery—and treatment rooms for outpatients. Along here to the left are rooms where children who need intermittent chemo come for treatment, or those who need minor surgery to repair a venous access port.'

'Do you have much trouble with the ports?'

It was an intelligent question, but it was easier to just rattle off information than actually speak to this man she'd said she'd marry.

But she did stop her spiel and turn to him, look at him, as she answered.

'We used to have some trouble with infection, but the new ports, plus more hands-on instruction with the parents or caregivers, has lessened it considerably.'

'Hands-on instruction?'

A serious question, no teasing smile lurking in his eyes, but just looking at him was causing her any number of problems, ninety-nine percent of them physical.

'With new parents—well, parents new to the apparatus—we not only show them what to do and what to look for—slight reddening or a hint of swelling around the port—but we have our own large doll, complete with port, in the children's room so parents can feel the bump beneath the skin. For parents on outlying properties, we have syringes they can use to practise flushing the port themselves, rather than returning here every four weeks so a nurse can do it.'

'And hygiene?'

Lauren shrugged.

'Once the wound has healed where it was inserted, and the dressing removed, it's normal skin care, really. With very young children, we usually keep them overnight after the port's implanted, just to check there are no reactions, but with the older ones, it's day surgery.'

'At home the danger would be infection.'

'Not if the wound is kept dry until it heals,' Lauren emphasised, then his words echoed in her head and she asked, '*Would be* infection? You're not doing it already?'

He sighed.

'I explained our hospital needed money spent on *it*, not hotels. I have made what improvements I can, but for children, particularly those needing chemo, well, I would not allow them to be treated in it. They were sent to a neighbouring country, but now I have a new children's hospital just opened and a dedicated oncology centre within it.'

They were walking on, Malik peering into the different rooms as Lauren spoke.

'Most of the treatment rooms have monitors, so children here for three or four hours while chemo drips into them can watch a variety of television programmes, the older ones have popular computer games they can play and for the younger ones, there are cartoons or simple touchscreen games.'

They took the elevator up, Lauren glad it already had passengers when they entered it, although their presence didn't lessen the physical bombardment his body was causing in hers.

It's a marriage in name only, her head kept telling her, yet the slightest brush of sleeve on sleeve, a hint of his aftershave in the air, could start a flurry of sensations within her, not palpitations exactly, or goose-bumps, but tingling stuff that totally unsettled her…

'Up here, it's a bit of a free-for-all!' she said, as they left the elevator, but Malik could already see that for himself. The place was a riot of colour, not only the walls with bright murals, but balloons seemed to dance across the ceiling, children's artwork was tacked up everywhere, and a couple of older boys, their mobile drip stands in one hand, were playing football in an open space.

He watched Lauren as she took up her tour-guide spiel again, admiring the sure way she moved, the smiles and sometimes quiet words or gentle touches she gave individual children.

'As you can see, this ward is for older children. Some of them participate in the morning television program they run that is shown throughout the hospital, a few have lessons—we have two teachers—and, generally speaking, it's as homelike as we can make it.'

'It's certainly that,' he said, putting out his foot to kick the straying ball back to the players. 'And younger children?'

'This way,' Lauren said, and Malik followed her again, wondering as he did so why asking her to marry him should have affected him the way it had—as if this would be a normal marriage and his body was already anticipating, well, carnal delights.

He liked the way she moved, this small, determined woman, and as she swept ahead of him, pausing now and then to speak to a patient or staff member, he was seeing her in his new children's hospital, bringing the caring attitude that was obvious with every word she spoke, as well as a wealth of experience.

But thinking this way was folly! Not about the hospital but about attraction. Attraction could lead to love and he was done with that. Romantic love had left him both hurt and humiliated, back when he was young, then seeing the dance Lily had led his brother had put him off the thought of it for ever.

A marriage in name only, that was the idea.

He caught up with her as she paused at one of the handwash dispensers, squeezing some foam onto her hands and spreading it thoroughly.

'I'll introduce you to a special friend of mine,' she said. 'Eve has JMML, so bloody rare you wonder why the most vulnerable should end up with it.'

Malik heard the passion of anger in her voice. JMML—juvenile myelomonocytic leukaemia—was very rare indeed. But vulnerable?

Because it attacked children?

Or something else?

Lauren had entered a room so Malik washed his hands and followed to see a small, dark-eyed child with a mop of dark curly hair smiling up at Lauren from her bed.

She was so slight she barely made a bump in the bedclothes.

'Hi, Evie, I've brought you a visitor,' Lauren was saying quietly. 'His name is Malik.'

The dark eyes turned to study him, then her face changed completely as she smiled. It was as if a light had been lit behind her translucent skin, and he could see the vibrant little girl she'd been before her body had betrayed her.

'Eve's family live a six-hour drive from the hospital, and she has three siblings, so it's difficult for even one of her parents to stay here for any length of time,' Lauren explained.

Explaining vulnerable at the same time—the child alone in a strange city with long separations from her family.

'But I have my phone—see,' the little girl said, reaching out a skeletal arm to lift a phone, with a bright pink case encrusted in sparkling stones, from the table beside her. 'And when I want to talk to them I turn it on and press just here, and at home it comes up on someone's phone or computer and tells them I'm there, and I can do…'

Anxious eyes turned to Lauren.

'What can I do, Lauren?'

Malik saw the fondness for the girl in Lauren's eyes.

'It's called FaceTime, sweetie. Press it to show Malik how quickly your family knows you're waiting to see them.'

Malik watched as the frail fingers manipulated the phone, and within seconds three children's faces appeared on the phone's screen, and excited voices yelled, 'Hello, Evie!'

Malik closed his eyes for an instant and swallowed hard, seeing this sick child connecting with her family so far away.

'How can I help?' he said, aware his voice was rough with the unexpected emotion.

Lauren smiled at him.

'Do you do miracles?' she asked quietly as various people—adults now as well—yelled through the phone to Evie.

He waited.

'The chemo used for AML resulted in a small remission. When she relapsed, she had a splenectomy and again was okay for a while. But now we're waiting for a stem-cell donor. The latest search was hopeful and the donor is being tested now but…'

She was the emotional one now. Malik could hear it in her voice.

'But?' he said, and Lauren shrugged, then visibly brightened.

'Even with the new cells, there's only a fifty percent chance of success, so we're all hanging out for our girl to be in the good half of that statistic.'

'And being positive,' she added, although he sensed she had to try harder for that.

He'd have liked to touch her, rest his hand on her shoulder in a show of support and empathy, but something inside him whispered no, and he looked back at the child who had shut off her phone and appeared to be sleeping.

The tour continued through the rest of the second floor, where there were younger children, play areas with colourful toys, televisions showing children's programmes, the music from them clashing with music from small computers some of the children had.

'It's very special,' he said, already adapting ideas to those that would fit in with his people's culture, his mind ranging ahead to the specialists he'd need for his hospital to become the top children's cancer unit in the region.

And he'd have Lauren—what a bonus! For he understood that this had been four years in the making and in recent years she'd been part of the consulting team when it came to the practicalities of making it a special place. The experience she would bring to his hospital was something he hadn't foreseen when he'd come to find her and Nimr.

And into his head came a vision of the future—he and Lauren working together for the good of his people, his country.

He and Lauren together…

'Thank you,' he said, and meant it in more ways than one, when she finally led him back to the front door. 'I shall see you tonight?' She looked startled.

'I could help you pack,' he offered hopefully, though why seeing her again, as herself and not a nurse, had suddenly become so important he didn't know. Unless the thought of their marriage had sparked an unexpected attraction. Actually, not so unexpected. He'd felt that unfamiliar tug the first time he'd seen her, tired and grubby, her eyes spitting fire at the man who'd organised their meeting.

Whatever, the thought of taking her back to Madan with him was suddenly every bit as important as taking Nimr…

The question threw Lauren, who was far from convinced this mad idea was real, let alone achievable.

'I'm on duty until ten,' she said. 'Joe's staying in to mind Nim…'

She paused.

'You *could* go to the house,' she said slowly. 'Then you could look at the Madan book with Nim and explain far more about the pictures than I can.'

'You have a book on Madan?"

Lauren nodded.

'Lily sent it when she first went there, and because Nim—well, I thought he needed to know about his father's heritage. He loves it, and looks at the pictures often. He can pick out his father among a group of, to me, anonymous men wearing white gowns. He has a picture of Tariq and Lily and him as a baby, so he knows who to look for.'

'I would enjoy that, and perhaps see you later?'

For some reason the simple question accelerated Lauren's heart rate.

Did he actually *want* to see her?

Or was it for assurance that she hadn't changed her mind?

More likely that, she told herself. This was a practical arrangement after all.

'I'm working until ten, which means it could be midnight

before I get home, if there's a problem or a lengthy handover. And believe me, by that time all I want to do is have a quick shower and fall into bed.'

There! That settled any silly heart rate acceleration.

'Of course,' he said politely, further squashing any excitement with his matter-of-fact acceptance of her explanation. 'I shall contact you tomorrow about arrangements.'

She watched him walk away, wondering what on earth she was getting into.

Worse still, wondering why the man was affecting her—no, *attracting* her…

This was to be a business arrangement, not a man-woman thing.

Would the attraction make that harder for her?

Too hard?

She remembered the passion with which Malik spoke of his country, and the things he wished to achieve in order to hand over to Nim a proud country to rule.

And as that was Nim's rightful heritage, would it be fair of her to take it from him?

She glanced at her watch. She could have a quick lunch then see someone in the personnel office to give in her notice.

This time her heart rate slowed—just thinking about such a definitive step made it pause.

'You're doing this for Nim,' she reminded herself, and headed for the canteen.

CHAPTER FIVE

IN THE CABIN of the luxurious private jet the real world seemed far away, far enough away for Lauren to relax. She listened as Malik answered Nim's questions about Madan, and told him stories of Tariq's childhood.

Lauren found herself relaxing, dozing even, until lunch was served, and Nim fell asleep before he'd finished eating.

'He's been so excited about all this,' she told Malik.

He smiled, and said, 'And you?'

'I've barely had time to think, there's been so much to do.'

He smiled again, and said, 'Which I'm certain you managed with great efficiency.'

'Not entirely,' she told him, aware how quickly he could sneak under her defences with a little compliment like that.

To forestall more of them, she added, 'Tell me about Madan.'

And he did, his voice full of pride as he spoke of the past, of passion as he spoke of the future, and of pain when he spoke of Tariq.

She heard truth in his voice as well, and knew, for all her doubts, that this man would never have harmed his brother.

But as they talked—the subjects ranging further now to work, and current affairs, even—she began to feel more and more at ease with him, and sensed he too was relaxing, their togetherness beginning to feel almost natural somehow…

Seen from the air as they came in to land, Madan was an unbelievable landscape of ochre mountains, endless desert, and there, at the top end, the vivid green of the oasis, with towering new buildings clustered around one end of it.

Nim was so excited to be nearing the country of his book he ran from one side of the plane to the other to catch different glimpses of it.

'Time to sit, Nimr,' Malik said, and Nim, already enslaved to this man who'd read his book and talked to him of his father, ran to his seat and buckled his seatbelt.

But as the plane descended, Lauren's misgivings returned, and the questions that haunted her nights—whether she was doing the right thing being the foremost of them—hammered in her head.

Had she spoken aloud? Malik reached over across the aisle and rested his hand on her shoulder.

'Please don't worry, everything will work out for the best.'

Don't worry? she wanted to yell at him.

How could she do that when she was not only stepping into a completely different way of life, language and culture, but in another day or so, according to Malik's well laid-out plan, she'd be a married woman.

And when that simple touch on her shoulder had sent warmth through her skin, how could she do anything but worry? She'd be married in name only, she reminded herself, but somehow that knowledge didn't help to settle the warmth, *or* the turmoil in her stomach, *or* the panicked fluttering of the thoughts inside her head.

They touched down and walked through a crowd of

white-robed figures towards a blue and white building, with tall minarets rising from it on all four corners, and a welcoming arched dome painted blue, to mimic the sky, above the entrance door.

Lauren held Nim's hand—probably too tightly—but while he was entranced by all the fairy-tale stuff he saw, she was terrified.

It's just a building, she told herself, *and this is nothing more than another country. People are people everywhere, both good and bad, sick and well. At least work will be familiar...*

'Relax!'

He was by her side, and the word had the sharp note of an order.

But perhaps that's what she'd needed, as she did begin to feel more at ease, smiling as people murmured greetings, releasing Nim so he, too, could be introduced.

Except now the same people she'd smiled at were bowing their heads to Nim as Malik introduced him, and there was something obsequious in the manner of the movement.

Something that unsettled Lauren once again.

'Do they have to do that?' she demanded quietly of Malik as he opened the back of an enormous black car for her.

'Do what?' he asked, his eyes catching hers, arrested by the question.

'Bow and scrape in front of him!' she retorted, angry now. 'We *talked* about it. I told you he should grow up like other boys—' she broke off to tell Nim, who was bouncing on the soft seats to sit still '—not like—oh, I don't know! Someone who should be bowed to!'

Then, exhausted by the strangeness of it all, the travel and her sudden spurt of temper, she slumped into the car beside Nim, pulled on a seatbelt, and tried to calm her breathing.

Go with the flow, she reminded herself, having decided that was the only thing to do from the day she'd handed in her resignation.

But she hadn't imagined the flow could be interrupted so soon after her arrival.

Or that Malik wasn't travelling with them, for he'd shut the door and the car was sliding silently away from the terminal, through huge golden gates, past the towering hotels, then into the shadows of the mountains she'd seen from the plane, apparently skirting the oases, for on one side of the road was vivid green and on the other the mountains, stark in shadow—*forbidding?*

Lauren shook her head at the fancy in time to turn to see the camels Nim was pointing out so excitedly.

Leaving the mountains behind, they entered an avenue of what Lauren took for date palms, tall and thickly leaved, their fronds almost forming a canopy over the road.

A long road, leading eventually to a high wall, and man squatting outside who stood to open the gates—into a miracle. Before them was the most beautiful garden Lauren had ever seen or imagined, carefully laid out in formal patterns, fountains reflecting a million tiny rainbows.

And roses—everywhere there were roses. There were other shrubs and bushes too, but predominately there were roses in every possible size and colour.

'Gosh, Mum, is this a palace?'

Lauren raised her eyes from the beauty of the garden and saw the magnificence in front of her. Golden domes and minarets, an arched colonnade around the building, sun glinting off the marble of its floor.

Huge wooden doors were, she could see now that she was closer, intricately carved.

'We were supposed to go somewhere else, not to the

palace,' she said to the driver, and he must have understood, for he shook his head.

'No palace, no palace,' he said as he alighted and came around to open her door.

A tall, well-built older man, in a black robe trimmed with gold, descended the four steps in a stately manner then bowed to her.

Dear heaven, not the bowing thing again—not to me.

But with Nim he held out his hand, and Nim released his grip on his mother's arm to shake hands with the man.

'Ahmed,' the man said, and Lauren forgot her nerves and stood taller and proud when the four-year-old boy said, 'Nimr,' rolling the final 'r' so beautifully Lauren guessed he'd had some coaching.

Ahmed led the way up the steps, Nim chattering to him about the camels he had seen, unaware he might not be understood.

A young woman, in long loose trousers and a long tunic, stepped out of the shadows of the entrance and came towards them.

'I am Aneesha, I am here to help you.' And with that she took Lauren by one hand and Nim by the other and led them inside. She paused briefly when Nim said, 'Don't forget to take off your sandals, Mum. Remember we read that in the book.'

Lauren had barely taken in the wide entrance hall, with its glorious carpets scattered about the marble floor and hung from many of the walls, when there was a disturbance outside and Malik appeared.

'I am sorry, so sorry. I wished to be here before you but was delayed with some business.'

He'd taken her hand as he spoke, and kept it enclosed in his as he spoke briefly to Aneesha, who nodded to the new arrivals and disappeared on silent feet into the depths of the building.

'Why are we here?' Lauren asked Malik, aware that her hand was responding to his by clinging a bit—well, maybe more than a bit—because somehow holding hands with this man seemed to make everything all right. 'Isn't this the palace?'

He smiled, responding to the movement of her fingers by pulling her a little closer to him, which made her feel even better, though surely that was silly when they barely knew each other.

'This little place? Oh, no, my mother might have insisted on a certain grandeur, but nothing would ever rival the palace, which must be four or five times the size of this humble dwelling.'

'Humble dwelling indeed!' Lauren muttered at him, aware that she should take back her hand but doing nothing. 'And have you been teaching Nim to roll that "r" on the end of his name?'

His only answer was a smile, and as it eased the frightened bits inside her, she also wondered why it had ever made her think of crocodiles.

'Here you will be safe. These people are my people—Tariq's people, too. They will watch over both of you and feel honoured to look after Nimr. But let me show you to your rooms, you must be tired after the journey, then later, perhaps, we can go to the hospital?'

For the first time since he'd burst into her life he sounded a little uncertain as he made that last suggestion.

Almost as if it was important to him that she go, but he was unwilling to push.

Malik uncertain?

She pushed the silly idea away, removed her hand from his and said, 'Then we'd better get going, hadn't we?'

He smiled again, his eyes crinkling at the corners, and for some reason that small, crinkly smile eased a lot of the tension that had been building inside her since the people who were obviously servants had appeared.

But 'rooms' hardly covered the accommodation they would have, her bedroom lined with silk, hung with draperies, carpets so soft underfoot she was glad she'd left her shoes outside the front door.

A huge bathroom with a range of luxury products from bath salts to not-so-humble toothpaste, a dressing room hung with outfits ranging from jeans—top brands—and silk shirts to colourful trousers and tunics like the ones the local women seemed to wear.

'Come and look at my room, Mum!'

Nim came bursting through a door she hadn't noticed, and she went through it to find a room that would have filled any small boy with delight.

So much for her hope of bringing him up as a normal child!

The bed was in the shape of a racing car, spaceships and satellites hung from a ceiling painted with stars—probably in their correct astronomical positions, she guessed—while the shelves held toys and games and large soft animals, particularly tigers in various sizes.

'We don't have tigers living here,' Aneesha was saying in her soft voice. 'But in the garden the sheikh is running a breeding programme for the desert leopard, which has come close to extinction. Would you like to see the baby cubs?'

Even in his wild excitement, Nim *did* turn to Lauren for a nod of permission, and although her heart quailed as her son disappeared through another door into the vast unknown depths of this enormous building, she had to believe Malik's promise to keep him safe, or she'd go mad with worry.

'So you trust me?' he said, having come into the room so quietly she gave a start.

'I *have* to!' she said. 'Who else is there?'

Had she sounded as tense as she felt that he touched her gently on the shoulder?

'Every person in this building would give his or her life for your son, and you, too, can be sure of their loyalty and protection,' he said quietly, then he drew her unresisting body into his arms and held her against the hardness of his chest, his enclosing arms adding their own promise of security.

And because it was such a relief to have someone else worrying about Nim, she stayed for probably an instant too long, and when he spoke her name she looked up at him, saw something she couldn't read in his eyes, at least until he kissed her.

Just gently, on the lips, a fleeting brush of skin on skin—then he was gone—striding briskly away, pausing at the door to look back at her.

'I will send someone to show you around, or, if you'd prefer to rest, perhaps some tea. I wouldn't leave except there is much to do, and unexpected problems that have arisen in my absence.'

And with that he was gone.

Lauren shook away the silly thoughts chasing through her mind, silly thoughts about that kiss…

It might have come out of nowhere, but it had been reassurance, that's all it had been.

And though it had caused a myriad of sensations in her body, she could put that down to her unease in this totally new and very, very different situation.

He'd given her a reassuring hug and kiss. What could be more natural?

'Keep telling yourself that,' she muttered, then looked around to check no one could hear her.

She was uncertain what to do. Should she go back to her rooms—her prison?

No way! She was going to have a quick wash, perhaps a coffee if she could find one, then go exploring.

A soft tap at the door was also reassuring. Someone to show her around, perhaps? Offer her tea?

She crossed the vastness of the sitting area and opened the door to find another smiling woman there.

'I am Keema,' the woman said. 'Aneesha, her English better than mine, so she can look after Nimr and teach him our words, and I will look after you.'

Uncertain what to do, Lauren held out her hand.

'I'm Lauren,' she said, and although she'd have liked to add, 'And I can't believe all this is happening,' she thought she might confuse her new friend, so simply ushered her in.

'You would like something before I show you the Sheikh's house?'

'I'd give my—'

And having discarded various things she'd normally have offered to give, like her firstborn—should she ever have one—or her right hand, she went with plain, rather than colloquial, English.

'I'd love a coffee.'

As Keema disappeared, Lauren looked around the room again, discovering her clothes and books had been unpacked and put neatly away in cupboards or on shelves.

Another country, another life…

'Coffee for my lady,' a deep voice said, as once again she chased tremors of trepidation from her mind.

Malik set the small tray on a table in the sitting area, took Lauren's hand again, and led her to a soft couch, settling beside her, which immediately dismissed any remnants of uncertainty.

She'd think why this was so later, but right now he was explaining something.

'I realised I couldn't just walk away and leave you here. It is my job to show you your new home, my job to see that you are comfortable. I have already been away, so affairs of state can wait a little longer.'

He poured the thick black coffee into tiny cups and handed one to her.

'It is not coffee as you know it, and I have that type of coffee should you find this distasteful, but I would like you to try it, if only once.'

A slight smile accompanied the words, and it was that which prompted Lauren to lift the tiny, delicate cup to her lips and take a sip.

Too sweet, was her first thought, and grainy, somehow, but a second sip produced such a feeling of well-being she felt herself relax.

'I could grow used to it,' she said, smiling for the first time since they'd arrived—well, smiling *genuinely*.

'I hope you do,' he said, face serious this time, and she knew behind the words he was telling her he hoped she'd stay.

Because of Nim?

Of course it was!

Their marriage would be one of convenience, which meant she should ignore that tiny spurt of happiness his words had prompted. Ignore the warmth she'd felt when he'd said it, sounding as if he really *did* want her to stay.

Her as well as Nim, perhaps?

But realistically a marriage of convenience would suit

both of them, she decided as she took another sip of coffee. They'd both lost loved ones and knew the pain of love…

But as they walked through the vast residence after the coffee he took her hand and tucked it into the crook of his arm, and she began to feel more at ease with this man she didn't know, so by the time he led her along a passage and out into a garden where Nim was playing with two small…kittens? No, these were pale beige little cats with a hint of spots to come. She felt relaxed enough to laugh at the antics of the threesome.

'These are the fourth cub twins we have bred here,' Malik explained to her, before going to kneel by Nim and take one of the cubs gently into his hand.

He lifted the kitten up for her to pat, and as her fingers brushed the silky fur, their fingers met—*eyes* met…

The moment passed, if there was a moment, for now he was speaking to Nim.

'When they are bigger, Nimr, we will take them out into the mountains where they belong, but before that we have to teach them how to look after themselves, so they can hunt for their food in the desert.'

Lauren held her breath, praying Nim wouldn't ask what they ate, but he was already telling Malik the cubs' names and how he could tell one from the other.

'These are better than rabbits, Mum,' he said happily, and Lauren closed her eyes and prayed again, this time that he would have plenty of that happiness in this new life.

'And now I *must* leave you for a while,' Malik said, returning to Lauren's side. 'But I shall return to eat dinner with you and Nimr, and tomorrow, if he is happy to be here with the staff and animals, that is time enough to show you the hospital.'

He put his hand in the small of her back to guide her

back indoors, back to her room, where he for stood a moment, looking at her, then touched a finger to her cheek and left.

And, no, she hadn't been waiting for another kiss—or so she told herself…

But she touched her finger to her cheek where his had been, and wondered how things might have been had the two of them met under different circumstances.

It was a foolish thing to think given it was unlikely he'd have even noticed her—and *that* practical thought doused the fluttering flames the touch had left behind.

Dinner, it appeared, was to be in one of the smaller dining rooms, or so Keema said as she pulled outfits from the wardrobes, holding them up for Lauren's inspection.

Did she have to wear one of them?

Would her own good slacks and a shirt not do?

For a moment she wished Malik was there so she could ask him, then she remembered how disturbed he'd left her feeling and cancelled the idea.

'Look, Mum, I've got a dress!'

Nim burst into the room, in a snowy white, long-sleeved tunic.

'Do you like it?'

Nim nodded.

'I look like the little boys in my book,' he explained. 'I can still wear my other clothes, Aneesha said, but for dinner or going out I wear this.'

He stopped, looking anxious.

'Do *you* like it?'

Lauren smiled at his excitement, although her heart quailed at the speed with which this transformation of her son was happening.

And just her son?

She looked at the outfits Keema had now laid on the bed, and knew she'd have to choose. Her good slacks and a shirt wouldn't cut it at all.

'I'll wear the blue,' she told the young woman, who swiftly removed the other garments.

'That's lovely, Mum.'

Nim stood by the bed, reverently touching the fine material of the dark blue tunic, decorated with silver thread around the neckline and hem.

She slipped into the dressing room to put it on, returning, arms out held for his approval.

'Beautiful!' was the response, only it was Malik there admiring her, and she could tell from the gleam in his eyes that it *was* admiration—and maybe something else?

'Now we're Madanis,' Nim told her, coming over to take her hand, a little shy, probably because she looked like a stranger.

She certainly felt like one, arrayed in dark blue silk with silver threads. Fairy godmothers and pumpkins came to mind and she smiled to herself.

Malik battled to contain the surge of excitement that had fired his body when he'd seen her.

Marriage in name only?

How could he possibly have thought that would work when something about this woman had attracted him from their first meeting? He remembered the way she'd fired up at the pompous managerial type who'd introduced them, scorn glittering in her eyes!

Now seeing them, the woman and the boy, there in front of him, he knew for certain he had done the right thing. It was personal now. These two were meant to be in his life...

* * *

But explaining to Nimr, over dinner, that he was going to marry his mother threw up unexpected difficulties—as far as Nimr was concerned.

'But then you'll be my father,' the little boy said, 'and you can't be my uncle and my father, can you?'

'If that's the worst of his worries, he'll be fine with it,' Lauren said later, when they'd seen Nimr tucked up in bed and were walking in the rose garden.

'He's very accepting of change,' Malik said, 'and I suspect that's your doing. You are his security, and while you are there, he knows everything will be all right.'

'If only it had been that simple for both of us,' Lauren said, and he heard in her voice the fear she'd lived with since the accident.

'It will be now,' he said, slipping an arm around her shoulders and drawing her closer. 'Did I not promise you?'

And as they wandered into the shadows of a rose arbour, he turned her in his arms and kissed her—again a gentle, barely-there brush of lips on lips, only this time, perhaps because the burden of Nim's safety had been lifted from her shoulders, Lauren found herself responding.

Kissing him back, her hands slipping around his chest to keep him close, her lips parting to his questing tongue…

'Marriage in name only?' he said, some time later, as they continued their stroll through the garden. And the teasing quality of his voice sent heat coursing through Lauren's body, until she wondered how they'd tell Nim about the bed-sharing part of what lay ahead, and coldness replaced the heat.

'Marriage in name only!' she said firmly, and hoped she was going in the right direction as she headed back to the house.

'He'll understand—well, maybe not understand but accept,' Malik said, when he'd caught up with her and once again pulled her close, demanding to know what was worrying her.

How could he be so certain, he who'd never had to worry about what lay ahead for a beloved child every minute of every day?

But when he kissed her again, she didn't pull away.

She'd just have to work it out, she decided as she slid into the unexpected delight just kissing this man could bring…

CHAPTER SIX

THE FOLLOWING MORNING, telling herself it was useless to be waiting in her room when she had no idea when Malik might appear, Lauren went out into the back garden, where there were apricot, pomegranate and orange trees, to watch Nim have his first camel ride, then co-opted Keema to give her another tour of the house, this time with local words for each room thrown in.

Walking through it with Malik, she'd counted about ten guest suites like hers, and at least four reception rooms, ranging from ballroom size to a more intimate one that opened onto the colonnade around the house, and would be a pleasant place to entertain.

Dining rooms, too, ranged in size, but one large formal one was set up in what must be a traditional style—no table and chairs but cushions set around a very long mat.

'And the kitchens?' Lauren asked, thinking she might at some stage need to make a snack for Nim.

'Oh, you don't want to go there. There are men—chefs—and they are not family and shouldn't see your face.'

It took a moment for the words to sink in, and when they did register Lauren could only shake her head. Here she'd been, thinking things were not so different from home—

except the place was so enormous—then suddenly she was bang up against a local custom.

'But if I wanted to go in?' she asked, and Keema shook her head.

'You must ask for anything you or Nimr need, and we shall bring it to you.'

Lauren thought about arguing—explaining that as an Australian it didn't matter if men saw her face, but Malik appeared from nowhere *and* she completely lost the conversational thread.

And a great deal of composure because one glance at his lips and that second kiss—the one she'd responded to—was front and centre of her mind. Her cheeks turned pink just thinking about it.

'Shall we go to the hospital?' he said. 'I have seen Nimr and explained where I am taking you. He's off to see where the baby camels are kept and be introduced to my birds, so he won't be worried, and Aneesha will see he eats his lunch.'

'And with so many people to take care of my son, I no longer need to be worrying about him?'

Malik smiled.

'I doubt you'd stop no matter how many carers he had or how much assurance I give you.'

She nodded and returned his smile with a small one of her own—small because, while she should feel free to have someone else caring for Nim, she also felt a sudden pang of loss.

Was this how it would be in this new future?

'He will still have time for you,' Malik said, as if he'd read her mind.

And caught something of her feelings, for he put a comforting arm around her shoulders—so much for forgetting about the kiss when just one touch sent her senses spinning—and led her to the car.

It was a smaller car this time—less intimidating but still a sleek and beautiful vehicle.

He drove well, not towards the tall towers of the city but on a road curving back from the mountains and around the outer limits of the oasis to where many squat, brown mud buildings stood, many of them with panels of woven leaves forming parts of the walls, all with intricate balustrading around the roofs, where, from the glimpses of greenery she'd glimpsed, there could be gardens.

'This is how we lived, though the leaders of the tribes always had far bigger places—more like forts than houses. And up ahead, where you see the scaffolding, is my new hospital being built.'

He pulled up on the side of the road so she could see the scaffolding already reaching four or five stories high, and a smaller building at the base of it.

'That's the old hospital—built by the first oil company that came to work our oilfields. It has been adequate for our needs, with a radiology department, pathology department, two operating theatres, with surgeons and trained theatre staff, and many wards.'

'And your staff?'

'They are mainly expats, but we have local doctors who have trained in the UK, including our chief radiologist. Because of having to bring in most of the staff from outside, English is the common language in the hospital. Some of the registered nurses are locals, but most of them aren't, although we have developed an in-hospital training system for enrolled nurses and another one for aides. We also have many aides who work as translators for the expats.'

'I imagine that's important, not to mention easier—

having people who can speak to the patients in their own language and carry on proper conversations.'

'You are right, which is why it's important to get our university up and running. I have some friends working on this, but while flashy hotels remain the priority for spending, it is difficult.'

She heard him sigh and wanted to reach over and rest her hand on his thigh, but after last night's kisses, which had left her feeling a bit befuddled, the less she touched him the better.

Had she really responded so readily?

Fiercely might be a better description.

She was considering whether it was a reaction to not having kissed a man for so long, rather than this man in particular, when she realised he was speaking again.

'Many tribal people still use traditional medicine so their doctors have been a wise man or woman in the tribe, who was taught by their predecessor.'

He paused and turned to look at Lauren.

'And I don't know whether it was the outdoor life our ancestors led, or if the traditional medicine worked, but apart from accidents—broken limbs and such—most people lived to a good age.'

'The new hospital will they come to that?'

'I do hope so, if I ever get it finished. I've been using my own money, but now Nimr is here, I should be able to get government funding for it. But…'

'But?' Lauren echoed, as he started the car again and drove towards the buildings.

'Since the discovery of oil and the wealth that came with it, most of the members of the ruling family and those close to them have been travelling to Europe—England and Germany in particular—for their medical needs.'

'Long way to go to see a GP,' Lauren said, and he smiled.

'Exactly! But that is why my father's generation has never felt the need to spend money on health care here—'

'When *they* had access to it overseas!'

'Exactly!' Malik said. 'Though the first hospital has problems, as you will see, it was still adequate. The oil men left it to the architects who built their hotel, so although they must have looked at plans of hospitals in other places, they didn't see the need for separate facilities and wards for men and women and, more specifically, for children.'

'So?' Lauren asked, guessing there was more.

He paused. Looking into the future?

'So I built the children's hospital first, before starting on the big one. We still use the laboratories in the old hospital—they are in good order—but eventually those in the new building will cover both and the old building can be demolished.'

He'd pulled up at the side of the old building and led the way inside.

'This was originally a grand entrance foyer, like the hotels have, then behind it, to one side, was—well, still is—the reception desk, and on the other side the emergency department. Unfortunately, many people saw this big space as ideal for a market—somewhere to sell their wares to patients and their families or other visitors. So now we use a side entrance for the ED and the main hospital, although some people still try to get in through this maze.

Lauren looked around. Fans whirred overhead and people milled around the great space, bargaining, shouting, chattering—so much noise and confusion.

'There's a man selling pomegranates over there!' Lauren said, indicating the man with a nod of her head.

'That's nothing,' Malik said gloomily. 'We had a patient from Pakistan in here once—many of the oilfield workers are expats—and his visitor was a snake charmer, complete with snake. The problem is, our people are not used to the hospital concept. They are family-oriented, so they want to be close to the patient. Ideally, they would like to stay with the patient in the ward or room, and if they can't they are likely to camp close by, so the market does a thriving business.'

'And in your new hospital? Will it be different?' Lauren asked.

He smiled at her.

'I hope so! My idea is that when it is completed, the old one can be turned into a kind of hotel, where families of the patients can stay free of charge.'

'And the market?' she asked, still enthralled by the madness of it.

'Will probably remain,' he said, so gloomily she had to laugh.

'It's not funny,' he told her sternly, but she caught the twinkle in his eyes, and laughed some more.

He led her around to the side entrance, but the tour was perfunctory, little more than hand-waving in one direction or another, rooms and wards labelled but not investigated.

'You'll see it all eventually,' he said as they came out through another side door at the other end of the market, 'but if you decide you want to work, it will be with the children. So now I'll show you my children's hospital.'

And the pride in his voice was enough to tell her it would be very special.

They walked around to the side of the new building where a gleaming white structure stood.

Lauren had to blink and look again but, no, her first impression had been right. It looked like a castle from a fairy story, with a big golden dome and tall, slender spires decorated with pink and blue—even what looked like a fort built at one side.

'It's a hospital?' she asked, unable to hide the wonderment in her voice.

Malik paused and turned towards her, guiding her into the shade of a tree where they could talk and see the incredible building.

'We had a sister, Tariq and I, who was very ill from the time she was born. I was too young to know details of her illness, and neither my mother nor my father ever spoke of it, so even later, when I began to study, I couldn't really work out what it had been.'

'She died?' Lauren asked, and he nodded.

'But for many years she was in and out of the hospital—which was new then. She was even flown overseas to see specialists. And one time when she was home and we were playing by her bed, and talking with her, she told us how horrible hospitals always looked and asked if they had to look like that.'

'Poor kid!' Lauren said, giving in to the need to touch his arm.

He smiled at her, laid his hand over hers, and continued, 'So we asked her what a children's hospital should look like. Tariq was good at drawing and he found paper and coloured pencils and she told him what to draw.'

'And this is *it*?' Lauren asked, shaking her head in disbelief that this magic castle could possibly be a hospital.

Malik smiled.

'It is my memorial to a brave little girl,' he said, his voice deep with emotion. 'The original drawing is framed on a wall inside, and we didn't put it on a mountain-top, as she'd have liked—that was a bit too inconvenient.'

He smiled again, apparently delighted at her reaction.

'Come, I'll show you around,' he said. 'It's spread out

because with children it really *had* to be ground floor so the families from out of town can camp close by, so it sometimes seems, at the end of the day, that you've walked many miles.'

Was he talking too much because he was worried she might not like his ambitious project?

But as he led her through the doors and she saw the bright painting of a camel train threading its way around the walls, she couldn't stop smiling, her face radiating delight as she turned to him.

'It's fabulous!' she said, and it took a great deal of willpower to remain all business in the face of her delight. What he'd really have liked to do was take her hand and walk around the walls with her, explaining the intricately woven camel bags hung on the camels and telling her stories of the past.

Just to see that smile again?

Of course.

But also just to be with her as man and woman without all the complications in his life and those he'd forced into hers. To see her smile, and feel the heat inside him that a simple smile could generate—to see where the attraction he knew was between them could lead…

'And this is just the entry,' he told her. 'Emergency is through this way.'

They entered, and he was barely through the door when someone called to him.

'Dr Madani!'

It was a nurse he knew and trusted, so he headed to the cubicle to see a small boy, about two, lying on the bed.

'A seed of some kind up his left nostril. I don't want

to try to dislodge with the crocodile clips, in case I push it further in.'

She handed him the otoscope, which was used for both nose and ears, and, after greeting the anxious mother beside the bed with a smile and a brief chat with the small patient, he bent over to have a look.

Such a young child—they could really only do it under anaesthetic, and he avoided anaesthetising children whenever possible.

'Do you know the trick that sometimes works?' Lauren said. 'I saw a doctor do it once and have used it many times since.'

He smiled at her—he might have known she'd come up with something, for he was beginning to realise that this woman was special in every way.

And his heart was smiling, too, as if this very ordinary conversation was a personal confirmation of the rightness of their match…

'Do tell,' he said, and she explained how she could block the free nostril while the mother blew hard into the child's mouth.

'You'll have to translate and tell her it might not work, but it's worth a try before anaesthetic.'

He explained to the woman, who was reluctant at first, but now Lauren was at the child's level, stroking his arm and playing with his fingers, the mother agreed.

And as Lauren pressed the free nostril shut and the mother blew, the seed *did* come out, to the delight of all.

'I can't have spent enough time in emergency rooms to have learnt that trick,' Malik said, when mother and son had departed.

'It's an old one and a good one, so now you know,' Lauren told him, her smile again causing a response in his heart.

* * *

He showed Lauren around the wards, which were sparsely occupied.

'Parents are wary about coming to the hospital in case they discover their child will have to stay, even for a short time. It is not their way, but they will learn in time. Attendance in Emergency is doubling every month, and we have arrangements so at least two people—usually the mother and grandmother, or an aunt—can be with any child in the wards at all times.'

He was leading the way into a wing off the main foyer, nodding and greeting staff as they passed.

'It's not big enough yet to have designated post-op or ICU wards, but these rooms are set aside for those purposes.'

He knocked and opened a door into a small, bright room, the two women in it adjusting their head scarves to cover all but their eyes but nodding to him, their eyes telling Lauren they were both smiling, too.

The patient lay on his back—a small boy about Nim's age, she guessed. His right foot and lower leg were in a cast and suspended in a cradle above the bed.

Broken ankle? she wondered, watching Malik as he tickled the boy's toes to make them wiggle, talking quietly to him at the same time, before turning to speak to the women, presumably about the child's treatment.

Although the conversation was going on for some time, now it must be about her, for both women were nodding and smiling in her direction.

Lauren smiled back and waved to the little boy, who hid his face behind his hands, then waggled a couple of fingers at her as Malik ushered her out of the room.

'I was telling them you are a children's nurse,' Malik explained. 'Abu, our patient, was born with a club foot and although that would have been something he could live with in another age, we now have proper facilities and a paediatric surgeon who will fly in when necessary.'

'Did gentle stretching and a cast soon after birth not help?' Lauren asked, as she'd assisted in such manoeuvres herself.

Malik shook his head.

'We didn't meet Abu until a fortnight ago, when someone persuaded his mother to bring him here. The foot was badly deformed by then because of the way he'd been walking on it and was causing him a lot of pain.'

'Poor kid, but at least they *did* come, and it won't be something he has to put up with for the rest of his life.'

They'd reached an open area, where beds could be separated by curtains. Two young girls in pyjamas, one with a tiara on her head, were playing on the floor in one corner, an array of toys around them.

'I've been told this open ward is a mistake for Madan, but children enjoy the company of other children, and I believe that as parents get used to the idea of hospitals, there will be less insistence on being present at all times. Most of the children we've had in here are children of expats working here, and if it is a local child then you'll see the curtains drawn around the bed most of the day and night.'

'Because the women visitors can't be seen by men who aren't related?'

Malik nodded, then shook his head.

'Not that many of the men come to visit—fathers sometimes do but generally it is felt that children's illness is women's business.'

'Things aren't that much different at home,' Lauren told him. 'The fathers come because they love their children, but some of them find it very difficult to see their child sick or hurting.'

Malik nodded.

‘Already I would feel that with Nimr,’ he said, sounding as if the thought had surprised him.

They walked through two more wards, meeting nurses and doctors on the way and stopping to speak to children so Lauren could get some idea of the patients she would have.

‘And this is Graeme Stewart,’ Malik said, pausing in front of an older man. ‘I trained under Graeme in London and as he is now semi-retired, he kindly agreed to hold the fort here for me while I sort out the family business.’

Lauren smiled at the man, enjoying the still distinctive Scottish burr beneath his English voice.

‘You might be coming to work here?” he asked, and Lauren nodded.

‘As soon as I know my son is settled in and happy with his carers,’ Lauren told him.

‘I will look forward to it. I would like to see more training going on with the young enrolled nurses, and you would be a great help there.’

The flutter of excitement Lauren felt at getting back to work—of having something normal in her life—must have shown on her face, for Malik said, ‘You love it, don’t you? Nursing?’

She nodded, unable to deny it, knowing how much she’d missed it in the two years she’d spent running with baby Nim.

‘He will be safe if you wish to start immediately,’ Malik said. ‘And he seems happy outside, playing with the animals.’

‘He is,’ Lauren replied, although inside she knew she wanted more for him—some other children to join the play so he had the socialisation he’d had at kindy.

Not that she'd worry Malik with that now, when he obviously had problems of his own.

'And you?' Malik asked. 'Are you feeling settled?'

Lauren laughed.

'Hardly,' she told him. 'We've been here barely twenty-four hours, but I think when I go back to work, it will seem more normal.'

Best not to mention that any unsettled feeling she was having was to do with him more than his country.

'That is good,' he told her, 'for there is something I must explain. I spoke of our marrying within days of arriving here, but there are problems within our council of elders that must be sorted out. A question of the succession…'

He spoke so gruffly she knew the problems must be worrying him. Succession?

Wasn't she here to ensure he would have the position of regent to Nim?

Wasn't that the succession?

Should she ask him about it?

She shook away the thought. She might not have been here long, but she'd picked up some of the cultural differences in the lines drawn between men and women. If he wanted her to know, surely he would tell her…

'You must do what you have to do,' she told him, resting her hand on his shoulder. 'With the helpers you have given us, Nim and I will be fine.'

He nodded and touched her hand where it still lay on his shoulder—a thank-you kind of touch, she knew, for all it sent a cascade of shivers down her spine.

'I'll drop you home,' Malik said quietly, and although the word evoked images of the home she'd had and the life she'd led, she knew, given time, she could get used to their new 'home'. Especially once she went back to work and life began to feel normal…

* * *

Malik literally dropped Lauren at the house, feeling bad that he did no more than open the car door for her and kiss her lightly on the cheek, before heading back to the council chambers in the palace where things were in such turmoil he wondered if he really wanted the job of sorting it all out.

But apart from it being the right thing to do—taking Lauren to the hospital—he'd also *wanted* to.

Wanted to spend a little time in her calming presence, to feel her close to him, smell the lingering scent of roses in her hair.

He groaned to himself, aware there'd be less turmoil in the council if he went along with marrying a Madani woman, aware also, if he pushed through his marriage to Lauren, the decision could make life here difficult for her.

And that was the last thing he wanted, for the more he saw of her, the more he respected and admired her—loved her, even?

No way! It was attraction he was feeling, and her response to his kiss the previous evening suggested it wasn't all one-sided.

But love?

It was a concept that sat uncomfortably in his mind, for love—apart from his love for Tariq and their younger sister—hadn't featured much in his life.

Besides which, he'd lost both of them—both the people he'd loved.

Would he risk it again?

He shook his head, more to shake away the thoughts than to answer an unanswerable question.

So, back to the endless arguments, *and* back to his search through the palace occupants for the person who had killed his brother, because while that person was alive and still plotting, Nimr could be in danger.

He drew up at the palace, aware that the place where he'd grown up had changed.

Or had his own suspicion charged the atmosphere around him?

The day dragged on, with arguments and counter-arguments, the council breaking into small discussion groups—talking, talking, talking, something his people loved to do.

And all he could think about was getting back to his mother's house in time to sit with Nimr while he had his dinner, read him a bedtime story, then maybe persuade Lauren to dine with him, to spend some time alone with her, walk in the rose garden, perhaps.

Excitement stirred, and he forced his mind back to whatever discussion was currently raging around him.

'Is there trouble?' Lauren asked, seeing the lines of tiredness in Malik's face.

'I will sort it,' he said, but Lauren knew when they'd sat with Nim while he'd had dinner, then read the bedtime story together, that something had been worrying Malik.

Would he tell her?

Let her share the burden?

It was what she wanted if they were to have a real relationship—a sharing of concerns as well as joys.

And just where had the idea of a 'real' relationship come from? A few touches? A kiss?

But as she asked herself the question, she knew, for whatever reason, that was what she wanted.

'I will handle it,' he said again when she asked over dinner. 'Let's talk about Nimr. Who are these friends he spoke of?'

So he wasn't going to share, but that was okay—they were still virtual strangers, really.

Added to which, this was a very different culture from her own, and even in the short time she'd been here, she had become very aware of that.

She changed the subject, talking about Nim, hoping some general chat might help him relax.

'Keema's sister has two boys, one a year older than Nim and one a year younger. The sister brought them over to play and Nim just loved having the company, although he's turning into a show-off, acting as though the leopard cubs, and camels, and even your falcons are his.'

'Boys have their own way of levelling things out,' Malik said, smiling at some memory of his own. 'But that is good. He needs some friends and I know Keema's family.'

'Is that important?' Lauren asked. 'Will you always have to be aware of who his friends are? Is it because you think he's still in danger?'

And if Malik had looked weary when she'd first seen him, he looked exhausted now.

'My instinct—no, my belief—is that no one would openly attack a member of the royal family here in Madan. We are too revered by the people. There would be public outrage, and that is why I wanted you here, not in Australia. But until I find who harmed his father, I cannot take any chances,' he said, anger twisting through the tiredness in his voice.

Lauren waited, knowing there was more—wishing she could do something, help him in some way.

'So, until I *do* find the person behind Tariq's death, Nimr will be guarded, not by soldiers with rifles but by people who will shadow him at all times. Ordinary people in appearance—unobtrusive, but still there.'

He turned to her with a tired smile.

'Did I not promise you that?'

He sounded so stressed she was sorry she'd brought it up, so she stood up and held out her hand.

'Let's walk in the garden—forget all the bad stuff and just enjoy the peace and beauty.'

They walked in silence, arm in arm, Lauren happy to be with him, this man she was getting to know. She'd seen him as a caring professional at the hospital, had watched his gentle interaction as he eased himself into Nim's life, and read his tortured soul when he'd spoken of his brother and of the plight of his people as they entered a new age.

But as they walked the scented paths, she felt him relaxing, and when they kissed in the shadowy colonnade she knew he wasn't thinking of his country's problems, or of revenge, for his body told her of his need for physical comfort—something that had been missing from her life too in recent years.

'We are not married yet, but I *will* marry you—even if it means leaving my country to live in yours, or anywhere you choose.'

He'd interrupted her in mid-kiss so it took her a few seconds to catch on to what he was actually saying.

She drew back far enough to see his face, although their arms still linked their bodies. And although it had shaken her, she'd leave the last bit of his explanation for another time. Right now, tired and worried as he was, he needed reassurance, and something inside her wanted to give it to him.

'I don't need a promise of marriage from you to take this further, Malik. We're both adult enough to admit there's an attraction between us—our kisses have proved that—so what's to stop us finding pleasure in each other without strings, or ties, or any thought for the future?'

He kissed her again, so deeply and thoroughly Lauren

felt herself melting, sagging against his body as her body demanded more.

Lifting her effortlessly into his arms, he strode with her along the colonnade and in through filmy curtains to a room in one of the smaller suites.

A lamp glowed faintly beside a massive bed that enveloped them both as he set her down and lay with her, kissing, murmuring words she didn't understand, hands learning her body as hers learned his.

But for all they'd slowed their pace, in the end desire took control and it was a frantic coupling, both of them half-dressed, until they lay exhausted, still entwined, their bodies exchanging silent messages where skin met skin, or pulse met pulse.

'This is *not* how it should have been!' Malik muttered, what seemed like a long time later but was probably just as soon as he could breathe normally enough to speak.

'You didn't enjoy it?' Lauren teased, and he took her in his arms, turning her to lie on top of him, holding her close.

'More than I could ever say,' he murmured against her neck. 'But I must go, and Nimr will want to find you in your own bed in the morning. Shall we walk together before we part?'

It was more than a question, yet not quite entreaty. This man, she knew for certain, would never beg.

But she understood he needed her to walk with him, to normalise things once again.

'Of course,' she teased. 'However would I find my bedroom if I don't come in the front door and count the rooms I pass until I come to mine?'

He laughed and held her closer.

'You are special,' he said, and the unexpectedness of the words—not a declaration of love or even desire—warmed her body in a way she'd never felt before.

An everyday word, but it drove deep into her heart and banished the bits of uncertainty his earlier words had left behind.

And much as she longed to know what was going on in his world, she knew he was a man brought up to protect the womenfolk in his life from trouble and concerns.

Sharing these with a woman would be totally alien to him, which didn't stop her hoping that one day he might.

Malik drove back to the palace where he was staying until they could marry. Back to the discord and scheming and some people's determination he should not marry Lauren.

He'd kind of let that slip tonight when he'd spoken of marriage, but doubted she'd picked up on it. He hoped she hadn't as he didn't want to worry her. She'd already carried fear as her shadow for four years—did she not deserve some peace and security?

And how could he explain the council of elders to a newcomer anyway? Explain that while he might eventually be regent and head of the country until Nimr came of age, the elders acted more like a Western parliament with the right to make laws.

In this case a particularly divisive and inexplicable law.

But could he leave his country?

Betray his people by leaving when they needed him most?

He knew he couldn't—wouldn't—for all it would be the easiest of solutions.

So he'd have to fight, and after tonight, and a taste of what could be between Lauren and himself, how could he not?

CHAPTER SEVEN

THE MEASLES EPIDEMIC struck swiftly and viciously, five children presenting at the hospital with a rash giving warning of what was to come.

'Five in one day—how bad *is* it out there?' Malik growled at Lauren, who'd come in answer to an urgent summons, leaving Aneesha and Keema to entertain Nim.

'Has no one been vaccinated?' she asked, and saw him shake his head gloomily.

And much as she'd have loved to touch him on the arm, to offer comfort of some kind, they were at the hospital, there were people everywhere, and a touch was out of the question.

Which was probably just as well, considering how his touches distracted her.

'I did set up a vaccination programme when I first returned from my specialty four years ago, fired up with enthusiasm to save the children of my country. But my father was ailing and the elders didn't push it. I should have overseen it but, with Tariq missing and then dead, and the new hospital being built, it was all I could do to keep working at my job, let alone think of other things.'

'And the hospital staff?'

'At least they have all had every vaccination and inoculation available.'

'That's great! Can we get a good supply MMR vaccine flown in?' Lauren asked. 'If we can get enough from outside sources, we can start vaccinating now, children first, then the adults because it won't spare anyone. School children we can do at school.'

Offering practical help was better than touching, but he paled and said, 'Nimr, he's vaccinated?'

He really, really needed that touch.

She made do with a nod.

'Me too, and you should have been before you worked in a hospital. What about palace staff? The staff at your mother's house?'

'I did them myself, back when I started it.'

'So some of them can help by going out and convincing people to come. Have we staff enough to cover the actual vaccinations?'

Malik had to smile at the passion in this woman, who had leapt on the problem like a—well, tiger—and was following thought alleys he hadn't even considered.

And much as he'd have liked to drag her into the nearest broom cupboard for a quick kiss—or just a hug—he ignored the physical sensations that being near her always brought, and went with practical instead.

'I will get whatever we need. Some vaccine is on the way, but you are right. Using the media to tell people to come will not be enough, we need women talking to other women. Adults who contract it can be at more risk of complications than children.'

'And maybe we can designate a space in a ward for the vaccinations or—'

She stopped and looked up at him.

'Would they come to your mother's place? We could do

it in the garden—in the colonnade—so the children could play outside while parents waited in line.'

'And we'd be keeping them well away from the hospital where the infection could easily be spread.'

He smiled at her, so aware of her it was a wonder she couldn't feel the heat.

'It will be an added incentive—visiting a big house and a garden. All people are curious.'

And Lauren, when she had time to think about it, had been amazed at just how quickly her idea turned into reality. Refrigerators were set up to hold the vaccine, experienced nurses brought in to administer it, house staff set to keeping order in the queues while others went out to markets and meeting places to hand out information and talk to families, both offering vaccinations for the well and explaining how to care for the sick, with plenty of fluids and bed rest until the rash began to disappear.

But that was happening in a different world, for at the hospital both children and adults with serious complications had been admitted, and the staff, Lauren included, were run off their feet caring for the influx of patients.

She saw Malik most days, though often he was there when she was snatching some sleep in the nurses' quarters at the back of the building while he took on the night duty. At least Nim was safe and happy, and over the last two years had become used to her odd hours. Sometimes, when she'd been on duty at home—especially on split shifts—she'd caught only glimpses of him for a few days, but had made it up to him on her days off.

Graeme was a constant daytime presence on the wards, dispensing both drugs and advice. The most common problems were flu-like symptoms and high fevers, although many of the children also suffered from sore eyes.

Their most complicated case was a young girl who'd had seizures brought on by her fever, and though she was stabilised, she was listless and pale—uncomplaining but far from well.

'Let's take some blood, there has to be something else going on,' Malik suggested, on a rare day he'd appeared on the ward while she was there.

And simply standing beside him as they looked at the child was enough to keep Lauren going.

'Encephalitis,' she said, remembering a list she'd read of possible complications. About one in a hundred children could contract pneumonia and one in a thousand encephalitis. 'Can we do a spinal tap for some cerebrospinal fluid?'

Malik nodded.

'I'll speak to her parents, get a brain scan too, to check for swelling, not that there is much we can do—although anti-viral medicines and immuno-suppressants might help.'

He moved towards the door of the darkened room, the blinds drawn to protect the child's eyes, then turned back to Lauren, who was checking on the bag that dripped fluid into the sick girl.

'I don't know how I would cope if it was Nimr,' he said, and the gruffness in his voice told Lauren just how deeply his feelings were for his new-found nephew.

'Nim will be fine,' she told him, keeping the arms she wanted to put around him firmly by her side. 'So let's get these other kids better.'

But as more people were answering repeated radio and television broadcasts to be vaccinated, the situation at the house became overwhelming. More vaccine was flown in, and Lauren, aware the children's hospital was managing—just—turned her attention to vaccination.

With Aneesha beside her to translate when necessary, she joined the nurses at the house, reforming the system so they had three orderly queues—women with children, men with children and adults on their own.

'In a story, romance could blossom in the adults' queue,' she said to Aneesha as they took a break on the edge of the fountain, eating watermelon from a tray, replenished often and left on a bed of ice, for everyone to help themselves.

'Is it my imagination of are there more children here than earlier?' she asked, and Aneesha smiled.

'Those at school come when it finishes at one o'clock. They want to play with Nimr in the garden.'

'Girls and boys?' Lauren asked as she peered at the children dancing along the garden paths, seeking the head of one she knew.

Aneesha smiled.

'At this age they are just children and it is good for them to play together. Your Nimr is a leader, see him there…' She pointed to the far corner where some kind of fort seemed to have appeared. 'He organised that old building into a pretend castle—I think a castle, although sometimes it is a spaceship. While I am with you, Keema watches from afar, while other staff are always nearby.'

Lauren closed her eyes, thinking how little she knew of her son's life these days. They still had their morning cuddles when he filled her in on what he'd been up to and most days she was home from work in time to sit with him at dinner—Malik joining them when he could—but it had been a shift in the level of their togetherness.

Her baby was growing up…

And perhaps that was a good thing, she decided as she faced the world again, finishing her watermelon and turning to wash her hands in the clear waters of the fountain.

As dusk fell, the queues didn't seem to have diminished.

'You've done enough,' she told Aneesha. 'Have a break,

I'll manage, but when you're ready, would you round up Nim and get him fed and into bed?'

'I shall not have to round him up, as you say,' Aneesha told her, 'for here he is.'

Two equally grubby boys had appeared from the garden, Nim beaming as he led his new, and apparently very shy, friend towards Lauren.

'Mum, this is my friend Najeeb, and he's four but he goes to school. Can I go to school too—please, Mum, please.'

His eyes were big with entreaty—this member of the ruling family wasn't afraid to beg.

'I'll find out about it,' she promised him. 'But now you're too dirty to be here where people are having their injections, so around the back with you. Aneesha will give you a bath and your dinner. I'll be in to say goodnight but these people need me right now.'

'That's okay, Mum. Najeeb's little sister is sick, and I know you're trying to stop other people getting it. Najeeb had his injection yesterday, that's when I met him.'

'And his mother or father? Who is with him?'

'His big sister. She's still in the queue.'

'Then let us find her,' Aneesha said. 'I will tell her I'll take you both for a bath and where she can come to eat with us.'

'Maybe find her and send her to me,' Lauren said. 'A little queue-jumping doesn't hurt once in a while, and I wouldn't want her becoming anxious for her brother.'

But the sister, when produced, was far from worried.

'I speak good English so I can help while Aneesha takes the boys,' she said. 'I want to be a nurse, and when I finish school I hope to start at the hospital for some training.'

Aware that many of the nurses she'd met had been

abroad for training, Lauren, in between patients, asked if that had been an option.

She shook her head.

'My father left and my mother has died. I must care for Najeeb until he comes of age.'

Lauren nodded. These things happened everywhere, she knew, but her heart ached for the girl who'd taken on such a burden.

By ten that night, they'd cleared the palace grounds of people wanting vaccinations and those who, Lauren suspected, simply came to look around. The girl and Najeeb had both been fed and sent home in a car, and as the servants cleaned up the debris of the day, Lauren took herself wearily to her rooms to shower and clamber into bed, ignoring the plate of pastries Keema brought for her, and the coffee, although she had to admit it had kept her going through the day.

The following day was not as bad, and two days later they could shut the gates, anyone still wanting vaccination told to report to the hospital.

Lauren was up and aware that she, too, should be heading to the hospital, *wanting* to be heading to the hospital, if only to see Malik.

Silly, really, how much she'd been missing him—how much her body had been missing him—and this after just one brief sexual encounter, a kiss or two, and touches that sent fire along her nerves.

She should be thinking about Nim, not Malik.

He was fixated on the school idea, and although she knew she'd have to discuss it with Malik, Lauren decided she could at least take a look.

'Is it far?' she asked Aneesha, who had offered her services again as translator, while Keema played with Nim.

'Not far,' was the reply, so they set out on foot, walking

for what seemed like miles to Lauren, with the sun growing perceptibly hotter as they went.

'I thought you said not far,' she complained to Aneesha. 'I thought that meant it was just around the corner. We should have brought water—no, we should have called a car.'

She knew she sounded cross and apologised, trudging on in the oppressive heat.

Malik picked them up as Lauren was certain she was about to die in the dry, desert heat, helping her into the soft leather seat in the front, where the air-conditioning washed around her like a cold shower.

'Why didn't you call for a car?' he demanded crossly. 'Only total idiots walk around in this heat! And where the hell did you think you were going?'

Lauren breathed in a little more cool air before answering.

'To a school, to check it out for Nim, but I think it will be too far for him to walk at his age, and I was only going to look, so I could talk to you about it.'

He'd handed her a bottle of cold water, and she stopped her explanations to drink thirstily.

'He has wanted to go to school for so long and it will be better for him to be with other children, instead of hanging around being spoilt by the servants.'

And having explained this, Lauren lay back in the, oh, so comfortable seat, then turned to check that Aneesha was still with her and had some water.

But Malik had also turned to Aneesha, who was now answering his questions.

'Forget that school, there are better ones, and I will sort one out for Nimr. Right now, I'll take you home,' he muttered to Lauren when the conversation finished. In spite of Aneesha's explanations, or perhaps because of them, he was still obviously angry.

'But his friend is at that school, we should at least look at it,' Lauren argued.

'Not when you're exhausted. Walking in the sun was madness, especially when you need to rest. You've been working practically non-stop for days, and I can't be there right now to keep an eye on you—there is just too much going on. I'll drive you straight home!'

Lauren straightened in her seat, fastened her seatbelt and said, '*After* we've seen the school. Nim is *my* child and I don't need you "sorting" his school!'

She was aware they shouldn't be having this argument in front of Aneesha but right now she was too tired to care.

'Anyway,' she continued, giving him no time for another objection, 'this is so much better, seeing it together. We'll be able to discuss it properly.'

Malik spoke to Aneesha again and with a sound that just might have been his teeth grinding took off along the road they'd been following.

The school was everything Lauren could have hoped for—a mix of local and expat children, most lessons in the native language, although English was also taught.

'He won't understand his lessons,' Malik grumbled.

'He's four—they're hardly doing algebra. It's more play learning, socialising, interaction with each other at that age. These things are important, Malik. Important to him, and important to me.'

To her astonishment, he looked at her and smiled, his anger gone.

Because she'd said it was important to her?

And although she could see he was exhausted, the smile he gave her as he agreed was warm enough to lift her spirits, to the extent that when they returned to the house she suggested they drop Aneesha off.

'I'll come back to the hospital with you. There'll be something I can do.'

He hesitated, then shook his head.

'I suppose if I don't take you, you'll set off on foot again.'

Lauren laughed.

'Oh, no, that's one lesson I *have* learned. I won't walk anywhere on these hot days.'

And just like that camaraderie between them returned, and beneath it, even in their less than upbeat state, hummed the attraction…

CHAPTER EIGHT

New cases of measles continued to come in to the hospital, the vaccinations taking time to work, and the airborne virus seemingly able to strike at will. But now Nim was going happily off to school each day, being at work where she was needed was a kind of antidote to this new stage of his life.

'Keema tells me there's a huge market not far from the hotels,' Lauren said, catching up with Malik in the hospital where she was still spending most mornings.

He'd looked surprised to see her, yet his tired face had softened into a smile.

'So?'

'I'm thinking those people might not have access to radio or television and aren't aware of the risks in crowds of people. Can we close it?' she asked.

'That market is the hub of the city. Closing it would be unthinkable.'

'So more people will get sick,' Lauren said. 'How fair is that? And look at you—when did you last sleep? You can't go on like this, you'll be ill yourself. I know the hospital is still coping with all the usual cases as well as the measles outbreak, but you need a break.'

His smile grew wider, glinting in his eyes.

'And is this the nagging wife I'll have if we marry?"

he teased, and she laughed, that glint in his eyes bringing her body to life with the usual rush of sensations just being near him could produce.

'I'll be far worse than this!' she told him. 'Now go and rest!'

But as he walked away she added, 'And close the market!'

But later, back in the children's hospital where the little girl had had the diagnosis of encephalitis confirmed, she paused by the child's bed, checking the fluid bag, the cannula, reading through the chart and thinking, in another corner of her mind, about the word Malik had dropped into their earlier conversation.

That tiny but, oh, so powerful word: *if...*

He's tired, it just sounded wrong, she assured herself, but still it jangled.

Was it a warning bell?

Maybe, but why was it worrying her? She hadn't been keen on the marriage idea from the start—*and* had told Malik he needn't promise marriage to act on their shared attraction.

So why worry now over one little *if*?

Because you're falling for him, that's why, she told herself. *The attraction was there from that first meeting, you know that, and in your head you've really grown to like the idea of marrying him...*

The medical situation eventually eased, although Malik was caught up with ensuring a regular vaccination program was set up, covering all the preventable diseases.

He'd call in at dinnertime to say hello to Nim, but as many of the people he had to speak to were in different time zones, he rarely stayed.

'I need vaccines but also places to store them safely,'

he said to Lauren, when they met in the staffroom at the children's hospital one morning. 'And staff to look after the storage facilities as well as trained staff to administer the drugs.'

'And no doubt another level of administrators at the top, to work out programmes and see they are carried out.'

He nodded grimly.

'Not to mention a committee of community leaders to advise people to take up the service for their own, and their children's, safety.

'All the things a health department does,' Lauren teased, and he agreed.

'We have gone past the time when a group of elders could handle all aspects of our people's private lives. We need to find some form of government acceptable to our people. Up until now, we've had the elders each tasked with a different job—one overlooking road construction, one liaising with the oil people, another in charge of schools, health and welfare, and so on. But with the nation growing at an unprecedented rate, these things must be formalised, and administrations put in place.'

'And you're the one who has to do it? Organise all this?'

She'd made coffee and found honey cake as he talked, and now she poured him a cup and eased him into a chair.

'Here, forget it all for a few minutes, just relax.'

She set the coffee beside him on a small table, and as she turned to get the cake, he caught her hand, held it, the look on his face telling her he had needed that touch as much as she had.

'I could not have done this without you,' he said, and, embarrassed at the rush of feeling she'd experienced, she laughed.

'Of course you could. You might have ended up even more tired than you are, though I doubt that's possible, but I've done nothing more than any nurse would do. And we've got through it, haven't we?'

She eased her hand from his for all she'd have liked to leave it there—warm and safe. 'And as for all this admin stuff, that will get done in time—it doesn't need to be done tomorrow, you know.'

He looked at her now, shadows in his dark eyes.

Was it tiredness?

Or something else?

She had no idea, but she had to drink her coffee and leave this room before she sat down on his knee and put her arms around him and told him everything would be all right.

Even though, since that little 'if' had entered her life she wasn't sure it would be.

And now it was at work she mostly saw him. With Nim happy at his school, she was working regular shifts, and although Graeme and a young registrar handled the doctors' duties, Malik appeared from time to time, usually inveigling her away to the staffroom so he could sit and spend a few minutes with her.

But this seeing and not touching grew harder with every visit, and her uncertainty about the future threw a shadow on the happiness that being with him here in Madan had so unexpectedly brought her.

Nim was happy, friends coming to play, chattering away in both languages with almost equal fluency. And her? Well, she certainly enjoyed her work in the fairy castle, enjoyed seeing children's faces light up as she came in, and loved the shy greetings from the mothers and aunts and grandmas usually in attendance on the sick children.

Even the fathers, and other male visitors, were accepting of her—perhaps seeing her uniform of loose trousers, tunic and cap as the armour she'd once fancied her uniform at home had been.

Not that it had worked against Malik.

And as if thinking his name had conjured his presence, suddenly he was there, in front of her.

'Come,' he said. 'I have caught up on my sleep, have begged Graeme to spare you to me, and I am taking you up the mountains. I have been a most remiss host, showing you nothing of my country, just setting you to work practically from the time you arrived.'

'And Nim, is he coming?'

'Not today, for this afternoon his class is coming to see the leopard cubs and his excitement—well, he will tell you.'

He paused, then added, 'He will be quite safe, you must believe that.'

And Lauren did, for she knew there were trusted men posted at the school to keep an eye on him, and within the walls of the big estate he would be carefully but unobtrusively watched. Had known too about the class visit to their house but had forgotten, as she did most things, when Malik had appeared.

She smiled at this man who had taken so much worry off her shoulders and brought her to this magical place. Yes, things had been hectic, and marriage seemed no closer, but the rare time they did spend together was—precious?

Certainly, it was drawing them closer, and as far as Lauren was concerned, yes, precious *was* the right word.

Forget the 'if' and live for the moment—go see the mountains.

'I'll just have a wash and be right with you,' she said, and darted off, wishing she'd had the forethought to bring a prettier outfit to the hospital just in case an occasion like this should arise.

But she washed her face and brushed her hair, noticing the curly mop longer now, framing her face more, tickling her neck.

I must ask Keema about getting it cut, she thought as she walked back to Malik, because thinking about mundane things was steadying the dizzy feeling of excitement in her chest.

She was so lovely, Malik thought, glancing at her when he could while she looked out the window, delighting in all she saw. Goats and camels mostly, until they left the fertile land around the oasis and began to climb the mountains.

'All our land was mountains once,' he told her, 'until wind and rain over thousands of years reduced the stone to sand. Only the strongest rock remained, but it too will one day disappear.'

The road wound upwards, Lauren still intent on the scenery, until he pulled up in the parking area at the top and she could look around, mostly at the vast sky above them and…

'An ocean of desert, the dunes the waves, stretching for ever…' she murmured.

The wonder in her voice touched something in his heart, but rather than bring him joy it caused an ache deep inside him.

How could he not have guessed that whoever it was who'd wanted Tariq dead would not also plot to thwart his plans for marriage?

Because that was what was happening. The whole 'marrying a Madani woman' thing the elders were debating hadn't just arisen out of nowhere. Their rulers had been marrying people from other tribes and nations right down through the generations, yet now when he wanted—really wanted—to marry Lauren, they were bringing in the new law.

He opened the car door and helped her out, putting his arm around her shoulders, leading her to the low wall surrounding the lookout.

'Oh, there's the oasis right beneath us,' she said, delight in her voice. 'And the hospital—the fairy castle, too—and way over there, glinting in the sun, all the big hotels waiting for their tourists.'

He laughed and pulled her closer, his body reacting to her closeness, wanting her, all of her, but this was hardly the place to be starting something they couldn't finish—hardly the place to be caught kissing in public should someone else arrive to see the view. Madan might be crawling towards modernisation, but public displays of affection?

The Madanis weren't ready for that yet.

'But tourists *should* come,' she said, easing away so she could look at him—following her conversation, not his thoughts. 'Because even the little I've seen of it is beautiful and special. Special interest tourism perhaps, so groups come to learn about the culture, and the people who have lived here since the days of the Silk Road. There's history here, and beauty, things beyond fast-food outlets and fancy hotels.'

Forget someone coming to see the view and local customs. Forget showing public displays of affection. The words she'd just spoken told him she was beginning to understand his homeland—maybe even beginning to love it.

And his joy was so great, how could he not think to hell with protocol and draw her into his arms, this wise woman he so wanted to be his? He kissed her, gently at first, a thank-you-for-those-words kiss, then he kissed her with his heart involved, trying to tell her how he felt—how much he—

Loved?

The word had certainly been there in his thoughts but he pushed it away, substituting wanted her, no matter the obstacles being put in the way.

Could he talk to her about it?

Explain?

But she had given up her old life for him—coming with him to Madan. How could he bother her with the shenanigans going on at the palace?

And was that really his reason for staying silent, for dealing with it on his own? Or was it the centuries of Madani blood in his veins that decreed such things were the business of the man of the family?

He had been educated in the Western world and believed in the equality of men and women, but that inbred Madani pride kept him from burdening her with problems that he, alone, could solve…

For Lauren, the kiss warmed all the places the 'if' had turned cold, and fired the senses Malik so easily aroused, but they were in a public place so they broke apart and walked around the outlook side by side, decorum keeping them a few inches apart.

But sensuality could zap across a few inches and her body ached for him.

He took her home after their brief tryst, and stayed to cat cakes with Nim and his friends from school, a picnic laid out by the kitchen staff on mats in the shade of a large apricot tree.

The children chattered around him, and Nim grew noticeably straighter and taller as his uncle, as he knew him, sat beside him.

And when the feasting finished, while Nim said farewell to his friends, Lauren walked with Malik back to his car.

'There is more than your concern about the state of your nation worrying you,' she said quietly, and he looked at her and smiled.

'I will work it out,' he said. 'I would speak of it if I could, but it is not our way, but I *will* work it out!

He kissed her swiftly on the lips.

'Trust me on that!' he said, and she found herself believing him.

Then he was gone and she could only wait, wondering how long it would be before she would see him again, how long before they could kiss again, make love again—slowly this time—enjoying the discovery of each other, skin on skin.

She shivered as desire coursed through her. It was probably better if they didn't kiss again—not until everything was sorted and they could be together properly…

For ever?

Right now, for ever didn't matter, though she longed for that with all her heart. But even a part-time relationship with Malik would be better than none at all.

Was this love?

Was this how Lily had felt about Tariq?

Had a kiss made her bones melt?

A touch send fire through her body?

At the hospital, with the measles epidemic waning, Lauren was now on regular shifts, and although previously she'd been called to wherever she was needed most in either of the hospitals, she was now back where she felt she belonged, nursing children.

The little girl with encephalitis was off her drip and

recovering slowly, but because she needed to be kept quiet for a few weeks, she was still in the hospital. The lad with the club foot was allowed home, his ankle and lower leg still in a cast so he moved, with surprising speed, on small crutches. The other children she'd met on her first visit had mostly been discharged.

Lauren, who even in the children's hospital was moved around, was on duty in the emergency department—depleted of a number of staff because of the overtime everyone had worked during the measles epidemic.

She wasn't even sure she had someone who spoke English to interpret for her, and, as her own lessons had been interrupted while they'd been so busy, she was worrying about this when a group of people, young and old, came in. She was used to the locals and their manner of dress—the women usually in the loose trousers and tunics, scarves around their heads, while the men wore much the same, only their trousers would be striped and their headgear a cap or intricately wound turban of some kind.

But this group were bright with colour, the women in flaring skirts of purple and orange, pretty blouses on the top, the men in the striped trousers but with bright jackets of red, or blue, or orange, while the barefooted children, pressed shyly against the adults' legs, all wore simple tunics in the striped material of the men's trousers.

As Lauren moved towards them, one of the men stepped forward and said something she didn't understand, but it was clear from his gestures he wanted to see someone else.

Graeme had been here long enough to know the language, but he was having some much-needed time off so Lauren gestured to one of the aides to speak to the group.

The aide spoke to a man who held a young child in his arms, the limpness of the little body suggesting he or she was far from well. Then, with the man in the lead, the group followed the aide to a cubicle, Lauren tagging along behind, aware she'd have to be the one to examine the child.

The child, a girl Lauren discovered when she pushed her way to the front of the group, lay on an examination couch, the man guarding her, the others still clustered around.

'They have to go,' Lauren said to the aide, waving her arms in a shooing motion and wishing she knew more local words, wishing she was a faster learner.

The aide proved her worth, although the protests were voluble enough for Lauren to know they objected to being pushed out.

The aide returned and together they removed the child's tunic. She was so hot to the touch Lauren knew drugs alone wouldn't reduce her temperature, so she mimed washing down the child while she dissolved some dispersible aspirin in water, drew it up into a syringe, and eased it into the child's mouth, sitting her up a little so she could swallow.

'We must cool her,' she said to the father as they worked, and wondered if the aide knew enough English to translate, for she was saying something to the man.

'Now I look at her throat,' Lauren said, opening her own mouth and pointing to the back of it. She lifted a spatula to hold down the tongue and shone a small torch into the mouth.

The tell-tale inflammation of the tonsils and white spots at the back of the throat suggested an infection and for the child to be so ill, a streptococcus infection was a good bet, but Lauren took a swab for testing to be sure.

She checked the girl's ears, but there was no apparent problem there, and all the while her mind worried around one word, penicillin.

Would the man—presumably her father—know if she

was allergic to it? The chances were she'd never had it, so no one would know.

But penicillin was the most effective treatment for strep bacteria, which might already be causing inflammation throughout the girl's body, particularly in the joints.

She left the aide sponging the girl down and went in search of the young registrar.

'So what do you think?' she asked him when she'd explained the dilemma.

'Phone Dr Madani,' was his reply, and Lauren couldn't blame the young man. He was only on a rotation through the children's ED, and probably had little hands-on experience with children.

Dr Madani's phone number was readily available, yet Lauren was reluctant to call. He knew her as a capable paediatric nurse—would he expect her to handle it?

And what matter of government business might he be involved in that she'd be interrupting?

Taking up his time when he'd already spent so much time at the hospital.

She phoned Dr Madani.

'Lauren, you are all right? Nimr?'

Wasted minutes with assurances, trying to brush away his concern so she could ask about the child.

'There's no one here to interpret,' she explained to him. 'I know she has a fever and what looks like a strep throat, but I'm wondering about using penicillin. I also need to know how she's feeling—if her joints are aching, that kind of thing.'

'Put the father on the phone,' Malik said, and Lauren sighed with relief, although deep inside she knew this wasn't good enough. She *had* to make more effort to learn the language—and practise more—in order to truly help these people.

But she passed the phone to the father, waited while Malik spoke to him, then the father handed back the phone.

'Were you thinking rheumatic fever?' he asked, and Lauren nodded, then realised she needed to speak and said yes.

'Go with the penicillin. Her joints *are* hurting, but admit her and we'll think about steroids for her joints when we see how she's doing. Keep up the aspirin until her temperature comes down, and, Lauren…'

He paused and she waited.

'They are tribal people, nomads, and it will be hard for them to understand she has to stay in hospital. I have told the father, but the two people only with the child policy isn't going to work.'

Lauren thanked him and pocketed her phone. She drew up penicillin and, explaining as best she could, injected it into the child. She started a drip to keep fluid levels up, and wrote up the instructions on the chart that would go with the child to the ward.

But when it came time to transfer the girl, she went along with the orderly, wanting to make sure she would be settled in a room so her family could stay with her.

'It's impossible,' Kate, the sister on duty in the ward, grumbled at her. Kate was South African, and was working here as part of a working holiday that would take her around the world, pausing here because she was now engaged to an American oil man. 'The family will give her whatever remedies they think will make her better.'

'If they've been doing it down through many generations, whatever they give her probably won't make her worse,' Lauren said. 'At least they've accepted that whatever they usually use hasn't worked because here she is in hospital.'

Kate continued to mutter under her breath, but Lauren

knew she'd see the girl was well looked after. But Malik had been right, there were at least eight people in the room with the patient, and that wasn't counting a tiny baby, hidden in a sling under one of the women's robes.

Her shift ended slightly later than it should have, and, knowing Nim would already be in bed, she went back to the ward to check on the young girl.

To her surprise, the crowd in the room had cleared, although the man she'd taken for the father remained there, sitting cross-legged on the floor, his back against the wall, his dark eyes constantly moving about the room as if some danger might lurk near his child.

'Has he eaten anything?' she asked the nurse who came in to check the drip.

'Not a thing,' she said, 'although we offered him some food.'

'But not food he would like,' a deep voice said, and Malik appeared in the doorway.

He spoke briefly to the man, who replied at far greater length, then apparently started to argue with Malik.

Lauren let it go on for a minute, but as their voices rose, she pointed to the child and ushered them both towards the door.

All this for a meal?

Finally, the voices stopped and Malik re-entered the room.

'He is particular about what he eats and his wife will have prepared his meal, but he felt he could not leave his child.'

Lauren caught on at once, and shook her head.

'So you have offered to stay with her while he eats?' she guessed. 'In spite of the fact you've hardly slept in more than a week, and are probably in need of feeding yourself!'

He smiled at her and shook his head.

'But you are also here,' he said, 'and that, for me right now, is more than food or sleep.'

Lauren could only smile and shake her head, the beauty of the meaning of the words flooding warmth into her innermost being—into her very soul…

And if the 'if,' whatever it might be, happened or didn't happen, she'd always have those words tucked into her heart to warm lonely nights and bring cheer on hectic days…

CHAPTER NINE

WITH THE MAN GONE, Malik examined the little girl, gently pressing on her knees and ankles, searching for signs of swelling.

He was reaching for the chart when Lauren said quietly, ‘I’ve sent a swab from her throat to the lab and asked for it to be put through as soon as possible, and I’ve booked her for Radiology tomorrow.’

She grinned at him.

‘So it’s a good thing you’re here so you can explain those things to the father when he comes back and he doesn’t think we’re kidnapping her when we take her across to the old hospital. I’ve asked for chest X-rays to check her heart and lungs, and an ECG in case it’s already affecting her heart.’

‘You don’t need me, then,’ Malik teased, because he wanted to see her smile again.

‘Oh, we definitely need you when it comes to explanations. I’ve come across men at home who’d prefer a man told them what was happening with their child because there are still men who think another man will know better, but this man? I couldn’t tell him the sun would rise in the morning, because even if I spoke the language he wouldn’t believe me.’

Malik reached out and touched her shoulder, wishing he could hold her, willing himself not to.

'That man and all the men that came before him *had* to be head of the family. Our people have always been aware of danger. And when there's danger, there must be a leader—one person who tells the others what to do so you don't get panic and mayhem. It is how they have always lived. How *we* have always lived.'

'And because there's been no one ruler since your father died, what you have now is panic and mayhem?' Lauren said.

'Total chaos,' he answered, and thought maybe he could take her in his arms, hold her for just an instant, but before he could move the door opened and the man returned, accompanied by an older woman.

The child's grandmother?

Malik explained about the tests they would do in the morning, about having to take the little girl through the corridor between the hospitals, and, yes, he could go with her.

'Are you off duty?' he asked Lauren, thinking even if she wasn't he'd find someone to replace her. He couldn't just walk away from her now he'd seen her.

'An hour ago,' she told him with a smile, and he touched her hand, just fleetingly, as they walked together to the desk for her to sign out.

'Then we shall go and eat,' he announced. 'We will go to the market—which, yes, I did close, but it has since reopened—and we will eat as our nomad friend will have eaten tonight. You and Nimr, because my mother fancied food of other countries and her kitchen staff reflect that in what they serve, haven't tasted many of our dishes.'

'You'd be better off grabbing a sandwich—which your

mother's staff do very well—and getting some sleep,' she said, concern for him evident in her eyes.

'I will sleep when we have eaten,' he promised. 'I will even send for another car to take you home, so I am not tempted to do other than sleep should I go first to your place.'

But as they were now in the shadowy dark of the car park he could put his arm around her shoulders and draw her close, feeling her body warm against his, feeling his own respond predictably.

He sighed.

This was not how it should be. They should be married by now, and he'd be taking his excitement home and bedding her—touching her, teasing her, learning what she liked, and what made her cry out—

Al'ama! What was he thinking?

He clicked open the car and opened the door for her, careful now not to touch her lest it inflame already overheated desires.

But to take her now—to lie with her at the house again, not married to him—would bring shame on her and, by implication, on Nimr. To do it once was bad enough and although the memory of that brief encounter was burned into his very bones so he ached whenever they were together, he would not, could not, repeat it.

His staff might be loyal, but gossip was the lifeblood of his people. He would not have her the subject of that, would not have her talked about in the market.

It had happened, yes—that heated, irresistible evening—but no more until they were married, and if that meant avoiding opportunities to be alone with her, then that was what he must do.

So why are you taking her to dinner?

He ignored the question that had whispered in his head, because he knew the answer.

He *needed* to be with her, needed it like he needed air to breathe and water to drink.

And he *was* rationing their contact, trying to see as little as possible of her.

He sighed as he slid behind the wheel, and she reached out and touched his knee.

'Is it so very hard, sorting out the problems you have at the palace?'

He rested his hand on hers, squeezed her fingers and turned towards her, tucking a wayward curl behind her delicate ear.

'Not nearly as hard as sorting out how I can be with you and not have you in my arms. Not holding you, making love to you, sharing talk, and love, and laughter with you.'

She returned the pressure on his fingers and said, 'You could always walk away, come back to Australia, live with us there as a normal family.'

He was wondering whether that could be a realistic option, when she leaned across and kissed him softly on the cheek.

'But I know you wouldn't,' she said softly. 'Back when we first met, you told me of the things you desperately wanted to achieve for your country. It was the reason you gave to need Nim back here in Madan. I heard the passion in your voice as you spoke of your plans, and it stirred something inside me.'

She touched her fingers to his cheek, his lips.

'To leave, to walk away from those dreams and aspirations, you wouldn't be that man who spoke with such passion of his people and their needs. You wouldn't be the man I've come to know so well and, I think, to love. So we stay, and pretend, and surely, one day, things will work out and we can be properly together.'

'A normal family,' he repeated, his voice gruff as a rarely felt emotion had tightened his throat as she'd told him of her love…

The markets were alive with lights, colour and music. Booths pushed against each other, selling everything from hair shampoo to enormous silver urns and vases, with clothing, car tyres, toys and radios in between.

'It's mad,' Lauren murmured, staying close to Malik as she feared she'd never find him in the crush should they be separated.

'Through this way,' he said, and steered her down a side alley to where the businesses were more substantial, tucked into the ground floor of buildings so they had doors that could be shut at night, if night actually closed the markets down.

Another alley then into a building and through a dark corridor that opened into a magnificent courtyard.

'I cannot believe that this is hidden away in here, in the midst of the madness that is the markets.'

'Most of the houses are like this, nothing but a building on the outside, but inside—'

He waved his hand to indicate the scene in front of them, the floor and walls bright with glazed tiles set in patterns as intricate as the carpets they walked on at the house, the potted palms and other small trees tucked here and there, the small fountain against one wall, and bright orange, and purple, and green cushions, large enough to lounge on, scattered here and there.

'There are tables if you'd rather,' Malik said, but seeing the small groups of people sitting on the cushions, each area made a little private by the potted plants, she opted for a cushion and they sat, Malik speaking to the woman who had greeted them.

'You will let me choose?' he said to Lauren, who smiled and nodded, still captivated by the beauty of the courtyard inside what had looked like a very drab exterior.

The woman returned to spread a mat, which looked far too beautifully woven to serve as a tablecloth, between them, then set down a silver jug, the outside frosted with beads of condensation, promising something cold inside.

She poured drinks, pale pink in colour and tangy with lemon, though the other ingredients Lauren could only guess at.

They raised their glasses in a toast, though to what she didn't want to think. It was enough to be with Malik, to sit a while, and eat and drink, and not worry about what might lie ahead.

Whatever happened, she knew that Nim was safe, and just knowing that had freed so much of the tension inside her that the future held no terrors.

Small nibbly things appeared—roasted nuts, dates, of course, but filled with a kind of soft cheese, olives, warmed in oil and lemon, flavoured with herbs that, again, she didn't know, and tiny, spicy meatballs, with delicious, cool yoghurt to dip them in.

'I've had to try everything and won't be able to eat anything else,' she told him, and he smiled.

'I think you will, when it arrives.'

Someone cleared away the dishes on the mat before the first woman returned with a strange-shaped earthenware dish and a bowl of couscous—pearl couscous Lauren remembered it was called—the bigger version. Pomegranate seeds and thin slices of preserved lemon skin decorated the top of the couscous, but as the woman lifted the lid of the other dish, the aroma of a very special meal had Lauren forgetting anything else.

There must be spices in it she didn't know, but she recognised saffron, and something sweeter.

'Try a little,' Malik suggested, putting a spoonful of couscous on her plate as the woman put a small amount of the stew—the only name Lauren had for it—with it.

She tried it, breathing in the spice-filled aroma. The meat was tender and delicious—lamb?—but with dried apricots, softened by long cooking, and tiny sultanas, carrot chunks, and another vegetable that Lauren couldn't name.

'It's delicious,' she said, passing her plate back to the woman's waiting hand, watching as she piled it high, holding up her hand so it didn't get even higher.

Malik was served, although Lauren imagined he would normally be served first, and together they ate, silent at first as they revelled in the exotic food.

But as appetite was satisfied they slowed, and talked, of food and the hospital and Malik's plans to get better education out to the far reaches of Madan, to build a university to train teachers and nurses and doctors.

'Shall we walk a little?' Malik suggested, when they'd finished their meal with a tiny cup of coffee.

He led her further into the market until they came out into the open, close by the darkness of the oasis, moonlight reflecting the palm grove in the still waters.

And hand in hand they wandered into the welcoming shadows beneath the thick-topped palms, the sweet smell of ripening dates filling the air with an intoxicating perfume.

And where a tiny trail led closer to the water, Malik took her in his arms and held her.

At first content to be close, Lauren's body remembering his, heating at the memory, until, inevitably, they were kissing, desperate kisses that told of yearning and frustration.

They held each other tightly, bound by their attraction.

Love?

But though she might not know details—would he ever share his concerns with her? See her as a full partner in their relationship?—she knew there were forces around them who could put an end to Malik's plans for his country, his hopes and dreams for Madan.

'I will sort it soon,' he promised when they eased apart, then kissed again because how could they not?

They walked back to the car, not through the markets but through the date palms, pausing now and then to kiss—to be together. But when they reached the car, Lauren's mind turned back to work.

'We should give the girl and all her family the measles vaccine. We're still getting a few cases,' she said, and Malik laughed.

'What's so funny?' she demanded.

'My mind is still on you—on kisses—and you? You're thinking work!'

'I was thinking there could still be some infection around and those people will be vulnerable, the young girl particularly so. Would it hurt to give her the vaccination while she's already fighting off the staph infection? Her body will see the vaccine as a further invasion and might fight it.'

Malik forgot about discretion and gave her a hug.

'Yes, we'll vaccinate the family, and the girl too, but as you say, not yet. And I'll find out from the leader where other tribes might be. They all come into the city from time to time, so they should all be protected, preferably before they arrive. How to do it is something I've been puzzling over, but with the need right now, I'll figure something out.'

He spoke lightly, but the idea excited him, for it had thrown up possibilities he hadn't considered.

He was getting nothing but frustration from the council, and the trade route the nomads still travelled was close to the lodge he had built when they had been setting the first of the young leopards free in their natural habitat.

He wouldn't leave until they had the results of the tests on the young girl and had stabilised her, but after that…

'I'll arrange vaccinations for the family and track down where some of the other nomadic tribes might be. They are very regular in their travel so we should be able to go out to the camps and vaccinate them before they get too close to town.'

He walked beside her to the car, his mind racing and excitement burning in his body. He would leave his two most trusted men with Nimr, let the housekeepers who lived at his lodge know that they were coming so they could open up the lodge and get in food.

Should he tell Lauren of his plans?

He shook his head at the thought. He'd already brought her here with a promise of marriage that, up until now, he'd been unable to keep, and in the current warring climate in the palace, who knew what might arise to thwart that plan.

So he hugged his excitement to himself, although as he kissed her goodnight in the shadows of the colonnade, he hoped his kiss told her of his feelings, if not his plans…

CHAPTER TEN

WITH YET ANOTHER meeting of the council of elders set down for ten days' time, Malik made his plans. He had loyal men who would lobby council members while he was away, and already he had close to a majority to vote against the new motion.

Graeme was delighted with the idea of having the nomadic people vaccinated, suggesting they might do other inoculations at the same time and organising all the equipment and drugs they would need.

'You'll take Lauren?' Graeme asked, and Malik studied his old mentor for a moment, wondering how much he knew or guessed about the situation—the delayed marriage, and his, Malik's, growing passion for the woman he'd brought so far.

Malik nodded.

'She did well organising everyone at the house,' he said, and wondered if it had sounded like an excuse and whether he should have said nothing.

But Graeme just smiled.

'That's good, she needs a break,' he said. 'She's bonded well with the family of the little girl—she seems to understand the people she'll be dealing with.'

Was that another dilemma? Something that might thwart his plan?

Malik shook off any doubts. Once the rheumatic fever diagnosis had been proved by tests, Lauren had been spending most of her on-duty hours with the child and her family.

But no one worked twenty-four hours a day, so other nurses were familiar with the case, and as the penicillin had reduced the swelling and pain in the girl's throat and she was eating well, there was little nursing to do.

Nevertheless, it was Lauren's first objection when he came to her with his idea of taking her out to the nomad camp on the old Silk Road to vaccinate the people there before they came into town.

'We'll be away a few days,' he told her, 'and I have already explained to the family of the sick girl that another nurse will be with her. And you can be sure Nimr will be well cared for. He tells me he would like his friend Najeeb to stay, so perhaps this would be a good time to have him over so he doesn't miss you so much.'

Lauren smiled at him.

'You don't leave much for me to do, then. Nim hasn't stopped talking about having Najeeb to stay, and you're right, this would be an ideal time.'

She guessed there was more to this than a simple trip out into the desert, that Malik had everything so organised before she'd even known about it. But whatever lay ahead, with Nim happy with the arrangements, it was a trip she'd love to make.

The two boys would have both Aneesha and Keema to look after them, and Lauren knew there'd be trusted men around them all the time.

'So,' she finally said, when she'd settled all of this in her head and faced Malik again, 'exactly what are you planning?'

The smile he gave her and the reaction of her body to that smile told her all she needed to know.

She closed her eyes to take it in, and tamped down the excitement that frustration had been building in her body.

'We stay in the camp?' she asked, and received an even more explicit smile in reply.

'You will see,' he said. 'It will be a surprise for you.'

And it was all she could do to *not* leap into his arms and hug him, hold him, kiss him…

Most unseemly behaviour in a hospital corridor.

She saw no more of Malik that day, eating dinner with Nim, who was so excited about having his friend to stay over he could barely eat his food.

But the excitement proved enough to send him straight to sleep, and Lauren was free to sit in her bedroom and consider what she should pack for a few working days with, as far as she could make out, a little extracurricular excitement thrown in.

Gloom set in. Okay, so she had plenty of respectable loose trousers and tunics like the ones she now wore all the time, but they were far from sexy.

For the past four years, her life had revolved around Nim and keeping him safe, so sexy underwear had been the furthest thing from her mind. But hers were so darned functional they made her want to weep.

So she did, just a little, and was drying her eyes when Keema entered to tell her Malik would like to see her.

He was waiting, very properly, in the small salon where she and Nim usually watched television.

'I thought I might see him to say goodbye, but it seems he's asleep already,' he said as she came into the room.

Then as she came closer he took her hands and drew her to him, looking down into her face.

'You have been crying? You are worried about leaving Nim? *Al'ama*, I am so stupid. I think only of myself and my own desires to be alone with you for a little time. It is too hard for you?'

He sounded so concerned Lauren put her hand to his cheek and kissed him swiftly on the lips.

'No, I'm fine, and Nim is so happy about the arrangement, he will not realise I'm gone.'

They talked a while and then he left, finalising the time he would send a car for her, explaining they would travel in his helicopter to the camp.

Another quick kiss and he was gone.

She shut away the doubts, packed her case, then showered and washed her hair, uncertain about what facilities a desert camp might have.

The nomad camp, when they arrived, made Lauren shake her head in disbelief. The tents themselves, large rounded affairs, were black, made from some kind of tanned animal skin, but all around was a swirl of colour.

Bright carpets were spread on the sand, women and children in brilliantly coloured outfits moved around outside the tents, while more carpets and mats hung from the anchoring ropes.

Camels wandered nearby, hobbles between their front feet preventing them from straying, and further out, a makeshift fence and a number of small boys kept goats and horses corralled.

A tall man, his head covered in a black turban with a long tail, appeared from the larger of the tents, and came towards the helicopter.

'You are welcome in my camp, Abdul-Malik,' he said, with a slight bow of his head.

'I am honoured to be here,' Malik replied, and while Lauren was trying to work out why the pair was speaking English, Malik spoke again.

'You will have heard many people in the city have been ill with the measles epidemic, a number of them seriously ill. I have brought a nurse to help me and we will vaccinate your people so they need not fear that illness or many others.'

'I have heard that too, and that you were coming,' the man said. 'You and the nurse from Australia, I believe.'

He turned to bow his head at Lauren, who held out her hand.

'I am Lauren,' she said, smiling at the man. 'And do you hear these things through some age-old tradition of listening to the wind, or do you have mobile phones these days?'

He laughed and dug into the pocket of his gown, to produce one of the latest models of phone.

'Easier than listening to the wind, although we still listen to it as well, for it tells us other things.'

Intrigued, Lauren couldn't help herself.

'Like sandstorms?' she said, and the man nodded once more.

'Those, and other travellers in our vicinity—the wind also tells us that.'

It was Lauren's turn to nod. She had read enough to know that in times when wars had been fought over territorial rights or bridal dowries, knowing an enemy was close would be important.

Malik was explaining how they planned to carry out the vaccinations, and the man had sent several young men to the helicopter to collect the ice boxes and medical equipment.

The man strode away to organise his people.

'His English is so—English, I suppose. Was he educated there?'

Malik smiled.

'He was at school with me in England. He lives this life

by choice, but also so he can indulge in his love of archaeology. He doesn't look for treasure but for everyday things people in the past made use of in their daily lives. One day he hopes to set up a museum that will track the lives of all who used the Silk Road over the centuries.'

Lauren shook her head in amazement.

'That would surely take more than one man's lifetime!'

Malik smiled at her.

'Ah, but you do not know this man,' he said.

He was certainly a good organiser, Lauren realised when he returned to show them to a small shelter that had been erected, with a folding table and chairs and two young women standing by, presumably to fetch and carry anything she or Malik might need, and to keep records of the patients.

And queues were already forming outside the shelter, women with small children at the front, then the men and boys, and at the end older people, possibly reluctant to be there.

'So, I have explained and you may start,' the leader said to them when he appeared from nowhere in front of them.

Lauren unpacked the equipment box, setting alcohol wipes in front of each of them, the ice boxes of vaccines between them, and two sharps containers behind those. They had a jar of hand sanitiser each and a box of gloves, and, tucked down in a box she left between the two chairs, jars containing jelly beans to give the children.

'At least we've had some practice at mass vaccination,' she said to Malik as they began—the measles, mumps and rubella vaccine the first they gave to everyone.

The young girls brought each patient forward and instructed them to roll up his or her sleeve, then, with the injection done, ushered the patient out through the open back of the shelter before writing in their notebooks.

In the early afternoon the queues disappeared. There one minute and gone the next.

'Lunch,' the headman announced. 'Come!'

Once out of the shelter, Lauren realised how hot the day had become.

'You will rest when you have eaten,' the man commanded, and Lauren knew it was a good idea.

'For an hour,' Malik said. 'No longer, for we wish to finish all the MMR vaccinations today. Tomorrow we will start on triple antigens for the babies and children, and for those to be effective we will need to return again and again.'

'And tetanus?' Lauren asked, ashamed she'd been so caught up in her longings for sexy lingerie she hadn't thought to ask Malik the details of the inoculations they'd be doing.

He smiled at her.

'I did that many years ago—when I was still a student. A group of us, friends of mine, used it as a holiday placement. We had a four-wheel drive bus and set out along the nomadic tribes' favoured routes. We had no hope of covering all the camps, but it's a tradition that's continued, and at each camp we would train a couple of people to give the injections and leave a small supply. Now they can replenish that supply when they are camped close to a town or city.'

Lauren could only shake her head, imagining the young medical students on their trek across the wild, uninhabited plains.

They rested in the main tent, on rugs piled on each other, made more comfortable by fat cushions. The two young women reclined by Lauren, who realised with an inward smile that Malik was ensconced on his throne of mats on the far side of the tent.

He was speaking with the headman and Lauren sensed the talk, in their own language, was a serious one.

The rest hour ended with cool drinks and sweet pastries, then it was back to work until the sun began to set, its red orb turning the desert into a field of flame.

'There is a solar-powered freezer where the cool boxes can be stored,' the headman told them. 'And I have asked my driver to take you to the lodge. He will collect you in the morning.'

He held up his hand to forestall Malik's protest.

'I know you know the way, but these days you are a city man—let me keep you safe.'

He bowed quite deeply as he spoke and Lauren guessed Malik had spoken to him of his problems with the palace.

If so, it was evident he had this man's support—but would that count in palace circles? Was this man even a citizen of Madan, or were nomadic tribes stateless, governed by the rule of the tribe?

'We will sit in the back,' Malik said, as he led Lauren to the big four-wheel drive vehicle. 'To do otherwise would embarrass our driver.'

He opened the door and took Lauren's hand to help her up, felt the tremor in her fingers as he touched her, and his own nerves respond immediately.

But what he'd planned would not be hurried. They were greeted at the lodge by the couple who lived there, looking after the place and also tracking the released leopards through small transmitters placed under the animals' skin. In the main room, a large map took up most of the wall, and Malik led Lauren to it, explaining its purpose and showing her the paths the released animals followed.

And as he watched her follow one track with a finger, her face showing her fascination in this, his pet project, he knew he loved her more deeply than he'd known he could love, and refused to consider there could be any other option than marrying her.

Marla led her to the guest bedroom, and Malik smiled to himself as he imagined her reaction to the palatial space, with the huge, netting-shrouded bed and gleaming bathroom beside it.

'You have all this out here in the desert?'

He heard the disbelief in her voice and walked over to the doorway, Marla ducking out as he stood there.

'My mother loved this place and, as you already know, she wasn't one to stint on luxuries. With bores sunk deep into the desert for water and solar panels for power, this was my mother's idea of camping.'

'Are all the rooms like this?' Lauren asked, then he saw colour rise to her cheeks, and he guessed she was wondering where he would sleep.

'Not quite as luxurious and the beds are definitely not as comfortable,' he said, stepping towards her and putting an arm around her shoulders to draw her close. 'So perhaps we'll have to share.'

She shivered and he wondered just how inexperienced she probably was. Before Lily's death there'd probably been boyfriends but the last four years, when she might have been learning more of the ways of men and women, had been stolen from her by her need to keep Nimr safe.

He kissed her cheek, her nose, her forehead and finally her lips, which parted like a parched man's seeking water. And through their tunics he felt the hard nubs of her breasts, and heard the tiny sigh she gave when his tongue touched hers.

And for a moment his determination to make love to her slowly and sensually wavered and he pictured himself lifting her through the screens around the bed and—

'I will leave you here to have a bath and rest before dinner,' he said, easing her away from his body and dropping a parting kiss on her lips. 'There is a deck out front, we can sit there to eat, so come through when you are ready.'

By the time Lauren joined him on the deck, wearing the blue trousers and tunic that was Nim's favourite, a nearly full moon was rising in the sky, turning the sands silver with its light.

Malik was seated at a low table, and he stood, hand outheld, to help her to a chair, so they could sit together and look out at the magic of the desert at night, where flashes of shadow suggested small animals might be hunting in the cool air of the evening.

The table was laden with silver platters, all with domed silver covers over them.

'It's like a game—lifting the covers to see what's underneath,' Lauren said, and Malik smiled at her, his eyes telling her things she longed to hear from his lips.

Or maybe she was just carried away, and it was nothing more than moonlight glinting in his eyes…

Until he touched her, just lightly on the shoulder, and said the words.

'I love you!'

But now the words she'd longed to hear sent her into a panic. What to do? What to say?

And did he mean it?

Was that question the reason why the words had thrown her so much? Shouldn't she have been thrilled, excited, throwing herself into his arms and telling him she loved him too?

She'd accepted some time ago that what she felt for him was love, but she'd never considered his care of her, his consideration, even the attraction between them might be signs of his love for her…

Thoughts and words chased through her head and she shook it to clear it, but that didn't help.

Maybe he had guessed at her confusion that he said, 'Let's eat,' and lifted one of the covers to show a mound of golden rice, speckled with currants and toasted almonds. He spooned some on a plate and then uncovered a meat dish—tantalisingly spicy—and added a spoonful of that.

'You can help yourself to anything you'd like with it,' he said, as if the 'I love you' had never been said. 'You will find preserves and pickles under the smaller covers.'

But Lauren was shaking too much to lift a single cover, shaking so much she used two hands to reach for the plate he'd served for her.

'Relax,' he said. 'We will be all right—that I promise you.'

And even though that little 'if' still hovered in the back of her mind, the words did help her relax, and she thanked him—for the words, the food, and for his love.

She set the plate on the table in front of her, then leaned across to kiss him on the lips.

'I love you too,' she said. 'And, yes, we'll work it out.'

Her own lie, really, that last part, for doubt about the outcome of their relationship was alive and well deep inside her, but for now she'd eat and love, and love and smile, and the love would leave her with happy memories, if nothing else…

Well, probably a broken heart, but she wouldn't think about that now, especially as he'd served himself some food but wasn't eating. Instead he was running his finger up her arm, beneath the sleeve of her tunic, and she knew, had her arm been bare as it would have been at home, the feeling could not possibly have been as erotic as this delicate touch beneath her clothing.

CHAPTER ELEVEN

MOONLIGHT FILLED THE room with its silvery magic, making Lauren's skin lustrous as he slipped off her tunic and trousers, the silk material making soft noises as it slid across her skin.

And as he'd promised, Malik took his time, wanting to see her, all of her—the gleaming skin, her pert breasts, a tiny waist and flaring hips.

He touched her, just to feel that skin—feel the warmth of it as the desire he could read in her eyes heated her body.

'My turn to strip you,' she said, but her voice trembled just a little and he knew she was uncertain. So he took her hands and guided them, removing his long tunic and the cloth he wrapped around his hips, so she couldn't help but see how ready for her he was.

But he'd promised to go slowly—to tease and tantalise—and he began with kisses that started on her lips but soon slipped lower to her neck and then her breasts—one and then the other, feeling her tremble now, though the hands that held his head to her were fiercely strong.

He lifted her to the bed and set her down, trailing his fingers now as well as his kisses up and down her body, her legs, her thighs, her belly button, lips kissing still, fingers teasing, touching, prying—opening her to further exploration as she twisted on the bed and uttered little cries that fired his own need even more.

But only when she cried out for him to stop, to not stop, to stop the torment, did he enter her, taking her slowly and carefully, feeling her moist warmth tighten around him, her body in rhythm now with his, until they finally crested the wave of desire together, gasping, crying out, clinging to each other like the survivors of a shipwreck.

He held her, wanting to stay like this for ever, their bodies bonded, their need satisfied for now.

Turning her so she lay by his side, she nestled closer, murmuring his name, looking into his face with a kind of wonder. Then her dark-lashed eyelids drooped and closed and she slept, while he watched over her, and wondered what lay ahead for both of them.

By morning they were sated with love, sleepily holding, touching, stroking each other, reluctant to leave the cocoon of the canopied bed, although work was waiting for them.

As was breakfast when, showered and fresh and slightly shy, Lauren made her way out onto the deck. There were baskets of fresh fruit, platters of cut melons, dishes of yoghurt spiced with nutmeg and sweetened with honey, and silver plates with their domed covers hiding spicy meat dishes and couscous or rice.

She knew her way around the Madan breakfast feast by now, and stuck with the yoghurt and fruit, Malik joining her as she selected a ripe, red strawberry.

He plucked it from her fingers.

'Open wide!'

And popped it in her mouth, so she tasted his skin with the sweet burst from the fruit.

She looked up into his eyes and saw him smile—knew she was smiling too.

* * *

For three idyllic days they worked together at the camp, exploring in the late afternoons, hoping to catch sight of a leopard, happy just to be together, with the curtained bed waiting for them in the lodge.

But that third night Malik was distracted, taking phone calls late into the night, collapsing into bed beside her, holding her tightly to him before turning on his side to sleep, lovemaking lost in his distraction.

She turned towards his unyielding body in the bed they'd shared with such joy and slid her arms around his waist, resting her head against his shoulder.

'Why can't you talk about what's worrying you?' she whispered to him. 'I probably can't help but sometimes talking about a problem will make things clearer. Talk to me—try it?'

Felt his shoulder move as he took in a breath and heard the sigh as it came out.

'Through all our generations there has been a divide—'

He stopped as if he had no idea how to continue.

'Between men and women?' Lauren guessed. 'Between what was men's business and what was women's business?'

She felt his nod and held him close, hoping she could find the right words.

'But the old ways are already changing. You have spoken so passionately about bringing Madan into the twenty-first century.'

'Over time,' he said gruffly, but she could feel his body relaxing.

'So talk to me. I'm already there—I'm a twenty-first-century woman. To me, you sharing your problems would be a gift—a sign of trust. And without trust, how can there be love?'

He turned and took her in his arms.

'It's such a mess that I cannot get it straight in my own head, let alone explain to you or anyone else. I've told you the elders can make laws and right now they are discussing a law that would sabotage our marriage, which has already been delayed far too long. I know who is behind it—my uncle, spurred on by his wife.'

'And you *know* this?'

'I do, but what I cannot work out is why. If I knew that, I could probably sort it out, but it doesn't make sense because I cannot connect it to Tariq's death. Yet I know from information my informants have given me that the two *must* be connected.'

Lauren wrapped her arms around him and warmed him with her body, her own head trying to make sense of things.

'Are you sure Tariq was the target?'

Malik pulled away from her as if to search her eyes for answers, although the moonlight would reveal little.

'The police—your police—were certain the accident wasn't set up to kill your parents. They looked into that quite deeply.'

It was Lauren's turn to sigh.

'I know all about that part of it—he was the only heir and chief target—I fielded many hours of questions myself. But if it wasn't Tariq or my parents, that only leaves Lily,' she said. 'Although why anyone would want to kill her, I cannot imagine.'

'Lily!'

He breathed the name, but his arms tightened around Lauren, clasping her to him so he could drop a quick kiss on her lips.

Then he was gone, out of bed and out the door, back on his cell phone, his voice urgent, questioning—demanding?

* * *

They returned to the city in the morning, Nim and Najeeb welcoming her with cries of delight, both wanting stories about the nomadic tribe and their camp—and life returned to normal, although a new normal now.

Aware that Malik had been neglecting things while they'd been away, she accepted that she wouldn't see much of him, and their time was reduced to brief glimpses in hospital corridors, hurried consultations over a sick child.

But even in these almost stolen moments she knew the bond of love was there between them, and now she understood a little more of the ways of this new country—understood the traditional places held by men and women in it. Now he'd spoken to her once about the problem, perhaps he would again, but if not, she wouldn't pester him—wouldn't force cultural change on him too suddenly. Loving him as she did, she was content to wait until the business that was troubling him had been resolved.

He came early one evening to see Nim before he went to bed, and to walk with her among the roses.

But his face was drawn with worry, his eyes deeply troubled, and though his hand touched hers as they walked, he didn't take it, didn't hold her and kiss her in the shadows of the colonnade.

Instead, he pulled a small pocket knife from somewhere and cut some roses as they walked—white and yellow, pink and red, a huge bouquet of colour and perfume by the time they were back at the front steps.

And there he handed them to her, his handkerchief wrapped around the stems to protect her hands from thorns.

'I caught the scent of roses in your hair that first day we met,' he said, so serious Lauren felt a quiver of fear in her heart. 'Now, for ever, you'll be tied to me through roses—roses and love.'

He took her free hand, lifted it and kissed her fingers, then departed, the quiver in her heart now a shard of ice, for his words had sounded like goodbye…

Malik walked away, aware he should have spoken—trusted her to understand. But how could he tell her that the information was pointing more and more to a member of his family—his uncle's wife—being behind the deaths of her family? *And* the abduction of the child she loved?

How could she, knowing this, hold him in her arms again, make love with him again?

Although not telling her was surely worse.

He shook his head. As yet it was merely suspicion and there was still the vote to be faced, one way or another.

He argued, fought, cajoled the council, but the force behind the clutch of elders wanting the new law was backed now by three of his uncles.

As family they would normally stand behind him, whatever his decision. But this time they couldn't be swayed, so the arguments went back and forth, and the need to shore up *his* supporters was constant, for many of them would prefer to take the easy way out of any decision.

Added to all that was his concern over information still coming in—information that tied, if not his uncle, at least his uncle's wife to the death of Tariq.

Surely not his uncle?

No, that was impossible—wasn't it?

They were family.

He had to try to work it out, to force himself to think beyond the imminent decision to what his uncle could have gained by removing Tariq from the family equation.

Nimr would still have been the heir, although maybe they'd hoped he, too, would have been in the vehicle. A two-week-old infant—of course he'd have been with his mother.

Except that Lily had hardly been the maternal type and leaving Nimr with Lauren had meant she could enjoy herself more.

But after Nimr, he, Malik, would have succeeded to the throne—he *was* his father's second son. Would he, too, have been targeted if that had happened?

He pounded his head with an open hand, trying to make his brain chase down through tangled pathways of deceit.

As things stood now, if the proposed change was made to the law, he couldn't marry Lauren *and* rule as regent for Nimr. The suggested law was that the ruler must have a Madani wife, but because it would not be retrospective, Nimr was still the heir.

And in danger?

Malik sighed—there was so much he didn't know, couldn't even guess at.

But what *was* certain was that a regent acted as the ruler, and marriage to Lauren would mean someone else would be appointed regent for Nimr, probably one of the uncles, all of whom were unheeding of the needs of the country.

And one of whom might have been implicated in Tariq's death…

If nothing else, what he was going through now had shown him how archaic their so-called government was—the country run by a group who took care of their own interests first, and could be swayed by favours, gifts and possibly even bribes.

There were only two days now to the vote and Malik wondered how long it would take, should he defeat the motion, to bring democracy to his people so everyone could have a say in how Madan was governed, instead of leaving all important decisions to the ruling tribe.

Lauren was aware that gossip was now rampant in the house, but her language lessons were proceeding slowly.

In the end, she had to ask, seeing Nim off to school then going in search of Keema, wondering how to broach the subject.

But it seemed Keema had already guessed at Lauren's new closeness with Malik, for her voice, as she answered, was heavy with regret.

'There is a new law,' she said. 'The ruler or the regent must marry a Madani woman.'

The words hit Lauren with the force of a lightning bolt, sending her head into a whirl and her heart into palpitations.

Stupid, of course, when she hadn't wanted to marry him in the first place. She'd agreed because of Nim…

But acknowledging stupidity didn't take away the pain.

For herself, for Malik, and for the country he'd hoped to help.

No, that was stupid—he could still rule for Nim, get things organised as he'd intended. Couples broke up all the time, and they'd been together so briefly they probably hadn't reached couple status.

She thanked Keema for her trust in passing on the information, and resolutely set her mind to getting somewhere close to normal. She was on a late shift. She'd go to work and come home, check on Nim, play with him in the morning, then go to work and come home again, and again, and again.

She could handle a simple existence, like the one she'd set herself when she'd stopped running and been determined to lead a normal life for Nim's sake.

But for all she'd been determined to stay strong, after two days all she really wanted was to see Malik—to tell him that it didn't matter.

Should she hold out a hand, stop him, take him somewhere quiet and explain this to him?

But the opportunity failed to arise, and even Nim was asking where he was…

Then one night he was there—early morning, really—pale and shaking by her bed, a sound as slight as a sigh waking her, so she stood up and took him in her arms, dragged him down and loved him all she could, with kisses and touches, and whispers of passion, taking his body and giving hers in return.

He slept then, in her arms, a deep and dreamless sleep, she hoped, but was gone when she awoke, alone and naked in her bed.

Was *this* goodbye?

Was this how her recent dreams of love and marriage would end?

No, she was wrong! She may not have known the man long, but she knew him well. He would not just walk away from her without a word.

He would do what had to be done about the deaths of their families, and he'd sort out the mayhem going on with the elders, because his country depended on him to take it forward. These were his most pressing concerns—and his duty.

And with duty done, he'd come for her.

All she had to do was wait.

He came again, late one afternoon, as she was wandering through the roses. He took her hand and walked with her in silence, until it was time to go inside and have dinner with Nim, who wasn't hesitant in complaining about what he thought had been such a long absence—although it had been all of four days.

'I have been busy,' Malik said, though the lines of strain on his face had already told Lauren that much. 'You know I would have come if I could.'

He included Lauren as he spoke, and she read the agony of uncertainty in his eyes.

He read Nim's bedtime story and they both kissed him goodnight, and as they left the room he took Lauren's hand in his.

'Can we talk a while?' he asked quietly.

And although inside she was such a mess she didn't want to hear his words, she had to know what was going on—and had to hear from him that the dream was over.

'Let's sit outside,' she said, and they walked along the colonnade to where soft cushioned cane chairs were set around small tables.

'Would you like coffee?' she asked, a polite hostess in what really wasn't her home.

He shook his head.

'I'm coffeed out,' he muttered. 'May never touch the stuff again.'

But before he sat he turned towards her, took both her hands and leaned in to kiss her.

Just gently, on the lips—a single kiss—but he kept her hands and somehow they were both sitting on the small lounge chair, hands clinging to each other.

'Have you heard about the law—the vote?' he said, and before she could reply added, 'How could you not—it would have been all over the house, if not the hospital. I know they've talked of nothing in the marketplace for days.'

He sounded so tired she slipped one hand out of his grasp to put it around his shoulders and pull him close.

And waited.

CHAPTER TWELVE

IF ONLY HE could find the words, Malik thought.

If only the decision he'd finally come to didn't hurt so much!

But he had to tell her, explain, find out what would make her happy.

He groaned then straightened his spine, put *his* arm around *her* shoulders, and held her to him.

'The new law makes it impossible for me to marry you and act as regent for Nimr,' he began. 'And the leader of the group that voted for it was one of my uncles. He—all my uncles—are easily bent to stronger wills, which my eldest uncle's wife certainly has.'

He paused, seeking words that weren't full of rage. None of this was Lauren's doing, although he believed now it had revolved around her sister.

'It was you who made me think more clearly about Tariq's death—think it through without emotion. And the question you asked—was I sure he was meant to be the victim?—made me realise that none of us had known he was in Australia. As far as we were all concerned, he was in the US.'

'But the local police ruled out my parents as the target,' Lauren reminded him.

He took a deep breath—there had to be truth for there to be trust.

'And Lily? Did anyone consider her?'

He put his palms against her cheeks, framing her face so he could see her eyes as he explained.

'When I considered Lily, it all became clear. My uncle's wife is from another powerful family, and she and Tariq had been promised to each other as young children.'

Grey eyes widened as she took this in.

'Then Lily came along,' she whispered, and he held her close and smoothed his hands across her hair.

'My information is that she sent three members of her family—distant relatives but trusted—to America and from there they travelled to Australia. Two of them—the couple who took Nim—are still in jail in Australia, and the third could be anywhere for he never returned to Madan.'

Lauren pulled away from him, needing to see his face.

'You *know* all this or is it just supposition?'

'I know most of it,' he said, his voice deep with the sadness this knowledge had brought him. 'She had no idea Tariq would be there—she was simply intent on getting rid of the woman who'd taken the man she thought of as hers.'

'And your uncle married her?'

Now he frowned and shook his head.

'There was dishonour in the family, you see. Although the arrangement wasn't set in stone, to renege would have brought on bad blood between the families. My uncle sorted that by marrying her himself so the families were united, just in a different way.'

'But she wants more?'

He sighed.

'Marriage to Tariq would have made her the wife of the ruler. Without the law, you, the sister of the woman she so hated, would take that role—though as wife of the regent. I think she could not bear that, especially as the realisation that she'd killed Tariq as well as Lily must have haunted her for the last four years.'

'Poor woman!' Lauren said. 'To be in so much pain she was driven to murder.'

'Poor woman indeed,' Malik snorted. 'I doubt she's felt a single moment of remorse. It is power she wants—power that motivates her.'

'And still wants, if she has persuaded your uncle and his supporters the new law is a good thing for the country. Would it be your uncle who takes control if you were not available?'

Malik nodded.

'Who *will* take control—for I will not be available!'

He spoke so determinedly Lauren shivered.

'Of course you will,' she said, hoping she had kept the pain and anguish she was feeling out of her voice.

Malik held her for a moment, held her close, before telling her the decision that had caused him so many sleepless nights but which was, he felt, the only way to go. 'I have decided we will leave.'

She stiffened against him, opened her mouth to protest, but he closed it with a quick kiss.

'Well, *I* will leave and hope you and Nimr will come with me. We will go back to Australia, or to another country if you wish—go together, marry and become a family—maybe have more children, who knows. I will work and you too if you wish, and we will make a new life for ourselves and forget this place.'

He heard a long sigh, then Lauren turned so she could take his face in the palms of *her* hands and look deep into his eyes.

'You are such a bad liar,' she said, almost smiling at the same time. 'You know you could never forget this place—this is your home, your country.'

'Maybe deep down in my heart I could not,' he admitted, 'but with you and Nimr we can build a new life and I can grow to love a new country.'

'Nonsense!' Lauren said. 'You'd be useful in another country, doctors always are, but you are *needed* here, by the country, and by the people that you love. You are needed here to help them come to terms with a new future—to help the country grow and develop into a modern society. And you know, in every fibre of your being, that if you go, that will not happen.'

Unable to deny her words, he could only look at her, aware she'd read his answer in his eyes.

Anger twisted inside him—anger at Lauren for making this so hard, anger at himself for failing to secure the vote.

'I won't stay here and watch them spend the country's money on trivia,' he growled. 'That is not an option. Neither would I leave my brother's son here to become a pawn in their power games.'

'But you can stay here—the answer's simple, you stupid man. You can marry a local woman—I've met dozens of wonderful Madani women—and you can rule as regent for Nim, and get to work on your dreams that have been put on hold for too long already.'

She paused, and the dread that had begun in his heart with her talk of his marriage to a local woman grew heavier.

'I will not leave Nim,' she continued, although she hadn't needed to put that into words to him, 'but he and I can live somewhere else, maybe close to the hospital, and I promise that there is no way I'd put your marriage or your reputation into any danger, neither would I do anything to hurt the woman you marry.'

'You don't love me?'

What else could he think when she spoke so calmly, so coldly?

'Of course I do. And I always will, but we have had our time together and I'll always have those memories.'

Another pause.

'Actually, I was thinking—those health outposts you want to set up along the nomadic tribes' regular route, the places where they always stop. You thought a nurse and perhaps an aide could operate them, doing regular health checks and vaccinations as the people come through. I'd be happy to do that. I already love the desert country. Nim and I can live out there. With the necessary books, I can homeschool him until he is old enough to go wherever older boys go to school.'

'You have it all worked out,' he said bitterly. 'You could walk away like that—as easy as you like—without a backward glance?'

'I didn't say it would be easy,' she snapped, 'but it would be a damn sight easier than living in town and seeing you, being near you, but not with you. Be reasonable, Malik, marrying someone else is what you have to do, so there's no point in getting all maudlin and lovesick about it. Your country needs you more than ever now there's been this split in the ruling parties.'

Malik just sat, trying to take in all she'd said, to process it so it made sense.

Which, of course, it did, even without much processing.

'You'd walk away from me?'

That was the hardest part to understand. What they'd had—to him at least—had been somehow more than love.

It had been unique, sublime, so special words failed to do it justice.

'I wouldn't walk,' she said, so quietly he barely heard the words. 'I'd run!'

Then she bent her head and he knew she was crying.

He put his arms around her and pulled her onto his knees, and sat there, holding her, feeling her misery in his bones, feeling loss right through his body.

And for a long time there was silence, and the perfume of roses in the air.

And as she shifted, about to move, he tightened his hold as a new solution burned in his brain.

'I can have two wives,' he said. 'I suppose they'd insist the Madani one was the number one, but you could be my second wife—my real wife.'

She stood up now, looking down at him.

'As long as you treat both of them equally,' Lauren reminded him. 'Even I know that that is the law about multiple marriages. And quite apart from that, do you think I'd ruin another woman's life? She'd know herself a token bride, a political wife—how would that make her feel?'

Lauren wandered down the steps, and plucked a yellow rosebud from the nearest bush.

'My way is the best, Malik. You know that. Do it for Nim if not for yourself—so you have a wonderful, stable, happy country with healthy and educated people to pass on to him.'

And clinging to her last tattered remnants of self-control, she walked away from him, through the gardens to the front door, and hastily along the passages that led to her room.

There, at least, she could cry properly, although that wouldn't do much good.

But what she could do was look back on her memories of Malik and the special time they'd shared. She could wrap each one carefully then tuck it into a box deep down in her brain, to be taken out so far into the future that looking at them would bring pleasure rather than tears.

Work was the answer. Waking after a troubled sleep, Lauren showered and dressed for work, checked that Nim was up and ready for school, pretended to eat with him while he had breakfast, then asked Keema to call for a car to take her to work.

The young girl with rheumatic fever was her first stop on the ward. As she slowly recovered, more and more of her family were sneaking in, so the room now resembled one of the smaller nomad tents she'd seen in the desert.

Lauren checked the girl as the father spoke, a young family member, a lad of about twelve, now acting as interpreter.

'Your man, he is well?'

My man? she'd have liked to say, but if this man had obviously sussed out the tie between her and Malik it would demean what they had had for her to deny it.

'His problems are affairs of state,' she said quietly. 'He will do what is right.'

As the boy spoke the man gave a bow of his head. The simple gesture was eloquent with understanding, and gave Lauren a warm feeling of support.

She turned her attention back to the child, the lad translating rapidly so the conversation felt almost normal.

'Has someone told you that the tests show no damage to the heart, and because of that she will be able to go home soon?'

A different nod this time—all business.

'But she must rest until she feels ready to play again,

and you will have to give her penicillin injections every four weeks—every twenty-eight days—for many years so she doesn't get it again.'

'Malik has told me this, and my sister, who trained as a nurse, will come back to live with us for a few months until I feel confident of doing the injections myself.'

Lauren smiled at him and waved her hands around the room where everyone, even the small children, was being very quiet.

Trying not to draw attention to their presence when the place looked like a fairground?

'Family is very special,' she said to the man. 'It is good your sister will help you for a while.'

'Family is everything,' the man said, and Lauren had to swallow hard and say a quick goodbye so she could escape before they saw her tears.

'You're stronger than this!' she told herself as she drew deep breaths in a cubicle in the bathroom. 'You *have* family, you have Nim. And Joe and Aunt Jane are as good as family—better even, considering all they have done for you.'

And now silently chastising herself for giving in to tears of self-pity, she returned to work, checked on the other children in the ward, made arrangements for a little boy with a broken leg who was returning home, spoke sternly to a mother who was feeding her recently diagnosed diabetic daughter with nougat, and generally fell into the routine that was work.

But as she talked with the aide who usually translated for her, and used some of the new words she was learning, she realised how much she'd grown to like this place—the hospital, the oasis, the country and its people.

For some reason, it had begun to feel like home, and although she knew, if she stayed, she'd be living in one of the small hospital accommodation units or a rented house, not a mansion with a rose garden bigger than a football field, she also knew that didn't matter. She could be happy here, she and Nim.

Malik would be too busy putting all his plans into practice to be at the hospital very much, and not seeing him would make things easier for her to bear.

Or maybe Malik would go ahead with his idea of the health outposts—and she could live in the desert with Nim—that would be wonderful.

She shook her head.

No, it wouldn't—not for Nim. Not now she really thought about it. Even if he grew to love the desert as much as she did, he'd have no friends out there except when one of the nomadic tribes was camped there. But even those friends would move on.

She had to smile at how far her thoughts had wandered in the time it took for the aide to write out instructions for the storage of penicillin. Smile?

She'd actually smiled?

Well, she damn well wasn't going to *not* smile!

This was how it had to be, for these people she was just getting to know and admire, and for the country that was unique and needed to be protected.

And *she* was going to go about her work as if nothing had happened, no matter how hard that might be.

And at night, instead of dreaming of the man who'd brought her such joy, she'd plan the future—hers and Nim's.

She was in the staffroom, and as Malik walked in her head was already into planning mode.

Which was fortunate as it gave her a good defence against all her physical reactions to his presence and to the spasm of pain it caused in her heart.

'I'll need a house near his school and not too far from the hospital. I'm sure you'll do whatever has to be done about keeping Nim safe, and as long as it's not too expensive I can pay rent out of my hospital wages until I can organise to transfer money over here. And it would be good if we could move soon so there will be less chance of silly talk and scandal. And if we could keep Aneesha for Nim's language lessons and to help me learn as well, that would be good.

He stared at her as if she was an apparition, shook his head, then walked away, whatever he'd come to say forgotten in her torrent of words.

But having said the words, and heard them in her own ears, the situation became far more real.

She could do this. Hide her broken heart and explain to Nim they were moving, learn how and where to shop for food, pack their things—could she take the trouser suits she'd been wearing for work, and maybe the lovely blue one...?

She sniffed hard, hoping to drain away the moisture collecting behind her eyes.

She *could* do this—she *would* do this...

Malik walked through the hospital in a daze. Knowing she was in the hospital, he'd hoped to find her and put his idea of them leaving to her once again—persuade her with love. Surely love would change her mind?

And he'd been met with a barrage of words that had stopped him in his tracks, and as he'd walked away, he'd realised she was deadly serious.

She would remain here in Madan, so he could rule for Nimr until he came of age.

Which left him where, exactly?

He tried to block out the answer to that question because it came in Lauren's voice.

He had to find a Madani bride!

How *could* he when he loved and wanted only Lauren?

What could he offer to another woman?

Certainly not love…

But Lauren was removing herself from the equation—and doing it deliberately because she was thinking of this woman—because without Lauren around he could least give his wife respect.

He groaned—aloud, it seemed, as several nurses passing by turned to stare at him.

Were they pretty?

Should he start to look?

He groaned again but kept it inside this time…

Nothing happened.

No new place of residence suddenly appeared, and Lauren had no idea where or how to start looking for something.

She could ask Keema for help, but it seemed disloyal to Malik to be discussing their personal lives, although everyone in the big house must know what was going on.

CHAPTER THIRTEEN

A FIRE IN a market on the edge of town brought in enough patients to keep all the staff busy for the next week, and although she didn't see him, Lauren knew Malik had been working every night because she saw his writing on the charts.

Well, she looked for it, and often looked just a little too long and touched it with her fingers when she did see it, as if somehow his written words could connect her to him again.

If you're going to stay here for ever you'd better get over this, she told herself one morning, but next morning looked again.

'Take some time off,' Graeme said to her, as she went off duty early the following week. 'The crisis is over—the children who need more care have been air-lifted out—and we're down to the ones who still need fluid replacement and their dressings changed.'

Lauren knew he was right. They were nearly back to normal, and she knew she was probably too exhausted to go on without a break.

She could look for somewhere new to live.

She needed sleep first, then she would look.

Her financial future wouldn't be a problem. She'd bought the duplex back home with money from her share of the sale of her parents' house but there was more. It was simply a matter of organising the sale of some shares and transferring some capital to a bank here.

At least Malik wouldn't have to pay her rent or, worse, buy her a house. How would his wife feel about that?

The word 'wife' still hurt, but she refused to not think about the unknown woman. It was for Nim, and the country he would one day rule, that she, Lauren, had made her decision, and she had every intention of sticking to it.

She was in the rose garden—could she plant roses in her new home, she wondered—when Keema found her. A Keema more excited than Lauren had ever seen her.

'Come, come, you must look and listen,' Keema said, taking Lauren's hand and practically dragging her into the house.

The television was on in the small salon, the screen showing a man in snowy white robes and white headdress on a platform in front of a large crowd.

'It is Malik,' Keema pointed out, although a glimpse of his shadowed face, and a flip of Lauren's heart had already told her that.

'He is speaking to the people—I will tell you his words,' Keema added, so Lauren stood and watched as Malik raised his hands and the excited crowd grew silent.

He began to speak, and while she didn't know the meaning of the words, Lauren heard a quiet determination in his voice.

'He talks of the new law,' Keema said. 'Talks of it being a bad law, for do we not live in a great wide world and should we not mix with the people of the whole world, whether for business, or pleasure—even marriage?'

Keema paused, and Lauren moved closer to the television, peering at the screen as if that would help her understand what was going on.

'He says the law tells him he must take a Madani bride, but is that the right thing to do, the good thing to do, if he loves another? He says he wants to marry and rule the country for his nephew, so Nimr will inherit a country that has good education—a university—and good care for sick people. I get the words muddled—'

Keema stopped, apologising for the delay. Listened again, then continued.

'He says that if it were not for the woman he loves, Nimr might not be alive, for the people who killed his father had been looking for him, although he was still only a tiny baby.'

Another pause, this time because the crowd had started shouting and Malik had to raise his hands to silence them again.

'He says the people who killed his brother also killed the family of the woman he loves—the brave woman who became a nomad to protect Nimr.'

Keema stopped again, turning to Lauren to ask, 'Did you do that?"

But Lauren was beyond speech. She had no idea where this was going, but tears were rolling down her cheeks as the man she loved with all her heart and soul spoke of his love for her…

'He says he wishes to do what is right for the country, but the new law says he cannot rule if he marries the woman he loves,' Keema whispered, tears running down her cheeks now.

On the television screen, Malik had stopped speaking for the noise from the crowd had grown so loud he could no longer be heard.

'What are they yelling?' Lauren asked, as the crowd waved their arms in the air and chanted a slogan or something else—the same words over and over again.

'They are crying out, "Marry her." They will not listen any more, they only cry *marry her, marry her, marry her*, all the time.'

And Lauren gave a rueful smile. Maybe if Malik became ruler and slowly brought in some form of democratic government, then the people would have some say in matters such as this—but for now, she knew, they had no power to alter the law passed by the council of elders.

But the words of the people warmed her heart and confirmed her decision to stay in this very different country—to stay and hopefully contribute to its future, to stay and make a difference if she could…

With Keema beside her, she was driven around the area—would it be called a suburb?—between Nim's school and the hospital. The houses were small, and of mud-brick construction, covered with earth-coloured plaster of some kind so they looked as if they'd been part of the landscape for thousands of years.

But inside many of them were new and modern, with two small bedrooms, kitchen and bathroom, living room and laundry, and, best of all, a large back garden, hidden from the front, but many of them already planted with fruit trees and roses.

'I live with my parents,' Keema explained, 'but I will ask my father about how you can buy one.'

'Could I rent one for a while?' Lauren asked, and Keema shook her head.

'I do not know that word but I will ask my father.'

And true to her word, she appeared the next afternoon with her father, a polite, middle-aged man in a business suit.

He bowed over Lauren's hand, and spoke to her in impeccable English.

'How can I help you?' he said.

'I need somewhere to live. Sheikh Abdul-Malik was kind enough to let me stay here while I found my feet, but now Nimr is settled in school and I am happy with my work at the hospital, I would like my own home.'

He bowed his head again, although she knew he must know there was more to her decision than she'd told him. After Malik's speech the entire country knew. Knew, also, that the law was the law.

She explained to her visitor that she must arrange money transfers from Australia before she would have the money to buy a property here but for now would like to rent one.

'And the Sheikh is not willing to make these arrangements for you.'

The implication of the words shocked Lauren. Keema's father was seeing her as a discarded mistress, believing it was Malik's duty to provide for her.

Well, in one way she was, she supposed, but…

How to explain?

'It is *my* decision to leave Abdul-Malik's house—mine, and mine alone. I wish to be independent, as I was back in Australia, but already I love your country and would be happy to remain working here. And I must think of Nimr, this is his heritage.'

And although inside she was a quivering mess, she managed to roll the 'r' on the end of Nim's official name quite well.

Then remembered Malik correcting her when first they'd met, and felt pain slice into her heart.

'You can lease our houses—this is something we have learned since the oil men came,' Keema's father was explaining. 'And more houses have been built for this purpose. But Keema tells me where you are looking—that is not a suitable place for you. There is an area where the ex-pats live—the houses there are better, more like Western houses.'

Which wasn't at all what Lauren wanted.

'Nimr is already at school here, and I would like to live close to his school. I believe he should grow up among his peers, the people he will one day rule—not among foreigners, no matter how convenient that might be.'

Keema's father bowed his head again.

'I shall find out what is available in the area where you wish to live,' he said, but Lauren had a feeling there was something behind his giving in without further argument.

She was proven correct when Malik arrived late that afternoon, a Malik she had never seen—coldly radiating anger.

'You have spoken to an outsider of our affairs,' he said, the words carrying the harshness of ground glass.

'Only Keema's father,' Lauren said. 'No one else. And it wasn't about you and I but about me finding somewhere to live.'

'And you did not think I would provide for you? Did you believe I would cast you both out of my home like so much unwanted rubbish?'

He stormed up and down the colonnade for a few minutes, perhaps so he wouldn't strangle her he was so angry.

Returned to stand in front of her.

'I have already had this house made over to you. It is your home—you will live here, not sneak off to some tiny house near the school.'

Maybe it was the 'sneak off' phrase that annoyed Lauren, but her temper was certainly rising when she said, 'Oh, for heaven's sake, Malik, have some sense. How's your wife going to feel if I'm still living in your home—living like a queen or, worse, a mistress? Will she believe you don't visit me, don't see me when you should be with her? I said I wouldn't harm your marriage in any way—and staying here would do that.'

The sudden flare of anger had burnt out quickly, and all Lauren felt was exhaustion.

So much had happened and she was tired and miserable. Heartbroken, in fact, but no way would she let Malik see that.

She turned away from him and wandered down into the garden, but even the abundant roses failed to give her solace.

Malik subsided into a chair and watched her in the garden, aware she was hurting as much as he was, regretting his anger, although he still felt it was justified.

Did she not really love him that she could just walk away like that?

Especially now things might change.

It was that he'd come to tell her.

He still could…

He stood up and followed her into the garden.

Stopped in front her, by a bush of pale lilac roses—his mother's favourite.

'I am sorry I was angry,' he said when she looked up at him, eyes blank of all emotion. 'I came to tell you the law might change—will change, I think. Or simply be deleted so the right to marry whomever one wishes will stand.'

He waited for a reaction, but none came.

'If that happens, we can marry,' he said, anxious now about her lack of response. 'I love you, Lauren, will you marry me?'

Her lips had moved, but as smiles went it barely fitted the description.

She walked away from him, pausing only to remove a dead rose here and there.

Then stopped and turned to him.

'The law hasn't changed yet,' she reminded him. 'And even if it does, would our marriage be the answer to the future? Won't the people who voted it in the first time be angered by the change—or more angered because they must already have been furious to have done that to you. Could it put Nim at risk?'

Malik shook his head.

She was right.

Changing the law changed nothing—except maybe to put Nimr back into danger.

He had information and supposition—some scraps of proof but nothing definite. Before they could move forward he had to prove his uncle's wife had been behind the so-called accident, and arrange for her to be detained or maybe exiled.

Which should have been his priority all along.

What an idiot he had been!

Here he was, running around trying to protect his own future when his brother's killers remained at large…

He bent and kissed her on the lips.

'Forget the house for the moment,' he said. 'Should you want one in another week, I will find one for you—where you want it, how you want it, I promise you.'

He kissed her again.

'But give me a week,' he said, then departed, because one more kiss and he'd have lifted her into his arms and carried her to bed.

Give him a week?

Two days into this allotted time—had she even agreed?—Lauren was no wiser as to what was going on. She was back at work so there was no time for house-hunting anyway, but of Malik there was no sign—not even a scrawled signature on a child's chart…

She worked, and at home continued her language lessons with Aneesha, going with her to the markets now and then to hear the language spoken all around her—steeping herself in it, and in the lives of the people.

She learned oranges were much prized, and that watermelons grew wild at some oases. She learned the names of many of the spices used in traditional dishes, and bought some beautifully embroidered, fine, silk shawls, even a few tunics that would go over the trousers she'd already been wearing.

But a shadow followed wherever she went, and as the days passed, it grew darker. To her way of thinking, Malik already knew who'd been behind the deaths. Was he concerned that his uncle might also have been involved?

His uncle was a blood relation, and the most important thing she'd learned in her time in Madan was the strength of family ties. For people who had begun as nomadic tribes, or were intermarried with such tribes, the family unit had always been their defence against outsiders—quite often in the past, it had been a physical defence.

So the last thing Malik would want to believe was that his uncle had been involved in his brother's death.

Lauren turned her attention back to work. She was in the nursery, in an isolation room, cuddling a baby with diphtheria.

'If Malik gets his way, your brothers and sisters will never get this horrible disease,' she told the baby as she rocked him to sleep in her arms.

She thought of all the good he could do for this country, and suddenly knew that staying here was probably *not* going to be an option. If *she* simply walked away—

or flew—changed Nim's citizenship to Australian, which would surely cut him off from any position in Madan, then Malik would have no choice but to marry a local girl and get on with his life.

He would be ruler rather than regent, and his children would inherit and Nim would be safe.

It was so simple she didn't understand why she hadn't reached that decision earlier.

Because you love him...

The days passed slowly. The leopard cubs were too big now for Nim to safely play with them and he was back to wanting a rabbit or a dog.

He was happy at school, but he'd been happy back home.

As she had been?

She shook her head, aware that 'kind of content' would be a truer description of her condition.

And I can be that again, she told herself, even with a pain that would lessen, but probably never leave her heart.

Again, it was Keema who hurried her into the small salon to see the local news.

'It is the wife of the sheikh's uncle,' she said. 'She is being banished from Madan.'

'And her husband?' Lauren asked.

Keema shrugged.

'They only talk of the woman, who must have done very bad things to be...you have a word, "exiled", I think?'

'Yes, exiled,' Lauren said, absentmindedly.

But that wasn't something she could talk about—not to Keema, or anyone at the hospital, although there too speculation was rife.

What could a woman have done to be exiled? people asked.

Had she cheated on her husband, which could, under local law, have had a much harsher penalty?

Lauren, aware of the answers, ignored the talk and gossip—and waited…

Malik came at dusk, playing with Nim in the garden, having dinner with the pair of them, talking of nothing much, his face so bland Lauren wanted to hit him for not telling her what was going on.

But with Nim in bed, they could wander into the garden, a place Lauren knew had become special to both of them.

'You saw the news?' he said, and she nodded, but when he said no more, she had to ask.

'She left alone. What of your uncle? Could he not have gone too? Will he not be heartbroken?'

Malik smiled at her.

'I tell you something and you think of someone else—someone who might be hurting.'

'I know about hurting,' she snapped, 'so of course I think of it. Was your uncle not part of it?'

'No! Not at all. In fact, he was horrified when she came to him a few days ago with a plan to hire someone to plant a bomb in a car to kill me, you and Nimr—to get rid of any opposition once and for all.'

'Horrified?'

Malik took her hands in his and drew her closer.

'He came straight to me, beside himself that his wife should think such a thing, let alone plan it, but the similarity to Tariq's death was what hurt him most, and he demanded to know if she'd planned that as well.'

'Did she admit it?'

Malik put his arms around her.

'Not right away, but when she saw his reaction she sneered at him, called him old and worthless, and demanded to know if he'd never realised how powerful it would make him to be rid of all his brother's children. He arrested her himself—called the palace guards and had her taken to the police station, but you're right, I couldn't let him see her face a public trial, so we chose this way.'

'We?' Lauren asked, needing to know the whole story for all she'd rather just be in his arms.

'My uncles and myself—the elders all agreed. To do more would embarrass my uncle and the country would look bad in the eyes of the world.'

'Oh, Malik,' Lauren whispered, and now she did move into his arms, hugging him to her, the week that had seemed more like a year finally over.

It was a long time before they spoke again—apart from whispered promises of love.

But as they lay together in Lauren's bed, watching the dawn light creep slowly into the room, aware they had to part before Nim woke, Malik spoke of their future, of a wedding, of wanting to present the woman he loved to his people.

'We don't need to make a fuss,' Lauren said, but he kissed her opinion off her lips.

'I *want* to make a fuss!' he told her. 'I want the world—well, our part of it—to see the wonderful woman I am marrying. The woman who will help me achieve all my dreams for this country.'

He turned and took her face in his palms.

'I couldn't do it without you,' he said. 'I know that now. I knew it as soon as you sent me away and told me to marry a Madani woman. It was as if I'd lost my dreams as well as you. As if nothing mattered any more. I would happily have taken you and Nim back to Australia and lived there with you both, but you refused to let me run away. And you were right.'

He kissed her lips, a deep kiss of commitment, and gratitude and love, all wrapped up in the touch of lips to lips.

CHAPTER FOURTEEN

As preparations for the wedding began, Lauren had to wonder what she was letting herself in for. To begin, Malik took her to the palace, an enormous, almost fantasy building, once again set in beautifully designed and kept gardens.

She was shown the state rooms that would be their new home, the huge salons where they would entertain both local and foreign dignitaries, then into a guarded and securely locked vault of some kind—as big as a bedroom—with golden treasures, precious stones, tiaras, necklaces, bracelets and rings set out along the shelves.

'Before we had oil—or knew we had oil—this was our bank, our insurance against bad times. For thousands of years the people have traded back and forth, and the ruling tribe has always kept enough of the treasures to add to this collection, so there would always be something to sell in order to provide food for the people, even in the leanest years.'

Lauren could only shake her head in disbelief at the beauty of the objects arrayed in front of her.

'A lot of these things were gifts—from one tribe to another—gifts exchanged. Other things were bought from travellers, either for their beauty or their value. But the personal things, they have been kept for the family, so you must choose a ring—it is tradition.'

'I couldn't choose one of these rings,' Lauren said, waving her hand at an array of dazzling rings in a glass case. 'I'd be uncomfortable wearing any of them.'

Malik smiled at her.

'Of course you would,' he said, 'but maybe this?'

He reached up high and pulled down a small box, opening it to show a beautifully cut sapphire, set in tiny diamonds.

'This is more you,' he said, and took her hand to slip the ring on her finger.

Where it fit perfectly!

'You planned this,' she said, grinning at him then checking the ring again to make sure it was real.

'I did,' he said, looking pleased with himself. 'I had Keema bring me the ring you sometimes wear that was your mother's to get the size and I knew this one was meant for you, so I had it sized and cleaned and there you are.'

'And Keema never said a word. She took me to look at houses, and still never said anything,' Lauren complained, but Malik just grinned at her, then kissed her, and held her left hand very tightly, as if he had to feel the stone on her finger to make it real.

The tour continued, and though Lauren looked around in wonder, there was a growing disquiet deep inside her.

Until finally she had to ask.

'Do we have to live here? Could you not be regent just as easily living where I am now?'

Malik shook his head.

'This is where the people expect me to be,' he said. 'This is where they wish to see me. Come!'

He led her down more corridors, back towards the front of the building, as far as she could make out, until they came to a huge room—more like a concert hall but open along the front and one side.

'This is where, on the first day of each month, people come to me with their problems. Ordinary people—school teachers, doctors, shopkeepers and street sweepers—anyone can come.'

'And you listen?' Lauren asked, thinking of the many times she'd visited her local councillor back at home for shade sails over the play equipment in their nearest park. He'd listened, agreed even, but as far as she knew there were still no shade sails…

'I listen, and do something to help if I can,' Malik assured her with a smile. 'I can't remember every request but I have some very efficient advisors who stand behind me and make notes of what needs to be done.'

'And can most things be done?' Lauren asked.

He nodded.

'Tariq and I, we often stood behind our father, listened to requests, then checked later if this system worked. We saw new wells sunk, and canals cleaned out in some of the suburbs, even once took a camel to a man who needed it as a dowry for his daughter so she could get married.'

Lauren laughed.

'Now, that I can believe you'd do.'

She thought about it for a while.

'Do women come? Or only men?'

'Mostly men, but I have been thinking—maybe we could begin a new tradition. The women could come and speak to you. We would have to find a suitable area—'

'In the garden,' Lauren said. 'They would be more relaxed there, and the children could run around.'

He reached out and hugged her.

'How could you have ever thought I could do this without you?' he demanded.

They wandered out into the gardens, finding an area shielded by hedges that would make a fine audience area.

'Thank you for this idea,' she said to Malik. 'Now I feel I can really help you follow your dreams, but right now I should go back to the house so I can organise more language lessons with Aneesha.'

He held her again, looking into her eyes, his own dancing with amusement.

'Am I not a good language teacher?' he teased.

And although she tried to remain cool and calm, she knew she was blushing.

'I already know the words you can teach me,' she said, and put her arms around him to hold him close, to rest her head against his chest and draw in the essence of the man she loved with all her heart.

But though he returned her hug, it was only momentary for there was far too much to be done.

'We need a date, and I must introduce you to the people as my future bride, and you must consult with Aunt Jane and Joe about when it will be convenient for them to come—and any friends of yours or theirs as well. We will send a plane. You will need a dress, no, two dresses, I think, one for the parade through town and the ceremony and one for the wedding feast with just friends and family and the council of elders and their wives—maybe a few hundred people, no?'

The words swirled around in Lauren's head like papers caught in a whirlwind.

So much for a small wedding!

They made their way back to the state apartments, and this time Lauren looked around the dark rooms ostentatiously decorated with treasures from the vault.

'May I change these rooms?' she asked, and Malik kissed her.

'Do whatever you like. My father's second wife decorated them like this, but as well as the vault there are rooms full of carpets and furnishings in the palace, and shops in the city should you need something special. I must go to work—work here, not at the hospital. I shall send someone to bring Keema and Aneesha to you to help.'

'Thank you,' Lauren whispered as he kissed her goodbye.

Over the next days, with help from the two women, Lauren organised for all the treasures in the entire apartment be returned to the vault, for surely they belonged to the people, not to individuals.

'They should be put on display in the public rooms,' she told the women, 'but we'll get on to that later.'

She looked around.

'The curtains have to go,' she said. 'Heavy gold damask is hardly the perfect choice for this climate. And all the furniture, too. It is too heavy and ornate.'

Aneesha gave orders and strong men miraculously appeared to remove things, and while Aneesha stayed to supervise, Keema and Lauren wandered through the palace, peeking into all the rooms, seeking things Lauren was sure she'd recognise as right when she saw them.

It took a week, between shifts at the hospital, to get the apartments emptied and painted in a sand colour, so pale it looked white in some lights but golden in others.

And then the furniture Lauren had found in her hunt around the palace began to appear. Low divans, piled high with colourful cushions, a huge bed with a carved headboard that looked as if it might have come from China millennia ago. Snow-white sheets and an ornately embroidered silk coverlet Lauren had found hanging on a wall in a dark corridor. A small table and two chairs were set beside the window, dressed now with sheer cream curtains that billowed into the room in the wind.

With her two patient helpers, she then scoured the palace for carpets, knowing what she wanted for the bedroom—hand-woven silk on silk that was blissful beneath bare feet.

Her search took her to the back regions of the palace where, to her surprise, she found what could only be described as a village. Out beyond all the state apartments and housekeeping and catering sections of the palace she found the staff housing, with children running around kicking footballs and riding bicycles.

And although she was pleased, for Nim would surely find some friends among these children, it was an old woman that she sought. A weaver and expert on all traditional carpets and mats and camel bags who, she was told, knew every rug the palace owned.

Aneesha introduced them and translated, and the old woman, now retired, stood up and beckoned them to follow her.

She chatted to Aneesha as they walked through corridors unknown to Lauren and into a darkened room.

'She says these carpets are not for everyone,' Aneesha explained. 'She says the last woman could not have these carpets. She, the old woman, would not allow.'

Lights came on and Lauren stared in wonder at the beautiful carpets, piled on each other according to size, their dazzling colours a feast for the eyes.

'This one she made herself,' Aneesha said, and Lauren knelt to examine it, running her hands over the unbelievable softness, tracing the intricate patterns with her finger.

'May I have it?' she asked, aware just how special it was.

Aneesha translated and the woman beamed at her and nodded.

'She would be honoured,' Aneesha said, then followed

the old woman to where she was turning back some carpets at the top of another pile, stopping at one in particular that sang with the colours of the desert in pale cream and gold and red.

Lauren smiled and nodded, then asked Aneesha if the woman would be willing to select all the carpets for her.

'Ask her if she will come with us to the apartments and have a look, so she will know what they need.'

It took some time, but eventually the apartment was finished, the muted colours of the furnishings Lauren had chosen allowing the carpets to reveal their full magnificence, and turning the rooms into places of restful and elegant beauty.

'So, you will show me what you've done?' Malik asked one evening when he called at the house for dinner with her and Nim.

She shook her head.

'That's a surprise for you on our wedding night,' she told him, then Nim was talking about his visit to the palace and the children he'd met and, of course, the dogs.

'They are called saluki hounds and could I have one, please?' he finished, and while Malik explained that they were hunting dogs and he would have to look after it himself, see it always had plenty of fresh water, and feed it, and take it for long walks for exercise, Lauren thought back to the first day they'd had dinner together—in her small kitchen back home.

Malik had spoken of these dogs then. How far they had come…

CHAPTER FIFTEEN

THE QUESTION OF the wedding was still to be settled, Lauren baulking at the idea of hundreds of guests and two different dresses and the other things Malik had suggested.

'It is how things are done,' he said. 'And it is my opportunity to introduce you to the people.'

She smiled at him.

'I think I've already met a fair cross-section of the Madani people during the vaccinations or at the hospital. And after your impassioned plea for support, they all know about me. Can't we just be married quietly? Maybe later have receptions for guests?'

'So how would you like to be married?' Malik asked. They'd stolen a few quiet moments to themselves in his office at the hospital, Lauren about to go off duty and he abandoning affairs of state to give Graeme a break.

'Now I have options?' Lauren teased.

'Of course you have,' he said. 'There's the palace without the pomp and ceremony if you that's what you'd prefer. There's plenty of choice there. Or any one of the big hotels would be only too happy to make the arrangements.'

'And the rose garden?'

Malik smiled at the woman he loved.

'Really?'

She nodded.

'Unless you really need to have all that fuss you spoke of earlier—a wedding befitting your position—what I'd really like is something small and private in the garden, because, if you think about it, it's about us, not other people.'

And although he'd thought his heart was already full of love for this woman, he felt it swell with the emotion once again.

'I'm not the King, just the caretaker, and I can get married however I like. You're right, we'll leave the pomp and ceremony for Nimr when his turn comes. So the rose garden it will be. We'll just have Aunt Jane and Joe, and Nimr, of course, and anyone else you'd like, and my uncles, who are so contrite at what they did with the vote it will be like forgiveness to them.'

'Aunt Jane and Joe?' Lauren whispered, as if she'd doubted what she'd heard.

He smiled at her.

'Of course! I'll arrange to bring them over, and you might ask them if they'd like to stay a while and see Madan. Other friends, if you'd like. Maybe Peter Cross and his family if Susie is well enough to travel—it might be a little treat for them after all they've been through. I can send a plane so numbers don't matter.'

Lauren shook her head in disbelief. He'd only heard of Susie that one evening and yet he'd remembered her name. Although, being Malik, he'd probably talked to Peter and learned a lot more…

So! A wedding in the rose garden.

'It's like a dream,' she said quietly.

'But not one we have to wake up from, surely,' he said, getting up from the piles of paperwork on his desk and coming around to hold her for a few minutes.

They talked of dates again—ten days away—and times—early morning when the dew was still on the roses—and Malik was filled with a deep inner peace and happiness, two things that had been missing from his life since Tariq's death.

Later that day he went out to the house to have dinner with 'his family', taking with him a gift for Lauren.

'What is it?' she asked, holding the light, tissue-wrapped parcel.

'Open it and see,' Malik told her, and she did, Nim hovering by her side to see what was inside.

A long shawl in fine, palest pink silk, heavily embroidered with silver thread.

'Oh, it's beautiful,' she said, touching the delicate material with soft fingers.

'It was my mother's,' he told her. 'She wore it on her wedding day.'

Lauren set it down and hugged him hard, her throat too thick with emotion for speech.

But, she realised later, looking at the treasured gift, it solved the problem of what to wear for her wedding. Once she'd dismissed the idea of a massive royal wedding and two dresses to get through it, she had been through the seemingly endless racks of clothes in her dressing room, and although many of them were obviously for evening or formal occasions, she'd been unable to decide.

But seeing this, she pictured a rose-pink tunic that had pale pink and silver embroidery. With the scarf wrapped around her head instead of a veil, it would be perfect.

The days flew by. Joe, Aunt Jane and the Cross family arrived, much to Nim's delight, and while Nim took Joe, Peter and Susie out the back to introduce him to the animals and the vet who cared for them, Lauren and the two women went through the clothes in the dressing room.

For Nim there was a new *thobe*, or long white tunic,

and a new cap for his head, although Lauren had to put a stop to him nagging Joe to also wear a 'dress'.

The day finally arrived, and Lauren and her 'family' walked through the garden to the arch where white roses grew from either side to fill the air with fragrance, their spent petals forming a carpet beneath their feet.

And Malik fit right in, garbed in his snowy robe and simple white square of headdress, held in place with a gold cord.

Lauren felt her breath catch in her throat at the sight of him, and for a moment she faltered. But she was close enough to see the sudden concern in his eyes so she smiled and kept walking, Nim by her side, Aunt Jane and Joe, the Cross family, and Keema and Aneesha close behind.

They stood and made their vows, which were blessed by an elder, then gathered in the small salon for a wedding breakfast of surely unparalleled magnificence.

Roses decorated the centre of the table with bowls piled high with fruit on either side. On the sideboard, an array of dishes with mouth-watering aromas were being kept warm over small heaters.

They ate and talked, and although Lauren would have liked nothing more than to slip away with her new husband, politeness insisted she stay.

But when they had eaten, coffee and sweet pastries were served in the colonnade, looking out over the roses, and she sat with Malik's uncles, assuring them she held no ill-will against them.

Malik had wandered off with Joe, and Nim was telling Aunt Jane about his school.

And there, in the garden, Lauren realised she'd found the place that she belonged—Madan. She was already planning how to set up the health posts along the routes of the nomadic tribes, a job Malik was only too happy for her to take over.

And Nim—she looked at his happy face as he explained about the leopards—had accepted this marriage with delight, assuring her when she'd stumbled through her explanation that he already knew people got married so they could sleep in the same bed…

She'd spoken to Aunt Jane and Joe, telling them she'd had solicitors draw up the papers to pass the ownership of her old home to Joe. Telling them also just how grateful she would always be to the two of them—taking care of her when she'd been broken by grief, coming to live with her to help with Nim—just being a family for her when she'd lost hers.

Telling them also that they were welcome to visit any time—that they would all love to see them…

Then Malik's voice broke into her rambling thoughts—Malik, her husband.

'And now,' he said, 'we come to the bride gift. It is customary in our family to give the bride a gift of money or jewellery that will provide for her should anything happen to me.'

He smiled at Lauren and added, 'Not that it will, my love, for how could I leave you?

'But my wife, who, as some of you already know, has decided views on many subjects, one of which, apparently, is not accepting such extravagant—as she calls them—gifts.' He paused to smile at his new bride. 'So I have been speaking to Joe, and with your permission, Lauren, I would like to give your bride gift to Joe for the organisation that he is now involved with—helping and training disabled defence force personnel, giving them a purpose in life and goals to aim for in the future, especially now the Invictus Games are growing into worldwide events.'

'Oh, Malik, that is a wonderful idea,' Lauren said, slipping down into the garden to give Joe a hug, then turning to hug Malik.

He held her close, just held her, but through the peace that being in his arms always brought another thought surfaced.

'Can we go soon?' she whispered, and his body, so close to hers, told her the answer.

And, as if by magic, the party dispersed. Aneesha had arranged a tour of the country for the visitors and Nim—trips to the lodge in the desert, and date farms, and oases, camel rides, and nights under the stars.

But Lauren and Malik had a shorter journey—to the apartment in the palace, where Malik shook his head in wonder at the transformation.

'It's like being in the lodge, but in the city,' he murmured as he took her in his arms, kissing her thoroughly before they tried the big old bed for size and comfort.

'I love you so much, Mrs Madani,' he whispered.

'And I you!' she said, as a deep feeling of peace and contentment settled into her heart—nestling up against the brimming love…

* * * * *

THE ITALIAN SURGEON'S SECRET BABY

SUE MACKAY

MILLS & BOON

PROLOGUE

'THAT WAS TOO CLOSE.' Nurse Elene Lowe shuddered and wiped the back of her glove-covered hand across her brow as she stepped back from the theatre table where five-year-old Joe Crawford lay, cast in so much plaster he wouldn't be moving for the foreseeable future.

'Too damned close.' Mattia Ricco, the surgeon, scowled. 'Can everyone ask their favourite child-whisperer or whatever to watch over this kid? He's going to need all the help going and some.'

'Sure will.' One of the other nurses grimaced over her shoulder as she left the theatre, closely followed by most of the team.

Beep. Once again the heart monitor was telling them Joe had gone into arrest.

Mattia swore as he snatched up the paddles. 'Stand back.'

Elene's own heart stalled. 'So not fair.' The little guy had arrested twice during the hours of surgery he'd just undergone to deal with two fractured legs and one smashed arm, and to wire his jaw back together.

His little body jerked upwards as Mattia applied an electric jolt.

Beep. Beep. Beep.

'I'll tell you what's not fair,' Mattia growled. 'A mother

driving through the city on a busy Friday night with her son lying down on the back seat asleep instead of belted securely into a car seat.'

He was right. Why would any loving parent do that? The drunk driver who took out the car at speed might not be Joe's mother's fault, but surely not protecting her child was? Elene swallowed the sour taste in her mouth. She understood Mattia's need to let rip, and as there was only her and the anaesthetist to hear him he was safe from condemnation. 'I'll take Joe through to Recovery and bring them up to speed on what's been happening.'

'I'm coming with you,' Mattia muttered. 'Not because I think you need me to fill in the gaps as you report everything, but I'm reluctant to hand him over until I know his heart's not going to stop again.'

Exactly her feelings. 'It's hard, but he'll be monitored and looked after as well as he was in here. No one's going to take their eyes off him for a long while.'

Forty minutes later Mattia said. 'The obs are the best they've been, though not how I'd like them.' He turned to Elene. 'Coffee? I want to be within calling distance in case…'

No surprise there. The Italian specialist on contract for a year had won the admiration of all Wellington's orthopaedic department's staff for his dedication and high standards. He'd also won the heart of every female in the whole hospital with his good looks and charisma, including hers. 'Tea for me.' She followed him into the cramped space that was the staff tea room beside the theatre. In her head she could still see Joe's little face smothered in the mask supplying him with oxygen and the small body being gently put back together. The heart failures. She wasn't ready to be alone with her thoughts. 'Who'd be a parent?'

'It's enough to put you off, I'll agree.

'But hell.' Mattia rammed his fingers through his thick, wavy hair. 'A five-year-old having cardiac arrest is beyond description. How was I going to tell his parents if we hadn't brought him back?' His Italian accent had thickened, making his words harder to decipher.

Elene's stomach turned to acid. 'This is when I wonder if I've chosen the right job. I hate having to be a part of so much agony and distress.' She'd spoken in Italian without thought. Reverting to English, her native tongue, she continued, 'Not even saving Joe takes away the nightmare of what we witnessed tonight.' Quickly spooning coffee granules into one mug and dropping a teabag into another, Elene tried to find something good to think about.

'Don't believe that. You're an exceptional nurse. We all have those doubts at times like this.' Mattia reached around her with the milk.

'Yeah,' she sighed. 'I guess.' A hint of the wild tickled her nose. Aftershave? Nope, there was light stubble on that sexy chin behind her. She tried to step away to put a gap between them and bumped against Mattia's chest. A solid, muscular wall that filled his scrubs top to perfection. Jerking away, she moved again, only to find him standing rock-solid in front of her, those intense dark eyes locked on hers—with something like lust spiralling through them. Did he need to blot out the last two hours too? In an instant common sense deserted her as excitement rose, filling her lungs, her stomach, her centre—tipping her forwards, towards that body she'd eyed more than once with a sense of wonder. Shutting down everything but the need to press close and feel—*feel* his strength, the tone of his worked-out muscles, his sex, to forget the horrendous scenes imprinted on her brain.

Hands were on her waist, bringing her closer to her goal. Firm, warm, sensual hands. Then she forgot the hands as

Mattia's head descended until his lips were close, so close, teasing, flirting—waking her up as she hadn't been in all the years since she'd left her ex. As she hadn't wanted to be for fear she'd repeat the same mistakes. But this was Mattia, the man she'd lusted after, and therefore argued with often to keep him at arm's length, for the eleven months he'd been working here.

This is the man your best friend's currently having a fling with.

Elene jerked out of those hands, away from that provocative mouth that could start her on a path to somewhere she must not go, and cursed the day he'd left Italy to work in New Zealand.

Mattia breathed deep, filling his depleted lungs and tightening his gut. Not for a nanosecond did his gaze leave Elene's face. She was swallowing as if her life depended on getting fluid down her throat. Her eyes were wide and filled with guilt. Guilt that was now creeping into his mind. While technically it wasn't a full-on relationship that would lead to something permanent, he was in the midst of a fling with another nurse, Danielle. Despite the casualness of their liaison he would not seek out another woman until it was over—probably at the end of his contract in four weeks.

But he'd come so close to kissing Elene. Too damned close. Driven by the need to blank out images of young Joe on the table, his heart stopping, his smashed bones, his innocence—yeah, damn it, falling into a kiss with a beautiful woman, even an out-of-bounds one, seemed the perfect distraction. Except it wasn't. She was right to pull away.

'Forget the coffee. I'm heading to PICU.' Hopefully the lad who had his mind going off track was now in there.

'No problem,' Elene answered in a tone that suggested it very much was.

He paused at the door. 'I apologise for my actions. I'm involved with your friend. It was wrong of me.' Playing the field didn't mean being callous and uncaring. He understood too well how that hurt others. Not that his ex-fiancée had done that to him. No, she'd found another way to decimate him, but despite the anger he'd never taken up deliberately hurting other women to ease his own pain. At the moment, Danielle was his latest conquest so other women were off-limits. Unfortunately. Because that near kiss— He'd never know. Yet now he understood why Elene had subconsciously been plaguing him on and off over the past months. She was hot, therefore dangerous to his equilibrium. But he was not about to change his thinking on women and relationships, not because this one set his heart racing as if it were being chased by a greyhound.

'I—' Her throat rose around another swallow. 'If you're apologising then I owe you one too. That shouldn't have happened. It certainly won't again. I can't believe I nearly let you kiss me.' She paused, drew a breath. 'I can only put it down to wanting to get as far away from the last two hours as possible.'

The two women were close, probably had an agreement not to look at each other's men, let alone kiss them. He stepped through the door, keen to get away and put this behind him. 'Elene, it's okay. Best we forget it ever happened though.' Like how? 'Believe it or not, I don't want to hurt Danielle any more than you do.'

Her head dipped. 'So we'll go back to being thoroughly professional around each other and no one will be any the wiser.'

He couldn't tell if that was relief or disappointment

flooding her eyes, and he wasn't hanging around to find out. They had to work together for another month. The idea of maintaining their usual aloof, sometimes argumentative façade was curdling in his stomach, despite being the right thing to do. Because it was a façade. On his part anyway. He wanted to know Elene—intimately.

But that's the last thing you're going to do, man.

CHAPTER ONE

'WHAT DO YOU MEAN? Double-booked *my* room?' Only the twelve-month-old in Elene Lowe's arms kept her from crumpling to a heap on the garish red carpet. Landing in a tangle of arms and legs would only exacerbate their distraught mood, and give the receptionist reason to be happy she had missed out on a room. Missed out? Elene slapped the printout of her confirmation lying on the counter. 'Booked and paid for. Six weeks ago. I am not going anywhere else.' If only her voice held the conviction required to back that statement, but she was all out of strength and energy. 'I need this room.'

'I understand, *signora*.' A quick glance at Elene's ring finger had the receptionist changing tack. '*Signorina*, I'm sorry, sometimes mistakes are made. The other people who booked and paid for the room arrived three hours ago and have signed in. We cannot ask them to leave now.'

'Yet you can ask me to go away.' Elene's hand tightened around her cherished bundle. All she wanted was to get Aimee settled so they both could fall asleep for hours. 'What am I supposed to do?'

Aimee began kicking her feet, a precursor to waking up. Long overdue. She'd woken when they'd disembarked at Naples International Airport, and instantly fell asleep again once in the taxi that brought them down to Sorrento, an expense well worth the money after more than thirty-four hours travelling from Wellington.

The receptionist seemed particularly interested in her fingernails as she muttered, 'There are no hotel rooms available in town. I know this from other people coming here looking for accommodation.'

Full of good news, wasn't she? 'I have to find somewhere.' Careful. Don't let the anger out. 'Can you suggest somewhere close by? Another town? My d-daughter.' She still tripped over that word. 'She's tired after a long journey and I need to settle her.'

'*Sì*, I understand, *signorina*. I will try the hostels, though you might have to share a room with other women.' The girl was already picking up the phone.

Hostels? As in backpackers' accommodation? With a toddler? Oh, that would be absolutely wonderful for everyone. Then again, what choice did she have? Sleeping outside the train station wouldn't be a good look; it'd probably scar Aimee for ever, and it would be a negative addition to the pros and cons list a certain doctor would no doubt draw up when he learned why they were here.

A high-pitched shriek reverberated in Elene's ear. Little legs kicked and hands pummelled her back and chest. Aimee had had enough.

'Shh.' Elene kissed her forehead. 'Shh, we're nearly there, sweetheart.' Lying to her girl was not good, but some people out there reckoned positive thoughts brought positive results. Lifting the writhing body above her head, she stared up and found a smile. 'Aimee, Aimee, wee, wee, wee.' Wonderful, even her singsong voice was off-key.

Another shriek bounced off the walls. Tears dripped down Aimee's red, scrunched-up face.

'Oh, baby, I know.' It was hard not to join in the crying. Digging into the backpack lying at her feet, she found the bottle of milk and tried to placate Aimee, but it was cold, and only achieved raising the noise level to extreme. Anyone would think she was murdering her little girl. Elene's heart swelled for this trusting little soul. None of this was *her* fault.

The receptionist had turned her back on them and was talking rapidly into the phone. Finding a bed in a hostel wasn't sounding promising either.

A bitter gust of breath crossed Elene's bottom lip. There was no avoiding it. She was going to have to front up early, unprepared, and on the back foot right from the start. Face it—she would never be prepared, didn't possess the elegance and sophistication required to look Mattia Ricco squarely in the eye as an equal, but she did have right on her side. And the backing of a loving, caring family in New Zealand. If only they were here. Except she had herself to blame for that one, having turned down every offer from both sisters and her mother to accompany her on this life-changing trip.

She tapped the counter. *'Mi scusi—taxi?'*

No, be strong.

'Please call me a taxi.' This time her voice wasn't a whisper.

The receptionist turned to point outside the front entrance. *'Dietro l'angolo.'*

'Grazie.' If only she had the energy to get around the corner.

'Ma-ma ma-ma.' Aimee's tiny fist banged Elene's shoulder and the bottle went flying, spraying a stream of white droplets over Elene's crumpled shirt and down to the carpet.

'Yes, baby girl, you're right. I need to get a grip.' She looked across to the receptionist with an apology. 'Excuse me.' Why hadn't she booked a hotel room in Naples for the night? Back in New Zealand, it had seemed such a good idea to get to Sorrento and settle in, catch up on sleep before tracking down her adversary. They hadn't stopped any longer in the places they'd landed on this endless journey than it took to catch the next flight because, back in the comfort of her cottage in Wellington, getting to the end and holing up until fit and ready for the upcoming confrontation had seemed the best way to go.

The receptionist came around the desk and picked up the bottle. 'Come on. I'll help you get a taxi. Where do you want to go?'

'The hospital.'

The young woman's eyes widened as she glanced at Aimee, remorse instantly filling her expression. 'I'm sorry we made a mistake with your booking. I'll heat the milk for your *bambino*.'

Elene couldn't lie. 'It's all right. Aimee's not sick. I know someone who works there who will help me out.' He'd have no choice. 'But if you can heat the milk I'd be very grateful.' Thank goodness Italian was her second language. How she'd manage otherwise didn't bear thinking about.

'My sister has a baby too.'

Aimee's not really mine. Make that not only mine. Because Aimee was hers in a complex kind of way. There was paperwork to prove it. Elene managed to keep the words behind closed lips. Having to explain was too complicated and time-consuming—and irrelevant. 'Aimee's had to put up with a lot of flying. She's been a champ.'

Finally settling into a taxi, she clicked the seatbelt into place, relieved there was a child's seat since she hadn't brought one with them, being too bulky and heavy with their other luggage. 'Don't go to sleep now, baby girl. Drink your milk instead. We're nearly there.' With every turn the taxi took her heart rate quickened. Should've stayed at home. Too late now. Or was it? Mattia had no idea she was in Italy, let alone about to knock on his door and burst his over-inflated bubble. She could still run away and forget all about keeping her promise to her best friend.

Aimee's little chest fell on a sigh as she scoffed the milk.

Elene's heart squeezed. 'Love you, baby girl. We're doing the right thing coming here.' What if Mattia—?

Don't go there. Take this one step at a time. This was what Danielle wanted, and what *she'd* promised to do for her. But she didn't plan on getting her heart broken. She was thinking about Aimee here, not Mattia's sexiness, which she'd not managed to forget as she should've.

So fight hard for Aimee, for both of you.

It could be a costly battle. Her family had money, but Mattia's was loaded to the point of being obscene. The smart thing would have been to stay in Wellington and pretend she hadn't made the promise of her lifetime. The smart thing, also amoral. Being abandoned by her biological father before she'd been born had skewed her thinking until she'd finally met him as a teenager. That was when she'd totally accepted as her father the man who'd raised her after marrying her mother and knew how lucky she'd been. Everyone needed, was entitled to, the unconditional love of good parents. 'Everyone, baby girl.'

The taxi stopped outside Sorrento's hospital all too soon. After settling Aimee into her stroller, Elene moved towards the lift that would take them up to Mattia's office, tugging their bag behind her. Despite the spring heat, her skin lifted in cold bumps. The time had come. Her hand tightened around the stroller handle. 'Please say I'm doing the right thing. It's what your mother wanted but I can't deny the fear of losing you to him blocking my throat.' She had to trust all the kind things Danielle said about him.

The lift must have been boosted by a rocket launcher. *Ping*, floor three. Then the doors slid open so fast she was spilling out into a corridor bustling with medical staff, orderlies pushing beds and patients on crutches. Sucking in her stomach, lifting her chin, she stepped into the office with the sign declaring 'Dottore Mattia Ricco' and up to the woman behind the desk and said, 'My name is Elene Lowe. I am here to see Dr Ricco.'

'You don't have an appointment,' responded the woman in a don't-fool-with-me voice.

'I don't, but I can wait until he is finished for the day.' Any time soon, surely? The clock outside the door had read eighteen-oh-five.

'The doctor doesn't see people without an appointment. He's a very busy man.'

'Please tell him I am here and let him decide if he'll see me.' Because if he refused she had his home address on her phone, and right about now she'd do whatever it took to find a bed for Aimee.

The woman glanced at the closed door to the side. 'I can't do that.'

Just then Aimee let out a shriek and began pummelling her thighs, pushing her little body against the stroller restraints.

'I think my baby needs changing.'

'There are public toilets on this floor.'

Elene's eyes suddenly stung. It was all too much. 'Please.'

'Sorry.'

Typical of Mattia to have a heartless lioness guarding his patch. Not that she had any right to complain, but there was no accounting for exhaustion and worry. 'I am going in to see the doctor now, and taking my child with me.'

The woman rose. 'You can't. He's unavailable right this moment.'

Of course. He'd be with a patient. She lifted Aimee out of the stroller. 'Then I'll sit here and wait. I am not going anywhere until I've talked to Mattia.' She wasn't risking him leaving while she was in a bathroom.

'I'll call Security.'

'That won't be necessary, Sonia,' came an annoyed command from behind Elene. 'I will see to this lady. You can go home. It is late for you to be here.'

'But—'

'No buts, Sonia. Please do as I say.' Mattia might be talking to his secretary but his gaze was fixed on Elene when she twisted around to face him. Those almost black eyes were wide with surprise. 'Elene.'

So he hadn't recognised her from behind. Nor her voice. Or he had and hoped he was wrong. 'Mattia,' she acknowledged. Let the show begin. Better yet, could it wait twenty-four hours? She might be more prepared.

'This is an unexpected pleasure.'

'I'm sure pleasure is the last thing you're feeling.' They had rarely got on well enough to have more than a professional relationship, and when he'd dumped her best friend in preparation to swan out of Wellington onto his next adventure they'd drawn battle lines.

'Still blunt, I see.'

'Only way to go,' she snapped, before remembering she was supposed to get on with him or there'd be no hope for her or Aimee. 'Sorry. It's been a long and arduous couple of days and my tongue's getting the better of me.'

His gaze alighted on her mouth, his eyes widening almost imperceptibly. She was hallucinating. Could he be remembering that awkward moment back in Wellington? But why would he? It wasn't as though he'd have been celibate in the intervening year after leaving Danielle. He asked, 'You've come all this way to see me?'

The disbelief was so tangible she could almost see it hanging in the air between them. She could certainly feel it. Not that she blamed him. Turn the situation around and she'd be reacting exactly the same. 'Can we talk in private?' Her arm tightened involuntarily around Aimee. *Here we go.* The stress expanded, spread through her like wildfire in a pine tree plantation.

The dark gaze that had been focused on her lowered to her precious bundle, and Mattia rocked on his feet. His wide mouth flattened, and all that arrogance she remembered rose to the fore.

'We should take this somewhere else,' she managed through a dry mouth.

Mattia raised his head to stare at her, shock beginning to shadow that gaze.

He knows. Without a word being said, he's seen what's before him.

Mattia stepped back from them—way back. 'Congratulations on your child. How old is she?'

Denial to the fore. 'This is Aimee. She's twelve months old.' *Do the sums. Believe your gut reaction.*

But Mattia wasn't playing that game. He had one of his own on the go. 'Twelve months, eh? You kept your relationship quiet. I thought you were sworn to a single life.'

She still was. Which was none of his business. *Careful, you have to talk with Mattia about some serious stuff in the coming days.* 'I wasn't dating anyone when you were with Danielle.'

'How is Danielle?' His gaze flicked to Aimee, immediately looked away.

Oh, no. She was about to leap right into the middle of the deepest pool without a lifebelt. Her heart was already diving. Inclining her head towards the door that led into his office, she whispered, 'Can we?'

'I think we must.' He turned to his secretary, who hadn't done as requested and left. 'Sonia, I'll see you tomorrow.' His tone brooked no argument, yet the woman didn't leap up to leave. Brave lady. Or did she have something on him?

Could she share it with me? Gathering strength from Sonia's attitude, Elene stepped past Mattia. Then faltered. He had never seemed so tall, nor his frame so solid and imposing. Not even when he'd held her, been about to kiss her. Then, when the office door clicked shut behind them, the air evaporated, leaving her lungs struggling to do their job. Without invitation, she sank onto the nearest chair and settled Aimee on her lap, an arm around her tiny waist.

Mattia crossed purposefully to his desk but didn't sit, instead staring down at her. At them.

Too late, Elene realised she should've remained on her feet. Down here, she was at a disadvantage. No change then. But, for a moment, under that unnerving gaze locked on her, she'd forgotten how to fight her corner.

Two words cracked across the silence. 'So? Danielle?'

No easy way to say this. 'Died. Cancer.' Two months down the track, it hurt like yesterday. The pain was a rock behind her heart. She missed her friend so much. There was anger at Danielle being taken so young, when she had so much to look forward to and a daughter who needed her and who'd barely got to know her mother.

A breath hissed over Mattia's lips. 'That I did not expect.'

'Who would?' Danielle had been thirty-four, fit, supposedly healthy, with everything ahead of her.

His fingers raked his dark hair. 'Can I ask what type?'

'Cervical. It was rapid.' And brutal. A familiar nausea

soured her mouth. Caring for her best friend in those last months had been the hardest thing she'd ever done.

Aimee squawked.

Grateful for the interruption, Elene lightened her grip and kissed Aimee's cheek. 'Sorry, darling.' When she looked up there was no avoiding that dark, inscrutable gaze fixed on them. She had to get this over with. 'The cancer was discovered before Aimee was born.'

One abrupt nod. 'So the child is Danielle's?'

You've already figured that out. 'Aimee. Her name is Aimee.' Elene leapt up and strode across to stand right in front of him. 'Get it?'

She had to give him credit. He didn't back away or make a dash for the door. 'Yes, I get it.'

That stole her thunder. Did he really understand what she'd been saying without putting it into words? Probably not. Why would he? It wasn't as though Danielle had rung and told him the instant she'd found out. She hadn't told him at all. But there'd been that moment of recognition in Mattia's eyes. Could be she'd misinterpreted it.

Returning to the chair, Elene sat down and tried to relax. Getting angry or upset wasn't going to achieve a thing, and she hadn't been kicked out—yet. 'Aimee's nearly one, was born on the third of May last year.'

'Taurus.'

'What?' This man with a scientific mind knew his star signs? She'd thought she was beyond being surprised.

'The bull. Deliberate in actions, methodical. Likes luxury.'

Surprise got the better of her. 'You know this how?'

'I too am Taurus. You've got your hands full with this one.'

'*We* have.' *I want Aimee full-time, but I can't deny your role.*

'Now we're getting to the crux of your visit.' Mattia parked his honed butt on the corner of his desk. 'Tell me exactly why you're here.'

Truthfully? Mattia did not want to know. He really, really didn't. Sure, he'd made a summation of the situation, but to hear Elene confirm it would mean there'd be no way out. No going back to the life he'd had up until ten minutes ago. At this moment, there was still hope.

So Mattia focused on Elene instead. The instant he'd seen her standing in his reception area, that long auburn hair all askew, escaping the band meant to keep it in place, the slump in her small shoulders, the curve of her hips against the light fabric of her baggy trousers, he'd felt something he shouldn't have. A wave of lust. For Elene? Couldn't be, when they'd kept each other at arm's length, especially after the night he'd come within a whisker of kissing her. Yet the tightening in his crotch was definitely the sensation that went with sexual need. The woman who'd done nothing but annoy the hell out of him had found another way to vex him.

Danielle Hicks had always laughed at how he got so uptight around her friend, said he should get to know Elene properly because she was the best. Sadness engulfed him. Danielle. No one deserved her fate. She'd been such a vibrant woman, bigger than life, fun with a capital F. Being a doctor, he knew there were no boundaries when it came to life dishing out bad calls, but that didn't mean he had to like them. 'I'm sorry about Danielle,' he told Elene with all sincerity. She must've been devastated, still would be.

'Thank you.' *Sì*, definitely a wealth of pain and passion in those two simple words.

Mattia found his eyes tracking to the child now starting to grizzle.

Instantly Elene was cuddling and kissing her, before placing her on the floor to crawl. 'There you go, sweetheart. Freedom at last. All that flying's over. For now.'

Mattia ignored the 'for now'. 'You came straight through?' That'd be some haul for anyone, let alone a toddler.

'Yes. It might've been better to stop overnight in Hong Kong, but I thought I'd get here, then relax. A prolonged stop mightn't have worked for Aimee. Then again, I could be wrong.'

The child sank onto her butt and stared around the room, finally bringing dark eyes to rest on him. *His eyes.* Mattia fought the stab of wonder hitting his belly. But she was *his*. No denying the toddler came from his gene pool. There were photos on his desk showing almost identical faces—only those belonged to his niece and nephew. Cute like Aimee. Some time in the few weeks he'd dated Danielle he'd created a child. His hands clenched against his hips. He was a *babbo*. Like it or not.

That he could accept—well, he would after time to think about it and absorb the truth of the matter. He wasn't going to admit as much to Elene though. Not yet. Not until he learned what was behind this visit. It wouldn't be straightforward—meet your child and get to know her.

Elene's sudden appearance without warning was a worry in itself. Back in Wellington, her snippy remarks about his womanising had rankled. She'd also pushed the guilt button for that hot moment with her when he was in the midst of a fling with her friend. In defence, he'd always been honest with women about what he required from a relationship and if they couldn't agree he moved on fast. Elene had never accepted that Danielle was happy to go along with the rules. Elene was a warrior when it came to protecting her friend. So it stood to reason she'd be the same with her friend's daughter. *My daughter.* No.

Don't accept it so readily. There had to be proof and legalities and a whole load of other things to consider first. His stomach clenched so tight it hurt. Because he already knew half the score. Aimee was his. He'd never walk away from her, no matter what.

He demanded of Elene, 'Why are you here?' *To ask for money? To hand over Aimee and leave, free of obligations?* No, even with his high level of distrust he knew she wouldn't do that. Or would she? Raising a child would interfere with her career, and he'd seen how serious she took nursing. Couldn't fault her there. He could use her talents here, with the ridiculous lack of suitable nurses at the moment.

'We don't have anywhere to stay.' She'd gone for the immediate situation, not the bigger one. 'I'm hoping you can look past our previous disagreements to help me out.'

Sì, she could still push his buttons. If he wasn't careful he could find himself enjoying that. Mattia studied the pale face in front of him. Shadows stained her cheeks, her mouth drooped, as did her whole body, really. She was shattered, and who wouldn't be after those long flights getting here from New Zealand? Throw a baby into the mix and it was a wonder she was conscious.

'Believe me, the last thing I'm feeling like is arguing.' Nor was he mentioning the unexpected heat lancing him internally from seeing her again. She was a breath of fresh, though angry, air.

'I'm sorry for turning up like this. I'd hoped for a night to recuperate,' she acquiesced, worrying him more than almost anything else she could've done.

'You came here directly from the airport?'

'Via the hotel that double-booked my room.'

Blink, blink.

Don't cry. You are a tough, snippy woman—you don't do tears.

Then her words swiped his brain. Elene meant it when she said she didn't have anywhere to stay. Got it wrong about what would worry him the most, hadn't he? She'd just handed him a grenade. Offering her a place to stay for a few days would mean seeing his daughter every day—bringing home the truth: bang, bang, bang. Having to spend endless hours in Elene's company was another problem that'd be equally difficult to handle. He breathed deep. Tossing her out on the street wasn't an option. His house was enormous; this mightn't be as difficult as he envisioned. Besides, it was said, keep your friends close and your enemies closer. At the moment Elene fell into the latter category. 'I believe you have a nappy to change.' He'd overheard her conversation with Sonia.

Her head dropped, rose, in a slow nodding gesture. 'I do.'

He took charge. 'I have a patient to check on. It won't take long, then we'll head home. Unless you want me to change the nappy first.' It wasn't as though he didn't know how.

She stared at him like there was no strength left in any part of her small frame. As if he'd offered her a gift she was waiting for him to snatch back. Finally she muttered, 'I'll do the nappy.'

Who'd have believed he could feel compassion for this woman? Right now he wanted to give her whatever she needed. *Anything.* He also wanted her back on the other side of the world, out of his hair.

'You can stay with me until you sort other accommodation. There's no rush. I have lots of space and bedrooms.'

Elene sagged further and he made to catch her and hold her upright, but as he took a step forward she began pulling herself together, one click at a time. 'Thank you,' she whispered.

'Don't thank me. It is why you turned up here, isn't it?' There. Bring this back to practicalities—definitely not about the child, not about Elene, not his unexpected reaction to her.

'I was desperate. Aimee was screaming the roof down. The hotel receptionist was struggling to find accommodation at a hostel and— I'm sorry. I couldn't think of anything else to do.' Just as it was for him, it was as though Elene was afraid to talk about what had brought her to Sorrento in the first place.

He'd go along with her. There was no way he wanted to delve into that particular mess. Not tonight. 'You did the right thing.' By Aimee, at any rate. He'd have been furious if they'd stayed in a room amongst strangers. His daughter deserved better. So did Elene, though he wasn't sure why he felt that way. Perhaps he'd extend the invitation to stay through to the end of her visit, but he'd wait on that decision. 'I'll be back shortly.'

Mattia strode away without a backward glance, despite his head pounding with incredulity. He was a *babbo*. Elene had brought his daughter to meet him. Sure, he wasn't naïve; there was a lot to get through, decisions to make about Aimee. But a fizz of excitement ran through his veins.

Except it was Elene's face popping into his mind, not Aimee's. Elene's expression when their lips had brushed that night, the sudden tightening in his blood and manhood when he'd breathed her in. That would not happen again. Not now that they had a child whose future needed sorting out.

He'd never seen Elene so exhausted, heard her voice so flat—not even after a day of emergencies and dramas in

Theatre. She'd run out of steam, and was unlikely to be back up to speed quickly. Jetlag was a killer of even the toughest souls, so he'd see she had everything she needed to get through it. If he lived to regret that, so be it. It wasn't in his nature not to help someone and, in this case, Elene was in a mess partly because of him. Even if he hadn't had a clue what had been going on with Danielle, he owed Elene for bringing his child across to him, and he hated owing anyone. Debts were repaid pronto. This particular one was too close for comfort, so the sooner it was dealt with the better.

Mattia charged along the corridor, trying to outrun the sight of Elene looking so lost. Normally a feisty woman who rattled his cage and annoyed the hell out of him, this was not Elene Lowe. Bring *her* back. She might push every button he had and some, but he'd prefer that any day. The feisty version heated his blood with anger, sometimes with lust; this version also made him sympathetic, warmed him towards her. Made him want her with him.

Mattia swore.

CHAPTER TWO

ELENE WAS ONLY vaguely aware of the mansion Mattia drove up to, barely noticed the wide expanse of wall hanging off the hill, her mind busy, racing from Mattia to Aimee to sleep and back again. Once inside, the heat fell away under the onslaught of air conditioning, but she couldn't find the energy to take in what was in front of her. In her arms, Aimee was busy squirming and staring around, making up for her lack of interest.

Ahead, Mattia paused. Her case swung from one large hand, the stroller from the other. 'I'll show you which bedroom you'll use. There's a cot in the basement my niece and nephew used when they were a similar age.'

'That's a bonus. Aimee will be safer in a cot than on a bed with pillows tucked around her. She's a restless sleeper.'

'Shall I put it in the same room as you?'

'Please. So far she's doing okay, but being in an unfamiliar room without me on hand could exacerbate her mood.' The last thing Aimee was about to do was go to sleep; not after the hours she'd put in getting here, while the only thing Elene wanted to do was pull bedcovers over her head and succumb to the lethargy tugging at every cell and not reappear for twenty-four hours. But, hey, that was never going to happen. Not now she was a parent.

'Let's get this sorted so you can relax.' Once again Mattia was striding away and she scurried to keep up.

How long this unusual politeness would last was anyone's guess. Elene looked around the bedroom he led her into. It was huge and even this late in the day still warm from the sun. A bonus was the attached bathroom. 'Perfect.' She'd better not get too comfortable. This was a short-term fix.

'Glad you're happy with it.'

'Why wouldn't I be?' No clues in that inscrutable face staring at her. 'I'll start phoning around hotels tomorrow so we can get out of your way as soon as possible.'

'Leave it for a day or two.'

So he wasn't inviting her to stay for the whole time she was here, but then he didn't know how long that was, or if she even intended returning to New Zealand. 'We're heading home in three weeks.'

His tense stance appeared to relax a fraction, but that could've been the play of light from the overhead lamp causing her to think so. Of course he didn't want her here, had yet to come to terms with Aimee—if he accepted his role in her life. There were many hours ahead for him to come up with lots of questions, demands and denials. The questions she was prepared for. The demands not so much; they worried her enough to make her shake in her shoes, but until she heard them she couldn't fight them. As for the denials, she'd wait and see.

'Are you intending staying in Sorrento the whole time?' He spoke as though holding his breath—as if her answer was important.

'That depends on you and how things go. I have family outside Florence I might catch up with.' The trains were reliable and fast, and would make travelling with Aimee a doddle. 'But this trip isn't about them.'

'I'll arrange transport if you decide to head up there.'

Typical. 'I am perfectly capable of organising a couple of train tickets, thanks all the same.' Take it easy. He mightn't be on the ward now, but there was no need to antagonise him when he was offering help. She wasn't thinking straight, there was so much fog in her head. Why else did she keep noticing that flat belly and wide chest? Presumably he'd had them when she knew him before and they hadn't impacted on her in any way then. *Oh, yeah? Who do you think you're fooling?*

'I wasn't thinking trains.'

They'd be beneath him. *Stop it.* 'Let's leave it until I've caught up on sleep and can think straight.'

'Done. I'll get the cot.' Within minutes Mattia returned with a large square bag which he emptied onto the carpet before assembling the cot like a pro.

'You've done that more than once.' Elene aimed for friendly as she plugged in the nightlight disguised as a plastic teddy. 'How many nieces and nephews have you got?'

'One of each, both aged two and a half, and there're two more *bambini* on the way.' He glanced sideways down to Almeo, now crawling towards her bed. 'She doesn't look much like her mother.'

'Except for the curls.' Those were definitely Danielle's.

'Danielle always complained about hers.' His tone was wistful. 'Despite what you thought, I liked her a lot. We got on well, but the *friendship* was never going further than those few weeks.'

Time to fess up. 'I know.' When his eyebrows lifted she hastened to explain. 'I didn't at the time. I truly thought you'd hurt her, but later Danielle explained she'd only wanted a fling, same as you.'

'She'd had a few flings. Why was it any different with me?'

Elene struggled to come up with an answer. She'd just

always been anti about Danielle and Mattia. Shrugging, she admitted, 'I don't know. She was happy, especially when you stood up to that drunk for her.'

Mattia nodded. 'He'd been ogling her all night in the pub, making her very uncomfortable. When he came across and made lewd comments I'd had enough and suggested we go out the back for a discussion.' Flicking his forefingers in the air, he emphasised 'discussion.' 'He declined.'

'Go you.' So chivalry wasn't dead. But she wouldn't expect it to be with a man like Mattia. One thing she couldn't dispute: he was a gentleman and treated women as they deserved. Except they'd always rubbed each other up the wrong way. Was she in denial? Had there been sparks at other times than that one night she'd tamped down hard because he was seeing her friend? He was tall, good-looking in a dark and dangerous way, intelligent, funny, and— No. She was not noticing anything like that about him. No way. She looked around for something else to focus on.

Aimee was using the cot to pull herself up onto her feet. She slipped and banged down on her bottom.

Elene waited for the indignant shriek that usually accompanied a fail. Instead Aimee turned on her toothless grin and reached for the cot to start over. 'She's happy to be free of constraints.'

Mattia was watching his daughter, disbelief and something else on his face. Longing? He hadn't touched Aimee yet. Not even a finger on her arm. Holding himself back until he'd thought through all the connotations? Afraid of where this might go? Still in denial? Who knew? She certainly didn't, and right now working it out was beyond her.

For her own sake Elene felt a little bit glad he wasn't rushing to fall in love with his daughter, if he accepted who she was. Being here was about deciding where Aimee should live and with who, though she was determined that would be her, but denying Mattia fatherhood wasn't happening either. Bending down, she swung Aimee up to hold her out to her father. 'Here. You look after her. I need to shower.'

Mattia automatically caught Aimee in his steady hands. Not that Elene would've let her drop, but he hadn't even thought about not taking her. Holding his daughter out, he watched her kicking her legs and banging her hands on his arms, her face split in a gummy smile as she eyed him up. *Hope I pass the test.* Gulp. Really? Of *course* really. He was her father. He didn't need a DNA test to prove that. Gut instinct brought about by the family likeness and Elene's honest demeanour, even without putting it into words, told him all he needed—or didn't need—to know.

'Hello,' he croaked around a tennis ball lodged in his throat.

'Ma-ma-ma-ma.'

'Is that right?' A smile was stretching his mouth without any input from his brain. 'You're beautiful.'

'She won't break,' came a crisp quip from behind.

What? *Oh, hold her against me.* Was that what Elene was telling him? 'Thought you were going for a shower.' He glanced over his shoulder and saw the apprehension blinking back at him. She was worried about this development. What exactly was her role in Aimee's life? Number one question to go on the list he suspected would be pages long before many hours passed. Elene's usually sparkly green eyes were now dark, like the ocean depths. Her tiny, curvy body had shrunk ever smaller.

Trying to reassure, not that he knew what he was comforting her about, he said softly, 'Go on. I'll take Aimee out to the family room. Promise I know what I'm doing.'

The tip of her tongue played with the corner of her

mouth, tightening his groin again. Then she nodded and headed to the bathroom. Those loose trousers did nothing to hide the curves of her butt, nor the slimmest of waists. An hourglass figure finished off with full breasts that he'd tried not to let his gaze linger on when she'd held Aimee against them.

Aimee. Dragging his attention away from Elene he refocused, bending his arms slowly, bringing Aimee closer and closer until she was against his chest, wriggling like a worm on hot concrete. This was so different to holding Marco or Giulia. This was—parenthood with a capital P. He jerked. *I really am Papà.* Being a parent meant being involved with a woman, a need Sandy had permanently finished off. Though apparently life had other ideas for him.

Air whooshed out of his mouth, ruffling the curls on top of his daughter's head. He dropped a kiss on them. 'Let's get you some dinner, little one.' Elene might like a meal too. He was starving. Lunch had been a quick bite hours ago, between a hip replacement and a shoulder reconstruction.

After placing Aimee on the floor out of harm's way, Mattia poured two glasses of Sangiovese, put one on the table for Elene and studied the contents of the fridge. Anna, his housekeeper, kept it well stocked and there was a prepared meal to reheat, but not enough for two. It'd do for tomorrow's lunch. Tonight he'd make comfort food, using the pasta dough Anna had also prepared earlier. Elene deserved a little care and attention. That was some trip she'd undertaken with a toddler. For her friend. For him? Something about that deep sadness in her eyes suggested yes to both. Bet she was wondering what he'd do, and where that'd leave her.

Hell. He combed his fingers through his hair. As reality trickled into his brain he tried not to overthink things.

They had a lot to process. But not tonight. Because Elene was tired, and lovely and gorgeous. Don't forget the snippy woman behind that exhaustion. She wouldn't have stayed back in Wellington while this softer, kinder version made the trip.

Checking Aimee was still happy playing with the coloured wooden blocks he'd given her, he set about putting together the ingredients for an Alfredo sauce. The clock boomed out eight o'clock. Half an hour had passed since he'd brought Aimee through here. Had Elene fallen asleep in the shower? Should he check on her? Entering the bathroom might bring back the more familiar version.

'Sorry.' Elene burst through the doorway, her chest rising and falling as though she'd run through the house. 'That's one powerful shower. I've probably used all your hot water, but it was worth it. All the aches gone, leaving me feeling normal again.'

She certainly looked it. Standing tall for someone so short, her face was relaxed for the first time since he'd discovered her in his waiting room, her gaze clear of worry; she looked alert. Hot and sexy normal. The spoon he stirred the sauce with clattered into the pot. *This is Elene. She doesn't do sexy.* Not around him, any rate. *She did once.*

With effort he rolled a shoulder. 'There's a glass of Sangiovese on the table. One of Italy's best secrets.' Getting back on track was essential. For his sanity, for the days ahead when they'd no doubt be battling over childcare issues. She'd once called him a fly-by-night. *Well, Miss Lowe, I'm going to prove how wrong you were.* He had not liked her contemptuous opinion of him, even when he'd understood she was trying to protect Danielle.

Not that he'd deny he'd spent a year living loosely after his fiancée, Sandy, had stolen from his charity and attempted to bring his esteemed family into disrepute by accusing him of taking the funds and setting her up to take the fall. Except Sandy was the one to languish in jail. His family had pushed him to take a year off and go live a little, put his mistake behind him. He'd gone reluctantly, the guilt heavy, but it seemed his parents knew what they were doing. New Zealand, with its great outdoors culture and the easy lifestyle, had been liberating and exciting. Yet from the day he'd landed back on Italian soil he'd been determined never to cause a ripple of trouble for his family again and got on with achieving his interrupted goals. With the exception of one—loving a woman enough to marry her and have *bambini.* His gaze drifted to Elene, now savouring the wine.

'Delicious.' Elene gave him a smile that slid under his skin as easily as cream over hot pie. 'I haven't had a Sangiovese since I was last in Italy.'

'How long ago was that?' Might as well learn as much as possible while she was in a good mood.

'Three years. I worked at a hospital in Firenze most of my stay. Loved every moment.' Another sip, and those full lips were momentarily rich, dark red.

Mattia's belly tightened. He took a large gulp from his glass. Should not have brought her here. Oh, yes, and what was he supposed to have done when she had nowhere to go? Another mouthful and he reached for the bottle. This was going to be a long night, followed by some long days, and more nights. 'You had a licence to practice here?'

'I did, and I've kept it up. Easier than having to redo it further down the track if I decided to revisit my family.'

That might come in handy for the future. 'Your mother's Italian, right?' He vaguely remembered something about Elene's heritage after she'd spoken to him in Italian once in Theatre.

Elene nodded. 'When she was two her parents moved

to New Zealand. Years later she met my dad, who owned a vineyard with his brother in Masterton. Now one of my younger sisters is the winemaker and my parents are happy dishing out advice and being grandparents.'

Grandparents? To *his* daughter? How did they feel about Elene bringing Aimee over here to meet him and his family? He wasn't asking. There'd been enough shocks for one day. Time to relax and enjoy dinner—and the company. 'So you'll be a pasta fan, then.'

'Duh.' Her deliberate eye-roll made him laugh.

'What about all that lamb and beef Kiwis seem to eat by the ton? You enjoy those too?'

'What's not to like about roast lamb leg or medium rare sirloin steak?' She grinned.

His stomach flipped. He'd never seen her grin before. Better for him if he didn't again. For some inexplicable reason that grin affected him deeply. It was cheeky, friendly, normal around him. This was not the Elene he thought he knew.

Elene glanced behind him. 'Your pot's boiling over.'

Whipping around, he rescued the pot before too big a mess was made on the stove top. Distracted, that was the problem. 'What about food for Aimee?'

'I've got that covered. I brought enough to get through the first days.' She was beside him, holding up a sealed packet with a teddy bear with oats in its paw on the front. 'Just need a small jug to heat this up.'

'I'll have to get her onto pasta quick-smart.' Handing Elene what she required, Mattia returned to concentrating on the pasta sauce. Burning it in front of her was not an option. Nor was letting the water boil over again.

Silence fell between them, occasionally broken by Aimee's mutterings as she placed block on top of block, only to have them tumble to the floor time after time. Patiently she'd start again, until Elene knelt down to straighten the stack after each placement. Finally all the blocks were used up and Aimee shrieked with delight, clapping her hands wildly and knocking the stack over.

Mattia watched them together. Two very different heads bent over the blocks. One with straight auburn hair, the other black and curly. Chalk and cheese. Elene and Aimee. 'Why did Danielle choose Aimee for a name?'

That auburn head flipped up, a challenge in her gaze. 'You don't like her name?'

'Did I say that? I was wondering if there was a connection to someone Danielle had been close to, someone special.' He liked the name even if it wasn't Italian.

She nodded. 'Danielle was raised by her Grandma Aimee.'

Mattia nodded. 'That's nice. Middle name?'

Defiance filled her eyes. 'Elene.'

'So she's got an Italian name. I like that. Surname?' *Shut up.* Mattia snatched up the pot and drained the water from the pasta. And waited for the explosion.

Elene knew Mattia must be bursting with questions, but right now she needed to take it easy. They'd been together for only a couple of hours and there were ordinary things to do, like feeding Aimee and playing with her until that pent-up energy wore off. Deliberately or not, he'd lured her into a false sense of security. Concentration was required so as not to miss anything.

'Don't tell me it's Lowe,' Mattia growled impatiently.

Her hackles rose in an instant. 'What would be wrong with that?' Her father would've been proud for Aimee to have the family name.

'Nothing, I suppose.'

'You suppose? Oh, buster, you suppose nothing. You

haven't got a clue what's happened since you left Wellington. What Danielle wanted for her daughter. What she suffered, knowing she'd never see Aimee grow up. All you're worried about is a name.' Where did those damned tears come from? She slashed at her cheeks and reached for Aimee to hug her tight, only Mattia was there, holding out a paper towel for her to wipe her face before he picked up his daughter.

'Tell me more so I *am* clued up.'

Reaching for her wine, Elene drew deep breaths. She and Danielle had tried to prepare for this moment, but it was always going to be difficult explaining her friend's reasons for refusing to tell Mattia about his child, and her own fear that he'd want full custody of his daughter.

'Elene?' He said her name softly, touching her deeply, questioning her determination not to fall in love again. 'I understand talking about her must be difficult.'

She nodded. 'Did Danielle ever mention her childhood to you?' She'd be surprised if she had.

Topping up her glass, Mattia said, 'Not a word.'

'Her mother ran away when she was three and her father brought her up. Make that dragged her up. There was little money, a continuous stream of women who were unkind to her, and she had few friends. At fourteen she got pregnant and her father tried to force her to have an abortion. Somehow, and I'm not sure of the details here, she avoided the termination, only to have her father make her sign the baby over for adoption.'

Mattia swore. 'That's cruel. How did he get away with it? It shouldn't have been his call to make.'

'He threatened to turn Danielle out on the street if she didn't do it. At fourteen, with no other family for support, she had no choice. The social welfare system let her down. Apparently her father charmed them into believing Danielle wanted to *give* her baby away.' Elene stared at the carpet. 'I don't think she ever got over that.'

'There are some real monsters out there.'

'There are. I've been very lucky.' Elene looked him in the eye. An explanation of her own wouldn't go amiss. 'The man who conceived me didn't want me but the man I've called Dad all my life more than made up for him.'

'More cruelty. I'm sorry to hear your stories. You and Danielle would've understood each other very well.'

'We did.' Needing to get Danielle's story over with, Elene continued. 'She intended letting you know about the pregnancy, but kept putting off the moment. She was so happy, so engrossed in having a baby you'd think she'd want to share the joy, but it was like she was holding it all to herself *for* herself.' Another mouthful of wine, another deep breath. 'Then the cancer diagnosis came and you didn't get a look-in.'

'She was afraid I'd take the baby away?'

Elene leapt in to negate that hurt. 'Not because she truly believed you were capable of such cruelty. She wanted every minute she could with her baby without having to fight for the two of them. Not involving you from the beginning was a by-product of her past. I don't think she ever trusted any man to look out for her.'

'Thank you for that. Danielle once told me you were the only person she felt completely safe about telling the things that mattered.' Mattia looked thoughtful.

Get it over with. 'Aimee Hicks-Ricco,' she told Mattia, watching for his reaction. 'The Ricco part yet to be confirmed by you.'

Mattia stared at her as if his last chance of escape had vanished. All the colour drained from his cheeks.

Guilt sneaked up on Elene unexpectedly. She had

whacked him over the head with this. 'I'm sorry. It's hard, you know?'

'Yes, I do. Very hard.' His stunned gaze dropped to Aimee and ever so slowly a glimmer of something she couldn't quite recognise crept into his expression. Hope? Longing? She waited quietly.

Mattia finally turned back to her. 'Hicks-Ricco. Aimee will always be aware of her mother. I like that.'

On hearing her name, Aimee banged a fist on her father's chin. 'Ma-ma-ma-ma.'

Elene sighed with relief. He wasn't denying the obvious, had accepted the truth far quicker than she'd given him credit for. 'I understand you're full of questions, but can we leave them for now? At least until Aimee's fed and gone down for the night. Please?' Now she was begging, and she hadn't begged since she ran away from her ex. Craig hadn't taken any notice so maybe Mattia wouldn't either. But since Aimee came into her life there was no end to the things she would do to get what the little girl needed. Except give her up.

Mattia was staring at her, not in a bad way, nor one that made her sit up with hope, just neutral, as though seeking answers without verbalising the questions. Finally, he nodded. 'I agree.'

Phew. She headed for the microwave that was regularly beeping the message that the jug of oats was ready. 'You've got milk?'

'Here.' With Aimee in one arm, he deftly opened the fridge to retrieve the cardboard container and pass it to her. 'Cutlery in that drawer to your right.'

How domestic—if bobbing on the top of a tsunami could be called homely. Getting through the coming weeks in this civilised fashion would be ideal. She'd try to keep her best game face on. Falling for Mattia's charms—those she'd seen him turn on other women, if not her—would create more problems, not less. He liked to control everything and everyone around him. Had he always been like that? Or was it a result of a past relationship?

She'd had the controlling partner, and it had taken her parents' and Danielle's support and a lot of courage to leave him. Craig had made it hard, swearing undying love while at the same time demanding her money, dictating her dress style, even her work hours. Everything to suit him. But once he'd started trying to keep her family and friends away she'd packed up her belongings and sneaked out of the sterile apartment Craig owned and into the cottage at the back of her parents' house until she was ready to branch out and buy her own home.

It'd been crippling, not being able to decide which outfit to wear or what to eat for breakfast, and without Danielle and her family she might never have found the courage to start down the path to freedom. She was not about to put herself into the hands of another controlling man. Which meant she and Mattia were destined to never be more than buddies because he liked to keep everything going his way.

While feeding Aimee, Elene watched Mattia put the finishing touches to the sauce for their pasta which, if the pleased expression on his face when he sampled it was anything to go by, he'd cooked to *al dente*. He was at home in the kitchen, didn't have any qualms about cooking dinner or cleaning up as he went. A self-contained man.

'You look after this place yourself?'

'No, I cheat. You'll meet Anna tomorrow. She cleans up after me and makes some meals. Be warned, she adores *bambini* and will want to spoil Aimee. There's a small apartment on the ground floor where she lives.'

He declined to look after his home? Like he didn't put in long hours at the hospital?

'We can handle that. Aimee loves nothing better. My mum and dad care for her some days when I'm at work, and she can't get enough of them. To counter that she goes to a crèche three days a week, which I admit to feeling guilty about.'

'What else can you do? You're the equivalent of a working mum.' Mattia was plating up dinner and her stomach was sitting up to attention. Aeroplane food had not been much fun.

'That smells wonderful.' She wiped Aimee's chin before placing her back on the floor by the blocks. The *equivalent* of a working mum? That stung, but it was true. She was the closest thing to a mother Aimee had right now and, while she'd always have that role, it was yet to be decided if it would be full-time or the days when Mattia was too busy to be with his daughter. *Eat, stop worrying over what you haven't discussed yet.* Food would shut up both her stomach and her head for a while.

The fragrance wafting up from her plate had nothing on the flavour exploding across her tongue. 'You'll have a battle on your hands if you think you can get me to leave your house before I head back home.' She'd found it in her to tease this man? The pasta must be even better than she thought.

'The day I put boiled potatoes and cheese sauce in front of you will be the message to pack.'

'The day you do that I'll bake lamb roast with all the trimmings.' If Mattia hadn't been smiling she might've worried he wasn't pulling her leg. He needn't worry. She'd start looking for a hotel tomorrow.

'The battle lines have been drawn.' He smiled to take the sting out of his words.

Elene struggled not to stare at those lips, winding up her imagination in ways she'd denied for a long time. Lips that might trail over her skin, leaving her wired and ready. Her libido shot into life, wanting more from Mattia. *Ah, hello? You're waking up after a long drought because of Mattia?* This was one diversion she did not need, or want. But his kiss would be like no other.

Her mouthful of wine went down the wrong way and she choked, then had to put up with the embarrassment of having her back slapped with one enormous—and warm—hand. It would be too easy to lean back into that unexpected gentleness and close her eyes. She sat forward, took another, more careful sip from her glass. 'Thank you.'

'Eat, relax. I won't hassle you with any more questions tonight.' To prove it, Mattia became intent on enjoying his pasta.

While worrying about that, Elene was struggling to keep her eyes open, despite the tasty food. The wine wasn't helping keep her awake, but she'd earned it. It was good to sit back and take a load off her feet, and her mind. But she couldn't get too comfortable. She had to stay awake long enough to put Aimee to bed when she was ready, and that looked like being a while away yet.

Mattia stood and cleared their plates, brought a bowl of enormous strawberries to the table.

Then Aimee looked up and threw a block across the floor, followed by a cry that had to be heard back in town. Another block followed the first and more cries filled the room.

'Here we go. Meltdown time.' At least it hadn't happened mid-flight. That would've been awkward.

Mattia was staring at Aimee as though he couldn't believe what was going on.

'Your niece and nephew don't have good old crying matches?' Elene reached down to lift Aimee into her arms, only to get belted on the nose with a flying fist. 'Ouch.' Her eyes filled at the pain. 'Careful, missy.'

The noise intensified. Aimee's little mouth was wide open, her eyes ferocious slits above her red cheeks.

'Shh, sweetheart.' Elene bounced her on her hip.

Aimee wasn't having anything to do with it. Her fists were flying and the crying changed to deep sobbing, tugging at Elene's heart with each gasp.

'Want me to heat some milk?' Mattia asked.

'You can try, but I suspect it's going to take some time to get her to quieten down. I can't complain since she never cried the whole trip.'

Surprisingly, Mattia's mouth twitched. 'Saving it for me, were you, little one?' He ran a hand over Aimee's head.

'I'll take her to the bedroom and leave you in peace.'

'Give her to me. I'll walk around the back yard for a while, see if that distracts her enough to quieten down.' Mattia stood with his arms out.

Elene gaped. The man was offering to take a crying toddler and try to soothe her? Seemed she knew nothing about him. 'If you're sure?' Already she was handing Aimee over to those large, safe hands, the relief enormous. She didn't know if she had it in her to walk and talk with Aimee now, for what could be hours. 'I'll take over when you've had enough. This might go on for a long time.' He'd soon be sick of the crying and kicking and want shot of Aimee.

'I'll manage.' His arms were cradling his daughter, rocking her slowly back and forth as he began striding across the kitchen. 'You heat the milk, eat some strawberries and make yourself some tea if you like. I'll be outside.'

The neighbours were going to love that. 'If you're certain.' But she was talking to herself, alone in Mattia's kitchen, the crying muffled behind the closed door. She should be glad to have someone to help with Aimee, but she felt as though she were stranded on top of a rock with the tide racing in. Could they make joint custody work?

Nearly an hour later the world became quiet. Elene went outside to take Aimee off Mattia to put her to bed, but she was wide awake, smiles having replaced the crying. 'You're supposed to fall asleep now.'

'Why don't you go to bed? If you give me a jumpsuit or whatever it is you call night attire for toddlers, I can put Aimee down when she's ready. She's going to outlast you by quite some time,' Mattia said.

It was tempting. So, so tempting. But she was meant to be caring for Aimee, not Mattia. Not yet.

'Let it go, Elene. You're exhausted, and staying up any longer isn't going to help anyone.'

'You're right,' she capitulated.

It wasn't until she was digging through the case for Aimee's clothes that it dawned on her that Mattia would be bringing Aimee in here while she was in bed. *So what?* She'd be out of it. It wasn't as if the man would have his wicked way with her. And that was not disappointment lapping at her periphery. Besides, the loose-fitting cotton PJs she'd shortly pull on would turn any red-blooded man off in a flash. Yeah, she could stop worrying on that score.

CHAPTER THREE

MATTIA STOOD BY the cot in the dim glow thrown by the nightlight, gentling Aimee into slumber, and sporadically glancing across to the spread-eagled form that was Elene in sleep mode. Sprawled wide, stretching to all points of the king-sized bed, with the pillow jammed around her shoulders. All the frustrations of earlier were gone, leaving a peaceful expression, occasionally tightened when a cute little snore escaped. *Sì*, very appealing.

He straightened his back. Elene might be cute when she was out for the count, but the moment those eyes opened and that brain started analysing him and the mess they were in, there'd be nothing adorable about her. This was Elene Lowe. Be warned. She'll fight to the death to get what she wants, which in this current predicament he presumed meant what was right for Aimee. What she *believed* to be right, and after hearing about the father she adored he understood where she was headed. He had to admire her for that. He was prepared to do the same. The difficulty being their requirements would differ enormously.

He already knew he wanted custody of Aimee. No argument. But Elene hadn't come to hand her over. Not at all. Beyond doubt, she loved his daughter.

A soft gasp came from the cot. Finally Aimee was asleep, her arms spread wide, her flushed face turned into the pillow. Gorgeous. Beautiful. His daughter. His heart tapped against his ribs. How could he fall for her so quickly? He knew nothing about her, hadn't known she existed until that afternoon, and yet she already had his heart. Gut instinct, a name from Elene and his deeply buried need for a family told him this little girl was his. Thank goodness no woman had ever had quite that impact on him. None other than Sandy, that was, and she'd made it easy for him never to want to fall in love again.

His gaze shifted back to Elene, and an alien warmth stole through him. Because she was looking out for his daughter, not because he wanted her. Having and raising his own child meant, in his book, having a wife. Except now he had a daughter without a wife, which didn't sit well. Children needed and deserved the safety and comfort and love that having two parents together brought. Would Elene marry him to be there for Aimee? Without love?

That night in Wellington Hospital had made him want more from her. Waves of shock rocked him. What the hell? How crazy did he think he was? He was not marrying a woman who took pleasure from sniping at him. Life would be tiring. Then again, he'd know exactly where he stood with Elene. There'd be no hidden agendas, no nasty surprises. They could go into a contract, eyes wide open, and his hand firmly on the family wealth. So unlike anything he'd thought necessary years back, when he still believed in love and sharing and caring.

Mattia stormed out of the room, closing the door behind him none too gently, then cursed in case he'd woken either female. Not hanging around to find out, he headed for the kitchen and that Sangiovese. Another glass might calm him enough to get some sleep tonight. And if it didn't then he'd be in fine form tomorrow. But at least he wouldn't be here. He'd be at the hospital, dealing with other people's problems, avoiding his own. Reality kicked in. He was a doctor, always available when needed. No more wine tonight.

Dropping into his large leather chair in the lounge, he stretched out and pointed the remote at the TV taking up a lot of space on the opposite wall. The news channel came up and he watched and listened without seeing or hearing a thing. Only his phone ringing brought him back to the room. '*Ciao.*'

'Mattia, it's Carla. Signor Familaro's struggling with pain. We can't get it under control. He's in a terrible state.'

If Carla couldn't calm him then no one could. 'What about Rose?' The woman was the consultant on call for the night.

'No one's heard from her since she left at ten.'

Strange. 'I hope she's all right, and not had an accident.' The tourist numbers were starting to build up and those who drove weren't always familiar with the Italian way on the roads, but at this time of night Sorrento was usually quiet.

'No reports from the emergency staff of a vehicle accident. They'd have told us if one of our own was brought in.'

It was a smallish, everyone-knows-everybody kind of hospital. 'I'm on my way.' Signor Familaro had had shoulder surgery that morning, and was on a strong regime of painkillers which obviously weren't doing their job. Sometimes a patient did need more, and he'd have to make the call whether to administer a morphine pump or not. If Aimee woke before he got back then there went Elene's sleep. He hoped it didn't happen, because he'd planned on being the one to soothe Aimee and prevent Elene being woken too soon. Caring too much about the wrong female? Bile was tart on his tongue. Both females.

Mattia left a note on the bench saying where he was in case Elene got up during the night and required something she couldn't place her hands on. Driving to the hospital, the vision he hadn't been able to avoid of Elene, starfish-like on the bed, went with him. A deep need made him squirm in his leather seat. If Elene had woken and seen him, all hell would have broken loose. She'd have called him a range of names, none of them friendly. He might have been making sure Aimee wasn't about to wake Elene up from much-needed sleep, but try telling her that. She'd have had him by his round things, twisting them out of use before he uttered a word. His body froze. Elene was not getting anywhere near his groin, whatever her mood at the time.

Arriving on the surgical ward, Mattia read the nurse's notes on the computer before approaching his patient. 'Stefano, I hear you're having more pain than is to be expected.'

'I need something stronger,' grunted the older man.

According to the notes, Stefano had first asked for more painkillers an hour ago. 'Did it come on suddenly, or was it a gradual build-up?'

'I don't know. Pain is pain, doc. All I want is something to get rid of it.' Sweat beaded the man's brow.

'Did the pain wake you?' Had Stefano rolled onto his shoulder while sleeping, despite the pillows in place to prevent that happening? 'Or did you move that arm abruptly without thinking?'

Stefano looked sheepish, unable to meet Mattia's gaze. 'I might've.'

The shoulder Mattia had operated on that afternoon needed to remain as still as possible. 'Despite the pain and strapping and lying on your back, it's very easy to make a move you've done all your life without hesitation. Unfortunately, it isn't good for your shoulder.' He was calculating dosages in his head. 'I'm going to put you on a morphine drip.'

The relief was instant. '*Grazie.* I'm sorry to cause trouble this late.'

Mattia smiled. 'You didn't.' Two females had done that. One in particular. The wrong one. The one with a figure that had his blood in a whirl and his hormones on the rampage. 'I'll check your shoulder in case you've done damage.' He hoped not, though dislocation was a possibility and would explain the excessive pain, except that would've taken a hard knock, not something likely to have happened while lying in bed. Moments later, he announced, 'All good.' They weren't going back to Theatre.

Carla had been alongside throughout this conversation and now told Mattia, 'The morphine pump's ready in the drugs room. Just need your signature on the paperwork.'

'Let's do it.' Once the pump had been set up on a stand at the head of the bed and the drip inserted into the large bore needle strapped to Stefano's lower arm, Mattia explained to his patient, 'Every time the pain is too sharp, squeeze this bulb and you'll get a dose of morphine. I want you to do it before the pain gets excruciating, but not until you start to get a niggle of discomfort. The doses are low but too many is not what we want here. Understand?'

His patient eyeballed him. '*Sì.* I don't want too much any more than you do.'

'Good, but don't hang out to be brave either. The idea is to keep the pain at a steady level where you don't feel it and it's not spiking all the time.' He could say the same for the heat in his blood whenever that image of Elene on the bed flicked into his head. Spiking was not good: a flat, steady line the only way to go.

'Thanks, again, Doc. See you in the morning?'

'Some time tomorrow.' Out at the nurses' counter he asked, 'Anyone else needing attention while I'm here?'

'No. Apart from Stefano, it's been quiet,' Carla answered.

'Any word yet from Rose?'

'Yes, she called to say she's got a stomach bug and is vomiting so she's staying away.'

'Very wise.' Though she could have let them know sooner. 'As long as she's all right and got someone to keep an eye on her. Let's hope she hasn't shared that around with the patients earlier in the day.' They didn't need staff falling by the wayside with a bug. Nurses were thin on the ground at the moment, and the two new ones due to start in a couple of weeks weren't going to be enough. *There's a very competent nurse residing in your house.* What? Bring the enemy into the one place he was free of her? Where he was away from those all-discerning eyes, the unspoken expectations? Not likely. Though it wasn't the only bolthole he had. There was the charity hospital in Napoli and its local surgical unit where he spent his weekends. The nursing shortage was taking its toll on care there too.

'Call Luigi if anyone else needs seeing.' Mattia knew he could cover call, sleep in the night staff's room and not go home to what faced him there. Or he could toughen up and be on hand to help Elene if required. His good side won out. Avoiding Elene went against his better judgement and, besides, he liked that she was in his house. He had yet to work out why he felt that way.

The house was in darkness except for the kitchen light as he drove up to the automatic door opening into the underground garage. The only sounds were the routine creaks of the floorboards and walls. It was as though he was alone. Yet he wasn't. The blocks Aimee had played with were still on the floor and in the kitchen an empty milk container sat on the bench.

In his room he stripped down to his boxers and slid

under the sheet, stretched his feet to the end and put his hands behind his head. He was wide awake—and tired beyond reason. The past week had been crazy busy; the coming one would be the same if he let it. But spending time with his house guests would go a long way towards getting to know them and making sensible decisions for the future based on facts, not on emotions.

A muffled cry broke into his thoughts and he was instantly on his feet. In the hall he strained for a repeat. Nothing. Had it been Aimee? Or did Elene cry out in her sleep? As he reached the bedroom he heard it again. Louder, angrier. Definitely childlike. Now a light shone under the door. He knocked, waited. 'Elene?'

The door opened a crack and she stood there, half asleep, with Aimee in her arms—looking wide awake and furious with the world. 'Sorry if she woke you.'

'She didn't. Want me to take her?'

'I've got it. I'll try another bottle.'

The shrieking was intensifying, and what had been a cute face was bright red and slicked with tears. He said, 'This isn't going to end quickly. I think she's still overtired.'

'I think you're right.'

Now there was a surprise—Elene agreeing with him. 'Let me hold her while you deal with the bottle.'

The next day Elene sipped coffee while watching Aimee crawling around the kitchen, smiling and gurgling as though she was used to being transported halfway around the world to a complete stranger's house. After that last outburst Aimee had slept through till nearly ten. Unheard of.

'Mattia has the magic touch with children,' Elene mused aloud.

'That he has,' the woman, who'd introduced herself as Anna when Elene finally made it out here, said around a smile, her soft gaze fixed on Aimee. If she had any queries as to whose daughter she was, she wasn't voicing them. 'Jetlag has unsettled her.'

'I agree. It's poleaxed me.' Her coffee cup was empty already.

'More?' Anna held up the coffee pot.

'Please. It's just what I need.'

'What you need is breakfast, young lady. You have to keep your energy levels up for running around after this little one. Bread rolls or *fette biscottate*? I have prepared both.'

'*Biscottate*, thank you.' Nothing like a sweet rusk to start the day. 'But let me get it. You don't have to look after me.'

'It's nice to have someone in the house. Mattia's rarely here, always working late, and at the weekends he has his other work.' Anna slid a plate laden with breakfast onto the counter. 'Enjoy.'

'I will.' But not the whole mountain of rusks. Just a couple. 'Mattia has another job outside the hospital?' Wasn't he busy enough? It wouldn't be for the money.

'Ask him about the Napoli Charity Hospital some time.' Anna's friendly open face suddenly closed down. Said too much? Remembered who she worked for?

Elene didn't press her, despite the intense need to learn as much about Mattia as she could. Knowledge about what made the man tick might come in handy when they got down to discussing where Aimee would live and with whom, but quizzing a reluctant Anna would create an enemy and lose her the chance of a friend. 'I will.'

Later she pushed the stroller with Aimee belted in down Strada Statale towards the town centre, where tourists were meandering through the shops or enjoying coffee and wine at the many cafés. Wandering through the crowds, hearing many languages, the overriding one Italian, made her feel at home in a way only Italy could. She was a Kiwi through and through, yet there was something about her mother's country that warmed and excited her. Growing up had been a mix of New Zealand and Italian cultures.

After getting her fix of shops and food she took Aimee down to the beach to get messy in the sand before heading home in preparation to front up to Mattia.

It didn't happen. She waited to have dinner with him, but at nine o'clock she conceded defeat and, disappointed, heated up a bowl of pasta to eat curled up on the couch in front of TV. When exhaustion got the better of her she headed to bed.

Over breakfast next morning Mattia apologised. 'I had hoped to get home so we could talk but there was an accident. A man walked across the train track without looking. I was in Theatre for hours.'

Elene shuddered. 'No wonder you look tired.' She could cut him some slack. 'I'm beginning to think I should've phoned to tell you I was on my way and why.'

'Why didn't you?'

'It seemed too impersonal for something so huge. Plus Danielle made me promise to come and see you without warning.' It was something she hadn't got to the bottom of before it was too late. 'There's a lot to sort through. Face to face must make it easier.' She was watching him and not once did he shrink from anything she said. 'I promise I haven't come here to cause trouble.'

Mattia's phone beeped. He was on his feet as he read the message. 'I've got to go. Last night's patient has suddenly lost consciousness. Talk to you tonight.'

Again Mattia didn't come home for dinner. Elene

started getting frustrated the later the night got. Mattia could not do this to her, to Aimee. Avoidance wouldn't solve a thing. But was she being fair? Turning on the TV, she flicked through channels looking for a diversion.

'Elene, wake up.' A firm hand shook her shoulder.

She blinked and shrugged Mattia away before that heat could unravel all her determination to keep her distance. 'So you're finally home.' Rubbing her eyes with the back of her hand, she glanced up at him, swallowed the longing pouring up her throat. Why did he have to be so good-looking? 'What time is it?'

'Nearly eleven. Why are you still up?'

'You said we'd talk tonight.'

'Unfortunately it didn't work out. Again.' His hands gripped his slim hips, his fingers marking time.

'What was it tonight?'

'A child who'd fallen down two flights of stairs breaking both legs.'

'I wish I'd known.' Then she could've stopped griping at him in her head.

'I'm here now.' Mattia left the room and moments later a plate was banged onto glass and the microwave started up.

When Elene entered the kitchen he was pouring a glass of wine. He waved the bottle in her direction. 'Want one?'

'No, thanks.' She put the kettle on. Fruit tea was what she wanted. And a discussion with Mattia. It was suddenly imperative they talked. Almost as though because he'd stayed away she had to get moving on it. Yes, that was it. They could talk, work out what was going to happen with Aimee, then she could go and visit her family in Firenze, taking Aimee with her. 'I'll be out of your hair as soon as possible.'

'Stay here until you leave for New Zealand.'

'That's hardly fair on you.' *Or me.*

'You're arguing for the sake of it, Elene. The town's busy with tourists—you're not going to find a hotel with a room available for as long as you'd require. At best, you'll be moving from one to another every few days. That's not good for Aimee.'

He was right. On all counts. The water boiled and she concentrated on filling her mug, remembering another night filling a mug before feeling Mattia's hands on her waist, his face so close.

'I'll take your silence as agreement.'

'Might as well. I've run out of arguments. Thank you. I do like it here, and it's easier with Aimee being able to run around as she wishes.' Her tired smile was a truce. If these last two days were anything to go by, she'd hardly ever see him, though that wasn't why she'd come this far. 'Do you work weekends as well? All of them?'

'Sometimes. Okay, mostly.' Mattia sipped his wine.

Didn't he have a life outside being a surgeon? This didn't compute when the man she'd seen in Wellington had spent hours having fun, always with a pretty female on his arm. Anna had hinted something about his weekends being busy. 'Not all your time is spent at the Sorrento hospital.'

'No.' The microwave pinged and he retrieved a plate of linguini.

'Mattia.' Elene wrapped her hands around her mug and watched him moving around the kitchen collecting cutlery and the pepper grinder, his movements defined and confident. He was a man who demanded attention just by being himself. Would he forgive her for dropping in as though from another planet, bringing life-changing issues with her? 'This is awkward.'

The stool legs squeaked across the tiles as he pulled one out from the counter. 'If you're still worrying how I feel about not knowing about Aimee before you turned up, then don't. Allowing for your promise to Danielle, I think you also went for high impact. I'd have done the same.' He lowered that gorgeous butt onto the stool, holding his plate in one hand, a fork in the other, his eyes fixed on her.

'Yet so far, when it comes to Aimee, we've basically discussed heated milk and dirty nappies.' How could she expect complete and utter frankness from him when she wasn't handing it out herself? 'Even in our drollest discussions Danielle and I didn't see that coming.' *Damn, Danielle, I'm making a right mess of this.*

Suddenly Mattia was standing directly in front of her, his hands reaching for her. 'I've already said it but I'm telling you again. I am so sorry about Danielle.' His hands covered her shoulders, engulfed them. Warm, strong, kind. 'She was a beautiful lady, inside and out.'

'She was,' Elene hiccupped. 'I miss her so much. We'd been friends for years and some days I don't how I'll get by without ringing her up and chewing her ear off over some silly thing that's happened.' *Or about her daughter and how cute she is, and how she's learned to crawl and say Ma-ma-ma-ma.*

'Maybe you'll never completely get over that, but that's not necessarily a bad thing. Good friends are to be treasured, and you've got a store of memories to draw on. Not the same as a real conversation, but they're there.' His thumbs were rubbing back and forth on the front of her shoulders, soothing, calming. Unbelievable.

She could get to like this. *Come on, you already do.* When she lifted her head he was watching her without the usual exasperation or questions. Instead his face was soft: not sharp but kind, not wary but friendly. It would be too easy to lean up and kiss him. And completely out of line. Instead she drew in air, leaned into those hands to gather strength from him and said, 'I take it you accept Aimee is yours.'

His hands fell away and he returned to his stool. '*Sì.* I do.'

Phew. That would save a lot of time. Elene dug deep for a smile. 'I'm glad.'

'I'm coming round to feeling like that.' His smile was slow and his eyes were confused. 'It's not that I don't like the idea of being a father, I just hadn't planned it to happen like this, if at all. But then, that's life.'

'Damned curve balls, eh? Didn't you want children some time?'

Mattia reached for his wine, took a deep drink, his gaze fixed somewhere in the distance. Even when he began talking he didn't look at her. 'I was once engaged, going for the whole family package. Life was sweet, my career going along as I'd planned, and I'd started a charity medical centre in Napoli that was beating all expectations. People were donating money and time from all over the place. It was incredible.' Then his voice took on an angry vibe. 'My fiancée ran the finances.'

Oh-oh. Trouble? Elene waited out his silence, knowing he'd finish his tale, no matter the pain.

Finally, 'Sandy was very good at what she did, and it took a year before anyone realised where those donations were going. And by then it was too late to save Charity Napoli. But facing up to her crime wasn't part of her plan. I was the intended scapegoat and for a while it looked as though I'd be charged with fraud.' His hand shook and wine sloshed over the rim of his glass. 'Eventually common sense and my family's reputation for philanthropy prevailed and the truth came out. Sandy went to jail and, because of her actions against me and the family, the judge gave her the maximum penalty.'

Elene's heart squeezed for this proud man who'd been dealt such a lousy hand. 'I'm glad she got caught and sentenced. You didn't deserve that at all. No one does. Thank goodness for families.' No wonder he didn't do trust very well, if at all. Something to remember whenever she felt the need to get close to him. He'd never again look at a woman twice.

'Without them I'd have been sunk.' Leaning back in his seat, he looked directly at her. 'Which is why I never thought I'd have my own children. Getting that involved with a woman is anathema to me. Except it's been taken out of my hands.' His mouth lifted into a small, wry smile.

Clunk. That was her heart dropping. 'You don't have to treat me as though I'm Sandy reincarnated. I am here for Aimee to meet you, and to put my side of the story.'

Forking up a mouthful of pasta, Mattia chewed thoughtfully. 'You're worried how I'm going deal with this.'

'Of course I am.'

The smile that had begun flicked off. 'Did Danielle make you a legal guardian of Aimee?'

'Yes. She intended me to be Aimee's mother.'

Still watching her, he nodded abruptly, leaving her to wonder if he approved or not. 'Am I named on the birth certificate?'

'No. But I've brought copies of all the pertinent documents.' The lawyers had put it all together so there wouldn't be anything missing. 'Shall I get them for you?'

'Sì.'

Elene had reached the door when the worry won over being fair. Spinning around, she said, 'I love Aimee. With all my heart. I would do anything for her.'

Except hand her over to you permanently. Not because you won't be the best dad, but because I can't live without her.

'That's obvious whenever you're together.'

'I want to be there for her as she grows up. All the time.'

In an instant Mattia again stood before her, taking her hand in his, looking down into her eyes with nothing but compassion. 'I know that. Give me time, Elene. That's all I ask of you for now. There's a lot to think about. Apart from the fact I am now a father, something that still shocks me and yet feels—' His hand curled around hers as he tapped his chest. 'Feels right in here.'

Some of the knots inside loosened. Her hand was warm in his strong one. Her heart thudded. Aimee was loved by her father. But as she began to smile other knots tightened, and her lips froze in place. Where did that leave her? Would she have to pack up and move over here to be with her little girl?

'I won't just walk away from her. She's a part of me too.' It had been her who'd bathed and changed Aimee almost from the day she was born, who'd heated milk when Danielle couldn't breastfeed, who'd got up during the night on every cry so Danielle mightn't wake.

'Time, Elene. Please.'

Fair enough. It was all she had to give him. 'I'll get those papers and leave you to unwind from your day.'

All she could hope was that he wouldn't start arming himself with lawyers before they discussed every possibility. Looking into those dark eyes, she couldn't find anything to suggest he'd take advantage of her legally, but she'd read Craig completely wrong so how could she trust her instincts?

She pulled away reluctantly. As his hands left her she felt a loss so deep it was frightening. As though she'd stepped back from something big, something deep. She couldn't have. This was Mattia, a man who'd given few concessions to those he worked with in Wellington, and especially her, and yet so far he'd given her plenty. Why did the memory of that almost kiss invade her right now? She'd have done anything to see that through, except for the fact Danielle was having a fling with him. But that was history. Yet it seemed she was still susceptible to men who liked to take charge.

When she handed Mattia the papers he kissed her cheek. 'Goodnight, Elene.'

A hint of the wild touched her skin, like once before. How sultry could two words sound? How tight could her insides coil from one chaste kiss on her cheek? Her skin flared pink, her stomach tightened and a flame of need burst into life at her core. Turning around so he couldn't see her face, read her eyes, she raced to shut herself in the bedroom and leaned back against the door, dragging in a lungful of air. This was not happening. That was Mattia out there. Not the man of her dreams. That man would be genuinely considerate and kind, not wanting to control everything around him. Not like Craig, who'd pretended to be considerate and kind, loving and giving. He'd turned into a monster.

Mattia was not someone she wanted to get to know intimately, because intimacy suggested a willingness to give herself up completely. She could still feel the debilitating powerlessness whenever Craig had yelled at her for cooking steak when he wanted chicken, for being five minutes late home from work because a patient needed her. Craig came first in everything. Yet her body, even her head, was telling her Mattia didn't use control to hurt people, that he used it to keep himself out of danger from others.

Another idea struck. Was this Mattia's way of undermining her so he could win his way with Aimee? That was more like the Mattia she knew. Before Danielle had told her otherwise. Before coming close to kissing him. Before a lot of things.

The Mattia standing in the kitchen with nothing but genuine kindness on his face, in his gaze fixed on her, was very different to what she'd anticipated on the long flights over.

It was time to get to know Mattia Ricco inside out. The good, the bad and the downright sexy. No, not that. Why not? He was gorgeous, inside and out. Yeah, but would he still be when she refused to step aside from Aimee's future?

No, he would not.

Hold onto that thought.

CHAPTER FOUR

'WANT TO GET CHANGED? We're going out for dinner on Via San Francesco, if that's okay with you?' Mattia smiled as he strolled out to join her and Aimee in the back yard the next night, hands in pockets, looking like he didn't have a worry in the world. But he did. Aimee. He also looked as though he didn't expect her to say no.

Elene looked up at him towering above her. 'You've forgotten something.'

'Not at all. Anna's more than happy to babysit.' Smug didn't suit him. 'She's happy to stay upstairs until we return.'

'I was thinking more along the lines of you didn't say please.'

Teasing him mightn't work but he'd asked her out to dinner so why not lighten up a bit? Just the two of them, taking an adult break despite the pressures on them, had a lot of appeal. Aimee had taken to Anna like mud to white shorts so no problem there. Which left the burning question: What to wear? The blue and white cotton dress with shoulder cuffs or the blue and white cotton dress with shoulder cuffs? Not haute couture, nor bargain basement.

Mattia might have a fit when he saw her ready to go out with him, considering the circles he moved in. What he wouldn't realise was three-quarters of the case she'd brought over was filled with tiny tee shirts and shorts, minuscule socks and jackets.

'Give me half an hour.'

Where was the iron kept?

'Take all the time you need. There's no hurry.' He knelt down by Aimee. 'Hello, my girl.'

Another knot let go inside. Elene gulped. *My girl.* He was finally acknowledging out loud to Aimee his place in her life, and even though she wouldn't have a clue what had just gone down, Elene certainly did. This had to be good. For Aimee at least.

A shadow crossed Mattia's face. He swallowed hard. 'Hello, Aimee.' His voice sounded as though someone had hands around his throat and was squeezing. He wasn't looking Elene's way. In fact she'd swear he wasn't seeing anything not inside his head.

'Mattia?'

'Go get ready,' he growled, reaching for a toy truck, rolling it back and forth, his gaze still somewhere other than in the room. 'Please.'

'Sure.'

After slipping into her dress Elene brushed out her hair so it fell over her shoulders, then pulled on her happy face along with her make-up. If she was going out to dinner with Mattia then she intended having a good time, no matter what they talked about. Which would be about Aimee's future, surely? What else was there? They weren't close friends wanting to share a meal and a bottle of wine in a relaxed atmosphere. He certainly wasn't attracted to her. *Nor am I attracted to Mattia.* She was not thinking about that heat nearly flooring her the night before. *Not, not.*

'You look lovely.' Mattia watched her step across the family room to pick up Aimee for a goodnight cuddle before tucking her into bed. He sounded genuine, but it had been a while since a man had paid her a compliment so she might be imagining it.

'Thank you.' Her mouth watered and another bout of heat tapped places best ignored as she glanced at Mattia. He'd changed into casual dark grey trousers and an open-necked white shirt which highlighted the sun-kissed tone of his skin. Good start to the evening. *Not attracted, remember. Not, not.* 'I'll take Aimee to her cot. Aimee, say goodnight to Papà.'

'Ma-ma-ma-ma.'

'Nice try.' Mattia kissed Aimee's cheek, then said to Elene, 'Good luck.'

'You can say that every time I need to put her down,' Elene told him ten minutes later. 'She's sound asleep.'

His eyebrows rose. 'That's a first. Let's go while we can.' He took her elbow. 'Anna, call me if there's a problem,' he said to his housekeeper-turned-babysitter.

'*Sì.* Have a nice time.' Anna's smile was endearing.

Elene nodded. 'Thank you for doing this.'

'No problem.'

'This is the locals' favourite restaurant. I'm sure you'll like it,' Mattia told her when he held her chair out at the ideally situated table overlooking the harbour with the lights of Naples in the background.

'I'm sure I will.' If she could swallow anything, because suddenly this felt like her first date as a teenager—butterflies in her stomach, fingers fidgeting with the napkin the waiter placed on her lap.

'The menu is limited, but superb,' he continued, seeming totally relaxed for the first time all night. Not for him any awe of the setting, or excitement about his companion.

Why feel like this when they had important issues to resolve? Looking around the restaurant, Elene let the warmth slide under her skin and tried to relax. It had been a long time since she'd last gone out with a devastatingly handsome man. Tonight she longed to enjoy Mattia as a date, forget he was a possible adversary.

'This is wonderful,' Elene sighed. 'Being in Italy, being Italian for now, it brings my two halves together. If you know what I mean,' she added on a whisper. He probably thought she was crazy and not suitable to mother his daughter.

'I can't imagine what it's like to have parents from two different countries. But I'd say it must broaden your outlook on most things.'

'Food especially, and wine.' She laughed before picking up the menu.

'Ah, wine. What type would you like? Red or white?' Mattia asked.

'You choose.' She wasn't up with the local wine. 'I'm having the shrimp salad.'

'Then we'll go for the Pinot Grigio.'

'Does your family live in Sorrento?' she asked after the waiter had taken their orders.

'My parents and two of my brothers and their families are in Napoli. My other brother lives further north, where he oversees the family vineyards. The house I'm living in has been in the family for five generations, and therefore not strictly mine. Any of the family can, and do, arrive to stay whenever the whim takes them.' Love softened his face.

'Obviously that doesn't bother you.'

'Why would it? It's how it's always been. My grandparents, their parents before them. Sometimes I think it's ridiculous I rattle around in such a large home on my own, but everyone's got their own place and likes their independence.'

'Think of the family history. Not everyone has that, not

so openly anyway.' Elene thought back to her childhood. 'I can't remember a time when my family hasn't always been there for each other either, but there isn't the depth, the same house steeped in family history.' She sighed. 'That's special.'

Mattia nodded. 'You're right. I never gave it a lot of thought, mostly took it all for granted: the houses, the comfort, the businesses that provide so much—the past, with its ups and downs, the people who came close to losing everything and those that lifted the company back to greater heights every time.' His gaze had wandered to the view beyond the window and a thoughtful expression tightened his face. 'After what Sandy did I came to fully understand and appreciate how lucky I am, and that I'd fight to keep it that way for all my family if necessary.'

Elene watched him, refraining from talking, letting him have this moment, and thinking about her situation. Had she just been issued with a warning? Or was Mattia telling her these things because of the custody problem? It didn't matter how relaxed she became or what they talked about, everything always came back to that. Aimee's future and her role in it.

Returning his attention to her, Mattia asked, 'You have siblings?'

'Two younger sisters. The one I mentioned before who manages the vineyards my father and his brother began many years ago, and the other a lawyer at a major firm in the city.' The firm who'd drawn up the papers for Danielle about the guardianship.

'Growing wine's something we have in common.' He leaned back in his chair, an elbow slung over one corner. 'You'll know your wines then.'

'The Sauvignon Blanc, Pinot Gris and Chardonnay, definitely, but not the Italian varietals. Though I put some effort into learning about them last time I was here.' She cracked a smile, determined to keep on the upside of happy. 'Too much effort.'

Mattia's laugh was sharp and unexpected. 'Go you.'

Inside she melted a little. When she wasn't worrying about why she was here she felt free and happy, as if there was a future to look forward to involving a man she might love. *Careful.* No, caution could take a back seat while they were getting on so well, when she was having plain old fun. Nothing to do with letting go the restraints on her heart.

'This shrimp is delicious.'

'Glad you like them.'

'What's not to like? Thank you for bringing me here. It's special.'

'You're welcome.' His chest rose, fell, and he asked, 'Have you ever been in a serious relationship?'

Her smile slipped away. 'Yes.'

'It didn't work out?' While she was trying to decide how to answer, he continued. 'You used to say you weren't interested in relationships.'

Tell him. He told you about his fiancée. They needed to know these things to understand each other better, and she had nothing to lose. Craig had already taken her pride. 'I lived with a guy for three years, got engaged, was about to be married, then I left him.' Her finger picked at the tablecloth. 'Craig liked to control everything about me. *Everything.* I succumbed because it was easier than fighting him, plus the guilt was horrendous whenever I let him down.'

Mattia sat back, his gaze soft, non-judgemental.

'Looking back, I can't believe I let him do that but it was like water dripping on stone; one drip doesn't alter a thing, many make an impression.'

'Yet you found the courage to leave.'

'You talk about your loving family. Well, mine and Danielle saved me. They didn't storm in and snatch me away, knowing that would probably make me draw up the barriers. Instead they refused to stay away, despite Craig telling them to, and if I didn't turn up for family dinners Dad would drive around to collect me. It was Danielle who told me I had to leave Craig because it was only going to get worse. She helped me pack while he was out at the dentist one morning.' She'd left most of her belongings behind, wanting nothing to do with Craig's choices of clothes and make-up, books and music.

'You pick good friends.' Mattia sat forward and placed his hand over her chilled one. 'Thank you for telling me. I know how hard it is to do that. Now enjoy the rest of dinner.'

From then on they talked only about the ordinary everyday things in their vastly different lives, until finally Mattia drained his glass and pushed his plate aside. Resolve began taking over in his countenance. 'Right, finished here?' He didn't wait for her reply, standing up and dropping a wad of notes on the table, suddenly looking impatient.

Just as well she wasn't craving that tiramisu on the menu. 'Sure.' She hurried after him. 'What's the rush?'

He slowed. 'Sorry. I need some air.' Had everything caught up with him?

Outside the restaurant Mattia turned right, paused to take her elbow before continuing with long strides that had her almost jogging.

Elene recognised the streets from her meanderings during the day. 'We're going to the beach?'

He glanced down at her shoes and shook his head. 'We'll stick to the paths running along the top of the escarpment. I can't see you managing the hundreds of steps down to the sand in those.'

'Then slow down.' She was wobbling like a bird trying to balance on an overhead wire in a full gale.

He did. Abruptly. Causing Elene to topple towards him. Instantly he caught her, held her by the waist until she'd righted herself.

'Thanks,' she muttered, failing to ignore the heat those hands created through the fabric of her dress. If only this was a normal date where they would kiss and cuddle and follow up with more back at the house. If only Mattia would see her as a woman he might like, might want to get close to, and not just Danielle's friend and Aimee's surrogate mother. But there was that fiancée in his past. Not to mention how Craig had changed her thoughts on relationships. Strange how she kept forgetting that around Mattia. Digging deep, she found the strength to pull away from those all-too-exciting hands.

Dropping his arms to his sides, Mattia asked, 'Are you warm enough?'

'Yes.' Her body was heavy with heat from his touch. Stepping sideways put a little distance between them but didn't cool her body any degrees.

Mattia shoved his hands in his pockets and his chin dropped to his chest as he began strolling along the pathway. After some minutes he stopped and turned to eyeball her. 'The papers from your lawyer prove you're Aimee's legal guardian. And state that I am her father. That's pretty much it.'

Now her temperature dropped to cool. The battle, if there was going to be one—and she'd be naïve to think differently until otherwise shown—had begun. 'As I told you.'

'So we're in a similar position to a divorced couple deciding where the kids live and who with.'

'Putting it bluntly, yes.'

Mattia stared at her for a long moment, then began to

walk again. 'Tell me why Danielle did that.' She must've made a sound because he added, 'I am not saying you aren't suitable.'

Okay. Not what she'd expected. Maybe she should stop trying to second-guess Mattia and just hear him out.

'She wanted me to be her mother. Also it was to prevent Aimee ever ending up in the welfare system if things went belly-up.'

'Why would they do that?' He sounded genuinely puzzled.

'Think about it, Mattia. How well did you two know each other? What if you weren't prepared to acknowledge you were Aimee's father?'

'I would never do that.'

'I know that,' Elene admitted. 'I overheard you talking to one of the doctors about a young patient—his father had left him in the care of friends while he went traipsing off on an extended holiday and he refused to come back when he heard of the accident that put the boy in hospital. You were angry, and said you'd always put your child before your own needs. I told Danielle but her past made her wary, hence my name on those papers as Aimee's mother.'

'That makes sense.' He nodded slowly. 'I remember that kid. He was heartbroken his dad wasn't there for him. I wanted to wrap him up and take him home, which wouldn't have helped at all.'

'You've got a big heart, Mattia.' Something she hadn't quite accepted before. Did it mean she could expect him to do whatever was possible to keep both Aimee and her happy as they resolved this? Because, as much as she feared losing Aimee, she also knew she'd never get in the way of the little girl's relationship with her father. Her own past proved the worth of a good dad.

'Did Danielle ever mention marriage? Before she became ill?'

'Only in the negative. I raised the idea and she said the fling with you was great but getting together permanently wouldn't happen because she never wanted to be beholden to a man.' Elene thought back to the day she'd found out about the pregnancy and how excited her friend was. 'She wanted the baby, very much. And then—'

Mattia's hand touched her lower back, his fingers spread wide.

'Then she learned she had cancer.'

Elene nodded, struggling to hold back the tears. A couple escaped and she let them flow so as not to draw attention to them. 'It was horrible. I was with Danielle when the doctors told her. We were in shock. It seemed impossible, even though we knew that these horrors happen. Just not to us.'

Mattia was making circular motions on her back as they walked slowly along the path. 'I presume surgery would've been risky for the baby.'

'It wasn't happening. Danielle was adamant, even when told of the likely outcome. Her baby came first. She would not risk its life.' Now she had to wipe away the tears; there were too many to ignore.

Mattia handed her a handkerchief.

'Thanks.' She sniffed. 'I didn't think anyone used these any more.'

'I find tissues aren't quite the thing when helping a crying woman.'

She gave a droopy smile. 'Someone brought you up to be a gentleman.'

'That family we were talking about earlier.'

They'd reached a park bench. Elene said, 'Mind if we sit down? I'd like to take in the view while we talk.' The distant lights of Naples were a balm to the anxiety building inside her as she reached the sensitive part of her story. Without waiting for a reply, she sank onto the wooden slats and crossed her arms under her breasts.

Mattia sat beside her, his legs stretched out interminably. Long, muscular, slim. An athlete's build.

Elene tried to drag up images of the man she'd kept at arm's length for her friend's sake in Wellington, and all that landed in her head was a picture of Mattia about to kiss her. They'd been wrong to get that far, but in the heat of the moment she hadn't known anything other than Mattia.

'Go on,' he urged.

'After the diagnosis everything changed.' Elene's arms tightened further. 'Danielle wanted the time she had left to be about her baby. She quit her job to focus on being as fit and healthy as possible. I moved into her apartment to help whenever needed. The being healthy bit didn't work out. The pregnancy mixed with cancer rapidly drained her. They found lesions on her lungs when she was at thirty-three weeks' gestation. Doctors suggested inducing the birth. Danielle refused, wanting the best start for her baby, and afterwards she focused entirely on Aimee for the time she had.'

Mattia waited quietly, making it easier to continue.

'We spent a lot of hours talking about the future.' Swallow. 'I believed she should've told you before Aimee was born. To me it wasn't just about Danielle's needs. Whereas she fully intended having that time with Aimee to herself, saying you'd have years with her if you wanted her, and making me promise not to get in touch with you until after.' After. That word still wrung her heart.

Not so Mattia. '*If* I wanted my child? What did she think I was?' He was up on his feet, hands on hips, staring at her as though she was the culprit here.

'Sit down, Mattia.' She refused to go on while he was hovering over her. 'You're making me uncomfortable.'

He made to comment, then must have thought the better of it. 'Fine.' The bench shook as he dropped down beside her.

'I'd never have prevented even a minute of that time for Danielle with Aimee.'

She gave him a smile. 'You'd have had to get past me.'

'There is that.' He returned the smile, followed by a sigh. 'You'd have been a hellcat.'

'Agreed. So, where do we go from here? We've dealt with the past, now there's the future to sort out. One thing you need to understand—I will never walk away from Aimee.'

'I already figured that out.' Mattia stared out across the bay for a long time. 'I suggest we take time getting to know each other.'

Not what she'd expected. Relief soared, then plummeted. Did Mattia have his lawyers determining what was required for him to gain full custody of his daughter? Her hands clenched against her ribs. Thinking like that might not be fair but she had to face facts. If Mattia wanted his daughter entirely for himself she would fight back hard, but her resources were minuscule compared to the Ricco fortune. 'You aren't saying how you want this to work.'

Mattia pulled her hand free, covered it with his warmth. 'Relax. I'm not going to do anything underhand. You will know every step I take, what I'd like to do, and I expect the same from you. I also will never walk away from my daughter. She's in my life for ever.' Dropping her hand, he continued. 'I think we've covered enough ground tonight. We're still talking, not arguing, which is a good way to finish. All I ask is that you trust me.'

Big ask when there was so much at stake. Yet she

couldn't find it in her to disagree. So far he hadn't left her in the lurch over anything. Being naïve again? Or learning to trust her instincts with this man? 'I'm not looking for trouble. We've got enough already.'

They'd nearly reached his car when Mattia asked quietly, 'One thing. So far I've only heard about Danielle and what she wanted for our daughter. What do *you* want from me? For yourself,' he added. 'Money? A home here? What?'

'Nothing,' she gasped, her blood running cold, her face feeling as though he'd physically slapped her. 'Absolutely nothing,' she cried through clenched teeth. He wanted her to trust him? How about returning the favour?

She was good, Mattia conceded. But good actor or genuinely honest person, he had yet to determine. 'Fine.' *Just checking, Elene. Because I won't be played for a fool again.* He didn't like what he'd done, but the need to know was a juggernaut that wouldn't be stopped. Not after Sandy stealing from his charity and then trying to get him arrested for misuse of donations. Being used came with the territory for his family. There were often people on the make, or trying to ingratiate themselves into the Ricco business in order to cruise through life. But Sandy? When she'd wanted for nothing? Even years down the track he didn't understand her motives. The only good thing to come out of it seemed to be that he'd become a father. And meeting the woman now storming ahead along the roadside, putting distance between them, going right past his car.

Acting as though he'd hurt her by his question? He shook his head. No acting about it. Her fury was all-consuming. Perhaps he'd got her wrong. If Elene wasn't interested in gaining anything from him out of this then he owed her an apology—once she calmed down. Try now and he'd get his head knocked off with one of those shoes swinging furiously from her hand. But how was he to be sure? 'Elene, stop. Get in the car.'

A finger was waved at him over her shoulder, leaving no doubt about what she thought of that suggestion.

'It's not safe to walk alone this late at night.'

Another wave, no friendlier than the first.

Fine. He'd follow her, all the way home if he had to. Slamming the door, he started the car to roll along behind her. Of course Elene wasn't going to give in and get in the vehicle after what he'd asked. Did that mean he could safely say she wasn't after anything more than to be Aimee's *madre*? Another can of worms. Her terms or his? Would they ever be able to agree on something so tricky? She had dropped into his life without warning. To catch him on the hop?

Pulling up alongside Elene, he lowered the window and asked, 'What did you hope to gain by turning up here unannounced?'

She didn't stop, didn't even falter in those long, angry strides, the soles of her feet slapping on the pavement with each step. 'Only to keep my promise to Danielle,' she shot over her shoulder.

What game had Danielle been playing? Surely she didn't think he and Elene could get together as a couple? As far as he knew, she'd never learned about that moment in the tea room—how it had rocked him deeply, and how hard he'd worked at forgetting it.

Now Elene stopped, whipping around to glare at him. 'What do you think? That I wanted to do it this way?' Her hand slapped the roof of his car. 'No, Mattia. Danielle was so ill I'd have promised her the moon if she'd asked for it.' With that she was off again, charging up the hill like a rocket.

He sighed. What a woman to have onside. The mother of his child had been very lucky to have such a friend. One in a million. One he'd like walking with him through life. If he ever got stupid enough to fall in love again, that was. And one thing was certain: he wasn't stupid. Not often.

He waited until she was nearly out of sight before engaging gear and cruising along behind her, pausing to let her get ahead, catching up, not once considering leaving her alone. It must've rankled when she had to wait at the gate to get inside the property and again for the garage door to lift so she could enter the house and make her way to her room. Not once did she acknowledge him. Not a nod, a word or a glance. Her back was straighter than the flagpole on the end of the deck, her chin sharper than a knife.

He was in too deep. And hating it. Elene had fought back hard, which he admired. She wasn't whimpering like a puppy, waiting to be forgiven, but telling him he'd have to do better if he was to gain her respect. Considering how her ex had treated her, it only showed how strong she'd become. He only had himself to blame. They'd been getting on so well before he'd gone and wrecked it. But learning the truth was imperative. Protecting his family came first. Elene had the perfect excuse for getting close, and that was his daughter. Her guardianship could be a ruse to obtain financial gain from his family, but unless that was the case he was loath to contest her legal role. Danielle had chosen Elene as Aimee's mother, and he'd respect that to the best of his ability—as long as he retained his rightful place in his daughter's life, which meant having her living with him full-time.

He was going to have to convince Elene to stay in Italy. Permanently. That was all there was to it.

That's all? He groaned. It'd be easier to run the Sahara Marathon, and he didn't even run to the hospital. This was

Elene Lowe he was talking about, remembered from working together in Wellington: stubborn, determined when she put her mind to it. He had to find a way through those barricades that she'd flung up when he'd accused her of wanting something from him. He had to do it for everyone's sake. Starting ASAP. He only hoped he had enough time to accomplish the right outcome before she left for home—taking Aimee with her.

He'd start by going to bed and not antagonising her any more tonight.

And tomorrow? He groaned. A full surgical schedule to deal with. A child to consider. An angry woman to placate. Bring it on. Really?

Sì. Mattia stopped pacing the kitchen. Placating Elene might be difficult, yet he wanted to, wanted to win her confidence and her trust—something she'd only half-heartedly given earlier. She had to be the most infuriating woman on the planet and yet he wanted to get on with her. Naturally he'd do all he could for his child. But… This wasn't only about Aimee. This was about getting to know, understand, care about Elene Lowe.

Oh, come on. This is about acknowledging the heat that tightens your groin whenever she's close, about that challenge in her eyes that has you wondering if you had a fling with the wrong woman back in Wellington.

Now he was really going to sleep well. Because he already knew the answer to that one.

'Damn it.' Striding down the hall, he rapped on Elene's door. 'Can I have a word?'

The door opened a crack. 'You had too many already.' The door closed.

Mattia gave another, sharper rap. 'Elene, I am sorry for what I implied. Truly sorry.' He couldn't countenance her thinking he might be a bully like that Craig character.

The door opened. Elene slipped through and closed it before leaning back against the wall, her arms folded beneath her breasts, those intense eyes locked on him. 'Did you mean what you asked?'

He had to be honest. It was the only way to go. But neither would he grovel. 'Yes.'

'Thank you. I understand why you had to ask.' He was being impaled with that look. 'Just not how you went about it.' Then her stance softened. Only a little, but it was enough. 'See you in the morning.' She left him standing in the hall feeling like a kid on detention outside the headmaster's office.

'Goodnight, Elene,' he whispered, more to himself than her. 'See you tomorrow.'

CHAPTER FIVE

ELENE WOKE TO a very quiet room. Jerking upward, she stared over at the cot. Empty. How had she slept through Aimee stirring and doing her morning routine of 'Ma-ma-ma-ma'? That she'd lain awake till after four might have something to do with it. Unless someone had taken Aimee away before she started? Mattia? Or Anna? She knew who she hoped it'd been, and it wasn't that tall, arrogant man who'd pushed every button she owned and then some last night. The thought of Mattia coming in here while she was comatose stirred her blood to simmering, just because he could and would.

His apology hadn't come naturally, but it had come. His belief she'd come all this way with a toddler in tow to see what was in it for her was understandable given what Sandy What's-Her-Face had done to him. Didn't mean he hadn't hurt her. The real reason she found it difficult to accept his apology was because Craig had only ever apologised after she'd left him and he'd wanted to win her back. *Mattia isn't Craig.* True. It was time to stop superimposing Craig onto every man she met, starting now.

Her phone showed ten minutes after nine. No wonder Aimee wasn't in her cot. But it might mean Mattia had left for work and Anna would be minding their little girl. *Their* little girl? Oh, boy, she was in trouble. There was no way she could ever give up Aimee so, however they resolved this, she was also always going to be a part of Mattia's life, even if from the sidelines.

Bang-bang. The pounding in her head intensified. She'd drop it for now. Try breakfast and coffee. Then take Aimee up to Pompeii town by train to get away from Mattia's house, the male scent that clung to his discarded jacket, the empty glass he'd leave on the kitchen counter—everything came with an undertone of something she daren't acknowledge. He had a way of getting under her skin that made her think of summer and heat and excitement.

Wandering into the kitchen, Aimee's excited shrieks from the deck told Elene her girl was happy. Snatching up an irresistible *biscottate* from the laden plate on the bench, she headed outside. 'Morning, baby girl.' Then the air stalled in her throat. Mattia had not gone to work. Waiting for her to resume her duties? No, Saturday or not, if he'd needed to go in he'd have called on Anna to take care of Aimee until she was up. Or banged on her door.

Mattia looked up from where he sat on the boards beside his daughter. 'Morning, Elene. You catch up on sleep?' So he was playing nice.

'A little.'

'Feel up to a drive down the coast?' Playing *very* nice.

'As in the Amalfi Coast?'

'Yes, I thought Positano for lunch. Have you been there?'

'A cousin took me on a quick trip that way, but it was over too fast. I've always wanted to go back one day.' She squelched the rising excitement, aimed for calm and reserved. She hadn't forgiven him *that* much. 'I'd love to go.' Okay, nearly reserved.

Mattia was on his feet. 'I'm making coffee. Want some?'

Oh, what the heck? 'Is this Mattia?' she asked around a sudden smile, feeling comfortable with him at last.

He grinned on his way past. 'Sure is.'

A Mattia grin was dynamite, exploding through her, impelling her knees forward. Locking her knees to stop herself from falling in a heap, she absorbed the sudden heat swamping her even as that grin continued to decimate her. Wow. More, please. 'I'll pack a bag for Aimee. She's coming with us.'

'Wouldn't dream of leaving her behind.' The smell of freshly ground coffee beans filled the air, teasing her taste buds. 'Have your breakfast first. There's no hurry.'

More *biscottate* wouldn't go amiss. Keep this up and she'd be buying new clothes. But how could she ignore the delicious treats? They were better than her mother's, and that was saying something. Standing in the doorway where she could keep an eye on Aimee and talk to Mattia, she asked, 'Won't we hit the tourist rush?'

'All part of the fun. Anyway, it's not too bad in April. Watch out next month.'

'Aren't you meant to be working?' Anna had mentioned Mattia working weekends somewhere other than the Sorrento Hospital.

'All taken care of.'

'What is this other job?' For a moment it seemed life was perfect, with Mattia preparing the coffee, those delicious *biscottate*, Aimee playing on the deck. Almost as if they were a family. Get a grip. *That's fantasy.* What was wrong with that?

'There's a surgical unit in town that's an outreach of a charity hospital in Napoli where I do orthopaedic surgery for those less fortunate. We have a roster of specialists who take turns putting their skills to good use, mostly at the weekends when no one's required at their regular positions.'

Even though he'd spent time outdoors in Wellington having fun on a bike and in a kayak, Mattia had worked long and hard, been available for many more hours than he was paid to cover.

'I heard you work there most weekends.'

'Someone's been talking too much.' His grin had retreated to a smile, but it was just as damaging. Today might prove hard on her emotions, yet she couldn't help feeling happy, excited even. Soon she'd be shrieking just like Aimee. This man came with a magical touch after all.

'You think?' She sipped the steaming coffee he'd placed on the nearest counter. 'How's this hospital staffed? Completely with volunteers? Or is there permanent, paid staff to keep it running smoothly?' Could she put in a few hours over the coming weeks and contribute to her stay in a roundabout way?

Mattia leaned against another counter, his arms crossed over that expansive chest, cup of coffee in one hand. 'Permanent and volunteer medical personnel keep the place going.'

'I'd like to see it.'

'I—' On the bench his phone rang. Picking it up, he wandered outside to the deck, talking about a patient.

Elene finished her breakfast and rinsed the plate and cup before delving into the fridge to prepare bottles and food for Aimee to take on their trip.

'You're in luck,' Mattia said when he returned. 'I have to see a patient at the unit before we go to Positano.'

'Coincidental?'

He shrugged with a smile. 'So it would seem. It also means we should get moving.'

'Onto it.' Excitement had her moving quickly towards

the shower. Finally she was going to see something of the coast, while visiting the charity unit Mattia devoted a lot of his time to was an added bonus. More than that, she would see another side to him in action. An interesting side. If she could persuade him to let her put in some hours at the charity unit, he might appreciate that she wasn't just a money-hungry woman with nothing more on her mind than causing trouble.

With Aimee in his arms Mattia led Elene into the surgical unit offshoot of the Naples charity hospital he'd made happen, pride expanding in his chest. His achievement hadn't been without the generous help and support of a lot of people, so he wasn't about to blow his own trumpet, but he needed Elene to understand what they were trying to achieve here—and succeeding. 'We have eight beds, four to a room, and it's a rare day they're not all full.'

Elene walked beside him, taking in everything, and approving. 'You cover all surgeries?'

'Except the ones requiring sophisticated equipment. Those cases not covered by the health system we find the funds to operate next door at the hospital.'

'It's wonderful.'

Warmth crept in under his ribs. He wanted her approval, he realised. Seeing what was important to him, she'd understand how moving to the other side of the world wasn't an option. If she realised a fraction of the effort he put in here he'd be pleased, because she'd know more about him. He needed that. Don't ask him why, he just did. Hearing about her bully fiancé had loosened something inside him, had him wanting to make the Aimee situation work as well for her as him. If only he hadn't had that brain fade and voiced his distrust. Then again, it could be a good thing he'd got it out there, done and dusted. Except now he had to earn Elene's trust. Ironic, really.

'You must spend every spare minute here.' Elene's smile was full of approval and wonder. 'What about time out for you?'

'I had that in Wellington. Now I'm home, I'm focused on doing as much as possible for others. Though—' he looked down at his daughter and smiled '—I'll have to change my ways for my girl. Can't have her growing up thinking I was too busy working to notice her. Can I, little one?' He dropped a light kiss on Aimee's cheek, felt love for her expand.

'I'll teach her not to let you get away with anything.' Elene was still smiling, which had to be good, didn't it?

'No surprise there. Come on, I'll introduce you to everyone.' This visit wasn't only about checking up on Gino, but also about letting Elene into his life in a way no other woman had been since Sandy. In the same environment—a charity medical centre. Caution flickered in his veins. Women knew he ran this unit, they just didn't know how much of himself he put into it, how he gave his heart for those people far less fortunate than him. Elene understood that already if the admiration in her eyes was a clue. Ignoring the nudge of guilt because he was trying to manipulate her, he led her into the nurses' office.

The interest flaring in the nurses' expressions amused Mattia. Until their gazes shifted from Elene to him and onto Aimee, and the interest became an ah ha moment. Ouch. 'Elene is a nurse in the hospital where I worked in New Zealand. I dated her best friend.'

Elene's look was pure enjoyment, suggesting she'd recognised his discomfort. Couldn't blame her for that.

Jiggling Aimee on his hip, cuddling her and breathing in the baby scent, Mattia felt a moment of pure happiness.

This was what being a father was about. Then he noticed the bemused looks coming his way from the nurses, knew there was a long way to go. Biologically he was Aimee's dad, but in all other ways he had yet to work things out with Elene before he told the staff what they were surmising was correct.

'Come on, Elene. My patient's along here. He won't mind you tagging along.' *That way I get to keep you away from prying nurses with nothing better to do than ask unwanted questions.*

'You'd better give me Aimee. Hanging onto her while talking to a patient might be going too far.' Elene reached for the wriggling bundle he was holding.

As much as he wanted to hold onto his girl, he handed Aimee over. Elene had a point. 'You realise everyone thinks you're her mum.'

'They're not far off the mark,' she said, and followed up with one of those stunning smiles that warmed him to the tips of his toes.

This was all wrong. He should not be feeling any warmth brought on by Elene. But he was. No denying the softening in his belly, the increased speed of his heart. The same feelings he'd known that night in Wellington. Being careful was paramount. Elene had been hurt before. He wouldn't be the next guy doing that to her.

Taking her elbow, he led her towards the middle-aged man who lived in a tiny house with his wife and eight kids. 'Gino, I heard you wanted to see me. This is Elene, a friend from New Zealand.'

Under Mattia's fingers Elene's soft skin felt like velvet, making him want more of her. About to whip his hand away, he paused. This astute woman would instantly know something was up if he let go abruptly. No, nothing was up, but he couldn't deny there was some tightening going on beyond his belt.

Gino was giving Elene the once-over. '*Ciao*, Elene. Nice to meet you. The doctor's one wonderful man for all the good work he does for people like me.'

'That's enough, Gino. Show me where this pain is.'

Elene was smiling at the other man, ignoring his attempt to divert the conversation to more basic needs. 'I hear this unit does good things for lots of people.'

'So you're the doctor's wife. Your daughter is the spitting image of him.'

The colour fled Elene's cheeks. 'No, not his wife.'

'Excuse me, everyone. Can we get down to business?' *I'm the doctor around here, which means I'm in charge.* Not that these two were taking the slightest bit of notice of him. About to step away from Elene, Mattia hesitated. *Support her, man. Don't leave her to deal with this.* 'Like I said, we're friends. Now, Gino, what's the problem with your surgery?'

Either Elene hadn't heard him or she chose to ignore him. 'I'm going to talk to Dr Ricco about putting in some hours here while I'm in town.'

'You want to work here?' Mattia asked before putting his brain in gear. It shouldn't surprise him. Nursing was in her blood. She wouldn't be able to walk away from patients in need. What's more, they'd love her in here.

'Why not? I'm sure you can always use an extra pair of hands. I have a current licence to nurse in Italy. I don't need a visa since I've got dual citizenship.' Her smile was devastating, no doubt designed to suck him in and get the answer she was holding out for.

'You have?'

She nodded. 'Mum thought it a good idea in case I decided to return to her roots.'

'That could work out for everyone.' Things were beginning to fall into place. Elene could move to Sorrento without any legal difficulties. But did he want her working here? It was one thing to show her what drove him to get up every day, quite another to have her working in his space. Or was it? He wanted her to move to Sorrento, so letting her into his domain was a given. Keep your enemies close, remember? Except he struggled to think of her as anything but a friend. Um, make that a woman who rattled his emotions, set his body humming and didn't take him at face value. A woman he could all too easily get beyond liking—if he hadn't already started down that track. 'We'll talk about it later.'

The expectation in her eyes didn't falter. 'I'll hold you to that.'

'Thought you might.' He watched her wander away, presumably to give Gino some privacy to talk about what was bothering him. Elene was a great nurse; his patients in Wellington always had nothing but good words for her. Nothing would be any different here, so why *was* he hesitating? *Because I feel vulnerable around her.* And that was so alien it floored him.

'Dr Ricco?' Gino spoke loudly.

Vulnerable to a woman? To Elene? How was that possible?

'Doctor?' Louder still.

He reluctantly turned away from that tempting sight of Elene's straight back, pert butt and the long hair swishing back and forth over her shoulders, and refocused on who he'd come to see in the first place. He definitely couldn't have her working here. His patients would be in jeopardy every time he got distracted.

'Sorry, Gino. What did you say?' Over the phone, the

nurse had mentioned the man's reluctance to get out of bed and start working that new hip.

'The nurse says I have to walk with one of those geriatric walking frames. I only had surgery yesterday. I need to rest.'

'Not at all, Gino. The best thing you can do to help yourself is get out of bed and start moving. Not big steps or long walks, just back and forth across the room like the physio showed you, and the exercises.'

The man grimaced. 'Won't I damage the wound?'

Getting too cosy? That happened in here sometimes, and who could blame the patients? A comfortable, warm bed, meals at regular intervals and clean pyjamas—all things most people took for granted were luxuries for many of this unit's patients.

'Not if you follow the rules. There might be a little pain, which the nurses can give you something for, but if you don't do this the thigh muscles will tighten and hurt far more later on.'

Gino sighed and sat up, grunting as no doubt that wound reminded him why he was here.

Mattia brought the walking frame closer. 'Those exercises for tightening and relaxing your thigh muscles while lying in bed will have you back on your feet quicker than you can believe.'

'Mattia, can you take a look at some results that've come through from the lab?' a nurse called from the desk.

'Sure. You take over here.' Mattia crossed to the desk and studied the computer screen in front of him, then picked up the phone and dialled the pharmacy down the road. Next he visited Signora Esposito. So much for a quick drop by before hitting the road to Positano.

A glance across the ward had him smiling. Elene was now with Gino as he balanced awkwardly on the walking frame. 'That's it. One small step, then another. See, you can do it.'

'My legs are feeble,' Gino grumbled before taking another step.

Elene told him, 'You'll be on crutches before you know it, and able to give the nurses cheek as you go past their desk.'

His progress picked up from a snail's pace. 'Why are nurses always so chirpy?'

'Hassling patients is part of our job. No, don't turn around. You can make it to the other side and back. That's it. You're doing great.'

Mattia sat on the corner of the desk and watched Gino hanging off every word Elene uttered, doing his best to impress her. Yes, they needed her here. Everyone except him, that was. Though that was getting harder to believe by the day.

'I don't think I could ever be brave enough to drive along this road.' Elene stared at the car in front that had just cut across the front of Mattia's vehicle. It wasn't the first of the morning. 'Look at all those dents in the bodywork.'

'I was going to offer you the use of my car whenever I'm at work.' Mattia laughed. 'Not a good idea?'

'Not if you want it back in pristine condition.' She laughed too, then winced as a car coming in the opposite direction overtook and sent everyone sideways in avoidance mode. 'That was close.'

'That's Italy. Toughen up and enjoy it. The driving does get a little chaotic on popular roads like this one, especially when tourists are thrown into the mix.'

'I'll take the bus or train while I'm here.' Especially since she had a toddler to think of. She looked beyond the sharp bend they were approaching and gasped. 'That's so beautiful. All those houses painted pretty shades of yellow and pink and red and white, with the sea at the bottom. How they remain attached to the steep hillside is beyond me.' This was what she'd wanted to see again. Also to wander along the streets of Positano and poke around in the shops, pick up some souvenirs to take home.

'Let's go for a walk on the beach before having lunch, give Aimee some freedom after being strapped into her seat for so long.' Mattia glanced in the rear-view mirror. 'Though she's happy enough, no grizzling at all.'

'She never complains when she's in a car. I think the movement past the window fascinates her. Dipping her feet in the water will have her smiling even more.'

Mattia slipped into a parking space right at the beginning of the walkway down to the beach. 'Perfect.'

'How lucky can you get?'

'Who says luck had anything to do with it?' He grinned and got out.

Watching Mattia unbuckling Aimee from the seat and setting her on his hip with such aplomb had a lump forming in Elene's throat. Of course he was used to doing the same for his niece and nephew, but this was different. This was fatherhood. His hands were gentle as he settled his daughter just right, his eyes observant as he closed the car door and pinged the locks. Mattia was a natural dad. No denying he already loved Aimee.

'You coming?' he called over his shoulder.

Give me a minute to get myself together. 'Sure. Nothing like sand between my toes.' The moment she reached the beach she stuffed her thongs in her backpack.

Mattia took Aimee to the water's edge, slipping her sandals into his pockets before standing her in front of his long legs. She clung to him, swaying back and forth, his hand on her arm steadying her. Her mouth was split into a wide grin. 'Ma-ma-ma-ma.'

Elene stood watching him, hoping her sunglasses hid the direction of her gaze. He was a sight. That masculine build, the covert strength and not so covert confidence—the perfect picture. A picture dreams were made of. Even hers. Until she acknowledged this hunk was Mattia Ricco, a man who could destroy her happiness if he chose to fight her for Aimee.

But the dream didn't fade, instead remained steady in her mind. Mattia was laughing as he held Aimee so her feet were in the sea, feet that were kicking and covering his shorts in salt water. He was bonding with his daughter. And that was as sexy an image as any Elene had noted about him.

Sinking down on the sand, she pulled her knees up to her chin, wrapped her arms around her legs and watched father and daughter having fun. She couldn't find it in herself to be jealous or worried. It was the perfect picture. It was how this trip was meant to unfold.

Aimee shrieked with delight as she kicked more water in the air.

Yes, Elene thought, Aimee's meant to be with this man. As she's meant to be with me. Which meant being positive and taking each day as it came, listening to Mattia as he worked through his role in all this and giving her point of view in return. So she'd try for relaxed and enjoying the moment.

Reaching into the backpack, she tugged a small towel free. 'You're both going to need this,' she called to Mattia, who was wearing an enormous smile as he dragged Aimee along the top of the water.

'What I need is a pair of earplugs,' he said with a laugh.

When Aimee got bored, Elene changed her thoroughly

wet clothes, then they headed across the road to a lunch restaurant where the staff had no qualms about a toddler joining them. This was Italy.

The Margherita pizza they shared was fragrant and delicious. 'You can't beat this.' Elene licked up a strand of mozzarella.

Strolling along the road afterwards, Elene ducked into a shop to buy Aimee a cute sunhat, then herself an irresistible blouse at another.

When Mattia said, 'Let me get that,' she scowled at him.

'No, thank you.' Then she remembered she was supposed to be positive and not looking for arguments. 'But thanks for offering.'

He saw through her. 'It was genuine: a present, not a test.' A hint of guilt was mixed with the honesty in his voice.

'It's okay. Buying clothes is my "can't resist" passion.' He'd struggle to believe her if he saw how few she'd brought on this trip.

Mattia laughed. 'Find me a woman who doesn't think the same.'

'Glad to think I'm normal.'

'Define normal.'

Now the man was joking with her? A good sign, surely?

Another shop tempted her in. 'I won't be a minute.' She was lying. She needed space to settle her emotions—she was getting too complacent with Mattia. Because today she'd started believing in the impossible. Had begun thinking they might have a future together, and not only one that involved Aimee. But she had to be fooling herself. It could not work.

CHAPTER SIX

'TOO MUCH SUN and excitement for one little lady,' Elene muttered as she rocked Aimee on her lap once they were back home.

'It's been a big day for her,' Mattia agreed.

The look on Elene's face as she gazed down at Aimee was pure love. His gut clenched. What were they going to do about this? Aimee had already lost her mother—to have Elene taken out of the picture was not an option. It would be cruel. But Aimee was also his daughter. How to make it work for everyone? So far the only solution he could come up with was working hard at convincing Elene he couldn't leave Sorrento, not for his sake as much as for his family, who would hate for him to go so far away. More clenching was going on in his gut. Not that Elene's family would thank him for coercing her into moving to Italy, despite her having roots here. One day at a time, he told himself. They needed to be sure of each other when final decisions were made and the only way to do that was getting to know each other thoroughly. But the days were going by fast.

He poured a glass of Sangiovese and took it across to Elene. 'How serious are you about working at the charity unit?'

'If I can work out a plan for Aimee I'd like to help out a few hours each day, Monday to Friday.'

Her lips on the edge of the glass were full, soft—the kind that hot dreams were made of. Trailing over his feverish skin dreams. The kind he could not have about Elene. At least not until they'd got through what faced them with Aimee. 'Anna would be happy to mind her. So—wages. I'll pay you the same as the other nurses get.'

Her head jerked up, those love-filled green eyes now spitting arrows at him. 'I won't be paid, thank you very much. And if that's another test you can stick it where the sun never reaches.'

It had been a test, one designed to shut down the sudden hope and need that had surged through him as he'd dwelt on her mouth. Instead, he'd angered Elene all over again. He was wrong to keep pushing her. She was not interested in his wealth. Or she was aiming for the bigger package. Why was he so distrustful? Sure, Sandy had taught him a massive lesson, but he didn't usually feel so driven to test women like he did Elene. Was there a need to protect himself from a sense of coming home he'd begun feeling around her? Because of that flare of longing she made happen? It was time he spent a night with a woman. Just not this one. He continued to dig the hole he'd soon be buried in. 'Most of the nurses draw wages. There's no reason you shouldn't.'

Standing up, she held a now quiet Aimee out for him to kiss goodnight. 'I'm going to put her to bed.' At the door she paused to look back at him. 'You're not the only person who likes to help others less fortunate. Who do I see to arrange hours that fit in with the staff and my other commitment?' Her eyes dropped to her precious bundle, before returning to bore into him.

'I'll tell the staff you'll be on duty nine to twelve, starting Monday. You can work out the days with them. I'll also let Anna know.'

Elene nodded softly. 'Thank you.'

As she stepped through the doorway Mattia felt the strings holding them connected pull and tighten. Their lives were getting more entwined by the day. At the moment Elene had the upper hand. It had been a long time since *anyone* had done that to him.

'Elene,' he called softly.

Reluctance was in every angle of her body, in the steps she took to come back and confront him. 'Yes?'

If only she'd relax fully around him. 'Tomorrow I'm going to Napoli for lunch with my family, and I'd like to introduce you and Aimee to them. Will you come with me?'

Her eyes widened. 'Yes, of course.'

'They don't know anything about this situation yet.'

'Oh, man, you've got to deal with that sooner rather than later.'

'You're right. I just haven't been able to find the right moment so far.' He wanted to snatch Elene to him, hold her close so he didn't give in to the temptation to shake her until she smiled at him again, until she looked pleased to be meeting his family, till she stepped up beside him so they were united in whatever happened tomorrow. But he couldn't show uncertainty to this woman. He had to be strong. It was all he had. While he believed his parents would accept Aimee—and Elene—without reserve, that thread of doubt lurking in the back of his mind was a leftover from the days of Sandy's treachery and how she'd brought disrepute on his family, however briefly. Hurting them again would not be happening on his watch. 'I'll phone them now.'

'I'll wash my dress.'

As in the dress she'd worn to dinner last night? Was that the only dress she'd brought? A woman who enjoyed fashion had one outfit to wear somewhere special? Come to think of it, she'd worn the same two sets of shorts and blouses every day, one set on the washing line, one covering her mouthwatering body.

He'd remedy that as a way of showing her he was sorry for being such an oaf, of saying thanks for all she was doing for his daughter, and for him. It had cost her emotionally to bring Aimee to him. There was no doubt how much she loved Aimee so she had to be worried sick about the outcome. He needed slapping around the ears. He'd only been thinking about what was happening to him, and how to get her to fit in with his life.

'Say goodnight to Papà.' Elene held Aimee out to him.

Taking his girl into his arms, he stared down at her and wondered how he'd believed his life was perfect before. He'd been so far off the mark, it was unreal. Then his gaze shifted to Elene. She *was* a part of this new picture. Now that they were in Italy, not Wellington, and he wasn't having a fling with anyone, it was almost impossible to deny he wanted to know her better. Kissing Elene would make this day into something special. Instead he kissed Aimee's forehead and hugged her lightly, before handing her back to her mother. 'Goodnight, little one.' Then to Elene, he said, 'After I've talked to my father I'll cook dinner.'

'I'm not hungry,' she called over her shoulder as she disappeared into her bedroom.

'We'll see about that.' Carbonara was a favourite of hers, and he was a dab hand at putting it together. He picked up the phone slowly, staring around the casual lounge room. Baby shoes lay in the middle of the floor, a discarded tiny singlet in a crumpled mess on the couch. The scent of summer roses that was Elene mingled with the tang of the Sangiovese. He'd never taste that particular wine again without being reminded of her. From down the hall came baby giggles and adult chuckles, and inside he melted a little bit more.

His house had never felt so—so enjoyable. A family home, not a huge house that echoed when he made a sound. He'd spent most of his life inside these walls with his grandparents and parents and brothers, as a child and an adult, enjoying laughter and in-depth conversations about anything and everything. Since returning from his year in New Zealand he'd lived here on his own, and not once had he felt alone, yet now, with Elene and Aimee here, he understood he'd been lonely. There were a lot of wonderful memories in each of the rooms—family ones, time with playmates and later with teenage friends. Even an occasional girlfriend came into that collection, but over the last few days a sense of missing out on what was most important had begun sneaking up, making him look beyond the comfort and effortlessness of his solitary life. Making him want to get involved with special people to share everything.

Down the hall Aimee shrieked, bringing him out of his stupor. He had a phone call to make. Or he could go say another goodnight to his daughter. He'd still have to make that call, tell his parents what was going on, but—

Dropping the phone back on the table, he headed for the bedroom which nowadays looked like a nursery and not a sterile area waiting to be messed up. He preferred it with toys and clothes covering all the surfaces. 'Hey, little one. Got another goodnight kiss for Papà?'

'Your phone call was over quick.' Elene lifted Aimee up to him from the change table where she'd been buttoning up the all-in-one pyjamas covered in teddy bears.

'I haven't made it yet.' He ignored the surprise on Elene's face. The small, warm, wriggling body in his arms brought a large smile to his face. Tickling Aimee's tummy, he laughed. 'It's bedtime, my girl.'

'I think you're waking her up, not quietening her for sleep.' Elene didn't sound hassled, just accepting.

More accepting of him? That had to be good for whatever came next. 'I'll tuck her in shortly.' When he'd had his fill. 'She's cute, isn't she?' He heard the pride in his own voice. He was in big trouble. Or on notice that he had to resolve all the difficulties between him and Elene so he didn't miss out on time with Aimee. *And Elene.* His grin faded. Elene. He wanted lots of time with her. His eyes drifted from Aimee to Elene, scoping out that compact, curvy figure, those full lips, the orange-tipped toes.

Thump. A small fist caught him a blow on the chin.

'Hey, minx, careful.' Mattia blew bubbles on Aimee's cheek until she laughed and then he placed her in the sleeping sack and kissed her forehead. 'See you in the morning.'

Elene appeared on the other side of the cot and leaned over to do the same, except she said, 'Night, night, gorgeous. Love you.'

Together they left the room, Elene turning off the light and he closing the door softly. Walking side by side down the hall felt right, which only made it all the more awkward when what he'd like to have with Elene and what he'd get were very different things.

'Sorry, I haven't started on dinner,' he managed around the sudden lump of annoyance at her for putting him in this situation—even when it wasn't her fault. 'And I have my parents to deal with first.'

'You're hungry?' Green eyes met his. 'I can prepare something.'

He'd been going to do that for her. 'You've got a dress to wash.'

'I don't think toasted sandwiches will take all night.'

He stared at her. Toasted sandwiches? People came to Italy in their droves to eat pasta and pizza, not sandwiches. From deep inside a bubble built up, pushed upward, exploded across his tongue. Laughter filled the air. 'You're amazing.' Then he spun away and with something resembling a spring in his step headed for that damned phone and the call he'd been putting off. Elene was doing strange things to him. No doubt about it. One moment he was annoyed, the next, happy. Bizarre.

'You're amazing.' Those two words bounced around Elene's skull as she pressed the dress into warm, soapy water. Why had Mattia said that? They were poles apart in most aspects of their lives.

You think Mattia's wonderful about certain things, like his care for his patients. Oh, please. It's his body and looks and kindness and fun that've got your knickers in a twist. Patients have nothing to do with it.

He probably meant she was amazing because she'd offered to save him the effort of cooking when she'd said she wasn't interested in food. Tell that to her starving stomach. It had been the thought of sitting down at the same table with Mattia while fancying him that put her off wanting to eat.

In the kitchen she could hear Mattia's carefully modulated voice through the wall, but not what he was saying. He'd shut himself in his office, presumably so she wouldn't be privy to what he told his family about her unexpected arrival on his doorstep. Her heart squeezed for him. How did he tell those nearest and dearest that there was another member of the family that no one had known about? It wouldn't be easy, even when they seemed close.

Tomorrow he was introducing them to her. Would she get an interrogation? Be hauled over hot coals for bringing Aimee over without warning? Her mouth dried while her pulse quickened. Looking around the kitchen, she focused on normality, regained her composure. She would not be afraid of their reaction. She had right on her side. She was looking out for Aimee, after all.

Why did you make me promise to bring Aimee here unannounced, Danielle? What was wrong with phoning to tell Mattia he was a father? Did you want us to catch up, maybe get together for Aimee's sake? As usual, there were no answers descending upon her. Not so usual, despair didn't follow. Strange.

Opening the fridge, she debated what to fill the sandwiches with. Not that there was a lot of choice, the contents being more suited for a pasta sauce. So—tomatoes, ham, cheese.

An arm whipped around her and lifted out a water bottle.

She sucked in a breath, got a wave of male smell. Snatching up packets of food, she twisted around and elbowed the fridge door shut and came to a halt, inches from Mattia. Being this close, so in his sphere, had her blood fizzing. He was bigger than she'd remembered, making her feel petite. Fragile almost. Breathing had become a problem. 'Excuse me.' She needed air, fast.

'Certainly.' But he didn't move. Not a centimetre.

Raising her head, her breath clogged her sluggish lungs. His gaze was fixed on her, his mouth barely open, those lips teasing and tempting. Too tempting. *Careful what you wish for.* A kiss from Mattia. And afterwards? When they still had a long way to go, sorting out Aimee's future? She knew from last time how long it took to get over his kisses—and he hadn't actually kissed her. He'd only have to crook his finger and she'd do whatever he wanted. 'Move. Now.'

'Certainly,' he repeated, only this time he did as she demanded.

Relief warred with regret. Regret that she'd never get to try out those lips, feel that mouth covering hers. Relief that he'd never make love to her and find her lacking. Because this man was experienced. Without a doubt. He'd played the field in Wellington, and there'd never been a bad word spoken about him. While she had had one long-term relationship with a man who'd put her down, no matter how much she gave of herself when making love. Letting Mattia find out her failings wasn't happening. How humiliating would that be? But— If only. Those pecs were made for touching, caressing, kissing, licking.

The bag of tomatoes hit the floor with a soft plopping sound. The container of ham followed, making a harder cracking noise.

'Are you all right?' Mattia asked as he bent down to pick up the items.

No. Not at all. 'Why wouldn't I be?' *Don't answer that.* Because he'd probably be an expert at mind-reading as well, and boy, was her mind a mess of need and denial, of longing and regret.

He watched her as he moved to the counter to place the now bruised tomatoes on a dish. 'We're all set for lunch. My parents are looking forward to meeting you.'

I bet they are. 'I'm looking forward to it.' In a way it was true. It was another step closer to resolving everything—one way or another.

Then Mattia asked, 'What's your family's take on this? Are they okay with you raising someone else's child?'

'They've been nothing but supportive.'

'Would they be happy if you moved to Italy? Permanently.'

He didn't need to add that last word. She got his meaning in spades. 'My parents will back whatever decision I make.'

'We make, Elene. We.'

'You're right. I keep wondering when we're going to get around to talking about the crux of the matter.' Leaning back against the fridge, she watched him try and wriggle his way out of that.

'We're making inroads by going slowly, getting to know each other in a stronger, more realistic way than we did in Wellington when I was involved with your friend. Introducing you and Aimee to my family is the next step. If I'm wrong, I apologise, but there're no ground rules to follow here.'

That apology showed how hard Mattia was working with her. She nodded. 'It's okay. I'm nervous, that's all. How did they take the news they have another grandchild?'

'Surprisingly well. But then I think my parents are beyond being shocked by anything me or my brothers do. I'm guessing you can't have four boys and not get a few knocks along the way.'

'Lucky you, having brothers. My sisters are both louder and more outgoing than me.'

'Trust me, brothers can be a pain too.'

Which brought her back to reality. 'We still have a lot to learn about each other.' She'd be gone in a couple of weeks.

Mattia laughed. 'By this time tomorrow you'll know more about me than you'd have imagined. And probably more than I want you to find out.'

'So they're not going to hogtie me and snatch Aimee away?' The question was out before she'd thought of being prudent.

'That's what's putting that frown on your brow.' Mattia crossed and laid a hand on her arm. 'I promise you no one's going to grill you, throw you out the door or remove Aimee from your arms.' The eyes locked on her were almost black with intensity. 'I won't let that happen.'

Knock me down. Mattia would stick by her, support and look out for her. They had come a long way. Though it was in his nature to look out for others, she sensed he was more involved with her, with the need to care for her. A man who'd stand by her, especially against his beloved family, was the sort she'd been looking for all her life. Her father had set the benchmark, and she should never have got involved with Craig. Mattia was beginning to understand her better than she could have imagined.

'I don't intend coming between you and your family.' She drew a shaky breath. 'But thank you. It means a lot that you'd stick up for me.'

He scowled. 'Why wouldn't I?' He was studying her, that intensity ramped up even higher. 'Sure I like getting my own way, but I'd never bully you to achieve my own gain.'

She swallowed, staring at him. 'I know that.'

When she tried to move away Mattia put his hand on her other arm, gently held her in place. 'What Craig did—is that why you were so against me and Danielle? You thought I'd hurt her badly. Like you've been.'

Sucking her lips back against her teeth, she nodded. 'Danielle didn't bruise easily, yet when you came along I thought she might. I was wrong. There are times I struggle to believe not every male is a bully.' *Why did I ever feel the need to protect Danielle from Mattia?* Again she wondered if even then she'd been protecting *herself* from him because he was out of bounds, having chosen to date Danielle.

'It's completely understandable.' Those large hands were unbelievably tender on her skin.

Don't move in case he takes them away. She enjoyed being touched by Mattia. He was so sexy, and kind, and caring. The swear word that rose in her mind was blunt. Followed by a blunter thought. *You were jealous of Danielle. You wanted Mattia yourself.* A shiver tripped up her spine. Had she really? No denial was rushing at her. Elene lifted her eyes to Mattia's face, drank in the chiselled chin, the dark stubble, the laughter lines at the corners of his mouth. Quite the package. No wonder she'd lusted after him. And now? Now nothing. That had to remain in the past. Now they needed to become friends. Sex with a friend wasn't a recipe for success when there was so much at stake.

'Elene.' Her name was molten chocolate on his tongue, slipping off in a single low breath. 'Elene,' he repeated.

Heat flooded her. Because of her name on his lips. Her toes were lifting her towards him, narrowing the gap between their bodies, aided by his hands pulling softly on her arms until her breasts were against his lower chest. Still gazing up at him as if she'd been struck by lightning, she didn't consider backing away, only knew the longing deep inside to kiss him, to taste him, to know his mouth on hers.

Lowering his head slowly, as though giving her the chance to pull away, Mattia's mouth came tantalisingly close before he hesitated. His eyes were smoky, watching her, waiting for what?

Not pulling away. Not this time. Elene stretched those last few centimetres to place her mouth on his, feeling the strength and gentleness, the fullness, the need his lips invoked.

A groan spilled between them, escaping from Mattia as he kissed her back. Kissed her deep, sensually. Making her hope, beg, that she could return the favour equally as mind-blowing, as heating as what having Mattia's mouth devouring hers was doing to her. A kiss was a kiss—so wasn't true. The kisses she'd known never produced sparks and made her boneless, hadn't sent torrents of mindless need racing to every inch of her body and especially to that place now throbbing with such longing.

Pressed up against him, his arms wrapped around her keeping her there, Elene lost track of everything except those lips, that slick tongue venturing into her mouth, the strength of his body she was so entwined with they'd become one. A hunger opened wide, had her feasting harder.

'Mattia,' she whispered around their kiss. Mattia. Mattia? She was kissing Mattia when they had so much to resolve? The heat chilled, her skin lifted in bumps. The need remained, not building, not dying—just there, tormenting her in its persistence. 'Mattia.'

Immediately he jerked his mouth away, brought his hands to her upper arms to hold her steady. 'Elene,' he gasped. 'That—' He stopped, staring at her as if an alien had entered his home.

Considering everything, she probably was one. Or had her inexperience been that obvious? She shrugged away from him, found the strength to walk across the room to the other side of the counter, putting space between them before she did something silly like grab him and start all over with another bone-melting, brain-exploding kiss. 'That shouldn't have happened. I'm sorry.'

Anger reflected back at her as he growled, 'Don't you dare apologise. We're adults and know what we're doing.'

'We do?' She sure as eggs didn't. All she could definitely say was she'd loved every moment of the kiss and would do anything for another—except she knew she couldn't. Not if she wanted to survive intact.

'I guess.' The fingers he dragged through his dark hair were shaking.

She'd rattled him. Good. She wasn't in this pickle alone. His indecision was heart-warming, showing yet another side to a man she'd always believed beyond indecision. Especially about something as simple as a kiss. But it hadn't been a simple kiss. Not in her book, any rate.

'See you in the morning.' There'd be no avoiding it since they were going to see his family. Her heart squeezed. The Ricco family on top of that kiss was stacking up to be insurmountable trouble. Why had she instigated it? Why, why, why? Hey, it had been the kiss of a lifetime, worth any amount of trouble. She snatched up her half-full glass of wine as she went past the table. She needed it. Badly. To soothe her messed-up mind. Not to mention to cool her deliciously bruised lips, to calm her rapid heartbeat, something to sip as she meditated on what just happened.

I kissed Mattia Ricco. That was what happened, no more, no less. Oh, yeah? There was plenty more to it, otherwise why were her legs like logs, her feet chunks of floppy rubber?

She should've grabbed the bottle. There wouldn't be any sleep going on tonight and imbibing would be a pleasurable way to fill in an hour or two. There'd be some cruising through her mind for ideas on how to handle meeting the Ricco clan. Mattia might have said he had her back, but making a fool of herself wasn't an option. Nor did she want to be answering awkward questions, but how to prepare for them when she couldn't be certain what they'd be?

Settling back against the headboard of the enormous—made for two and sex—bed, she sipped wine and looked across the room to where Aimee's cot had been until that morning, when they'd shifted her to another room since she'd settled in so well. Elene sighed. Tracing the outline of her mouth brought X-rated ideas of what she would like to do with Mattia next time they kissed.

Except there wasn't going to be a next time.

Elene was quiet on the drive up to Naples. She was exhausted, having lain awake until the early hours, her head spinning with a long litany of all things Mattia.

He'd woken her with a mug of strong coffee and some ciabatta with tomatoes before getting Aimee ready for the day. One day he'd make the perfect husband for some lucky woman. Just not her.

He'd told her in a quiet, let's-forget-last-night voice, 'We're going to Via Toledo in the city before heading to the family house.'

'Right. I'll be quick,' she'd answered, not knowing what Via Toledo was about, but seeing any part of Napoli was a bonus. She'd never been there; the airport didn't count.

Now she asked into the uncomfortable silence that had fallen as Sorrento dropped behind them, 'What's on Via Toledo?'

'Shops.'

'Mattia.' She hadn't meant to snap but they were in a car together, going to visit his relatives, and tension was increasing inside her with every passing minute. She took a deep breath. They needed to be getting along, not scrapping. 'What kind of shops?'

'All kinds. Especially clothing and shoes, and all the things women love.'

'You spilt red wine on your white skirt?'

He didn't even laugh. 'You need some clothes. I'm taking you shopping.'

'Oh, no, you don't.' First he kept testing her to see what she was trying to get out of him, and then he'd decided to buy her a new wardrobe. A test or a gift she was supposed to accept with gratitude? Forget being the peacemaker. 'If I want clothes I'll buy them.'

'It's my way of saying thank you for bringing Aimee across to meet me.'

She gasped. Never had she expected him to say that. Never. 'Low blow.'

The car lurched sideways as Mattia aimed for the verge, where he hauled on the brake and twisted in his seat to face her. 'I meant it.'

'All you had to do was say thank you.'

Those dark eyes were fierce. 'I'm a man of few words, especially the important ones.'

She had noticed. 'Yet you said them the moment I got mad at you.'

A wry expression came across his face. 'I reacted without thinking. Something you tend to cause me to do too often.'

She affected Mr Always in Control? Not likely. 'Save it—' *Gulp.* There really was a hint of remorse in his gaze. Reaching out, she touched his hand. 'Take me to Via Toledo. I'd love some new clothes.' It wasn't like her to get around with so few choices. 'But I'll pay for them.'

A reluctant smile lifted that delightful mouth. 'Let me buy one outfit.'

Would it be selfish to say yes? That look said not. 'All right.' A pair of shorts and a blouse wouldn't be excessive.

Except she hadn't factored in the high-end fashion shop Mattia took her to. As for getting away with a casual outfit, forget it. The dress the assistant held out for her to try on after Mattia told her to find something that wasn't elaborate or formal but could be worn just about anywhere took Elene's breath away. And probably cost more than a week's salary back home. 'I can't take that.'

'You haven't tried it on yet.' Mattia grinned and jiggled his daughter in his arms. 'Move, woman. We haven't got all day.'

Slipping into the slinky red thigh-length dress, Elene stared at the image in the mirror before her and watched the shape of her figure come to life as the assistant closed the zip. Who was this stranger?

'Wow…' she croaked.

'Wow, indeed,' came that deep, sexy voice she knew she'd miss when she left Sorrento.

She flicked around. 'Mattia?'

'The assistant opened the curtain.' His gaze roved over her. 'Thank goodness.'

'Try these on.' The woman was back, brandishing a pair of red stilettos with fine straps, the shade a perfect match for the dress.

'Ah, no, thank you. I've got shoes.' *Nothing quite like these.* But she had to be sensible. Didn't she? Not that she often was when it came to fabulous shoes and dresses.

'One dress doesn't make an outfit,' Mattia drawled.

He was impossible when he was winning. But for once she couldn't find it in her to argue. He was being kind, and arguing would be petty. Besides, she *had* to have those shoes. And the dress. Reaching for the shoes, she sank onto the couch and rubbed the soft leather with a fingertip, before slipping her feet inside. Bliss. So, so comfortable straight up. Standing, she twirled before the mirror, her gaze fixed on the shoes. 'They're beautiful,' she said in wonder. Never before had she known such perfect footwear.

'They're yours,' Mattia grunted, his eyes fixed on them too. Then slowly his gaze travelled up her legs to pause on her thighs, where the hem of the dress cut a line. His eyes widened, darkened. With lust? For her?

Elene felt her stomach drop and that spot at the top of her legs moistened. Turning away, she couldn't help but glance in the mirror for another look at him. There was something magic about Mattia, something that woke her up in ways she'd thought would never happen again. In ways she didn't want because they only led to trouble and hurt.

If Mattia made to kiss her again would she run away? Or stay to kiss him back with all she had?

Grabbing the edge of the curtain, she went to pull it shut.

'Don't take the dress off,' Mattia said.

'I'm not wearing it and risking dribble stains.' Aimee had been rubbing her mouth a lot since waking up and the resultant mess wouldn't be a good look on the soft, clinging fabric.

'My shirt can handle those. But if you really don't want to wear something new and exciting then that's your call.'

Put like that, how could she not? Her hands slid over her waist and down her hips, Mattia's eyes following, making her blush. When she didn't do blushing. 'Right, then, thank you. Shouldn't we get going?'

Mattia blinked and looked around. 'I won't be a moment,' he said as he headed to the discreet counter in the far corner of the shop.

Elene took one more look at herself in the mirror and sighed. Wearing something so lovely made her feel very feminine, and boosted her confidence to face whatever the lunch with Mattia's family brought. Was that why Mattia had splashed out? To help her? She hoped so, and was prepared to give him the benefit of the doubt there was no other ulterior motive. He'd said he'd be on her side with his family, and she had to believe him without question. Today was about Aimee. And her. And Mattia.

Back on the road, Mattia again cranked up her wariness. 'Who paid for your airfares to come here? And you've taken time off work for this trip, and I'm sure there are a lot of day-to-day expenses around raising Aimee. I'd like to help with those.'

Since he wasn't accusing her of trying to get money out of him, she could relax. 'Danielle left me everything she had for Aimee's welfare, and expressly demanded I use her money to visit you.'

'I see.' He left it at that.

Not that Elene believed for one second the discussion was over. Only on hold. But she'd go along with him. Today already held enough hurdles.

CHAPTER SEVEN

WITH HIS HAND on Elene's waist, Mattia ushered her inside his parents' home. 'Relax, no one's going to bite.' Not her anyway. If anyone was getting an interrogation it would be him.

'Easy for you to say,' she muttered, her hands clenched at her sides.

He should've let her carry Aimee to boost her confidence, but this was his daughter he was bringing home for the first time and he wasn't going to hide behind Elene. 'It's me who'll be in the hot seat.'

Tipping her head back, she stared at him. Slowly a smile grew, softening those lush lips, lightening the intense green in her eyes. 'This I want to see.'

He laughed, some of his tension dissipating. His parents had been shocked to learn about his child. Not that their shock had registered nearly as high as his when he'd first set eyes on Aimee. Now they'd had time to absorb the sparse facts he'd given there'd be endless questions for him, and for Elene. He'd protect her if it got too relentless and personal. Elene wasn't the enemy here. No one was. This was about family and doing the right thing. And loving his girl. Which one? Air whizzed across his tongue. Aimee, of course. But his eyes were on Elene.

'Your niece and nephew are here?' She glanced up at

him and his heart thudded. She was beautiful, and definitely getting to him. 'I can hear young children,' she added.

'I'd say the whole tribe's turned up.' No such thing as a quiet introduction to the Ricco family for either of these two. 'It's normal for everyone to come together for Sunday lunch, but two of my brothers are meant to be in London attending a business conference.'

'They still could be.' Hope laced her voice.

'Not likely.' Pressing his hand more firmly against her back and absorbing her softness, he said, 'Maybe I should've gone about this another way, but I figured it best to have everyone here while I tell them the facts.'

'Say it once?' Elene nodded. 'I understand. But couldn't I have stayed in Sorrento while you did it?'

'You'd really have done that? Let me take Aimee to meet my family without you there to comfort her if she gets upset?'

'You know I wouldn't.'

He'd hoped that would be her reply, would've bet on it even, but he was still grappling with getting to know her and could be horribly wrong about a lot of things. Relying on instinct had got him into trouble before.

'In here.' They'd reached the large family room where loud voices interspersed with children's shrieks were coming from. '*Ciao*, everyone.'

Silence fell instantly as all eyes turned towards him and the child in his arms, and then to the woman at his side. Introducing anyone, even a woman he was dating, to this lot had never been so awkward. The questions and rebukes were flying back and forth from him to Elene. Nothing like his usually happy and welcoming family, except for his sisters-in-law. They were relaxed and intrigued.

Mattia squared up to the room. 'Everyone, I'd like you

to meet Elene Lowe. Elene, this is my mother and my father.' He went on to introduce his brothers and sisters-in-law.

His father stepped forward and kissed Elene on both cheeks before giving her one of his soft dad smiles. 'Welcome to our home, Elene.'

On that the room erupted, with everyone wanting a piece of the action and flinging hugs and kisses in all directions. All except his mother, whose kisses for Elene were more formal. He wouldn't have expected any different, but it still stung. For Elene. Yeah, and for him.

Mattia leaned close to Elene and muttered, 'This is more like it.'

Her returning smile hit him in the belly. 'Just like home.' There was a modicum of worry in those riveting eyes, but she was coping with the onslaught. Then she turned away and said in flawless Italian, 'Hello, everybody. It's lovely to meet everyone.'

Mattia dragged his gaze away and sucked in a breath. His mother was watching them too closely. If Elene had noticed, she wasn't letting it get to her, was returning an embrace from one of his sisters-in-law with enthusiasm. This might work out fine. Then he glanced back to his mother and knew there was a way to go yet. Starting with the reason they were in this predicament. He lifted Aimee around on his hip, holding her protectively. Protecting her from what? His family adored children, and no one would hurt her. But at this point she was an unknown. He hadn't realised how difficult today might be. 'And this is Aimee.' He barely got the sentence out without choking on the lump that suddenly lodged in the back of his throat. 'My daughter.'

Arms and kisses were flying again. Elene stood back from the fray, out of the way of everyone wanting their first touch of his daughter. His hands were gentle yet firm as he held her, aware of how Aimee's eyes were widening in shock. Dropping a kiss on her forehead, he murmured, 'There, there, little one. It's all right.'

It wasn't. A shrill cry erupted. 'Ma-ma-ma-ma.'

In an instant Elene was there, reaching for her, tucking her against her breast, rubbing soothing circles on her back. 'Shh, sweetheart, I'm here. It's okay.' Her eyes were full of love and completely focused on Aimee, ignoring his family completely.

He liked that. Elene's priority was his daughter. *Their* child. While at times he struggled to believe she wanted nothing from him that wasn't to do with Aimee, he knew with absolute certainty she would always put Aimee first, regardless of her own needs.

Aimee quieted immediately, snuggled further into Elene, adding a dash of slobber mixed with tears to the new dress.

Elene must have noticed, but did she care? Not at all, Mattia decided. It was all about keeping Aimee happy. Another knot of worry unravelled. Right from the start, Elene's love for Aimee had never been in doubt, and that had become a problem for him to find a way around. If she loved the child that much then how were they going to resolve who was the constant parent and who was the part-time one? Watching her bringing a goofy smile to Aimee's face, he understood Elene would never leave her life. He could relax on Aimee's behalf. Where that left him was something else, but right now, amongst his family who'd willingly step up to help him out as a solo parent, he still wanted Elene to be in the picture permanently. In his picture, in his life in some way. Didn't he mean in Aimee's life? Not his?

Shock rattled him. He wasn't falling for Miss Green

Eyes. He mustn't. He'd decided long ago that if he was going to marry and have children it would be with a woman from his background, who knew what being wealthy meant and how to live the life with class—not someone who only saw the possessions and endless stream of toys and friends and what was in it for her. Not a woman like Elene, who could steal his heart and leave him in a mess if he was too vulnerable, as Sandy had done.

Except he was coming to believe Elene could live his way. She certainly wasn't overawed by his background, more like his sisters-in-law, who'd come from middle class families. So was there hope for him and Elene? Could he risk getting his heart broken again? Hell, if not for Sandy's deceptions, he wouldn't have gone off down under to New Zealand, wouldn't have met Danielle and Elene, certainly wouldn't be the father of the cutest, noisiest little girl he'd ever laid eyes on. Maybe he owed Sandy for that. *Not likely.*

Small hands were pulling at his trousers, reminding Mattia he belonged to more than his parents and siblings. 'Hey, Giulia, Marco. Got a kiss for Uncle Mattia?' He scooped them up in his arms and blew loud, noisy kisses on their cheeks. 'Want to meet someone special?' Mattia turned to Elene. 'See that little girl? Her name's Aimee and she's your cousin.' He'd put it out there. No taking it back. Not that he'd ever do that, but still. The old urge to protect himself had risen to the fore, despite being amongst his family, and it was hard to ignore.

Elene stepped closer, her smile for him full of encouragement. Then she focused on his daughter. 'Aimee, sweetheart, look who's here.' She shifted her bundle of arms and legs to look across at her cousins. 'Do you want to play with them?'

Mattia gave both his girls a smile. 'Giulia's got some

dolls and Marco likes playing with trucks. What do you think, Aimee?'

Her little legs were kicking into Elene, her need to get down apparent to everyone. The moment Elene placed her on the carpet she was crawling towards him, her focus entirely on her cousins, whom he set down beside her. Giulia raced to get her dolls while Marco got down on his knees and reached over to touch Aimee on the arm. Then he touched her back, her curls, her face.

Everyone gasped, and laughed, and there were a few tears in some of the gazes Mattia observed before looking to Elene. Happiness brightened her face, followed by a sharp intake of breath. Seeing how easy it was for Aimee to fit in, did she worry about when it came time to take her away again? Did she wonder if she'd be able to return to New Zealand with Aimee? He did not want to let them go. Intended for them to live with him permanently, as friends with a daughter.

When Elene turned to him a look of awe was reflecting out at him. 'I can see how alike the three of them are. No wonder you—' She stopped.

'The Ricco genes are strong,' he said, glad she hadn't finished that sentence. He didn't want his family learning how he'd guessed his role in Aimee's life. He didn't need to share that particular meeting with anybody. It was between him and Elene. He hadn't been as welcoming and kind as he could've been and it still made him uncomfortable. Offering her somewhere to stay might've been generous but he'd done it for mostly the wrong reasons, which cancelled any generosity he thought of claiming.

Giulia returned with an armful of dolls and plopped down with the other youngsters, totally unaware of all the adults watching every move they made. No longer shy or upset, Aimee took the doll her cousin offered and started pulling off the dress.

The underlying tension went out of the room, everyone suddenly talking non-stop, as per normal, and his father headed to the table where glasses and bottles of wine stood. 'Elene,' he said as he passed her. 'What would you like to drink?'

Papà had accepted her, no matter what. He could do worse than to follow his father's example. He owed Elene better than he'd managed so far. 'Papà, is the company plane booked for the end of April?'

Elene longed to run after Mattia, glue herself to his side. They mightn't have sorted out anything to do with Aimee and their future lives, but she felt safer with him than with these strangers who obviously had questions fizzing at the edge of their tongues, in their voices, their sideways glances at her and Aimee. Even Mattia wasn't immune, but he strolled through it all with the confidence that being a loved member of this family gave him. While being a wimp wasn't going to help her cause, nor Aimee's, it was very tempting to hide. Yet these people were her daughter's relatives and she had to—and would—respect that. After all, it was one of the reasons she'd come all this way.

Finding everyone watching her, she wondered what she'd missed. Digging deep, she smiled around the room and said, 'I hope you'll all be patient with Mattia and me while we work our way through things.' Her main focus was on his mother, Maria, since the woman hadn't relaxed with her as everyone else had. Not even close. Protective mother hen to the fore. She'd have witnessed Mattia being hurt once, wouldn't want that happening again. *Relax, Maria, it isn't on the cards.*

Though there'd been a sharp intake of breath at Elene's

words, Maria's slim shoulders relaxed a little and she asked in a kinder tone, 'Would you like to sponge your frock before it stains?'

'Yes, please. It's brand-new and I'd hate to ruin it already.'

'It's a gorgeous dress, and you look stunning in it.' A friendly arm slid around hers. 'Come on, I'll show you where the bathroom is,' Sofia, Mattia's sister-in-law, said.

'I'm coming too,' Alessia, the other sister-in-law piped up.

'No show without Ali,' said Sofia with a laugh. 'Papà, make that another glass of wine, please. We can't remove stains without a glass of wine in hand.'

So this wasn't going to be a short trip to clean her dress. Elene took the proffered glass. *'Grazie.'* She might need it because, sure as chocolate eggs at Easter, she was in for a grilling. All she hoped was she survived intact.

Mattia caught her eye and winked, as though saying she'd be fine, these two wouldn't behead her. Showed how little he understood females. But she returned his smile before following the women down an enormous hall and into a bathroom the like of which she'd never seen in her life. Marble fixtures, shining taps, gleaming mirrors and a couch on one wall. Who had a couch in their bathroom?

The Riccos, obviously. Her mouth dried as she looked around, well aware she was giving herself away, but unable to stop the sense of sinking into a deeper pool of problems than she'd ever envisaged. She wanted out, fast. This was not her, and never would be. Her family were well off, but wealthy beyond her imagination? No. And that was how she liked it. It was what she was comfortable with. *Hey, you're not part of this family, and so none of this matters.* True, but she might have to see a fair bit of them over the years ahead. All those Sunday lunches loomed in her brain.

'You're stunned.' Sofia laughed and took her hand to pull her over to one of the basins. 'You'll get used to it. The first time Marco, my husband, not my son, brought me here, I thought he was having me on, playing games with me and that I'd wake up back in reality.'

'It was similar for me,' Alessia told her. 'But don't worry, the family's not snobby, and almost don't care about what they have. Well, they do, but they share it, give it away to others who need it, and downplay it all the time.'

Elene looked from Alessia to Sofia, then around the room again. 'It's daunting. I really didn't understand before.' If she was giving away too much about herself, then too bad. Her reaction was honest. 'Where do I find a cloth?'

Sofia opened a couple of drawers before extricating what was required. 'Is it true you and Mattia are not lovers?'

If she hadn't put her glass on the counter the whole lot would've tipped down the front of her dress, and there'd be no saving the fabric from red wine. 'Yes.'

'Yes, you are, or yes, you're not?' Sofia's tone was friendly and fun.

'Not.' Elene wanted to believe Sofia meant no harm with these questions, but this could be a clever way of finding out more about her and her position in Mattia's life than either of them were willing to share. Not that they'd worked it out for themselves yet, but she was certain becoming lovers wasn't on Mattia's agenda. Though that kiss hinted it was possible. *Down, hope, down.*

Alessia took the cloth from her lifeless fingers and held it under a tap. 'Sofia, leave Elene alone. Give her a chance to get to know us a little. We're not her tell-everything-to girlfriends. Yet,' she added with a gleam in her eye.

'You two are that close?' Why did Alessia hope they'd form a friendship with her? Did she want to see Mattia settled down? Nothing made sense and she wasn't about to delve into things that in the long run would have nothing to do with her. Fingers crossed, she'd be back in New Zealand in two weeks, getting on with her life. *You'll more likely be packing up to return here so Aimee can be close to Mattia.* Her heart squeezed for her little girl. And for Mattia. He already loved Aimee unreservedly, which was the best outcome of this trip. But where did it leave *her*? Because he had said he wanted Aimee with him permanently. Would he move to New Zealand for that? Maybe she would need these two on her side.

Alessia tapped her arm to get her attention. 'We're very close. Sofia was engaged to Marco when Jon introduced me to the Riccos. If it weren't for Sofia I'd probably have run and never stopped. It was scary.'

'You were a shy little rabbit.' Sofia laughed. 'Now look at you. No one in this family would dare argue with you.'

Alessia gave an exaggerated shrug. 'Take no notice of her, Elene.'

'So you didn't come into this bathroom full of questions?' Sofia asked, still laughing. 'Mattia hasn't been serious about any woman he's brought to family functions in the years I've known him and yet here he is with a child—his, apparently—and he's also brought Elene along. Who's beautiful, by the way.'

'Stop it, you're embarrassing Elene,' Alessia said.

'And—' Sofia paused for effect, locking her eyes on Elene '—I've never seen him look at a woman the way he does you.'

A thrill of excitement rippled through Elene. How did Mattia look at her? Other than when he was angry or wanted something she wasn't prepared to give, she couldn't imagine what Sofia might be referring to. Not that she was asking. That would encourage the woman's curiosity, but boy, did *she* ever want to know. A sudden image of the intensity in his eyes as he withdrew from kissing her last night shook her. But he wouldn't be looking at her like that in front of his family. Would he?

Alessia's laughter broke through Elene's disturbing thoughts.

'The cloth?' She held out her hand. These women were warm towards her, but she had to remember whose family they were a part of, whose side they'd take if it all turned out bad. 'If you really want to know, Mattia and I couldn't stand the sight of each other when he was working at the same hospital as me in Wellington.' Um, there was that night. Yeah, but one night didn't a relationship make. Not a good one, anyway.

'That was more than a year ago. Anything can change in that time.'

'Until I turned up last week we've had nothing to do with each other since then.' Sponging the fabric carefully, she was relieved to see the dribble disappear. 'Hopefully that'll dry back the way it was.' She looked across to the two women watching her and saw nothing but friendship in their faces. Her hand shook when she raised her glass to her lips. That she had not been expecting.

Sofia leaned over and tapped her glass against Elene's. 'To you and Aimee.' She sipped, then added, 'And to Mattia. Now, we'd better join the others before Mamma drags us out there.'

'She hates lunch to be held up for anything,' Alessia agreed. 'Or anyone.'

And today that'd be especially me, Elene mused as she followed the women to the dining room and took the seat indicated beside Mattia. 'Where are the children?'

'There was hell to pay when we tried to seat them at the children's table. They're having too much fun playing so it's been agreed to leave them to carry on, and we'll give them food when they're ready.'

'So they've got you wrapped around their tiny fingers.' She grinned. 'I like that.'

'It's a special occasion.' Mattia grinned back.

How to get Mattia wrapped around *her* finger? He was slowly—okay, not so slowly—getting under her skin, and it would be hard to fly away at the end of her stay. Did she have to go? As in not return? That seemed less likely by the day. Mattia had so much to lose by leaving Sorrento, while she could work anywhere. But what about her family? That was a question for another time.

When Elene glanced across the table, Sofia was smiling at her and Mattia with satisfaction. *No, Sofia, we are not lovers, and chances are remote.* Her stomach dived. Unfortunately. Just because he could kiss like the devil didn't mean he'd ever follow it through, and there was more to a relationship than hot kisses that led to even hotter movements. Yes, but a relationship had to start somewhere and getting the bedroom stuff right was as good a place as any. Heat was crawling up her cheeks. Sitting at a table, surrounded by Mattia's family, and she was thinking about sex with him.

A slug of wine did nothing to calm her; instead it went down the wrong way and she had to suffer the indignity of having Mattia gently slapping her back for the second time in two days. With a strong, warm—make that hot—hand. Oh, boy. She was in trouble. And it seemed everyone knew it, if the way they were all watching her and Mattia was any indication.

She took the glass of water he passed her and tried not to gulp it down.

Mattia came to her rescue. 'Eat, everybody.'

Grateful for the laden dishes passing up and down the

table, Elene spooned steaming food onto her plate, then when everyone was ready to eat hid behind enjoying the meal. With each mouthful she enjoyed it more and more, and relaxed muscle by muscle until finally her stomach gave up protesting and accepted every mouthful gratefully.

Mattia's father leaned forward to get her attention. 'You speak Italian like a native. Were you born here?'

Here we go. Question number one. She wasn't counting Sofia's attempts. 'No, I'm a Kiwi.' She was putting it out there so no one could say she'd tried to hide her true feelings of home. 'My mother was born in Panzano, outside of Florence, and her family moved to New Zealand when she was two. She came back to Italy when she was eighteen, but returned home within a few months. She's never been back.' *My dad adopted me when he married Mum, and I was fifteen months old.* 'I was brought up to speak both languages, and cook Italian and Kiwi food, and to spend many hours around the table talking about anything and everything.'

'So your father's a New Zealander?'

Her real father, not her biological one. 'Dad's great-great-grandfather came out to New Zealand from Britain, which is a common history for many New Zealanders. Irish, Scots, English, Welsh—we're all mixed up.' None of this had anything to do with anything.

'I'd like to be fluent in more than one language,' Sofia said around a mouthful of *tortellini*. 'Maybe I should take lessons in Japanese.'

Everyone laughed. 'You?'

Mattia explained to Elene, 'Sofia's a chef at one of Napoli's top Italian cuisine restaurants, but that's where her cooking talents stay.'

Maybe, but she had diverted everyone's attention. Elene

smiled across to her. Somehow, without any input on her behalf, she'd made a friend.

'I was a chef. Now I'm a mum with another *bambino* on the way.' She nodded across to Elene as she rubbed her tummy.

'Thank you,' Elene mouthed, and got up to help clear away the plates now that everyone had finished the main course.

'You don't have to do that. You're a guest,' Mattia's mother said.

Exactly, and she didn't like the role when she was trying to fit in. 'At home we all knuckle down to help.'

'Then you can put those dishes in the dishwasher.' Maria had got the message, though Elene could see she wasn't quite happy with it. Not yet, at any rate.

She began rinsing plates and looking through the large windows to the expansive vegetable gardens beyond. 'Who looks after the gardens? They're wonderful.' The rows stretched as far as she could see, with every vegetable imaginable growing strong.

'Mostly I do the vegetables. They're my passion, for the cooking. Being able to eat what I produce is rewarding.' There was pride in Maria's voice.

'My father always grows far too many vegetables because he doesn't know where to stop, and the local charities are the winners, especially since he retired. As for the rest, it's hit and miss who mows the lawns or weeds the flowerbeds.'

'I can understand that. I'm lucky we have a permanent gardener for everything else.'

Mattia arrived between them with an armful of dirty plates. 'These'll keep you quiet for a while.' He nudged Elene.

'I could hand over to you,' she retorted. 'I know your

mother taught you how to clean up. I've been in your kitchen, remember?'

His mother was watching them with that guarded expression once again in place. It was getting a little tiring.

'Is there something in particular you'd like to ask me?' Elene asked tightly.

The woman stared at her for a long moment, then nodded. 'All right. Now's as good a time as any. What do you want from my son?'

Like son, like mother. 'Nothing other than to make it work for Aimee in a way that is agreeable to the three of us.'

'Why didn't you phone to tell Mattia about his daughter instead of arriving unannounced?' Maria glanced at her son. 'Yes, we presume that's what happened even if you didn't say so.' Those sharp eyes returned to Elene. 'You wanted to shock him? Show him how you could look after Aimee for him?'

'Mamma.'

'No, Mattia. We need to know you're not being taken for a ride.'

The woman was protective of her son, as any good mother should be. Like Elene was trying to protect Aimee. 'Signora Ricco, I am the messenger.' *Don't shoot me.* 'Danielle asked that I bring Aimee to Italy without warning to meet her father, and at the time I promised to go along with her wish. She had her reasons, but I agree there were also better alternatives.'

'So why not take one of them?'

'I don't break promises lightly. If at all.' A quick glance at Mattia showed how invested in this conversation he'd become. Was this how they were going to break the ice about starting the process of planning the future? It was what she needed to happen. They all did. The how was irrelevant if it got them somewhere. A little explanation to Maria wouldn't go amiss. 'Danielle and I were best friends from the day we started our nursing training. We clicked immediately and there was nothing we couldn't tell each other, and nothing either of us wouldn't do to help the other.' Hopefully, Mattia heard and truly understood everything. 'I didn't approve of Mattia as her lover. I thought he was using her. Danielle finally told me if anyone was using anyone it was her. She enjoyed Mattia's company and the fact he didn't want commitment.' Which had hurt because *she*'d have wanted all of that with him when she'd admitted her lust for him.

The silence stretched out, Maria waiting not so patiently for her to continue. Mattia handed her a glass of water.

After taking a sip, she put it aside. 'When Danielle learned she had cancer while pregnant there wasn't much I wouldn't have done for her.' As his mother opened her mouth, Elene held up her hand. She needed to get this finished before her voice cracked up completely. 'She asked me to be Aimee's guardian. I couldn't say no. Every child needs people in their lives to cherish and fight for them. She had no one else at home to do that for her daughter, and I'd do anything for my friend's child.' The last words were choked out over another lump that blocked her throat. 'She insisted I tell Mattia only after she was gone.'

'Why didn't this Danielle tell Mattia herself?' Maria glared at her as if it was her fault.

'She was afraid he'd come and take over with Aimee, and she wanted every moment she had left with her baby.' A tear escaped, followed by another. Swiping at them with the back of her hand, she reached for the glass. She needed help here.

'I can understand, though I don't agree. She could've written a letter for you to forward to Mattia. My son deserved that.' The look became suspicious. 'Or did she, and you chose to ignore it for your own gain?'

Elene closed her eyes and swallowed the pain those acidic words wrung out of her. Fair enough. This woman had Mattia's back. But Mattia wasn't rushing in to defend her as he'd said he would. So he didn't entirely trust her despite everything he'd said so far. Opening her eyes, she stared in turn at both of them. 'I want nothing from Mattia than for him to accept my role in Aimee's life. I am her registered guardian. Believe it or not, I am not interested in your wealth. I have a happy life and want for nothing. I will always be there for Aimee, will continue to raise her, along with Mattia. How or where we make that work is yet to be determined. But—' she fixed her eyes on Maria '—Mattia and I will make those decisions.' With that, she took her glass and headed to the door opening into the garden, to wander blindly along the narrow paths.

Behind her, Mattia was saying in a sharp tone, 'Elene's right, Mamma. This is for us to work out.'

So he had backed her. Yet there'd been that question in his eyes as he'd waited for her answer to what she wanted from him. After what his ex had done to him, could she blame him? Probably not, but it still hurt. What a mess. With one hand she rubbed the opposite arm, where her skin was chilled. She'd gone and made an enemy of the woman who Mattia more than likely turned to for advice on family matters. But she had been true to herself.

Mattia strolled outside to find Elene. There were things to be said, yet it wasn't as simple as opening his mouth and uttering them. One thing he was coming to believe was that Elene had not come to Italy with the intention of getting something out of this for herself, other than to be Aimee's mother.

Even then she was prepared to share, to accept she had no choice in the matter, and was working to make it happen in a way that suited everyone. Doing better than him at it. She'd stood up to Mamma without hesitation. Her fierce loyalty to one little girl came from somewhere deep within, no doubt because of the love her own adoptive father gave her.

At the far wall stood the woman putting his normally calm, controlled life in turmoil. Elene had the power to trip him up, to make him revisit all the plans and controls he'd put in place in his life after Sandy's perfidy. This woman was disturbing him in the most unexpected ways. He needed to get some control back or he was lost for ever. 'Tell me about your biological father.'

Her mouth dropped open, was quickly slammed shut. Behind the shock flaring in her eyes, he sensed her mind was racing. The glass in her hand was in danger of spilling water all over her dress. A deep breath. 'I grew up wanting to be acknowledged by him. It never happened. When I came over here to meet my mother's family I looked him up. It was an unpleasant meeting, and made me so glad to have my real father. I returned home with my tail between my legs, and continued receiving nothing but love from Dad.'

'Hell, Elene. That's awful.'

'It was, but at the same time I have the most loving dad anyone could ask for.' Twirling the half empty glass in her fingers, she seemed to ponder how much to tell him. 'My mother was eighteen when she became pregnant with me. Her boyfriend immediately dumped her so she flew home and not long after met Jeff Lowe.'

A sour taste filled Mattia's mouth. No woman should ever be treated so ruthlessly.

Her mouth twisted into a small smile. 'Jeff Lowe is

my real dad, and has been there for me all my life. When each of my sisters came along I was still daughter number one. He treats me how a father should treat his daughters.'

He couldn't argue with the loyalty and fierceness in her voice. 'Aimee's one lucky little girl. You keep your word.' Convincing Elene to move to Italy to be near him had just got harder. But they'd leave it for now, go inside and join his family. Mamma had softened towards Elene after that blunt statement earlier, saying to him that she was a gutsy lady who wasn't afraid to state her mind. He agreed. Aimee would always be watched over, cared for, loved unconditionally wherever she was.

He wanted some of that. Hell, he wanted all of that and more. And not just with Aimee. But letting go the things that kept him on the straight and narrow wasn't coming easily when there was so much mistrust in his past. He reached for her arm, removed the glass from her shaking hand and said, 'Come on. Dessert and the family are waiting for us.'

Doubt filled her face and eyes, her stance. 'Really?'

'Really. You don't think Sofia and Alessia would've dragged you off for a conflab if they didn't want to get to know you better in the nicest possible way, do you?'

'They were very friendly.'

'Bet they had a hundred questions that weren't all about why we're here.' Those two had formed a strong bond from the moment they'd met, as if they needed each other to keep from being swamped by his over-enthusiastic and demanding family. Elene could do worse than joining their ranks. A lot worse.

CHAPTER EIGHT

THE SUN WAS bright and her feet skipped as Elene made her way down the hill on Monday morning. The Tyrrhenian Sea was so blue it looked like something off a paint chart. Ferries were shuttling back and forth along the coast, moving the first waves of eager tourists. Mattia had offered to drive her to the unit for her first day on the job but she liked being out amongst the locals, taking in the sights and sounds of Sorrento. Being Italian.

The smell of freshly brewed coffee had her stopping at the café where locals were ordering their morning fix. She chattered to people as she waited for her cappuccino, happy to be a part of the scene. Could she do this on a regular basis? Live here, become involved with the community, raise Aimee as a local? It wouldn't be impossible, or uncomfortable. Danielle had hinted she wouldn't object to her daughter growing up in Italy.

The moment Elene walked onto the ward she felt at home. Nursing did that to her, no matter where she was. People in need of care were her specialty, and it didn't matter if they were young or old, rich or poor; pain and illness affected everyone the same. Being here added to the sense of being in the right place. Sorrento was pulling her in with its promise of sun, laughter, friendly people—and Mattia. The real sticking point. Falling under his spell, she could almost believe she might be able to risk her heart again, while his mountain of distrust would take a monumental leap to get over. Might pass on that. She'd probably miss the landing spot.

'Hi, Colleen,' she said to the charge nurse she'd met briefly yesterday when Mattia brought her in on their way home from Naples. 'Where do you want me?'

'Hello, did you bring two of those?' Colleen nodded to the take-away coffee in her hand.

'Tell me how you have it and I'll get you one tomorrow.'

'Black. Let's find you a uniform before I introduce you to our patients. I've rostered you to look after Gino since he hasn't stopped singing your praises. Then there's Joanna, who had pancreatic surgery yesterday. But how it works around here, we all keep an eye on everyone.'

'No problem. Is Gino walking on those crutches yet?'

'No.' Colleen shook her head. 'That's another reason he's yours this morning. You had him moving once Mattia got him out of bed so I'm hoping you'll be able to continue with that.'

'Why doesn't he want to get walking?' Most people who had hip replacements couldn't wait to be up and about after months or years being incapacitated.

Colleen sighed. 'Some of our patients don't have much to go home to. Having three decent meals a day can be a huge step up. Others don't have someone at home to look after them while they recuperate.'

'That's sad.' She'd never known what it was like to go without, but she had done her share of helping those who did by working in the second-hand goods shop to raise funds. 'Everyone's entitled to the basics.'

'Entitled, maybe, but getting them is another story. Which is why Mattia is fierce about keeping this place going. Here, put these on.'

Another reason he'd loathe to relocate to her side of the world. The list was growing in his favour. Strange how that wasn't tipping her into despair, instead focusing her on what was most important—Aimee. 'How long have you worked here?'

'Nearly two years. I was working full-time at the main hospital and decided to volunteer here instead. My husband's a general surgeon and contributes time when required. We moved out from Ireland for the warmth and lifestyle, and have no intention of ever returning.'

'Why would anyone when it's so beautiful?' *Remember that in the bleak moments. Living here wouldn't be hard.* She could rent an apartment nearby, work paid hours at the hospital and put in some extra here. And miss her family. Elene's heart squeezed. Last night she'd talked to her mother for nearly an hour, and then one of her sisters rang and it had been late when she finally went to bed Her youngest sister was turning twenty-one tomorrow and she wouldn't be there for the celebrations. Homesickness hit, then she remembered why she was here and pushed it away. Aimee would never know what it was like to be rejected by those nearest and dearest. Never.

'You're staying with Mattia, right?'

'I am.' That was all she had to say on the matter. 'Right, let's go see Gino.'

He saw her coming from across the room. '*Buongiorno*, Elene. They told me you were coming in today. I'm glad to see you.'

'Told you he's a fan.' Colleen left her to get on with cajoling Gino out of bed and onto his crutches.

'Come on, Gino. We're going for a walk.'

'But it's nearly time for the tea trolley to come round, and I can't miss out on that,' he griped.

'You won't. I'll make you a cup myself if necessary. Have you had your blood pressure taken this morning?'

'It was high.'

Elene had to swallow the laughter his delaying tactics brought on. She *would* have him up and walking before she left for the day. 'I'll get the monitor while you sit up and swing your legs over the side.'

The two short walks over the morning were interspersed with exercises to strengthen the damaged muscles and bed rest, which seemed to be Gino's favourite part of the morning.

'You know how to get them moving.' Mattia surprised her as she helped Gino back onto the bed for the last time.

'Aren't you meant to be at the hospital?' she asked.

'Next surgery's at two. I thought I'd come see how you were doing. And check on Gino. How's your morning gone?'

'I've been in my element.' A glance at the wall clock showed she should've signed off half an hour ago. 'No wonder my stomach's jumping up and down.'

'You going straight home?'

'I should in case Aimee's fretting.' She'd grab a pastry at a café on the way.

'She's happy playing in the sandpit.' When she raised an eyebrow at him he shrugged. 'I rang Anna on my way here. Let's grab that bite to eat together.'

'Sure,' she said to his retreating back. He just expected her to agree. So what? Her spirits were soaring. A few minutes with Mattia were always minutes to enjoy. Usually, anyway. When she came out of the changing room he was waiting at the main entrance.

Outside, they walked towards the bus station where there were many cafés. Mattia led her down an alley into a tiny, dimly lit café where the talk was all in Italian and old men were playing *dama.*

Elene laughed. 'I grew up playing Italian checkers.'

'You fit right in here,' Mattia said. 'What would you like to eat?'

Settling for a sandwich, Elene sat at the only vacant table, which was crammed into a corner, and watched Mattia chat casually to a couple of elderly men. His height dwarfed anyone standing, and brought the walls in even closer, making the café feel small and cosy. She'd seen his charm in action in Wellington but outright friendliness hadn't been so apparent, though he was usually with patients when she'd been near him.

Mattia tugged his phone from his pocket, holding it to his ear. Waving to her to join him, Mattia told the girl to put their lunch in bags and cancel the coffee. 'Gino's fallen and possibly dislocated his hip.'

'Not good.' Grabbing their lunch bags, Elene hurried after him. 'What's the plan?' Mattia had surgery in thirty minutes at the hospital.

'We'll take him into Theatre immediately. You can work with me. An anaesthetist is on her way, so it shouldn't take long.' He punched a number on his phone and told someone that he'd be a little late for the operation scheduled for two.

Elene ran to keep up with his long strides. 'I'll call Anna and explain I'll be late. Hopefully Aimee won't get upset.'

'You think? When Anna spoils her rotten? Aimee never cries around her.'

'True.' Relief relaxed Elene.

'Gino.' Mattia didn't slow down as he entered the ward. 'What happened? Colleen, I'm back and Elene's with me.' He was at the bed, pulling back the cover. 'Now, my man, I'm going to take a look at your hip. If you have dislocated it then we have to give you an epidural, numb you from the chest down, and then I can put it back in place.'

'Will I be all right, Doctor?' Gino was pale, and looking stunned. 'I was only doing what Nurse Elene said. I wanted to show her I could do it on my own. Then I twisted around when someone called my name.'

Elene winced. 'It's all right, Gino.' She took the man's shaky hand and held tight. 'Dr Ricco will have you up and about again in no time at all.' She'd bet Gino would be afraid to get back on those crutches for a while. 'I'll be here to help you every day until you've got your confidence back.'

Mattia gently felt the muscles around Gino's hip, but the abnormal angle of the hip joint said it all. 'Definitely dislocated. Right, we'll go scrub up. Colleen will bring Gino through to the prep room and we'll do this in Theatre. It's a safer environment. Not that we have any alternative, spare rooms being in short supply.'

Standing at a basin next to Mattia, scrubbing her hands, she couldn't help but smile. This was like the days in Wellington when she'd worked with him, but today she was completely at ease with him, wasn't looking for things to argue about. 'No wonder you always look exhausted at the end of the day if this is what happens to your schedule.'

'The life of a doctor, eh?' He elbowed the tap off.

'Not all doctors take on another unit on top of their regular work.'

'Whatever.'

He'd pulled on vinyl gloves and was aiming for the door, but stopped to face her. There was an intensity in the eyes now locked on hers. But after a moment all he said was, 'Let's do this,' and the door he'd elbowed open swung shut behind him.

Elene followed, and began taking obs. 'BP one-thirty-five over eighty-five.'

A woman rushed in and introduced herself as the anaesthetist before quickly and efficiently putting Gino into La-la

Land, from where he uttered tiny snores and looked as though nothing was wrong.

Elene lifted Gino's hospital gown away from his lower body and Mattia stepped up to lift the injured leg. He was fast and strong, and it was done, the hip back in place. Mattia felt around all the muscles in the hip area. 'He's going to hurt for a while.'

'This'll set back his recovery,' Elene agreed. 'BP's one-thirty-five over ninety-eight.'

Mattia nodded. 'Don't be too quick to get him back on crutches. Start with the walking frame tomorrow, and then only for short stints over the next couple of days.' He looked down at his patient. 'He didn't want to leave the unit, but I bet he'd give anything to be heading home now.'

'It must've been some fall to dislocate that hip.'

'He twisted very abruptly,' Colleen told them as they wheeled the bed out of Theatre. 'I heard him cry out, then there was an almighty crash and I found him lying on the floor.'

'Didn't he know not to twist his body?' Mattia asked, looking ready to tell someone off.

'Yes, he did,' Colleen growled. 'But it's one of those movements people make without thought.'

Elene smiled. Another nurse not prepared to let Mattia boss her around. 'I'll sit with him until he comes round.' She could eat her sandwich there. 'I'll give Anna another call. I hope she doesn't change her mind about looking after Aimee. This is day one and I haven't been near home yet.'

'I'll call her,' Mattia said. Then, 'Home, eh?'

A blush raced up her cheeks. 'As in the place I'm staying for a while. Home is a shorter way of saying the same thing.'

'Here I was, thinking you were settling in.' He didn't

sound annoyed that she might've been. Surely he didn't want that? No, he was talking without thinking it through. Except Mattia never did that, always knew what he was saying.

Elene relented. 'It's a lovely place and I am happy to be there.'

'Get as comfortable as you like.'

'Careful. I mightn't want to leave again.'

'Exactly.'

She'd walked right into that one. 'Are you suggesting we could continue cohabiting and sharing Aimee indefinitely?'

'It's one way of moving forward.'

But what if they bumped into each other in the kitchen and it led to another kiss? Or took them down the hall to a bedroom? 'I don't know about that.'

'Give it some thought.' Then he was gone, heading out of the door and off to the hospital and the surgery he'd postponed.

She'd been daydreaming about kisses while Mattia had been getting down to the nitty-gritty of why they were even in the same space, the same town, country.

I'm not fit to be a mother if I'm that easily distracted.

Checking Gino's pulse did nothing to help with the turmoil now erupting in her head. Her pulse was probably way higher than his. How serious was Mattia about her staying on in his house for longer than her original schedule? Had he thought it through? She'd have to find a proper job that would pay her bills—board and groceries at least. They'd be sharing so much, but everything would be on Mattia's terms because it was his house, his territory. No, she couldn't stay on indefinitely under the current terms.

'Nurse?'

'Hey, Gino, you're awake. That's good. You're not

going to feel anything in your lower body for a few hours. There'll be no getting out of bed for the rest of today.'

'You're not going to make me walk?'

'You're off the hook till tomorrow, and then we'll take it slowly, starting with the frame again.'

'I'm sorry I made a mistake and hurt myself. The doctor wasn't too pleased with me, I think.'

Wrapping the BP cuff around his upper arm, she laughed. 'Dr Ricco was worried about you, not angry. But you're going to have to be more careful from now on. No sudden movements. The walking was going so well, and that's a good thing, but crossing your legs, twisting your hips or making sudden turns is not allowed. Understand?'

'Yes, Nurse.'

'Yes, Elene,' she emphasised. Until now he'd always used her name. 'You're not in trouble with me either.'

Her patient relaxed into his pillow. 'That's good.'

'The better news is there's rabbit stew for dinner.'

She got a wobbly smile in return.

Ripping the cuff away, she told him, 'Blood pressure's almost normal. Now, go to sleep and let that hip start mending. I'll be right here if you need to go to the bathroom or want a drink of water.'

Less of a wobble in the next smile. 'You're good to me. I don't deserve it.'

'Everyone's allowed a second chance.' Care of Mattia, that one. But he was right. People made mistakes, but it didn't mean they should be punished for ever. So could she think of getting into a relationship again and making a go of it next time? Could that be her second chance? Why did an image of Mattia flit across her mind just then? He was not the man for her second-chance relationship. She knew he was nothing like Craig, but he liked being in control too much. Though those kisses did make up for that, for a while. And, truly, he didn't demand she be subservient like Craig had. Though that had taken time to become apparent with Craig. No. Mattia was nothing like him. It should work. Hello? To hell with second chances, huh? Mattia would not give himself one after the Sandy fiasco so there went hers.

'I'll get you a cup of tea.' She stood up, not waiting to see if Gino wanted one or not. Keeping busy would get her mind back in order, and hopefully put a stop to those stupid images and ideas floating around her brain like they had every right to be there.

Thursday was going to be another hot, clear day. Elene knew that from the quick drive to the unit with Mattia at five-thirty that morning as they responded to an emergency. 'Fill me in on the details,' she said to him.

'Our patient's a teenager, six months pregnant and homeless. Her friends brought her in when she slipped on the steps leading up from the beach, where they apparently spent the night under the stars. Euphemism for nowhere else to go.'

'There's no shelter for the homeless?'

'Yes, but some teenagers avoid it, not wanting to answer the questions or be sent into care.' Mattia pulled into the unit's car park.

'Why bring her here and not the hospital?'

'You'd have to ask them that. But, from what I've been told, we'll transfer her as soon as it's feasible.' His door opened. 'We're dealing with a broken arm and torn blood vessels, not the pregnancy.'

'She'll need checking thoroughly if she fell very far.' That baby could've taken a hard knock.

'I agree. But first things first. Stop the bleeding.'

There was a lot of bleeding to stop, and most of it nothing to do with ruptured blood vessels. Mica was haemorrhaging. According to her friends, the baby had taken the brunt of the fall. The shattered ulna and radius in her left arm with a torn vein only added to their woes.

'Elene, I'm going to call in the obstetrician and then operate on Mica's arm. Get ready to assist.'

'Yes, Mattia,' she answered with a smile as she sponged blood off Mica's arms.

Mica was sent to Radiology while everyone prepared for Theatre. Elene felt right at home, despite not knowing the others crowded around the table—except for Mattia. And sometimes she wondered how well she knew him. But not in here. Watching Mattia, working alongside him, while he operated always had her in awe. But that wasn't the man she had to get along with.

'Those bones aren't broken,' Mattia muttered as he scanned the X-ray of Mica's arm before the anaesthetist put her under. 'They're shattered.' Stepping closer to the young girl, he asked quietly, 'Mica, can you hear me? I'm Dr Ricco.'

The girl nodded once, opened frightened eyes to stare at him.

'I know your arm is hurting. Are you in pain anywhere else?'

Her good arm moved and her hand touched her ribs. 'There.'

'I want another X-ray,' Mattia announced. 'Can we get the portable machine in here *pronto*?'

'What's up?' Elene asked as she gently inserted a cannula in Mica's good arm in preparation for drugs and fluids.

'I don't like the condition of her bones where the fractures occurred.'

'Brittle bone syndrome?'

'Mica.' Mattia leaned close to the trolley. 'Do you have a history of broken bones?'

Another nod. 'Lots. Lately.'

So it wasn't something she'd had from birth. 'Dietary?'

'Could be.'

Elene placed the BP cuff above the cannula and took a reading. 'One-forty-two over eighty-eight.'

Mattia and the obstetrician discussed how to go about this without too much stress on Mica while dealing with all the injuries ASAP.

Elene heard a stifled gasp and bent over the trolley with a tissue to wipe the tears spilling down the frightened girl's cheeks. She was only a child herself. Sixteen, pregnant and in a terrifying situation. 'It's going to be all right, Mica.' She took her hand and leant close. With the doctors talking, nurses preparing for surgery, the anaesthetist getting ready, it was chaotic in an organised way, but very scary for their patient. 'Everyone's on your side.'

'My baby?'

That was a problem she couldn't answer. 'The doctors are monitoring Baby. Its heart's beating so that's good.' She wasn't about to outline what could be wrong. The baby had been quiet for a while, no kicking—possibly dealing with shock. 'We're going to give you something to make you go to sleep for a little while.'

'Keep my baby safe,' Mica sobbed. 'Please.'

Elene froze, her hand hovering above Mica's. 'Keep Aimee safe. Please. Don't let anything bad happen to her.' Danielle on the birthing table, haemorrhaging due to low platelet numbers, tears streaming down her pale cheeks, fear in her eyes.

'Elene?' Then, 'Elene, focus.' Mattia was beside her, his hand on her shoulder. 'You're in Theatre with Mica. Mica, remember?' He'd spoken in English.

She shivered and looked up into his concerned eyes. 'Sorry.'

'It's okay. Think you can see this operation through?' No censure marred his question. He understood.

Finding a wobbly smile, she nodded. 'Yes, I can.'

'Great.' Then Mattia looked around the team lined up. 'Let's do this.' On the nod from the anaesthetist he picked up a scalpel, his focus entirely on the fractured arm and putting the bones back together. Elene, now under control of her emotions, passed instruments as he required.

An hour later they left Theatre, Mica's shattered bones wired together, the bleeding stopped and her arm stitched. She was still in the care of the obstetrics team who had managed to stem the haemorrhage but were concerned about the baby's lack of movement.

Mattia scrubbed his hands and turned to Elene. 'You did well in there.'

'Thanks to you getting me back on track. That's not happened before.'

Mattia stepped closer, laid a hand on her shoulder. 'You are allowed to grieve.'

'Not in Theatre with a seriously injured young girl desperate to save her baby.' A tear escaped and slid down her cheek, followed by another, and another

'Don't torture yourself.' He drew her against his length, his arms winding around her. 'You're coping with a lot and doing it brilliantly.' He leaned close, his lips brushing her cheek. 'Brilliantly.'

The air was suddenly filled with man scent overlaid with antiseptic. And Elene's head seemed to be floating, blanking the pain, absorbing the warmth, the kindness, the *understanding* from this man. She pressed closer to the source of comfort and security.

Then those lips were on hers, skimming across her

mouth before possessing her, taking the kiss deeper and deeper, his tongue owning hers, until she was afraid to breathe in case she woke up to find this all a dream. Which would be the right thing to happen. But she didn't want right. She wanted this—Mattia's kisses. Mattia himself. Wanted him burying himself inside her and obliterating the pain for ever.

'Hmm.' Someone cleared their throat behind her and she leapt back, away from that mouth, from those slumberous eyes suddenly sparking into amusement.

Mattia straightened and looked over her shoulder. 'Hello, Jeremy. I don't believe you've met Elene. She's been putting in hours at the unit. Elene, this is Colleen's husband, Jeremy.' His hand caught her elbow, drew her closer to him.

'Hello, Elene. Colleen's mentioned you, but have to say I wasn't expecting to meet you here this morning.' He really meant as in kissing Mattia, surely?

With Mattia's hand supporting her Elene didn't feel awkward. Having him at her side made her feel special and cared for. 'I'm about to change out of this uniform and disappear back to the unit.'

Mattia's grip tightened. 'Why don't we get breakfast before clocking on at our respective wards?'

'Sounds good to me.' More than good. This was starting to feel like a relationship, even if only friends. 'Give me five minutes.' Actually, friends didn't cut it. They'd kissed again. Mattia had moved past friend category. She just didn't know which one to put him in next.

Mattia watched Elene haul her slouched body out of the room like she was lost.

'I hear she's a great nurse and a lovely lady.'

Mattia shrugged casually. 'All of that.' And some. But

he wasn't saying. Of course he shouldn't have kissed her, but he was a man, and Elene was beautiful and womanly, and in need of comforting. Jamming his hands into his pockets, he nodded at Jeremy. 'See you around.'

Jeremy might think twice before reporting what he'd interrupted to his colleagues, but Colleen would know before the day was over. It couldn't be helped. Besides, kissing Elene under any circumstances was the perfect start to his day.

Once in clean clothes, he sauntered out to the corridor to wait for her. He could get used to this. What? He stopped, stared around. Everything was how it always was. He was in Sorrento, soon to be at the hospital where he spent most of his days. He hadn't had a brain aberration. So how did he explain the fact he enjoyed waking to Elene in his house, to working alongside her on occasion, to sharing meals? *Turn around, head to the ward early, forget you offered breakfast.*

Elene appeared further along the corridor, that sadness still lurking in her stance despite that kiss. He began moving in her direction. He would not go back on his invitation. He wanted to spend time with Elene. Whatever the future brought as far as how he managed full-time parenthood while keeping Elene around, it could only be a plus if they were getting along. Nothing to do with the heat simmering in his veins.

Dressed in those fitted shorts and the sleeveless blouse she wore every second day, Elene looked stunning. His heart flapped around like a stranded fish, unable to behave sensibly. Below his belt things were stirring. *This is Elene, someone you have to convince to move here permanently, not take to bed.*

Tell that to his lower regions. The fact was that from

the moment he'd seen her outside his office the day she'd arrived in Sorrento he hadn't been able to put her back in the box labelled 'snippy annoying female.'

But how was a man to resist those curves, that swell of her breasts, the full lips that his imagination had tripping over his skin? When Elene looked over at him her green gaze whispered across him, lifted bumps on his arms and further tightened his manhood. He fell deep into that labyrinth, unable to fight the attraction, knowing he was on a hiding to nowhere and still wanting to go there. Time to do something about gaining control while he still could.

'Sorry, but I can't make breakfast. I've got an emergency with one of yesterday's patients,' he lied before abruptly heading away, unable to watch disappointment overtaking the sadness in her face. *Sorry, sorry, but someone has to look out for my heart, and the only person available right now is me.*

Damn Elene. She'd done this. It was all her fault he'd begun falling for her, had started wanting the whole happy family, cosy home scenario. Her fault. Not his. Not when he'd locked away those expectations long ago. Even after he'd come close to kissing her in Wellington he'd managed to stay focused. He was doing perfectly well on his own, without having anyone special to love. His extended family supplied all the love he needed. Or so he'd thought until the advent of Elene Lowe, non-snippy version. And his daughter. They were a package. He could not sever one from the other. It wouldn't be right, nor fair. Nor did he want to. They went hand in hand, and it would be perfect if he could add his hand to that mix.

It wasn't going to happen. While Elene hadn't shown signs of wanting to set up house with him so that she could live in the lap of luxury, he'd been duped before, no longer trusted his judgement completely. Only time would allow him to work through this, and time wasn't available. Aimee needed structure in her life, plus security and unbridled love. Aimee needed him to make up his mind—should he carry on living in Sorrento and convince Elene to join him on a platonic footing, or move to Wellington and start over on the career ladder, set aside the charity for someone else to run? Except the charity was no longer the important issue in his life now. He had a daughter.

He and Elene needed to sit down over a meal and talk, make plans, bring this indecision to an end. This weekend.

The next morning Elene bought two coffees on the way to the unit.

'Gino's still feeling sorry for himself,' Colleen told her, flipping the lid off her take-away cup to let the coffee cool. 'I'm sure that won't stop you getting him on the move.'

'Slowly, slowly, today. Mattia said to stay with the walking frame for now.' That man knew how to wind her up. Yesterday he'd been so understanding and then that kiss. Her cheeks flamed. Then he'd cancelled breakfast. There hadn't been an emergency. How he'd thought she wouldn't find out was beyond her. Colleen had talked to him on the phone ten minutes into their shift. He'd gone from kissing her to suggesting breakfast to walking away on a lie. Last night he hadn't come home until nearly midnight, missing out on goodnight kisses with Aimee. She'd been in bed, reading because sleep was elusive. The temptation to rush out and confront him had been strong, but she'd managed to stay put and hold onto the words that might set them back.

'Jeremy says Mica's been asking for you,' Colleen said with a grin on her face.

Obviously that wasn't all Jeremy had told his wife. Elene wasn't taking up the gauntlet. 'I'll drop in to say hello when I've finished here.' Mica had been transferred and slowly recovering. Baby was still in utero and under constant monitoring.

Colleen only grinned more. 'Whatever.'

'Right. On with the day.' She was bursting to talk to someone about Mattia and the mess they were in but Colleen, lovely as she was, wasn't the right person when she worked with Mattia. If only she had time to call home. But there was no such thing as a short conversation with her sisters. Anyway, she didn't want short; she needed deep and long—with answers that'd soothe her stress levels, and there wasn't time.

Digging out her phone to check for messages, just in case Mattia had grovelled for forgiveness, she gasped. Not Mattia, but there was a message from Maria Ricco. She had to be seeing things. But no—the name *Maria Ricco* flashed at her. Was she calling to say *Don't go near my son, you're poison*? Elene wouldn't put it past her after that interrogation on Sunday. Though they had been talking on more friendly terms by the time she and Mattia had left for Sorrento. Only one way to find out. Elene pressed return and held the phone to her ear.

It only rang once. 'Elene, thank you for calling me back. I know you're at work so I wasn't sure if you'd see I'd tried to get hold of you.'

'I'm about to start. Were you trying to get hold of Mattia?' The moment she asked she knew she couldn't be further from the truth. Maria would have every number Mattia possessed.

'I wanted to talk to you.' There was a laden pause. 'I'll start again. Would you let me come down and spend time with Aimee today? I won't take her away from the house.

It's just that, well, she's my granddaughter and I'd like to get to know her.'

Elene sank onto a chair. Here we go. It'd started. The family getting close to Aimee. But that was good, it was right, and she couldn't deny the request. Where did it leave her? *Being selfish. This is about Aimee, not me.*

'I'd understand if you'd prefer to be there at the same time. In case she gets upset.' The self-doubt in Maria's voice tugged at Elene. This woman wasn't as tough as she'd made out.

Drawing a breath, Elene said, 'Aimee rarely gets upset, and I'm sure you can cheer her up if she does.'

'Does that mean you'll let me visit?' Hope replaced the doubt.

'I would never stop you. You're her *nonna*.'

'Thank you, Elene. I was thinking I could stay on so you and Mattia can go out for dinner. Alone,' she added with a tight laugh.

'You think Mattia and I should go out together?' Elene blurted. This woman had been a tigress on her son's behalf and now she was suggesting they go on a date? 'I think you've got the wrong idea about how well we get on.'

'Have I, though?'

'Yes, definitely.'

Or did Maria have a point? When they'd been caught kissing, Mattia hadn't been ashamed or embarrassed, and had stood by her when Jeremy turned up.

'You need some time together. I'll see you later.'

Back to that strong woman who spoke her mind. But Elene had seen another side to her now. Maria and her son had a lot in common.

Elene found herself smiling. 'I look forward to catching up.' She surprised herself by meaning it.

Texting the news to Mattia, she wondered if he'd bother to answer, if he had time that was.

Ping.

That's great. Would you like to go out to dinner tonight?

He had to be between operations.

Ah, hello? You've got over your snit? Not wanting to play the role of injured party, she answered him.

Definitely. We've got babysitters.

We're sounding like an ordinary couple. X

A kiss? Mattia had sent her a kiss?

Aren't we just?

Her finger hovered over the X key. What the hell? She liked his kisses, those of the touching, feeling kind.

X

Then she went to see how Gino was getting on.

CHAPTER NINE

MATTIA PRESUMED DINNER was superb, because he'd eaten at the Tyrrhenian Hotel before and not been able to fault the food or service. Tonight he could've been eating dust for all he knew. With Elene sitting opposite, that red dress highlighting the figure he'd spent all day trying to stop wondering about, nothing he put in his mouth had flavour. Even his favourite wine tasted bland. Elene, on the other hand, was anything but.

For once her hair wasn't tied back in a knot but flowing over her shoulders. He wanted to get lost in those auburn locks. Her make-up was flawless, yet he preferred it when she didn't wear any, her skin blemish-free and lightly tanned. Tempting. The shade of the dress highlighted the creamy skin of her shoulders and neck.

'So, what are we going to do about you, Aimee and me?' Elene asked.

Her question should've brought his mind to order, focused on the important. It didn't. Showed how far gone he was.

Ignoring his half-full plate, he lifted his glass. It was necessary to pretend nothing was disturbing him, otherwise Elene would pounce with a zillion questions, though she was watching him, her gaze searching. 'I hope you find what you're looking for,' he quipped, suddenly afraid he'd be found lacking.

So like Elene, she didn't drop her gaze. She wasn't afraid of him. 'Wouldn't you like to know?' Someone was obviously totally in control of *her* mind—and her body.

Damn her. It wasn't right he was the only one suffering. 'Let me see. You're wondering what it would be like to make love under the stars on my deck.'

She blanched. Now her eyes lowered. Her teeth dug into her bottom lip. And the hand holding the wine glass shook. 'Where did that come from?' she whispered.

He should feel lousy for taunting her. He didn't. It was the mating game and he'd never played it with Elene. Hadn't wanted to before. Make that—hadn't been prepared to give in to the relentless need. But tonight? Oh, man, he didn't know how not to. Because none of what had happened over the past ten days had done a thing to turn off his attraction to Elene. She'd done what no other woman had for a long time—got to him in every way.

Pull back. Talk about the weather. Don't let her any closer. You'll only regret letting her in. It's a road to pain. But nothing would stop him pushing harder. Removing her glass, he wrapped his hands around her hand. 'It comes from that kiss yesterday.' And the previous one, and all the ones he'd dreamt of in between. 'It isn't enough. I want to know what's behind it. To discover you.'

Colour rose in her cheeks, her lips curved into a smile so encouraging he wanted to haul her across the table and have her right then.

Mattia stood, still holding her hands. 'Come on. We're going home.' He was making a habit of cutting dinner short.

Even as she said, 'Your parents are there,' she was running beside him in a familiar way, her fingers gripping his as though afraid he'd let go.

'Not for long,' Mattia muttered. It was a bonus Papà had joined his mother for babysitting duties because now he could drive Mamma back to Napoli as soon as he and Elene got home. He wasn't changing direction this time. He was going to make love to Elene.

Later, he couldn't remember driving up the hill, or parking, or saying goodnight to his parents, who seemed extraordinarily happy and quick to leave after telling them Aimee was sound asleep and that Anna had gone to her sister's for the night. The only memories he retained were of carrying Elene to his bedroom and standing her on her feet by the massive bed. Of pausing to ask, 'Are you sure?'

And Elene murmuring, 'Absolutely,' before pressing her peaked breasts against his chest.

Memories of kissing her, of losing time and everything else except them, their bodies, their lovemaking. Of pulling the zip of her dress down, notch by notch, then smoothing away the fabric from her shoulders, feeling her come alive under his palms, down over those unbelievable breasts to her trim, curvy waist, beyond to her hips, until it fell in a pool at her feet, still wearing the wicked shoes that did a number on him all by themselves.

'Let me see you,' she said in a throaty voice that sent more ripples of longing through him.

When her fingers were too slow undoing the buttons of his shirt he leaned back to haul it over his head and toss it aside without taking his eyes off those lace-enclosed breasts. Then he bent forward and licked her nipple through the lace.

She cried out, and a shudder rocked her.

He bit gently.

Her cry was louder, the shudder stronger, and her hands were on his shoulders, gripping tight, her lower body pushing against his, where his need for her was apparent. Hot and hard.

He gave the second breast the same treatment, got the same reaction. Elene was whimpering, and they'd hardly started.

'Look at me,' he commanded. 'I want to see your emotions.'

It seemed to take for ever for her eyelids to lift, and the eyes that focused on him were slumberous with desire. No doubt a mirror image of his own.

Her hands were on his hips, then moving to his manhood, wrapping around him, sliding down his shaft, up, down again.

'Not yet,' he growled, his eyes still intent on hers, reading every reaction as he cupped her breasts and rubbed his thumbs across her nipples.

Her hand tightened on him.

Scooping Elene up into his arms, he kissed her in an attempt to slow things down. Should've known better. Their previous kisses had always been incendiary; this one was no different. They fell onto the bed, Mattia aware of the soft mattress that absorbed their bodies, of the low light spilling across her face, his arms—knowing that soft mewing sound Elene uttered every time he touched her, the tension in her muscles at the top of her legs, the need pulsing through her veins.

'Elene,' he whispered as he brought her to a climax.

'Mattia,' she whispered in return as she took him in, gave back to him.

'That's getting to know each other on a whole new level,' he muttered as his breathing returned to normal afterwards.

Elene laughed, a deep, rich sound that made his toes curl with emotions he wasn't ready to explore. 'Not sure where it takes us but right now I don't care.' She snuggled close, a hand splayed across his chest.

He covered her hand with his. 'Closer.' Perfect, really.

That was all he remembered until he awoke later and reached for Elene. He had to have her again. But the bed was empty. She was gone.

The en suite bathroom's light wasn't on. When he placed his hand on the sheet it was cold. She'd left his bed while he slept. That was new for him. They'd hardly started; there were hours to go before they had to get up for work.

Flinging the sheet aside, he stood up and headed for her bedroom until he noticed a light showing under the door of Aimee's room. Shoving the door wide, he stepped in and faltered to a stop. Aimee was tucked into Elene's arms, her sweet face pushed against those beautiful breasts. Air leaked over his lips. This was parenthood. It interrupted everything, held mums and dads to ransom. It was changing his life abruptly—no slowly getting used to having to put Aimee, and Elene, before everything else. He'd thought he'd be the full-time parent, with Elene and Anna picking up the slack. It was possible, though it wasn't how he wanted to raise his daughter—to be remembered by his absences and not playtime before dinner, bedtime stories before sleep.

'When did she wake?'

'Shh,' she warned, finger to her lips, her arm wound around Aimee as she rocked back and forth.

Aimee stirred.

Elene was holding her breath.

Mattia eased down beside her, wrapped his hand carefully around one tiny covered foot and enjoyed being with his girls, hoping his action wouldn't wake Aimee but unable to resist her.

Slowly Aimee settled again.

As did Mattia's heart. This was special, being part of his own family. Yet there was something hovering in the back of his head like a warning. *Get real. You're already including Elene in every picture you have of Aimee's future. Aimee and Elene and you. Stop hiding behind your daughter and accept Elene means the world to you. Get over the past.*

Swallowing hard, he croaked, 'Aimee woke you?' This was such a normal family scene—he wasn't used to it but he wanted more. Lots more.

Elene nodded, that messed-up hair covering half her face. 'About forty minutes ago. She needed changing. When that didn't settle her I gave her milk which, fingers crossed, has worked.'

'I was out of it.'

'I thought I was, but seems I've developed the mothering instinct.'

So this was what his brothers meant when they said having kids changed everything and yet everything remained the same. He wanted Elene in his bed again, yet knowing he'd have to wait wasn't a problem.

'Can I do anything?' he whispered.

Her swollen lips cracked into a big smile. 'Probably not what you're used to post-coital, but I'd die for a cup of tea.'

'You're right, haven't had that request before. But then I haven't had my own child, or anyone else's, to wake me after I've been having amazing sex.'

'You're not looking too concerned about it.'

'Surprising, isn't it?' Aimee looked so cute, snuggled against Elene, her little chest rising and falling on each noisy breath. He risked running a finger over his little girl's arm, felt her vulnerability. A lump formed in his throat. 'You know what? I like having her here. With you,' he added. 'You're a pair.' *My pair.* 'I'm glad, relieved, happy, to know Aimee's got you.'

A solitary tear rolled down Elene's cheek, and he followed it with his finger.

'I mean it. You're her mother now, and always will be. We've a way to go making this work but I believe we will.' His lips brushed her cheek, where that tear had left a trail. 'I promise to do all I can to achieve it.'

Elene wanted to lean into Mattia and accept his promise without thought. It would be so easy. He accepted her role in Aimee's life. He accepted Aimee for his own, and wanted to share her life. What more could she want? It was her turn to give back, and she was more than willing. They'd spent the most magical time in his bed. She was halfway to being in love with him. Did she say now that she'd move to Sorrento permanently? When she'd missed her family these past days more than she'd have believed? Could Mattia and Aimee become her new family? He hadn't offered that. She'd be foolish to leap in and show all her cards. Or would she? Part of her wanted to. Her past warned her not to. 'Thank you,' was all she managed.

'I'm not sure where that leaves me,' he said. 'So I'll go make that tea, just to show I can be of use when required.'

'Mattia.' Elene reached for his hand. 'You've paid me a huge compliment. I feel it in here.' She tapped her chest beside Aimee's head. 'I arrived in Sorrento expecting—and looking for—a fight, for your reactions to be about what you wanted, with little regard for me and how I felt about Aimee. I was wrong. Sorry.'

His smile could've lit up a town. It certainly lit up her heart. 'We're doing fine, Elene. Just fine. There's a way to go, but I'm liking the journey so far.'

Her return smile came from her heart. 'You just want more sex.'

'There is that.' His hand splayed across his chest and his smile became a wicked grin. 'Before or after the cup of tea?'

Aimee chose that moment to open her eyes and stare up at them. Elene felt her heart expand. Then she looked at Mattia and saw the love shining out of those dark eyes, and her heart grew to include him. She was lost to him. Fight it, argue with herself, whatever—she loved Mattia. Probably had begun to since that night back in Wellington. He was handling this so well, and he wasn't as closed to accepting what life tossed at him as she'd believed. It made sense for her to make the major sacrifice over where to live. He had more to give up and, while moving here would bring difficulties, it wouldn't be all bad.

'Ma-ma-ma-ma.' Aimee interrupted her thoughts.

'Hey, sweetheart. Say Papà.'

'Ma-ma-ma-ma.'

'Okay, we'll get there.' Standing, she stretched up to kiss Mattia. 'Let's skip the tea.' He was never going to fall in love with her. Because of what Sandy had done to him, the shackles weren't going to fall from around his heart. So she'd love him from the sidelines, and hope that was enough. But for the next week there was nothing stopping her having a good time, while getting to where they needed to be on a wave of optimism and not through a mire of disagreements and second-guessing.

She got her tea an hour later, sitting up in Mattia's bed, her muscles barely able to function enough to keep her upright. If that was what great sex did then she'd been missing out all along. Until Mattia. Man, oh, man. Did he know what he was doing? Her doubts over being good enough had fled. Mattia made her lose her inhibitions, turned her more adventurous and willing to give as good as she got.

Lying beside her, hands behind his head, staring at the

ceiling, Mattia took her breath away. Then his next words tightened her throat. 'Please don't take the timing of this next question the wrong way. I'm feeling more relaxed than I have since the moment I set eyes on you nearly two weeks ago, and I want to ask you something important.' His gaze moved from the ceiling to her. 'Is there any possibility that you would move to Sorrento permanently? I think we've shown we can make it work.'

D-day. Make that D-hour. She should be getting in a pickle, but she'd already reached the decision, found her answer. Deep down she'd accepted what Mattia wanted, and there weren't enough reasonable arguments to put up against him. She'd miss her family not being close by on a daily basis. Her job, her cottage, her sports groups? Replaceable. Her closest friend was gone, and there weren't others so much a part of her life she couldn't move away. 'Yes.'

'That's it? Yes?' Hope started rising in his eyes.

Hope she understood because she felt it every day. For her, the hope was that Mattia wouldn't fight her over the joint custody issue, that they'd share. If that meant moving to a country she wasn't exactly a foreigner in, then getting brave and stepping up had to happen. 'Yes.'

'Thank you.' He sat up and wrapped an arm around her shoulders. 'We can decide how this all comes together over the next few weeks. Thank goodness for phones, eh?'

She smiled through the doubts already creeping in and shoved them aside to get on with her new life. 'Not quite as good as face-to-face though.'

'I want you to be completely happy with whatever arrangements we make.'

Throwing in some unbelievable sex would make it that much easier. Though that would stop soon. Mattia didn't do permanent, and she was only just coming round to the idea of trying for permanency herself. Except she'd gone and fallen in love with the man. The truth had been niggling away at her for days. Now it was right in front of her eyes, in her heart. She was in trouble. Warm tea sloshed onto her chest.

'Hey, careful.' He handed her the box of tissues to wipe up. 'What were you thinking about that got you all jumpy?'

You. Me. Love.

'All the stuff I'll have to pack and shift over here.' It was the best she could come up with and not spill her heart.

Mattia took her chin between his fingers and turned her head so she had to look at him. 'I'll let you off this one, but let's try and stay truthful with each other. It'll make everything that much easier.'

Like why you couldn't make it to breakfast?

Elene sighed. She wasn't getting into an argument. 'Just my nerves getting in the way of logic.' She put her mug aside and slid down the bed, tugging Mattia to join her. If they weren't going to be this close for ever then she would take what she could while it was available. She chuckled. Overnight she'd become insatiable, and so far she couldn't fault it.

Sunday morning brought more sunshine. 'Doesn't it ever rain here?' Elene was thinking of the storms that regularly lashed Wellington. Her home town wasn't known as Windy Wellington for nothing, and while this endless sunshine was wonderful she could almost wish for a small storm. Almost.

Mattia laughed. 'Are you seriously saying you'd prefer to be back home with winter screaming across the Cook Strait?'

'It's not that bad.' In fact it could be invigorating. And wet, and cold, and—home. But she wasn't missing home.

Not when Mattia was taking her and Aimee to Napoli for the family lunch later in the morning. Sofia had phoned for a chinwag yesterday, talking about anything and everything as friends did. She'd made Elene feel welcome and homesick for her sisters at the same time.

'Want to go shopping again?' Mattia asked from where he was loading the dishwasher.

She'd love to. She was so over the few clothes she'd brought with her. But Mattia might offer to pay for her and that would be a slippery slope. It could become a habit and then he'd be right in thinking that she wanted to get what she could from him. 'Not today.'

'I won't ask the other female in the house. My mother's already bought out the shops for her.'

It was true. Aimee now had more outfits than she'd ever wear before she outgrew them. Maria enjoyed indulging her grandchildren. If Sofia hadn't told her Maria did the same for Giulia and Marco, Elene might've suspected her of deliberately overdoing it to show what Aimee could have if Elene brought her to live here full-time. Mattia had suggested they shouldn't say anything about what they'd agreed while they worked out the details or his mother would want a say in everything.

'Aimee looks gorgeous in that dress Maria brought on Friday.' Elene hadn't been able to resist dressing her girl in the pretty dress for their outing.

The day went without a hitch, and Elene felt as though she'd been dropping by on Sundays for ever. Sofia and Alessia had as many questions as the previous week while they sat in the back yard with their wines, watching the kids play and laughing and talking nonstop.

Mattia regularly checked that Elene was happy and had whatever she needed. 'He's just as attentive as Marco,'

Sofia said around a laugh. 'Watch out, Elene. The man's getting serious.'

'Don't go getting ideas,' she warned. About to say more, she looked up to find Mattia standing in the doorway watching her. It was obvious he'd heard Sofia's comment and her reply—and he didn't seem upset at her answer.

Her heart banged. Which was silly when she knew there was no hope in that direction. Typical. When she'd finally moved on from the past she'd fallen for a man who had his own issues to deal with before he'd reciprocate her feelings, if he could. Homesickness swamped her. Her sisters would know what to say, would tell her to get Mattia out of her system and find someone to love her properly. Neither of them had had their hearts broken yet and believed moving onto the next man was a matter of putting one foot in front of the other. Long might that last for them. But if only they were here. Or she was at home, sitting around the table catching up on family news and nonsense. But they weren't, and she wasn't. She was in Naples with Mattia and his family, being made to feel she might belong. She should be grateful, not sad. Deep breath then. 'Where's the best place in Napoli to buy shoes? I promised myself I'd take a couple of pairs home with me.'

Alessia sighed and did an eye-roll. 'Now I know we're best friends. I'll take you to my favourite shop this week.'

'We could have lunch at Prego's,' Sofia said.

'Knew you'd want to come,' Alessia laughed.

'Sisters united,' Sofia scoffed.

Elene wasn't so sure about sisterhood yet. 'I work most mornings, and then there's Aimee to think about.'

'We'll have a late lunch. Maria can look after all three children.' Sofia was checking her diary on her phone. 'I can do Wednesday.'

'Works for me,' Alessia said. 'Elene?'

She gave up pretending she didn't want to go out with these two. 'Wednesday's good. I'll catch a train up so I'll be a while getting to the city.'

'Anna can drive you and Aimee up,' Mattia said from behind. So much for thinking he'd returned inside.

'Done. Thank you, everyone.' Then Elene thought about the housekeeper. 'If it's all right with Anna.'

'It will be.' Then Mattia said, 'Lunch's ready,' and waited to take Elene's elbow to lead her inside.

On Tuesday Maria came down to Sorrento to spend time with her granddaughter, and stayed on while Mattia again took Elene out to dinner.

'Seems your mother can't get enough of Aimee,' Elene commented halfway through the entrée.

'You're heading home on Saturday. Naturally she wants to spend time with her granddaughter.'

'Fair enough.' Mattia had relented and told the family on Sunday that Elene would be moving to Sorrento permanently. Everyone was genuinely thrilled. She had yet to break the news to her family.

Mattia put down his fork. 'I've been thinking about where you should live. There's plenty of room in my house for us not to get under each other's feet all the time.'

Elene ignored the tightening of her heart. He'd only said what she already knew. They were not going to be sharing the same bedroom. She suspected the nights of passion wouldn't be picked up when she returned to live here, that Mattia would use the break to end the fling. He was a flings man, not one for commitment. 'I think I'd prefer a small place of my own, an apartment, maybe.'

'The problem is finding one that isn't rented out to vacationers in summer. There'd be more opportunity in the towns between here and Napoli, but then you wouldn't be close for me to drop by after work.'

'But living in your home won't work long-term. We'd want privacy to come and go as we please, with who we please,' she added to see how he reacted.

He gulped down the mouthful of seafood he'd been chewing. 'True.'

'What would it cost me to buy here? Ballpark figure.' She could sell her cottage back home since she wouldn't be living there. Plus she had an investment from her grandmother that could be used.

'That won't be necessary.'

'I'd prefer that to renting long-term. I'd need your advice on the best areas for safety and weather.'

'I repeat, that won't be happening. If there's any property purchase happening I'll do it.'

'Mattia, without starting an argument, I get to decide where to live, and to choose my own home.' One moment she believed they were on the same wavelength, the next Mattia proved her wrong. Indignation rose. 'I can afford this.' *I think.* Shouldn't have said that until she'd checked out prices. Not that she'd let him pay.

'You don't know the system here, won't know what to look out for in a property.'

'Then you can help me, or put me in touch with a realtor you trust.'

'Why don't you give me a list of what's important to you and let me do the job?' He didn't give up easily.

But she'd known that. It was one of his endearing characteristics when it wasn't aimed at wrecking her requirements. 'Because I can't tell you what the X factor will be, what that undefinable something that ticks my boxes will be. When I bought the cottage it had everything I was looking for, as did most of the places I'd seen, but the cottage touched me in some way. Its warmth, quirky kitchen, the tree out the back. Things I hadn't believed I'd care about.'

'I've never bought a house so I don't understand. I presumed it was all about getting value for money, the right location, sun angles, not quirky anything.' His smile said he was trying to understand her need to make her own choices.

'If I found a property I loved I'd certainly want your opinion, and someone to make sure it wasn't going to get washed off the hill in the next rain deluge.' She'd worked too hard to get where she was, and wasn't about to toss it away.

'If you're giving up your home to move to my side of the world then you must let me make it as easy as possible for you. If that means buying you a property then I will. And—' he held his hand up '—I want to give you something back for all you've done for Aimee and me.'

Her tongue stuck to the roof of her mouth. This was still Mattia, with his kindness and thoughtfulness, but he liked, maybe needed, because of what Sandy had done, to be in charge. A sip of her wine loosened her tongue enough to speak. 'Bet you never thought you'd be saying that to me.' She had to go for the light-hearted approach or spill her heart, and he wasn't ready for that.

Already there was withdrawal going on in his eyes. 'Funny how life flips you on your head when least expected.'

Lifting her fork, she watched him. Whatever he was thinking, he wasn't about to turn into a monster. If only he wanted to share more with her than raising a child. A shiver caught her. Mattia might be feeling close to her but he didn't love her. She had to accept that or living here would be hell.

Starting now with accepting how it would be, she said,

'This *gnocchi* with four cheese sauce is divine.' It really was. One thing she'd never complain about in this country was the food. 'Just like Mum makes.' Talking on the phone to her mother wasn't the same. She needed to see her expressions, feel her warmth, love. Love. She had it in abundance back home. Now she'd have to cultivate some here. Her eyes lifted to the man sitting opposite her, wanting to see and feel his love.

Don't waste your time. You'll only break your heart all over.

I, Mattia Ricco, a sane and intelligent man, have just offered to buy Elene a home of her own.

He who didn't trust women to accept him for who he was and not want to grasp everything going, totally believed in Elene not to hurt his family, not to pull his heart out and stamp all over it. How did he explain this to himself? Had he gone and fallen in love with her? Couldn't have. He wasn't doing that ever again. He wanted a word with the clown who said *never say never.* These emotions about Elene had been growing slowly out in left field and he needed to resist them. Only then would his life get back on track. A long and lonely track.

Mattia turned his focus to Elene and away from the questions and shocks tripping his brain. Something was bugging her. She kept glancing at him then out over the now dark sea beyond the road. He'd upset her by insisting he'd buy her a home, but that couldn't be what was putting a scowl on her beautiful face. Was it about moving away from her home turf to his? She'd hate leaving her family permanently. During his year in New Zealand there'd been times when he'd have given anything to have one of his brothers there to tease him, give him cheek, to take away the emptiness created by being away from all he knew and loved.

Reaching for her hand, he squeezed gently. 'Elene, I'm coming to Wellington with you for a week.'

Her smile was uncertain. 'Why?'

'Two of us looking after Aimee on the flights will make for an easier trip for you.'

'I survived last time.'

'Exactly. Survived. You were a wreck when you arrived.' The company plane wasn't available next week so he'd get first class tickets for the three of them. Anything to make her journey more comfortable.

'What about work?'

'They'll manage, one of the other surgeons returned on Thursday.'

'I won't be returning here that quickly. I have to work out my notice at the hospital, for one.'

'I understand. There's lots for you to do.' Her hand was warm under his. A simple gesture shouldn't hold so much care and concern, friendship and…

Mattia jerked his hand away, sat back in his chair. 'Everyone here understands and will do what they can to help. You've completely won over my family, and the sisters-in-law think of you as a special friend.' But they weren't *her* friends, *her* family. He got that. It worried him. What if Elene got so homesick she couldn't remain in Sorrento? Then he'd have to make the move, and deal with similar problems. He'd go talk to the specialists he'd worked with while in Wellington last time. No harm in putting out feelers in case he found himself moving down there.

'Sofia and Alessia do make it easier for me.' She drew circles on the table with her forefinger. 'I'm looking forward to our lunch tomorrow. Girl time.'

'All talking nonstop so you can't hear each other.' The

girls would make Elene see her new life didn't have to be lonely.

'I intend getting a job when I come back.'

'That won't be hard. There're always part-time positions available at the hospital, especially in the winter months.'

'Did I say part-time? That's my decision to make, not yours.' Picking up her fork again, she played with the last piece of *gnocchi* on her plate, shoving it through the sauce, back and forth. 'Accept that I will do what's best for Aimee, and we'll get along just fine.'

'But…' He paused.

'No buts, Mattia. I am making most, if not all, of the concessions here. Be warned, I will not become subservient, nor will I live how you expect. I do have a mind of my own and intend using it.' Stabbing the *gnocchi*, she pushed it into her mouth. So there.

Fair enough. He chuckled. Seemed nothing could dampen his spirits tonight. 'We should have some interesting conversations over the coming years.' Elene wasn't a simpering fool who'd do anything to keep onside with him. He'd hate that with a vengeance. Feisty women knew their own minds, which was a big attraction for him.

A vision of her naked body wrapped around his flashed before his eyes. Their lovemaking was out of this world. It wasn't just sex. Did that mean attraction beyond the physical? Every morning he woke up with a smile and a sense of wonder at a new day bringing any amount of happiness and fun with Elene and his daughter. Getting excited about life with a woman should be worrying. Or it could be exciting if he took the risk and gave her his heart. Not today. Not in one solid hit. Piece by piece, the barricades were cracking, which was a more manageable way to move forward with this.

'Would you like dessert, *signor*? *Signorina?*' The waitress hovered at the table.

Mattia raised an eyebrow. 'Elene?'

'No, thanks.'

Tipping his head at the waitress, he told her, 'Me neither.' As the girl walked away he rose, reached for Elene's elbow. 'Time to go home.'

To bed to make wild, passionate love? Or to separate rooms to think about everything they'd discussed tonight? Or did he waste time thinking about Elene getting under his skin and how to go about removing her before he got in too deep? If he wasn't already too late.

CHAPTER TEN

ELENE LAY BESIDE MATTIA, one leg between his, her arm on his chest. Making love just got better every night. There was a rawness to Mattia that drew her in, made her want to give him so much.

He'd been badly hurt in the past so handing over his heart again would take something major to happen. Love was the only thing that might break the shackles he'd tightened around that particular organ. If she'd learnt anything about Mattia these past weeks, the main one was he wasn't about to let love near. Except for Aimee, who'd stolen her father's love without a blink. As children did. If only it was that simple for *her* to win him over.

There were times when they got along so well that hope rose. But like at dinner earlier, that hope often got a dose of cold water. Mattia wanted to tell her how to run her life, and no one would ever be allowed to do that again. That was her slippery slope to avoid. She might've agreed to move here but it'd been her decision. She hadn't been following orders. Like tonight there'd be more demands and like tonight she'd refute them. She was capable of making her own choices and living with the results.

'You planning on lying awake all night?' Mattia asked. 'What's your problem? You're tense as a wire strop on a boat.'

Shuffling sideways and withdrawing her leg and arm, Elene lay on her back and stared at the darkened ceiling. 'I'm not sleepy.' Though after their lovemaking she should be comatose.

'Problem?'

You. 'Just a lot of things going round and round in my head.' *Again, you.*

'Don't make mountains out of everything, Elene. It's hard enough as it is. I do understand what you're giving up to come here.'

'Do you though?' She paused, but when Mattia said nothing she continued. 'When I return, what will our relationship be?'

The bed rocked as he sat up and leaned against the headboard. 'Why do you ask?'

'Because I want to know. No grey areas. These past few nights have been special, but I suspect you won't want to continue for ever.'

'You know I don't do commitment. It is what we argued about back in Wellington when I was going out with Danielle.'

She swallowed the hurt. 'Yes, I hadn't forgotten, and still chose to sleep with you.'

'I am sorry, Elene. Truly sorry.'

'So I'll return to Sorrento, and we'll carry on as though this never happened.'

'I don't imagine I'll be forgetting it in a hurry.'

Her head flipped around so she could see his face, but there wasn't enough light to really read what was racing through his eyes. 'Nor will I,' she whispered. 'Which is why I don't think I can live in your house, not even temporarily until I find my own place.'

'You'll be lonely in an apartment with only a toddler for company.'

'I'd be just as lonely here.' Having Mattia in her face day in, day out, would not mean companionship. She sat up beside him and reached for his hand. When she threaded her fingers between his they didn't curl around her hand. 'Let's leave it at that.'

'There's a lot to think about.' His fingers loosened around hers. Did he realise they were holding hands? 'I should've expected this. You're always blunt when it comes to clearing the air.'

She'd hardly started, but telling Mattia she'd fallen in love with him was not happening. She had her pride. So did Mattia, and out of habit, or because he needed to protect himself, he'd put up a wall so high and deep they'd never make their way through it. For Aimee's sake, she wouldn't risk trying. Pulling her hand free, she slid down the bed again and lay staring up at the ceiling. 'We're getting better at talking.'

His laugh was self-mocking. 'You think?'

'Yes, Mattia, I do.' But they were still a long way from being close. As friends or lovers, or partners for life? They needed to stay close, again for Aimee's sake. And theirs if the way forward was to be comfortable and they'd be able to consult each other on all the important issues that bringing up a child would raise. 'It's progress.'

'You're right.'

She grinned in the dark. 'Say that again.'

'Don't push your luck.' He slid down beside her. 'Roll over and I'll cuddle you till you relax.'

Exactly what she wanted, yet it would make her long for more. Couples cuddled, not short-term lovers. Hadn't he just made it clear as crystal where they were going with this…relationship? Friends, single parents sharing raising a child, whatever. They didn't do cuddling naked in bed. That was too loving and close, too wonderful to be happening.

'Think I'll get up and read for a bit, distract my brain.' She rolled out of bed before she could give in to those tempting arms.

'Elene?'

Mattia would hate for her to say what was on her mind and it would drive a wedge between them. 'Go to sleep. I'm fine,' she lied.

Out in the family room, she checked her phone for messages, felt her eyes water when the screen showed blank. Not even the usual banter from her sisters, but they'd be at work. Homesickness overwhelmed her, pushed her into the cushions. Better get used to it. When she returned here, keeping busy would be an antidote to some extent, but nothing beat having people around who loved her unconditionally. Pressing her mother's number, she held the phone to her ear and waited, and waited. Okay, not at home and, Mum being Mum, her phone was probably still on the bench.

Swiping the back of her hand across her face, Elene reached for a cushion and hugged it to her breasts. Breasts that not so long ago were responding to Mattia's hands and tongue, tightening and aching with need. She shouldn't have left his bed. She'd had to, or fall deeper. It was going to be hard enough stepping away without adding other memories of tenderness to the picture.

Next week she'd fly out of Naples, bound for Wellington and all the packing that needed to be done. Only days left for making love with Mattia, of knowing his body, of sharing hers—if they continued after their discussion tonight. Silly woman that she was, she wanted to have those last nights together. When she returned she'd never leave her room in the middle of the night to get into bed with

Mattia. They'd never again make love against the bench in the kitchen while waiting for the kettle to boil. How was she going to be able to return to all those memories?

Mattia quietly observed Elene as she bounced a grizzly Aimee on her hip and gripped shopping bags in her other hand. She looked shattered.

'Been busy?' He nodded at the logo-covered bags she was dropping onto the kitchen table.

'I'm definitely out of practice. Once Sofia and Alessia get started they don't stop. I swear there isn't a shop on Via Toledo we didn't go into.' She jiggled her human bundle to no avail. If anything the shrieking got louder.

'Give me Aimee so you can take a load off your feet.' He reached into the fridge for the wine. 'Pour yourself one of these while you're at it. Dinner is prepared for cooking so we can eat whenever.'

'That'll be when missy decides to quieten down and go to sleep.'

'I'll run her a bath.' Though his girl wasn't fond of getting wet, once she was in and playing with her toys she usually calmed down.

'Good luck with that. She's been wound up all the way home. Too much excitement visiting with Nonna and her cousins.' The glass shook in Elene's hand as she poured a small drink.

Worry hit Mattia. 'Are you all right, other than tired?'

She huffed out a breath. 'Yes. I didn't get much sleep last night.'

'You didn't choose the most comfortable of places to crash.' He'd found her on the couch amongst the cushions when he'd come out to turn on the coffee maker at six that morning. 'Why weren't you in bed?'

Another huff. 'I was restless.'

Something wasn't ringing true. But the shrieking in his ear was serious so he left Elene to wind down with her wine while he dealt with madam. 'Come on, little one. Let's play splish-splash.'

Pushing boats through the water and tickling Aimee on the ribs quickly quietened her and Mattia relaxed. Until he lifted her out and began to dry off the bath water. Then the crying started again. 'Guess we're going out to the deck next.'

'I'll heat the pumpkin mash,' Elene called as he strode past. 'Food might help.'

It did for a while, but as soon as Mattia tried to wipe her face and hands Aimee let rip with more screams. 'You have a future as an emergency siren, little one.' Back to pacing the deck.

'Let me take her.' Elene stood in front of them a long time later. 'I'll see what I can manage.'

Within minutes the shrieks had dulled to occasional snorts and hiccups. 'The mother touch,' he noted. 'I'm impressed.' He also loved how domesticated this felt, and how much he was enjoying being beside Elene as they settled their child. He glanced around the deck at all the toys spread around. Could he get Anna to leave it as it was so it always felt like a family home?

'It doesn't work every time.' Elene smiled tiredly, her body sagging.

He walked beside them, round and round the deck, Elene obviously wary of trying to put Aimee down yet. 'I'd say give her back to me but that might prompt more trouble.'

'I agree.'

'I'd like to know what kept you awake last night,' he risked.

Another circuit of the deck. Then, 'What I'm undertaking is huge. What if I can't do it? Find that I miss home too much? What if Aimee can't cope with different children at crèche, all talking in a strange language? I mightn't be able to go to work and mix with adults.'

Where had the strong, take-no-prisoners woman gone? Elene didn't crumple at the first hint of difficulty. He wrapped an arm around her shoulders and tugged her close, counting off by raising his index finger. 'You've impressed the hospital staff and patients with your professionalism and kindness.' Second finger. 'The same goes for the charity unit people.' Another finger. 'My family think you're wonderful and want to do all they can to persuade you to stay and settle in. Anna adores you and won't hear a bad word about you.'

'What did you say for her to tell you that?'

'I mentioned your cooking skills.'

'Nothing wrong with them.'

'There was that duck confit.' It'd been a disaster.

'A gentleman wouldn't bring that up.'

'Too late.' He smiled down at her. Then he held up his thumb. 'Last, but not least, I'll have your back all the way. I want you to fit in for your sake, not just mine. This has to work for both of us or else it will end badly. So I will do all I can to make you happy.'

Instead of smiling at him, her face shut down.

What had he said? 'Elene?'

Twisting out of his arm, she headed inside. 'I'll try putting Aimee down. She's almost asleep.'

Mattia watched her rush away, putting distance between them. This wasn't making sense. Not at all. About to follow her, he changed his mind and headed to the kitchen to start cooking the tortellini. A break from whatever was bothering Elene might help. They could talk after dinner.

But when he went into the family room after cleaning up

from dinner and putting the dishes in the washer he found Elene was finishing up talking to her family.

'Everything all right?' he asked around a lump of worry.

'I've told them what we've decided so naturally they're full of questions. But overall they're happy for me. It's hard not being there to gauge their reactions.'

She'd miss that in the future.

'You talk to them most days.'

'It's not the same. I want the hugs and the laughter and crazy talk.'

Mattia's heart lurched. This was the crux of what faced them. What if they couldn't make it work? They had to. There was no other solution.

Mattia tried not to grip the edge of his seat as the massive plane lowered through the clouds to the tiny runway below. Wellington had turned on its biggest storm in a decade apparently and the airport had been closed all night, only opening after ploughs had cleared away the snow and hail. Flying had never bothered him before, but with his little girl smiling up at him, her face full of trust, he knew a fear like he'd never known. He was meant to protect her, not put her in harm's way. 'Hey, baby girl, isn't this fun?'

The bigger girl beside him grimaced. 'You think?'

Her white knuckles gave him an excuse to hold her hand. Not that he needed one. They were still lovers, though how that would play out now they were staying with her parents was anyone's guess. He wasn't ready to let Elene go yet. Somehow he doubted he ever would be. Which was why he was in this tin can shaking all over the sky instead of back in Sorrento considering his next operation. He loved Elene. Articulating that wasn't happening. He'd tried the night before they'd left Italy, had taken her out for a special dinner in a stunning location and opened his mouth to utter the words and nothing came out. At least she hadn't guessed what was on his mind and made him look a fool.

For now he'd continue showing his feelings, not telling her. It was the best he could manage, and better than nothing.

Thud. The plane made it onto the ground.

'Phew.' Elene wiped her brow. 'Welcome to my turf.' Her smile was wry. 'Thank goodness I packed jackets for Aimee and myself.'

'Minus three is a little cooler than twenty-four,' he admitted.

Elene had taken her phone off flight mode and messages were pinging. 'Dad's waiting in the terminal. Everyone else's stayed back at the house because of the appalling road conditions.'

The inquisition was on hold for a little longer. 'That's probably a wise move.' Mattia unbuckled his seatbelt and stood up to collect their gear from the overhead lockers while Elene unstrapped Aimee.

'Relax,' she admonished. 'No one's going to eat you.'

'Easy for you to say.' He wasn't too concerned about what Elene's family thought of him, but more how they felt about her moving to Italy permanently. They, and Elene, didn't know about his appointment with the head of the orthopaedic department at Wellington Hospital in two days' time. He never went without a back-up plan, in case things turned to custard.

'Done it all before.' She grinned. 'And lived to talk about it.'

'*Sì.* Let's go get another stamp in our passports.'

Transitioning from the plane to the luggage carousel to Immigration and out into the arrivals hall went smoothly and a lot quicker than he'd have believed. As he watched

Elene being engulfed in a hug from the man who'd raised her, Mattia felt a tug at his heart. He was asking her to give this up for him. Aimee would be happy growing up in Wellington or Sorrento, but Elene? He wasn't so sure.

Then his hand was being gripped and shaken by Jeff Lowe. 'Thank you for coming all this way with Elene. I know the flight over to Italy knocked her a bit.'

'A lot,' he told her father. 'But she's one tough biscuit.'

'I know.' Pride filled the older man's eyes. 'Come on. There are some very impatient females at home who've been texting nonstop for the past hour to see where you all are.' He took two of their bags and led them out to his car.

Accepting of him or not? Mattia wondered.

Elene talked all the way to the house and then ran up the path to the women rushing out to greet them, regardless of the cold.

Mattia held Aimee and felt his heart tighten as he watched this family reunite as though they'd been apart for months, not weeks. 'I can't do this to her.'

Beside him Jeff turned and said, 'You're not. It's Elene's choice. She'll only do what she wants, and what's right for Aimee.'

'What if the two are at opposing ends of her wish list?' He couldn't ask her to make that decision. She already had, though.

'Who says that?' Jeff asked. 'I know my girl and if she believed she couldn't make it work you wouldn't have stood a chance.'

'That's true. She's the only woman I know who rides roughshod over my expectations and demands.'

'You like that even if you're not admitting so.'

Damn, this man had him sussed in minutes. Words failed him and he was grateful for Rebecca Lowe approaching with her arms wide to take her granddaughter into her embrace. Except Rebecca included him in the hug.

'Welcome to our home, Mattia. It's lovely to finally meet you after all that's happened.'

He had to blink rapidly so as not to embarrass himself. 'I'm glad to be able to spend time with you too.'

Just like that, he seemed accepted. No one gave him a grilling about how he'd treat Elene in Sorrento or why he couldn't move to Wellington. No one tried to change their plans, or demand he bring Elene and Aimee to visit every so many months.

'Told you it'd be okay,' Elene gloated that night as they recovered from a fast but passionate lovemaking session.

'Your father didn't want to whip me for sharing your bed.' He grinned in the dark. They were in her cottage, two streets away from her parents' home, where they'd first planned on staying. And yes, he'd succumbed to Elene's wiles because…because he couldn't help himself. He was going to have to rethink not going anywhere with this relationship—fast.

'His way of keeping you on your toes,' she said with a laugh and ran a hand down his chest and on down, down, down…

'How am I going to get all my stuff to Sorrento?' Elene asked Mattia three days later. 'There's a ton of it.'

Yesterday, while Mattia had gone to the hospital to catch up with people he'd hung around with when working there, she'd taken an inventory of everything she'd like to take to her new life. There was a lot.

'I want to talk to you about that.'

He sounded so serious she stopped folding the washing and sat down at the table beside him. 'Please don't tell me you don't want me moving to Italy after all.' Her family had been wonderful the way they'd accepted her decision and hadn't pressured her to rethink it. They were adamant they'd find ways to be with each other regularly.

Mattia cleared his throat. 'I wasn't totally honest with you about why I went to the hospital. I had an appointment with Brent Underwood.'

'The Head of Orthopaedics? Why?'

'To see if there were any vacancies. Or if one might be coming up.'

Why? Hadn't they decided on living in Sorrento?

'Mattia, what are you saying? That you're moving here instead of me going north?'

'Exactly that.' He stood up and paced across the small room. Turning back to face her, he continued, 'I've seen how much you love your family, what you'll be giving up for me. I can't let you do that. You got homesick after two weeks. Expecting you to live in Sorrento permanently isn't being fair.'

This was not going the way she'd thought. 'What about your family? You're all just as close.'

'We are, but I'll cope. There's a new position opening up in August, and I'm going to apply with Brent's backing.'

'What about your position in Sorrento? Your charity work?'

'The charity board will replace me, and what's another change in my career?'

His shrug didn't fool her. 'I won't let you give it all up for me. You can't keep moving around changing jobs. Not when you worked so hard to get where you are now.' Standing, she crossed to wrap her arms around him. 'Don't do this.'

'I have to, Elene.' His arms caught her to him and his chin rested on the top of her head. 'I want to do it for you and Aimee. I can't have you being lonely in Sorrento on my account.'

She stood in his embrace, absorbing the warmth from his body, breathing his man scent, holding him tight. Mattia was prepared to do all that for her. Did he love her after all? Or was he just being the kind, considerate man she'd come to know? If that was the case then they wouldn't last long as friends. He'd get restless, would miss his family too much and start to blame her. Whereas she'd chosen to go to Italy, felt at home there and, while she'd miss everyone here, she'd have a family of her own with Aimee and Mattia. Mattia, as in the other parent for their little girl, not her husband.

Pulling away, Elene slapped her hands on her hips and stared up at him. 'No, Mattia. We agreed on me moving to Sorrento. You can't just change the rules to suit yourself.' He went to say something and she placed her hand over his mouth. 'Listen to me.' She was going to lay it all on the line. She had to. 'If we were a couple, as in married, with our Aimee, would you do this?'

'What's the difference?'

'Plenty. How much do you care for me?'

His eyes widened as he stared at her. 'A lot.'

A lot. Better than she'd expected, but nowhere enough. *Okay, heart, I apologise in advance if this turns pear-shaped and you get crushed but I'm not being honest if I don't tell him.* Her chest rose and fell as she struggled to gain composure. 'Mattia, I love you. As in with all my heart love you.' Shock registered in front of her. *No surprise. Keep going.* 'Will you marry me?'

Silence reigned. Mattia stared at her as though he'd never seen her before.

Her stomach squeezed in on itself, making her nauseous, and her head spin. Why had she proposed to him?

He was going to say no. Of course he was. There was no reason why he wouldn't. Once he got over the shock of her being so forthright, that was. He liked to be in control and she'd just taken that away. She needed to regain some control of her own. 'Right. Guess I know where we stand.' Stepping back, she had to hold herself from running out of the door and down the street, away from the most embarrassing mistake of her life.

'Elene.' The tenderness in his low voice caught her, made her look at him.

'Yes, Mattia?'

Slowly he reached for her hands. 'Please come closer.' When her hands were enfolded in his and her gaze on him, he cleared his throat. 'You always have the power to stun me, and I love that about you.'

Not the same as he loved her, but it was progress.

'Elene Lowe, thank you for your proposal, but—'

Her heart stopped.

'But I like to do my own proposing. Elene, I love you with every fibre of my being. Will you please marry me and live with me for ever, wherever we choose?'

If she'd been able to speak she'd have answered, *Yes, Mattia, I will marry you, love you for ever, and live in Sorrento.*

But the words were glue in her mouth so she leaned in and placed her lips on his and kissed him.

'Sì, sì, sì!'

Then Mattia swung her up into his arms and strode down to her bedroom to make love, slow and gentle and filled with love. Like no other time before.

On the way to dinner at her parents', where Aimee had spent the day, Mattia swung by the liquor outlet for bottles of champagne. 'We have some celebrating to do.'

Elene smiled, as she did all the time now. 'Bring it on.'

'I hope there are plenty of spare beds in your house, Mattia, because we'll always be visiting,' her dad told him when they'd made their announcement to the family. 'We are very happy for you both, but don't think we won't be coming over often to annoy you.'

'You're welcome. My family can't wait to meet you all, too.'

'About a wedding, Elene?' Georgie, her sister, asked. 'Where? Here or Sorrento?'

'Here,' she and Mattia answered together. They hadn't discussed it but she wasn't surprised at Mattia's response. He really did want everything to be perfect for her. 'You're both bridesmaids, by the way.'

'Like you had a choice.' Georgie grinned.

'Pa-pa-pa-pa!' Aimee had her say.

Mattia's chest exploded with love and he nearly smothered his girl with a hug. 'Oh, man,' he sniffed.

Jeff tapped a spoon against his glass. 'Raise your glasses, everyone. Let's drink a toast to the happy couple.'

'Cheers, Elene and Mattia. And Aimee.'

Mattia held his arm out and wound it round Elene's, their glasses held ready. 'To my beautiful fiancée.'

'To my man.' Bubbles burst across Elene's tongue as she sipped her champagne. This had to be the happiest moment of her life.

And then Mattia unwound his arm and took her free hand with his. 'There's one more toast I wish to propose.'

Elene stilled, instantly knowing. Her fingers tightened around Mattia's.

He raised his glass. 'To Danielle, without whom Elene and I would never have met up again. Without you, Danielle, we wouldn't have our wonderful Aimee. Thank you,' he croaked.

Tears spurted unbidden down Elene's face. 'Thank you, my dearest, bestest, most special friend. Thank you for trusting me.'

And for the first time since she'd held Danielle's hand at the end she felt the pain leaving her. It wouldn't go completely, but now she could live with it a little more comfortably.

Turning to Mattia, she said, 'I love you.'

He leaned in to kiss her, ignoring the wisecracks in the room. *'Ti amo.'*

* * * * *

MILLS & BOON

Coming next month

A SINGLE DAD TO HEAL HER HEART
Caroline Anderson's 100th book

'I can't offer you a relationship, not one I can do justice to, but I'm lonely, Livvy. I'm ridiculously busy, constantly surrounded by people, and I'm hardly ever alone, and yet I'm lonely. I miss the companionship of a woman, and I'd like to spend time with one who isn't either simply a colleague or my mother. A woman who can make me laugh again. I spend my days rushed off my feet, the rest of my time is dedicated to my children, and don't get me wrong, I love them desperately, but—I have no downtime, no me-time, no time to chill out and have a conversation about something that isn't medicine or hospital politics or whether the kids want dippy eggs or scrambled.'

His mouth kicked up in a wry smile, and he shrugged, just a subtle shift of his shoulders that was more revealing than even his words had been, and she forgot the coffee, forgot her foot and her common sense, and walked up to him, put her arms round him and hugged him.

'Scrambled, every time,' she said, her voice slightly choked, and it took a second, but then he laughed, his chest shaking under her ear, and he tilted her head back and kissed her. Just briefly, not long enough to cause trouble, just long enough to remind her of what he did to her, and then he rested his forehead against her and smiled.

'Me, too. Preferably with bacon and slices of cold tomato in a massive club sandwich washed down with a bucket of coffee.'

'Oh, yes! I haven't had one of those for ages!'

He laughed and let her go. 'I'll cook you brunch one day,' he said, and it sounded like a promise.

'Is that a promise?' she asked, just to be sure. 'Not that I'll hold you to it, and I'm not in a position to do a relationship justice either for various reasons—work, health…'

'Health?'

She shrugged, not yet ready to tell him, to throw *that* word into the middle of a casual conversation. 'Amongst other things, but—whatever you want from me, wherever you want to take this, I'm up for it.'

'Is that what you want from this? An ad hoc affair?'

She held his eyes, wondering if she dared, if she had the courage to tell him, to let him that close, to open herself to potential hurt. Because she'd have to, if this was going any further.

But there was nothing in his eyes except need and tenderness, and she knew he wouldn't hurt her. She nodded. 'Yes. Yes, it is, if that's what you want, too.'

His breath huffed out, a quiet, surprised sound, and something flared in his eyes. 'Oh, Livvy. Absolutely. As long as we're on the same page.'

'We're on the same page,' she said, and he nodded slowly and dipped his head, taking her mouth in a lingering, tender kiss. And then he straightened, just as it was hotting up, and stepped away with a wry smile.

Secrets in the Boardroom

FIONA BRAND

ALISON FRASER

CHARLENE SANDS

MILLS & BOON

Published in Great Britain 2018
by Mills & Boon, an imprint of HarperCollins*Publishers*
1 London Bridge Street, London, SE1 9GF

ISBN: 978-0-263-26634-4

09-0718

MIX
Paper from responsible sources
FSC™ C007454

This book is produced from independently certified FSC™ paper to ensure responsible forest management.

For more information visit: www.harpercollins.co.uk/green

Printed and bound in Great Britain

A PERFECT HUSBAND

FIONA BRAND

"...each of the gates is a single pearl,
and the street of the city is pure gold,
transparent as glass."

Revelation 21:21

One

Dark hair twisted in a sleek, classic knot... Exotic eyes the shifting colors of the sea... A delicate curvy body that made him burn from the inside out...

A sharp rapping on the door of his Sydney hotel suite jerked Zane Atraeus out of a restless, dream-tossed sleep. Shielding his eyes from the glare of the morning sun, he shoved free of the huge silk-draped confection of a bed he'd collapsed into some time short of four that morning.

Pulling on the jeans he'd tossed over a chair, he dragged jet-lagged fingers through his tangled hair and padded to the door.

Memory punched back. An email Zane had found confirming that his half brother Lucas had purchased an engagement ring for a woman Zane could have sworn Lucas barely knew. *Lilah Cole: the woman Zane had secretly wanted for two years and had denied himself.*

His temper, which had been running on a short fuse ever since he had learned that not only was Lucas dating Lilah, he was planning on *marrying* her, ignited as he took in glittering chandeliers and turquoise-and-gold furnishings.

The overstuffed opulence was a far cry from the exotic but spare Mediterranean decor of his island home, Medinos. Instead of soothing him, the antiques and heavily swagged drapes only served to remind him that he had not been born to any of this. He would have to have a word with his new personal assistant, who clearly had a romantic streak.

Halfway across the sitting room the unmistakable sound of the front door lock disengaging made him stiffen.

Lucas Atraeus stepped into the room. Zane let out a self-deprecating breath.

Ten years ago, in L.A., it would have been someone breaking in, but this was Australia and his father's company, the mega wealthy Atraeus Group, owned the hotel so, of course, Lucas had gotten a key. "Ever heard of a phone?"

Closing the door behind him, Lucas tossed a key card down on the hall table. "I phoned, you didn't answer. Remember Lilah?"

The reason Zane was in Sydney instead of in Florida doing his job as the company "fixer" and closing a crucial land deal that had balanced on a knife's edge for the past week? "Your new fiancée." The tantalizing beauty who had almost snared him into a reckless night of passion two years ago. "Yeah, I remember."

Lucas looked annoyed. "I haven't asked her yet. How did you find out?"

Zane's jaw tightened at the confirmation. "My new P.A. was your old P.A., remember?" Which was why Zane had chanced across the internet receipt for Lucas's latest purchase. Apparently Elena was still performing the role of personal shopper for his brother in her spare time.

"Ahh. Elena." He glanced around the room. Comprehension gleamed in his eyes.

Now definitely in a bad mood, Zane turned on his heel and strolled in the direction of the suite's kitchenette. A large ornately gilded mirror threw his reflection back at him—darkly tanned skin, broad shoulders and a lean, muscled torso bisected by a tracery of scars. Three silver studs, the reminder of a misspent youth, glinted in one ear.

In the lavish elegance of the suite, he looked uncivilized, barbaric and faintly sinister, as different from his two classically handsome half brothers as the proverbial chalk was from cheese. Not something he had ever been able to help with the genes he'd inherited from the rough Salvatore side of his family, and the inner scars he had developed as a homeless kid roaming the streets of L.A.

He found a glass, filled it with water from the dispenser in the fridge door and drank in long, smooth swallows. The cold water failed to douse the intense, unreasoning jealousy that seared him every time he thought of Lucas and Lilah, the picture-perfect couple.

An engagement.

His reaction to the idea was as fierce and surprising as it had been when he had discovered Elena admiring a picture of the engagement ring.

The empty glass hit the kitchen counter with a controlled click. "I didn't think Lilah was your type."

As gorgeous and ladylike as Ambrosi Pearls's head jewelry designer was, in Zane's opinion, Lilah was too efficiently, calculatingly focused on hunting for a well heeled husband.

Two years ago, when they had first met at the annual ball of a charity for homeless children—of which he was the patron—he had witnessed the smooth way Lilah had targeted her escort's wealthy boss. Even armored by the formidable depth of betrayal in his past, Zane had been oddly entranced by the businesslike gleam in her eyes. He had not been able to resist the temptation to rescue the hapless older man and spoil her pitch.

Unfortunately, things had gotten out of hand when he and Lilah had ended up alone in a private reception room and he had given into temptation and kissed her. One kiss had led to another, sparking a conflagration that had threatened to engulf them both. Given that he had been irritated by Lilah's agenda, that she was not the kind of woman he was usually attracted to, his loss of control still perplexed him. If his previous personal assistant hadn't found them at a critical moment, he would have made a very big mistake.

Lucas, who had followed him into the kitchen, scribbled a number on the back of a business card and left it on the counter. "Lilah has agreed to be my date at Constantine's wedding. I'm leaving for Medinos in a couple of hours. I was going to arrange for her to fly in the day before the wedding, but since you're here—" Lucas frowned. "By the way, why are you here? I thought you were locked into negotiations."

"I'm taking a couple of days." A muscle pulsed along Zane's jaw.

Lucas shrugged and opened the fridge door.

The shelves were packed with an array of fresh fruit, cheeses, pâtés and juices. Absently, Zane noted his assistant had also stocked the fridge with chocolate-dipped strawberries.

"Good move." Lucas examined a bottle of very expensive French champagne then replaced it. "Nothing like making the vendor think we're cooling off to fast-track a sale. Mind if I have something to eat? I missed breakfast."

Probably too busy shuttling between women to think about food. The last Zane had heard Lucas had also been having a wild "secret" affair with Carla Ambrosi, the public relations officer for Ambrosi and the sister of the woman their brother, Constantine, was marrying.

"Oysters." Lucas lifted a brow. "Having someone in?"

Zane stared grimly at the platter of oysters on the half shell, complete with rock salt and lemon wedges. "Not as far as I know."

Unless his new assistant had made some arrangement.

If she was helping Lucas with his engagement during her

lunch breaks, anything was possible. "Help yourself to the food, the juice…"

My girl.

The thought welled up out of the murk of his subconscious and slipped neatly past all of the reasons that commitment could never work for him. Especially, with a woman like Lilah.

Since the age of nine, relationships had been a difficult area.

After being abandoned by his extravagant, debt-ridden mother on a number of occasions while she had flitted from marriage to marriage, he had definite trust issues with women, especially those on the hunt for wealthy husbands.

Marriage was out.

Lucas took out the bowl of strawberries and surveyed the tempting fruit.

"It doesn't bother you that Lilah's on the hunt for a husband?"

An odd expression flitted across Lucas's face. "Actually, I respect her straightforward approach. It's refreshing."

Despite every attempt to relax, Zane's fingers curled into fists. *So Lucas had fallen under her spell, too.*

Try as he might, now that Zane had acknowledged that Lilah was his, he could not dismiss the thought. With every second that passed, the concept became more and more stubbornly real.

It was a fact that for the two years following the incendiary passion that had almost ended in lovemaking, he had been tormented by the knowledge that Lilah could have been his.

He had controlled the desire to have a reckless fling with Lilah. He had controlled himself.

Lucas selected the largest, plumpest strawberry. "Lilah has a fear of flying. I was hoping, since you're piloting the company jet that you could take her with you to Medinos when you leave."

Zane's jaw tightened. Everything in him rejected Lucas's

easy assertion that Zane would tamely fall into place and hand-deliver Lilah to his bed.

He fixed on the first part of Lucas's statement. In all the time he had known Lilah she had never told *him* she had a fear of flying. Somehow that fact was profoundly irritating. "Just out of curiosity, how long have you known Lilah?" Lucas did spend time in Sydney, but not as much as Zane. He had never heard Lilah so much as mention Lucas's name.

"A week, give or take."

Zane went still inside. He knew his brother's schedule. They had all had to adjust their plans when Roberto Ambrosi, a member of a once-powerful and wealthy Medinian family, had died. The Atraeus Group had been forced to protect its interests by moving on the almost bankrupted Ambrosi Pearls. A hostile takeover to recover huge debts racked up by Roberto had been averted when Constantine had stunned them all by resurrecting his engagement to Sienna Ambrosi. The impending marriage had gone a long way toward healing the acrimonious rift that had developed between the two families when Roberto had leveraged money on the basis of the first engagement.

He knew that, apart from a couple of flying visits in the last couple of weeks—one to attend Roberto's funeral—that Lucas had been committed offshore. He had only arrived in Sydney the previous day.

Zane had spent most of the previous week in Sydney in order to attend the annual general meeting of the charity. As usual, Lilah, who helped out with the art auctions, had been polite, reserved, the tantalizing, high-priced sensuality that was clearly reserved for the future Mr. Cole on ice. She had not mentioned Lucas. "Why not take Lilah with *you?*"

Lucas seemed inordinately interested in selecting a second strawberry. "It's a gray area."

Realization dawned. Lilah had not been subtle about her quest of finding a husband. He had just never seen Lucas as a candidate for an arranged marriage. "This is a first date."

A trace of emotion flickered in Lucas's gaze. "I needed someone on short notice. As it happens, after running a background check, I think Lilah is perfect for me. She's talented, attractive, she's got a good business head on her shoulders, she's even a—"

"What about Carla?"

Lucas dropped the ripe berry as if it had seared his fingertips.

The final piece of the puzzle fell into place. Zane realized what the odd look in Lucas's eyes had been just moments ago: desperation. Hot outrage surged through him. "You're still involved with Carla."

"How did you know? No, don't tell me. Elena." Lucas put the bowl of strawberries back in the fridge and closed the door. "Carla and I are over."

But only just.

Suddenly the instant relationship with Lilah made sense. When Sienna married Constantine, Carla would practically be family. If it came out that Lucas had been sleeping with Carla, intense pressure would be applied. Under the tough exterior, when it came to women, Lucas was vulnerable.

He was using Lilah as a buffer, insurance that Carla, who had a reputation for flamboyant scenes, would not try to publicly force him to formalize their secret affair with a marriage proposal.

That meant that love did not come into the equation.

If Lucas genuinely wanted Lilah, Zane would walk away, however that was not the case. Lucas, who had once been in the untenable position of having a girlfriend die in a car crash after they had argued about the secret abortion she'd had, was using her to avert an unpleasant situation. As calculating as Lilah was with relationships, she did not deserve to be caught in the middle of a showdown between Lucas and Carla.

Relief eased some of his fierce tension. He didn't think Lilah had had time to sleep with Lucas yet. Somehow that fact was very important. "Okay. I'll do it."

Lucas looked relieved. “You won’t regret it.”

Zane wasn’t so sure.

He wondered if Lucas had any inkling that he had just placed a temptation Zane had doggedly resisted for over two years directly in his path.

Two

Heart pounding at the step she was taking, her first bona fide risk in twelve years of carefully managed, featureless and fruitless dating, Lilah Cole boarded the sleek private jet that belonged to Ambrosi Pearls's new owner, The Atraeus Group.

The nervy anticipation that had buoyed her as she had made her way through passport control ebbed as the pretty blonde stewardess, Jasmine, seated her.

Placing the soft white leather tote bag that went with her white jeans and comfy, oversized white shirt on the floor, Lilah dug out the discreet, white leather-bound folder she had bought with her. She had been braced for another stress-filled encounter with the dark and edgily dangerous Zane Atraeus, the youngest and wildest of the Atraeus brothers, but she was the sole occupant of the luxurious cabin.

Fifteen minutes later, with the noise from the jet engines reaching a crescendo and a curtain of gray rain blotting out much of the view from her tiny window, Lilah was still the only passenger.

She squashed the ridiculous idea that she was in any way disappointed as she fastened her seat belt with fingers that were not entirely steady.

Flying was not her favorite pastime; she was not a natural risk taker. Like her approach to relationships, she preferred to keep her feet on the ground. A stubborn part of her brain couldn't ignore the concept of all that space between the aircraft and the earth's surface. To compound the problem, the weather forecast was for violent thunder and lightning.

As the jet taxied through the sweeping rain, Lilah ignored the in-flight safety video and concentrated on the one thing she *could* control. Flipping open the folder, she studied the profiles she had compiled.

Cole women had a notorious record for falling victim to the *coup de foudre*—the clap of thunder—for falling passionately and disastrously for the wrong man then literally being left holding the baby. Aware that she possessed the same creative, passionate streak that ran through both her artistic and bohemian mother and grandmother, Lilah had developed a system for avoiding The Mistake.

It was a blueprint for long-term happiness, a wedding plan. She had found that writing down the steps she needed to take to achieve the relationship she wanted somehow demystified the whole process, making it seem not such a leap in the dark.

When she did eventually give herself to a man, she was confident it would be in a committed relationship, not some wild fling. She wanted marriage, babies, the stable, controlled environment she had craved as a child.

She was determined that any children she had would have two loving parents, not one stressed and strained beyond her limits.

Over the last three years, despite interviewing an exhaustive number of candidates, she had not managed to find a man who met her marriage criteria and appealed to her on the all-important physical level. Scent in particular had proved to be a formidable barrier to identifying someone with whom she could have an intimate relationship. It was not that the men she had interviewed had smelled bad, just that in some subtle way they had not smelled *right*. However, things were finally taking a positive turn.

Lilah studied the notes she had made on her new boss, Lucas Atraeus, and a small number of other men, and the points system she had developed based on a matchmaking website's recommendations. She spent an enjoyable few minutes reviewing Lucas's good points.

On paper he was the most perfect man she had ever met. He was electrifyingly good-looking and used a light cologne that she didn't mind. He possessed the kind of dark, dangerous features that had proved to be an unfortunate weakness of hers and yet, in terms of a future husband, he ticked every box of her list.

For the first time she had found a man who was her type and yet he was safe, steady, reliable. The situation was a definite win-win.

She should be thrilled that he had asked her to a family wedding. This date, despite its risky nature, was the most positive she'd had in years and, at the age of twenty-nine, her biological clock was ticking.

She didn't know Lucas well. They had only met in the context of work over the past few days, with a "business" lunch at a nearby cafe tossed in, during which he had told her that not only did he need an escort for his brother's wedding, but that he was looking for a relationship with a view to marriage.

Like her, she didn't think Lucas had succumbed to any kind of intense physical attraction. He preferred to take a more measured approach.

If it were possible to control her emotions and fall in love with Lucas, she had already decided she would do it.

She checked her watch and frowned. They were leaving a little earlier than scheduled. If the pilot had only waited a few more minutes, Zane might have made it.

She squashed another whisper of disappointment and

snapped the window shutter closed. Witnessing the small jet launching itself into the dark, turbulent center of the storm was something she did not need to see.

The liftoff was bumpy. During the steep ascent, wind buffeted the jet and lightning flickered through the other windows of the cabin. When they finally leveled out, Lilah's nerves were stretched taut. She had taken a sedative before she had left her apartment, but so far it had failed to have any effect.

The stewardess, who had retreated to a separate compartment, reappeared and offered her a drink. With the cabin to herself, sleeping seemed the best option, so Lilah took another sedative. According to her doctor, one should have worked; two would definitely knock her out.

She was rereading Lucas's compatibility quotient, which was extremely high, her lids drooping, when a heavy crack of thunder shook the small jet. Lightning flashed. In that instant the door to the cockpit popped open. Zane Atraeus, tall, sleekly broad-shouldered and dressed in somber black, was framed in the searing flicker of light.

The jet lurched; the folder flew off her lap. The clasp sprang open as it hit the floor, scattering loose sheets. Lilah barely noticed. As always, her artist's eye was riveted. Zane's golden skin and chiseled face—which she had shamelessly, secretly, painted for the past two years—could have been lifted straight out of a Dalmasio oil. Even the imperfections, the subversive glint of the studs in his lobe, the faint disruption to the line of his nose, as if it had once been broken, were somehow… perfect.

She blinked as Zane strolled toward her. Her vision readjusted to the warm glow of the cabin lights. Until Zane had moved, she had not been entirely convinced that he was real. She thought she could have been caught up in one of the vivid, unsettling dreams that had disturbed her sleep ever since The Regrettable Episode two years ago.

Unlike the temporary effect of the lightning flash on her

vision, the events of that night had been indelibly seared into her consciousness. "I thought you missed the flight."

His steady dark gaze made her stomach tighten. "I never miss when I'm the pilot."

Aware that the contents of the folder had spilled into the aisle, and that the topmost sheet which held the glaringly large title, *The Wedding Plan,* was clearly visible, Lilah lunged forward in an attempt to regather the incriminating sheets. Her seat belt held her pinned. By the time she had the buckle unfastened, Zane had collected both the folder and the loose sheets.

Her cheeks burned as he straightened. She was certain he had read some of the contents, enough to get the gist of what they were about. She took the sheets and stuffed them back into the folder. "I didn't know you could fly."

"It's not something I advertise."

Unlike the lavish parties he regularly attended and the endless stream of gorgeous models he escorted. Although, flying did fit with his love of extreme sports: diving, kitesurfing and snowboarding, to name a few. Zane had a well-publicized love for anything that involved adrenaline.

It occurred to Lilah, as she jammed the folder in her tote bag, out of sight, that she didn't know what Lucas liked to do in his spare time. She must make the effort to find out.

Zane shrugged out of his jacket and tossed it over the arm of the seat across the aisle. "How long have you been afraid of flying?"

Lilah tore her gaze from the snug fit of his black T-shirt and the muscular swell of tanned biceps. She was certain that beyond an intoxicating whiff of sandalwood she could detect the scent of his skin.

Her blush deepened as she was momentarily flung back to the night of The Episode. Zane had suggested they go to an empty reception room so they could indulge their mutual passion for art by studying the oils displayed on the walls.

She couldn't remember much about the garish abstracts. She would never forget the moment Zane had pulled her close.

The clean, masculine scent of his skin and the exotic undernote of sandalwood had filled her nostrils, making her head spin. When he had kissed her, his taste had filled her mouth.

Somehow they had ended up on a wide, comfortable couch. At some point the bodice of her dress had drifted to her waist, a detail that should have alarmed her. Zane had taken one breast in his mouth and her whole body had coiled unbearably tight. She could remember clutching at his shoulders, a flash of dizzying, heated pleasure, the room shimmering out of focus.

If the door hadn't popped open at that moment and Zane's date, who was also his previous personal assistant, a gorgeous redhead called Gemma, hadn't walked in, Lilah shuddered to think what would have happened next. She had dragged her bodice up and clambered off the couch. By the time she had found her clutch, which had ended up underneath the couch, Zane had shrugged into his jacket. After a clipped good-night, he had left with Gemma.

The echoing silence after the heady, intimate passion had stung. He had not suggested they meet again, which had put The Episode in its horrifying context.

Zane had not wanted a relationship; he had just wanted an interlude. Sex. He had probably thought they had been on the verge of a one night stand, that she was *easy*.

Embarrassingly, she *had* forgotten every relationship rule she had rigidly stuck to for the twelve years she had been dating.

Zane walking out so quickly then never bothering to follow up with a telephone call or text had been a blessing. It had confirmed what she had both read about him and discovered firsthand—that no matter how attractive, he could not be trusted in a relationship. If he couldn't commit to a phone call, it was unlikely he would commit to marriage.

Another shuddering crash of thunder jerked her back to the present.

Aware that Zane was waiting for an answer, she busied herself fastening her seat belt. "I've been afraid of flying forever."

Instead of sitting where he'd slung his jacket, Zane lowered himself into the seat next to hers.

She stiffened as he pried her hand off the armrest. "What are you doing?"

His fingers curled warmly through hers. "Holding your hand. Tried-and-true remedy."

Nervous tension, along with the tingling heat of his touch, zinged through her at the skin-on-skin contact. There was something distinctly forbidden about holding hands with Zane Atraeus.

Illegitimate and wild, according to the tabloids, Zane had been the instant ruination of hundreds of women, and promised to be the ruination of even more in the future. She had the shattering firsthand knowledge of exactly how that ruination was achieved.

She flexed her fingers, but his hold didn't loosen. "Shouldn't you be in the cockpit?"

"Flight deck. There's a copilot, Spiros. He doesn't need me yet."

Her stomach clenched as she was suddenly reminded that they were twenty-eight thousand feet above the ground. "How long is the flight?"

"Twenty hours, give or take. We land in Singapore to refuel. If you don't like flying, why are you going to Medinos?"

Trying to arrange her future with a steady, reliable husband who would not leave her. Trying to avoid the Cole women's regrettable tendency to fall victim to the *coup de foudre*.

Her head started to swim, and it was not just the dizzying effect of the sandalwood. She remembered that she had taken two sedatives. "Trying to get a life. I'm twenty-nine."

She blinked. She was beginning to feel as if she was swimming in molasses. Had she actually told him her age?

"Twenty-nine doesn't seem so old to me."

She smothered a yawn and frowned at the defensive note in his voice.

"What did you take?"

Her lids slid closed. She gave him the name of the sedative.

"They'll knock you out. I can remember having them as a kid. After my father found me in L.A., we flew to Medinos. I was a handful. I didn't like flying, either."

Curiosity kept her on the surface of sleep, caught in the net of his deep, cool voice and fascinated by the dichotomy of his character. She had read his story on the charity website. One of the things she admired about Zane was that he happily revealed his past in order to help homeless kids.

"Put your head on my shoulder if you want."

The quiet offer sent a warning thrill through her. She considered leaning against the window, but the thought that the shutter might slide open and she would catch a view clear down to the ground was not pleasant. "No, thank you." She struggled to stay upright. "You're nicer than I thought."

"Tell me," he muttered, "I'm curious. You've known me for two years. How did you think I would be?"

Her lids flickered open. Exactly how he had been the night of the ball. Dangerous, sexy. *Hot.*

With an effort of will, she controlled her mind, which had shot off on a very wrong tangent. Zane had probably been in intimate situations with more women than he could count. She doubted he would even remember how close they had come to making love. Or that she had actually—

She cut short that disturbing thought and searched for something polite to say. As an Atraeus, Zane was one of her employers now. She would have to adjust to the new dynamic.

Her stomach tensed at a thought she had cheerfully glossed over before. If she and Lucas married, their relationship would be even closer; he would be her brother-in-law. "Uh—for a start, I didn't think you even liked me."

"Was that after what happened on the couch or before?"

The flashback to the sensations that had flooded her that night was electrifying. From the knowing gleam in Zane's gaze, she was abruptly certain he knew exactly what had happened.

Embarrassed heat warmed her cheeks. He had been lying on top of her at the time. She would be naive to consider that he had not noticed that she had lost control and actually had an orgasm.

He had to know also that if Gemma hadn't turned up dangling car keys and making them jump guiltily apart, that she had been on the verge of making an even bigger mistake. "I'm surprised you remember."

"Lucas won't marry you."

The sudden change of topic jerked her lids open. The dark fire burning in Zane's eyes almost made her forget what she was about to say. "Lucas isn't the only one with a choice."

"Choose someone else."

Lilah's heart slammed against the wall of her chest. For a split second, she'd had the crazy thought that Zane had been about to say, "Choose *me*."

From an early age she had discovered that men liked the way she looked. Something in the slant of her eyes, the curve of her cheekbones, the shape of her mouth, spelled sexual allure. On occasion attraction had spilled over into an uncomfortable fascination, although she had never thought that Zane Atraeus would find her more than ordinarily attractive.

She dragged in a lungful of air and tried to deny the heart-pounding knowledge that behind the grim tone Zane Atraeus really did want her. "What gives you the right?"

"This."

Zane bent toward her, his head dipped. Her pulse rate rocketed.

For two years she had tortured herself about her loss of control. Now, finally, she was being offered the chance to examine what, exactly, had gone wrong.

She caught another enticing whiff of clean skin and exotic cologne. Dimly, she noted that the concept of her ruination had receded, a dangerous sign, although she was still in control. She had time to shift in her seat. If she wanted she could turn her head—

Warm fingers gripped her chin. The pressure of his mouth on hers almost stopped her heart.

Suddenly, the electrical hum every time he looked at her coalesced into stunning truth. The double whammy of her ticking biological clock combined with prolonged celibacy was the reason she was having such a difficult time controlling her responses to Zane.

Relief surged through her. She didn't know why she hadn't thought about that two years ago. It was the logical explanation. Zane had caught her at a vulnerable moment at the charity ball. She simply hadn't had the resources to resist him.

Jerking back from the seductive softness of the kiss, Lilah gulped in air.

The experience had been so riveting that the harder she had tried to suppress the memories, the more aggressively they had surfaced—in her dreams, her painting.

She had to get a grip on herself. She could not afford to take him seriously. According to the tabloids, the youngest Atraeus brother was the dark side of the mega wealthy Atraeus family, wild and dangerous to know, the bad as opposed to the good.

Which only went to prove that her judgment when it came to men was no better than her mother's or her grandmother's before her.

A little wildly she decided that the attraction was no bigger a deal for Zane than it had been two years ago. But that didn't change the disturbing knowledge that, if anything, she was in an even more vulnerable position now. The sensations already coursing through her body had the potential to destroy the future she had mapped out for herself.

She could not let that happen.

She was strong-willed. She had steered clear of intense emotions and casual flings all of her adult life. She was not going to mess up now.

With a younger man.

Zane was twenty-four, twenty-five at most, and with no sign of tempering his fast, edgy lifestyle with the encumbrances of a wife and family. He could say what he liked about his brother, but on paper, Lucas *was* perfect. He was older, more mature, ready to commit and without the wild reputation.

Those minutes on the couch with Zane and the experience of losing control and almost giving herself to a man who had demonstrated that he did not care for her had been salutary.

She knew the danger of her weakness now. On top of the healthy sex drive that came with her Cole genes, her biological clock was ticking loudly in both ears.

The thought that Zane could make her pregnant sent a hot flash through her that momentarily welded her to the seat before she managed to dismiss the notion.

Zane was not husband material. All she had to do was ignore the magnetic power of the attraction and her raging hormones, ignore the destructive impulse to throw her wedding plan away.

And throw herself beneath Zane's naked body.

Three

After a formal family dinner at the Atraeus family's Medinian castello the following evening, Lilah excused herself from the table while coffee was being served. Lucas had left some twenty minutes earlier, during dessert. His defection had been no great surprise because through the course of the evening she had become grimly certain that he was involved with another woman.

After obtaining directions from one of the kitchen staff, she paused by the door to Lucas's private suite. Stiffening her shoulders against the chill of the Mediterranean fortress walls, she rapped on the imposing door.

Lean brown fingers manacled her wrist. "I wouldn't go in there if I were you."

Lilah spun, shocked by the deep, cool voice and the knowledge that Zane had left the dinner table and followed her.

Snatching her wrist back, she rubbed at the bare skin, which still tingled and burned from his grip.

She dragged her gaze from his overlong jet-black hair and

the trio of studs glinting in one lobe. An unwanted surge of awareness added to the tension that had gripped her ever since she had arrived at the castello that evening and seen Lucas in the arms of Carla Ambrosi.

Lucas and Carla had a short but well-publicized past, which Lilah had mistakenly believed to be invented media hype. To further complicate things, Carla was Lilah's immediate boss.

Zane indicated the closed door. "Haven't you figured it out yet? Lucas is…busy."

The startling notion that, beneath the casual facade, Zane was quietly angry was shattered by the distant sound of laughter and the tap of high heels. More guests leaving the dining table, no doubt in search of one of the castello's bathrooms.

Suddenly, the stunning risk Lilah had taken in traveling thousands of miles for a first date with an extremely wealthy man whose love life was of interest to the tabloids came back to haunt her. He had fulfilled all of the criteria of her system. Now things were going disastrously wrong.

Zane jerked his head in the direction of the approaching guests. "I take it you don't want to be discovered knocking on Lucas's bedroom door?"

A wave of embarrassed heat decimated the chill. "No."

"Finally, some sense." Zane's fingers curled around her wrist again.

The startling intimacy of the hold sent another tingling jolt through her. A split second later, heart pounding with nerves, she found herself crushed against Zane's side and flattened against the cold stone of an alcove. She inhaled, bracing herself against the effect of the sandalwood and the sudden, nervous desire to laugh.

As unpleasant as the evening had been she couldn't suppress a small thrill that Zane had come to her rescue. Now they were hiding like a couple of kids.

Zane leaned out and peered around a corner. When he settled back into place she discovered that she had missed the warmth of his body.

His dark gaze touched on hers. "What I don't get is why Lucas asked you."

Lilah stiffened at the implication that she was the last person Lucas should have asked to partner him at a family wedding.

Determinedly, she stamped on the soft core of hurt that had haunted her since she was a kid—that her illegitimate birth and the poverty of her background made her less than respectable. "You certainly know how to make a girl feel special."

He frowned. "That wasn't what I meant."

"Don't worry." She dragged her gaze free from the dangerous, too-knowing sympathy in his. "I have no problems with the reality check."

She just wished she had thought things through before she had left home. Labeled "Catch of the Year" in a prominent women's magazine, Lucas *had* been too good to be true.

Somewhere in the distance a door snapped shut, cutting off the sound of footsteps and laughter. The abrupt return to silence made Lilah doubly aware of the masculine heat emanating from Zane's body and that the pale pearlized silk of her gown suddenly seemed too thin, the scooped neckline too revealing.

Hot color flooded her cheeks as the stressed uncertainty that had driven her to go in search of Lucas, and the truth, gave way to the searing memory of the kiss on the flight out.

The sedatives she had taken had kicked in shortly afterward. She had not seen Zane again until they had landed in Singapore, where two more passengers, clients of The Atraeus Group, had boarded the jet. Courtesy of the extra passengers, the rest of the flight had been uneventful. During the customs procedures, aware that Zane had been keeping tabs on her, she had managed to separate herself from him and had taken a taxi to her hotel.

Zane checked the corridor again. "All clear, and your reputation intact."

"Unfortunately, my reputation is already shredded."

That was the risk she had accepted in traveling thousands of miles on a first date with her billionaire boss. She hadn't yet had time to formulate the full extent of the damage this would do to her marriage plan. Her only hope was that the other men on her list didn't read the gutter press.

Jaw locked, she marched to the door of Lucas's suite and rapped again.

Zane leaned one broad shoulder against the door frame, arms folded across his chest. "You don't give up easily, do you?"

Lilah tried not to notice the way the dim light of an antique wall lamp flared across his taut, molded cheekbones, the tough line of his jaw. "I prefer the direct approach."

"Just remember I tried to save you."

The door eased open a few inches. Lucas Atraeus, tall and darkly handsome in evening clothes, was framed in the wash of lamplight.

The small flare of anger that had driven her back to his door leaped a little higher. She had expected Lucas to be somehow diminished in appearance. It didn't help that he still looked heartbreakingly perfect.

The conversation was brief, punctuated by a glimpse of Carla Ambrosi, the woman Lilah realized Lucas truly wanted, hurriedly setting her clothing to rights. In that moment any idea that she could retrieve the situation and persevere with Lucas dissolved.

Gripping the door handle, Lilah wrenched the solid mahogany door closed, cutting Lucas off. In the process the strap of her evening bag flew off her shoulder. Beads scattered as the pretty purse hit the flagstones.

Silence reigned in the corridor for long, nervy seconds. Lilah tried to avoid Zane's gaze. She was so not grieving for the relationship. Somehow she had never managed to get emotionally involved with Lucas. "You knew all along."

He picked up the purse and a number of glittering beads and handed them to her. "They've got a history."

Lilah slipped the little beads into the clutch. “I read the stories two years ago. I guess I should have included the information in my—”

“Wedding planner?”

Her gaze snapped to his. “*Process*. My woman’s intuition must have been taking a mini-break.”

He lifted a brow. “Don’t expect me to apologize for being in touch with my feminine side.”

The ridiculous concept of Zane Atraeus possessing any feminine trait broke the tension. “You don’t have a feminine side.”

A sudden thought blindsided her. Zane in his position as The Atraeus Group’s troubleshooter *was* used to handling difficult situations. And employees. “You’re running interference for Lucas.”

It made perfect sense. With Carla in the mix, Lucas had hedged his bets and asked Zane to fly her out. Now Zane had stepped in to stop her making a scene. It placed her in the realms of being “a problem.”

“No.”

The flatness of Zane’s denial was reassuring. His motives shouldn’t matter, but suddenly they very palpably did. She couldn’t bear the thought that she was just another embarrassing, or worse, scandalous, situation that Zane was “fixing.”

In the distance a door opened. The sharp tap of heels on flagstones, the clatter of dishes, broke the moment.

Zane straightened away from the wall. “You could do with a drink.” His hand cupped her elbow. “Somewhere quiet.”

The heat of his palm against her bare skin distracted Lilah enough that she allowed him to propel her down the corridor.

Seconds later, Zane opened a door and allowed her to precede him. Lilah stepped into a sitting room decorated in the spare Medinian way, with cream-washed walls, dark furniture and jewel-bright rugs scattered on a flagstone floor. A series of rich oils, no doubt depicting various Atraeus ancestors, decorated the walls. French doors opened out on to one of the many stone terraces that rimmed the castello, affording expansive views of a moonlit Mediterranean sea.

Zane splashed what looked like brandy into a glass. “When did you realize about Lucas and Carla?”

She loosened her death grip on her clutch. “When we arrived at the castello and Carla flung herself into Lucas’s arms.”

“Then why go to Lucas’s room when you had to know what you would find?”

The question, along with the piercing gaze that went with it, was unsettling. She was once again struck by the notion that beneath the urbane exterior Zane was quietly, coldly angry. “I’d had enough of feeling uncomfortable and out of place. Dinner was over and I was tired. I wanted to go back to the hotel.”

He pressed the glass into her hands. “With Lucas.”

The brush of his fingers sent another zing of awareness through her. “No. Alone.”

She sipped brandy and tensed as it burned her throat. She was not about to explain to Zane that she had not gotten as far as thinking about the physical realities of a relationship with his brother. She had assumed all of that would fall into place as they went along. “I put a higher price on myself than that.”

“Marriage.”

She almost choked on another swallow of brandy. “That’s the general idea.”

Fingers tightening on the glass, she strolled closer to the paintings, as always drawn by color and composition, the nuances of technique. Jewelry design was her trade, but painting had always been her first love.

She paused beneath an oil of a fierce, medieval warrior, an onyx seal ring on one finger, a scimitar strapped to his back. The straight blade of a nose, tough jaw and magnetic dark gaze were a mirror of Zane’s.

Seated beside the warrior was his lady, wearing a parchment silk gown, her exotic gaze square on to the viewer, giving the impression of quiet, steely strength. Lilah was guessing that being married to the brigand beside her, she would need it. An exquisite diamond and emerald ring graced one slim finger; around her neck was a matching pendant.

She felt the heat from Zane's body all down one side as he came to stand beside her. The intangible electrical current that hummed through her whenever he was near grew perceptibly stronger.

Lilah swallowed another mouthful of brandy and tried to ignore the disruptive sensations. The warmth in the pit of her stomach extended to a faint dizziness in her head, reminding her that she had barely eaten at dinner and had already sipped too much wine. She stepped closer to study the jewelry the woman was wearing.

"The Illium jewels."

Lilah frowned, frustrated by the lack of fine detail in the painting. "From Troy? I thought they were a myth."

"They got sold off at the turn of last century when the family went broke. My father managed to buy them back from a private collector."

Lilah noticed the detail of a ship in the background of the painting. "A pirate?"

"A privateer," Zane corrected. "During the eighteen hundreds his seafaring exploits were a major source of wealth for the Atraeus family."

Lilah ignored Zane's smooth explanation. After a brief foray into Medinian history, she had gleaned enough information about the Atraeus family to know that the dark and dangerous ancestor had been a pirate by any other name.

She stepped back from the oil painting in order to appreciate its rich colors. The play of light over the warrior's dark features suddenly made him seem breathtakingly familiar. Exchange the robes, soft boots and a scimitar for a suit and an expensive black shirt and it was Zane. "What was his name?"

"Zander Atraeus, my namesake, near enough. Although my mother didn't have a clue about my father's family history." He turned away. "Finish your drink. I'll take you back to your hotel."

She followed Zane to the sideboard and set her empty brandy glass down. She noticed the glint of the seal ring on the middle finger of Zane's left hand. "Your ring looks identical to the one in the painting."

"It is." His reply was clipped, and she wondered what she had said to cause the cool distance.

Suddenly she understood and busied herself extracting her cell from her clutch. She knew only too well what it was like to be an illegitimate child and excluded from her father's family. As much as she had tried to dismiss that side of the family from her psyche, they still existed and the hurt remained.

"You don't have to take me back to the hotel. I can call a cab." Unfortunately, the screen of her cell was cracked and the phone no longer appeared to work. It must have happened when her purse had gone flying.

Zane checked his watch. "Even if the phone worked, you wouldn't get a cab after midnight on Medinos."

Her stomach sank. She was a city girl; she loved shops, good coffee, public transportation. All the good-natured warnings friends had given her about traveling to a foreign country that was still partway buried in the Middle Ages were coming home to roost. "No underground?"

A flash of amusement lit his dark gaze. "All I can offer is a ride in a Ferrari."

Her stomach tightened on the slew of graphic images that went with climbing into a powerful sports car with Zane Atraeus. It was up there with Persephone accepting a ride from Hades. "Thanks, but no thanks. You don't need to feel responsible for me."

Zane's expression hardened. "Lucas won't be taking you back to the hotel."

Her chin jerked up. "I did get that part." She had been stupidly naive, but not anymore. "Okay, I'll accept the lift to my hotel, but that's all."

Zane's fingers brushed hers as he took her empty glass. "Good. Don't throw yourself away on a man who doesn't value you."

"Don't worry." She stepped back, unnerved by how tempted she was to stay close. "I know exactly how much I'm worth."

She realized how cool and hard that phrase had sounded. "I didn't mean that to sound…like it did."

His expression was neutral. "I'm sure you didn't."

Another memory surfaced. Two weeks after "the kiss," at another function, Zane had found her politely trying to fend off her friend and escort's boss.

She could still remember the hot tingle down her spine, the sudden utter unimportance of the older man who had decided she was desperate to spend the night with him. For an exhilarating moment she had been certain Zane had followed her because he wanted to follow up on the shattering connection she had felt when they had kissed.

Instead, his gaze had flowed through her as if she didn't exist. He had turned on his heel and left.

In a flash of clarity she finally understood why she had agreed to travel to Medinos with a man she barely knew.

The date had been with Lucas, but it was Zane she had always wanted.

In her search for Mr. Dependable she had somehow managed to fixate on his exact opposite.

Lucas had been an unknown quantity and out of her league, but he was nothing compared to Zane. With Zane there would be no guarantees, no safety net, no commitment. The exact opposite of what she had planned for and needed in her life.

Four

Ten days later, Zane stepped into the darkened offices of The Atraeus Group's newest acquisition, Ambrosi Pearls in Sydney. He took the antique elevator, which matched the once-elegant facade of the building, to the top floor.

It was almost midnight; most of the building was plunged into darkness. Zane, who was more used to mining and construction sites and masculine boardrooms, shook his head in bemusement as he strolled into Lucas's office. The air was perfumed; the decor white-on-white. It looked like it had been designed for the editor of a high-end fashion magazine. He noted there was actually a pile of glossy fashion magazines on one end of the curvy designer desk.

Lucas turned from his perusal of downtown Sydney. His hair was ruffled as if he'd run his fingers through it, and his tie was askew. He looked as disgruntled as Zane felt coming off a long flight from Florida.

Zane checked his watch. It was midnight. By his calculations he had been awake almost thirty-six hours. "Why the cloak-and-dagger?"

Lucas stripped off his tie and stuffed the red silk into his pocket. “I’ve decided to marry Carla. The press is already on the hunt. I’ve been trying to do a little damage control, but Lilah’s going to come under pressure.”

Zane’s tiredness evaporated. Now the midnight meeting at the office made sense. Lucas’s apartment had probably been staked out by the press. “I thought you and Lilah were over.”

If he had thought anything else he would not have gone back to Florida to close the land deal. He would have sent someone else.

Lucas paced to the desk, checked the screen of an ice-cream pink cell as if he was waiting for a text, then rifled through a drawer. He came up with a business card. “We are over, but try telling that to the press.”

He scribbled a number on the card. “Lilah came to my apartment. She was followed.”

Zane took the card. If he thought he had controlled the possessive jealousy that had eaten into him ever since Constantine’s wedding, in that moment he knew he was wrong. “What was Lilah doing at your apartment?”

Lucas frowned at the pink cell as if something about it was stressing him to the max. “I’m not sure. Carla was there. Lilah left before I could talk to her. The point is, I need you to mind her for me again.”

In terse sentences, Lucas described how a reporter had snapped photos of him kissing Carla out on the sidewalk, with Lilah looking on. The pictures would be published in the morning paper.

Every muscle in Zane’s body tensed at the knowledge that Lucas and Lilah were still connected, even if it was only by scandal.

During Constantine’s wedding, which Lilah had attended because she had not been able to get a flight out until the following Monday, she had made it clear she was “off” all things Atraeus. Zane had not enjoyed being shut out, but at least he’d had the satisfaction of knowing Lilah was over Lucas.

He wondered what had changed her mind to the extent that she had actually gone to Lucas's apartment. Grimly, he controlled the cavemanlike urge to grab Lucas by his shirtfront, shove him against the wall and demand that he leave Lilah Cole alone. "She won't like it."

Lucas's expression was distracted. "She'll adjust. She's being well compensated."

Zane went still inside. "How, exactly?"

Lucas shuffled papers. "The usual currency. Money, promotion."

Zane could feel his blood pressure rocketing. "Carla won't like that."

"Tell me about it." Lucas shot him a tired grin. "Women. It's a juggling act."

And one in which Lucas, with his killer charm, had always excelled.

Suspicion coalesced into certainty. Despite the engagement to Carla, Zane was certain that Lilah *was* still in the picture for Lucas. Maybe he had it all wrong, but he couldn't allow himself to forget that Lucas had bought Lilah an engagement ring.

He could still see the catalog picture Elena had shown him. The solitaire had been large and flawless. Personally, he had thought the chunky diamond had been a mistake. He would have chosen something antique and lavish, maybe with a few emeralds on the side to match her eyes.

Zane's jaw clenched against the fiery urge to demand to know why, now that Lucas was engaged to Carla, he couldn't leave Lilah Cole alone.

Irrelevant question. Atraeus men had a long, well-publicized history of womanizing. He should know; he was the product of a liaison.

Letting out a breath, Zane forced himself to relax. "How long do you want me to mind her this time?"

Lucas shrugged. "The weekend. Long enough to get her through the media frenzy that's going to break following the announcement at the press conference—" he checked his watch "—today."

Zane's temper frayed at the possessive concern in Lucas's voice. "Sure. We got on okay on Medinos." He drilled Lucas with another cold look. "I think she likes me."

Lucas looked relieved. "Great, I owe you one. I know Lilah isn't your normal type."

Zane's brows jerked together. "What do you mean, not my type?"

Lucas placed his briefcase on the desk and began loading files into it. "Lilah's into classical music; she's arty. I think she paints."

"She does. *I* like art and classical music."

He snapped the case closed. "She's older."

Lucas made the age gap sound like an unbridgeable abyss. "Five years is not a big gap."

Lucas's cell broke into a catchy tango.

Jaw compressed, Zane watched as Lucas snatched up thc phone. "Nice tune. Bolero."

Lucas shrugged. "I wouldn't know. This is my secretary's phone. Mine's, uh, broken." He held the cell against his ear and lifted a hand in dismissal. "Hey, thanks."

"Not a problem." Jaw taut, Zane took the creaking elevator to the ground floor. If he had stayed in the office with Lucas much longer he might have lost his temper. He had learned long ago that losing control was the equivalent of losing, and with Lilah Cole he did not intend to lose.

He had to focus, concentrate.

A whole weekend. Two days, *and nights.*

With a woman so committed to marriage she had written a blueprint for success and developed a points system for the men who had scored highly enough to make it into her folder.

Lilah slid dark glasses onto the bridge of her nose and braced herself as she stepped out of her taxi into the midmorning heat of downtown Sydney. Two steps toward the impressive doors of the hotel where the press conference was being held, and a maelstrom of flashing cameras and shouted questions broke over her.

Cheeks hot with embarrassment, she tightened her grip on the ivory handbag that matched her stylish suit, and plowed forward. Someone tugged at the sleeve of her jacket; a flash blinded her. A split second later the grip on her arm and the reporter were miraculously removed, replaced by the burly back of a uniformed security guard. The mass of reporters parted and Zane Atraeus's dark gaze burned into hers, oddly calm and assessing in the midst of chaos. Despite her determination to remain calm in his presence, to forget the kiss, a hot thrill shot down her spine.

"Lilah, come with me."

For a split second she thought he had said, "Lilah, come to me," and the vivid intensity of her reaction to the low, husky command was paralyzing.

She had already had two negative experiences with Atraeus males. Now wasn't the time to redefine that old cliché by fantasizing about jumping out of the frying pan and into the fire, again.

The media surged against the wall of security, an elbow jabbed her back. She clutched Zane's outstretched hand. He released her fingers almost immediately and scooped her against his side, his muscled heat burning into her as they walked.

Three swift steps. The glass doors gleamed ahead. A camera flashed. "Oh, good. More scandal."

She caught the edge of Zane's grin. "That's what you get when you play with an Atraeus."

The hotel doors swished wide. More media were inside, along with curious hotel staff and guests. Lilah worked to keep her expression serene, although she was uncomfortably aware that her cheeks were burning. "I didn't 'play' with anyone."

"You went to Medinos. That was some first date."

The nervy thrill of Zane turning up to protect her evaporated. "I didn't exactly enjoy the experience."

As first dates went it had been an utter disaster.

Zane ushered her into an open elevator. The heat of his palm at the small of her back sent a small shock of awareness through her. Two large Medinian security guards stepped in on either side of them. A third man, blocky and muscled with a shaven head, whom she recognized as Spiros, took up a position by the door and punched buttons.

Lilah's ruffled unease at Zane's closeness increased as the elevator shot upward. "I suppose you're in Sydney for the charity art auction?"

"I'm also doing some work on the Ambrosi takeover, which is why Lucas asked me to mind you."

The last remnants of the intense thrill she had felt when Zane had come looking for her died a death. "I suppose Lucas told you what happened last night?"

"He said you found him with Carla at his apartment."

Lilah's blush deepened. Zane made it sound like she had been involved in some kind of trashy love triangle. "I didn't make it to his apartment. Security—"

"You don't have to explain."

Lilah's gaze narrowed. The surface calm she had been clinging to all morning, ever since she had seen the morning paper, shredded. "Since Medinos, I haven't been able to get an appointment to see Lucas. I got tired of waiting. I was there to resign."

The doors slid open. Adrenaline pumped when she saw the contingent of press in the lobby of the concierge floor, although these weren't the sharp-eyed paparazzi who had been out on the street. She recognized magazine editors, serious tabloids, television news crews.

She took a deep breath as they stepped out of the elevator in the wake of the security team.

Zane's fingers locked around her wrist. "If you run now, what they'll print will be worse."

"Any worse than 'Discarded Atraeus Mistress Abandoned on Street'?"

Zane's expression was grim. "You should have known Lucas was playing out of your league."

Something inside her snapped. "Is it too late to say I wish I'd never met Lucas?"

The moment was freeing. She realized she had never actually connected with Lucas on an emotional level. Marriage with him would have been a disaster.

Zane's gaze captured hers, making her heart pound. "How worried are you about the media?"

Lilah blinked. The focused heat in Zane's eyes was having a mesmerizing effect. "I don't have a TV and I canceled my newspaper subscription this morning. Dealing with the media is not my thing."

"Is this?"

His jaw brushed her forehead. Tendrils of heat shimmered through her at the unexpected contact. His hands framed her face. Dimly, she registered that he intended to kiss her. In the midst of the hum of security, press and hotel staff, time seemed to slow, stop. She was spun back two years to the seductive quiet of the empty reception room, eleven days ago to the flight to Medinos.

She dragged in a shallow breath. She needed to step back, calm down, forget the crazy attraction that zinged through her every time she was near Zane. Constantine and Lucas had both gone through gorgeous women like hot knives through butter, but Zane had a reputation that scorched.

His breath feathered her lips. She closed her eyes and his mouth touched hers, seducingly warm and soft. A shock wave of heat shimmered out from that one small point of contact.

He lifted his head. His gaze, veiled by inky lashes, locked on hers. Instead of straightening, his hands dropped to her waist. The heat from his palms burned through the finely tailored silk as he drew her closer.

The motorized whirr of cameras and the buzz of conversation receded as she clutched at Zane's shoulders and angled her jaw, allowing him more comfortable access. This time the kiss was firmer, heated, deliberate, sizzling all the way to her toes. By the time Zane lifted his mouth, her head was spinning and her legs felt as limp as noodles.

The smattering of applause and wolf whistles shunted her back to earth. She stared at the forest of microphones trying to break through the wall of security, her wild moment of rebellion evaporating.

The phrase "out of the frying pan and into the fire" once more reverberated through her. "Now they'll think I'm sleeping with you as well."

Zane's arm locked around her waist as he propelled her through the reporters and into the room in which the press conference was being held. "Think of it this way, if you're with me, at least now they'll wonder who dumped whom."

Forty-five minutes later the official part of the press conference was over. Lucas and Carla, Lucas's mother, Maria Therese, and Constantine's P.A. Tomas had left in a flurry of publicity over their engagement announcement and the further announcement that Sienna and Constantine were expecting a baby.

Zane flowed smoothly to his feet. "Now we leave."

Relieved that Lucas's announcement had taken the unnerving focus of the press off her, Lilah hooked the strap of her handbag over her shoulder.

Two steps onto the still crowded floor and an elegant blonde backed by a TV crew shoved a mike at Zane. "Can we expect another engagement announcement soon?"

"No comment." Zane lengthened his stride, bypassing the TV crew and the question as he propelled her toward the elevator.

Even though Lilah knew that Zane's lack of response was the only sensible option, his comment left her feeling oddly flat and definitely manipulated.

The end of the nonrelationship with Lucas had not mattered. Standing on the pavement the previous evening while a reporter had snapped her witnessing Lucas and Carla locked in a passionate clinch had not been a feel-good moment. But, as embarrassing as her association with Zane's brother had turned out to be, after the toe-curling intimacy of the kisses in front of the media, in that moment she felt the most betrayed by Zane.

Five

Zane hustled Lilah out into a private underground parking lot and opened the door of a gleaming, low-slung black Corvette. He waited for Lilah to climb into the passenger-side seat then walked around the vehicle and slid behind the wheel.

He had been annoyed enough with Lucas to want to stake a claim on Lilah, although he hadn't planned on doing it in quite such a public way.

He also hadn't expected Lilah to kiss him back quite so enthusiastically. Although ever since they had hit the elevator on the way down she had been cool and reserved and irritatingly distant.

He lifted a hand as Spiros and the two security guards climbed into a black sedan.

He fastened his seat belt. The back of his hand brushed Lilah's. The automatic jolt he received from the brush of her skin against his increased his irritable temper. A temper that, just days ago, he had not known he'd possessed.

The dark sedan the bodyguards had climbed into cruised

out of the parking building. Seconds later, Zane followed, emerging into the glare of daylight.

He transferred his gaze to the woman beside him. Dressed in her signature ivory and white, her hair smoothed into a loose, elegant confection on top of her head, smooth teardrop pearls dangling from tiny lobes, Lilah looked both cool and drop-dead sexy. The fact that he had kissed off her lipstick, leaving her lips bare, only succeeded in making her even more sensually alluring.

Grimly he noted that the same addictive fascination that had tempted him to lose his head two years ago was still at work. Lilah Cole was openly and unashamedly husband-hunting. She was the kind of woman he couldn't afford in his life, and yet it seemed he couldn't resist her.

Lilah stared straight ahead, her purse gripped in her lap. "I know I've been invited to lunch with your family, but with everything that's happened, maybe that isn't such a good idea. If you drop me off, I can get a taxi back to the office."

Zane's jaw tightened at the subdued, worried note in Lilah's voice. Lucas should have known better; he should have left her alone. "It's lunchtime. You need to eat."

She looked out of the passenger window. "I had cereal and toast for breakfast. I'm not exactly hungry."

Zane found the thought of Lilah crunching her way through cereal and toast before facing the press oddly endearing. He wondered what kind of cereal she ate then crushed his curiosity about her.

He braked for a set of lights. "Lucas would probably be relieved if you didn't show."

The words were ruthless, but he had gotten used to seeing Lilah calm and businesslike, with all her ducks in a row. For two years it had been a quality that had irritated him profoundly. Incomprehensibly, he now found himself looking for ways to get her back to her normal, ultraorganized self.

Her gaze snapped to his. "What Lucas wants or does not want is of no concern to me."

Zane felt suddenly happier than he had in days. The lights changed, he put the car in gear and accelerated through the intersection. "I can take you somewhere else to eat if you want."

Her head whipped around, her green gaze shooting fire. "On second thought, no."

"Good. Because we're here."

He watched Lilah study the elegant portico of the Michelin star restaurant as if the fluted columns represented the gates of Hades. "You're a manipulative man."

"I'm an Atraeus."

"Sometimes I forget."

He found himself instantly on the defensive. "Because I'm also a Salvatore?"

He did not voice the other lurking fear that had reared its head since his conversation with Lucas, that it was because he was only twenty-four.

She frowned, as if his shadowy past had not occurred to her. "Because sometimes you're…nice."

"Nice." His brows jerked together.

She looked embarrassed. "I read the article about you on the charity website. I know that you wear those three earrings to help kids relate to you when you do counseling work. You can try all you like to prove otherwise but, from where I come from, that's *nice*."

Lilah breathed a sigh of relief when Zane pulled in at her apartment's tiny parking area. Lunch had been just as stilted and uncomfortable as she had imagined. Thankfully, the service had been ultraquick and they had been able to leave early.

Zane walked around and opened her door. Lilah climbed out of the low bucket seat, acutely aware of the shadowy cleavage visible in the V of her jacket and of the length of thigh exposed by the shortness of her skirt. When she had dressed that morning, the suit had seemed elegant and circumspect but it was not made for struggling out of a low slung 'Vette.

Zane's gaze locked with hers, making her feel breathless.

She clamped down on the uncharacteristic desire to boldly meet his gaze.

Arriving at the front door of her apartment with a man was what she liked to refer to as a dating "red zone." She and Zane were not dating, but the situation had somehow become more fraught than any dating scenario she had ever experienced. After the kiss earlier, it would not be a good idea to allow Zane inside her house.

She gave him a bright, professional smile. "It's okay, you don't have to see me in. Thanks for the lift."

Zane closed the 'Vette's door and depressed the key lock. "Not a problem. I'll see you to your door."

"That won't be necessary." She aimed another smile somewhere in his general direction as she rummaged in her handbag for her door key.

Zane fell into step beside her. "If I'm not mistaken, that's a reporter staked out over there."

Lilah's head jerked up. She recognized the car that had been parked outside of Lucas's apartment the previous night. Her heart sank. "He must have followed us."

"The car was here when we arrived. According to Lucas, *you* were the one who was followed last night. The press has probably been staking you out ever since you returned from Medinos. In which case, I'd better see you safely inside."

Resigning herself, Lilah walked quickly to the large garage-style door, her cheeks warming as she saw the down-at-heel building through Zane's eyes. A converted warehouse in one of the shabbier suburbs, she had chosen the building because it had been cheerful, arty and spectacularly cheap. The ground floor apartment included a huge light-filled north-facing room that was perfect for painting.

Zane, thankfully, didn't seem to notice how shabby the exterior was, a reminder that he had not spent all of his life in luxurious surroundings.

Unlocking the door, she stepped inside the nondescript foyer, with its concrete floors and cream-washed walls.

Zane slid the door to enclose them in the shadowy space. "How many people live here?"

"A dozen or so." She led the way down a narrow, dim corridor and unlocked her front door. Made of unprepossessing sheet metal, it had once led to some kind of workshop.

She stepped into her large sitting room, conscious of Zane's gaze as he took in white walls, glowing wooden floors and the afternoon sun flooding through a bank of bifold doors at one end.

"Nice." He closed the door and strolled into the center of the room, his gaze assessing the paintings she'd collected from friends and family over the years.

He studied a series of three abstracts propped against one wall. "These are yours."

Her gaze gravitated to the mesmerizingly clean lines of his profile as he studied one of the abstracts. "How do you know that?" She had gotten the paintings ready for sale, but hadn't gotten around to signing them yet.

Faint color rimmed his cheekbones. "I've bought a couple at auction. I also saw your work in a gallery a few weeks back."

A small shock went through her that he had actually bought some of her paintings. "I usually sell most of what I paint through the gallery."

He straightened and peered at a framed photograph of her mother and grandmother. "So money's important."

Her jaw firmed. "Yes."

There was no point in hiding it. Following the recent finance company crashes, her mother's careful life savings had dissolved overnight, leaving her with a mortgage she couldn't pay. Subsisting on a part-time wage, which was all her mother could get in Broome, money had become vital.

Lilah hadn't hesitated. The regular sale of her paintings supplemented her income just enough that she was managing to pay her mother's mortgage as well as cover her rent, but only just.

Her failure to present her resignation to Lucas the previous evening was, in a way, a relief. Resigning from Ambrosi Pearls now would not be a good move for either her or her mother.

A crashing sound jerked her head around. Dropping her bag on the couch, she raced through to her studio in time to glimpse a young man dressed in jeans and a T-shirt, a camera slung over his shoulder, as he clambered out through an open window. A split second later, Zane flowed past her, stepped over a stack of canvases that had been knocked to the floor, and followed the intruder out of the window.

Zane caught the reporter as he hung awkwardly on her back fence. With slick, practiced moves he took the memory stick from the camera and shoved what was clearly an expensive piece of equipment back at the reporter's chest.

The now white-faced reporter scrambled over the fence and disappeared into the sports field on the other side.

While Zane examined the fence and walked the boundary of her tiny back garden, Lilah hurriedly tidied up the collapsed pile of canvases.

Her worst fears were confirmed when she discovered a portrait of Zane she had painted almost two years ago, after the disastrous episode on the couch. Zane had practically stepped over the oil to get out of the window. It was a miracle he hadn't noticed.

Gathering the canvases, she stacked them against the nearest wall, so only the backs were visible. She'd had a lucky escape. The last thing she needed now was for Zane to find out that she had harbored a quiet, unhealthy little obsession about him for the past two years.

Zane climbed back in the window and examined the broken catch. "That's it, you're not staying here tonight. You're coming with me. If that reporter made it into your back garden, others will."

Lilah's response was unequivocal. Given that Zane seemed to bring out her wild Cole side, going with him was a very bad idea.

Her cheeks burned as he stared at the backs of the paintings. "That won't be necessary. I'll get the window repaired. I've got a friend in the building who's handy with tools."

She led the way out of the room, away from the incriminating paintings.

His expression grim, Zane checked the locks on the windows of her main living room. "Your studio window is the least of your problems. You've got a sports field next door. That means plenty of off-road parking and unlimited access. Even with a security detail keeping watch front and back, the press won't have any problems getting pictures through all this glass."

"I can draw the curtains. They can't take pictures if there's nothing to see."

"You'll get harassed every time you walk outside or leave the house, and that fence is a major problem. Put it this way, if you don't come with me now, I'm staying here with you." He studied her plain black leather couch as if he was eyeing it up for size.

Lilah's stomach flip-flopped as images of that other couch flashed through her mind. There was no way she could have Zane staying the night in her home. The kissing had been unsettling enough. The last thing she needed was for him to invade her personal space, sleep on *her* couch. "You can't stay here."

Her phone rang and automatically went to the answering machine. The message was audible. A reporter wanted her to call him.

Lilah's gaze zeroed in on the number of messages she had waiting: twenty-three. She didn't think the machine held that many. "I'll pack."

Six

Minutes later, Lilah was packed. Zane, who had spent the time talking into a cell phone, mostly in Medinian, the low, sexy murmur of his voice distracting, snapped the phone closed and slipped it into his pants pocket. “Ready?”

The easy transition from Medinian to American-accented English was startling, pointing out to Lilah, just in case she had forgotten, that Zane Atraeus was elusive *and* complicated. Every time she tried to pigeonhole him as an arrogant, self-centered tycoon, he pushed her off balance by being unexpectedly normal and nice.

While he took her suitcase, Lilah double-checked the locks. On impulse, she grabbed one of her design sketchpads then stepped out into the sterile hall, closing the heavy door behind her.

Zane was waiting, arms folded over his chest, a look of calm patience on his face.

“I’ll just leave a message for a neighbor and see if he’ll fix the window.”

Taking a piece of paper out of her purse, she penned a quick note. Walking a few steps along the dingy corridor, she knocked, just in case Evan was home. She didn't expect him to be in until later in the day, so she slipped the note under his door. The door swung open as she turned to walk away. Evan, looking paint-stained and rumpled, stood there, the note in his hands.

"I didn't think you'd be here until tonight."

Evan was a high-end accountant and painter, and was also a closet gay. The apartment was something in the way of a retreat for him. She had been certain he would stay clear until the press lost interest.

Evan stared pointedly past her at Zane. "It's my day off. I thought I'd come over early just in case you needed a shoulder."

"She doesn't," Zane said calmly.

Evan's expression was suspiciously blank, which meant he was speculating wildly. "Not a problem." He transferred his gaze to Lilah. "Don't worry, I'll fix the window. Call me if you need *anything* else."

Zane held the front door of the apartment building for her. "So, you're still seeing Peters."

Lilah shielded her gaze from the sun as she stepped outside. "How do you know Evan's name?"

Zane loaded her case into the limited rear space of the Corvette. "Peters has a certain reputation with commercial law. So does his boss, Mark Britten."

She could feel her automatic blush at the mention of Evan's boss, the man who had been convinced she was dying to sleep with him before Zane's appearance had ended the small, embarrassing scuffle.

She descended as gracefully as she could into the Vette's passenger seat. "Evan is a *friend*." It was on the tip of her tongue to tell Zane that Evan was gay, but that would mean breaking a confidence. "He paints in his spare time. He doesn't live here. This is just where he keeps his studio."

When they pulled away from the curb, Lilah noticed that Zane's security pulled in close behind them. The ominous black sedan, filled with blocky, muscular men—the leading henchman, Spiros, behind the wheel—looked like something off a movie set. A cream van splashed with colorful graphics idled out of the shadows and slotted in behind the sedan.

Zane glanced in the rearview mirror and made a call on his cell. When he slipped the phone back in his pocket, he glanced at her. "The van's a press vehicle."

"And Spiros is taking care of it?"

Zane's gaze was enigmatic, reminding her of the gulf that existed between his life and hers. "That's what he's paid to do."

Zane inserted the key card in the door of his hotel suite and allowed Lilah to precede him into the room.

Unlocking his jaw he finally addressed the topic that had obsessed him from the moment he had recognized Evan Peters and realized that not only were he and Lilah "friends" of long standing, they were practically living together. "How long have you known Peters?"

There was a moment of silence while she surveyed the heavy opulence of the suite. "Six years. Maybe seven. We met at a painting class."

"When did he move in next door?"

His question was somewhat lost as Lilah strolled through the overstuffed room. The suite, he realized, with its curvy furniture, swagged silk drapes and gilt embellishment might not suit him, but it was a perfect setting for Lilah. Even dressed in the modern suit, she looked lush and exotic, like the expensive courtesans that, before Medinos had become a Christian nation, had been kept closeted in luxury behind lacy wrought iron grills.

She trailed one slim hand over the back of a brocade couch. "As a matter of fact, I was the one who moved next door to him. Evan knew I was looking for a bigger place. When the apartment became available he let me know. It was ideal for what I wanted, so I snapped it up."

His jaw tightened. "And it was a bonus living so close to Peters."

Lilah dropped her purse on the couch and paused to examine an ornate oval mirror. She met his gaze in the glass. "Evan and I are not involved. As you put it, he has a certain reputation in the business world. His painting and some of his artistic friends don't fit the profile, so he keeps that part of his life under wraps."

Involvement or not, it was the knowledge that Peters had likely shared Lilah's bed that bothered him.

Although it had not been the blond accountant's portrait lying on the floor in Lilah's studio. Or Mark Britten's, or Lucas's.

The portrait had been his.

Before he could probe further, his new P.A., Elena, who occupied a single room down the corridor, appeared. Plump but efficiently elegant in a dark suit and trendy pink spectacles, Elena had a clipboard in hand. Spiros appeared in Elena's wake and carried Lilah's bag through to the spare bedroom.

Zane made brief introductions and signed the correspondence on Elena's clipboard. He suppressed his irritation at Elena's bright-eyed perusal of Lilah and the fascinated glances she kept directing his way. No doubt she had read some of the more lurid stories printed about him, which would explain why she seemed to think he needed chocolate-dipped strawberries and oysters on the half shell in his fridge. If she knew how he had lived over the past two years, he thought grimly, she would not have bothered.

When both Elena and Spiros were gone, Zane shrugged out of his jacket, tossed it over a nearby chair and strolled to the doorway of Lilah's room.

The pressing questions surrounding the portrait she had painted of him were replaced by a sense of satisfaction as he watched her unload clothing into a huge, ornate dresser. In *his* suite.

Maybe his personal assistant wasn't so far off in her opinion of him.

According to the history books, on his various raids, Zander Atraeus hadn't confined himself to stealing jewels. At that moment, he formed a grim insight into how his marauding ancestor must have felt when he had stolen away the woman he had eventually married.

Lilah glanced up, a stylish jewelry case in one hand. "Your P.A. doesn't approve."

He settled his shoulder against the door frame, curiously riveted by the feminine items she placed with calm precision on top of the dresser. "Elena had a traditional Medinian upbringing. She would probably prefer you in a separate suite for propriety's sake."

Her expression brightened. "Great idea."

"You're staying here, where I can keep an eye on you. All the suites and rooms at this end of the corridor are booked out to Atraeus staff. It's safe because no one comes in or out without security checking."

"What about the publicity?"

He shrugged. "Whether you have a separate room or share this suite, after what happened this morning, the story they print will be the same. This way, at least, *I* know where you are."

She zipped her empty case closed and placed it in the closet. "What I can't figure out is why that should be so important to you."

"I made a promise to Lucas."

Hurt registered briefly in her gaze. "Silly me," she muttered breezily. "I forgot." Pushing open the terrace door, she stepped out onto the patio.

Zane caught her before she had gone more than a few feet. "Not a good idea. The terrace isn't safe."

On the heels of the hurt that Zane was only following Lucas's orders in looking after her, Zane's grip on her arm sent a small shock of adrenaline plunging through her veins.

She took a panicked half step, at the same time twisting to free herself. In the process her heel skidded on the paver. A sharp little pain signaled that she had managed to turn her ankle.

"What is it?"

She balanced on one heel. "It's not serious." It was the shoe that was the problem; there was something not quite right with the heel.

A split second later she found herself lifted up, carried back inside and deposited on the bed.

Zane removed the offending shoe, which had a broken heel, tossed it on the floor then examined her ankle. The light brush of his fingers sent small shivers through her. "Stay there. I'll get some ice."

"There's no need, honestly."

But he had already gone.

Wiggling her foot, which felt just fine, Lilah stared at the ornately molded ceiling, abruptly speechless. Gold cherubs encircled a crystal chandelier, which she hadn't previously noticed.

She pushed up into a reclining position, and eased back into the decadent luxury of a satin quilted headboard and a plump nest of down pillows. She wiggled her ankle. There was barely a twinge, nothing she couldn't walk off.

Before she could slide off the bed, Zane appeared with a plastic bag filled with ice cubes. The enormous bed depressed as he sat down and placed the ice around her ankle.

She winced at the cold and tried not to love the fact that he was looking after her. "It's really not that bad."

He placed a cushion under her ankle to elevate it. "This way it won't get bad. Just stay put."

He rose to his feet, his expression taking on a look of blunt possession that was oddly thrilling, and that soothed the moment of hurt when she had thought he viewed her as a problem. She decided that in the rich turquoise-and-gold decadence of the room, and despite his kindness over her ankle, she had no trouble placing Zane at all.

When someone looked like a pirate and acted like a pirate, they very probably were a pirate.

An hour on the bed without anything to read and no chance of drowsing off because she was on edge at being in Zane's suite, and Lilah had had enough.

Pushing into a sitting position, she swung her legs over the edge of the bed. She put weight on the foot. A few steps, with the barest of twinges, and she judged it was perfectly sound. The ice pack, which she had taken into her bathroom as soon as Zane had left the room, was melting in the bathtub.

She checked the sitting room, relieved to see that it was empty, and noted the sound of water running, indicating that Zane was having a shower. After changing into jeans and a white camisole, she brushed her hair and wound it back into a tidy knot. Collecting her sketchpad and a pencil, she slipped dark glasses on the bridge of her nose and stepped out onto the terrace. A recliner was placed directly outside her room.

Flipping the pad open, to her horror she discovered that she had picked up the wrong pad. Instead of her latest jewelry sketches, ornate pearl items based on a set of traditional Medinian pieces, she found herself staring at a charcoal sketch of intent dark eyes beneath straight brows, mouthwatering cheekbones and a strong jaw.

Flipping through the book, she studied page after page of sketches, which she had done over a two-year period. Slamming the book closed, she stared at the blank office buildings and hotels across the street. Until that moment she hadn't realized how fixated she had become.

She had simply drawn Zane when she had felt the urge. The problem was the urge had become unacceptably frequent. It was no wonder that in the past two years she'd had trouble whipping up any enthusiasm for her dates. She had even begun to worry about her age; after all she was nearly thirty.

She had even considered dietary supplements, but clearly food wasn't the problem.

A shadow falling over the sketchpad shocked her out of her reverie.

Zane, wearing black jeans that hung low on narrow hips, his muscled chest bare. "You shouldn't be out here. I told you, it isn't safe."

Lilah dragged her gaze from the expanse of muscled flesh, the intriguing tracery of scars on his abdomen. She was abruptly glad for the screen her dark glasses provided. "We're twenty stories up, with security controlling access to this part of the hotel. I don't see how this terrace can not be safe."

"For the same reason I have bodyguards. The Atraeus family has a lot of money. That attracts some wacky types."

"Is that how you got the scars?"

He leaned down and braced his hands on the armrests on either side of the recliner, suddenly suffocatingly close. "I got the scars when I was a kid, because I didn't have either money or protection. Since my father picked me up, no one's gotten that close, mostly because I listen to what my chief of security tells me."

She stared at his freshly shaven jaw, trying to ignore the scents of soap and cologne. "Which is?"

"That no matter how sunny the day looks, there are a lot of bad people out there, so you don't take risks and you do what you're told." He lifted her dark glasses off the bridge of her nose.

She released her grip on the sketchpad to reclaim the sunglasses. Zane let her have the glasses, but straightened, taking her sketchpad with him.

Irritation at the sneaky trick, followed by mortification that he might glance through and discover her guilty secret, burned through her. "Give that back."

She caught the edge of his grin as he stepped into the shadowy interior of the sitting room. Launching off the recliner, she raced after him, blinking as she adjusted to the dimness of the sitting room. She made a lunge for the pad. Zane evaded her reach by taking a half step back.

"Why do you need it so badly?" His gaze was curiously intent, making her stomach sink.

"Those sketches are...private."

And guiltily, embarrassingly revealing.

The drawings cataloged just how empty her private life had been. He would know just how much she had thought about him, focused on him and how often.

He handed her the pad but instead of letting it go, used it to draw her closer by degrees until her knuckles brushed the warm, hard muscles of his chest.

The relief that had spiraled through her when she thought he hadn't checked out the drawings dissolved. "You *looked*."

"Uh-huh." Gaze locked with hers, he drew her close enough that her thighs brushed his and the sketchpad, which she was clutching like a shield, was flattened between them.

He lifted a dark brow. "And you would be drawing and painting me because...?"

Lilah briefly closed her eyes. The old cliché about wishing the ground would open up and swallow her had nothing on this. "You saw the painting in my apartment."

"It was hard to miss."

She drew in a stifled breath. "I was hoping you wouldn't."

"Because then you could avoid admitting that you're attracted to me. And have been ever since we met two years ago."

Gently, he eased the sketchpad from her grip. "You don't need that anymore." He tossed the pad aside. "Not when you have the real thing."

Seven

Lilah was frozen to the spot, gripped by the inescapable knowledge that if she wanted Zane, he wanted her. "Maybe I prefer the fantasy."

"Liar." His head dipped, his forehead touched hers. "What now?" The question was soft and flat.

"Nothing." She swallowed, unable to take her gaze from his mouth, or to forget the memory of the kisses that morning.

Just that morning. In the interim a lot had happened. The passage of time seemed wildly distorted, as if days had passed, not hours.

And that was when she understood what had happened.

Somehow she had done the very thing she had worked to avoid. She had allowed herself to get caught in the grip of a physical obsession. And not just any obsession.

She stared into the riveting depths of Zane's eyes. She had followed a path well-trodden by Cole women. She had fallen victim to the *coup de foudre.*

That was why she had ended up on the couch with Zane.

It explained her inability to say "no" to kissing Zane on the flight and during the press conference.

Somehow, without her quite knowing how, she had allowed sex to sabotage her life.

Zane's gaze narrowed. "Don't look at me like that."

"Like what?" But she knew.

Her guilty secret had been exposed, the emotions and longings she had kept quietly tucked away—all the better to deny them—had been forced to the surface.

And Zane wasn't helping the process. Instead of backing off, he was making no bones about the fact that he liked it that she wanted him.

He dipped his head to kiss her. Lifting up on her toes, she wound her arms around his neck and met him halfway.

It was crazy. She hardly knew him, but already she knew how to fit herself against him, how to angle her jaw so his mouth could settle against hers.

With a stifled groan, he wrapped her close. Half lifting her, he walked her backward across the sitting room. Somewhere in the distance, Lilah registered the phone ringing, then they were in his room. The back of her knees hit the edge of his bed.

He came down beside her. Conscious thought evaporated as his mouth reclaimed hers. Long minutes later, he rolled and pulled her on top of him, his fingers tangling in her hair. Charmed and utterly seduced by the clear invitation to play, to kiss him back, she framed his face and lowered her mouth to his.

His palms smoothed down the curve of her spine, pressing her against him so that she was intimately aware of every curve and plane of heated muscle, the firm shape of his arousal. On the upward journey, he peeled her camisole up until he met the barrier of her bra.

Murmuring something short and soft beneath his breath, he fumbled at the fastening then shifted his hands around to cup her breasts.

The distinctive sound of the front door opening cut through

the dizzying haze. Elena, dressed in a shimmering, ankle-length black dress and looking like a sleek well-fed raven in spectacles, appeared in the doorway to Zane's room.

Zane muttered something short beneath his breath and rolled over in an attempt to shield Lilah from his assistant's view.

Cheeks flushed, Lilah dragged her camisole back into place.

Elena dragged her fascinated gaze from Zane's chest and seemed to remember herself. She checked the dainty watch on her wrist and addressed Zane in rapid Medinian.

Zane rose to his feet and pulled on a shirt that was draped over a nearby chair. "English, please, Elena."

"The car is ready. Gemma, your, uh, *date*—" she directed an apologetic glance at Lilah "—is waiting. Providing we reach the museum in the next twenty minutes, we won't be late."

Gemma. Lilah jackknifed. She was Zane's previous personal assistant and the pretty redhead he had escorted to almost every function the charity had held over the last two years.

Hurt shimmered through her. Above all the gorgeous girls Zane had dated, Gemma reigned supreme. Zane always went back to her. If Lilah had been tempted to fantasize about any kind of a future with Zane, this was exactly the wake-up call she needed.

A second salient fact registered. The museum. And an auction of a private art collection that had been donated to the charity.

Somehow in the craziness of the past few days, she had forgotten she was supposed to attend. Frantically, she checked her wristwatch.

She should have been dressed by now and calling a taxi.

Another thought occurred to her. "Howard."

Zane's head snapped around as he shrugged into a shirt. He gave her a questioning look.

"My date." She scrambled off the bed. She was supposed to be meeting Howard outside the museum in fifteen minutes.

She dashed into her room, snatched an uncrushable cream dress off its hanger, dressed and fixed her hair. She slipped into cream heels and applied a quick dash of mascara and lip-gloss, a spray of her favorite perfume and she was ready.

Picking up her clutch, she joined Zane and Elena. The venue wasn't far away, but there was no way she would make her rendezvous with Howard in time. To compound matters, this was a first date recommended by the online dating agency she had started using just weeks ago. She had never physically met Howard. All she knew was that he had ticked all the boxes in terms of her requirements in a husband.

Now that Lucas was history, Howard was number one on her list of eligible bachelors and her most likely prospect for marriage.

She dragged her gaze from the riveting sight of Zane in a black tuxedo, and tried to gloss over the fact that she had just climbed out of his bed and was now going to meet a prospective husband. "I need a lift to the museum."

Lilah was five minutes late.

Howard White was waiting in the appointed place in the museum foyer, although at first she had difficulty picking him out because he was older than the photograph he had supplied. Mid-forties, she guessed, rather than the age of thirty-two, which he had given.

Flustered and ashamed at herself for her loss of control with Zane, and for forgetting she was even meeting Howard, Lilah resolved to overlook his dishonesty.

Howard smiled pleasantly as they shook hands. "I feel like I know you already."

Guilt burned through her as Howard continued to study her in a way that was just a little too familiar for comfort.

Her picture *had* been splashed across the tabloids. Her only hope now was that he wouldn't put two and two together when he saw Zane. She would have to do her best to make sure that they were not seen together.

As he released her hand, she couldn't help but notice that he had a pale strip across the third finger of his left hand, which seemed to indicate that Howard had been recently married.

The evening progressed at a snail's pace.

Burningly aware of Zane just a short distance away with Gemma clinging on his arm, Lilah found it hard to focus on Howard and his accounting business.

Howard placed his empty mineral water on a nearby side table and beckoned a passing waiter. "Are you sure you wouldn't like some champagne?"

"No. Thank you." Lilah was beginning to get a little annoyed at the pressure Howard was applying with regard to alcohol, especially when he had not touched anything alcoholic himself.

"Very sensible." He put his wallet away.

She tried to think of something else to say, but the conversation had staggered to a halt.

Howard jerked at his collar as if it was too tight. "My—uh, mother doesn't agree with alcohol, especially not for women."

Lilah dragged her gaze from Zane's profile. She had barely paid Howard any attention, but all of her Cole instincts were on high alert. She had received the strong impression that Howard had been about to say "wife." "Your *mother?*"

Howard's gaze shifted to the auctioneer, who was just setting up. He dragged at his tie as if he was having trouble breathing. "I live with my, uh, mother. She's a fine woman."

Feeling suddenly wary of Howard, Lilah excused herself on the grounds that she needed some fresh air before the auction started.

She stepped outside onto a small paved terrace dotted with modern sculpture. A footfall sounded behind her. Zane. Light slanted across his cheekbones, making him look even tougher and edgier.

She had been aware that he had been keeping an eye on her the entire time and had hoped he would follow her.

He jerked his head in the direction of the crowded room. "When did you meet him?"

"Tonight."

His expression was incredulous. "A blind date?"

She stared at the soaring, shadowy shape of a concrete obelisk, as if the outline was riveting. "More or less."

It was none of Zane's business that Howard had contacted her through her online dating service. His application was very recent. It had appeared in her in-box just before she had gone to Medinos. She had felt raw enough on her return that she had agreed to her first actual date.

"I don't like him, and you're not leaving with him." There was a vibrating pause. "He's old enough to be your father."

There was an oddly accusing note to Zane's voice. Lilah stared hard at a tortured arrangement of pipes at the center of the small courtyard, a piece of art that, according to a plaque, had something to do with the inner-city "vibe." "He is older than I thought."

She rubbed her bare arms against the coolness of the night, suddenly desperate to change the subject. "Where's Gemma?"

"Gemma won't miss me for a few minutes. Is that why you dated Lucas, because he was older?"

Her gaze connected with Zane's. She didn't know why he was so stuck on the issue of age. "I don't see what this has to do with anything."

"I've read your personnel file. I know how old you are, I also know that you seem to date older men. Is that a requirement for your future husband?"

Despite the chilly air it was suddenly way too hot. She tried to whip up some outrage that Zane had accessed her personal information, but the implications of his prying were riveting. She couldn't think of any reason for Zane to focus on the age of her dates unless it affected him personally. The thought that

Zane was comparing himself with her dates and that he was actually worried that he was too young, was dizzying. “No.”

Something like relief flickered in his gaze. “Good.”

His fingers linked with hers, drew her close.

Lilah swallowed against the sudden dryness in her mouth. After the disaster on Medinos followed by the deadening effect of Howard’s company, Zane’s interest in her was fatally seductive. “This is a bad idea. You’re with someone else.”

In theory so was she, but Howard, with his sneaky lies and deceptions, had ceased to count.

“Gemma works for The Atraeus Group. She just helps me out on occasion.”

Zane’s head dipped, his breath wafted over her cheek, and suddenly, irresistibly, they were back where they’d been less than two hours ago—on the verge of…something.

His lips touched hers. Heat shivered through her, she lifted up on her toes. Her palms automatically slid over his shoulders, fingers digging into pliant muscle. His hands closed on her waist.

The sound of the auctioneer taking bids flowed out into the night, but even that faded as she stepped closer, angled her chin and leaned into the kiss.

Something shifted in the shadows, flashed. Zane’s head jerked up.

A second shadow flickered. A night security officer with a flashlight in one hand nodded as he walked past.

Confused, Lilah stepped back from Zane. For a moment she was certain someone had used a camera flash. She couldn’t stop the gossip and the sensationalized stories, but that didn’t mean she had to like the sneakiness of the reporters. “I’d better go back inside. Howard will be missing me.”

Zane was still watching the shadowy figure of the security officer as he stepped into a concealed side entrance. “Are you serious about him?”

“Not anymore.” Feeling a wrenching regret at leaving the courtyard, Lilah made her way back into the crowded room.

Howard was still engrossed in conversation with a knot of older men. He didn't bother to look her way. Lilah decided that Zane was right; he looked depressingly paternal.

Zane fell into step beside her. His fingers closed on hers.

Pleasure and guilty heat shooting through her, Lilah jerked her fingers free. Zane's teasing grin made her heart pound. She resisted the almost overpowering urge to smile back. "What do you think you're doing?"

The wicked grin faded. "Something I should have done before, checking out your date. I want to make sure Howard doesn't have an agenda."

"He does. I realized tonight that he's married."

Zane's expression went from irritated to remote as he slid his cell out of his pocket and spoke briefly into it.

He snapped the phone closed. "Go to the car with Gemma and Elena. Spiros has just pulled up to the curb outside. I'll deal with Howard. Your boyfriend was also out in the courtyard with a phone camera."

Lilah stared at Howard who she noticed, was now knocking back something that looked extremely alcoholic. She remembered the shuffling sound, the extra flash.

Zane inserted himself into the jovial male group with the confidence and ease that came from being a supreme predator in the business world. She saw the moment Howard realized he had been made, the automatic reach for his pocket as if he wanted to shield his cell phone.

Howard's wild gaze connected briefly with hers. With calm deliberation, Lilah turned her back on Howard and walked through to the museum lobby. She noted that she didn't feel in the least shocked or depressed by the betrayal. On the contrary, there had been something highly satisfying in watching Zane go into battle for her. Unfortunately, along with her new ruthless streak, she seemed to have also gotten used to leading a life of notoriety.

Gemma and Elena strolled out directly behind her. Spiros held the door for them while they climbed into the limousine.

Elena chatted with Spiros in Medinian, leaving Lilah with a clearly unhappy Gemma.

Seconds later Zane joined them. Gemma beamed and patted the vacant space beside her. Instead of climbing in, Zane glanced across at a group of boys Lilah had noticed loitering a small distance away from the limo.

He glanced at Lilah. "I won't be long."

Gemma, looking distinctly irritable as Zane walked over to the boys, extracted a cell from her clutch and within seconds was deep in conversation about her new job and a move overseas. Elena retrieved a romance novel from her clutch, attached an efficient looking little LED light to the back pages, and was promptly engrossed.

Lilah decided she clearly hadn't lived, because she hadn't thought to bring an activity with her that was suitable for downtime in a limousine. Absently, she noted Howard slinking off to his car, which turned out to be a sleek little hatchback with a personalized licence plate that read "HERS."

Zane terminated a cell phone conversation as he walked back to the car. "I can't come back to the hotel with you right now. I have to take care of these kids. They saw the posters for the charity auction—that's why they came."

Lilah stared across at the lean wraiths clustered around a park bench as if that small landmark was all they had. "What can you do?"

"Get them in a house for the night with state foster care. That doesn't guarantee they'll stay, but at least it's a start. I'll see you later."

Lilah watched as Zane walked back to the kids, seeing the instant brightening of their faces. She hadn't realized how personally involved he was, or how much kids liked him.

She felt like she was seeing him for the first time, not the quintessential bad boy or the exciting, elusive lover the media liked to publicize, but a committed, protective man who would make an excellent father.

With the rest of the night in Zane's hotel suite looming,

it was not a good time to discover that Zane had somehow managed to transcend the list of attributes she was searching for in a husband and had made her requirements seem petty and flawed.

Eight

Lilah's cell phone rang as she stepped in the door of the suite. It was Zane. She remembered that she had given him her number earlier.

"Stay in my room. I won't be late."

She stiffened at the invitation, as if Zane was already so sure of her he assumed she would be sleeping with him. "No."

There was a hollow pause. "Why not?"

"For a start, you already have a girlfriend."

"Gemma is not my girlfriend. Like I said, she's a company employee and she fills in as my escort on occasion. Tonight's date was organized a few weeks ago. I would have canceled if I'd had time."

Lilah's fingers tightened on the phone. "I know this might sound silly to you, but I made a certain…vow. I might have forgotten it for a few minutes this afternoon, but that doesn't change the fact that it's important to me."

There was a ringing silence, punctuated by raised voices in the background.

"I have to go," Zane said curtly. "Whatever you do, don't leave the suite. Spiros will be out in the corridor if you need anything. And don't use the hotel phone. It's not secure and the press are still camped in the foyer."

The phone clicked quietly in her ear.

Feeling suddenly flat and a little depressed, Lilah walked through to her room and showered in the opulent marble bathroom, which not only contained a large walk-in shower, but a sunken spa tub. After slipping on a silk chemise, she belted one of the fluffy hotel robes around her waist and walked back out to the kitchen.

She found a bowl of fruit and a basket of fresh rolls on the counter. The fridge was groaning with food.

Abruptly starving, because she had been too wound up to eat anything but a few canapés from the buffet at the auction, Lilah helped herself to bread and cheese and a selection of mouthwatering dishes from the fridge. To balance out the decadence, she made herself a cup of tea.

Loading her snack onto a small tray, she carried it through to the sitting room and set it down on an elegant coffee table. She flicked through TV channels until she found a local news station.

Wrong choice. She stared at the live footage of Zane with Gemma at some point during the charity auction that evening. Her arm was coiled snugly around his. Young and fresh, with an ultrasexy fuchsia gown, Gemma was the perfect foil for Zane's dark, powerful build.

Suddenly miserable, she flicked to another channel and stared blankly at an old black-and-white movie. At eleven o'clock, she turned the TV set off. Too restless to sleep and worried that her apartment might have been broken into, she decided to call Evan and check if he had managed to fix the window. She retrieved her cell from her handbag and discovered the battery was dead. In her hurry to pack, she had not included her cell phone charger.

She spent another half hour kicking her heels. Her irritation at her isolation in the fabulous suite was edged by the dreaded notion that maybe Zane hadn't yet returned because he was now with Gemma.

It wasn't as if she had a claim on Zane, or should want to make one. Despite the attraction that sizzled between them, the crazy, inappropriate sense of attachment, Zane Atraeus did not fit into her life.

The one area in which they were in complete harmony was the most dangerous part of their relationship. No matter how tempted she was to fall into bed with Zane, she couldn't forget that sex had gotten her mother and her grandmother into trouble, literally.

At eleven-thirty, she retreated to her bedroom, climbed into the Hollywood fantasy of a bed and tried to sleep.

At midnight, tired of tossing and turning in a tangle of silken bedclothes, she pushed out of bed and walked back out to the kitchenette. On impulse, she picked up the hotel directory, found out how to dial out and called Evan, who was a night owl and didn't normally go to bed until one or two o'clock.

Evan was terse and to-the-point. He *had* fixed the window, but now he was busy, entertaining a *friend*.

Cheeks burning, Lilah apologized. She was on the point of hanging up when Zane walked through the door.

Zane shrugged out of his jacket and tossed it over the back of a chair. "I thought I told you not to use the hotel phone."

Lilah said goodbye and hung up. "I had to make a call. My cell phone battery was dead."

He frowned. "Who is it? Howard?"

"No."

"Lucas?"

"I called Evan to see if he'd fixed my window."

He removed his bow tie and jerked at the buttons of his dress shirt. "Peters. Just how many male friends have you got?"

Annoyance zinged through her. "I don't know why that

should worry you, when you've got so many 'friends' yourself."

Zane's expression cleared, as if she had just said something that had cheered him up immeasurably. "I've spent half the night with a bunch of scared kids."

She stared resolutely at his jaw, desperate to avoid the softening in his gaze. "It's after midnight."

Comprehension gleamed. "And you thought I was with Gemma."

He closed the distance between them and framed her face so she was forced to meet his gaze, and suddenly there was no air. "Why do you think I became the patron of a Sydney charity, when I've been based in the States?"

Zane answered his own question. "Because I wanted you."

Zane logged the moment Lilah accepted that he genuinely wanted her.

Desire burned away the jealousy that had gripped him when he had found her talking on the phone.

He didn't *get* jealous. Ever since his early teens, he had controlled his emotions and his sex drive. He had been selective in his bed partners.

For two years, since he had severed his last short liaison, he hadn't needed a woman at all. It was not unusual for him to have periods of celibacy, but this one had stretched beyond personal preference.

Lilah's sea-green gaze locked with his.

The attraction didn't make sense. He didn't want Lilah to matter to him, but it was a fact that she did.

Bending his head, he touched his mouth to hers.

Long, drugging seconds passed. He lifted his head before he lost it completely. He was male, he loved women, their softness and beauty; he just didn't trust them.

Until now, he'd had no interest in changing.

The thought that he could change, that he wanted to trust Lilah, made his heart pound.

Her fingers slid into his hair. The faint, tugging pressure

as she lifted up and pressed her mouth to his was stunningly erotic. A wave of intense, dissolving pleasure shimmered through him. Dimly, he noted that he was on the edge of losing control.

Lilah lifted up on her toes, pressing closer to Zane. Subconsciously, she realized she had been waiting for this ever since Elena had interrupted them that afternoon.

With a stifled groan, Zane took a half step forward, pinning her against the edge of the counter.

She felt him tugging at her thick, fluffy robe, the coolness of the air against her skin as the robe slipped to the floor. He dipped his head and took one breast in his mouth through the silk of her chemise, and sensation jerked through her.

A split second later, the room tilted as he swung her into his arms. Depositing her on the soft cushions of one of the elaborate, overstuffed couches, he came down alongside her.

Blindly, she fumbled at his shirt until she found naked skin. She tore open the final buttons and impatiently waited while he shrugged out of the shirt.

She felt the heat of his palms gliding along her thighs, the warm silk of her chemise puddling around her hips.

In twelve years of dating, this was the closest she had come to feeling anything like the intensity that friends wept over and talked about, that she had absorbed second hand through books and movies.

Being desired, she discovered, was infinitely seductive; it undermined her defenses, dissolved every last shred of resistance. Even the idea of holding on to her virginity seemed vague and abstract. Especially in light of the fact that she had already more or less surrendered to Zane two years ago. After grimly hanging on to that bastion of purity for so long she couldn't help thinking it might actually be a relief to get rid of it.

Zane's fingers hooked in the waistband of her panties. Driven by desire and an intense curiosity, instead of resisting, Lilah lifted her hips and assisted the process. Cool air was instantly replaced by the muscular heat of Zane's body as he came down between her legs.

As wrong as her logical mind told her it was to allow Zane to make love to her, the man who was holding her, cradling her as if she was precious to him, *felt* right. She had never felt more alive; she couldn't help adoring every minute. In that moment she understood why both her mother and grandmother had risked all for passion. She couldn't believe she had waited this long to find out.

In an effort to help out, she tugged at the fastening of his pants, and felt him hot and silky smooth against her. His heated gaze locked with hers. For a moment, time seemed to stand still. Then he surged inside her.

Zane froze.

His gaze locked with Lilah's again. Comprehension sliced through the spiraling pleasure that for the past few minutes had numbed his brain. "You're a virgin."

Her expression was distracted, although she didn't seem overly upset. "Yes."

He wasn't wearing a condom. That was another first.

Zane's jaw clenched as wave after wave of raw desire washed through him. He had never lost control before. He needed to pull free and call a halt to the primitive rush of satisfaction that Lilah had only ever been his.

Lilah moved restlessly beneath him, the subtle shimmy easing the pressure and drawing him deeper. He gritted his teeth. "That's not helping."

Every muscle tensed as Lilah tightened around him, locking him into her body. Incredibly, he felt her climax around him. Burning, irresistible pleasure swamped Zane again. His jaw clenched as his own climax hit him, shoving him over the edge.

Long minutes passed while they lay sprawled together on the couch. Eventually, driven by an electrifying thought, Zane lifted his head.

He could make Lilah pregnant.

Not "could make," he thought grimly. That was something that happened in the future. He was pretty sure they were in the realm of "making pregnant" as in *now*.

Lilah was loathe to move, loathe to separate herself from Zane because she was certain that, as singular and devastatingly pleasurable as the lovemaking had been, despite a little initial discomfort, Zane was less than impressed.

He hadn't liked learning that she was a virgin.

Guilt flooded her when she remembered the shameless way she had clenched around him, holding him in her body.

A reflexive shiver went through her at the memory.

Zane's gaze was oddly flat. "Why didn't you tell me you were a virgin?"

Warm color flooded her cheeks. "There wasn't exactly time for a conversation."

"If I'd known, I would have done things…differently."

"I hadn't exactly planned on this, myself."

He propped himself on his elbows. "Neither had I. Otherwise I would have used a condom. Which is the second issue. How likely are you to get pregnant?"

She felt her flush deepen, although this time the surge of heat wasn't solely because of the very pertinent pregnancy question. "Don't worry, there's no danger of a pregnancy." She tried for a breezy smile, a little difficult when she had just tossed away what her grandmother had always termed her Most Valued Possession. "I take a contraceptive pill."

There was a moment of vibrating silence. Somewhere in the hush of the suite Lilah could hear the ponderous tick of a clock. Outside, somewhere in the distance a siren wailed.

Zane's expression was oddly frozen. "It's a relief someone was in control of the situation. For a minute there I thought we could be parents."

"No chance." She tried not to be riveted by the three very fascinating studs in his lobe. "The one thing I've never planned on being is a single parent."

There was another heavy silence. She got the impression that Zane was not entirely happy with her answer.

"Since you've taken care of the protection so efficiently..." He dipped his head and lightly kissed her then systematically peeled off the chemise. Satisfaction registered in his gaze as he tossed the scrap of silk onto the floor and cupped her breasts, his thumbs sweeping across her nipples.

Lilah's eyes automatically closed as the delicious sensations started all over again.

The rapid shift back into mind-numbing passion set off alarm bells. It occurred to her that now that they had made love, she was in a very precarious position with regard to marriage. Zane was not an option. He had never been an option. His aversion to relationships in general and marriage in particular was well publicized. *She* still wanted marriage, and she couldn't in all good conscience continue with her marriage plans while she had a lover. Regretfully, she did her utmost to dampen down on the desire.

She felt as if she was surfacing from a dream. She had been shameless and had acted with abandon. Her face burned at the memory. She had actively *encouraged* Zane to have unprotected sex with her.

She had clung to him when he had wanted to put a stop to the process and withdraw, then it had been too late and over in seconds.

It was as if, in a weird way, even though she had been sensible enough to guard herself with contraception, a wild, irresponsible part of her had actually courted the very thing she feared most.

Guilt and fatalism churned in her stomach. The sheer weight of her family history and conditioning, the years of guarding against these types of liaisons, should have been enough to stop her.

"We can't do this again." Pressing at Zane's shoulders, she wriggled free, grabbed at her chemise and dragged it on.

Zane's gaze seared over her as she belted the thick robe

around her waist. "All you had to do was say no." The tinge of outrage in his voice stopped her in her tracks.

She flushed guiltily at the truth of that, since she had been the one who hadn't wanted to stop in the first place. She dragged her gaze away from the bronzed, muscular lines of his body as he pulled on dark, fitted trousers. With his strong profile, his black hair tumbling to his broad shoulders, he was beautiful in an untamed, completely masculine way.

Disbelief flooded her that she had actually made love with him. Although the evidence was registering all over her body in tingling aches and the faint stiffening of muscles.

Zane retrieved his shirt. "There's one other thing you don't have to worry about. STD's."

Frowning, Lilah dragged her gaze from the mesmerizing sight of Zane's six-pack.

Zane's gaze snapped to hers. "Sexually transmitted diseases. I don't have any. If tonight was a first for you, it was a first for me. I've never had unprotected sex with a woman before."

Her stomach tightened at the clinical mention of another danger she had failed to consider, and the relegation of their lovemaking to sex. "Um…thanks."

She could feel her face, her whole body, flaming. At twenty-nine, she was probably more naive than the average fifteen-year-old and Zane's reputation with women was legendary. She had been so wrapped up in what she was experiencing she had failed to consider what Zane had to be thinking—that she was hopelessly gauche and naive.

Depression settled around her like a shroud. *Way to go, Lilah Cole. Living up to the family crest. Abandon all thought of responsibility until it's too late.* "If you'll excuse me, I'm going to bed now."

He folded his arms over his chest, his gaze cool. "I'll see you in the morning."

Not if she could help it.

Lilah closed her bedroom door behind her, relieved that

she was finally alone. She checked the bedside clock and an unnerving sense of disorientation set in. It wasn't yet one o'clock. Barely thirty minutes had passed since Zane had walked through the door. Thirty minutes in which her life had drastically altered.

She used her en suite bathroom to freshen up, this time hardly noticing the gorgeous fixtures. Instead of climbing into the elegant four-poster, she changed into jeans, a cotton sweater and sneakers, her fingers fumbling in their haste to get into casual, everyday clothes and restore some semblance of normality.

When she was dressed, she rewound her hair, which had ended up in an untidy mass, into a coil, stabbed pins through to lock the silky strands in place and systematically packed. Twenty minutes after entering her room, she was ready to leave.

Forcing herself to calm down, she sat on the edge of the bed and listened. She had heard Zane's shower earlier, but now the suite was plunged into silence.

Taking a deep breath, she walked to her door and opened it a crack. The sitting room was in darkness. There didn't appear to be any light filtering under the door of Zane's bedroom or flowing out on to the terrace, signaling that he was still awake.

Lifting her bag, she tiptoed to the door and let herself out into the hall. She was almost at the elevator when Spiros loomed out of an alcove and stopped her.

His fractured English almost defeated her. When he picked up his cell and she realized he was going to call Zane, she summoned up a breezy smile, as if the fact that she was sneaking out in the middle of the night was all part of the plan. "Nessuno." She jabbed at the call button and carefully enunciated each word as she spoke. "No need to call Zane, he's sleeping."

He frowned then nodded, clearly not happy.

Forty minutes later, Lilah paid off the taxi that had delivered her back to her apartment and walked inside.

She checked the messages on her phone. They were all

from tabloids and women's magazines wanting interviews. She had expected that Spiros, who had been uneasy about the fact that she had left at such an odd hour, would have caved and woken Zane up. Clearly, that hadn't happened, because there was no message from Zane.

Feeling oddly let down that she hadn't heard from Zane, she deleted them all.

Pulling the drapes tight, just in case someone was lurking outside with a camera, she changed into a spare chemise in pitch darkness and fell into bed.

She slept fitfully, waking at dawn, half expecting the phone to ring, or for Zane to be thumping on her door.

She got up and made a cup of tea, collapsed on the couch and watched movies. By ten o'clock, when Zane hadn't either called or come by, exhausted from waiting, she dropped back into bed and slept until two in the afternoon.

When she got up, her stomach growling with hunger, she checked her phone. There were a string of new messages but, again, they were all from reporters.

Stabbing the delete button, she erased them all and finally decided to put herself out of her misery by taking the phone off the hook. On impulse, she checked her cell phone, but it wasn't in her bag. She must have left it in Zane's suite.

To keep the cold misery at bay that Zane didn't appear to have any interest in contacting her, she opened a can of soup and made toast. Evan knocked on her door, wanting to return her spare key and check that she was okay. At four o'clock a second visitor knocked.

A courier. He handed her a package and requested she sign for it.

She scribbled her name, closed the door then ripped the package open. Her stomach dropped like a stone as her fingers closed around her cell phone.

From the second she had left Zane's suite, she realized, she had been waiting for him to come after her, to insist that he wanted her back. That what they had shared had been as special for him as it had been for her.

That clearly wasn't the case.

Zane hadn't even bothered to include a note with the phone. All he had done was return her property in such a way that made it clear he no longer wanted contact.

Feeling numb, she put the phone on charge. Almost immediately, it beeped. Crazy hope gripped her as she opened the message.

It was Lucas, not Zane. He wanted her to call him.

Using the cell, she put the call through. Lucas picked up immediately. The conversation was brief. Thanks to her boosted media profile, she had just won a prestigious design award in Milan, which would give Ambrosi an edge in the market. A week ago, she had applied for the job of managing the new Ambrosi Pearl facility, which was to be constructed on the island of Ambrus, one of the smaller islands in the Medinian group. If she wanted the job, it was hers.

The job was a promotion with a substantial raise in her salary plus a generous living allowance. If she took it, paying her mother's mortgage would no longer be a problem. She would even be able to save.

The only problem was, Zane lived on Medinos. Although, with the amount of travel he did, most of it to the States, she doubted their paths would often cross.

A bonus would be that she could leave Sydney and all of the media hype behind. She would have a fresh start.

Away from her latest sex scandal.

Taking a deep breath, she took the plunge and affirmed that she would take the job.

Lucas rang back a few minutes later. He had booked a flight, leaving in two days. Her accommodation, until a house could be arranged, was the Atraeus Resort on Medinos.

Reeling from the sudden change of direction her life had taken, Lilah rang her mother and told her the good news, carefully glossing over the bad parts.

After she had hung up, she cleared her answering machine and disconnected the phone. She also turned her cell phone off. She didn't know how long it would take the media to discover that Lucas had offered her a job on Medinos, but given the added hype behind the Milan award, she didn't think it would take long.

Too wound up to try and relax again, she decided to take one of her finished paintings to the gallery that handled her work.

When she walked into the trendy premises, the proprietor, Quincy Travers, a plump, balding man with a shrewd glint in his eyes, greeted her with open arms.

With glee he took the abstract she'd painted and handed her a check for an astounding amount. "As soon as I saw the story in the paper I contacted some collectors I know and put an extra couple of zeroes on the price of the paintings. I sold out within thirty minutes."

"Great." Lilah's delight at the check, which was enough to pay off her mother's mortgage and still leave change, went into the same deep, dark hole that had snuffed out her delight at the Milan award and her promotion.

She shoved the check in her purse. Just what she needed to brighten her day. Like her jewelry design, any value her art now had was tied to her notoriety.

Quincy propped the painting on an empty display easel and rubbed his hands together. "No need to put a price on this. I've got buyers waiting. Sex sells. What else have you got, love? You could scribble with crayons and we'd still make a fortune."

"Actually, I'm leaving town for a while, so that will be the last one for the foreseeable future."

Quincy looked crestfallen. "If I'd known that, I would have asked more for the other paintings." He rummaged beneath his counter and came up with a battered address book. "But all is not lost. If the buyers know this is the last one, they'll pay." He flipped it open and reached for his phone. "By the way, did you really, er, *date* both brothers at the same time?"

Lilah could feel herself turning pink. She was suddenly fiercely glad she was leaving town in two days. "No." Ducking her head, she walked quickly out of the gallery.

She had just slept with the one.

Nine

Two days later, fresh off a flight from Broome in Western Australia and frustrated that he had not been able to get any reply from either Lilah's work or home phone, or cell, Zane swung the Corvette into the parking space outside her building.

He buzzed the apartment. While he waited for a response, the electrifying moments on the couch replayed in his mind. The enthusiastic way Lilah had clung to him, the explosive moment when he had known for sure that she had never made love with Lucas, Peters or any other man. The fierce way she had locked him into her body when he had attempted to withdraw, as if she hadn't wanted to let him go.

The brain freeze that had hit him, because he hadn't wanted to stop, either.

When he'd discovered that Lilah had sneaked out on him during the night, he had been both furious and relieved.

The fact that he had made the monumental mistake of making love to her without protection, that he could have made her pregnant, still stunned him.

It had been right up there with finding out that she had been a virgin.

A day spent kicking his heels, trying to decide if those out-of-control moments had been unscripted and spontaneous or if he had been neatly manipulated by a consummate operator had been enough.

Every time he had examined what had happened, he had come to the same inescapable conclusion. Whatever Lilah's motives had been in surrendering her virginity to him, she had taken care of the contraception, which argued her innocence.

He had done a background check on Lilah, even going so far as to fly to her hometown, Broome. When he'd found out that, like him, she was illegitimate, several pieces of the puzzle that was Lilah Cole had fallen into place.

He knew how a dysfunctional upbringing could influence decisions. Lilah had been brought up by her single mother, whose health was poor. Consequently, the financial burden had now fallen on her. She not only paid her own costs in Sydney, she paid her mother's mortgage and medical bills.

The knowledge put Lilah's search for a well-heeled husband into an irritatingly practical light. It had also exposed how potentially vulnerable Lilah could be to an "arrangement" should some man try to step into her life.

He leaned on the buzzer again. Since Lilah wasn't answering any calls, he had reasoned that she had most probably taken some time off work and was inside, hiding out from the press.

His frustration level increasing when there was still no response, he cut through the adjacent property, another shabby warehouse, and pushed through the broken fence into Lilah's backyard.

He examined the bifold doors and windows, which were locked and blanked out by thick drapes. He rapped on the door and tried calling. When there was no answer he walked back around to the front door and pressed buzzers until he got an answer from one of the other apartments.

A voice like a rusty nail being slowly extracted from a sheet of iron informed him that Lilah had left the country. Her apartment was now empty, if he wanted to rent it.

Zane terminated the conversation and strode back to the Corvette. A quick call to Lucas answered the question that was threatening to aggravate his newly discovered anger problem.

"Lilah has flown to Medinos. She's agreed to head up the new Ambrosi Pearls facility."

Zane's fingers tightened on his cell. "Who made the arrangement?"

"I did. I'll be flying out to Medinos in the next few days to check that she's settling in."

A snapping sound informed Zane that he had just broken one of the hinges that attached the LCD screen to the body of his phone. "Carla won't be happy."

That was an understatement. Carla Ambrosi was known for her passionate outbursts. But whatever Carla might feel about Lucas's continuing involvement with Lilah didn't come close to Zane's level of unhappiness.

"After the crazy stuff the tabloids have been printing," Lucas said grimly, "the less Carla knows about Lilah the better. I'm organizing for her to spend some time with her mother here when I fly out to Medinos."

Zane's stomach tightened. Which meant Carla would be conveniently out of the way for Lucas's meeting with Lilah. "When did Lilah leave?"

"Today."

Zane terminated the conversation and placed a call to Elena. Within seconds she had located the information he wanted. The only flight out of Sydney to Medinos that day had already departed.

Tossing the phone on the passenger seat, Zane slid behind the wheel and accelerated away from the curb. Lilah had left that morning, but her flight was long, with a three-hour stopover in Singapore and another shorter stop in Dubai. Using the Atraeus private jet, he would easily reach Medinos before her.

Whatever ideas his brother might have of conducting a clandestine affair with Lilah, Zane was certain of one fact. Lilah hadn't chosen to give herself to Lucas; she had given herself to him.

He, also, had made a choice when he had made love with Lilah. He wanted her, and after two years, one night had not been enough. One thing was certain: he was not about to let Lucas entice Lilah away.

Satisfaction curled in his stomach as the decision settled in. If he'd had any reservations, in that moment they were gone.

The complication of Lilah's virginity and marriage plan aside, he was finally going to live up to the reputation of his marauding ancestor.

Lilah was his, and he was taking her.

Lilah stepped into the air-conditioned terminal on Medinos. Almost immediately she was accosted by a uniformed security guard, a holstered gun on one thigh.

Exhausted from the long nerve-racking flight, during which she had only been able to sleep in snatches, she accompanied the officer to a small, sterile interview room. Several fruitless questions later, because the guard's English was limited and her Medinian was close to nonexistent, she resigned herself to wait. The one piece of information she had gleaned was that, apparently, they were waiting for a member of the Atraeus family.

Minutes later, her frustration levels rising, her luggage, along with a foam cup of coffee, was delivered to the interview room and an airport official showed up to personally process her arrival papers. As the official handed her stamped passport back, the door opened. Zane, dressed in dark jeans and a loose white shirt, his hair ruffled as if he'd dragged his fingers through it repeatedly, strolled into the room.

For a confused moment Lilah had difficulty grasping that

Zane was actually here, then the meaning of his presence sank in. "You're the Atraeus who had me detained."

The official left, the door closing quietly behind him.

Zane frowned. "Who were you expecting? Lucas?"

The flatness of Zane's voice was faintly shocking. Lilah couldn't help thinking it was a long way from the teasing grin and the seductive huskiness of Saturday night. "As far as I know, Lucas is still in Sydney."

Zane placed a newspaper, which had been tucked under one arm, down on the desktop.

The glaring headline, *Lucas Atraeus Installs Mistress on Isle of Medinos,* made her bristle. When she had flown out of Sydney, she had hoped she was leaving all of that behind.

Folding the paper over, she threw it in the trashcan beside the desk. "I haven't seen that one. They don't hand out Sydney gossip sheets as part of the in-flight entertainment."

Zane perched on the edge of the desk, arms folded across his chest. "Who knew that you were flying out to Medinos?"

Lilah located her handbag and stored her passport in a secure pocket. Making a quick exit lugging a large suitcase, a carry-on bag, her laptop and her handbag would be difficult, but she was ready to give it a go. "Quite a lot of people. It wasn't a secret."

Zane looked briefly irritated as she tried to harness her laptop to the suitcase using a set of buckles that was clearly inadequate for the job. "That's not helpful."

"It wasn't meant to be." She hauled on a dainty strap and finally had the laptop secure.

"So who do you think could have leaked the information that you were moving to Medinos to the press?"

She moved on to the carry-on case, which posed a problem. She was going to need a trolley after all.

"You don't have to worry about the luggage. I'll carry it for you."

Anger flowed through her at the implication that *she* could have sold the story. "I prefer to manage on my own."

"You don't have to, since I'm here to pick you up." With efficient movements, Zane unhooked the laptop and used the straps to neatly attach the carry-on case to the large suitcase.

Lilah reclaimed her laptop. "I don't get it. You didn't come around or call, and now—"

"I called. Your phone didn't seem to be working."

She tried to get her tired brain around the astounding fact that Zane hadn't abandoned her, entirely. Although, there was nothing loverlike about his demeanor now. A lightbulb went on in her head. "Don't tell me you thought I could have leaked the story because I'm angling to be Lucas's mistress?"

"Or to break Lucas and Carla up."

For a vibrating moment she struggled against the desire to empty what was left of her coffee down his front. Instead, she set her laptop down and, stepping close, ran her finger down Zane's chest, pausing over the steady thud of his heart. "Why would I, when as you so eloquently put it, I've already got the real thing?"

Heat flared in his gaze. His fingers closed around her wrist, trapping her palm against the wall of his chest. "Past tense, Lilah. You were the one who walked out."

Shock reverberated through her that he could possibly have wanted her to stay. "I didn't think you were...serious."

His gaze was unnervingly steady. "One-night stands are not exactly my thing."

The heat from his chest burned into her palm. "So all those stories in the press about you and who knows how many gorgeous women are untrue?"

His free hand curled around her nape. He reeled her in a little closer. "Mostly."

Honest, but still dangerous. Distantly, she registered that this was what she had so badly wanted from Zane two days ago. He had finally come after her and in true pirate fashion was seemingly intent on dragging her back to bed. "So, in theory then, the press could have lied about me."

He leaned forward; his lips feathered her jaw sending a hot tingle of sensation through her. "It's possible."

"I'm not interested in breaking Lucas and Carla up."

"Good, because I have a proposition for you." He bit down gently on her lobe. "Two days on an island paradise. You and me."

Sensation shimmered through her, briefly blanking her mind. So that was what it was like, she thought a little breathlessly. She had read that the earlobe was an erogenous zone. Now, finally, she could attest to that fact.

She took a deep breath and let it out slowly. The idea of an exciting interlude with Zane before she started work and became once more embroiled in her search for a stable, trustworthy husband, was unbearably seductive. There were no good reasons to go, only bad ones. "Yes."

She caught the quick flash of his grin before his mouth closed on hers, and for long seconds she forgot to breathe.

Ten minutes later, Lilah found herself installed in the rear seat of a limousine, Zane beside her and the familiar figure of Spiros behind the wheel. A short drive later and they pulled into a picturesque marina.

She examined the ranks of gleaming superyachts, launches and sailboats tied up to a neat series of jetties. "This doesn't look like the Atraeus Resort."

"It's a nice day. I thought you might enjoy the boat ride."

Spiros opened her door, distracting her. When she turned back to Zane, the seat next to her was empty. Zane was already out of the limousine, his jacket off and draped over one shoulder. Following suit, she climbed out, wincing at the dazzling brightness of sunlight reflecting off white boats. Finding her sunglasses, she slid them onto the bridge of her nose.

By that time, Spiros, who she had noticed had not met her gaze once during the last few minutes, had her cases out of the trunk. Zane was already halfway down the jetty and untying ropes. The boat trip to the resort seemed to be a fait accompli, so Lilah followed in Spiros's wake, determined to enjoy the sunny day and the spectacular sea views.

By the time she reached the sleek white yacht, her cases were already stowed. Zane extended his hand and helped her climb aboard.

Almost instantly the engine hummed to life. Spiros walked along the jetty, released the last rope and tossed it over the stern. Lilah couldn't help noticing that he seemed to be in a hurry. When he didn't climb aboard she frowned. "Isn't Spiros coming?"

"Not on this trip." With deft skill, Zane maneuvered the yacht out of its berth.

Minutes later, they cleared the marina and the boat picked up speed, wallowing slightly in the chop. Feeling faintly queasy with the motion, Lilah sat down and tried to enjoy the scenery.

Twenty minutes later, her unease turned to suspicion. Instead of hugging the coastline they seemed to be heading for open sea. The coastline of Medinos had receded, and the island of Ambrus loomed ahead.

Dragging strands of hair out of her eyes, she pushed to her feet, gripping the back of her seat to stay upright. "This is not the way to the resort."

"I'm taking you to Ambrus."

"There's nothing *on* Ambrus."

His gaze rested briefly on hers. "That's not strictly true. There's an unfinished resort on the northern headland."

The yacht rounded a point and sailed into calmer water. Lilah stared at the curve of the beach ahead and the tumbled wreckage of the old pearl facility, which had been destroyed in the Second World War. It was, literally, a bombsite. In a flash, Spiros's odd behavior and his hurried exit made sense. Zane had planned this. She gestured at the looming beach. "I didn't agree to that. You said two days. Paradise."

Zane throttled back on the engine. "Maybe I wasn't talking about the scenery."

An instant flashback to the heated few minutes on Zane's couch made her blush. "I didn't exactly find paradise in your hotel room."

"There wasn't time. If you'll recall, you ran out on me."

Her jaw firmed. When she had landed on Medinos her life had been firmly under control. Somehow in the space of an hour everything had gone to hell in a handbasket again. "I'm booked in at the Atraeus Resort. That's where I'm staying for the next few weeks."

"You agreed. Two days." His jaw tightened. "Or did you want another media furor when Lucas arrives tomorrow?"

She stared at the tough line of his jaw. The dazzling few moments in the customs interview room when she'd been weak enough to allow him to kiss her replayed in her mind. That had been her first mistake. "I assumed you were taking me to my suite at the Atraeus Resort."

"I apologize for the deception," he said bluntly, although there was no hint of apology in his gaze. "I'll take you to Medinos in two days' time. Once Lucas leaves."

She stared at the deserted stretch of coastline then back at the distant view of Medinos. She had wanted out of the media circus and she had wanted peace and quiet. It looked like now she was getting both, with a vengeance. "Is there power, an internet connection?"

"There's a generator. No internet."

"Then we need to go back to Medinos. I'll be missed. People will be concerned. Questions will be asked."

Zane frowned. "Who, exactly, is going to ask these questions?"

Lilah stared fixedly at the horizon, aware that the conversation had drifted into dangerous waters. "I have…friends."

"It's only two days."

A little desperate now, Lilah tried for a vague look. "Online friends. I need to keep in touch."

Zane's gaze was unnervingly piercing. "And being away from an internet connection for two days is an issue?"

She crossed her arms over her chest, refusing to be drawn. "It could be."

After the disappointment with Lucas she had felt an urgency to move along with her marriage project and had committed to a series of dates with her list of potentially perfect husbands. Howard had only been the first. Up until that moment she had been too busy with making arrangements to leave Sydney, and preparing herself for a new life and a new job, to stop and think about the upcoming series of dates she had arranged for a scheduled holiday back home in two weeks' time.

The sound of the engine changed as they neared shore. The reality of what was happening sank in as the huge, deserted sweep of the crescent bay underlined their complete isolation. "You're kidnapping me."

Zane's brows jerked together. "That's a little dramatic. We're staying at a beach house where we can spend some time together, uninterrupted."

Against all the odds her heart thumped wildly at his bad-tempered, rather blunt statement, which definitely indicated a desire to keep her to himself. She guessed she could excuse him, although not right away.

He had *kidnapped* her.

She clamped down on the dizzying delight that he wanted her enough to actually commit a crime. After Zane's behavior in Sydney and her misery when he had failed to come after her, it was a scenario she hadn't dared consider.

The engine dropped to a low hum. Zane stabbed at a button. The rattle of a chain cut through the charged silence as he dropped anchor.

Lilah watched the grim set of Zane's shoulders as he studied the chain for a few seconds to make sure the anchor had taken hold. "I suppose on Medinos, trying to get a conviction against an Atraeus is impossible."

Zane went very still. When he straightened, she realized

the faint shaking of his shoulders was laughter. He grinned, suddenly looking rakish. "Not impossible, just highly improbable."

Ten

The inflatable boat scraped ashore on the pristine white-sand beach. With a fluid movement, Zane climbed out and held it steady against the wash of waves. Ignoring the hand he offered her, Lilah clambered over the side, shoes in one hand, handbag gripped in the other.

Ankle-deep water splashed her calves, surprisingly cold as she stepped onto the firmly packed sand at the shoreline. With muscular ease, Zane pulled the inflatable higher on the beach, unwound rope and tied it to an iron ring attached to a weathered post.

Shielding her eyes from the sun, which was almost directly overhead, Lilah examined the bay. Beyond the post was an expanse of tussock grass interspersed with darker patches of wild thyme and rosemary. Farther back, and to the right, she could see, following the broad curve of an estuary, the remains of sheds. To the right, flanked by a grove of gnarled olive trees, was the ivy-encrusted remnant of what must have once been a grand villa. She instantly knew that this had to be

Sebastien Ambrosi's villa. Sienna and Carla Ambrosi's grandfather had left Medinos in the 1940s and settled in Broome, Australia, where he had reestablished the Ambrosi Pearls business. "The house looks smaller than I imagined."

"You knew Sebastien Ambrosi?"

"My mother used to work for him in Broome, seeding and grading pearls. He was very kind to us." She lifted her shoulders. "I've always been fascinated by Ambrosi Pearls, and I've always longed to see Ambrus."

While Zane unloaded their cases, she walked along the beach. From here nothing was visible except the misty line where sea met sky, no land, no Medinos or any other island, just water and isolation.

She studied the Atraeus beach house, which was set back into a curve in the jagged cliffs. Built on three levels, it wasn't, by any stretch of the imagination, a cottage. Planes of glass glinted in the sun. The teaklike wood and the jutting curves and angles gave it the appearance of a gigantic ship flowing out of the rock. Sited higher than the beach, it no doubt commanded a magnificent view.

"Are you all right?"

She whirled. "You're holding me prisoner. Other than that, I guess everything is just fine."

Any hint of amusement winked out of his gaze. "You are not a 'prisoner.' I've asked a Medinian couple, Jorge and Marta, to stay over for a couple of days. Jorge is a trained butler, and Marta is a chef. I'm trying to keep this as PC as I can."

"A PC kidnapping."

His jaw set in an obdurate line. "If you're hungry, Marta will have lunch ready up at the house."

Zane breathed a sigh of relief when Lilah appeared, fresh and cool after showering and changing into a white shift, to join him on one of the enormous decks for lunch.

Marta had set out a tempting array of salads and meats. As Zane watched Lilah eat, curiously at home in the wild setting, a sense of possessiveness filled him.

The house on Ambrus was a luxury retreat. He could have brought any number of women he had known here, but he had never been even remotely tempted. Lilah was his first guest. Not that she had seen it that way.

He realized he wasn't just attracted to Lilah; he liked her, even down to the way she pushed his buttons. She had given him a hard time from the minute he had caught up with her in the airport.

His decision to do whatever it took to keep her with him settled in. She wasn't ready to admit it yet, or surrender to him, but he was confident he could change that. Deny it as she might, she couldn't hide the fact that she wanted him.

Until that moment, he hadn't known how this would work, but now the equation was simple. Lucas had had his chance, and made his choice. He was no longer prepared to allow his brother, or any other man, near her.

Emotion expanded in his chest. After living an admittedly wild, single life, it was something of a U-turn. Until that moment he hadn't known how much he wanted to make it. He still didn't know how exactly they would work out a relationship, how long it would last—or if Lilah was even prepared to try, given her agenda—but he was finally prepared to try.

Lilah placed her fork down and smothered a yawn. "I think I'll go take a nap."

Zane watched her walk back into the house and determinedly squashed the desire to go after her.

After detaining her at the airport then kidnapping her, carrying her to bed would not improve on the impression he had made. Given that he wanted more than a short-lived liaison, he needed to take a different, more mature, approach.

As much as he wanted to follow up on the promise of those rushed few moments on the couch, he would have to wait.

She didn't trust him yet. At this point trust was a commodity neither of them possessed.

When Lilah woke, the sun had gone down and she could smell something savory cooking. Pushing back the sheet, which was the only covering she had needed in the balmy heat, she walked through to the lavish marble en suite bathroom to freshen up.

It seemed that even when the Atraeus family holidayed at the beach, it was done with style. After washing her face, she ran a comb through her hair and coiled it into a loose knot on top of her head. Eyes narrowed, she surveyed her crumpled wardrobe. If she was launching herself into a two-day venture of passion, she needed to dress the part.

In the end she changed into a simple but elegant ivory cotton dress with an intriguingly low cut neckline that she usually teamed with a thin silk camisole.

She inserted pearl studs in her ears and spent a good ten minutes on her makeup. The results weren't exactly spectacular, but Zane hadn't given her much notice. Feeling buoyed up but more than a little on edge, she strolled out to the main sitting room.

For the next two days she had a guilty kind of permission to put her marriage plans to one side and immerse herself in a passionate experience. Unfortunately, she was going to have to play it by ear. Nothing in her extensive research on dating with a view to marriage had prepared her to cope with a rampant love affair with a totally unsuitable man.

Zane was already on the deck dressed in fitted dark pants that outlined the muscular length of his legs and a loose, gauzy white shirt. On another man the semitransparent shirt might have looked soft and effeminate, but on Zane the effect of muslin clinging to broad shoulders was powerful and utterly masculine. With his hair sleeked back in a ponytail, the studs in his ear were clearly visible, making him look even more like his piratical ancestor.

Somewhere classical music played softly. Marta had set the table, but this time it was glamorously romantic with white damask, gleaming gold cutlery and ornate gold candlesticks. Lit candles provided a soft, flickering glow, highlighting the Lalique glassware. With the deck floating in darkness above the rocks and the sea luminous and gleaming below, it was easy to fantasize that she was standing in the prow of a ship.

Dinner was a gazpacho-style soup with fresh, warm rolls, followed by a rich chicken casserole with pasta. Desert was a platter of honeyed pastries, fresh figs and soft white cheese.

Marta and Jorge cleared away. When Zane indicated they should go inside, she preceded him gladly, grateful for the distraction from the growing awareness that they were finally alone.

Feeling even more nervous now, Lilah walked around the huge sitting room, studying the artwork on the walls. She stopped at a beautifully executed watercolor of a rocky track, which culminated in a cave.

Zane's deep, cool voice close to her ear sent a tingling jolt of awareness through her. "That came from the old villa. One of the few possessions that survived the World War Two bombing."

She forced herself to study the familiar signature at the bottom right-hand corner of the painting, although with Zane behind her she was now utterly distracted. "Of course, one of Sebastien's."

"You might recognize a couple of landmarks." He reached past her to indicate a familiar headland, then farther in the background, a high peak. "It's a painting of an area behind the old villa."

She tensed at Zane's proximity. It was ridiculous to be so on edge. It wasn't as if they hadn't kissed a number of times, made love.

The warmth of his breath on her nape sent a shivery frisson down her spine. "Would you like a drink?"

When she turned, he had already moved away and was at the drinks cabinet, a decanter of brandy in one hand, a balloon glass in the other. "No. Thanks."

He splashed brandy in the glass and gestured at the comfortable leather couches. "Have a seat.

Lilah chose an armchair close to the fire, sank into the

cloud of leather and tried to relax. She blushed when she registered Zane's gaze lingering in the area of her neckline, and tried to brazen out the moment.

"Why didn't you tell me that Peters was gay?"

She stiffened at the question. "And how would you know that?"

"I was interested. I made a few inquiries."

Outrage stiffened her spine. She knew what Zane did for a living. He was The Atraeus Group's fixer. If there was a difficult situation or a problem with personnel, Zane took care of it along with a sinister clutch of characters, one of whom happened to be Spiros. "You mean you had me, and Evan, investigated."

Irritation gleamed in his dark eyes. "I asked a few questions in the Ambrosi office. That girl who works in PR? What's her name?"

"Lisa."

"That's it. She told me."

Lilah let out a breath. She should have guessed. Lisa, who was a romantic at heart, would have been dazzled by Zane. She would have hemorrhaged information in the belief that Zane was truly interested in Lilah. "I agreed to be Evan's date on a few occasions to help him keep up the charade that he was straight for his accounting firm, that's all."

Zane positioned himself to one side of the fireplace, the brandy balloon cradled in one hand. "And what about Evan's boss?"

Her mind flashed back to a moment at the charity's annual art auction two years ago when Zane had found her fending off Britten after she had asked him a few leading questions on the subject of marriage and he had gotten the wrong idea.

"I thought you were involved with both Peters and Britten."

"Climbing the corporate ladder?" Which explained why he had practically ignored her for two years.

"Something like that." He finished his brandy and set the glass down on the mantel.

Lilah kept her gaze glued on the flames. "And after we made love, when you knew I hadn't slept with Evan or Britten, or Lucas, why didn't you bother to contact me?"

"I figured we both needed some time. Besides, I needed to go out of town. Broome, to be exact."

Lilah's head came up at the mention of her hometown. "To check out the pearl farms?"

"I wasn't interested in the pearls on that trip. I went to see your mother. I needed her permission."

For a moment she actually considered that Zane had done something crazily old-fashioned and had declared his intention to ask for her hand. Almost instantly she squashed that idea. Firstly, he hadn't asked her anything remotely like that, and since he'd walked into the interview room at the airport there had been plenty of time. Secondly, he would have to both want her *and* love her to propose marriage. "Permission to do what?"

"To pay off your mother's mortgage and outstanding loans."

She shot to her feet, any idea of a romantic idyll gone. "You've got no right to meddle in my family affairs, or offer my mother money."

"The agreement has nothing to do with you and me. Or our relationship."

"We don't *have* a relationship, and my mother is in no position to repay you."

"I don't want the money back."

She went still inside. "What do you want, then?"

"I already have it. Peace of mind."

She frowned. "How can paying off my mother's house give you peace of mind?"

"Because it takes financial pressure off you. Your mother was worried about you." Reaching into his pocket, he produced a slip of paper.

Lilah recognized the check she had written out and expressed to her mother so she could make arrangements with her bank to pay off her mortgage. Clearly, the check had never been cashed.

He dropped the check on the coffee table. "You can give that back to Lucas."

The coolness of his voice jerked her chin up. "It isn't Lucas's money. Although indirectly he, and you, did help me earn it."

Zane's brows jerked together. "The money didn't come from Ambrosi, I made sure of that."

"No. Some of my paintings sold. With the notoriety of my being involved with Lucas, then you, the gallery owner put huge prices on the works and sold out in one day." She picked up the check. "This was the result."

He took it from her fingers, crumpled it in his fist and tossed it into the fire. "Do you know what it did to me to see that check? I thought Lucas was helping you out financially."

Lilah was on her feet now. "And that it was…what? Some kind of down payment on my becoming his mistress?"

"Maybe not right now, but it could have been, eventually."

She let out a breath and tried to calm down. So…okay. She could understand his thinking, because she knew something of his background. She knew his mother had fallen from the glamorous life of an A-list party girl into drug addiction and had depended on a string of less than A-list men to support her and her son. It had been a precarious existence, and Zane had been forced to live it until he was fourteen. "What I don't get is, why you could think that?"

He stepped close and threaded his fingers through her hair. She felt the pins give, moments later her hair slipped down around her shoulders. "You traveled to Medinos for a first date with Lucas. Now you're here, a resident, and Lucas is planning on having a couple of days on Medinos…without his bride-to-be."

She frowned. "Lucas is my boss, that's all. The only thing I really liked about him was that he looks like you."

The bald statement hung in the air, surprising her almost as much as it surprised Zane.

"You hardly knew me."

She gripped the lapels of his shirt and absently worked a button loose. "But then that's how it works."

Zane tilted her face so she was looking directly at him. "You're losing me."

"Fatal attraction. The *coup de foudre,* the clap of thunder."

"Still lost."

"Sex," she muttered baldly. "As in…an affair."

His expression turned grim. He released his grip on her. "A dangerously unstable affair. With a younger man."

She blinked at the grim note in his voice. "Uh—more or less."

A split second later she was free altogether and Zane was several feet away, gripping the back of a leather chair. "Before we go any further let's get one thing clear. I didn't bring you here for a quick, meaningless thrill. If you want me to make love to you, we're going to go about it in a normal, rational, *adult* way."

Instead of throwing herself at him like some desperate, love-starved teenager. The way she had the last time.

The way she had been about to do about thirty seconds ago.

Lilah's cheeks burned. Zane was still gripping the back of the chair. As if *he* needed the protection.

She had known this was going to be a sticky area, and she had messed up, again. She was beginning to understand what had gone so disastrously wrong for Cole women over the years. With their naturally passionate natures they tried too hard to be "good" then got caught in an uncontrollable whiplash of desire. "Now that you mention it, I don't think this is the greatest time to make love."

His gaze was as cool and steady as if those heated moments had never happened. "Then, good night. If you need anything, I'm just down the hall. Or, if you prefer, you can call on Jorge and Marta who are sleeping in the downstairs apartment, although they don't speak any English."

The words *But what if I change my mind?* balanced on the tip of her tongue. She hastily withdrew them as he padded across to the ornate liquor cabinet and splashed more brandy into a clean glass.

She had already made a string of rash decisions with regard to Zane. Before she made even more of a fool of herself, she needed to think things through.

Although the fact that she *was* going to make a fool of herself again was suddenly, glaringly, obvious.

Eleven

The following morning, Lilah woke, exhausted and heavy-eyed after a night spent tossing and turning.

She had lain awake for hours, listening to the sounds of the sea and Zane's footsteps when he had finally gone to bed in the small hours. Aware of Zane, a short distance away in the next bedroom, she had eventually dropped off, only to wake periodically, thump her pillow into shape and try to sleep again.

Kicking the sheet aside, she padded to her bathroom and stared at her pale face and tangled hair in the mirror.

Zane's withdrawal had created an odd reversal in her mind. Sexually, the ball was in her court. If she wanted him, it was clear she would have to make the first move. No more excuses or deception about who was driving what.

His demand had succeeded in focusing her mind. Now, instead of trying to talk herself out of a wild fling with Zane, she was consumed with how, exactly, one went about asking a man for sex.

Lilah showered and dressed in a white camisole and a pair of board shorts, a bikini beneath, in case she felt like a swim.

After applying sunscreen, she walked out to the kitchen, only to discover that the nervous tension that had dogged her all morning had been unnecessary. Zane had left the house early. According to Marta's gestures and the few words Lilah could recognize, he had gone sailing.

Feeling relieved and deflated at the same time, she walked out on the deck where the table was set for breakfast. One glance at the empty sweep of the bay confirmed that the yacht was gone.

After breakfast she walked down to the beach and went for a swim. After sunbathing until she was dry, she walked back to the house, showered off the salt and changed back into the camisole and boardies.

To fill in time, she strolled through the house, examining the art on the walls, pausing at the watercolor that had been done by Sebastien Ambrosi.

Zane had said the painting was an actual place on the island, behind the villa. From the distant peaks included in the landscape, the cave was set on high ground. On impulse, she decided to see if she could find the cave and, at the same time, see if her cell phone would work.

Pulling on a pair of trainers, she slipped her cell in a pocket and indicated to Marta that she was going to walk to the place in the painting.

A few minutes exploring around the old villa site and she found the entrance to a narrow track that ran up through the steep hills behind the villa.

Twenty minutes of intermittent walking and climbing and she topped a rise. The view was magnificent. In the distance she could even make out hazy peaks that formed part of the mountainous inland region of Medinos. She hadn't seen any evidence of the cave.

Sitting down on a rocky outcropping, she tried the phone, but the screen continued to glow with a "No Service" message.

Instead of feeling trapped and frustrated, she felt oddly

relieved. She had done her duty, attempted to make contact with the outside world, and had failed.

She was clambering down a steep, rocky slope when she saw Zane's yacht dropping anchor in the bay. Her heart skipped a beat as she watched Zane toss the inflatable over the side. In the same instant her foot slipped. A sharp pain shot up her ankle. She tried to correct her footing and ended up sliding the rest of the way down the bank.

Sucking in a breath, she tested her ankle, the same one she'd turned in Sydney. Annoyed with the injury, which, while minor, would make the trip down slow, she began to hobble in an effort to walk off the injury.

It started to rain. She was congratulating herself on traversing the narrowest, most precipitous part of the track with steep slopes on both sides, when she glimpsed Zane walking toward her and slipped again, this time landing flat on her back. She lay on the wet ground, eyes closed against the pelting rain, and counted to ten. When her lids flipped open, Zane was staring down at her, water dripping from his chin, wet T-shirt plastered to his torso faithfully outlining every ridge and muscle. "Two days. Paradise, you said."

"It would have been if we'd spent the time in bed."

"Huh." She pushed into a sitting position and checked her ankle and in the process realized that the white camisole she was wearing was now practically invisible.

Zane crouched down beside her. Lean brown fingers closed around her ankle.

"Ouch. Don't touch it." Despite the slight tenderness, a jolt of purely sensual awareness shot through her.

His expression was irritatingly calm. "It's not swollen, so it can't be too sore. How did you do it?"

"I saw you and slipped. Twice."

The accusation bounced off him. "Can you walk?"

"Yes."

"Too bad." He pulled her up until she was balanced on one foot then swung her into his arms.

The rain began to pelt down. She clutched at his shoulders. "I'm heavy."

He glanced pointedly at her chest. "There are compensations."

He continued on down the hill but instead of taking a broad track to the beach, he veered left heading for a dark tumble of rocks. They rounded a corner and a low opening became visible. "Sebastien's cave."

"I thought it might be near."

The mouth to the cave was broad, allowing light to flow into the cavern. Ducking to avoid the rock overhang, Zane set Lilah down on one of the boulders that littered the opening. He shrugged out of the rucksack he had strapped to his back, unfastened the waterproof flap and extracted a flashlight. The bright beam cut through the gloom, revealing a dusty brass lantern balanced on a natural rock shelf and an equally dusty brass lighter lying beside it.

He crouched down and examined her ankle again. "A bandage would help."

She retracted her ankle from his tingling grip. "I can wait for a bandage. Really, it isn't that bad."

"Bad enough that it's starting to swell." He peeled out of his T-shirt.

Murky light gleamed on ridged abs and muscled pecs, the darker striations of the two thin scars that crisscrossed his abdomen. One was shorter and lighter, as if it hadn't been so serious, the other more defined and longer, curling just above one hip.

She dragged her gaze from the mesmerizing expanse of bronzed, sculpted muscle, abruptly aware that he knew exactly the effect he was having on her and that he was enjoying it. "Don't you need to wear that?"

"It's either my T-shirt or your top. You choose."

She concentrated on keeping her gaze rigidly on the wadded T-shirt. "Yours."

"Thought you'd say that."

Using his teeth, he ripped a small hole near the hem of the shirt then tore a broad strip, working the tear until he ended up with a continuous run of bandage. Clasping her calf, he began to firmly wind the bandage around her ankle.

"Don't tell me, you were a Boy Scout."

"Sea Scout." He ripped the trailing end of the bandage into two strips and tied it off.

"*Ouch*. Figures."

He wound a finger in a damp strand of her hair and tugged. "Goes with the pirate image?"

She reclaimed her hair and tried to repress the brazen impulse to wallow in the jolt of killer charm and flirt back. "Yes."

Rising to his feet before he gave in to temptation and kissed Lilah, Zane examined the lantern, which still contained an oily swill of kerosene.

He found a plastic lighter in the rucksack and tried to light it. Frustratingly, the lighter wouldn't ignite. On closer inspection he discovered that the cheap firing mechanism had broken. Tossing the lighter back in the rucksack, he tried the old brass lighter, which had to date back before World War II. It fired instantly. Seconds later, the warm glow of the lantern lit up the cave. "Close on seventy years old and it still works. They should keep making stuff like this."

Zane caught the quick flash of Lilah's smile, and held his breath at the way it lit up her face, taking her from pale and gorgeous to high-voltage, sexily gorgeous.

She held his gaze with a boldness that took him by surprise and made his heart race then looked quickly away, her cheeks pink.

She shrugged. "Sometimes I forget you're an Atraeus."

He shrugged, his jaw clenched in an effort to control the sudden hot tension that gripped him, the desire to compound his sins by grabbing her and kissing her until she melted against him. He had to keep reminding himself he was trying for a measured, adult approach, in line with his desire to try an actual relationship. "Before I was an Atraeus I was a

Salvatore. In L.A. that meant pretty much the opposite of what Atraeus means on Medinos."

"And that's when you got the scars?"

He found himself smiling grimly. "That's right. Pre-Spiros."

Picking up the lantern, he held it high. "Wait here. I'm going to check out the rest of the cavern."

And take a few minutes to regain the legendary Atraeus control that, lately, was losing hands down to the hotheaded Salvatore kid he used to be.

When he returned, Lilah was on her feet. Automatically, he set the lantern down and steadied her, his hands at her waist.

She released the rock shelf she'd grabbed and clutched at his shoulders. "Every time I see you lately, I seem to lose my balance."

"I'm not complaining."

With a calm deliberation formulated during a sleepless night and several hours out on the water, he eased a half step closer, encouraging her to lean more heavily on him. "That's better."

She wound her arms around his neck with an automatic, natural grace that filled him with relief. Despite the disastrous conversation the previous night, she still wanted him.

Her breasts flattened against his chest, sending another jolt of sensual heat through him, but he couldn't lose his cool. He had said that the next time they made love they were going to go about it in a rational, adult way, and he was sticking to that.

Lilah met his gaze squarely. "Why did you sail away on your own?"

A chilly gust of wind laced with rain swept into the cave.

"I wanted to give you time to think things through. If you had wanted off the island that badly, I would have taken you, but—"

"I don't."

His mouth went dry at her capitulation. A split second later thunder crashed directly overhead.

Lilah lifted a brow.

"Come and see what I found." An uncomplicated satisfaction flowed through Zane as he picked up the lantern and helped Lilah through to the rear part of the cavern, which narrowed and curved then widened out to form a second room.

The cavern was furnished with a table and two chairs, a small antique dresser and a chaise longue. As dusty and faded as the furniture was, the overall effect was elegant and dramatic, like a set for an old Valentino movie.

"What is this place?"

Zane set Lilah down on one of the chairs and stripped what proved to be a dustcover off the chaise longue revealing red velvet upholstery. "I'd guess we've found the location of Sebastien Ambrosi's love nest."

Lilah touched the velvet. She had heard the tale from her grandmother, who had known Sebastien quite well. According to Ambrosi family history Sebastien had asked for Sophie Atraeus's hand, but in order to save the then failing Atraeus finances, Sophie had been engaged to a wealthy Egyptian businessman. "Where he was supposed to meet with his lover, Sophie Atraeus."

"You know your history."

Zane's gaze was focused and intent as he pulled pins out of her hair. Heart pounding, she clutched at his sleek shoulders. With slow deliberation, his mouth settled on hers. Automatically, she lifted up on her good foot and wound her arms around his neck.

The kiss was firm, but restrained. After a night of tortured wrestling with her values, all undermined by a fevered anticipation that had kept her from sleeping, it was not what she had expected.

Wry amusement glinted in his eyes. "I'm trying to slow things down a little."

"Under the circumstances, it's a little late to worry about being PC."

His hands closed on her hips, pulling her in close against him. "Is that un-PC enough for you?"

She buried her face against his throat, breathing in his scent, reassured by his tentativeness, charmed by his consideration and the touches of humor. "What are you afraid of? That you might lose control and we'll end up having unprotected sex?"

He reached into his pocket. Moments later he pressed a foil packet into her hand. "That won't happen again."

Suddenly the murky afternoon was hot and airless.

His mouth captured hers again, this time frankly hungry. She felt the hot glide of his palms on her chilled skin as he peeled the damp camisole up her rib cage. Obligingly, she lifted her arms so he could dispose of the garment altogether. Moments later her bra was gone.

She braced herself against his shoulders as he unfastened her shorts and peeled them along with her panties down her legs.

When he straightened, she unfastened and unzipped his jeans. He assisted by toeing off his trainers and stepping out of damp, tight denim.

Lacing her fingers with his, he pulled her close. Heat flooded her at the intimacy of skin on skin.

The sound of the wind increased, damp air stirred through the cavern, raising gooseflesh on her skin. Zane wrapped her close. "This is no place to make love."

She buried her face in the muscled curve of shoulder and neck and breathed in his scent. "It was good enough for Sebastien and Sophie."

"Almost seventy years ago." He cupped her nape and fastened his teeth gently on the lobe of one ear, sending a bolt of heat clear through her. "I was thinking modern-day bed, silk sheets, soft music."

"Where's your sense of adventure?"

"Back in L.A.," he said drily.

Releasing her, he pulled her down with him onto the chaise

longue, their legs tangling, the weight of him shatteringly intimate. The chaise longue was narrow and unexpectedly hard, but the discomfort was instantly forgotten as the heat of his body swamped her.

She kissed him, wanting him with a fierceness that shook her. She could feel the heat and shape of him against her inner thigh and remembered the foil packet, which she was still holding. “I might need some help with this.”

His teeth gleamed. He relieved her of the condom. “Leave it to me.”

With expert movements, he sheathed himself, reminding her that while she was a novice, Zane operated at the other end of the scale. His experience and conquests were legendary. Seconds later, he moved between her legs. She felt the hot pressure of him, a moment of shaky vulnerability at what she was allowing, then the aching rush of pleasure.

For long seconds she couldn’t think, couldn’t breathe. Zane simply held himself inside her, his gaze locked with hers. And endless moment later he began to move. Not hurried and edged by anxiety, but a slow, tender rhythm that squeezed her chest tight, gathered her whole being. Lovemaking as opposed to the stormy few seconds they had shared in Sydney.

Zane’s gaze locked with hers as sensation drew them to gether, swept her in dizzying waves, shoving her over an invisible precipice as the coiled intensity shattered.

For long minutes Lilah floated, disconnected and content, happy to wallow in the intimacy of Zane’s solid weight, the heart-pounding knowledge that there was much more to lovemaking than she had ever imagined.

As if he’d read her thoughts, he lifted his head and braced himself on one elbow. He framed her face with his free hand, stroking his thumb across her bottom lip. “Next time, we’re making love in a bed.”

Twelve

The vibration of Zane's cell broke the warm contentment.

He extracted his phone from his jeans and checked the screen. "Sorry. Work call. The downside of a satellite connection." Pulling on his jeans, he walked out into the first part of the cavern to take the call.

Cold now that Zane was gone, Lilah found her damp clothes and quickly dressed. The squall had passed and watery sunshine filtered into the cave, relieving the oppressive gloom.

Curious about the meeting place of the two lovers who apparently had been forbidden to see each other, she studied the room. When Sophie had disappeared during a bombing raid during the war, it was rumored that Sebastien had taken her with him to Australia. Sebastien had denied the claim. The unresolved questions had been a bone of contention between the two families ever since.

Lilah opened a cupboard in the dresser and found a small wooden box and a letter. The box contained a missing set of bridal jewels that she instantly recognized. She had designed jewelry based on Sebastien's sketches of this very set. They had belonged to the Atraeus family, and Sebastien had been blamed for stealing them.

Heart speeding up, she extracted a piece of fragile, yellowed paper. She could read a little Medinian, better than she could speak it, enough to know she was looking at a love letter.

Zane strolled in, sliding the phone into his jeans pocket. She showed him the jewels then handed him the letter.

"Sophie Atraeus's final love letter to Sebastien Ambrosi." He set the letter down beside the casket of jewels. "Well, that solves the mystery. Sophie boarded one of the ships that sank with all hands. She was lost at sea."

"And she left the bridal jewels here."

"Probably for safekeeping. When the islands were evacuated, a lot of families hid their valuables in caves. To Sophie it would have made perfect sense."

Lilah touched her fingertips to a delicate filigree necklace. "These are more than jewels, they're history. And a record of love."

Zane's dark, assessing gaze rested on her.

Feeling faintly embarrassed, she closed the box and tested her weight on her sore ankle. "I think I can walk now."

Zane took the box from her, set it down on the table and drew her close. "Not yet. Later."

By the time they left the cave, the storm had cleared and it was twilight. A slow walk down the hillside, heavily assisted by Zane, and they reached the house on sunset. The fairy-tale quality of the afternoon extended into the evening with another candlelit dinner beneath the stars.

The tension of the previous night seemed a distant memory as the dishes were cleared away. When Zane pulled back her chair and linked his fingers with hers, it seemed the most natural thing in the world to go to bed together.

When Lilah woke the next morning, she was alone. Feeling disappointed, because she had looked forward to waking up with Zane, she quickly showered and dressed in a white halterneck top and muslin skirt. When she walked out onto the deck, still limping slightly, Zane was seated at the table, drinking coffee and answering emails.

Zane got to his feet and held her chair. "Your ankle's still swollen."

"Only a little. The stiffness should wear off while I walk." Feeling let down that he hadn't kissed her, but reasoning that Zane was probably distracted by whatever work situation he was dealing with, she sat and poured herself a glass of freshly squeezed orange juice.

"You won't need to walk much." Zane bent down and kissed her on the mouth.

The warm pressure, the sudden intensity of his gaze, broke her tension. The dire suspicion implanted by a number of women's magazine articles, that now they had made love and she was a "sure thing" Zane was losing interest, receded.

Zane checked his watch as he returned to his seat. "We're going back to Medinos. I've called in a ride.

By ride, Zane had meant the Atraeus family's private helicopter. Concerned about her ankle and despite her objections, Zane insisted she should get it checked out by a doctor. The helicopter set them down in the grounds of the Castello Atraeus. Zane transferred their luggage to his car and drove her to a private clinic located in downtown Medinos.

They were greeted by a plump and cheerful doctor. A few minutes later they were back out on the street. Lilah, now almost free of the irritating limp, walked as briskly as she could toward the car.

Now that they were back on Medinos, she was aware that as wonderful and earth-shattering as her time with Zane was, it had to be over. She couldn't afford to abandon her arrangements just because Zane wanted to be with her for a few days.

Zane insisted on helping her into the passenger-side seat then slid behind the wheel with a masculine grace she doggedly ignored. She would have to get used to viewing him as one of her bosses again, although with the sleek width of his shoulders almost brushing hers and the hot scent of his skin it was going to be difficult.

"Okay," he said flatly. "What's wrong?"

Lilah ignored the flash of irritation in his eyes and tried to focus on her happy place, which at present was the bland fence that encircled the parking lot. "Nothing. I need some processing time."

He actually had the gall to pinch the bridge of his nose as if he was under extreme stress. "This would be a feminine thing."

Her gaze clashed with his and the fact that she had not only made love with Zane *a number of times* but was actually considering canceling the series of blind dates she had set up for next week, for him, hit her forcibly.

She stared at the masculine planes of his face, the narrowed eyes and tough jaw, the moment of disorientation growing.

He was too wealthy, too attractive and too used to getting exactly what he wanted. The wild fling had been a mistake. She must have been out of her mind thinking that she could ever control any part of a relationship with Zane. "We've had the two days, it has to be over."

His brows jerked together. "We could spend a few more days together. I know you have vacation time coming up, but you don't fly back to Sydney until the end of next week."

She felt her brain scramble. "An affair wasn't on my priority list. I have things to do—"

"Like checking out online marriage prospects."

There was a ringing silence. "I don't know how you knew that, but yes."

"Stay with me until the end of the week." He started the engine and put the car in gear.

Her chest squeezed tight as he turned on to the spectacular coast road with its curvy white-sand beaches and sea views. After which time she would seldom see Zane, if at all, because he worked mostly in the States.

"Talk to me, Lilah."

She turned her head, which was a mistake, because Zane's gaze was neither cool nor distant, but contained a flash of vulnerability that tugged at her heart. For a split second she was filled with the dizzying knowledge that Zane truly wanted to be with her. "I don't know that it's a good idea to continue."

Lilah's fingers clenched on her handbag. The last thing she had expected was that Zane, with his freewheeling approach to love, would try to keep her with him, even if only for a few days.

She should hold firm and finish it now. Staying with Zane could wreck her plans for the secure marriage she needed. She was already distinctly unmotivated at the thought of meeting the men in her file.

But it was also a fact that since she had undertaken the search for a husband a great many things had changed; *she* had changed.

She was now financially secure and no longer based in Sydney. The financial pressure of her mother's mortgage was gone.

She was no longer a virgin.

The difference that made was unexpectedly huge. She now knew that if she was not passionately attached to her prospective husband, she would not be able to go through with the physical side of the relationship.

She was aware that this restriction would drastically reduce her chances of finding someone. She was almost certain that none of the men on her list would fulfill her new requirement, but she was no longer worried. She could marry, or not. It was her choice.

The sense of freedom that came with that thought was huge.

She still wanted a stable marriage, but she no longer felt she *had* to marry in order to be happy or secure. Now she had a much more important goal: she wanted to be loved.

Zane turned into the drive that led to the Atraeus Resort and pulled in under the elegant portico.

Lilah signed the register then followed Zane to the bank of elevators. "What if I say 'no' to more time together?" The instant the question was out she knew it was a fatal mistake.

Elevator doors slid open.

Zane gestured that she precede him. "I'm counting on the fact that, when it comes to us, you don't have a big track record with 'no.'"

The abrupt switch to teasing charm, and Zane's use of the word *us* threw her even more off balance. "A gentleman wouldn't say that."

He hit the button to close the door. "But then, as we both know, I'm no gentleman."

No. He was mad and bad and dangerous to know. He had turned her life upside down, and he was still doing it.

Almost a whole week with Zane before she committed herself fully to the tricky business of finding a husband. The thought was dizzying, tempting.

She couldn't say no.

"All right," she said huskily. "Six more days."

"And then it's over."

She tensed, stung by the neutrality of his tone, the implication that he would be relieved when the affair came to an end. "You make it sound like the resolution to a problem." One of his troubleshooting projects.

Zane bent his head and brushed her mouth with his. "It is a problem, and it has been for two years."

Six days.

She no longer wanted to concentrate on the men she had planned to meet and date next week. But neither could she afford to abandon her series of interviews altogether.

Zane was not abandoning his life for her. She still needed to plan for the future. She would need something to hold on to when he had gone.

The doors of the elevator opened. Lilah stepped out into the expensively carpeted corridor of the penthouse level. Zane opened the door to a suite.

Decorated in subtle champagne-and-pink hues with elegantly swagged curtains, the suite was both gorgeous and spacious. A glass coffee table held a display of lush pink roses, tropical fruits, a plate of handmade chocolates and an ice bucket with champagne and two flutes.

There were two bedrooms.

Lilah was aware of Zane talking to a bellhop who had delivered their luggage.

While Zane tipped the bellhop she continued to check out the rooms.

Except for the colors, the suite was a mirror image of the one they had shared in Sydney. The separate bedrooms contained identical four-poster beds swathed in diaphanous champagne silk and gorgeous en suite bathrooms. Everything was carefully arranged so that two people could live separate lives in the same suite.

She sensed his presence behind her a split second before she heard the sound of her case being placed on the stand just inside the door. She caught Zane's reflection in a large ornate mirror and her heart turned over in her chest.

When she turned, one broad shoulder was braced against the door frame. He had brought just the one suitcase, she noted, hers. She realized he had already placed his case in the other bedroom.

She set her handbag down on the end of the bed. "This is a two-bedroom suite."

His gaze was neutral. "I prefer to sleep alone."

Her stomach and her heart plunged.

Desperate for a distraction, Lilah switched her gaze to her cases. "Oh good, you've brought my laptop."

She forced a bright, professional smile and grabbed the lifeline of an internet connection.

"You're going to work?"

Blinking back a sudden urge to cry, she picked up the computer case. "I have some private correspondence to see to."

Blindly, she walked past Zane out into the sitting room

and headed in the direction of an elegant writing desk. Placing the case on the glass-topped surface, she busied herself setting up the laptop.

Zane's clinical approach to their sleeping arrangements, his rejection of any depth of intimacy, was a reminder she badly needed. Now more than ever, she needed to carry through with her schedule for the following week.

Zane frowned as he watched Lilah. The blank look in her eyes tugged at him, warring with his habit of carefully preserving his emotional distance. He was almost certain she was crying.

Instead of backing off, he found himself irresistibly drawn as she booted up her computer. "I thought we could go out for lunch."

"That sounds nice."

Zane frowned at the brisk note in Lilah's voice. He glanced at her laptop screen. The separate rooms dilemma suddenly evaporated. "Are these online 'friends' all male?"

"As it so happens, yes."

The emotional calm he had worked so hard to maintain since the riveting hours in the cave was abruptly replaced by the same fierce, unreasoning jealousy he had experienced when he had found out that Lucas was taking Lilah to Constantine's wedding. "Have you dated any of them?"

She fished spectacles out of her handbag, pushed them onto the bridge of her nose and leaned a little closer to the screen as if what she was reading was of the utmost importance. "Not yet."

Dragging his gaze from the fascinating sight of the spectacles perched on the delicate bridge of Lilah's nose, he studied the list of men she was perusing. The lineup of photographs portrayed a selection of Greek gods, some flashing golden tans and overly white teeth, some dressed with *GQ* perfection. The one exception was a slightly battered, bleach blond surfer type.

Lilah scrolled and he glimpsed the logo of the matchmaking agency. The lightbulb flared a little brighter. "But you intend to?"

"That's right. Next week when I have my annual vacation."

His gaze snagged on the four men who had withdrawn. He noted the dates. Just days after the scandal had erupted into the newspapers.

He also noted that the flood of new applications had all come in at a similar time. "How many?"

"Fifteen so far." She scrolled down to a chat page, which had several comments posted. "Seventeen if two other very good prospects come on board."

The corporate-speak momentarily distracted him. He had to remind himself that the businesslike approach was entirely consistent with Lilah's view of marriage. She didn't just want a man, she wanted a paragon, someone who would tick every one of the boxes on her corporate marriage sheet.

Someone who possessed all of the steady, reliable qualities that he clearly did not. "This is why we only have a week. You're fitting me in before you go back to Sydney to find a husband."

Her gaze remained glued to the screen. "If I'm seeing someone from the agency I can't be involved."

Involved. He suddenly knew the meaning of stress.

Lilah could feel Zane's displeasure as he studied the emails pouring into her mailbox.

Abruptly, she found herself spun around in her chair. Irritation snapped in his gaze and she realized she had pushed him too far with the list.

"Is that all this is?"

She dragged her spectacles off. "You said it yourself. Marriage doesn't come into our equation."

"I thought we had an agreement."

"We do, but long-term commitment is the one thing I do want. The reason I haven't been able to settle on anyone is because you've always been in the picture just often enough to blot out any other prospects."

The expression in his gaze was suddenly remote. "Are you saying I'm responsible for your decision to advertise for a husband?"

"No." *Yes.* She stared at the screen and tried to pinpoint what had driven her to such an extreme. It had been after the last charity auction, she realized. Zane had been there with Gemma.

Lilah had spent an entire agonizing evening trying not to be aware of Zane and failing. Afterward, she had decided she needed to deal with the fixation by making plans for the future. It had been a relief to come up with a workable plan.

It was not a good time, she realized, to acknowledge that her approach had been naive and too simplistic. The strength of her plan had relied on the screening process of a matchmaking company and the integrity of the men who had replied, which was a fatal flaw. With her family history, she should have known better. "I've tried normal dating. This seemed a more…controllable option."

Grimly, Zane decided that he shouldn't be pleased he had effectively blotted out the other men in Lilah's life. Neither should he be annoyed that Lilah dismissed him as secure relationship material, when that was the stance he had always maintained.

He should be more concerned with distancing himself. Given that they only had six days left to douse the fatal attraction that threatened to ruin both of their lives, it was not a good time to feel fiercely possessive.

Emotionally, he did not get involved; he had learned the hard way that love had conditions. It literally took him years to trust anyone, and he could count those he did trust on one hand.

That ingrained wariness of people made him good at his job. He didn't take anything for granted. His approach was often perceived as clinical and heartless. Zane didn't bring emotion into the process; he simply did the job he was paid to do.

But somehow, despite his background and his mind-set, he *was* involved. "Just what do you think every one of those guys who answered your ad wants?"

"A steady, stable relationship."

"Do you believe in the tooth fairy?"

"This is not a good time to be sarcastic."

"Then don't believe in this. It's not real."

He straightened and stabbed a finger at one of the photos of a bronzed, sculpted torso. The handsome, chiseled face rang a bell. He couldn't be sure, but he had a suspicion it belonged to a male model, probably from some underwear billboard. "*They* are not real."

"Which is exactly why I intend to conduct one-on-one interviews next week. If they're not genuine, I'll know."

There was a moment of vibrating silence. "This is the reason you have to be back in Sydney?"

"Yes."

"Where, exactly, do you intend to conduct these interviews?"

"At restaurants and cafes. They're not interviews exactly. More a series of…blind dates. After I conduct online interviews to screen candidates."

Blind dates. Suddenly Zane needed some air.

Thirteen

Pacing to a set of French doors, he jerked them open, although he was more interested in Lilah's reflection in one of the panes than the sun-washed balcony. "Did you give them your real name?"

"Yes. And a photograph."

"Along with your occupation." Lilah was nothing if not thorough. His tension ratcheted up another notch. "When the recent publicity hit the newspapers, they would all have instantly recognized you."

Lilah could feel herself going cold inside. Of course she had considered that angle, but she had been guilty of hoping that the original list of five steady, reliable men she had assembled would be too sensible to read the gutter press, or to connect the wild stories with her resume.

Zane's gaze, reflected in the glass, was neutral enough to make her feel distinctly uncomfortable. "The whole point of the exercise is marriage. What did you expect me to do? Pretend to be someone I wasn't?"

"Like the guys who replied."

Her gaze was inescapably drawn to a couple of the photos, which she suspected were of male models and not the candidates. In the case of one particularly stunning man, she was almost certain she had seen him on an underwear billboard. "I'm well aware that some of the applications are not honest."

There was a vibrating silence. "I have resources. If you want I can have them screened by the private investigative firm The Atraeus Group uses in Sydney."

For long seconds she wavered, but given the media exposure that had made her temporarily notorious, she couldn't afford not to have Zane's help. He was in the business of checking and double-checking on the integrity of businesses and personnel. She did everything she could to research the candidates, but with limited time and resources, she couldn't hope to do any in-depth checking in the span of a few days. "Okay."

Lilah brought up her file of applicants and vacated the chair. Zane sat down and began to scroll through, the silence growing progressively deeper and more charged as he read. "Do you mind if I email the file to my laptop?"

"Go ahead."

Seconds later, he exited her mail program and rose from the chair. "I'm going to have these names checked out. The firm I use has access to criminal files and credit records. I'll order lunch in, it shouldn't take more than a couple of hours to get some basic details back." An hour and a half later, Lilah stared at the list of men on her dating site, her stomach churning at the thought of what Zane could turn up. While she had waited for the results of his investigation, she had eaten one of the selection of salads that had been delivered by room service then made herself coffee in the small kitchenette.

She sipped the coffee, barely tasting it. Six days together. She blinked back a wave of unexpectedly intense emotion. It wouldn't be six days of making love; it would be six days of saying goodbye.

Jaw set, she forced her attention back to her laptop screen and began reading through all of the mail. She had expected to have a few withdrawals—what she hadn't expected was for four of her five vetted men to have quit her page and the raft of new applications.

A prickling sense of unease hit her. She had compiled her previous list of stable, steady men over months from the unenthusiastic trickle of replies to her dating agency application. In the span of two days she had lost four of the five steady prospects she had intended to meet the following week and had received fifteen new "expressions of interest." Not good.

She scrolled through the emails, flinching at some of the subject lines.

Clearly, it had been an easy matter to connect the scandalous stories in the press with her matchmaking page. Most of her solid prospects had quit and she was now being targeted by men attracted by her notoriety.

Zane strolled into the suite. "A handful of the applicants checked out." He tossed a pile of papers down on the desk. "Don't reply to any of these. If you do, you can count on my presence at any interviews you conduct because, honey, I'll be there."

Lilah swallowed the impulse to argue a point she was in one hundred percent agreement with herself. She did not want to end up at the mercy of some kind of kinky opportunist or worse, a reporter trying to generate another smutty story. "I don't see how. You won't be in Sydney next week."

Zane strolled toward his bedroom, unbuttoning his shirt and shrugging out of it as he walked. "For this, I'll make a point of it."

Lilah dragged her gaze from Zane's broad back, and the unsettling, undermining intimacy of watching him undress. With an effort of will, she squashed the impulse to walk up behind him, wrap her arms around his waist, lean into his heady warmth and breathe in the scent of his skin. "I don't see why when you made it clear you don't want anything more than a temporary arrange—"

"You want more than the one week time limit?"

Lilah tried to squash the heart pounding thought that they could extend their affair for weeks, maybe months. The reason she was keeping the time so short was to get the fixation with Zane out of her system. She couldn't in all honesty enter into a marriage with someone else if she was still attracted to Zane.

Although, she was already certain she had made a fundamental mistake. The desperate fixation *had* faded somewhat, but it had been replaced with something much more insidious.

She was beginning to *like* Zane. Neither her mother nor her grandmother had ever mentioned liking their lovers. There had simply been the dangerously out-of-control passion, which had been dispensed with when the pregnancies had become apparent.

She avoided answering him and instead stared at the papers Zane had tossed down on the desk. On the top was the underwear ad guy. In reality, he was a forty-five-year-old, twice-divorced mechanic who had somehow managed to make his application from a minimum-security prison cell.

According to the detective firm Zane had employed, he was currently serving a two-year sentence for car theft. With time out for good behavior, he could be out in six months.

The sound of running water in Zane's shower broke the heavy silence that seemed to have settled around her. She skimmed the information on the rest of the applicants Zane had blacklisted. Logging back on to the matchmaking site, she deleted them from her page. That left her with six applicants in total, one from her previous batch of applicants, and five new ones. Three were depressingly unsuitable, so she deleted them. That left her with three.

The sound of the shower stopped.

She tried to concentrate on the photos and profiles of the three remaining men on her dating list. Jack, Jeremy and John, the three J's.

They were all pleasant, attractive men in solid jobs. John Smith, wearing a crisp, dark suit, looked like an ad for *Gentleman's Quarterly*. Listed as the CEO of his own company, he fitted the profile she had put together for a husband perfectly.

The one applicant who had not deserted her following the scandal in the newspaper, Jack Riordan, had been high on her list. He wasn't perfect, but it was heartening that her top pick apart from Howard, who had not worked out, was still on board.

Taking a deep breath she decided she needed to reward Jack Riordan's loyalty for sticking with her despite the scandal, take the plunge and commit to an initial date.

She typed in a suggested meeting time and place and hit the return key. Her computer made a small whooshing sound as the reply was sent. A split second later her message appeared on her page.

Stomach tight, pulse hammering, she stared at the neat print. After months of lurking online, reluctant to commit to anything more than a little window-shopping, she felt she was finally moving forward with her plans. She ought to feel positive that, while she wouldn't have Zane in her life, at least she had the possibility of having *someone*.

There were no strings, she reminded herself. Half an hour in a coffee shop or over a lunch table, and if she didn't like Jack, or vice versa, they need never contact one another again.

The thought was soothing. On impulse she quickly typed in affirmatives for the other two men. Now more than ever, with the end of her time with Zane set and the knowledge that hurt was looming, it was important to stay focused.

She stared at the three messages on screen and her stomach did a crazy flip-flop. The decision shouldn't feel like a betrayal of Zane, but suddenly, very palpably, it did.

With a jerky movement, she pushed back from the desk, rose from her seat and strolled to the French doors. She stared out at the serene view of sea and the distant, floating shape of Ambrus.

A shiver went through her as she remembered the hours spent making love to Zane on Ambrus, then further back to the stormy interlude in Sydney.

Unhappy with the direction of her thoughts, she walked through to the bedroom and began to unpack. Long seconds ticked by as she emptied her suitcase and tidied it away in a large closet.

Despite trying to put a positive spin on the process of finding a husband, every part of her suddenly recoiled from the idea of replacing Zane in her life.

In her bed.

She walked back out into the sitting room and began to pace, too upset to settle. Her stomach was churning; she actually felt physically sick. She had the sudden wild urge to erase the messages she had sent, because she knew with sudden conviction that no matter how wonderful or perfect any one of the three J's might be she was no longer sure she was ready to offer any of them a relationship. The thought of sharing the same intimacies with another man that she had shared with Zane made her recoil. She couldn't do it.

The truth sank in with the same kind of absolute clarity she experienced when she knew a painting was finished or a jewelry design was completed. It was a complication she should have foreseen. She had tried to get Zane out of her system, but she had done the exact opposite of what she had planned to do. She had fallen wildly, irrevocably in love with him.

In retrospect, the damage had been done two years ago when she had first met him at the charity art auction.

She wondered why she hadn't seen it from the first. Clearly she had been so intent on burying her head in the sand and denying the attraction that she had failed to recognize that it was already too late.

She had been a victim of the *coup de foudre*. Struck down somewhere between the first intense eye contact when she had strolled into the ballroom that night over two years ago and the passionate interlude at the end of the evening.

With her history she should have sensed it, should have *known*. Her only excuse was that neither her mother nor her grandmother had ever mentioned a lingering fascination or liking coming into the equation. Cole women were notoriously strong-willed. As soon as the pregnancies, and their lovers' unwillingness to commit, had become apparent, the relationships had ended.

If she'd had any sense, as soon as she had registered the unusual power of the attraction she would have gotten as far away from Zane Atraeus as she could. Instead, she had offered to donate more paintings to his charity, gotten involved with fundraising, even volunteered to help with the annual art auctions. Every step she had taken had ensured further contact with Zane.

It was no wonder she had not been able to let go of the fixation. In her heart of hearts that was the last thing she had wanted. She had hung around him like a love-struck teenager, secretly sketching and painting him.

She had compounded the problem by legitimizing the affair as an exercise to get Zane out of her system. Instead she had succeeded in establishing him even more firmly in her life, to the extent that now she didn't want anyone else.

She had been in love with Zane for two years. There was no telling how long she would remain in love, but given the stubborn streak in her personality, it could be for years. Quite possibly a *lifetime*.

She still wanted a stable marriage and a happy family life. She wanted love and security and babies, the whole deal. But she no longer wanted them with some unknown mystery man in her future.

She wanted them with Zane.

Zane strolled out as she headed back to the desk, dressed in a soft white shirt and a pair of faded, glove-soft jeans.

Aware that the screen of her laptop portrayed the appointments she had made, and which she was now desperate to retract, Lilah made a beeline for the desk.

Zane, who clearly had the same destination in mind, reached her laptop a split second before she did.

The scents of soap and clean skin and the subtle, devastating undernote of cologne made her stomach clench.

Zane touched the mouse pad. The screen saver flickered out of existence, revealing the three postings she had made.

To Lilah's relief there were no replies, yet. In Sydney it would be midmorning. All three J's would be at work.

"You've made times to meet." Zane's voice was soft and flat.

Lilah stiffened at his remoteness; it was not the reaction she had expected. The lack of annoyance, or even irritation, that she was progressing with her marriage plans was subtly depressing.

With the suddenness of a thunderbolt his cool neutrality settled into riveting context. She had seen him like this only once before, when he had been dealing with a former treasurer of the charity who had "borrowed" several thousands of dollars to pay for an overseas trip. Zane had been deceptively quiet and low-key, but there had been nothing either soft or weak about his approach. Potter had taken something that mattered to Zane, and he wasn't prepared to be lenient.

Zane had quietly stated that if the money wasn't back in the account and Potter's resignation on his desk by the end of the day, charges would be laid and Zane would personally pay for and oversee the litigation.

Potter had paled and stammered an apology. He hadn't been able to write the check fast enough.

Lilah had always been aware of Zane's reputation for taking no prisoners in the business world. The element that had struck her most forcibly was that the charity had mattered to him *personally.*

Hope dawned. She knew she mattered to Zane; he had admitted as much. As hard as she had struggled to stay away from him, he had struggled to stay away from her, and failed.

Because she mattered to him on a level he could not dismiss.

By his own admission, he had become more involved with the charity than he had planned because she was there. They had ended up together on Medinos and in Sydney. They'd had unprotected sex. For a man who was intent on staying clear of entanglements, that in itself was an admission.

Then there was the small matter of Zane virtually kidnapping her for two days.

She felt like a sleeper just waking up. She had been so involved in the minutiae of day-to-day events and her own plans for marriage that she had failed to step back and look at the bigger picture.

Zane cared for her. He said he cared about who she was with next. Although it was a blunt fact that Zane did not have a good track record with helping her to find love. He had gotten rid of Howard and a raft of dating applicants. He had effectively made sure that Lucas remained in her past.

There was only one conclusion to be drawn: Zane was jealous.

The tension that gripped Lilah eased somewhat as possibilities she hadn't considered opened up, expanded.

If Zane was jealous, then maybe, just maybe, there was a chance that he could overcome his phobia about intimate relationships and commit to her.

The possibility condensed into a breathtaking idea.

Relationships were not her strong area; hence the marriage plan. It had not been successful, but at least it had given her a framework—a system—to move forward with, and that was what she needed with Zane.

Not a marriage plan. The stakes were suddenly dizzyingly, impossibly high. She needed a strategy to encourage Zane to fall in love with her.

It was a leap across a fairly wide abyss, but in that moment of realization she had already mentally taken that leap. The future stretched out before her in dazzling, Technicolor brilliance. Not just a steady, reliable marriage, but one based on true love.

Once Zane fell for her, she was confident the whole marriage thing would take care of itself. There was a risk involved, but when Zane succumbed to love, the intensity of the emotion should be powerful enough to dissolve whatever objections he had to marriage.

Heart pounding, Lilah stared at the incriminating dates on the screen. It occurred to her that the proposed dates had a positive angle. They could generate the pressure that was needed to convince Zane that he couldn't bear to let her go.

The about-face in thinking was a little disorienting but she was already adjusting to the new direction. The sudden itch to sit down with a pad and pen and start formulating a plan was the clincher.

She could do this.

She had no choice.

She would begin by waiting a day or so before she canceled with the three J's. Taking a deep breath, she smiled pleasantly and answered Zane's question. "I didn't see much point in waiting around."

Zane's brows jerked together. "There's every point. You should have waited for the in-depth security checks."

Lilah's mood soared at his bad temper. "You didn't mention a further check. In any case, other than the very thorough checks you've already conducted there's nothing more that can be done unless you intend to put them under twenty-four-hour surveillance—"

She was caught and held by the complete absence of expression on Zane's face. "That is what you were planning on doing, isn't it?"

Zane's gaze met hers for a searing moment. "Yes."

The small, delighted shock wave she felt at his admission was replaced by a sudden breathless anticipation as he studied the screen. Lilah felt like a kid at Christmas, waiting to unwrap a gift. The surveillance only proved her point. It was the kind of extreme thing one did when they were falling in love.

The discovery made her feel like dancing a jig around the sunny room. She had clung to the depressing view that Zane was elusive and superficial and absolutely not good husband material. Now wasn't a good time to feel that, despite all the areas they did not fit, crazily, he was perfect for her.

Zane stabbed a key and began studying profiles. "You've chosen Appleby, Riordan and Smith. I wouldn't trust Smith. His first name's John—that makes him close to invisible in terms of security information."

Lilah kept her expression smooth and professional. "The initial dates, are just a meet and greet, they do not imply commitment."

There was a vibrating silence, broken by the near silent sound of an indrawn breath. With controlled movements, Zane picked up the hotel folder, which lay next to her laptop and flipped to the page of restaurant listings as if food was suddenly paramount. "You could withdraw from the process."

The barely veiled command in his voice made her want to fling her arms around his neck and hug him. To prevent herself from looking deliriously happy, she picked up a pen and pad and started working on her new plan of action by making an important note. She could not afford any over-the-top displays of affection until Zane capitulated. She allowed her brows to crease, as if she had just remembered that Zane had said something but was too distracted to recall his exact words. "Why should I do that?"

Zane, who seemed more interested in the restaurant he was choosing than their conversation, picked up the sleek phone on the desk, although his grasp on the phone was gratifyingly white-knuckled. "Given the recent publicity, I'm not inclined to trust any of the three. If you won't accept surveillance reports then I'm going to have to insist on being present at the interviews."

Lilah tapped her pen on the notepad. "Let me get this right.

You don't want a relationship with me, yet you'll take time off to make sure I'm..."

"*Safe* is the word you're looking for."

Lilah was momentarily sidetracked by the stormy look in Zane's eyes. A quiver of anticipation zinged down her spine then she registered Zane's emphasis of the protection angle. She was certain he was using it as a handy excuse to avoid admitting to anything else. "You can't come to the interviews."

She had no problem being firm on that point since she intended to cancel all three dates. "What would I tell the applicants?"

Zane froze in the act of dialing the hotel restaurant. "Tell them you're no longer available."

Fourteen

Zane allowed the singular truth that he was burningly, primitively possessive of Lilah to settle in.

With a sense of incredulity, he realized that he had made the kind of rash, male, territorial move he had only ever observed in other men.

He had crossed a line and now there was no going back.

He eased his grip on the phone and set it back on its rest a little more loudly than he had intended.

Lilah, who was in the process of shutting down her computer, was oddly composed. There was a distinct air of expectation that made his jaw compress.

She closed the laptop with a gentle click. "What exactly do you mean by 'no longer available'?"

Her gaze was carefully blank, but he detected the hopeful gleam in her eye. He knew with utter certainty that she wanted him to say marriage.

Bleak satisfaction that he had finally made it on to Lilah's list of marriage candidates was tempered with irritation that it had taken so long, and the old, ingrained wariness. He could feel the jaws of Lilah's feminine trap poised to snap shut.

As much as he wanted Lilah, he would not be maneuvered into a relationship that would leave him vulnerable. Years had passed since his mother had abandoned him, not once, but a number of times in pursuit of well-heeled lovers or husbands. He would never forget how it had felt to have the rug pulled out emotionally, to be relegated to last place on her list when he had needed to be first. By the time his father, Lorenzo, had found him at age fourteen, he'd had difficulty forming any relationships at all.

Remembering the past was like staring into a dark abyss. The level of trust involved in committing to any kind of intimate relationship still made him go cold inside. The progress he had made over the past few years was monumental but he was not capable of moving any further forward with Lilah now unless he could be absolutely, categorically certain of her love.

Unfortunately, Lilah's continued focus on finding a steady, reliable husband suggested that he was not even close to being number one in her life.

Grimly, he realized that part of his wariness revolved around the certainty that, because of his shadowy past and inner scars, a breakup was inevitable. And when it happened, *he* would most likely be the instigator of the betrayals.

"What exactly do you mean by 'no longer available'?"

Grimly, he examined Lilah's question, and the demand that had surprised them both.

Unlocking his jaw, he answered her question. "I think we should try…living together."

"For how long?"

Zane, arrested by Lilah's calm response, watched as she strolled to the kitchenette and extracted a bottle of water from the fridge. He had the sudden, inescapable feeling that he had ventured into a maze and was being herded by a master strategist.

To his surprise he found there was an element of relief to

the thought that Lilah would try to ruthlessly manipulate him into an even deeper commitment. He had always viewed her methodical approach to getting what she wanted from relationships as calculating. Now, it occurred to him that with his past he could not afford to go into a relationship with a woman who was too weak or too frightened to try to hold on to him. "I don't know."

She poured a glass of water and walked sedately in the direction of the bedroom. "Let me think about it."

The door to her bedroom closed quietly behind her.

Zane stared at the closed door for long seconds.

His heart was pounding, his jaw locked. He was aware that Lilah had just pulled off a feat that no one in either his professional or his personal life had attempted in a good ten years.

She had put him on hold.

She had kept her three agency dates, with him on the side.

For the first time since he was a teenager on the streets he experienced what it felt like to be shut out, although the feeling was somewhat...different.

As a teenager, he had been running on survival skills and desperation. That was not the case now. In his job as the Atraeus Group's troubleshooter, he had spent years dealing with people who were intent on closing doors in his face.

Probably the most important skill his father had taught him was that when it came to negotiating there was always a way. He either found another door or he made his own, whatever got the job done.

It was an odd moment to realize that his time as a homeless kid had created qualities in him that had uniquely fitted him out for problem solving. For one thing, he did not give up easily. He was also used to operating from a losing position, and winning.

Something in him cleared, healed.

He was aware of a sense of lightening. He was no longer fourteen and at the mercy of forces and people he could not control. Ten years on, he had a certain set of life skills and a considerable amount of money. Those two factors provided him with an edge that had been formidably successful in business.

A sense of relief filled him. In the business arena he had never been defeated no matter how unpromising the situation. He did not see why he couldn't apply the same strategies that had been so successful in business to a relationship. The only wonder of it was that he had never thought of that before.

His decision made, he strolled to his computer and found the details the security firm had supplied for the three men Lilah had chosen.

Strolling into the kitchenette, Zane opened the fridge. It was depressingly empty. He had missed lunch and his stomach felt hollow and empty. Now hungry as well as frustrated, he pulled out a beer and called down to room service for a pizza.

He walked back to his computer, intending to catch up on some correspondence. On the way, he noticed that Lilah had forgotten to take the bridal-white leather-bound folder with her.

The last time he had seen the contents of the folder had been when Lilah had dropped it on the floor of the jet on her first flight out to Medinos. He had only read snatches; just enough to understand that it contained the kind of inside information that would be very useful to him right now.

The sound of the shower in Lilah's en suite bathroom was the decider. The phrase "all is fair in love and war" took on a new resonance as he picked up the folder and carried it out to the terrace to read.

Setting the beer on the table, Zane pulled out a chair, sat down and began flipping through the pages. There was a formatted set of profiles, complete with photographs, a series of neatly handwritten notes including underlined notations highlighting domestic prowess, and a punitive points system.

A failed marriage carried a penalty of ten points. The total any one man could earn was twenty. Divorce wasn't complete disaster, but close.

* * *

Lilah had expected dinner in the hotel restaurant to be a little tense after she had left Zane strategically hanging. However, instead of the frustration she had glimpsed that afternoon, Zane seemed relaxed and oddly preoccupied, as if his mind was on other things.

Twice he had taken calls on his cell, getting up from the candlelit patio table to pace around the enormous floodlit infinity pool, looking taut and edgy in black pants and a loose black shirt.

To make matters worse, Gemma, who Lilah had thought was based in Sydney, was seated at a nearby table. According to Zane, his former P.A. had just transferred to a position on Medinos, and now worked for the manager of the resort. She started her new job at the end of the week.

Looking young and sexy in a minuscule hot orange dress that should have clashed with her titian hair but somehow didn't, Gemma succeeded in making Lilah feel staid and old-fashioned in the classic white silk sheath she had chosen.

Every time Lilah's gaze was drawn to Gemma, the weight of every one of her twenty-nine years seemed to press in on her. Gemma looked far more Zane's type than she could ever be. It was a depressing fact that in the dating game, classic Hepburn just did not cut it with Lolita. Her sexuality had finally been released, but it was clear that if she wanted to keep Zane's eyes on her, she was going to have to update her wardrobe.

She stared bleakly at the exquisite table arrangement of pink roses. Panic gripped her at the thought that she *had* overplayed her hand. That instead of giving their relationship a discreet nudge toward marriage, she had pushed too hard and Zane was now cooling off.

Zane finished his call and returned to the table. Their dessert, an island specialty he had insisted on ordering, was delivered with a flourish. Lilah tried to show an interest in the exquisite platter of almond pastries and sweetmeats sprinkled with rose petals, but she had lost her appetite.

A wine waiter materialized beside the table with a bottle of very expensive French champagne. As if they had something to celebrate.

Candlelight, roses, champagne, all the classic elements of a grand romantic gesture.

The depression that had settled on her like a dark shroud dissipated, wiped out by a sudden dizzying sense of anticipation. Her heart began to pound. She felt like she was on an emotional roller coaster ride. Her instincts were probably all wrong, but she couldn't blot out the sudden, wild notion that Zane was about to propose.

Zane leaned forward and the subtle but heady scent of his skin and the devastating cologne made her head swim. "Do you see anything you like?"

Her gaze was caught and held by the piercing quality of his eyes. In the candlelight his irises were midnight dark with an intriguing velvety quality. He frowned and she realized he wanted her to look at the dessert that had just been delivered.

She surveyed the dessert tray. Almost instantly, she saw the glitter of jewels in the center.

Her excitement evaporated. Not an engagement ring; a diamond bracelet.

The standard currency for mistresses.

At that moment, Gemma, who was leaving with her escort, stopped at their table.

Her gaze moved from the discreet pop of the champagne cork to the bracelet. She smiled brightly. "Diamonds." She waggled one slim, tanned wrist, displaying a narrow gold bangle that shimmered with tiny stones. "Doesn't Zane give the *best* presents?"

While the waiter poured flutes of champagne, Gemma lingered, introducing her date. She eventually left in a flurry of lace ruffles and floral perfume.

Zane handed Lilah a flute of champagne, which she noted

was pink, to match the rose petals. She tried to be upbeat about that fact. Zane had gone to a great deal of effort to create a special occasion, and he had brought her a gift, which was significant.

Unfortunately, somewhere between discovering the bracelet and the conversation with Gemma, the sizzle of excitement had gone.

His gaze held a hint of impatience. "Do you like it?"

Lilah set the champagne down without tasting it. Grandma Cole had gotten a diamond bracelet from her lover, shortly before he had left her. She had used it as a down payment on a small cottage for her and the baby.

Reluctantly, she extracted the bracelet from its nest of confectionary and petals. It was unexpectedly heavy for such a delicately, intricately constructed piece. Her breath caught as she noted the cut and the quality of the emeralds interspersed between the diamonds. Not new, but old. Make that *very* old.

She frowned. The design was hauntingly familiar. She was certain she had seen something like it before, although, in the flickering light of the candles, she couldn't be sure. Curiosity briefly overrode her disappointment as she studied the archaic design.

She itched to put her spectacles on and examine the bracelet more closely, but she couldn't afford either the professional or the emotional attachment. Not when it looked like a bracelet was Zane's standard form of dating gift.

Despite all of the reasons she could not accept the bracelet, a small part of her didn't want to relinquish it. The value of the stones didn't come into it. The bracelet could have been made of plastic. What mattered was that Zane had thought to give her a gift, a keepsake of their time together.

Unfortunately, old or new, she couldn't risk accepting the bracelet in case Zane took that as her tacit agreement to a relationship with him on his terms.

As his temporary live-in lover.

After the way he had interfered with her dating program

that afternoon, she knew that if she weakened, Zane would be relentless.

Reluctantly, she placed the bracelet on the table.

Zane frowned. "Aren't you going to try it on?"

"It's lovely, but I can't accept it."

"If this is about Gemma, you don't have to worry. She was my personal assistant, nothing more."

"I don't think she sees it that way." Gemma's attitude toward Zane had always been distinctly proprietorial. So much so that for most of the past two years, Lilah had thought she *was* Zane's steady girl.

He looked impatient. "Which is why she isn't my P.A. anymore. The bracelet was a goodbye gift."

Lilah made an effort to calm emotions that were rapidly spiraling out of control. She had to keep reminding herself that she was with Zane now, not Gemma. "Goodbye, and she transfers to Medinos?"

It would not have been the way she would have handled the situation.

"I couldn't fire her, and she liked Medinos. It was a solution."

Lilah's fingers clenched. Gemma had clearly gotten emotionally involved and Zane had found a way of shifting her out of his work space, while still letting her have her way and stay close.

And think that she still had a chance.

It was a perfect example of Zane's nice side. From her dealings with him in the charity, Lilah knew he didn't like seeing anyone in a vulnerable situation get hurt. He would go out of his way to personally help. She loved that evidence of his compassion but she couldn't help wishing that Zane had been a bit more ruthless with Gemma.

Another unsettling thought occurred to her. If Zane had not given Gemma a definite "no" she had to wonder how many other discarded women still lingered on the fringes of his life in the hope that a relationship was still possible.

It was not a happy thought. Zane was nothing like the irresponsible, self-centered men who had abandoned her mother and grandmother, nevertheless the scenario with Gemma was unsettling in a way she hadn't quite worked out.

Ignoring the champagne and the dessert, Lilah got briskly to her feet.

Now visibly annoyed, Zane slipped the bracelet into his pocket and rose to his feet. He fell into step with her as she threaded her way between the tables, easily keeping pace.

His palm cupped her elbow, sending tingling heat up her arm. His gaze locked on hers. "Why won't you accept the gift?"

Lilah ignored the gritty demand and the pleasure that flooded her that, finally, Zane was responding in the way she had hoped. She focused on a bland section of beige wall in an effort to control the wimpy desire to give in, fling her arms around his neck and melt against him. "It's…too expensive."

"I'm rich. Money is no object."

They emerged from the restaurant. A little desperately she eyed the bank of elevators ahead. "It's not about the value, exactly."

Zane released her elbow as they reached the elevators. She caught a flash of his expression in the glossy steel doors. He looked disbelieving and grimly annoyed.

"Do I get points for trying?"

Her gaze snapped to his. "You *read* my folder."

"I needed to see what I was up against."

Lilah jabbed the elevator button. A door slid open. "That would be commitment."

After a night of passion that was curiously unsatisfying, Lilah rose early and spent time alone, adapting elements of the marriage plan to suit the new strategy. She decided the best way to show Zane that she was not fretting over the way their brief fling, apart from the heart-pounding sex, seemed to be disintegrating was to throw herself into her work.

During the early hours, she had given herself a pep talk

about the positives. Zane had responded to her elusiveness with a gift. It had been the wrong gift and he had cheated by reading her folder, which was a blot. She was prepared to overlook his behavior on the basis that he had not thought things through. The one shining factor was that he had made his choices based on the desire to win her. It was progress.

For the next two days she got up early and walked to Ambrosi's new retail center, a charming, antiquated building situated on the bustling waterfront. Interior decorating wasn't her job, but the retail center would be her temporary office until the facility on Ambrus was completed. Lilah figured that if she had to work there for the next six months she needed to like her surroundings, so she pulled rank and inserted herself into the process.

Zane, who had had to spend long hours closeted with Elena working through the raft of paperwork on a deal in Florida, had become even more remote. Despite their lovemaking, the abyss between them seemed to be widening.

With her strategy seemingly in tatters, it was hard to concentrate on paint colors and curtain samples when all she wanted to do was take a taxi back to the resort and throw herself into Zane's arms.

To avoid weakening, she had taken herself shopping during the long, somnolent lunch breaks the Medinians enjoyed. Instead of eating, she had spent a large amount of money on filmy, sexy clothes and a daring hot orange bikini that she gloomily decided she would probably never get the opportunity to wear.

New makeup that made her eyes look smoky and exotic, subtle caramel streaks in her hair and a fake tan completed the makeover. Every time she caught her reflection in glass doors or looked in a mirror, Lilah was amazed at the difference the subtle changes had made, although Zane had barely seemed to notice.

Tempted as she was to bluntly declare that she was in love with him and put an end to the tension, Lilah made a grim effort to appear sunnily content. She couldn't shake off the dreadful conviction that the instant Zane knew she had fallen for him, he would put an end to any hope of long-term commitment.

That was how it had worked with her mother and her grandmother. Once the prize was won, the passion had cooled. Their lovers hadn't been able to leave fast enough.

Zane strolled into the building chaos just short of noon. Wearing dark narrow trousers and a loose white shirt, sunlight slanting across his taut cheekbones, he managed to look both dangerously sexy and casual.

Lilah was instantly aware of her own attire. Instead of her usual low-key neutrals, today she was wearing one of her new purchases, a filmy orange blouse teamed with a tight little black camisole that revealed just a hint of cleavage and tight, white jeans. Combined with strappy orange heels and iridescent orange nail polish, the effect was unexpectedly striking.

Zane's gaze glittered over her. Lilah registered the gratifying flare of shock that was almost instantly shuttered.

Zane had finally noticed her. Although, it could simply be the orange color, which she had developed something of a fetish for lately. Orange was hard to miss.

Just minutes ago she had felt warm, but comfortable. Now, beneath the weight of Zane's gaze, despite all of the doors and windows flung wide admitting the balmy sea breeze, Lilah felt flushed and overheated.

"Are you ready to go?"

That afternoon Zane had planned a boat trip to survey Ambrosi's old oyster beds and the site for the new processing plant. The trip would be followed up by a launch function for the new enterprise at the castello.

Lilah ignored the faint edge to Zane's voice and kept her attention on Mario, the builder. She had spent the morning directing a number of contractors as they had fitted air-conditioning and lighting fixtures and erected partitioning. Mario was a little on the short side, but outrageously handsome. On a purely intellectual level she had thought she should feel something for such a good-looking man. Depressingly, the only thing she had felt had been the battle of wills as Mario had tried to improve on her floor plan. "Almost."

Zane's gaze shifted to the bronzed contractor who was hefting a dividing panel into place. Mario had already repositioned the panel for her twice. Both times the angle had not been quite right. As a consequence he was sweating, his T-shirt clinging damply to his chest.

Mario placed the partition and finally got it right. She rewarded him with a smile. "*Bene*."

Zane's fingers interlaced with hers. A split second later she found herself pulled into a light clinch. Her heart pounded as Zane's gaze settled on her mouth. The move was masculine and dominant and, in front of the contractors, definitely territorial.

His mouth brushed over hers, sending a hot pulse of adrenaline through her. It was a claiming kiss, the kind of reaction she had wanted two days ago.

Two days. Panic made her tense. Time was sliding away, only four days left. Suddenly, it didn't seem nearly enough time for Zane to fall in love with her.

Zane's hands settled at her waist, making her feel even hotter. This close she could see the nicks of long-ago scars, the faint kink in a nose that should have been perfectly straight, the silky shadow of his lashes. She drew in a breath and just for a few seconds, gave herself permission to relax.

Zane cocked his head to one side. "Is this a 'yes'?"

She stiffened at the lethal combination of pressure and charm. "Yes, to the boat trip."

The midday sun struck down, glaringly hot on the marina jetty, as Lilah walked on ahead while Zane unloaded dive gear from the trunk of the car. She rummaged in her new string beach bag for a pair of dark glasses as she strolled, drawn by the bobbing yachts and the aquamarine clarity of the sea.

Movement on Zane's yacht drew her gaze. The bleached

surfer hair on one of the men rang an instant alarm bell, although neither of the other two men on the yacht were remotely recognizable.

Although, if it was the three J's she was looking at, she shouldn't be surprised. If most of the applicants had been scammers, the odds were not good for the three she had picked.

Suddenly any idea that Zane had been suffering the agonies of an emotional crisis for the past two days was swept away. The entire time she had been playing her waiting game, he had been busy working on a preemptive move.

By the time Zane appeared, stripped down to a pair of sleek black neoprene dive pants, his chest bare, a gear bag filled with diving equipment, there was no doubt.

Jaw set, she met his gaze. "How did you get them here? Wait, let me guess—Spiros."

What was the point in having a henchman unless he could do useful things like kidnap all three of her potential husbands?

Fifteen

The lenses of Zane's dark glasses made him look frustratingly remote and detached. "You make it sound like Spiros kidnapped them. All he did was pilot the jet."

That was like saying that all Blackbeard did was sail the ship. "How did you get them?"

The idea that they had been coerced in any way evaporated as she took in their collective grins, the clink of beers. A definite holiday air pervaded the yacht. "No wait, don't tell me, it was a corporate kidnap." She slid her dark glasses onto the bridge of her nose. "Two days. *Paradise*."

Zane shrugged. "They could have refused."

"Hah!"

His gaze narrowed. "If you don't want to spend time with them just say the word. Spiros can take them out for the afternoon, no problem."

Which was, she realized, exactly what he wanted. He hadn't brought the men here so she could get together with them. His plan was much simpler than that. He was intent on ruthlessly cutting them out of her life.

She squashed the thrill that shot through her at his un-PC behavior and jabbed a finger in the direction of his chest. "You had no right—"

He caught her hand and drew her close, his hold gentle as he pressed her palm against his bare chest. "While you're with me, I have every right. I told you I wanted to be present when you met them."

Lilah's toes curled at the fiery heat of his skin against her palm, the thud of his heart, the sneaky, undermining way he had gotten around the issue of crashing her dates. "I didn't agree."

Although, she realized that none of that mattered now, because it was clear Zane had never considered any of the men as serious contenders. If he had, he would not have brought them to Medinos.

She stared at the obdurate line of his jaw. In a moment of blinding clarity, she recognized the flip side of the situation, an even more important truth. Zane wanted her enough to eliminate the three J's in the first place. Far from ignoring her for the past two days, Zane had been focusing his energies on systematically clearing away all opposition so he could have what he wanted. As if her agreement to his proposition was a forgone conclusion.

He jerked his head in the direction of the yacht. "It's your choice. If you don't want to spend time with them, you don't have to."

Tension hummed through her along with an undermining, utterly female sense of satisfaction. It was difficult to stay mad at Zane for completely subverting her strategy when a part of her adored it that he had gone to such lengths to cut out the competition.

He wanted her, enough that he couldn't bear the thought of her having other men in the picture. It was exactly the result she had wanted; it just hadn't panned out the way she had thought.

A dazzling idea momentarily blotted out everything else. She was suddenly glad for the concealment of the dark glasses. "Not a problem," she said smoothly.

Mentally, she ticked off a number of new, exciting options all based around having three extra men in close proximity for the afternoon. "Now that they're here, why not meet them?"

Seconds later, Zane handed Lilah onto the yacht.

Jack Riordan, clearly an outdoors kind of guy and at home on the yacht in a pair of board shorts and a tank, looked exactly like his photo. Jeremy Appleby did not. Instead of tall and dark, he was blond and thin, with a goatee. He also had an impressive camera slung around his neck, which put Lilah on instant alert.

Zane's gaze touched on hers. The knowledge that he had also noted the camera formed a moment of intimacy that sent pleasure humming through her. Despite everything that was wrong between them, in that moment she felt utterly connected to Zane, as if they were a couple.

She also felt protected. Next to Zane's and Spiros's tanned, muscular frames, Appleby looked weak and weedy. Lilah would not want to be in Appleby's shoes if he tried to take photos or file a story.

Like Appleby, John Smith did not look anything like the *GQ* photograph he had supplied. With his plump build, balding head and glasses, he didn't come close.

A blond head popped out of the cabin, breaking the stilted conversation. Lilah recognized the pretty flight attendant from the jet. Though she was dressed now in a bright pink bikini teamed with a pair of low-slung white shorts, evidently Jasmine was fulfilling the same role, because she had a tray of cold drinks.

Lilah noticed that Jack Riordan seemed riveted by Jasmine's honey-blond hair and mentally crossed him off her now-defunct list.

After casting off, Spiros took the wheel. To Lilah's relief, Zane didn't leave her alone with the three men, but stayed glued to her side. Her relief was short-lived as Zane systematically questioned each of the three J's about their lives, concentrating on their finances.

An hour into an agonizingly slow trip, which bore more of a resemblance to the Spanish Inquisition than a pleasure cruise, they reached Ambrus.

Zane dropped anchor. Spiros heaved the inflatable raft into the water, preparatory to rowing to the beach. The three J's trooped below to change into their beachwear.

Lilah clamped down on her frustration and helped Jasmine take glasses and bottles to the galley. When she emerged on deck, Zane was securing the inflatable. She checked that the three J's were still below. "You had no right to interrogate them like that."

Apart from the fact that it had been embarrassing, it had utterly nixed any opportunities to make Zane jealous. She had barely been able to get a word in edgewise.

Zane knotted the rope to a cleat and straightened. "Did you really believe Appleby owned his own software company?"

When he had not seemed to know the difference between a megabyte and a gigabyte, it hadn't seemed likely. "No."

"Or that John Smith is the CEO of an accounting firm?"

She had not caught on to all of the jargon Zane, who had a double degree in business administration and accounting, had dropped into the conversation, but she had understood enough to know that John Smith had failed the test. "Jack Riordan seems genuine." His knowledge of the yacht at least seemed to back up his small boat-building business.

At that moment, the three men emerged on deck, ready to board the inflatable. Appleby and Smith, their alabaster skin slathered with sunblock, appeared to glow beneath the brassy Mediterranean sun.

If Lilah had been fooled, even for a second, that Zane was

doing this out of the kindness of his heart, that notion would have now been completely discredited.

First the inquisition, now the swimsuit contest.

When they reached the beach, Jasmine tossed her shorts on the sand, laid out a bright yellow towel and lay down to sunbathe. While Zane and Spiros assembled snorkeling gear, Lilah strolled behind a clump of shade trees to change. Setting her beach bag down on the sand, she extracted the hot orange bikini, which she had been reluctant to change into on the yacht.

Before her courage deserted her altogether, she quickly changed then knotted the turquoise sarong that went with the bikini around her hips. She frowned at the lush display of tanned cleavage and considered changing back into her white jeans, camisole and shirt.

Even as the thought passed through her mind she knew she could not afford to do that now. She had lost the leverage of the three J's and she was almost out of time. Unfortunately, the bikini was now a crucial part of her strategy.

Zane almost had a heart attack when Lilah emerged onto the beach. He was glad Spiros had taken the three J's on a snorkeling expedition. It was an easier solution than the medieval threats he would have been forced to issue just in case any one of them decided it was okay to look.

The cut of the outrageously sexy bikini somehow managed to make Lilah's narrow hips and delicate curves look mouth-wateringly voluptuous. Added to that, after just a few days on Medinos, her skin had taken on a tawny glow that made her green eyes look startlingly light, her cheekbones even more exotic. In the span of a few minutes, Lilah had gone from mysterious and reserved to lusciously, searingly hot.

If she had bought the bikini for the specific purpose of driving him crazy, Zane thought grimly, she had achieved the result. "When did you get the bikini?"

Lilah, who seemed more interested in laying out a bright turquoise towel and rummaging through her trendily matching beach bag, gave him a distracted, too innocent look as if she hadn't quite registered who had spoken.

Zane's jaw clamped tighter as she abandoned arranging a neat line of possessions, one of which, suspiciously, was a *red* folder, and finally seemed to become aware of his presence.

She directed a smile in his general direction. "Two days ago."

After their discussion.

Zane folded his arms across his chest so that he wouldn't repeat the cavemanlike behavior he had displayed on the jetty and simply grab Lilah. He eyed the red folder and wondered what new scheme she was cooking up now. "Have you come to a decision yet?"

She lifted a hand to her eyes and stared out to sea as if she was more interested in the four heads bobbing in the water than having an actual conversation with him. "I'm still thinking it over."

His jaw clamped. If he wasn't mistaken the smile she had given him was the same smooth, professional smile she had given the builder earlier on in the day. "The way I see it, we have three days left." He jerked his head in the direction of the swimmers. "And we're wasting time."

Lilah's cheeks went instantly pink. "Is sex all you're interested in?"

He noted with satisfaction, any suggestion that she was disinterested in him evaporated. "At the moment, yes."

Lilah glanced around distractedly. Her gaze came to rest on Jasmine, who was flipping through a magazine.

Zane frowned. It was not the response he had wanted. Living with Lilah for the past two days had been like living with a professionally cheerful automaton. The passionate nights aside, he was now officially frustrated. "Jasmine can't hear a thing. She's listening to her iPod. If she registered anything short of an explosion it would be a miracle."

She glared at him and he realized something else that was different about Lilah. She'd had light streaks put in her hair.

His hold on his temper slipped another notch. He had never thought of himself as a controlling person; his motto was Live and Let Live. However, when it came to Lilah he didn't feel anything that came even remotely close to flexibility. He found himself supremely irked that she had changed her hair without even bothering to mention it to him. "You've changed your hair."

From her beach bag Lilah fished out another object, which seemed much more rivetingly interesting than the conversation he was trying to have with her. "Yesterday. I didn't think you had noticed."

The bright turquoise iPod, which signaled that Lilah had found a new way to block him out, was the last straw, literally. In two years Lilah had never been trendy; she had remained tantalizingly, coolly the same. "Honey, I'm noticing now."

Lilah's gaze flashed to his, the deep anger in their depths electrifying, and suddenly the air was charged.

For two years he had been burningly aware of Lilah's underlying sensuality, the latent feminine power buried beneath the tempting reserve and bland, virginal white.

The reserve, like the white clothing, was long gone, replaced by hot, passionate colors, cutting-edge fashion and way too much skin.

He had been so absorbed with his own reactions to the new confident, sexy Lilah that he hadn't stopped to think about what was driving the change.

The answer was terrifyingly simple. Lilah was no longer a virgin. Thanks to him, she was now a mature woman of experience. Single. Available. And, if he wasn't mistaken, ready to shop around for what she wanted.

Taking into consideration the wish list in her white folder, he had to assume that the kind of man she would want to extend her sexual experience with would not be a man with a dysfunctional past and an inability to commit.

He did not think she was calculatingly aware of the power

she could wield. She was still feeling her way, but he was grimly certain that it would not take her long to find out.

It was a dangerous state of affairs.

Suddenly the color of the new folder—red—took on an unsettling meaning. The thought that if he could not satisfy Lilah's needs that she could start experimenting with men—plural—made him go cold inside.

Jack Riordan popped out of the surf, a speargun in one hand, a silvery fish flapping on the end.

Feeling embattled, Zane studied Riordan with new eyes. He was the least good-looking of the three, but he had a lean, rugged build and the kind of mature dependability that even Zane liked.

Riordan had one other advantage; he was a mature man who was clearly looking to settle down.

It was an advantage he should have taken more note of before he had risked bringing Riordan to Medinos.

His jaw tightened. This wasn't working.

His aim had been to protect Lilah and eliminate the competition. Unfortunately, Lilah seemed to *like* Riordan, in which case his plan could have backfired.

The thought that she might start dating Riordan was a defining moment.

Over my dead body.

Flashes of white caught his eye; Smith and Appleby were also exiting the water. He scooped up the beach bag, which, if he wasn't mistaken, contained Lilah's clothes. He had played a waiting game long enough.

Lilah realized Zane's intent a bare second before he swung her up into his arms. She noted where the expensive little iPod, which she had been on the verge of working out, had fallen and clutched at his bare shoulders. She tried to repress the automatic thrill that he was actually carrying her.

She was still angry and deeply depressed at the thought that had occurred to her, that she had made a dreadful mistake in thinking that Zane cared for her. That her entire strategy was flawed.

If Zane was even the tiniest bit as obsessed as she had become, he should have noticed her hair before now.

She stared at the approaching tree line. "Where are you taking me?"

"Somewhere you can get dressed."

"I'm *wearing* clothes."

His gaze burned over the expanse of silky skin bared by the skimpy bikini, the length of her legs visible beneath the transparent gauze of the sarong. "Couldn't prove it by me."

"I'm wearing more than Jasmine." In point of fact she was wearing a great deal more. Jasmine had a microscopic bikini, with no sarong.

"What Jasmine does or does not wear is irrelevant."

Cool shade slid over her skin as he rounded the clump of trees she had changed behind earlier. Lilah blinked as her eyes adjusted to the dim light. "I don't see why."

He set her down. "Because Jasmine doesn't interest me. Which brings me to the subject of Smith, Appleby and Riordan. Get rid of them."

There was a moment of vibrating silence.

Zane was jealous.

Lilah kept her expression carefully blank, but a part of her was melting and ridiculously happy because even if Zane wasn't showing any signs of being in love with her yet, he wanted her enough to bully and coerce and demand.

And he wanted the three J's out of the picture.

"I haven't agreed to anything yet."

His gaze was hot and distinctly irritable, signaling that the cool reserve that had grown between them when she had refused to agree to his relationship terms was finally and definitely gone. "Take as much time as you need. But *we* have an agreement and we are not wasting any more time." Both hands were wrapped around the soft flesh of her upper arms now. With a slow, inevitable movement, he pulled her close. His mouth brushed hers, heat zapped through her.

Drawing in a deep breath, she planted her palms on his chest, created a small amount of overheated space and tried not to notice how gorgeous his chest looked. "I've decided to finish with the three J's."

There was a moment of tense silence. "Will you stay with me at the castello tonight?"

For a shivering, delicious second she drowned in the stormy depths of Zane's eyes. Of course, she would be present at the launch party at the castello, but Zane was asking her to stay with him at his family home. "Yes."

The last blaze of a fiery sunset illuminated the evening sky as Zane showed Lilah to her suite at the castello.

He was acutely conscious that the guest suite he had allocated Lilah, the only one next to his, also happened to be next door to Lucas's suite.

Zane unlocked the door and handed her the key.

Lilah glanced at Lucas's door, a faint flush to her cheeks. Zane's jaw tightened as he pushed the door open and stepped inside. He had been on the verge of asking Lilah to stay with him in his private suite a number of times that afternoon, but every time he approached the subject his jaw had locked and the words wouldn't come.

He carried her suitcase through to the bedroom.

Lilah unzipped her case. "What time do you need me downstairs?"

Zane checked his watch. Frustrated, he noted he was overdue at a press interview.

He had spent valuable time driving Appleby, Riordan and Smith to the airport and making sure they boarded their commercial flight out. In light of the discovery that Appleby had been a journalist, and that he had somehow gotten photos of Lilah in her bikini, wiping the memory stick of his camera had been a job he had not wanted to entrust to Spiros. "In one hour."

Zane couldn't help noticing there was no sign of Lilah's normal low-key wardrobe as she shook out a jewel-bright array of clothes and hung them in the closet.

His gaze snagged on an outrageously sexy pair of red heels. He had never been obsessed with women's clothing, but as he left the suite, Zane found himself wondering what Lilah would wear tonight. After the revelation of the orange bikini, he decided, he couldn't bank on one of the modest cream cocktail dresses she had alternated wearing to a number of charity functions.

Unlocking his own suite door, he walked into his room, which, for the first time, did not feel like a refuge. Instead it felt oddly blank and solitary. He changed into evening clothes and walked downstairs in time to meet Constantine and Lucas, who had decided to stay on Medinos for the opening of the new pearl facility.

Even knowing that Lilah didn't want Lucas, Zane would have been profoundly annoyed by his brother's presence if he hadn't known that Carla was supposed to be joining him.

As they walked into the small reception room where the interview was being held, for the first time in years Zane's mind was not on business.

He wondered how far Lilah would push him tonight.

Grimly, he decided that his biggest problem was one that had never bothered him before. Because they hadn't established firm grounds for a relationship, he didn't have any rights.

Until that afternoon he had not understood how important it was to make it very clear, publicly, that Lilah was his.

Sixteen

Lilah showered and spent some time smoothing an expensive body moisturizer into her skin. With her skin pampered and glowing, she wrapped herself in a robe and confronted her wardrobe.

Instead of wearing the classic cream cocktail dress she had originally planned on, she took out an uncrushable red halterneck she had bought the previous day. Not her usual color, or style, the curve-hugging dress was transforming, bringing a glow to her skin and deepening the color of her eyes.

After dressing, she carefully applied her makeup, following the instructions she had been given by the beautician who had sold her the products. Instead of confining her hair in its usual coil, she brushed it out, letting it swing in loose silky waves down her back. She inserted red crystal earrings in her lobes and fastened a gold pendant around her neck. The fine gold chain was almost invisible, leaving a single red crystal suspended just above the shadowy cleavage of her breasts.

She slipped into red heels and walked over to the closet door, which had a full-length mirror.

Her heart rate, which was already too rapid, pounded a little faster. It was going to take some time getting used to the glaringly available siren who stared back at her.

She consulted her red folder, which was open at a page she had entitled “Seduction” then quickly worked through her list. Her fingers shook slightly with nerves as she draped a red silk negligee over the bed then unpacked a box of richly scented votive candles and placed them at strategic points around the room.

They had made love enough times that she shouldn’t feel nervous about the idea, but she had never set out to deliberately seduce Zane before. She wanted to make everything, herself included, as irresistible and gorgeous as possible. The last touch was a bottle of very expensive French champagne in the small bar fridge.

She surveyed the room with an eagle eye. The scene was set.

If Zane finally made the kind of emotional breakthrough she had been hoping for, he could even propose. The thought made her pulse race even faster.

Taking several deep breaths to calm herself down, she remembered to spritz herself with a waft of an exotic perfume she’d bought to go with the dress, picked up a matching red clutch and strolled downstairs.

Lilah’s heart sank when the first person she saw as she entered a large, elegant reception room hung with chandeliers and festooned with white roses, was Gemma.

She was mentally braced to brazen out the evening with Zane; she didn’t know if she could cope with another feminine dueling match with Zane’s former P.A.

Before she could slide past the younger woman, Gemma waved her over to her group and insisted on introducing her.

Lilah already knew the two buyers from a high-end European chain of stores. She kept a smooth, professional smile in place while she chatted and tried to pretend that the way she looked was not wildly different to her usual low-key style.

Gemma was bubbling over with enthusiasm for the Atraeus family, who had moved her from Sydney to Medinos.

As Gemma's enthusiasm for all things Atraeus continued unabated, including the fact that she *loved* Medinos so much she intended to settle there permanently, Lilah felt again the sense of unease that had swept through her the previous evening. It wasn't jealousy. Although Gemma was bluntly intent on making her aware of just how much she wanted Zane. The tension that gripped her was more elusive and disturbing. She couldn't quite put her finger on—

The deep cool register of Zane's voice sent a hot tingle down her spine. Bracing herself for his reaction when he saw the red dress, she turned.

The voice belonged to Lucas, not Zane. The embarrassment of the moment was limited by the fact that Lucas was talking on his cell. Judging from the blankness of his expression, he had not even recognized her.

Zane's oldest brother, Constantine, an imposing figure, was just feet away, his arm around his new wife, Sienna Ambrosi, who was pregnant and glowing.

Out of nowhere, longing, unexpected and powerful, hit Lilah. For years the idea of a pregnancy had been something she had avoided thinking about, beyond taking extreme measures to make sure it never happened to her. Now, in the space of a few seconds, everything had changed.

Sienna, Lilah realized, was the picture of everything she wanted: the protective husband, the well-loved glow, the baby. Bleakly, she faced the fact that if Zane didn't fall in love with her, it was possible that she would never achieve any of those things. If she could not imagine replacing Zane with another man, she did not see how she was ever going to progress to the point of having a baby with someone she did not love.

She refocused beyond Lucas's shoulder. Her breath caught in her throat. Zane, looking edgily gorgeous in a tuxedo, was heading straight for her.

A prosaic little fact that had been the stumbling block of

Cole women for fifty years, and which she had happily glossed over in her pursuit of Zane, was suddenly glaringly highlighted.

She could try any number of strategies and tactics, but she could not *make* Zane fall in love with her.

Zane cut through the room, his gaze caught and held by the intensity of Lilah's.

Something had happened; something had changed.

His jaw locked as he took in the spectacular red dress that clung to every curve, the lavish, silky fall of dark hair.

The only time he had seen Lilah's hair out of its neat coils had been when he had pulled out pins and threaded his fingers through it. To his knowledge she had never voluntarily undone her hair for anyone, himself included.

His attention shifted to the man standing nearby.

Lucas.

The suspicion he had never entirely managed to wipe from his mind shot to the surface. If he'd had any doubts about the concept of marriage, which he had been tossing around like a hot coal for the past hour, they were gone.

His decision to examine the whole process from a business point of view had been a major turning point. He didn't know why he hadn't thought of the idea earlier. He had never had any problem negotiating complex legal agreements and, at the end of the day, the binding nature of marriage was similar to a business contract.

The emotional side was the tricky part but, since he had already decided he wanted Lilah to live with him, he figured that with her systematic, logical approach, they could negotiate their way to an understanding.

He was clear on the main point: Lilah belonged to him and before the night was out he was determined that she would have his ring on her finger.

If she would accept him as a husband.

His jaw clenched. The thought that, after years of avoiding sexual lures and marriage traps, he would literally have to force a woman to marry him should have been amusing.

Unfortunately his sense of humor had died that afternoon on a hot beach on Ambrus.

"Zane, *babe!*"

Zane's jaw locked as Gemma, all flowing red hair and sexy black lace, blocked his view of Lilah and Lucas.

Her arms coiled around his neck. His hands clamped her waist preventing full body contact.

She winked and grinned good-naturedly. "I've been calling, but you haven't answered."

That was because he had a block on her number. "I've been busy."

Calmly, he disengaged himself and declined her invitation to join her for a drink out on the terrace.

If he had known how complicated it was going to be taking Gemma along to charity functions in Sydney as his casual date, as insurance that he wouldn't lose his head over Lilah, he never would have crossed that particular line.

Zane finally managed to disentangle himself, only to discover that Lilah had disappeared.

Lucas snapped closed the cell he had been talking into, a grin lighting his face. "Carla has just arrived at the airport. I'm on my way to pick her up."

Zane swallowed the blunt warning he had been about to deliver. If Lucas, who had entered the room just seconds before, had been on the phone to Carla then he would not have had time to talk with Lilah.

Zane skimmed the well-dressed crowd, looking for a spectacular red dress and a silky fall of dark hair. "I thought Carla wasn't well."

Lucas dug car keys out of his pocket. "She's feeling better, which is good. I've missed her like crazy."

For the first time Zane noticed the changes in Lucas. He looked relaxed and carefree. Even his clothing was different. The suit he was wearing was a cutting-edge departure from his usual classic style. The changes could mean only one thing. He had seen the phenomena often enough in friends. Relief loosened some of Zane's tension. "You love Carla."

Lucas tossed the keys in one hand and clapped him on the arm. "I'm *in* love with her. There's a difference."

Zane watched his brother leave, transfixed by the thought of all the changes Lilah had recently made. He had been so concerned with his own issues, he had somehow managed to miss the fact that Lilah had literally blossomed while they'd been together.

He wondered how he could ever have been so blind.

Lilah joined the small knot of guests and stared blindly at an exquisite display of antique Ambrosi pearls. She should have been upset at the clinch she had just witnessed. She was *not* good with the body contact, but Gemma sidetracking Zane wasn't what was upsetting her. The thing that had struck her most was Gemma's single-minded pursuit of Zane. That was, she realized, the basis of the cold unease that gripped her. Gemma's determination reminded her forcibly of herself.

Taking a deep breath, she tried to concentrate on the jewelry display. One strand of outstanding iridescent pearls, the signature product of Ambrosi, was said to be the first ever produced by the inventor of the process, Dominic Ambrosi, an alchemist who had lived in the eighteenth century.

Symbolic of the business merger, an entire section of the display was devoted to Atraeus jewels. A blank space in the display had been filled by a photograph and description of The Illium Cache, the ancient set of diamond-and-emerald jewels that for some reason had not made it into the case. Frowning, Lilah bent closer to study the photograph.

She caught a flash of Zane's reflection in the mirrored display case. Heart suddenly pounding, she straightened.

Zane's gaze seemed riveted by the red crystal suspended in the valley between her breasts. "I see you've found my ancestor's treasure trove."

Lilah blushed, acutely aware of the revealing neckline. It

wasn't as revealing as Gemma's black lace dress, but it was uncomfortably close. "Unfortunately, the most important pieces are missing."

"Ah. The fabled Illium Cache."

Off to one side of the room, a flash of red caught Lilah's eye. Gemma's hair, as bright as a flame. She paused just short of the corridor that lead to the bathrooms and the castello's private suites. Her gaze was fixed on Zane as if she was waiting for him to make eye contact. To Lilah's eyes, she looked a little desperate.

The hollow feeling she had experienced when she had seen Gemma winding herself around Zane came back to haunt her. "I just saw you with Gemma."

Zane, who barely seemed to notice Gemma's attempt to get his attention, looked impatient. "We need to talk, and we can't do it here."

Zane's grip on her elbow distracted her from the lonely figure of Gemma, waiting for Zane to notice her, as he steered her away from the jewelry cases.

Minutes later he showed her into what looked like a study filled with heavy dark furniture and an oversized desk. An entire wall was lined with leather-bound volumes; the remaining walls were decorated with oils. When she saw Zane's laptop sitting on the desk, she realized that this was his office.

Zane perched on the edge of the desk, arms folded across his chest. "You're in love with me."

The soft, flat statement took her breath. She thought she had done a thorough job of covering up her feelings. Clearly she had slipped up badly. Now that Zane knew she loved him, that didn't leave her with much leeway. "That doesn't mean I'll agree to live with you on a temporary basis."

"Because I'm terrible husband material?"

"I never said that."

"Not directly, but it's a fact that I didn't make it on to your list. Would you stay if I offered marriage?"

Lilah's fingers tightened on her clutch. She stared at the

closest painting, one of a girl holding a bunch of bright flowers. The soft expression on the girl's face as she looked directly at the painter radiated tender promise. She was in love.

As Lilah knew, firsthand, that tended to change things. "I'm not sure what you mean exactly by 'marriage.'"

His expression shifted, as if she had surprised him. "A legal marriage. I thought that was what you wanted."

Her heart pounded in her chest. Marriage was her goal—with Zane, if he could love her. "I do."

She saw his flicker of relief. "Good. If we marry, I won't touch another woman while we're together."

While we're together.

The qualifier made her stiffen. It implied an end.

In other words he was still talking about the same, temporary arrangement he had mentioned in their hotel suite, but ratified by marriage.

Suddenly Zane's businesslike approach fell into its correct context. He was not registering emotion because this was not an emotional discussion. He had reverted to business tactics in order to control the terms of the relationship.

The thought that Zane felt he needed to control her love so he could be with her was subtly wounding. She of all people could understand his emotional fears and vulnerabilities because for years she had shared them, although to a lesser degree. "Just out of interest, how long do you think this proposed marriage will last?"

Silence reigned for long seconds, filled by the tick of a mantel clock, the distant strains of music.

"I can't answer that question, but if you think I'm going to fall in love with someone else, you don't have to worry. That won't happen."

For a split second she almost managed to twist the meaning of Zane's comment into a declaration of his love for her, then his flat denial that he could fall in love registered.

As if the thought of surrendering to love was not on his personal horizon.

It was not a new concept. It was Zane's modus operandi with relationships. The fact that she could not make Zane fall in love with her was the basis that had undermined her entire strategy. "It's a common enough scenario. Women fall for you on a regular basis."

Irritation registered in his gaze. "I get partnered with women on a regular basis through company business and charitable events. That's mostly what the tabloids pick up on. The only woman I know who has certifiably fallen for me is you."

The knife twisted a little deeper. "And that makes me a sure bet."

His hands curled around her upper arms, his palms shiveringly hot against her skin. "You were a virgin, and you've got a logical, methodical approach to relationships. That's what I trust."

Jaw set, Lilah resisted the gentle pressure to step closer to Zane. She would not muddy this process any further with passion. They had already been that route. And what Zane proposed was sounding more like a business deal than a relationship.

The vibration of his cell phone broke the taut silence.

Frowning, Zane released his grip and checked the screen. He looked briefly frustrated. "I have to go. There's something I need to take care of before the official part of the evening begins."

Lilah strolled back to the party and circulated, chatting with buyers and contractors. She checked her wristwatch. Long minutes had passed since Zane had excused himself.

She walked out on the terrace just in case he had come back and she had somehow missed him. The terrace was windswept and empty.

She strolled back inside and surveyed the reception room again. Zane was not in the room.

It suddenly occurred to her that neither was Gemma, and with her flaming red hair and white skin, the younger woman was unmistakable.

The last time she had seen Gemma, she had been heading toward the part of the castello where the private suites were located, and suddenly she knew what the desperate look she had sent Zane had meant.

Feeling like an automaton, Lilah stepped out of the reception room. A ridiculously short amount of time later she found herself in the castello's darkened hallway, the chill from the thick stone walls seeping through the silk of her red gown.

She paused at the door of Zane's private quarters and lifted her hand to knock. The chink of glass on glass signaled that the suite was occupied.

A grim sense of déjà vu gripped her. She rapped once, twice.

It occurred to her that this time, unlike the incident with Lucas, Zane could not rescue her because, in a sense, she was confronting an aspect of herself that she did not like very much.

The door swung open on a waft of perfume. Gemma's tousled red hair cascaded around her white shoulders. Slim fingers clutched a silky black negligee closed over her breasts, the defensive gesture making her look young and absurdly vulnerable.

Lilah couldn't help thinking that it looked like they had both had the same idea about setting the scene for seduction.

She felt the weight of every one of her twenty-nine years crushing down on her. Her irritation with Gemma evaporated. "You should stop trying and go home. Sex won't make Zane, or any man, have a relationship with you."

"How can you know that?"

Because it had been burned into her psyche by both her mother and her grandmother. Unfortunately, she had temporarily forgotten that fact. "Logic. If you couldn't make him fall in love with you in two years, then it's probably not going to happen."

Gemma's expression went blank, as if she didn't know what to say next.

A split second later, the door snapped shut in Lilah's face.

Lilah fumbled the key into the lock of her door and let herself in. The door closed with a soft click behind her.

She stared at the glowing lamp-lit room, the sexy, filmy negligee draped over the bed.

The preparations were wrenchingly similar to Gemma's, and the end result would be the same. She could not make Zane love her, either.

She had changed, through falling in love with him, but she had to accept that for Zane the past might never be healed.

Feeling numb and faintly sick, she jammed the negligee out of sight in the case, picked up the phone and made a quick call to the airport. She managed to secure a flight to Dubai, which was leaving in an hour. She would have several hours to wait before she could get a connection to Sydney, but that didn't matter. She could leave Medinos tonight.

She arranged for a taxi then changed into clothes suitable for a long flight—cotton pants and a sleek-fitting tank, a light jacket and comfortable shoes. She caught a glimpse of the red crystal earrings dangling from her lobes in the dresser mirror as she packed. She removed them with fingers that were stiff and clumsy, wound her hair into a knot and secured it with pins.

She did a final check of the room then tensed when she realized she was lingering in the hope that Zane would come looking for her.

Swallowing against the sudden pain squeezing her chest, she walked down to the lobby of the castello. She didn't have time to stop at the hotel and collect all of her things. That would have to wait until she returned to Medinos at the end of her vacation.

Not a problem.

By the time she came back, Zane, who was involved in a set of sensitive negotiations in the States, would probably be gone. The retail outlet would be almost ready to open and construction of the pearl facility on Ambrus would be underway.

She would be busy interviewing and training staff. In theory she wouldn't have time to think.

When she reached the forecourt the taxi pulled into a space. A chilly breeze blew off the ocean, whipping strands of loose hair around her cheeks as she climbed into the backseat. She checked her wristwatch. Time was tight, but she would make her flight.

Her throat closed as the taxi shot away from the castello. She was still reeling from the speed with which she had made the decision to leave, but she could not have done anything else.

She was not a "glass half full" kind of girl and now she was in love.

Until Zane, she hadn't been even remotely tempted to break her rule of celibacy. It would have taken a bolt of lightning—literally a *coup de foudre*—to jolt her out of her mindset, and that was what had happened. She had seen Zane and in that moment she had lost her bearings. She had committed herself emotionally and now she didn't know how to undo that.

She could not accept the marriage agreement he had been clearly working toward. She refused to die a lingering emotional death, like Gemma.

She stared bleakly ahead, at the taxi's headlights piercing the dark winding ribbon of road.

There was no going back. It was over.

Seventeen

Zane knocked on Lilah's door. When there was no answer, he walked inside. A quick inventory informed him that she had packed and left.

He strode to his suite. Any idea that Lilah had made an executive decision and moved in with him died an instant death. The moment he opened the door and caught the scent of Gemma's signature perfume, his stomach hollowed out and he understood exactly what had gone wrong.

A split second later, Gemma emerged from his bedroom, fully dressed, but the filmy negligee clutched in one hand told the story.

Suppressing the raw panic that gripped him, he strode past Gemma and found his wallet and his overnight bag. "How long ago was Lilah here?"

Gemma watched from the safety of the sitting room as he flung belongings into the bag. "Fifteen minutes." She stuffed the negligee into her evening bag and sent him an embarrassed look. "You don't have to worry, I won't do this again."

Zane zipped the bag closed and walked to the door. He couldn't be angry with Gemma, not when he was responsible for this mess. He had been guilty of the same sin Lucas had committed when he had tried to keep Carla at a distance. Now his strategy had backfired on him. "Good. You should keep dating that guy you were with the other night. He's in love with you."

"How do you know?"

Zane sent her a stark look.

Gemma blinked. "Oh."

He waited pointedly at the door for Gemma to leave. He knew the boyfriend was somewhere downstairs, because Spiros had run a standard security check on him before the invitation to the castello was issued.

Once Gemma was gone, he headed for the front entrance.

He resisted the urge to check his watch. Lilah had been gone a good fifteen minutes. It only took ten minutes, max, to get a taxi out to the castello.

He reached the forecourt in time to see the red taillights of a taxi disappearing down the drive. There had been a lone occupant in the rear seat.

Constantine's aide, Tomas, who was greeting late guests, confirmed that the occupant had been Lilah.

Zane strode to the garage, found his car and accelerated after the taxi.

The repercussions of Gemma's stunt kept compounding. He hadn't touched her, but with his past and his reputation, no one, least of all Lilah, would believe him.

He reached their hotel suite and walked quickly through the rooms, long enough to ascertain that Lilah was not there, nor had she returned. That meant she had gone straight to the airport.

Using his cell, Zane checked on flights as he took the elevator down to the lobby. There was an international departure scheduled in just under an hour. He made a second call. The Atraeus Group owned a significant block of shares in the airport itself. Enough to ensure that when Zane needed assistance it was never a problem.

He reached the airport in record time and strode to the airline desk. As he spoke to the ticketing officer, his fingers automatically closed around the small jewelry case he had retrieved from the family vault before he had discovered that Lilah had left.

She loved him. He could hardly believe it.

And all he had been prepared to offer her was a loveless marriage, a business deal that would allow him to stay safe emotionally.

In retrospect the offer had been cowardly, a cover-up for his own failings and a situation he would not have been able to sustain, since a business arrangement was the last thing he wanted from Lilah.

His chest felt tight, his heart was pounding. For years he had been focused on the betrayals in his past. After all of *his* betrayals of Lilah, he was very much afraid that he had finally lost her.

The boarding call for Lilah's flight was announced as she strolled toward the gate. Buttoning her jacket against the air-conditioned chill, she joined the line of passengers.

A male voice with an American accent sent hope surging through her. She checked over her shoulder. For a split second she thought she saw Zane then she realized the man was shorter, darker.

Until that moment, she hadn't realized how badly she had wanted Zane to come after her.

Blinking back a pulse of raw misery, she kept her gaze pinned on the flight board, which was now showing a "delayed" message, and shuffled forward. She dug her boarding pass out of her purse as she neared the counter.

Behind her there was a stir. The deep register of another masculine voice that sounded even more like Zane made her tense. Determinedly, she ignored it.

Someone said "Excuse *me,*" in an offended tone.

Her head jerked around, her gaze clashed with Zane's.

His eyes were dark and intense, his expression taut. "I didn't touch her."

A hot pulse of adrenaline that he *had* come for her momentarily froze her in place. "I know."

He looked baffled. His hand closed on her elbow.

Despite the fact that her heart was pounding so fast she was having trouble breathing, Lilah gently disengaged from his hold. She knew how this worked. Once Zane got her out of the line he would start taking charge and she would melt; she would have trouble saying "No."

"She wasn't there at my invitation and there never was a 'me and Gemma.' She was only ever a…convenient date."

Lilah blinked, then suddenly she knew. "For the charity functions."

Zane's gaze was level. "That's right."

She suddenly felt short of air. "If you felt you needed protection from me, why did you even bother to come?"

"The same reason I'm here now. I couldn't stay away."

An announcement came over the speaker system that the flight was delayed. Lilah made another heart-pounding connection. "*You* delayed the flight."

"Being a member of the Atraeus family has its uses."

Lilah dragged her gaze from the sexy five o'clock shadow on his jaw and tried to concentrate on the bright hibiscus-printed sundress of the woman ahead of her. "Why did you have the flight delayed?"

The woman wearing the flowered dress gave her a fascinated look.

Zane's dark gaze held hers with a soft intensity. "Because there's an important question I need to ask you."

Panic gripped her, because hope had flared back to life and she couldn't bear it if he presented her with another variation of a loveless marriage.

Boarding resumed. "I have to go and you can't come with me."

He held up his boarding pass.

There was a smattering of applause.

Lilah dragged her gaze from the grim purpose in Zane's eyes. So, okay, he could board the flight, she couldn't stop that. "What did you want to talk about?"

"It's uh—private."

A nudge in the small of her back from the passenger behind prompted her to move forward another step. She was only feet from the counter now, but boarding the jet had ceased to be a priority. Every part of her being was focused on Zane, but she was afraid to read too much into his words. "I can't accept a temporary relationship. I still need what I've always needed—commitment."

His brows jerked together. "I'm capable of commitment. Don't believe everything the tabloids print. I've dated, but since I met you there hasn't been…anyone."

For a fractured moment the ground seemed to tilt and shift beneath her. She was certain she had misheard. "Are you saying you haven't slept with *anyone?*"

He frowned, his gaze oddly defensive. "It's not unknown for men to be celibate."

Heads turned. There was a visible stirring in the gate area. Somewhere a camera flashed.

Lilah's stomach churned. Just their luck, there was a journalist in the queue.

Zane's arm curved around her waist. "Is the fact that I was celibate so hard to believe?"

Still stunned by the admission, Lilah didn't protest when he hustled her out into the relative privacy of the corridor. "No. *Yes.*"

The thought that he hadn't wanted to be with another woman since he had met her was dizzying, terrifying.

"I don't lie."

Her mouth went dry. It explained why he had lost control in Sydney. Despite her resolve to stay distant and cool, she was riveted by the thought. “What I don’t get is, with all the women you could have, why me?”

Zane sent her a frustrated, ruffled look as if he was all at sea. “You’re sexy, gorgeous. We have a lot in common with the business, art, our pasts. I like you. I *want* you.”

Her heart squeezed in her chest. Liking and wanting, not *loving.*

He drew a velvet box from his pocket and extracted a ring.

The jewelry designer in her fell in love with the antique confection of diamonds and emeralds. The ring was heart-breakingly perfect.

And he wanted to marry her.

Lilah swallowed against the powerful desire to cave and say yes. “You chose a ring you knew I couldn’t resist.”

“I’ll do what I have to, to get you.”

Her jaw tightened at the neutral blankness of his approach. “What if I say, no?”

“Then I’ll keep asking.”

Once again the neutrality of his tone hit her like a fist in the chest then suddenly she saw him, suddenly she *knew.*

At age thirteen, he would have used that tone on the streets: with the gang that had cornered him and beat him; with the police and welfare workers who had shifted him from place to place; with his mother when she had finally decided to come looking for him.

It wasn’t that he didn’t care. It was because he did.

The strain of his expression, the paleness of the skin beneath his tan registered as he gripped her left hand, lifted it, the movements clumsy.

Raw emotion flooded her when she saw the unguarded expression in his eyes. When she didn’t withdraw from his grip the flash of relief almost made her cry.

He slid the ring onto the third finger. The fit was perfect.

Lilah stared at the glitter of diamonds, the clear deep green of the emeralds, the ancient, timeless setting. But mostly what she saw was the extreme risk Zane had just taken with a heart that had been battered and bruised, and for a few years, lost.

Somewhere in the recesses of her mind, she registered that the ring he had slipped onto her finger was a part of the priceless Illium Cache of jewels that his buccaneering ancestor had once claimed as booty.

The ring matched the bracelet he had tried to give her.

She swallowed. He had been trying to tell her then.

According to the material she had read tonight the cache was a bridal set; there had always been a ring to match the bracelet. More than that, they were heirlooms: family jewels.

As a jewelry designer she knew the message of the gems themselves was purity, eternity. Love.

She met Zane's gaze and the softness there made her heart swell. "This belongs in your family."

"Which is exactly where it's staying, if you'll marry me." For a moment he looked fiercely, heartbreakingly like his ancestor.

His fingers threaded with hers, pulled her close. "I wanted to give it to you before the opening ceremony tonight. That's why I had to leave when I did. Constantine has the combination to the vault, which is down in the cellar."

He had wanted her to wear the ring in front of his family and all of their business colleagues. Her chest squeezed tight. It explained why Zane had left just when they had seemed to be getting somewhere.

"It's beautiful." Everything she could ever have wanted and more, but it was nothing compared to the real treasure Zane was offering her: his heart.

The hurt that had filled her when she had thought Zane couldn't care for her drained away. Out of self-defense she had clung to the picture the press had painted of him, but it was no more real than the picture they had painted of her.

Zane was everything she had been looking for in a husband and more. "Yes, I'll marry you."

He muttered something rough in Medinian and pulled her

close. “Thank goodness. I don’t know what I would have done if you’d refused.” He buried his head in her hair. “I love you.”

The relief of his husky declaration shuddered through her. She wound her arms around his neck and simply held on. They had been walking toward this moment for two years, both stumbling, both making mistakes.

Zane wrapped her even closer, so tight that for a few seconds she could barely breathe. She didn’t care. She was having trouble concentrating on anything but the shattering knowledge that Zane *loved* her.

His hold loosened as he talked in a low husky voice. He had been afraid that he had lost her, that he had finally driven her away with his old fear that she couldn’t simply love *him,* that there would be a catch—something to be gained—that she would turn out to be dishonest and manipulative. He could bear anything but that. He had been in a terrible situation, unable to stay away from her, but afraid to be with her and discover that she had an agenda, and it wasn’t loving him.

He lifted his head, looked into her eyes and the air seemed to go soft and still. “I love you.”

And this time he kissed her.

Epilogue

A year later Zane proudly escorted his wife of ten months to the opening of the Ambrosi Pearl facility on Ambrus.

The ceremony, which was to be followed by champagne and a traditional Medinian celebration, with local food and music, was timed for sunset. The whole idea was that the extended twilight would bathe the new center with its large, modern sculpture of a pearl, with a soft, golden glow to celebrate the homecoming of Ambrosi Pearls. Unfortunately, clouds were interfering with the ambiance.

A large crowd of Atraeus and Ambrosi family were present along with locals, clients and of course the media. Constantine and Sienna were there, happily showing off their dark-eyed, definitely blond baby girl. Unbearably cute, Amber Atraeus had clearly inherited the luminous Ambrosi looks and a good helping of the Atraeus charisma.

Lucas and Carla, who had been married for several months, had just returned from an extended holiday in Europe. Looking happy and relaxed, they hadn't started a family yet, but Zane privately thought it wouldn't be long.

Lilah frowned at the gloomy sky, squeezed his hand and checked her watch. "It's time to start."

Glowing and serene in a soft pink dress, her hair coiled in a loose knot, she stepped up to the podium and welcomed the guests.

After providing a quick history of Ambrosi Pearls, Lilah asked a priest to bless the building then handed the proceedings over to Octavia Ambrosi, the great-aunt of both Sienna and Carla.

The oldest living Ambrosi, Octavia, affectionately known as Via, had been Sebastien Ambrosi's sister. She had lived on Ambrus with Sebastien, seen the destruction of the war and the rift that had torn the Atraeus and Ambrosi families apart when Sophie Atraeus and the bridal jewels had disappeared.

In the moment that Via was helped up to the white satin ribbon strung across the front doors of the center the sun came out from behind a cloud, flooding the island with golden light. With great grace Octavia cut the ribbon.

Later on in the evening, when guests had started to leave by the luxury launches that had been laid on by the Atraeus family, Lilah was surprised when Carla made a beeline for her. Since the tension which had erupted between them over Lilah dating Lucas, they had barely spoken, although that was mostly so now because they lived in different countries.

Carla gave her a quick hug and handed her a battered leather case. "This belonged to Sebastien. Since you and Zane will be living on Ambrus in the refurbished villa, we thought you should have it."

Zane's arm came around Lilah, warm and comforting, as she opened the case. Her eyes filled with tears as she studied the silver christening cup engraved with Sebastien's name.

Carla's expression softened as she looked at the cup. "It's of no great monetary value—"

"How did you know?" Zane said abruptly.

"That Lilah's pregnant?" Carla smiled. "It was an informed guess. You two shouldn't look so happy."

Lilah closed the case and tried to give it back to Carla. "This is a family treasure."

Carla smiled as Lucas joined them, followed by Sienna and Constantine with a sleepy Amber tucked into the crook of his arm. "In case you hadn't noticed, you are family."

* * * * *

THE BOSS'S SECRET MISTRESS

ALISON FRASER

CHAPTER ONE

'LUCAS RYECART?' Tory repeated the name, but it meant nothing to her.

'You must have heard of him,' Simon Dixon insisted. 'American entrepreneur, bought up Howard Productions and Chelton TV last year.'

'I think I'd remember a name like that,' Tory told her fellow production assistant. 'Anyway, I'm not interested in the wheeling and dealing of money men. If Eastwich needs an injection of cash, does it matter where it comes from?'

'If it means one of us ending up at the local job centre,' Simon warned dramatically, 'then, yes, I'd say it matters.'

'That's only rumour.' Tory knew from personal experience that rumours bore little relationship to the truth.

'Don't be so sure. Do you know what they called him at Howard Productions?' It was a rhetoric question as Simon took lugubrious pleasure in announcing, 'The Grim Reaper.'

This time Tory laughed in disbelief. After a year in Documentary Affairs at Eastwich Productions, she knew Simon well enough. If there wasn't drama already in a situation, he would do his best to inject it. He was such a stirrer people called him The Chef.

'Simon, are you aware of your nickname?' she couldn't resist asking now.

'Of course.' He smiled as he countered, 'Are you?'

Tory shrugged. She wasn't, but supposed she had one.

'The Ice Maiden.' It was scarcely original. 'Because of your cool personality, do you think?'

'Undoubtedly,' agreed Tory, well aware of the real reason.

'Still, it's unlikely that you'll fall victim to staff cuts,' Simon continued to muse. 'I mean, what man can resist Shirley

Temple hair, eyes like Bambi and more than a passing resemblance to what's-her-name in *Pretty Woman*?'

Tory pulled a face at Simon's tongue-in-cheek assessment of her looks. 'Anyone who prefers blonde supermodel types… Not to mention those of an entirely different persuasion.'

'I should be so lucky,' he acknowledged in camp fashion, before disclaiming, 'No, this one's definitely straight. In fact, he has been described as God's gift to women.'

'Really.' Tory remained unimpressed. 'I thought that was some rock singer.'

'I'm sure God is capable of bestowing more than one gift to womankind,' Simon declared, 'if only to make up for the many disadvantages he's given you.'

Tory laughed, unaffected by Simon's anti-women remarks. Simon was *anti* most things.

'Anyway, I think we can safely assume, with a little judicious eyelash-batting, you'll achieve job security,' he ran on glibly, 'so that leaves myself or our beloved leader, Alexander the Not-so-Great. Who would you put your money on, Tory dearest?'

'I have no idea.' Tory began to grow impatient with Simon and his speculations. 'But if you're that worried, perhaps you should apply yourself to some work on the remote chance this Ryecart character comes to survey his latest acquisition.'

This was said in the hope that Simon would allow her to get on with her own work. Oblivious, Simon remained seated on the edge of her desk, dangling an elegantly shod foot over one side.

'Not so remote,' he warned. 'The grapevine has him due at eleven hundred hours to inspect the troops.'

'Oh.' Tory began to wonder how reliable the rest of his information was. Would Eastwich Productions be subject to some downsizing?

'Bound to be Alex,' Simon resumed smugly. 'He's been over the hill and far away for some months now.'

Tory was really annoyed this time. 'That's not true. He's just had a few problems to sort out.'

'A *few*!' Simon scoffed at this understatement. 'His wife

runs off to Scotland. His house is repossessed. And his breath smells like an advert for Polo mints… We do know what that means, Goldilocks?'

At times Tory found Simon amusing. This wasn't one of them. She was quite aware Alex, their boss, had a drink problem. She just didn't believe in kicking people when they were down.

'You're not going to do the dirty on Alex, are you, Simon?'

'*Moi?* Would I do something like that?'

'Yes.' She was certain of it.

'You've cut me to the quick.' He clasped his heart in theatrical fashion. 'Why should I do down Alex…especially when he can do it so much better himself, don't you think?'

True enough, Tory supposed. Alex was sliding downhill so fast he could have won a place on an Olympic bobsleigh team.

'Anyway, I'll toddle off back to my desk—' Simon suited actions to his words '—and sharpen wits and pencil before our American friend arrives.'

Tory frowned. 'Has Alex come in yet?'

'Is the Pope a Muslim?' he answered flippantly, then shook his head as Tory picked up the phone. 'I shouldn't bother if I were you.'

But Tory felt some loyalty to Alex. He had given her her job at Eastwich.

She rang his mistress's flat, then every other number she could possibly think of, in the vain hope of finding Alex before Eastwich's new boss descended on them.

'Too late, *ma petite*,' Simon announced with satisfaction as Colin Mathieson, the senior production executive, appeared at the glass door of their office. He gave a brief courtesy knock before entering. A stranger who had to be the American followed him.

He wasn't at all what Tory had expected. She'd been prepared for a sharp-suited, forty something year old with a sunbed tan and a roving eye.

That was why she stared. Well, that was what she told herself later. At the time she just stared.

Tall. Very tall. Six feet two or three. Almost casual in khaki trousers and an open-necked shirt. Dark hair, straight and slicked back, and a long angular face. Blue eyes, a quite startling hue. A mouth slanted with either humour or cynicism. In short, the best-looking man Tory had ever seen in her life.

Tory had never felt it before, an instant overwhelming attraction. She wasn't ready for it. She was transfixed. She was reduced to gaping stupidity.

The newcomer met her gaze and smiled as if he knew. No doubt it happened all the time. No doubt, being God's gift, he was used to it.

Colin Mathieson introduced her, 'Tory Lloyd, Production Assistant,' and she recovered sufficiently to raise a hand to the one stretched out to her. 'Lucas Ryecart, the new chief executive of Eastwich.'

Her hand disappeared in the warm dry clasp of his. He towered above her. She fought a feeling of insignificance. She couldn't think of a sane, sensible thing to say.

'Tory's worked for us for about a year,' Colin continued. 'Shows great promise. Had quite an input to the documentary on single mothers you mentioned seeing.'

Lucas Ryecart nodded and, finally dropping Tory's hand, commented succinctly, 'Well-made programme, Miss Lloyd…or is it Mrs?'

'Miss,' Colin supplied at her silence.

The American smiled in acknowledgement. 'Though perhaps a shade too controversial in intention.'

It took Tory a moment to realise he was still talking about the documentary and another to understand the criticism, before she at last emerged from brainless-guppy mode to point out, 'It's a controversial subject.'

Lucas Ryecart looked surprised by the retaliation but not unduly put out. 'True, and the slant was certainly a departure from the usual socialist dogma. Scarcely sympathetic.'

'We had no bias.' Tory remained on the defensive.

'Of course not,' he appeared to placate her, then added, 'You just gave the mothers free speech and let them condemn themselves.'

'We let them preview it,' she claimed. 'None of them complained.'

'Too busy enjoying their five minutes' fame, I expect,' he drawled back.

His tone was more dry than accusing, and he smiled again.

Tory didn't smile back. She was struggling with a mixture of temper and guilt, because, of course, he was right.

The single mothers in question had been all too ready to talk and it hadn't taken much editing to make them sound at best ignorant, at worst uncaring. Away from the camera and the lights, they had merely seemed lonely and vulnerable.

Tory had realised the interviews had been neither fair nor particularly representative and had suggested Alex tone them down. But Alex had been in no mood to listen. His wife had just left him, taking their two young children, and single mothers hadn't been flavour of the month.

Lucas Ryecart caught her brooding expression and ran on, 'Never mind...Tory, is it?'

Tory nodded silently, wishing he'd stuck to Miss Lloyd. Or did he feel he had to be on first-name terms with someone before he put the boot in?

'Tory,' he repeated, 'in documentary television it's always difficult to judge where to draw the line. Interview the mass murderer and are you explaining or glorifying his crimes? Interview the victims' families and do you redress the balance or simply make television out of people's grief?'

'I would refuse to do either,' Tory stated unequivocally at this mini-lecture.

'Really?' He raised a dark, straight brow and looked at her as if he were now assessing her as trouble.

It was Simon who came to her rescue, though not intentionally. '*I* wouldn't. I'd do anything for a good story.'

Having been virtually ignored, Simon thought it time to draw attention to himself.

Ryecart's eyes switched from Tory to Simon and Colin Mathieson performed the introductions. 'This is Simon Dixon. Alex's number two.'

'Simon.' The American nodded.

'Mr Ryecart.' Simon smiled confidently. 'Or do you wish us to call you Lucas? Being American, you must find English formality so outmoded.'

Tory had to give credit where credit was due: Simon had nerve.

Lucas Ryecart, however, scarcely blinked as he replied smoothly, 'Mr Ryecart will do for now.'

Simon was left a little red-faced, muttering, 'Well, you're the boss.'

'Quite,' Ryecart agreed succinctly, but didn't labour the point as he offered a conciliatory smile and hand to Simon.

Simon—the creep—accepted both.

It was Colin Mathieson who directed at them, 'Do you know where we might find Alex? He isn't in his office.'

'He never is,' muttered Simon in an undertone designed to be just audible.

Tory shot him a silencing look before saying, 'I think he's checking out locations for a programme.'

'Which programme?' Colin enquired. 'The one on ward closures? I thought we'd abandoned it.'

'Um...no.' Tory decided to keep the lies general. 'It's something at the conception stage, about...' She paused for inspiration and flushed as she felt the American's eyes on her once more.

'Alcoholism and the effects on work performance,' Simon volunteered for her.

She could have been grateful. She wasn't. She understood it for what it was—a snide reference to Alex's drinking.

Colin didn't seem to pick up on it, but Tory wasn't so sure about Lucas Ryecart. His glance switched to the mocking smile on Simon's face, then back to hers. He read the suppressed anger that made her mouth a tight line, but refrained from comment.

'Well, get Alex to give me a bell when he gets in.' Colin turned towards the door, ready to continue the guided tour.

Ryecart lingered, his eyes resting on Tory. 'Have we met before?'

Tory frowned. Where could they have met? They were unlikely to move in the same social circles.

'No, I don't think so,' she replied at length.

He seemed unconvinced but then shrugged. 'It doesn't matter. We probably haven't. I'm sure I would have remembered you.'

He smiled a hundred-watt smile, just for her, and the word handsome didn't cover it.

Tory's heart did an odd sort of somersault thing.

'I—I…' Normally so articulate, she couldn't think of a thing to say.

It was at least better than saying anything foolish.

He smiled again, a flash of white in his tanned face, then he was gone.

Tory took a deep, steadying breath and sat back down on her chair. Men like that should carry around a Government Health Warning.

'"I'm sure I would have remembered you."' Simon mimicked the American's words. 'My God, where does he get his lines? B movies from the thirties? Still, good news for you, ducks.'

'What?' Tory looked blank.

'Come on, darling—' Simon thought she was being purposely obtuse '—you and the big chief. Has he got the hots for you or what?'

'You're being ridiculous!' she snapped in reply.

'Am I?' Simon gave her a mocking smile. 'Talk about long, lingering looks. And not just from our transatlantic cousin. Me think the Ice Maiden melteth.'

Tory clenched her teeth at this attempt at humour and confined herself to a glare. It seemed wiser than protesting, especially when she *could* recall staring overlong at the American.

Of course it hadn't lasted, the impact of his looks. The moment he had talked—or patronised might be closer to the mark—she had recovered rapidly.

'Well, who's to blame you?' Simon ran on. 'He has at least

one irresistible quality: he's rich. As in hugely, obscenely, embarrassingly—'

'Shut up, Simon,' she cut in, exasperated. 'Even if I was interested in his money, which I'm not, he definitely isn't my type.'

'If you say so.' He was clearly unconvinced. 'Probably as well. Rumour has it that he's still carrying a torch for his wife.'

'Wife?' she echoed. 'He's married?'

'*Was,*' he corrected. 'Wife died in a car accident a few years ago. Collided with a tanker lorry. Seemingly, she was pregnant at the time.'

The details struck a chord with Tory, and her stomach hit the floor. She shook her head in denial. No, it couldn't be.

Or could it?

Lucas could shorten to Luc. He was American. He did work in the media, albeit a quite different area.

'Was he ever a foreign correspondent?'

She willed Simon to ridicule the idea.

Instead he looked at her in surprise. 'As a matter of fact, yes, my sources tell me he worked for Reuters in the Middle East for several years before marrying into money. I can't remember the name of the family but they've Fleet Street connections.'

The Wainwrights. Tory knew it, though she could scarcely believe it. He'd been married to Jessica Wainwright. Tory knew this because she'd almost married into the same family.

How had she not recognised him immediately? She'd seen a photograph. It had pride of place on the grand piano—Jessica radiant in white marrying her handsome war reporter. Of course, it had been taken more than a decade earlier.

'Do you know him from some place, then?' Simon didn't hide his curiosity.

Tory shook her head. Telling Simon would be like telling the world.

'I remember reading about him in a magazine.' She hoped to kill the subject dead.

* * *

'Where are you going?' he asked, watching her pick up her handbag and jacket.

'Lunch,' she snapped back.

'It's not noon yet,' he pointed out, suddenly the model employee.

'It's either that or stay and murder you,' Tory retorted darkly.

'In that case,' Simon did his best to look contrite, '*bon appetit*!'

It deflated some of Tory's anger, but she still departed, needing fresh air and her own company. She made for the back staircase, expecting to meet no one on it. Most people used the lift.

Taking the stairs two at a time, she cannoned right into a motionless figure on the landing, bounced back off and, with a quick, 'Sorry,' would have kept on moving if a hand hadn't detained her. She looked up to find Lucas Ryecart staring down at her. Two meetings in half an hour was too much!

The American, however, didn't seem to think so. His face creased into a smile, transforming hard lines into undeniable charm. 'We meet again...*Tory*, isn't it?'

'I—I...yes.' Tory was reduced to monosyllables once more.

'Is everything all right?' He noted her agitation. He could hardly miss it. She must resemble a nervous rabbit caught in headlights.

She gathered her wits together, fast. 'Yes. Fine. I'm just going to the...dentist,' she lied unnecessarily. She could have easily said she was going to do some research.

'Well, at least it's not me,' he drawled in response.

Tory blinked. 'What's not?'

'Giving you that mildly terrified look,' he explained and slanted her a slow, amused smile.

Tory's brain went to mush again. 'I...no.'

'Check-up, filling or extraction?'

'Extraction.'

Tory decided an extraction might account for her flaky behaviour.

'I'll be back later,' she added, feeling like a naughty schoolgirl.

'Don't bother,' Lucas Ryecart dismissed. 'I'm sure Colin won't mind if you take the rest of the day off.'

He said this as Colin Mathieson appeared on the stairwell, holding up a file. 'Sorry I was so long, but it took some finding.'

'Good…Colin, Tory has to go to the dentist.' The American made a show of consulting him. 'Do you think we could manage without her this afternoon?'

Colin recognised the question for what it was—a token gesture. Lucas Ryecart called the shots now.

'Certainly, if she's under the weather,' Colin conceded, but he wasn't happy about it.

There were deadlines to be met and Alex was seldom around these days to meet them. Colin was well aware Tory and Simon were taking up the slack.

'I'll come in tomorrow,' she assured him quietly.

He gave her a grateful smile.

'Tory is a real workaholic,' he claimed, catching the frown settling between Lucas Ryecart's dark brows.

'Well, better than the other variety, I guess.' The American's eyes rested on Tory. He had a very direct, intense way of looking at a person.

Tory felt herself blush again. Could he possibly know why they were covering for Alex?

'I have to go.' She didn't wait for permission but took to her heels, flying down the stairs to exit Eastwich's impressive glass façade.

Having no dental appointment, she went straight back to her flat to hide out. It was on the ground floor of a large Victorian house on the outskirts of Norwich. She'd decided to rent rather than buy, as any career move would dictate a physical move. Maybe it would be sooner rather than later now Lucas Ryecart had descended on Eastwich.

Tory took out an album of old photographs and found one from five years ago. She felt relief, sure she'd changed almost out of recognition, her face thinner, her hair shorter, and her make-up considerably more sophisticated. She was no longer that dreamy-eyed girl who'd thought herself in love with Charlie Wainwright.

Coupled with a different name—Charlie had always preferred Victoria or Vicki to the Tory friends had called her—it was not surprising Lucas Ryecart had failed to make the connection. Chances were that all he'd seen of her was a snapshot, leaving the vaguest of memories, and all he'd heard was about a girl called Vicki who was at college with Charlie. Nobody special. A nice ordinary girl.

She could imagine Charlie's elegant mother using those exact words. Then, afterwards, Vicki had probably undergone a personality change from ordinary to common, and from nice to not very nice at all. What else, when the girl had broken her son's heart?

It was what Charlie had claimed at the time. Forget the fact that it had been his decision to end the engagement.

She took out another photograph, this one of Charlie's handsome, boyish face. She didn't know why she kept it. If she'd ever loved him, she certainly didn't now. It had all gone. Not even pain left.

Life had moved on. Charlie had the family he'd wanted and she had her career. She still had the occasional relationship but strictly on her terms with her in control.

She pulled a slight face. Well, normally. But where had been that control when she'd met Lucas Ryecart that morning? Lagging way behind the rest of her, that was where.

It had been like a scent, bypassing the brain and going straight for the senses. For a few moments it had been almost overpowering, as if she were drowning and had forgotten how to swim.

It hadn't lasted, of course. She'd surfaced pretty damn quickly when he'd begun to talk. She still bristled at his criticism on the single mothers documentary, regardless of whether it might be fair, and regardless of the fact that he'd bought Eastwich and along with it the right to express such opinions. She just had to recall what he'd said in that deep American drawl and she should be safe enough.

The question floated into her head. 'Safe from what?'

Tory, however, resolutely ignored it. Some things were better left well alone.

CHAPTER TWO

BY MORNING Tory had rationalised away any threat presented by Lucas Ryecart.

It could have been a simple chat-up line when he'd asked if they'd met before. Even if he'd seen a photograph of her, it would have left only the vaguest of impressions. And why should he make the connection between a girl student named Vicki and the Tory Lloyd who worked for him? She hadn't between Luc and Lucas until Simon had talked about his past and no one in Eastwich really knew about hers.

No, chances were he'd already forgotten her. He'd be like all the other chief executives before him—remote and faceless to someone in her junior position.

Reassured, Tory did as promised and went in to work, dressed casually in white T-shirt and cotton chinos. As it was Saturday, there were no calls to answer and, within an hour, she had dealt with most outstanding correspondence on her desk. The rest she took down the corridor for her boss's personal attention.

She didn't expect to find Alex Simpson there, not on a Saturday, and was initially pleased when she did. She imagined he'd come in to catch up on his own work.

That was before she noticed his appearance. There was several days' growth of beard on his chin and his eyes were bleary with sleep. His clothes were equally dishevelled and a quilt was draped along what he called his 'thinking' sofa, transforming it into a bed.

At thirty Alex Simpson had been hailed as a dynamic young programme-maker, destined for the highest awards. He had gone on to win several. Now he was pushing forty and, somewhere along the way, he had lost it.

'It's not how it looks.' He grimaced but was obviously relieved it was Tory and no one else. 'It's just that Sue's husband is home on leave and I've had no time to make other arrangements.'

Tory held in a sigh but she couldn't do anything about the disapproving look on her face. Officially Alex was lodging with Sue Baxter, a secretary at Eastwich, while he fixed himself up with more permanent accommodation. Unofficially he was sleeping with her while her Naval Engineer husband was on tour of duty. Tory knew this because *in*discretion was Sue Baxter's middle name.

She was a shallow, slightly vacuous woman, and what attraction Sue held for Alex was hard to fathom, but Tory kept her opinion to herself. Alex seemed intent on pushing his own self-destruct button and Tory felt ill-qualified to prevent him.

'You won't say anything, will you?' He smiled a little boyishly at Tory, already knowing the answer.

She shook her head, her loyalty guaranteed. She didn't fancy Alex, though many women did. Nor was she sure if she liked him at times. But he had a vulnerable quality that brought out a protective streak in her.

'You'd better not hang round here, looking like that,' she said with some frankness.

'I suppose not.' Alex made another face. 'I hear the new chief exec appeared in person yesterday.'

Tory nodded. 'I said you were out researching a programme.'

'I was, sort of,' he claimed. It was as unconvincing as his rider of, 'Pity I missed him.'

Tory looked at him sceptically, but refrained from pointing out that, had Lucas Ryecart met Alex while he was in this condition, Alex might not still be on the Eastwich payroll.

'Tory, I was wondering—' he gave her an appealing look '—if I could go to your place. Just to clean up. And maybe get my head down for an hour or two.'

Tory's heart sank. She told herself to refuse point-blank, but it came out as a less definite, 'I'm not sure, Alex. You know how tongues wag round here and if anyone saw you—'

'They won't,' he promised. 'I'll be the soul of discretion.'

'Yes, but—' Tory didn't get the chance to finish before Alex smiled in gratitude at her.

'You're a great girl.' He jumped up from his desk with some of his old enthusiasm. 'A wash and brush-up, that's all I need, and I'll be a new man.'

'All right.' Tory was already regretting it as she relayed, 'I have a spare key in my desk.'

Alex picked up the quilt from the couch and stuffed it into a cupboard, before following her back down the corridor to her office.

'You'll need the address.' She wrote it down on her telephone pad. 'You can use the phone to find a hotel or something.'

'Kind of you, Tory darling—' he looked rueful ' but I'm afraid hotels are out till pay day. My credit rating is zero and the bank is refusing to increase my overdraft.'

'What will you do? You can't keep dossing down in the office,' Tory warned.

'No, you're right. I don't suppose you could…' he began hopefully, then answered for himself, 'No, forget it. I'll find somewhere.'

Tory realised what he'd been about to ask. She also understood he was still asking, by not asking. His eyes were focused on her like a homeless stray.

She tried to harden her heart. She reminded herself that Alex earned a great deal more than her for doing a great deal less. Was it her problem that he couldn't manage his money?

'Never mind.' He forced a brave smile. 'I'll be back on my feet soon. I'm due my annual bonus from Eastwich next month—that's assuming this American chappie doesn't cancel it.'

Or cancel him, Tory thought as she looked at Alex through Lucas Ryecart's eyes. He was a shambolic figure whose past awards would be just history.

'Look, you can use my couch,' Tory found herself offering, 'until pay-day.'

'Darling Tory, you're a life-saver.' A delighted Alex made to give her a hug but she fended him off.

'And strictly on a keep-your-hands-to-yourself basis,' she added bluntly.

'Of course.' Alex took a step from her and held up his hands in compliance. 'No problem. I know you're not interested.'

He should do. Tory had made it clear enough in the beginning and Alex, philanderer though he undoubtedly was, respected the fact. He was also lazy; mostly he ended up with women who chased him. Being handsome in a slightly effete way, he drew a certain type of woman. Tory wasn't included in their category.

'Five days.' Tory calculated when their next salary should appear in the bank.

'Fine.' Alex gave her another grateful smile before turning to go.

'Alex,' Tory called him back at the door, 'try and stay sober, please.'

For a moment Alex looked resentful, ready to protest his innocence. Tory's expression stopped him. It wasn't critical or superior or contemptuous. It was simply appealing.

He nodded, then, acknowledging his growing problem, said, 'If I don't, I'll crash somewhere else. Okay?'

'Okay.' Tory hoped his promise was sincere. He wasn't a violent drunk but she still didn't want him round her place in that state.

After Alex had gone, she wondered just how big a mistake she'd made. She knew it was one. She trusted it would turn out to be of the minor variety.

Rather than dwell on it, she returned to her work, but was interrupted minutes later. Her door opened and she looked up, expecting to see Alex again. She stared wordlessly at the man in the doorway.

Overnight she'd decided it was a passing attraction she'd felt towards Lucas Ryecart. Only it hadn't yet. Passed, that was. Dressed in black jeans, white shirt and dark glasses, he was just as devastating.

'How's the tooth?' he asked.

'The tooth?' she repeated stupidly.

'Gone but not forgotten?' he suggested.

The tooth. Tory clicked. She'd have to acquire a better memory if she were going to take up lying to this man.

'It's fine,' she assured. 'Actually, I had forgotten all about it.'

'Good.' His eyes ran over her, making her feel her T-shirt outlined her body too clearly. 'You didn't have to come in. How do you usually spend your Saturdays?'

The same way, Tory could have admitted, but somehow she didn't think he'd be impressed, even if he now owned most of Eastwich. More like he'd think she had nothing better to do with her time.

'It varies.' She shrugged noncommittally, then glanced down at her work, as if anxious to get on with it.

He noted the gesture, and switched to asking, 'Has Simpson gone?'

'Simpson?' Tory stalled.

'*Alex Simpson.*' He leaned on the doorframe, eyes inscrutable behind the dark glasses. 'At least I assume it was Simpson and not some passing bum, making himself at home in his office.'

'Alex was here, yes,' she confirmed and went on inventively, 'He came in to catch up on his paperwork.'

'He was catching up on some sleep when I saw him,' countered Ryecart.

'Really?' Tory faked surprise quite well. 'He did say he'd been in very early. Perhaps he nodded off without realising.'

'Slept it off, is my guess,' the American drawled back, and, pushing away from the door, crossed to sit on the edge of her desk. He removed the glasses and appraised her for a moment or two before adding, 'Are you two an item? Is that it?'

'An item?' Tory was slow on the uptake.

'You and Simpson, are you romantically involved?' He spelt out his meaning.

'No, of course not!' Tory denied most vehemently.

It had little impact, as the American smiled at her flash of temper. 'No need to go nuclear. I was only asking. I hear Simpson has something of a reputation with women,' he remarked, getting Tory's back up further.

'And from that you concluded that he and I…that we are…' She was unwilling to put it into words.

He did it for her. 'Lovers?'

Tory found herself blushing. He had that effect.

He studied her, as if she were an interesting species, and her blush deepened. 'I didn't think women did that any more.'

'Possibly not the women you know,' Tory shot back before she could stop herself.

He understood the insult. He could easily have sacked her for it. Instead he laughed.

'True,' he conceded. 'I tend to prefer the more experienced kind. Less hassle. Lower expectations. And fewer recriminations at the end… Still, who knows? I could be reformed.'

And pigs might fly, Tory thought as she wondered if he was flirting with her or just making fun.

'What about you?' he said with the same lazy smile.

'Me?' she asked. 'Oh, I prefer the invisible kind. Much less hassle. Zero expectations. And absolutely no recriminations.'

It took the American an instant to interpret. 'You don't date?'

'I don't date,' Tory repeated but without his tone of disbelief, 'and I don't need reforming, either.'

He looked puzzled rather than annoyed, his eyes doubting her seriousness.

'Is that a targeted response,' he finally asked, 'or a general declaration of intent?'

'Come again?' Tory squinted at him.

'Are you just telling *me* to take a hike,' he translated, 'or are all men off the agenda?'

Tory debated how much she wanted to keep her job. Just enough to show some restraint, she decided, so she said nothing. Her eyes, however, said much more.

'Me, I guess,' he concluded with a confidence barely dented. 'Well, never mind, I can live in hope.'

He was laughing at her. He had to be. He wasn't really interested in her. It was all a joke to him.

He straightened from the edge of her desk, saying, 'Would you have some idea how I might contact Simpson? '

'I…I'm not sure.' Having denied any relationship with Alex, Tory could hardly reveal the fact he was holed up at her place. 'I might be able to get a message to him.'

'Fine. I've asked all senior department heads to meet me, nine a.m. Monday, for a briefing,' he explained. 'It would be advisable for Simpson to attend.'

Tory nodded. 'I'll tell him…I mean, if I get hold of him,' she qualified, anxious to dispel the notion she and Alex had anything other than a business relationship.

'Well, if you can't, don't worry about it,' he ran on. 'It's Simpson's problem if he can't give Personnel a current telephone number.'

Tory frowned. 'But you saw him this morning.'

'So why didn't I wake him up?' he asked the question that was clearly in her mind. 'Let's just say I thought the morning after wouldn't be the best time to meet a new boss. What do you think?'

Tory thought that remarkably fair of the American—to give Alex the chance to redeem himself. Of course, he might simply prefer to sack him when he was stone-cold sober.

'Alex is a very good programme-maker,' she declared staunchly. 'He won a BAFTA three years ago.'

'Simpson *was* a very good programme-maker,' Lucas Ryecart corrected her, 'and, in this business, you're only as good as your last show. Simpson should know that.'

Tory said nothing. Speaking up for Alex had cut no ice with this man.

He also suspected her motives. 'Why so concerned about Simpson? If he goes, it might do your own career some good.'

'I doubt it.' Tory wondered who he was trying to fool. 'Simon is more experienced than me.'

He frowned, making the connection only when she glanced towards the second desk in the room. 'More willing to promote his cause, too, as I recall. Is he the reason you're loyal to Simpson?'

'Sorry?'

'You don't want to work for this Simon guy?'

No, Tory certainly didn't, but she didn't want to do Simon down either.

'You're not homophobic, are you?' he surmised at her uneasy silence.

'What?' Tory was startled by his directness.

'Homophobic,' he repeated, 'Anti-gay, against homo—'

'I know what it means!' Tory cut in angrily, and, forgetting—or, at least, no longer caring—who he was, informed him, 'It might be hard for an American to understand, but reticence isn't always an indication of stupidity.'

'Being brash, loud-mouth colonials, you mean.' He had no problem deciphering the insult. He just wasn't bothered by it.

Tory wondered what you had to do to dent this man's confidence. Use a sledgehammer, perhaps.

'Simon's sexual preference is a matter of complete disinterest to me,' she declared in heavy tones.

'If you say so,' he responded, as if he didn't quite believe her.

'I am *not* homophobic!' she insisted angrily. 'Whether I'd want to work for Simon doesn't hinge on that.'

'Okay.' He conceded the point, then immediately lost interest in it as he looked at his watch, saying, 'I have to go. I have a meeting in London. I'll give you my number.'

He picked up her Biro and, tearing out a slip of paper from her notepad, leaned on her desk to write his name and two telephone numbers.

'The top one is my mobile,' he informed her. 'The other's Abbey Lodge. I'm staying there in the short term.'

Abbey Lodge was the most exclusive hotel locally, favoured by high-powered businessmen and visiting celebrities.

He held out the piece of paper and for a moment Tory just stared at it as if it were contaminated. Why was he giving her his telephone number? Did he imagine she'd want to call him?

'In case you have a problem tracking down Alex Simpson,' he explained, patently amused at her wary expression.

'Of course.' Now she almost snatched the paper from him.

'Still, if you want to call me, regardless—' his mouth

slanted '—feel free. I'm sure we can find *something* to talk about…'

'I…' On the contrary Tory couldn't think of a sensible thing to say. She'd been so presumptuous it was embarrassing.

'Meanwhile—' his smile became less mocking '—it's a beautiful day. Why not play hooky for once?'

The suggestion sounded genuine but Tory felt even more uncomfortable, recalling the fact she'd played hooky yesterday.

'I have some stuff to finish,' she claimed, sober-faced.

'Well, you know what they say: all work and no play,' he misquoted dryly, 'makes for a dull television producer.'

Tory realised he was joking but wondered, nonetheless, if that was how she seemed to him. Dull. What an indictment.

It put her on the defensive. 'I'm not the one travelling down to London for a business meeting on a Saturday.'

'Did I say business?' He raised a dark brow.

Tory frowned up at him. He had, hadn't he?

He shook his head, adding, 'No, this one's strictly personal.'

'I'm sorry.' Tory denied any intention to pry.

But he continued, 'In a way, it involves you. I'm having dinner with the woman I was dating until recently…a *farewell* dinner,' he stressed.

Tory met his eyes briefly, then looked away once more. There was nothing subtle about his interest in her.

'This really is none of my business, Mr Ryecart,' she replied on an officious note.

'Not now, maybe—' he got to his feet '—but who knows what the future might hold?'

He afforded her another smile. Perfect white teeth in a tanned face. Too handsome for anyone else's good.

Tory tried again. 'I shouldn't think we'll meet very often, Mr Ryecart,' she said repressively, 'in view of your considerably senior position, but I'm sure I'll endeavour to be polite when we do.'

This time her message couldn't be missed. 'In short, you'd like me to take a hike.'

Tory's nails curled into her palms. The man had no idea of the conventions that governed normal conversation.

'I didn't say that,' she replied, through gritted teeth. 'I was just pointing out—'

'That you'd touch your forelock but nothing else,' he summed up with breath-taking accuracy.

Tory felt a curious desire to hit him. It took a huge effort to stop herself, to remind herself he *was* her boss.

He held up a pacifying hand, having clearly read her thoughts. He might be brash, but he wasn't stupid.

'Tell you what, let's agree to dispense with the forelock-tugging, too,' he suggested and finally walked towards the door.

Tory's heart sank. What did that mean?

'Mr Ryecart—' she called after him.

He turned, his expression now remote. Had he already dispensed with her, altogether?

She didn't intend waiting to find out. She asked point-blank, 'Should I be looking for another job?'

'What?' Such an idea had obviously been far from his mind. He considered it briefly before answering, 'If you're asking me will Eastwich survive, then I don't know that yet. It's no secret that it's operating at a loss, but I wouldn't have bought it if I didn't feel turn-around was viable.'

It was a straight, businesslike response that left Tory feeling decidedly silly. She had imagined rejecting Lucas Ryecart might be a sackable offence but obviously he didn't work that way.

'That isn't what you meant, is it?' He read her changing expression.

'No,' Tory admitted reluctantly. 'I thought…'

'That I'd fire you for not responding to my advances,' he concluded for himself, and now displeasure thinned his sensual mouth. 'God, you have a low opinion of me…or is it all men?'

Tory bit on her lip before muttering, 'I—I…if I misjudged you—'

'In spades,' he confirmed. 'I may be the loud, overbearing American you've already written me off as—'

'That's not—' Tory tried to deny it.

He overrode her. 'And I may let what's in my pants overrule good sense occasionally,' he continued crudely, 'but desperate I'm not, or vindictive. If you leave Eastwich, it won't be on my account.'

Tory wanted the ground to swallow her up. She started to say, 'I'm sorry, I shouldn't have—' and was left talking to thin air.

Lucas Ryecart might not be vindictive but he had a temper. She experienced its full force as the door slammed hard behind him.

And that's me told, she thought, feeling wrung out and foolish, and wishing she'd kept her mouth shut.

He'd been flirting with her. Nothing more. Perhaps he flirted with all personable women under the assumption that most would enjoy it. He'd be right, too. Most would.

They'd know how to take Lucas Ryecart, realise that anyone that handsome, and rich, and successful, would scarcely be interested in ordinary mortals. They'd be slightly flattered by his appreciative gaze, a little charmed by his slow, easy smile, but they certainly wouldn't be crazy enough to take him seriously.

She glanced out of the window in time to see him striding across the car park. She didn't worry that he'd look up. She was already forgotten.

She watched him get into a dark green four-by-four. It was a surprisingly *un*flash vehicle. She'd have expected him to drive something fast and conspicuous—a low-slung sports car, perhaps. But what did she really know about Lucas Ryecart? Next to nothing.

She tried to remember what Charlie, her ex-fiancé, had said. He hadn't talked much of his dead sister but he'd mentioned her husband a few times. He'd obviously admired the older man who'd spent his early career reporting from the trouble spots of the world. Charlie's mother had also alluded to her American son-in-law with some fondness and Tory had formed various images: faithful husband, dedicated journalist, fine human being.

None fitted the Lucas Ryecart she'd met, but then it had been years since Jessica Wainwright's death and time changed everybody. It had certainly changed his circumstances if Eastwich was only one of the television companies he owned. He was also no longer the marrying kind, a fact he'd made clear. Arguably, his directness was a virtue, but if he had any other noble character traits Tory had missed them.

Time had changed Tory, too. Or was it her current lifestyle? All work and no play, as he'd said. Making her dull, stupid even, unable to laugh off a man's interest without sounding like prude of the year.

Tory felt like kicking herself. And Alex. And Lucas Ryecart. She settled for kicking her waste bin and didn't hang around to tidy up the mess she made.

She took the American's advice and spent the afternoon at the Anglian Country Club, a favourite haunt for young professionals. For two hours she windsurfed across the man-made lake, a skill she'd acquired on her first foreign holiday. It was her main form of relaxation, strenuous though it could be, and she was now more than competent.

Sometimes she took a lesson with Steve, the resident coach. About her age, he had a law degree but had never practised, preferring to spend his life windsurfing. They had chatted occasionally and once gone for a drink in the club but nothing more. Today he helped her put away her equipment and asked casually if she had plans for the evening. She shook her head and he proposed going for something to eat in town.

Normally Tory would have politely turned him down, but Lucas Ryecart's image loomed, and she said, 'Why not?'

Tory drove them in her car and they went to an Italian restaurant. They talked about windsurfing, then music and the colleges they'd attended. Steve was easy enough company.

They went on to a pub and met some of his friends, a mixed crowd of men and women. Tory stuck to orange juice, and, although declining a party invitation, agreed to drive them there.

When the rest had piled out of her car, Steve surprised her with a kiss on the lips. It was quite pleasurable, but hardly earth-moving and another man's image intruded when she closed her eyes. She broke off the kiss before it turned intimate.

Steve got the message. 'I don't suppose you'd like to go home to my place?' he asked, more in hope than expectation.

'No, thanks all the same.' She gave him an amiable smile and her refusal was accepted in the same spirit.

Steve bowed out with a casual, 'Perhaps we can go out again some time,' and followed his friends into the house where the party was.

Tory drove home without regrets. She'd enjoyed the evening up to a point, but she had no desire to have competent, athletic sex with a man whose *raison d'être* was windsurfing. She'd sooner go to bed with a mug of Horlicks and a Jane Austen.

She returned to find her flat empty and felt a measure of relief, assuming Alex had chosen somewhere else to doss down.

No such luck, however, as she was rudely awakened at two in the morning by a constant ringing on her doorbell. Pulling on a dressing gown, she went to the bay window first and wasn't entirely surprised to see Alex leaning against the wall.

'Lost my key, sorry,' he slurred as she opened the outer door and took in his swaying figure.

'Oh, Alex, you promised.' She sighed wearily and for a moment contemplated shutting the door on him.

'Couldn't help it,' he mumbled pathetically. 'Love her, really love her… Know that, Tory?'

'Yes, Alex. Now, shh!' Tory hastily propelled him through the hallway before he woke her neighbours.

'I'm not drunk.' He breathed whisky fumes on her as he lurched inside her flat. 'Just had a drink or two. Her fault. The bitch. Phoned her up but she wouldn't talk to me.'

Tory sighed again as he sprawled his length on her sofa. There would be no moving him now. She should have turned him away.

'Why won't she talk to me?' he appealed with an injured air. 'She knows she's the only one I've ever loved.'

'Her husband was probably there,' Tory pointed out in cynical tones.

'Husband?' He turned bleary eyes towards her, then rallied to claim belligerently, 'I'm her husband. Eyes of God and all that. Better or worse. Richer or poorer. Till death or the mortgage company do us part,' he finished on a self-pitying sob.

'Who are we talking about, Alex?' Tory finally asked.

'Rita, of course.' A frown questioned her intelligence, then he began to sing, 'Lovely Rita, no one can beat her—'

'Shh!' Tory hushed him once more. 'You're going to wake the woman upstairs.'

'Don't care,' Alex announced, this time like a sulky boy. 'All women are vile… 'Cept you, darling Tory.' He smiled winningly at her.

Tory rolled her eyes heavenward. She might have taken Lucas Ryecart too seriously that morning, but she was in no danger of it with Alex. Drunk, Alex would flirt with a lamp-post.

'I thought you were talking about Sue,' she stated in repressive tones.

'Sue?' He looked blank for a moment.

'Sue Baxter,' she reminded him heavily. 'Works at Eastwich. Husband in Navy. Woman you've been living with for the last month or two.'

Drunk though he was, Alex understood the implication. 'You think I don't love Rita because I've been shacking up with Sue? But I do. Sue's just…'

'A fill-in?' Tory suggested dryly.

'Yes. No. You don't understand,' he answered in quick succession. 'Men aren't the same as women, Tory, you have to realise that.'

'Oh, I do,' Tory assured him, and before he could justify his infidelity on biological grounds she stood and picked up the blanket and pillow she'd dug out earlier. 'You're an education in yourself, Alex,' she added, draping the blanket over him without ceremony. 'Lift.'

He raised his head and she thrust the pillow under him.

'You're not a woman, Tory,' he told her solemnly, 'you're a friend.'

'Thanks,' she muttered at this backhanded compliment. Not that she minded much. She didn't want Alex's roving eye fixing on her. 'Goodnight, Alex.'

''Night, Tory,' he echoed, already settling down for the night. Soon he would be out for the count.

It was Tory who was left sleepless.

After an afternoon spent windsurfing and an evening in company, she should be tired enough to sleep through a hurricane, yet she couldn't sleep through Lucas Ryecart.

Alex had provided a temporary distraction but now he was just another concern. How could she keep Alex sober tomorrow so he would be presentable on Monday for his meeting with Ryecart?

She tried telling herself it wasn't her problem. And it wasn't, really. After all, what did she owe Alex? He had given her a chance, taking her on as a production assistant when she'd had little experience, but she'd surely repaid him, covering up for him as she had over that last three months. It would be much the wisest thing to let Alex fend for himself.

Perhaps Alex might even hold his own with the American. After all, he was an intelligent, articulate man with a first-class degree from Cambridge and twenty years' experience in the television industry.

Whereas Lucas Ryecart, who was he?

The man who was going to wipe the floor with Alex, that was who, she answered the question for herself, and for the second night in a row fell asleep with Lucas Ryecart's image running round her brain.

CHAPTER THREE

TORY woke in an extremely bad mood, and felt not much better after taking a shower. Dressed in jeans and T-shirt, she went through to the living room to tackle Alex. She had decided: she wanted him gone, a.s.a.p.

Only he wasn't awake yet. With his arms tight round a cushion and his legs bent up on the sofa, he lay there muttering in his sleep. He looked a wreck and he smelled awful, of too much booze and nicotine. She'd never found Alex attractive; this morning he was positively repellent. No way was he going to get his act together by Monday.

But she realised that she wouldn't need to give him a hard time. When Alex woke up, he would feel sorry enough for himself.

She was right. When she woke him with strong black coffee, he was full of remorse.

He'd forgotten his promise not to return to her flat drunk. Apparently he'd had a whisky for Dutch courage before phoning his wife in Edinburgh. When she'd slammed the phone down on him, he'd had several more.

'So, basically it was all Rita's fault,' Tory concluded on a sceptical note, deciding a sympathetic approach wasn't going to help him.

He looked a little sheepish. 'I didn't say that, exactly.'

'Just as well,' Tory muttered back, 'because I haven't met many candidates for living sainthood, but your wife has to be one.'

He looked taken aback by her frankness, but didn't argue. 'You're right. I didn't treat her very well, did I?'

Tory's brows went heavenward.

'Okay, I admit it,' he groaned back. 'I was unfaithful to her

a couple of times, but it didn't mean anything. It's Rita I love. After twenty years together she should know that.'

'Twenty years?' Tory hadn't viewed Alex as long-term married.

'We met at college,' Alex went on. 'She was so bright and funny and together. She still is… If only I'd realised. I can't function without Rita,' he claimed in despair.

'Then you'd better try and get her back,' Tory advised quite severely. 'Either that, or get your own act together, Alex, before you lose it all.'

'I already have,' he said miserably.

Tory resisted the urge to shake him. 'Hardly. You have an exceedingly well-paid job doing something you used to love. Give it another week or so, however, and you'll probably be kissing goodbye to that, too.'

Alex looked a little shocked at her plain-speaking, then resentful. 'It's not that bad. Sure, I've missed a few deadlines and been absent for a meeting or two. But Colin understands. He knows I'll be back on track soon.'

'You've forgotten the American.' Tory hadn't.

'Ryecart.' Alex shrugged at the name. 'So, there's a new chief exec. He'll only be interested in the business side.'

'I don't think so.' Tory decided not to pass on Ryecart's comments about their last documentary but decided Alex still required a reality check. 'There's something you should know. He saw you yesterday morning, crashed on your office couch.'

'Damn,' Alex cursed aloud, before saying with some hope, 'Maybe he thought I'd been working all night.'

Tory shook her head again. 'This man's not stupid, Alex. He knew you were sleeping it off… He wants to see you first thing Monday morning.'

'Well, isn't that civilised of him,' Alex sneered, 'not waking a sleeping man? Making me sweat till Monday morning before sacking me.'

That scenario had already occurred to Tory, but she said nothing.

'He was probably too much a coward to do it on Saturday,' Alex ran on speculatively. 'Probably thought I'd turn round and punch his lights out for him.'

Tory sighed heavily. 'Men are ridiculous.'

That deflated Alex somewhat. They both knew he was as likely to punch someone as become celibate.

'All right, so I'm no fighter, but he wouldn't know that.'

'I doubt he'd care. He looks well able to take care of himself.'

'Big?' Alex deduced from her tone.

'Huge.' Tory reckoned the American was at least six inches taller than Alex.

'Upwards or outwards?'

'Both… Well, sort of. He's not fat. He's just…muscly, you might say,' Tory described him with some reluctance.

Alex slanted her a curious look. 'You don't fancy him, do you, Tory?'

'No, of course not!' she protested immediately. 'Whatever makes you say that?'

He shrugged, then smiled a fraction. 'The blush on your face, I suppose. I've never seen you blush before.'

'Rubbish. I'm always blushing. I'm like a Belisha beacon in hot weather,' she declared extravagantly and turned the conversation back on him. 'Anyway, we're not talking about me. It's you that has the problem. You're going to have to make an effort on Monday, Alex, to impress him.'

'Is there any point?' he asked rhetorically. 'Why go in and give him the satisfaction of firing me?'

'Oh, for God's sake, Alex!' She lost her patience. 'Stop being such a wimp!'

For a moment Alex looked seriously indignant. He was her boss, after all. Then he remembered he'd just spent the night sleeping on her sofa, and had pretty much surrendered his right to deference by offloading his problems on her.

'I'm sorry. I shouldn't have said that,' Tory added as his face caved in, exposing his vulnerability.

'No, it's all right. It's what Rita would have said to me. She couldn't stand people wallowing in self-pity.' He looked in admiration at Tory, and her heart sank. She didn't need Alex transferring his emotional dependence onto her.

'Well, it's up to you, Alex. I'm not going to tell you what

to do.' She rose abruptly to collect their coffee-cups and take them through to the small kitchen adjoining.

He followed her and watched as she rinsed them out in the sink. 'I could prepare a schedule of documentaries we propose to make in the coming months.'

Tory frowned. 'What documentaries?'

He shrugged. 'I'm sure we could come up with something.'

'We?' she echoed.

'I thought, well, that you might—'

'Give up my *one* day off?'

'Well, if you've plans…' He clearly believed she hadn't.

'You think my life is dull, too, don't you?' she accused, almost wiping the pattern off the saucer she was drying. 'Good old Tory, with nothing better to do at the weekend.'

'No, of course not,' Alex disclaimed quickly, realising he'd touched a sore spot.

Tory scowled, but not at him. It was Lucas Ryecart's comments that still rankled. She couldn't seem to get the man out of her head.

'I just know I'll work better with you as a sounding-board,' Alex added appeasingly.

Tory knew he wouldn't work *at all* if she didn't help him.

She gave in. 'You go wash, I'll make the coffee, then we'll get started.'

'Tory, you're a brick.'

Tory pulled a face as he went from the kitchen to the hall and the bathroom off it. She heard the shower running shortly afterwards and, above it, the sound of him singing. She pulled another face. What did he have to sing about?

Men were unbelievable. One moment Alex was confessing his undying love for his wife and his devastation at her loss, the next he was singing a selection of top-twenty hits from the seventies.

Compartmentalisation. That was the key to the male psyche. Everything kept in separate little cubicles. Love of wife and children. Work and ambition. Fun and sex. Duty and religion. Nip into one cubicle, pull the curtain and forget the rest. Then nip out and onto the next. Never mind tidying up what you've left behind on the floor.

Not all men, of course, but the majority. She thought of Lucas Ryecart. Another compartmentaliser. One moment she was a woman and he was making it damn plain he fancied her. The next she was one of his employees and he clearly had no problems treating her as such. Then he was gone, and no doubt she'd been forgotten the second he'd climbed into his car.

So very different from women. Women stood at windows, watching cars pull away while they sorted out what they felt and why. Women carried their emotional baggage between cubicles until they were bowed with the weight.

There were exceptions, of course. Her own mother was one. Maura Lloyd had a simple approach to life. Create what havoc you liked, then shut the door on it and move on. It had worked for her—if not for the people round her.

Tory had been Maura's only child. She'd had her at eighteen. Tory's father had been a married lecturer at art college. At least that was one of the stories Maura had told her, but at times he'd also been a famous painter, a cartoonist in a popular daily paper, and an illustrator for children's story-books. Tory was never sure whether these were total fantasy or a selection of different men who might have sired her or the same multi-talented many-careered individual. Whichever, Maura had consistently avoided naming the man throughout Tory's twenty-six years, and, having met some of Maura's later partners, Tory had decided to leave well alone.

At any rate, Maura had decided to keep her. After a fashion, anyway, as Tory had spent her childhood shuttling back and forth between gentle, unassuming grandparents who lived in a semi in the suburbs to various flats her mother had occupied with various men.

The contrast couldn't have been sharper, order versus chaos, routine versus excitement, respectability versus an extravagantly Bohemian lifestyle. Tory had never felt neglected, just torn and divided.

She loved her mother because she was warm and funny and

affectionate, but, in truth, she preferred living with her grandparents. When she'd become sick as a child, her mother hadn't pretended to cope. Grandmother Jean had been the one to take her to chemotherapy and hold her hand and promise her her beautiful curls would grow back.

It wasn't that Maura hadn't cared. Tory didn't believe that. But it had been a selfish sort of caring. When Tory had needed calm, Maura would be playing the tragic figure, weeping so extravagantly a ten-year-old Tory had become hysterical, imagining she must be dying.

She hadn't died, of course, and the childhood leukaemia was now a distant memory, although, in some respects, it still shaped her life. She supposed everything in childhood did.

She looked round her kitchen—everything in its place and a place for everything. Grandmother Jean's influence, although she'd been dead ten years and her grandfather for longer.

There was no visible sign of her mother but Tory knew she carried some of her inside. She just kept it locked up tight.

'Tory?' A voice broke into her thoughts. 'Are you all right?'

'Sure. I've made coffee.' She loaded a tray with the cafetère and cups and a plate of croissants.

Alex followed her through and, after a slow start, they began to trawl up some ideas for future programmes.

They worked all day, with only the briefest break for a sandwich lunch, and as Alex got into his stride the man who had won awards re-emerged. Tory remembered why she had wanted to work for him in the first place. When he wasn't bed hopping or pub-crawling, Alex Simpson was a fairly talented programme-maker.

In the end they came up with four firm proposals for future programmes and a promising outline of another. Alex sat back, looking pleased with himself, as well he might, while Tory had some satisfaction in imagining Lucas Ryecart's reaction.

'Where's your nearest take-away?' Alex asked, consulting his watch to find it after six.

'There's a Chinese a couple of streets away,' she replied. 'I have a menu list somewhere. We can phone in an order, then I'll collect it.'

She went to a notice-board in the kitchen and found the menu list for the Lucky Dragon. They made their selection and she did the calling.

Alex followed her through to the hall, saying, 'I should go,' as he watched her sling on a lightweight jacket.

'You don't know where it is.' Tory slipped out the door before he could argue.

The Lucky Dragon was, in fact, easy to find. The problem was one had to pass The Brown Cow pub on the way, and Tory wasn't sure whether Alex would manage to *pass* it.

She went on foot and the food was ready by the time she arrived. She walked back quickly so it wouldn't go cold. She didn't notice the Range Rover parked on the other side of the street or its owner, crossing to trail her up the steps to her front door.

'I'll do that,' he offered just as she put the take-away on the doorstep so she could use her key.

Tory recognised the voice immediately and wheeled round.

Lucas Ryecart took a step back at her alarmed look. 'Sorry if I startled you.'

Tory felt a confusion of things. As usual, there was the physical impact of him, tall, muscular and utterly male. That caused a first rush of excitement, hastily suppressed, closely followed by the set-your-teeth-on-edge factor as she realised a series of things. He had her address. Her address was on a file. He had her file. He owned her file. He owned Eastwich.

He just didn't own her, Tory reminded both of them as a frown made it plain he wasn't welcome.

'I wanted to speak to you,' he pursued. 'I decided it might be better outside work hours… Can I come in?'

'I…no!' Tory was horrified by the idea. She wanted no one, especially not this particular one, to find out Alex was using her flat as a base.

'You have company?' he surmised.

'What makes you say that?' Her tone denied it.

He glanced down at the plastic bags from which the smell of food was emanating. 'Well, either that, or you have a very healthy appetite.'

Sherlock Holmes lives, Tory thought in irritation and lied quite happily. 'I have a friend round for tea.'

'And I'm intruding,' he concluded for himself. 'No problem, this won't take long. I just wanted to say sorry.'

'Sorry? For what?'

'Yesterday morning. I was way out of line. Wrong time, wrong place, and I was moving too fast.'

Tory was unsure how to react to what seemed a genuine apology.

'I—I...this really isn't necessary,' she finally replied. 'We both said things. I'd prefer just to forget the whole incident.'

'Fine. Let's shake on that.' He offered her his hand.

'Right.' Tory took it with some reservations.

His grip was firm and strong and it jolted her, as if his touch were electric. Warmth spread through her like a slow fire. Quite alarming. To be turned on by a handshake. Even the thought brought a flush to her pale cheeks.

He noticed it and smiled. Did he know?

'You're very young,' he said, out of nowhere.

She shook her head. 'I'm twenty-six.'

'That's young.' He smiled without mockery. 'I'm forty-one.'

Tory's eyes widened, betraying her surprise. He didn't look it.

'Too old, I reckon,' he added, shaking his head.

'For what?' Tory asked rather naively.

'For girls young enough to be my daughter,' he concluded, laughing at himself now.

No, you're not. Tory almost said the words aloud. But why, when she wanted rid of him? Didn't she?

She looked down. They were still holding hands. She slipped from his grip. The warmth between them remained.

'Colin Mathieson told me you were in your thirties,' he recalled next.

Tory's heart sank a little. Colin *believed* she was in her thirties. It was a wrong impression fostered by Alex when he'd employed her for the job.

'Perhaps he was thinking of someone else,' Tory suggested weakly.

'Perhaps,' he echoed. 'Anyway, if I'd known your real age, I wouldn't have asked you out.'

It was Tory's turn to frown. Did he have some religious objection to women under thirty? Or did he imagine her too immature to interest him?

'You didn't,' she pointed out.

'Didn't I?' He arched a brow before admitting, 'Well, it had been my game plan. I guess I didn't get round to it.'

Now she was too young or inexperienced or whatever for him to bother, Tory surmised with some anger, surely irrational.

'It was Colin who gave me your address,' he went on. 'I told him I wanted to talk to you about Simpson.'

Alex? For a moment or two Tory had forgotten about Alex.

She could tell the American, of course. She could invite him in so he could meet a sober, industrious Alex. Did it matter if he jumped to the wrong conclusions about him being there?

Tory found it did matter, so she said nothing.

'Did you manage to locate him, by the way?' Lucas enquired directly.

She nodded.

'He's looking forward to meeting you,' she fabricated. 'I believe he has some future projects he wishes to discuss.'

Lucas Ryecart looked mildly surprised but didn't challenge it.

'Good.' He then began to say, 'I guess I'd better leave you to your meal—' when the door opened behind Tory.

She turned to see Alex and this time her heart plummeted. He was holding his jacket, obviously on his way out. On seeing her, his face clouded with guilt.

Tory was quick to realise where he'd been going. Tired of waiting for the meal, he'd been off in search of liquid refreshment.

'There you are.' Alex recovered quickly. 'I was worried you'd got lost and was coming to look for you.'

'No, I…' She glanced between the two men but made no effort to introduce them.

Lucas Ryecart, of course, knew exactly who Alex was. His eyes briefly registered the other man, then slid back to Tory and didn't leave her. Dark blue eyes, cold with anger.

'Sorry—' Alex picked up on the sudden drop in temperature '—I can see I'm in the way. Would you like me to disappear for an hour or two? Let you have the flat to yourself?'

Tory could have groaned aloud. Alex made it sound as if they were sharing the place.

'I…no, don't do that, Alex.' She'd spent all day getting his mind back on work. She wasn't giving him a chance to go AWOL on her.

It was the wrong answer as far as Lucas Ryecart was concerned.

'No, don't do that, *Alex*,' he mimicked her anxious tone, reading too much—far too much—into it. 'Miss Lloyd and I have finished any business between us for now.'

Having said his piece, he turned and walked away.

'Damn!' Tory swore in frustration.

Alex, having registered an American accent, began, 'Was that—?'

'Yes!' Tory confirmed and, half tripping over the Chinese take-away, picked the bags up and shoved them at Alex. 'Carry these in!'

Then she raced down the steps and across the street in time to catch Lucas Ryecart opening the door of the Range Rover.

'Wait, please,' she appealed before he could climb behind the steering wheel.

He stopped and turned. His expression was now remote, as if he'd already dismissed her from his mind, but, after a moment's deliberation, he closed the car door and leaned against it.

'Okay, I'm waiting.' He folded muscular sinewy arms across a broad chest.

Tory saw tension and anger beneath the apparently casual gesture. 'I…um…just wanted to clear up any possible misunderstanding. About Alex being there, I mean. You see…well, it's not—'

'How it seems?' he cut across her ramblings with a mocking lift of one dark brow.

'Yes, ' she confirmed, 'I mean, no, it isn't.'

'So that wasn't Alex Simpson,' he drawled on, 'and you aren't about to share an evening meal with him and he isn't currently staying at your flat and you haven't lied to me about your involvement with him.'

Tory saw from his face that she would be wasting her time, telling the truth. Any inclination on his part to kiss and make up had departed with Alex's appearance at the door.

'There's no point in this,' she muttered to herself and would have walked away if a hand hadn't shot out to keep her there.

She tried to pull her arm free. When she couldn't, she lifted her other hand, intending to push him away. He was too quick for her. He grabbed both her wrists and dragged her round until he had her backed against his car.

He did it with the minimum of force. Only her pride was really hurt.

She snapped at him, 'Let me go!'

'Okay.' He released her but stood so close she was still trapped and asked, 'Is Simpson's wife filing for divorce?'

She frowned at the unexpected question. 'Yes, possibly. Why?'

'Well, that explains the need to keep quiet,' he concluded, 'if not the attraction.'

His eyes narrowed in contempt and Tory found herself flaring back, 'You know nothing!'

'You're right. I don't,' he agreed in the same vein. 'I don't know why a bright, beautiful young woman would waste herself on a washed-up has-been with a wife, two kids and a drink habit to support… Perhaps you could enlighten me?'

'Alex isn't a has-been!' Tory protested angrily, recalling the programme outlines they'd prepared to impress this man. Some of their ideas were good, damn good. All futile, now, it would seem. 'And he doesn't have a drink problem.'

He threw her a look of pity.

'Who says love doesn't walk around with a white cane and guide dog?'

She threw him back a look of fury.

'I'm not in love with Alex Simpson! I never have been in love with Alex Simpson. I never shall be. I don't even believe in love!'

She spoke in no uncertain terms and speculation replaced pity in his gaze, but he still didn't release her.

'So you don't love Simpson,' he mused aloud. 'You don't love anybody. I wonder what gets you through the day, Tory Lloyd?'

'My work,' she answered, both literally and figuratively. 'That's what's important to me. That's *all* that's important to me.'

He shook his head, then leaned towards her to say in a low voice, 'If that's true, Simpson must be goddamn lousy in bed.'

Tory reacted with shocked disbelief. 'Do you have to be so…so…?'

'Accurate?'

'Crude!'

'I can't help it,' he claimed. 'I am American, after all.'

His tone was serious, but inside he was laughing. At her.

'Is that what you like about Simpson? Is he suitably refined?'

'More so than you, at any rate.'

Tory had, by this time, given up worrying about job security.

Lucas Ryecart had also abandoned any effort to be a fair, reasonable employer.

'I won't argue with that.' He shrugged off any insult, before drawling, 'But at least I have a certain homespun notion of morality.'

'Really?' Tory sniffed.

'Yes, really,' he echoed. 'If I were married, I wouldn't dump my wife and kids just because a newer, prettier model came along—'

'That's not the way it was,' Tory almost spat at him, 'and who knows what *you'd* do. You're *not* married, are you?'

'Not currently, but I was.' His face clouded briefly.

Tory could have kicked herself. She'd forgotten momentarily his connection with Jessica Wainwright.

'And when I was married, I was faithful,' he added quietly.

Tory believed him. He hadn't cheated on Jessica. He hadn't cheated because he'd adored her.

Her anger faded as she wondered if he still grieved but she didn't want to probe further. She was uncomfortable with the whole subject.

'Mr Ryecart,' she replied at length, 'I don't feel this is any of my business.'

'It will be, *Miss* Lloyd,' he mocked her formality, 'come the day I take you away from Simpson.'

'What?'

'I said—'

'I heard!' She just didn't believe him. Was it a joke?

Blue eyes caught and held hers. They told her it was no joke.

'I've decided I *am* interested, after all,' he stated dispassionately.

They could have been discussing a business deal. She was to be his latest acquisition. Take over, asset strip, move on.

'I thought you were too old for me,' Tory reminded him pointedly.

'I'd have said so, yes,' he agreed in dry tones, 'but as you're already living with someone of my advanced years, you obviously don't share my reservations.'

'I am *not* living with Alex,' she seethed in denial.

'You're simply good friends, right?' He slanted her a sceptical look.

Tory wanted to slap him. She longed to. She'd never had such a violent urge before.

'Oh, think what you like!' She finally snapped. 'Only don't take it out on Alex.'

'Meaning?' Dark brows lifted.

'Meaning: you may fancy me—' she continued angrily.

A deep, mocking laugh interrupted her. 'English understatement, I love it. I don't just *fancy* you, Miss Lloyd. I want you. I desire you. I'd like to—'

'Okay, I've got the picture,' she cut across him before he became any more explicit. 'But that's not my fault or Alex's. I haven't encouraged you. If this affects our positions at Eastwich—'

'You'll scream sexual harassment?' His eyes hardened.

Tory scowled in return. He was putting words in her mouth that weren't there. 'I wasn't saying that.'

'Good, because I've told you before,' he growled back, 'I am quite capable of separating my private life and my position as Chief Executive of Eastwich… If I decide to fire Simpson, you can be sure it'll be for a better reason than the fact he's currently sharing your bed.'

'He isn't!' Tory protested once more, only to draw a cynical glance that made her finally lose it. 'To hell with this! You're right, of course. Alex and I *are* lovers. In fact, we're at it like rabbits. Night and day. Every spare moment,' she ran on wildly. 'We can't keep our hands off each other.'

It silenced him, but only briefly before he drawled back, 'Now who's being crude?'

'It's called irony,' she countered.

'All right, so if you and Simpson aren't lovers…' he surmised aloud.

'Give the man a coconut,' she muttered under her breath.

He ignored her, finishing, 'Prove it!'

'Prove it?' she echoed in exasperation. 'And how am I meant to do that—set up a surveillance camera in my bedroom?'

'That would hardly cover it,' he responded coolly. 'Some couples rarely make it to the bedroom. I prefer outdoor sex myself. How about you?'

Tory didn't have to feign shock at an involuntary vision of a couple entwined in long grass under a blue sky. Not just any couple, either.

She shut her eyes to censor the image and heard his deep drawl continue, 'Not that I was suggesting it as an immediate option. A date will do, initially.'

Tory's eyes snapped open again. 'A date?'

'You know—' he smiled as if he could see inside her head '—boy asks girl out. Girl says yes. They go to a restaurant or the movies. Boy takes girl home. If he's lucky, he gets to kiss her. If he's very lucky, he gets to—'

'Yes, all right,' she snapped before he could warm any more to the theme. '*You're* asking *me* on a date?'

'That was the general idea,' he confirmed.

'To prove I'm not slee—having an affair with Alex?' Her tone told him how absurd she thought it.

'It isn't conclusive,' he admitted. 'But if you were my woman, I wouldn't let another man get too close. I reckon Alex Simpson will feel the same way.'

Tory doubted it. Even if she had been Alex's *woman*—how primitive it sounded—she didn't see Alex fighting anyone over her.

'Alex doesn't work like that,' she said disdainfully. 'He's much too civilised.'

'Really.' He glanced across the street towards her house and the bay window on the ground floor.

Tory followed his eyes in time to see Alex drawing back behind a net curtain. Evidently he'd been watching them. It was hardly surprising.

'He's curious, that's all,' she explained. 'He's realised who you are. It's nothing personal.'

'Yeah, I bet,' he scoffed in reply.

'It's true!' she insisted.

'Okay, so it's true,' he repeated, humouring her, 'in which case he won't mind if I do this.'

'Do wh—?' The question went unfinished.

The American leaned forward and kissed her before she could stop him. His lips touched hers with fleeting intimacy. It was over in a matter of seconds, but she was left feeling the imprint of his mouth on hers.

'I—I…' she stammered, wide-eyed '…you sh-shouldn't…'

'No, I shouldn't,' he agreed, gazing hard at her. 'But now I have…'

Now he had, he would have to kiss her again. His eyes told her that.

Tory had time to protest, turn her head, do anything but stand there looking up at him. Time to move away before his head blocked out the sun and his mouth covered hers, hard and possessive. Time to pull back as he began to kiss as if they were already lovers.

Only Tory had never felt like this before. Totally powerless, her eyes shutting, her lips parting, letting him in. Unable to resist as he stole the breath and the will from her. Boneless and fluid in strong arms wrapped round her waist, drawing her closer.

Passion flared so quickly, it caught them both unawares. Somewhere in the back of her head, Tory knew this was crazy, but she didn't seem to care. Her arms lifted to his shoulders and he dragged her body to his. They fell back against the side of his car, oblivious. He went on kissing her. He started touching her. They forgot where they were.

Her jacket was big for her. Just as well. It hid the movements of his hands, pulling out the T-shirt from her jeans, running up over her back, then round to her small, firm breasts. She wore a crop top rather than bra. He touched her above it, stroking a nipple erect through the material. She moaned in his mouth. He groaned back and tried to push aside the top. She didn't stop him. She wanted this.

Sanity returned only as the front door of the nearest house slammed and a voice exclaimed loudly, 'Look, Mummy, they're still kissing. Don't they know they'll get each other's germs?'

'Shh, Jack,' another instructed, 'and stop staring. Just get into the car!'

The first, childish voice penetrated the mush that Tory's brain had turned into, and the mother's had a sudden, sobering effect.

She pushed at Lucas Ryecart's shoulders. He'd already taken his hand from her breast but was slow to release her entirely. He lifted his head away and they both glanced in the direction of the woman hustling her child into a car parked some yards down the road.

Embarrassed colour filled Tory's cheeks but Lucas Ryecart was unflustered. He didn't hide his pleasure in the kiss but gave her a slow, sensuous smile.

'You'll come back with me.' It was a statement, not a question.

Tory looked blank.

'To my hotel.' He made his meaning clear.

And the blue eyes holding hers made it clearer still.

'I…of course not!' Tory finally mustered up some indignation.

He ignored it. 'Why not? We both want it.'

Tory shook her head, denying it.

He smiled, and the smile called her a liar. He thought her a pushover. Something to do with the fact she'd just acted like one.

Pride reasserted itself and she tried to pull free. He held her easily, large hands spanning her waist.

'You won't have to go back to Simpson,' he assured her. 'I'll help you move out on him tomorrow.'

Tory stared back at him. What was he suggesting?

'We've only just met.' Her tone told him he was absurd.

'So?' He laughed. 'How often does it feel like this?'

She could have said, *Like what?* but he might have reminded her. And she didn't need it. Her body was trembling from the simple touch of his hand on her waist.

'You don't have to move in with me,' he went on. 'Not yet, at any rate. But you can't keep living with Simpson.'

'I'm not living with Alex,' she repeated for what seemed like the twentieth time. 'It's my flat.'

'Even easier,' he reasoned. '*You* can kick *him* out.'

Tory discounted the kiss and finally asked herself why she was having this conversation with a perfect stranger.

'You're crazy,' she concluded with more than a vein of seriousness.

'No, *I'm* honest,' he countered, 'and I don't see much point in fighting the inevitable.'

Him and her in bed together. That was what he meant. Tory didn't need a translation. His eyes told her. His certainty was disturbing. He imagined she was so easy.

It was time to fight back.

'Mr Ryecart—' she gave him a look that would have soured cream '—you either think an awful lot of yourself or very little of me. Whichever, I would sooner walk over red-hot coals with a plastic petrol can in my hand than go to bed with you. Is that honest enough for you?'

Was it insulting enough? Tory asked herself.

Seemingly not as he made some sound of disbelief and she, losing her temper, pushed him hard on the chest.

Taken by surprise, he stumbled backwards but recovered in time to grab her as she tried to escape.

The smile was gone. His eyes glittered dangerously. 'You can't sleep with Simpson again. Do you understand?'

A shiver went down Tory's back at the unspoken threat. She pulled at her arm but he wouldn't release her.

'Do you understand?' he repeated.

'Yes,' she choked the word out.

He caught and held her eyes, insisting, 'You *won't* sleep with him,' even as he finally let her go.

For a moment Tory returned his stare, and saw something in it, dark and disturbing, that told her she didn't really know who this man was.

Then she was running, running as she should have done earlier, blindly across the road and up the steps, through the door Alex had left on the latch.

She didn't look back. If she had, she would have seen him.

Lucas Ryecart watched her until the moment she disappeared.

CHAPTER FOUR

TORY'S office looked out onto the main corridor. Monday morning she watched Alex and the other senior producers walk towards the conference room at the far end. They were in subdued mood for their first official meeting with the new big chief.

Two hours later she watched them return with a considerably more relaxed air.

Only Alex didn't. He didn't return for another half an hour.

Simon spotted him first. 'Here he is.'

Alex popped his head round the door. 'Tory, can I see you for a moment?'

His manner gave little away as he proceeded to his office.

'Maybe he wants help in clearing his desk,' suggested Simon on a hopeful note.

Tory muttered, 'Shut up, Simon,' in passing as she walked past him on her way to Alex's office, closing the door behind her.

'Everything all right?' she asked tentatively, then listened in bemusement as Alex began to enthuse over the American and his plans for Eastwich.

It was as if he had suffered a blinding conversion on the road to Damascus with Lucas Ryecart in the role of God.

'When he asked me to wait back,' Alex ran on, 'I thought, This is it. The axe is about to fall. But nothing. He just wanted to discuss the direction I envisaged our department taking.'

Tory's gaze was incredulous. Did Alex really believe Ryecart was interested in his opinions?

'Naturally I handed over the presentation package I'd prepared,' he declared smugly. 'He seemed impressed.'

'Really.' Tory tried to convey some of her scepticism.

Alex misunderstood. 'Don't worry, he knows you had a part

in it. He asked me how long we'd worked in such close liaison.'

Tory recognised sarcasm even if Alex didn't and could have groaned aloud. She wondered how she could bring Alex up to speed. The trouble was she'd worked hard to kill Alex's curiosity about Ryecart the evening before. She'd put their evident quarrel down to the American's belief that she'd been less than honest about Alex's whereabouts and fortunately Alex hadn't witnessed the kiss that had followed.

'I wouldn't take what he says at face value, Alex,' she warned at length.

But Alex refused to let her dampen his spirits. 'He seems straight enough to me… Anyway, I feel like celebrating. Come to lunch. Antoine's. My treat.'

Tory wondered how Alex could suddenly afford to pay for such extravagant dining.

'Thanks,' Tory replied, 'but I have an appointment in less than an hour. We could go to the canteen, if you like.'

Alex pulled a face, as Tory had guessed he would, and said, 'I'll pass, if you don't mind.'

'Not at all.' Tory trailed back to her office, still puzzling over Ryecart's game plan.

'Well?' Simon enquired as she returned.

'Everything's fine,' Tory said succinctly and went to pick up her bag from under her chair. 'I'm going to the canteen for lunch.'

'I'll come with you.' Simon wanted to hear more.

They walked along the corridor together and she relayed some of the phrases Alex had used about the American while Simon raised a sceptical brow.

'Miss Lloyd!' Someone called from behind them.

Tory kept walking for a step or two, pretending she hadn't heard. She had no need to glance round to identify the voice.

'Wait up.' Simon grabbed her arm. 'It's the man himself.'

'You don't say!' Her teeth were already clenched as she turned to find Lucas Ryecart bearing down on them.

It was a purely physical reaction. She knew she didn't like him. She'd told herself that a hundred times.

But it had changed nothing. Her heart still stopped for a beat or two, then raced like a runaway train. She heard its engine roar and tried to focus on her dislike, not his looks. Did all women feel the same? Was that why he'd been called God's gift?

Their absorption in each other was mutual and obvious, so much so that Simon said, 'Shall I make myself scarce?'

'Yes!'

'No!'

The answers were simultaneous, but Simon knew which side his bread was buttered. He smiled at Eastwich's new boss before strolling off down the corridor.

Deserted, Tory went on the offensive. 'What do you want?'

'We need to talk,' he responded in a low undertone, 'but not here. It's too public. Come to lunch.'

Tory shook her head. 'I can't.'

'Or won't?' he challenged in reply.

Tory had forgotten he had no time for social niceties. She abandoned them, too.

'All right, I won't,' she confirmed.

He nodded, then looked at her long and hard. 'If it's any comfort, you scare the hell out of me, too.'

Was he serious? Tory wasn't sure, but the conversation was already in dangerous territory.

She deliberately misunderstood him, answering, 'I don't know why you'd be scared of me, Mr Ryecart. It's not as if *I* could sack *you*.'

He made an exasperated sound. 'That's not what I meant and you know it! Can't you forget our respective positions for a single moment?'

'Shh!' she urged before they attracted an audience. 'But, no, since you ask, I can't forget. Neither would you, I imagine, if you were in my position.'

'Underneath me?' he suggested.

'Yes!' She'd walked right into it.

He smiled, giving it a whole new meaning, while Tory blushed furiously.

'If only you were.' His eyes made a leisurely trip down her body and back again.

'You—' Tory could think of several names to call him but none seemed rude enough.

'It's all right, I can guess.' He was more amused than anything.

Tory seethed with frustration and anger. If she didn't walk away, she would surely hit him.

She did walk away, but he followed her to the lift.

It took an age to arrive. She stood there, ignoring him. Which was hard, when she could feel him staring at her.

The lift arrived and a couple of women from Drama stepped out. They nodded at Tory, then glanced at her companion. Their gaze was one of admiration rather than recognition.

Lucas Ryecart was oblivious, stepping into the lift with her.

Tory wanted to step out again, but it seemed an act of cowardice. What could he do in the five seconds it took for the lift to reach the ground floor?

He could stop it, that was what. He could run a quick eye over the array of buttons and hit the emergency one.

Tory didn't quite realise what he'd done until the lift lurched to a halt.

'You can't do that!' She was genuinely outraged at his action.

'Why not?'

'I...you... Because...well, you just can't!'

He grinned, mocking her regard for authority, and she flashed him a look of dislike.

'Don't worry,' he assured her, 'I'll give myself a severe reprimand later... For now, let's talk.'

'I don't want to talk.' Tory eyed the control panel, wondering if she should make a lunge at it.

She rejected the move as overly dramatic until he drawled, 'Fair enough. Let's not talk,' and, with one step, closed the distance between them.

Sensual blue eyes warned her of his intention.

Tory's heart leapt. In alarm, she decided, and raised her arms to fend him off.

'If you touch me—'

'You'll scream?'

So she wasn't original. She was still serious.

'Yes!'

'Well, of course, what else would you do, the lift being stuck and all?'

Tory glowered at him. He had an answer for everything.

He stretched out a hand and lightly brushed a strand of hair from her cheek. Then, before she could protest, he stepped back to his corner of the lift.

'Don't panic. I won't touch you till you ask me to.'

He appeared confident she would.

'We'll both be dead before then,' she shot back.

The insult went wide. His smile remained.

He leaned back against the wall as if he had all the time in the world. 'You never told Simpson about our…our *conversation* yesterday, did you?'

'There was nothing to tell,' she retorted, the ultimate put-down.

He arched a brow in disbelief. 'It's fairly usual for you, I suppose, being propositioned by other men?'

'Happens all the time,' she claimed, deadpan.

He laughed, briefly amused, then regarded her intently before murmuring, 'I can believe it.'

He had a way of looking at a woman that made Tory finally understand the expression 'bedroom eyes'. She tried hard to conjure up some indignation.

He helped her along by adding, 'So why settle for a wimp like Simpson?'

'When I could have someone like you?' she replied with obvious scorn.

'I wasn't thinking specifics. Pretty much any young, free and single guy would be an improvement on Simpson,' he said in considered tones. 'But, yes, since you're asking, I reckon there's every chance you could have me.'

The sheer nerve of him took Tory's breath away. 'You…I…wasn't—'

'After you show Simpson the door, of course,' he stated as a condition.

Tory still didn't believe she was having this conversation. 'And if I don't?'

His eyes narrowed, even as he admitted, 'I haven't thought that far.'

But when he did? Would their jobs be in jeopardy?

Tory found it impossible to gauge. Lucas Ryecart was still a stranger to her.

She glanced across at him. Today he was dressed formally. In dark double-breasted suit, relieved by a white shirt and silk tie, he would have looked every inch the businessman if it hadn't been for his casual stance, hands in pockets, length resting against a wall of the lift.

He caught and held her eye and homed in on her thoughts as he continued, 'If I wanted to fire Alex Simpson, I could have done so this morning with no great effort. I believe he has already had the requisite number of warnings.'

Tory hadn't known that. She'd imagined the executive board of Eastwich ignorant of Alex's recent conduct.

'Had you and he *not* been cohabiting—' his mouth twisted on the word '—chances are I would have. Instead I felt obliged to keep carrying him, at least for the time being.'

Tory frowned, failing to follow his logic. 'I don't understand.'

'It's like this. I *wanted* to fire him and normally would have.' A shrug said it would have given him little grief. 'However, I wasn't a hundred per cent certain why. Most likely it was because he's a sorry excuse for a production manager, but it just could be because he happens to be living with the woman I want,' he pondered aloud.

'I—I...y-you...' His bluntness reduced Tory to incoherence.

'So I decided I'd leave it for now,' he concluded, 'and if he continues to mess up, I won't have the dilemma.'

'You'll fire him, anyway?' Tory finally found her voice.

'Correct,' he confirmed without apology.

'And what if he gets back on form?' she challenged.

'Then he has nothing to worry about it.' He met her eye and his gaze did not waver.

He was either a man of honour or a very convincing liar. The jury was still out on which, but Tory could see the situation was going to be impossible.

'Maybe I should be the one to leave.'

'Eastwich?'

'Yes.'

His face darkened momentarily. 'You'd do that for Simpson?'

The suggestion had Tory sighing loudly. 'You mean hand in my notice while quoting "It is a far, far better thing that I do," etc. etc.?'

His lips quirked slightly, recognising the irony in her voice. 'Something like that.'

'Well, I'm sorry to disappoint you, but self-sacrifice is not part of my nature,' she told him. 'Try self-preservation.'

'From me?' He arched a brow.

'Who else?' she flipped back.

Arms folded, he thought about it some, before querying, 'Do I bother you that much?'

'Yes. No… What do you expect?' she retorted in quick succession and masked any confusion with a glare.

It had little effect. 'I must say, you bother me, too, Miss Lloyd. Here I am, supposed to be rescuing Eastwich from economic collapse, and I can't get my mind off one of its production assistants… What's a man meant to do?' he appealed with a smile that was slow and lazy and probably intended to devastate.

But Tory was wise to him now. 'This is all a joke to you, isn't it?'

'A joke?' he reflected. 'I wouldn't say so. Well, no more than life is generally.'

So that was his philosophy: life was a joke. It was hardly reassuring. For her or Eastwich.

'It comes with age,' he added at her silence.

'What does?'

'The realisation that nothing should be taken too seriously, least of all life.'

'Thank you,' Tory replied dryly, 'but I'd prefer to make up my own mind—when I grow up, of course.'

'Was I being patronising?'

'Just a shade.'

'Sorry.'

He pulled an apologetic face and Tory found herself smiling in response.

'Rare but definitely beautiful,' he murmured at this momentary lapse.

Tory tried hard not to feel flattered and counteracted with a scowl.

'Too late.' He read her mind all too well.

'Could you restart the lift...please?' she said in a tight voice. 'I'd like to go to lunch.'

'Sure,' he agreed to her surprise and reset the emergency stop.

The lift geared into action rather suddenly and Tory lurched forward at the same time. She was in no danger of falling but Lucas Ryecart caught her all the same.

He held her while she regained her balance. Then he went on holding her, even as the lift descended smoothly.

She wore a sleeveless shift dress. His hands were warm on her skin. She still shivered at the lightness of his touch.

She could have protested. She tried. She raised her head but the words didn't come. It was the way he was looking at her—or looking at his own hands, smoothing over her soft skin, imagining.

When he finally lifted his eyes to hers, he didn't hide his feelings. He desired her. Now.

He drew her to him, and she went, as if she had no volition. Only she did: she wanted him to kiss her, willed him to. Needed it. Turned into his arms. Gazed up at him, eyes wary, but expectant.

The lift came to a halt even as he cupped her face in his hands and lowered his mouth to hers. By the time the door slid open, he was kissing her thoroughly and she was helplessly responding.

'Well!' The exclamation came from one of the two men standing on the other side.

Too late Tory sprang apart from Lucas to face Colin Mathieson and a tall, grey-haired man of indeterminate age.

Colin's surprise became shock when Lucas turned to face them also.

The stranger, however, appeared greatly amused.

'We've been looking for you, Lucas, boy,' he drawled, 'but obviously not in the right places.'

He chuckled and his eyes slid to Tory, openly admiring Lucas's taste.

'Chuck,' Lucas responded, quite unfazed, 'this is—'

But Tory, horrified and humiliated, wasn't going to hang around while he introduced her to his American buddy.

'Don't bother!' she snapped at him, and took off.

She heard Colin call after her, half reprimand, half concern. She heard the stranger laugh loudly, as if enjoying the situation. She heard nothing from Lucas Ryecart but she could well imagine that slow, slanting smile of satisfaction.

Yet again, he had proved his point. Good sense might tell her he was like a disease—seriously bad for her health—but she seemed to have little immunity. The only sane thing was to keep out of infection range.

She went to the staff canteen, certain he wouldn't follow her there.

'Where have you been?' Simon demanded when she sat down with a spartan meal of salad and orange juice. 'I was about to give you up for dead—or alternatively *bed*. I wonder if he looks at all women that way.'

'Shut up, Simon,' she muttered repressively.

But Simon was unstoppable. 'Talk about smouldering. I used to think that was just an expression. Like in women's novels: "He gave her a dark, smouldering look." But not since I saw Ryecart—'

'Simon!' Tory glanced round and was relieved to see no one within listening distance. 'You might think this sort of thing

is funny but I doubt Lucas Ryecart would. You have heard of libel, I assume.'

'Slander,' Simon corrected. 'I haven't written it down... Well, not yet.'

'What do you mean, not yet?' Tory told herself he was joking.

Simon grinned. 'I could scribble it on the washroom wall, I suppose. L loves T. Or is it T loves L?' he said with a speculative air.

'It's neither,' she replied, teeth gritted.

Simon arched a surprised brow at her tone, but he took the hint and changed the subject.

Tory didn't linger over the meal but returned on her own to the office and threw herself into work so she wouldn't have to think too hard about anything else.

Alex didn't return from lunch—it seemed he was bent on pushing his luck—but she told herself firmly it wasn't her problem. She worked late as usual and was emerging from the front door just as Colin Mathieson was stowing his briefcase in the back of his car.

As he was a senior executive his bay was right at the entrance and, short of going back inside, she couldn't avoid him.

'Tory.' He greeted her with a friendly enough smile. 'I'm glad I've run into you. I wanted a word.'

Tory waited. She didn't prompt him. She just hoped the word wasn't about what she suspected.

She hoped in vain and stood there, wanting the ground to swallow her up, as Colin Mathieson gave her an avuncular talk which, while skirting round the point, could basically be summed up as: You are lowly, young production assistant. He is rich, charming man of the world. Are you sure you know what you're doing?

It was well meant, which was why Tory managed to mutter 'yes' and 'no' in the right places and somehow contain her feelings until she could scream aloud in the privacy of her own car.

Because it was galling. To be thought such a fool. Colin actually believed she was so naive that she took Lucas Ryecart seriously.

The day she did that, she really was in trouble.

CHAPTER FIVE

AFTER the lift incident, Tory was determined to avoid Lucas Ryecart. It proved easy. The American spent the next day closeted in meetings with various departments before disappearing to the States for the rest of the week.

His absence put things into perspective for Tory. While she'd been fretting over their next meeting, he'd been on a plane somewhere, with his mind on deals and dollars. Perhaps he did want her, but in the same way he'd want any grown-up toy, like a fast car or a yacht. He'd spare a little time for it, enjoy it a while, then move onto something—or someone—new.

She'd almost managed to get him out of her head when the postcard arrived with a bundle of other mail on the Saturday morning.

There was no name on it, just a picture of the Statue of Liberty on one side and the words, 'Has he gone?' on the other.

'Are you all right?' Alex noticed her strained expression across the breakfast table.

'Yes, fine.' She quickly shoved it in among her other letters. 'It…it's just a card from my mother.'

'I thought she'd moved to Australia,' Alex commented.

Realising he'd seen the picture side, she was committed to another lie. 'She's on holiday in New York.'

Alex nodded and quickly lost interest.

Tory reflected on the words in the postcard. *Has he gone?* How she wished!

She slid a glance at Alex, currently unsetting all the stations on her radio. He was driving her crazy.

Fanatically *un*tidy, he left clothes on chairs, take-away cartons on tables and used towels on floors.

Tory had tried a few subtle hints, then more direct comments and he was suitably contrite—but not enough to reform.

Tory wondered if it were her. Maybe she wasn't suited to cohabitation, even on platonic grounds.

At any rate, she longed for Alex to depart. Or had until the postcard had arrived. Now she was torn. She didn't want to seem to be giving into Lucas Ryecart's demands.

In the end she let fate decide it and when Alex returned later that day from an unsuccessful flat-finding mission she surprised him with her concession to stay a little longer.

'You're a star. I'll try to look for a place mid-week,' Alex promised, 'although it might be difficult, with Ryecart returning on Monday.'

Tory pulled a face. 'He's definitely back?'

'Didn't I say?' Alex ran on. 'He sent a fax yesterday, setting up a meeting with our department. Monday morning at the Abbey Lodge.'

'No, you didn't say.' Tory struggled to hide her irritation.

'Don't worry about it,' he dismissed. 'He just wants to discuss the department's future direction.'

'Well, I'll keep a low profile,' she rejoined, 'if it's all the same to you.'

Alex didn't argue. Having been bullied into sobriety by Tory, he had regained some of his old ambition. He would be too busy promoting his own career to spare much thought for Tory's.

In fact, come Monday morning, it was a two-man contest between Simon and Alex.

Simon gained an early lead by simply turning up on time. Caught by roadworks, Alex and Tory were already fifteen minutes late when they reached the Abbey Lodge Hotel and entered the lion's den.

Tory refused to look at the lion even when he drawled a polite, 'Good morning,' in her direction.

It was a small conference room, mostly taken up with an oval table and eight leather chairs. She put Simon between her and the great man, and left Alex to sit opposite and run through a quick explanation for their tardiness.

It did have some semblance to the truth. Alex's car *was* in the garage. She *had* given him a lift. And they hadn't anticipated the council digging up a major section of the ring road.

But, of course, Lucas Ryecart knew the reality: that Alex and she had arrived together because they were living together.

He even gave Alex the chance to confess. 'Do you and Tory live in the same neighbourhood?'

'I…no, not really.' Alex slid a conspiratorial glance in Tory's direction.

He was doing as he'd promised by keeping quiet about their current arrangement.

Tory's heart sank as Lucas drawled, 'That was *generous* of you, Tory, to go out of your way,' and forced her to look at him.

It had been a week since they'd met and in the interim she'd put herself through aversion therapy. She *could* not like this man, brash egotist that he was. She *would* not like this man, even if her job depended on it. She *had* to look at him with dispassion and see the ruthlessness that underlay the handsome features.

This time she was ready—just not ready enough. She saw his age, written in his sun-lined face and the grey round his temples. She saw the imperfection, a scar tracing white down one cheek. She saw the mouth set in an irritatingly mocking curve. But then she met his eyes and forgot the rest.

A deep blue, bluer than a tropical sky, they drew her to him, those eyes, and made her realise that attraction defied any logic. The sight of him still left her senses in turmoil.

But this time she fought it, this involuntary attraction. She got angry with herself for such weakness. She got even angrier with him for causing it.

'Actually, it wasn't out of my way at all.' Her voice held a defiant note.

His mouth straightened to a hard line. He understood immediately. She was answering his postcard. No, Alex hasn't gone.

He went on staring at her until she was forced to look away, then he switched back to business.

He talked frankly of the direction he envisaged the department taking. He wished to concentrate on documentaries with a longer shelf-life. Previous programmes had suffered from delays and hence loss of topicality or duplication from other companies.

Alex clearly felt he was being told what he already knew. 'We are conscious of duplication,' he put in. 'We abandoned a project not so long ago because Tyne Tees was further along on it.'

'How much did that cost Eastwich?' Lucas Ryecart enquired.

'I can't remember,' Alex admitted.

'I can.' Lucas Ryecart stated a figure.

'Sounds right,' Alex said rather too casually. 'Budgets aren't normally my concern.'

Tory, assiduously contemplating the wood grain in front of her, flinched inwardly. Did Alex have to jump into the hole the American was digging for him?

There was a moment's silence before Ryecart returned briefly, 'So I gathered.'

Alex caught on then, and backtracked to make the right sounds, 'Not that I don't try to work within a budget framework. In fact, some programmes have been done on a shoestring.'

'Really.' Lucas Ryecart's disbelief was dry but obvious. 'Okay, surprise me!'

'Sorry?' Alex blinked.

'Which programme was done on a shoestring?'

'I…well…' Alex was left to bluster. 'That's an expression. Obviously I didn't mean it literally, but I believe we're no more profligate than any other department. Look at drama.' He tried to shift focus. 'It's common knowledge that their last period piece cost half a million.'

'And made double that by the time Eastwich had sold it abroad.' Lucas Ryecart pointed out what Alex would have known if he'd thought about it. 'Moving on, Alex has drafted some proposals for future programmes with which I assume you're all familiar.'

Tory assumed the same but, from his tight-lipped expression, Simon was still in the dark.

'I left a copy on top of your desk,' Alex claimed at his blank expression.

'Really.' Simon was clearly unimpressed with Alex's efforts, and Tory didn't blame him.

'Have mine.' She pushed the document towards him. 'I have a spare.'

'Simon, you can get up to speed while we discuss it,' Lucas Ryecart pressed on. 'Okay, folks, at the risk of riding roughshod over anyone's pet project, I propose we can items one and four from the outset.'

'Can?' Alex echoed in supercilious tones although Tory was sure he understood.

'Rule out, bin, expunge.' Lucas Ryecart gave him a selection of alternatives that somehow made Alex look the fool.

Certainly Simon allowed himself a smirk.

Alex came back with, 'Why…if I may ask?'

His tone implied the American was being dictatorial.

'You can ask, yes.' Lucas Ryecart clearly considered Alex pompous rather than challenging. 'Proposal one is too close to a programme about to be broadcast by BBC2 and the costs on four will be sky high.'

Tory watched Alex's face as he woke up to the fact that the American was going to be no pushover like Colin Mathieson.

'Costs are the only criterion?' he said in the tone of the artist thwarted by commercialism.

Lucas Ryecart was unmoved. 'With Eastwich's current losses, yes. But if you want to spend your own money on it, Alex, feel free.'

He said it with a smile but the message was plain enough. Put up or shut up.

Alex looked thunderous while Simon gloated.

'Proposal two…' Lucas Ryecart barely paused '…is also likely to attract mega-buck litigation unless we can substantiate every claim we make against the drug companies.'

'You know that's damn near impossible,' Alex countered. 'We'd have to rely on inside sources, any of whom could be less than truthful.'

'Exactly,' Lucas Ryecart agreed, 'so I'd sooner pass… However, should you wish to take the story elsewhere, I won't stand in your way.'

Alex went from indignant to disconcerted as the American threw him off balance again. He had yet to fully appreciate that behind the pleasant drawling voice there was a man of steel.

'So that leaves us two ideas still on the table,' he resumed. 'Racial discrimination in the Armed Forces and drug-taking in the playground. Either might be worth exploring… In addition, Simon and I both have an idea we'd like to pitch.'

Alex was instantly suspicious. 'The same one?'

'Actually, no.' It was Simon who answered. 'We don't all go in for the conspiratorial approach.'

His disparaging glance included Tory. He'd obviously lined her up on Alex's side. She might have protested, had Lucas Ryecart not been there and likely to scorn any claim of impartiality.

'Tory—' the American turned those brilliant blue eyes on her '—perhaps you have some idea you'd like to put forward as well.'

She already had: at least two of Alex's proposals had originated with her, but, in giving them to Alex, she had effectively lost copyright.

She shook her head, and wondered if he considered her gormless. She had certainly contributed little to the meeting so far.

'As you know, Tory and I worked quite closely on this document.' Alex imagined he was rescuing her from obscurity.

Instead he confirmed what Simon suspected: that they'd worked as a team, excluding him.

It also made Ryecart drawl, 'Very closely, I understand.'

'I…well…yes…' Alex couldn't quite gauge the other man's attitude.

Tory could, only too well. For *very closely* read *intimately*.

She was finally stirred into retaliation. 'Have you a problem with that, Mr Ryecart?'

He fronted her in return. 'Not at all. I look forward to working in close liaison with you myself, Miss Lloyd.'

And let that be a lesson to me, Tory thought, clenching her teeth at the barely hidden double meaning.

She looked to the other two men, but if she expected any support she was in for a disappointment. Alex had put the American's comment down to sexist humour and was chuckling at it, and Simon was enjoying her discomfort.

It was every man for himself.

'Returning to the matter in hand,' Lucas Ryecart continued, 'I suggest each of us pitch our idea for a limited period, say forty minutes.'

He took his watch off and laid it on the table. It was a plain leather-strapped, gold-rimmed affair, nothing ostentatious. If Lucas Ryecart was wealthy, he didn't advertise the fact.

He glanced round the table, waiting for someone to volunteer. No one did. In adversity, they were suddenly a team.

'We're not used to working with time restraints,' Alex objected for all of them.

'I appreciate that, but I find deadlines cut down on bull,' Ryecart said bluntly, 'and forty minutes is the air-time for most documentaries produced at Eastwich… I'll go first, unless anyone objects.'

No one did. Tory felt a little ashamed for them all. They were such rabbits.

'Okay,' he proceeded. 'My idea more or less dropped in my lap. One of our backers, Chuck Wiseman, is a major publisher in the US and is looking to spread his empire to the UK. Specifically, he's bought out two quality women's magazines—*Toi* and *Vitalis*. Anyone read them?'

Tory was the only one to say, 'Yes.'

'Your opinion?' he asked seriously.

She answered in the same vein. '*Toi* is a pale imitation of *Marie Claire*. *Vitalis* is mainly hair, nails and make-up, with the occasional social conscience article.'

'Cynical but accurate.' He nodded in agreement. 'Chuck intends amalgamating the two, keeping the best of both and hoping to create something more original. But it is something of a marriage of convenience, with neither in any hurry to get to the altar.'

'It'll never work,' Alex commented.

'Possibly not,' Ryecart echoed, 'but Chuck's determined and he's a man to be reckoned with.'

'So where do we come in?' Tory was intrigued despite herself. 'Fly-on-the-wall stuff, recording the honeymoon.'

'Sort of,' Ryecart confirmed. 'Chuck's sending both staff on a residential weekend in the hope that familiarity will breed contentment.'

'He's obviously not very hot on old sayings,' Alex commented dryly.

'Still, it might make for a good story.' Simon smiled as he considered the in-fighting that would ensue. 'Where's he sending them? If it's somewhere hot and sunny, you can put me down for that one.'

Ryecart smiled briefly. ''Fraid not, Simon, but I'll note your enthusiasm. It's an outdoor-activity course in the Derbyshire Dales.'

'He has to be kidding!' Tory exclaimed before she could stop herself.

'Yeah, that's what I thought,' Ryecart echoed, 'but Chuck reckons he'll end up with a solid team as a result.'

'If they don't kill each other first,' murmured Simon.

'Or kill themselves, falling off a mountain,' Tory added. 'These courses are fairly rigorous, physically and psychologically.'

'Which is where we come in,' Ryecart rejoined.

'An exposé?' Tory enquired.

He nodded. 'Assuming there's anything to expose. Who knows? The course might be as character and team building as it claims.'

'I would think it would be more divisive,' Tory judged, but saw what he saw, too—the makings of a good human-interest story. 'I mean, if the staff know it's a test, there's going to be tension from the outset.'

He nodded. 'Two groups of individuals spending a weekend in each other's company under difficult circumstances. As fly-on-the-wall TV, it could prove dynamite.'

Alex and Simon nodded too, warming to the idea, even though it wasn't theirs.

'What are we talking here?' Alex asked. 'One of us plus camera crew interviewing these women while they abseil down mountains?'

'No crew,' Ryecart dismissed. 'The centre has continuous camera surveillance and uses camcorders for outdoor events. This footage will be handed over to Chuck's organisation and then to us.'

'Is that legal?' Simon said doubtfully.

'The centre has already signed a waiver, handing over copyright to Chuck,' Ryecart explained. 'The plan is for an Eastwich reporter to go undercover as a new member of staff for *Toi*. They'll have to join the magazine pretty much straight away as the course is this weekend. Whoever goes—' he glanced between the three of them '—I'll drive him or her down to London today for the interview.'

Both Simon and Alex looked at Tory.

'Why me?' She dreaded the idea of a car journey spent with Lucas Ryecart.

'At the risk of stating the obvious,' Simon drawled, 'they're both *women's* magazines. You're a woman. Alex and I aren't.'

'Quite.' Alex supported Simon for once.

Heart sinking, Tory looked towards the American.

He just said, 'It can be decided later,' and switched subjects with, 'Right, who wants to pitch their idea now?'

'I will.' Alex got in before Simon and began to flesh out his idea revolving drugs in the playground.

Alex had a somewhat novel idea, centring his investigation around public schools and the suggestion that a new breed of parents, themselves party-going and pill-popping in their youth, were tacitly condoning their children's drug-taking.

He'd obviously done some research on the subject and claimed to have already made contact with a headmaster willing to co-operate.

Simon cast doubt on the likelihood of that, pointing out that no public school head was likely to help him if it put fees at jeopardy.

'And you would know this, having gone to somewhere like Eton yourself?' Alex threw back.

'I did go to a public school, yes,' Simon said in his usual superior manner.

'A minor, I bet,' Alex guessed, accurately.

'Whereas you, no doubt, were a state grammar school boy,' Simon sneered back.

Tory suspected Simon already knew that, too. Alex was very proud of the fact.

'So?' Alex eyed Simon in an openly hostile manner.

'It shows, that's all,' Simon smirked in reply.

Exasperated, Tory intervened with a dry, 'Well, if anyone's interested, I went to a London comprehensive. Unofficial motto: Do it to them before they do it to you… But I was hoping I'd left my schooldays behind.'

Both Alex and Simon looked taken aback, as if a pet lapdog had suddenly produced fangs.

But it drew a slanting smile from Lucas Ryecart as he realised she was ridiculing their one-upmanship.

She didn't smile back. Simon and Alex might be behaving like prats but the American was still the common enemy.

'Quite,' Alex agreed at length and resumed speaking on his pet project while Simon continued to snipe the occasional remark and Lucas Ryecart refereed.

Tory wondered what the American made of the antipathy between the two men. Perhaps he was harbouring some idea of sending *their* fragmented team on an outdoor-activity course. The idea of Alex and Simon orienteering their way round some desolate Scottish moor, with only one compass between them, made her smile for the first time that day.

'You don't share that view?' a voice broke into her thoughts.

Tory looked up to find Lucas Ryecart's eyes on her again. Having only the vaguest idea of what had gone before, she hedged, 'I wouldn't say that exactly.'

'No, but your smile was a shade sceptical.' It seemed he'd been watching her.

'Possibly,' she admitted, rather than confess she'd been daydreaming.

'So you don't agree with Alex that most adults under forty will have tried some kind of recreational drug?' he pursued.

Now she knew what they'd been discussing, Tory wasn't any more inclined to express an opinion.

'Tory won't have,' Simon chimed in. 'Far too strait-laced, aren't you, Tory? Doesn't smoke. Doesn't drink. Doesn't pretty much anything.'

'Shut up, Simon,' she responded without much hope he would.

'See… She doesn't even swear.' He grinned like a mischievous schoolboy. 'I somehow doubt her parents were pot-smoking flower children.'

'Well, that's where you're wrong!' Tory snapped without considering the wisdom of it.

She regretted her outburst almost immediately as all eyes in the room became trained on her.

'Would you care to expand on that?' invited Simon.

'No,' she ground back, 'I wouldn't.'

'But if it gives some insight into the subject—' he baited, amused rather than malignant.

'Simon.' A low warning, it came from Lucas Ryecart. 'Leave it.'

Tory should have been grateful. He'd seen her vulnerability. But didn't that make her even more vulnerable—to him rather than Simon?

'Sure.' Simon was wise enough not to want to make an enemy of the American. 'I didn't mean to tread on anyone's toes.'

'That makes a change,' Alex muttered in not so low a voice, then gave Tory a supportive smile.

Ryecart took control once more, 'Simon, would you like to pitch your idea now?'

'My pleasure.' Simon was obviously confident.

Tory listened to him outlining his idea for a docu-soap on

a day in the life of a Member of Parliament. It sounded pretty tame stuff until Simon named the backbencher he proposed using. A controversial figure, with intolerant views, he was likely to produce some interesting television.

'He's almost bound to be de-selected next time around,' Simon concluded, 'so he has nothing to lose.'

'Has he agreed to it?' Ryecart asked.

'Pretty much,' Simon confirmed.

'Know him personally?' Alex suggested.

'As a matter of fact, yes,' Simon responded. 'I was at school with his younger brother.'

Alex contented himself with a snort in comment.

Simon expanded on the approach he'd take and Lucas Ryecart gave him approval to progress it further. He had done the same for Alex.

He wrapped up the meeting by saying, 'All right, we'll meet again in three weeks and see where matters stand. Thank you for coming.'

They were dismissed. At least Tory thought they were, and was breathing a sigh of relief as she picked up her briefcase and led the way from the room. They were out in the hotel lobby when the American said, 'Tory, I'd like to talk to you.'

He didn't stipulate why but he didn't need to. He was her boss.

Alex looked ready to ask but Lucas Ryecart ran on, 'Simon, perhaps you could give Alex a ride back to Eastwich as his car is in the shop?'

'Sure, no problem.' Simon knew better than to object.

Alex, too, accepted the arrangement and Tory was abandoned altogether. That was how it felt, at any rate, as they walked out of the main entrance.

She guessed Lucas either wanted to talk to her about the magazine assignment or her current living arrangements, *vis-à-vis* Alex. Neither prospect was appealing.

'We can talk over lunch.' He began steering her by the elbow.

'In the dining room?' Tory wasn't dressed for five-star lunching.

'We could have a bar meal,' he continued, 'or call room service if you prefer.'

'Room service?' Tory echoed rather stupidly.

'I'm staying here,' he reminded her.

She stopped in her tracks. 'You expect me to go upstairs with you?'

'Expect, no,' he replied, 'hope, absolutely.'

His smile was more amused than lascivious. He just loved yanking her chain.

'So what's it to be?' he added.

'I'm not hungry!' she countered.

'Bar meal it is, then,' he decided for them and switched direction.

'I said—' She was about to repeat it.

He cut across her. 'I heard. You may not be hungry but I am, so you can sit and watch me eat while we talk business.'

Business. The word reminded her once more of their prospective positions. She wondered why she kept forgetting.

'Couldn't we just return to the conference room?' She wanted to keep things on a formal basis.

'And risk being alone together?' He raised a brow. 'Well, if that's okay with you '

'No.' She hastily changed her mind. 'Let's go to the bar.'

'Sure, if that's what you want.' He inclined his head, making it seem he was accommodating her.

He really was the most aggravating man, Tory thought as they entered the hotel bar.

Large and well lit, it lacked intimacy but was almost empty. He installed her into a corner booth and was about to go and order at the counter when a waiter appeared. Lucas ordered a steak and salad, and insisted she have at least a sandwich.

From the bowing and scraping that went on, Tory assumed Lucas Ryecart was a familiar face.

'Big tipper, are we?' She couldn't resist remarking as the young waiter disappeared.

'Not especially,' he said with a grin, 'but Chuck is, so I guess I get the obsequious treatment through association.'

'Your magazine-buying friend,' she recalled out loud. 'He's staying here, too.'

'Was,' he confirmed. 'A bit too rural for him so he's moved back into the Ritz.'

In London, Tory assumed he meant. 'You make it sound as if he's living there.'

'He is for the moment,' he relayed, 'there and the New York Plaza. He commutes between the two.'

It seemed an odd way of life, even for a successful businessman. 'Has he a family?'

'He's between wives,' Lucas said, 'and has no children apart from a grown-up stepson… You're looking at him, by the way.'

Had she understood correctly?

'Chuck is your stepfather?'

'Is or was—I'm not sure which. He's remarried a couple of times since then.'

'Was, I think,' Tory volunteered, 'otherwise I'd have a multiplicity. Or two officials, anyway.'

Tory was normally reticent about her background but it seemed she'd met a fellow traveller, parent-wise.

'How old were you when your parents divorced?' His enquiry was matter-of-fact rather than sympathetic.

She answered in the same vein, 'They didn't. They were never married.'

He studied her face. 'You find that embarrassing?'

'No!' she claimed a little too sharply. 'Why should I?'

'No reason,' he mollified. 'It's hardly unusual these days… So were they the original pot-smoking hippies?'

Tory resented that question, too. 'Is that relevant to my work at Eastwich?'

'It might be,' he responded evenly, 'if you were to work with Alex on his drug story. It's best to go into these things with an open mind.'

Tory was tempted to argue with him, to say she was as objective as any good documentary-maker should be, but she wasn't sure if she were in this case. The truth was her mother had done drugs in the past. So-called soft drugs, but they had made Maura more feckless than ever. Tory had been old enough to know and disapprove, but too young to do much about it. It was one of the times she'd voluntarily decamped and returned to her grandparents in Purley.

'I would prefer to work on another story,' she declared at length.

'Fine by me,' he acknowledged with a brief smile. 'How convincing do you think you'd be as a features editor for a woman's magazine?'

For a split second Tory thought he was recommending she seek alternative employment, then she realised he was referring to the programme he'd proposed.

'You want me to do the *Toi/Vitalis* job?'

'Well—'

'Because I'm a woman?' That had been Simon's rationale.

'No, not especially,' Lucas Ryecart denied. 'I just can't envisage Alex trekking over moorland unless there's a pub at the end of the road and I don't see Simon in the role of observer, blending quietly into the background.'

Tory couldn't argue with either statement but was left feeling the job was hers through default.

'Right,' she murmured, her expression saying more.

'You're not happy?'

'Do I have to be?'

'Well, yes,' he countered. 'I don't want a good programme sabotaged by a lack of commitment on your part. So, if you're not up to this assignment, I'd sooner you say so now.'

And that's me told, Tory thought as she once more glimpsed a hard businessman behind the easygoing charmer.

The food arrived, giving her a moment or two to consider her response.

'I am up to it,' she claimed in a more positive manner. 'When do I start?'

She'd intended to sound keen but she wasn't prepared for his answer.

'This afternoon. You have an appointment with Personnel at the offices of *Toi*.'

'In London?'

He nodded.

'What if I don't get the job?'

He smiled at her naïvety.

'You already have. The interviews were last month. You've been a feature writer on a regional newspaper and this is your first magazine post.'

While he ran through her proposed cover, Tory suddenly realised what she was really taking on. She was going to have to lie about herself and her background and keep those lies consistent.

'Will anyone know I'm not a bona fide employee?'

'Only the personnel director of the group, and he's aware of your role.'

Tory wasn't altogether sure if she was.

'You don't expect me to provoke trouble?' she asked uncertainly.

'Absolutely not,' he said with emphasis. 'We want no charges of *manufacturing* material otherwise Eastwich's credibility will be blown. Sit back and observe like you did today.'

Tory couldn't help asking, 'Is that a criticism?'

'A comment,' he amended. 'After Alex and Simon's self-promotion, your reticence was almost refreshing although potentially limiting, careerwise… That's advice, by the way, not a threat.'

Tory nodded, accepting what he was saying. She had to push herself forward more.

She did so now, telling him, 'I do have ideas, you know.'

'I'm sure you do,' he responded. 'The trouble is, you let them be appropriated by other people.'

'We work as a team,' she stated a little testily.

'Yeah?' He raised a brow in disbelief. 'Perhaps someone should tell that to Alex and Simon. They seem to be playing on opposite sides. And your loyalty…well, we both know where that currently lies.'

With Alex, he meant, and Tory found herself colouring as if it were true. But it wasn't. Not in the sense he was implying.

'Alex is my boss. That's all!'

'So you keep saying.'

'Because it's true.'

'Okay, I'm your boss, too,' he reminded her unnecessarily. 'Can *I* come and share your flat?'

He gave her a mocking smile.

Tired of defending herself, Tory replied in the same vein. 'Sure. Why not? You could pull rank and pinch the sofa from Alex.'

Their eyes met and his smile faded. 'You're trying to say you're not sleeping with Alex?'

'No, I *am* saying that,' she corrected. 'Ask him, if you like.'

'Then why the pretence that Alex is living elsewhere?' he challenged.

'Because sometimes *other people* take two and two and make five,' she countered pointedly.

His eyes narrowed. '*Other people* have heard of Alex's reputation with women. I understand he's tested out more than one sofa since his wife left.'

Tory knew that was true enough so didn't comment. She said instead, 'Look, I like to keep home and work separate. And as far as work goes, Alex is my boss, plain and simple.'

It begged the question, 'And home?'

Tory felt she'd already answered it, and said flippantly, 'An extremely annoying flatmate who leaves the top off the toothpaste.'

He smiled briefly but disbelief lurked behind his eyes. Why could he not accept the truth?

Tory shook her head and, to her relief, he finally moved the conversation back to the magazine project, briefing her in what he saw as her role—passive but observant.

'When do I actually start work there?' Tory asked with some anticipation.

'Tomorrow,' he replied succinctly.

'Tomorrow?' She hadn't been expecting such short notice.

He nodded. 'That'll give you four days at the magazine before the team-bonding weekend.'

'But the magazine's in London,' she protested faintly.

'Which is where we're going now,' he added, 'or as soon as we've finished lunch and you've gone home to pack.'

Pack?

'You want me to stay over?' Tory was wide-eyed with suspicion.

'Is that a problem?'

He looked back at her, all innocence.

'In London?'

She wanted to make sure she'd understood.

'That's the general idea, yes.'

He nodded.

'With you?' She stared back stonily.

'If you like, although I hadn't planned on it,' he revealed. 'It's certainly an interesting proposition.'

'I w-wasn't…I didn't…I—I…' Tory stammered on until she saw the grin spreading on his face.

'No, I know.' He let her off the hook.

But he still laughed.

Damn the man.

CHAPTER SIX

LUCAS RYECART went on to explain. Tory had her appointment with the magazine at four p.m. and the plan was for her then to stay at a London hotel while she worked the rest of the week at *Toi*. At the same time he had a meeting with an investment banker and would be staying overnight at an entirely different hotel. Both venues were in central London so common sense dictated they travel down together. End of story.

Chastened, Tory accepted his offer of a lift and he trailed her back to her flat so she could pack a case. He waited outside for her.

They then travelled at speed towards the capital and Tory stared out at the motorway embankment rather than engage in further conversation. Having virtually accused him of luring her to the big city for immoral purposes, she felt silence was now her best option.

They'd reached the outskirts of London when her mobile rang.

Taking it out of her bag, she recognised the number calling as her office one. She pressed the receive button and wasn't too surprised to find it was Alex, wondering where she was. She didn't really get a chance to answer before he launched into a diatribe against the American, based on that morning's meeting.

Tory quickly switched the phone to her other ear, hoping Lucas hadn't caught the words 'arrogant ass' as Alex warmed to his theme. It seemed his enthusiasm for the American had dimmed somewhat.

She repeated Alex's name a couple of times in warning tones before actually cutting across him to say, 'Actually, Mr Ryecart's here beside me if you want to speak to him.'

It stopped Alex in his tracks momentarily, then he dropped volume as he proceeded to play twenty questions. Most she managed to field with 'yes's or 'no's and kept her voice carefully neutral.

To say Alex wasn't best pleased at her sudden secondment was an understatement and, in typical self-centred Alex fashion, he began to wonder how he was meant to get to work in the mornings, before he realised her car would still be in Norwich and was, therefore, available. She should have refused, of course. She didn't altogether trust Alex to drive it in a sane, sensible, sober fashion, but he pleaded and cajoled and called her Tory darling until she finally surrendered, more to shut him up than anything else.

When he finally hung up, she waited expectantly for comment from the American. She didn't have to wait long.

'So do you agree with him?' Lucas Ryecart drawled. 'Am I an arrogant ass?'

'You heard.'

'I'm not deaf.'

Tory supposed he would have to have been not to have caught Alex's initial remarks.

She tried bluffing. She was almost certain Alex hadn't used Lucas's name once.

'You're assuming that Alex was talking about you,' she muttered back.

He glanced from the road, fixing her with a sceptical look. 'Unless he happens to have a beef with another *swaggering Yank*. That's always possible, I suppose.'

Tory coloured as she realised he'd heard even more than she'd realised.

'Well, you know what they say about eavesdroppers,' she replied with some idea of putting him on the defensive.

'What?' He gave a short, mocking laugh. 'That they should immediately pull over onto the hard shoulder and climb out of the car while their passengers take abusive calls about them?'

This time Tory didn't argue back. He was right, of course. It was absurd to accuse him of eavesdropping when he could hardly have avoided listening to Alex's rant and rave.

She switched tacks. 'I'm sorry if you've taken offence but it's par for the course to bitch about your boss and you have put Alex's nose a little out of joint.'

She felt she'd laid on the right degree of humility but he made a dismissive sound.

'You think I care about Simpson's opinion? Believe me, I've been insulted by better men than him. The question was: do you agree with him?'

Tory was tempted to say, Yes, she did, but it seemed an act of extreme recklessness in their present situation.

She plumped for a circumspect, 'I have no thoughts on the subject.'

To which he muttered, 'Coward,' but in an amused rather than unpleasant tone. 'By the way, I wouldn't inform Simpson I'd overheard him.'

'Why not?' She would have imagined he'd want the opposite.

'A man in his position has only two ways to go,' he continued. 'He'll either feel the need to climb down and so embarrass us both with an apology I don't want and he won't mean. Or he'll be compelled to back up his remarks with a show of machismo for your benefit which, at the very least, will support my gut instinct that Simpson isn't worth the trouble he causes.'

'Right.' Tory saw the point he was making and the wisdom of it. 'I'll keep quiet.'

'Smart move,' he applauded her decision, then ran on, 'You know what really sticks in my craw about Simpson?'

Tory assumed it was a rhetoric question so didn't volunteer an answer.

Lucas continued, 'Forget the anti-American insults or his pompous posturing, the worst thing is the fact that he's just not good enough for a girl like you.'

Tory sighed loudly, wondering what she could say back to that. She was weary of denying involvement with Alex.

She said instead, 'And who do you imagine is?'

'Pretty much any personable, intelligent man without a drink problem would be an improvement,' he drawled back.

Not himself, then. Did that mean he'd lost interest? Tory supposed she should have been pleased but perhaps she was female enough to feel piqued as well.

She was considering her reply when he switched to saying, 'I'll leave that thought with you. Meanwhile, let's test your navigation skills. There's an A to Z in the glove compartment. We're looking for a Hermitage Road, NW something.'

'Okay.' Tory was glad of a change of subject and did as he suggested.

She didn't have to make much reference to the A to Z because she knew this part of London, and she guided him to the offices of the magazine without too much trouble.

'You're pretty good at giving directions,' he commented as they drew up outside the offices of *Toi.*

'For a woman, you mean?' Tory read the unspoken words in the compliment.

'I didn't say that,' he claimed even as a half-smile admitted it.

'I come from London,' Tory confessed, and, seeing she had five minutes to her appointment, began to collect her things together. 'Is the boot open?'

'Boot?' he repeated, then translated, 'The trunk?'

'Possibly,' she replied dryly. 'I need my case.'

'Won't it keep till I pick you up?'

'You're coming back for me?'

He nodded. 'Sure. I'll take you on to your hotel.'

'There's no need,' Tory dismissed quickly. 'I can get a taxi.'

'To where?'

'My hotel.'

'Which is?'

Tory frowned. What game were they playing now?

'You tell me,' she countered.

'I will when I find out,' he agreed. 'I've left Colin Mathieson's secretary to arrange it.'

'Right.' She should have known he wouldn't bother with any matter so trivial. 'I'll wait here for you, then.'

'I'll give you a call when I'm on my way,' he suggested. 'What's your cell-phone number?'

'I'll write it down.' She started to look in her bag for paper.

'That's okay,' he dismissed. 'Just tell me it.'

She did as he asked, and he repeated it as if it was already committed to memory.

Tory had her doubts. She certainly couldn't memorise an eleven-digit number after one hearing. But who knew what this man could do?

'I'd better go.' She glanced at her watch again. 'I don't want to be late for my interview.'

'Good luck, then.'

'I thought the job was mine.'

'It is,' he assured. 'That's the easy part.'

Tory supposed he was right. Convincing the rest of the magazine staff that she was a bona fide features editor might prove more difficult.

She finally climbed out of the car and walked up the steps of the magazine office, conscious that Lucas had yet to drive away. She turned round and he saluted her briefly. She didn't wave back but went ahead through the revolving doors that opened out into a reception.

'Yes.' An elegant blonde looked her up and down from behind a desk.

Tory said her name and she noticed the blonde's eyes flicker with recognition but no warmth before she was asked to take a seat in Reception.

She'd barely sat and picked up this month's edition of *Toi* when another identikit blonde arrived to escort her upstairs to the personnel director's office.

The interview was, as Lucas had said, just a formality, but she sensed the director wasn't altogether enthusiastic about her reason for being there. He used the expression 'the powers that be' when he referred to the magazine's new owner, Chuck Wiseman, and just stopped short of calling the team-bonding weekend psychological claptrap. He also warned her that, due to the unusual circumstances surrounding her hiring, she might possibly encounter some hostility from the editorial staff.

'I'm not sure I understand,' she queried this statement. 'Do you mean some know why I'm here?'

'Not that, no,' the personnel director assured her. 'If they did, we might have a walk-out on our hands. In fact, I have warned the *powers that be* of just such a consequence if you are discovered.'

'Then why should they be hostile?' she pursued.

'I'm only speculating on the possibility,' he backtracked a little. 'After all, there were at least two junior editors who felt they were in line for your post plus the fact it was never advertised. To all intents and purposes, you appear to have been given the job purely on personal recommendation from, let's say, above.'

'I see.' Tory did, too. She was joining a woman's magazine—a notoriously bitchy work environment, anyway—already viewed as someone's protégé. 'Who do they imagine has imposed me?'

'There are various theories,' he hedged, 'which I won't go into. I just feel you should be warned that you may get a somewhat frosty reaction.'

'Thanks.' Tory pulled a face.

She sensed he wasn't in the least bit sympathetic. Someone had obviously ridden roughshod over him, too.

'I'm afraid there isn't much I can do to improve the situation,' he added in the same cool tones.

'Don't worry, I'll survive.' Tory was sure she would.

The mishmash of types found on a woman's magazine was hardly as scary as some of the loud-mouthed, disaffected girls with whom she'd gone to school. At least no one here was likely to threaten to beat her up for her lunch money.

'I'm glad you're so confident.' He clearly didn't share the feeling. 'Anyway, I'll show you round the editorial department.'

She followed him to the lifts and they went back down to the editorial floor which was largely open plan. Tory trailed in his wake, conscious of curious eyes on her.

They stopped at a closed office at the end and Tory was introduced to Amanda Villiers, the editor-in-chief, who was currently conducting a meeting with several staff.

If she hadn't been pre-warned, Tory would not have understood Amanda Villiers's attitude. While on the surface her new boss was all polite handshake and smiles, there was an edge to every remark she made.

'I read your résumé with interest,' she drawled. '*The Cornpickers Times*, that was your first job, wasn't it? Features editor of the women's page.'

'*Cornwall Times*,' Tory corrected, while knowing the mistake had been deliberate.

Amanda was playing to an audience and several of her staff had dutifully tittered at her remark.

'Whatever.' Amanda Villiers smiled tightly. 'I didn't come up the provincial route. What does one write about for farmers' wives? How to get sheep dye from under their fingernails? Or how to prepare the perfect *Boeuf en Croute*—after one's killed it first, of course.'

Tory laughed, having some idea she wasn't meant to, and Amanda looked a little surprised.

'You've forgotten knit yourself a designer sweater, using your own flock,' suggested Tory on the same theme and took the wind out of Amanda's sails.

'Yes, well, all very fascinating, I'm sure,' Amanda said with a dismissive air, 'but a national women's magazine is, of course, a whole different world. Not that I need to tell you that. You did two years on that French magazine…what's it called again?'

Good question. Tory had spent an hour of the car journey that afternoon memorising her CV but it evidently hadn't been long enough.

'I don't imagine anyone's heard of it,' she murmured evasively.

'No, I certainly hadn't—' Amanda sniffed '—but, do tell, darling, how does one go from the *Cornish Times* to some sub-porno in Paris?'

Tory considered declaring herself not the type of person to work on a sub-porno, but she was already having enough trouble building any credibility without discussing ethics.

'It's a long story,' she told the room at large, 'with which

I may bore everyone when we're lying in our sleeping bags listening to the wind whistling round our tents.'

'Oh, God, the adventure weekend.' Amanda groaned aloud. 'You know about it and you still want to work here? You must be desperate.'

'I'm sure the job will make up for it.' Tory forced some enthusiasm into her voice.

Amanda looked sceptical and turned to a younger woman on her right. 'What do you think, Sam? You've been doing the job for the last six months. Is it worth a weekend in some godforsaken spot in the dales?'

Sam, a woman of about thirty, glanced between her boss, Amanda, and Tory, before making some inaudible comment, then staring rigidly at the notepad in front of her.

The set of her shoulders betrayed anger barely held in check. The only question was, where was this anger directed: at Tory who'd prevented her from being promoted, or the taunting Amanda whom Tory herself already felt like pushing off a cliff, given half a chance?

'Anyway, I'd better introduce you round.' Amanda finally remembered her manners and rattled off names and job titles too quickly for Tory to assimilate. 'When do you start?'

'As soon as possible,' Tory replied briefly.

'In that case, grab a pew,' Amanda suggested and left Tory with little choice.

She couldn't count on rescue from the personnel director because he was on his way out, problem disposed of.

Still, what happened next was familiar territory after that morning. While Amanda conducted a brainstorming session on cosmetic surgery, Tory was once again made to feel part of the furniture. Ideas were thrown up for discussion, opinions sought, criticisms levied but no one sought to include Tory in any of it.

This was not altogether surprising as the rest took their lead from Amanda and, having humiliated Tory sufficiently for the moment, the editor now ignored her totally.

Just as well, Tory realised, because she had little positive to say on the subject of breast implants or liposuction. She accepted some women felt the need for self-improvement but it seemed a growing obsession, the quest for the body beautiful. Magazines were full of such articles and the only question was whether they were documenting or feeding the phenomenon.

'What about you, Victoria?' Amanda finally addressed her. 'Have you had any fine tuning? Boob job, perhaps?' She glanced towards Tory's moderately sized chest, before deciding, 'No, maybe not… That nose, however. Very retroussé. What do you think, girls?'

Two of the women laughed as if she'd said something witty but a young woman at the end of the table seemed to suppress a sigh.

It made Tory wonder just what hidden tensions would be exposed after so many unrelieved hours in each other's company over the weekend.

For herself, she was already glad she worked for Eastwich and Alex for all his faults rather than the autocratic Amanda.

When Tory's cell-phone interrupted the meeting, Amanda gave her a look of pity before drawling, 'A golden rule, darling, mobiles off during meetings. I thought you'd have known that.'

Tory grimaced—as far as she was going to get to apology—and read the number calling. It was another mobile. She guessed it was Lucas.

'Who is it?' Amanda asked impatiently.

'A friend, he's giving me a lift,' Tory explained.

'Man friend?'

'Yes.'

'Lucky you.'

Amanda actually sounded more sincere than usual but Tory waited for the punchline. When it didn't come, she offered, 'I'll ask him to call back later.'

'No, don't bother. Time to wrap up, don't you think, *mes enfants*?'

The others nodded and Tory wondered if any ever disagreed with Amanda. Perhaps any who had were long gone.

'Well, answer him,' Amanda instructed, 'before he gives you up for dead.'

'All right… Hi,' she said into the mouthpiece.

Lucas replied simply, 'I'm outside.'

'Okay, be there in a moment,' she promised and rang off.

'Masterful type, is he?' Amanda concluded from this brief exchange.

'You could say that.' Tory nodded back.

'Love those, myself,' Amanda commented, 'in bed, at any rate. Not so keen when they're strutting about, demanding their socks washed and their breakfast cooked.'

Tory forced a laugh and wondered briefly if it was in the job description—to laugh at Amanda's jokes.

'Well, run along, mustn't keep him waiting, Vicki, darling,' the older woman urged in mocking tones that had Tory gritting her teeth.

But she did as she was told, anxious to get away from Amanda and her coven.

Fortunately she remembered her way back to the lift because no one volunteered to escort her, although she did find herself waiting with one of the other sub-editors. She recognised the girl who went in for sighing rather than sniggering.

'So what's your opinion?' the girl asked as they descended in the lift together. 'Think you'll like it here?'

Tory shrugged. 'Early days.'

'She doesn't get any better,' the girl drawled back, 'and she seems to have developed a pretty instant dislike of you, if you don't mind me saying so.'

Tory actually did mind, especially as it reinforced her own suspicions that working for Amanda was going to be a nightmare. Thank God, it was only temporary.

'I'll live with it,' Tory said at length.

Her lift companion regarded her with a look that seemed to waiver between pitying and admiring before the doors slid open and they parted in the reception area.

Tory didn't hang around. In fact, she almost ran down the steps to Lucas's awaiting car.

'How was it?' he said as she climbed into the passenger seat.

She released a breath of pent-up anger, before responding, 'Don't ask!'

'That bad?' he concluded.

'Worse.' Tory shuddered even before she spotted Amanda emerging from the building.

He followed her gaze. 'Who's that?'

'The editor from hell.' She grimaced. 'Can we go?'

'Yeah, sure,' he agreed easily and, putting the car in gear, drove towards the exit. 'I take it you were introduced.'

'More than introduced,' she relayed. 'After the briefest of inductions, the personnel director abandoned me to the pack.'

'The pack?'

'Editorial staff,' she qualified, 'but, believe me, the lions of the Serengeti would definitely seem friendlier.'

He laughed, then saw from her face she wasn't really joking. 'You don't think your cover was already blown.'

She shook her head. 'More a case of noses out of joint. Apparently one of them has been Acting Features Editor for months so she's hardly overjoyed by my appearance and, as for the editor-in-chief, Amanda Villiers, she resents having some nobody from nowhere imposed on them through suspect channels.'

'Well, never mind,' he tried to console, 'you only have to put up with it for a few days.'

'It's going to seem like weeks,' she complained. 'Forget their open hostility, have you ever tried pretending to be someone you're not?'

'Actually, yes,' he replied. 'I once passed myself off as the deaf and dumb son of a goat-herder in Northern Afghanistan.'

'Is that a joke?' The amused note in his voice certainly suggested it was.

'Not particularly, although it had its humorous moments,' he confided, before explaining, 'I was covering the Russian/Afghani conflict when I ended up in a situation where being an American journalist wasn't good for the health… Mind you, neither's going without food for a couple of days, but I survived,' he finished with a dry laugh.

Tory realised it was a true story. She had forgotten his former life as a foreign correspondent. This was the first he'd alluded to it.

'All right, you win.' She picked up the not-so-hidden message. 'I admit working undercover at *Toi* hardly rates in the danger stakes, but I'm still nervous about blowing it. I mean, I only know in the vaguest of terms what a features editor does. I'm going to be as hopeless as they think I am.'

Lucas pondered the last remark before pointing out, 'But if they're expecting you to mess up, it won't matter if you do, will it?'

'I suppose not,' Tory agreed. 'I just don't want to give Amanda Villiers the satisfaction.'

'Yeah, I've heard she's pretty monstrous.'

'You've heard? From whom?'

'Chuck. At least, I'm guessing it's the same woman. He calls her Mandy.'

'To her face?' Tory didn't think that would go down well.

'I guess so.' Lucas nodded. 'He took her out for lunch once and I don't see Chuck calling her Miss Villiers.'

'A business lunch, you mean?' pursued Tory.

He shrugged. 'Could have been… Is she pretty?'

Tory blinked at the question, before saying, 'Possibly. That was her on the steps.'

'Maybe not business, then,' he judged. 'Chuck certainly has an eye for a pretty lady.'

Tory glanced in his direction and saw the smile slanting his lips. It seemed he admired his stepfather for this.

'Isn't he…well, isn't he…?' She found no tactful way to express her doubts.

He did it for her, saying, 'Too old? Yeah, probably. But women don't seem to mind that. Chuck has a lot of charm. A lot of money, too,' he added dryly.

'And it doesn't bother you?' Tory couldn't resist asking.

He thought about it for a moment, then shrugged. 'Chuck's smart enough to look out for himself.'

It didn't really answer her question. 'But what about your mother? Does she still care?'

He shook his head. 'Mom's been dead twenty years.'

'I'm sorry,' she said automatically.

He gave her a quizzical look. 'What for?'

'Being nosy, I suppose.'

'Don't worry about it. I took it as a good sign.'

'Sign?' She was wary once more.

'That you're at least interested enough in me to ask such personal questions,' he stated, a smile in his voice.

Tory just stopped herself from saying, Don't flatter yourself, and responded instead, 'I was making conversation. That's all.'

'Yeah, okay.' He made a pacifying gesture with his hand. 'But for the record I am a forty-one-year-old widower. Both parents dead. No dependants. Sane. Healthy. Solvent. No unusual vices.'

His autobiography sounded so like a personal ad, Tory pointed out, 'You missed out with G.S.O.H. and W.L.T.M. young, attractive female for fun relationship.'

It drew a laugh before he drawled back, 'I find people who claim to have a good sense of humour often don't, and I've already met the young attractive female, thanks very much, although I'm not sure she goes in for "fun relationships".'

He meant her, of course. At least, Tory assumed he did. But she could hardly know for certain unless she asked him and that seemed a very unwise thing to do.

Her glance found him wearing the amused expression that was pretty much a fixture on his face.

'No comment?' he prompted.

Tory gritted her teeth, 'I doubt she's *your* type, then.'

'We'll have to see,' he replied, smile still in place. 'Meanwhile, let's get you settled in your hotel. It's called The Balmoral, Kingscote Avenue and is somewhere in W10.'

Tory picked up the A to Z once more and located their current position. Finding the hotel was something else. For all its grand name it was tucked away in a back street of a rather down-at-heel part of Earl's Court.

Not that she was about to raise any objections. She'd lived in worse areas with her mother and, although the hotel looked down-market, too, Eastwich's budget didn't usually stretch to much better.

It was Lucas Ryecart who said, 'Don't bother getting out,' when she made a move to do so. 'You're not staying in this dump.'

'It's probably nicer inside.'

'It would have to be.' He pulled a face. 'See that guy who's just walked into the joint? Russian Mafia, I'd say, if I didn't think they could afford better.'

Tory had seen the gentleman. Leather-coated with an upturned collar, he'd had a lean, mean unshaven face and suspicious air, but was probably an innocent foreign tourist.

'Well, if he is,' she suggested, 'think of the story I could write for *Toi*: Russian Mafia plan gold bullion robbery from royally named hotel. That would give the magazine much-needed edge, at any rate.'

'May I remind you, you work for Eastwich, not *Toi*?' he threw back. 'And that if you write bad things about the Mafia, they don't settle for complaining to the Press Complaints Commission. Let's go.'

'Where?' she asked as he pulled away.

'You can have my room tonight,' he replied and, anticipating any objection, added, '*Have*, I said, not *share*.'

'What will you do?' Tory was still not convinced by the assurance.

'Don't worry about me,' he dismissed. 'I'm having dinner with a friend who can probably put me up for the night.'

Friend? Male or female? The question crept into Tory's head, and, when she opted for the answer female, she felt a pang of jealousy, pure and simple. But why? She didn't want to get involved with him, did she?

Every shred of sense said no, but that didn't diminish her attraction to him. It wasn't merely his looks. The sound of his voice stirred something in her, too, and the way he moved, and his directness, though it was often disconcerting.

'In fact,' he resumed, 'when I come to think of it, this friend could probably help you—or, at least, his wife might.'

His wife. A moment's relief was quickly followed by denial. She hadn't really been concerned, had she?

'In what way?' she queried.

'She used to work for a woman's glossy before the kids came along,' he explained. 'She could give you the low-down on what a features editor does on a day-to-day basis.'

'That would certainly be useful.' Tory seriously doubted her ability to bluff through four working days before the adventure weekend.

'Okay, come to dinner, and you can pick her brains.' It was a fairly casual invitation.

Tory still hesitated. 'Won't they mind—you turning up with a total stranger?'

'Why should they?' He shrugged. 'Unless you become a major embarrassment after a glass or two of wine.'

'Not as far as I know,' she stated heavily.

'That's all right, then,' he replied, and, turning into the parking space in front of one of the biggest hotels in London, announced, 'We're here.'

A doorman appeared to open the passenger door while Lucas climbed out and opened the boot. He indicated her case and his overnight bag to the hovering porter before handing over his car keys so the vehicle could be parked somewhere.

'I'm going to leave the car here,' he explained as they went through the revolving door into the lobby, 'and retrieve it in the morning rather than search South Kensington for a parking space.'

She nodded at this information but wondered why he'd let the porter take his bag. Did he imagine she could be persuaded to let him share the room? If so, he was in for a disappointment.

'Reservation in the name of Ryecart,' he announced as they approached the desk, and, when it was located, informed them, 'A Miss Lloyd will actually be using the room. Is it possible to extend the booking from one night to four?'

Four nights? Did he mean for her? It seemed so.

When he'd finished business with the desk clerk, he said, 'You might as well stay here for the duration. Save the bother of finding somewhere else.'

'But surely it's too…' She pulled a face rather than say the word expensive in front of the porter.

'It's on Eastwich,' he said as if that made the money irrelevant.

She supposed it was his decision. After all, he *was* Eastwich in a sense. But hadn't he been griping about budgets to Alex just that morning?

Lucas checked his luggage into the porter's office to be picked up later. 'Why don't you freshen up before we go to my friends for dinner?' he suggested to Tory. 'Take your time. I have some calls to make, then I'll wait in the cocktail bar.'

Tory didn't actually remember agreeing to this dinner date, but wasn't given much chance to object as he turned on his heel and walked off towards the hotel lounges. She was left in the care of the porter who guided her to her room on the fifth floor.

The room was every bit as luxurious as she'd expected and, after the porter had departed, tip in hand, she spent a little while looking across the London skyline. Then, still debating the wisdom of going with Lucas on any date, however innocuous it seemed, she showered, changed into a pale lilac shift dress and spent at least twenty minutes trying to sweep her unruly hair into a sophisticated style before giving up and letting it fall back into a mass of curls.

It wasn't a proper date, of course. It was more in the nature of work. That was what she told herself, even as she checked once more how she looked in the mirror, before draping a cream pashmina round her arms and venturing out to find him.

As it was early evening, the cocktail lounge wasn't crowded. From the doorway Tory noticed him at the bar, talking to a stunning brunette of supermodel proportions. She was considering retreat when he spotted her in turn. He made some final remark to the brunette before crossing to greet Tory.

He noted her change of outfit with a smiling, 'You look lovely.'

Tory replied with a less gracious, 'Humph,' and followed it up by muttering, 'We can pass on dinner, if you prefer.'

'And do what?' He arched an interested brow.

He'd misunderstood so Tory glanced pointedly towards the brunette. 'You could pursue new interests.'

He followed her gaze, then laughed dryly as he curled a hand round Tory's elbow to guide her to the front lobby.

'You're not jealous, are you?' he added in amused tones.

She gave him a repressive glance, claiming, 'Not even remotely.'

'Shame.' He pulled a doleful face. 'No need, anyway. Pros like her don't do it for me.'

Tory assumed he meant professional women and threw back, 'Too challenging, are they? Women in executive positions?'

He looked puzzled for a moment, then gave another laugh. 'I think we may have lost something in the translation. When I say "pro", I mean, well, to put it politely, a lady of the night.'

'Lady of the...' The penny finally dropped with Tory and left her round-eyed with disbelief. 'That girl...she was...no, she couldn't be.'

He nodded before switching subjects to say, 'I'll need your room key.'

'What for?' she queried.

'My overnight bag,' he reminded her slowly and indicated the porter's lodge tucked into a corner of the lobby. 'They'll have it stored under room number.'

'Oh.' She just had to stop reacting with suspicion to everything he said. 'Here.'

She produced it out of her clutch purse and waited while he retrieved his case.

They emerged from the hotel to find it still light and sunny on this summer's evening.

The liveried doorman assumed they'd want a taxi and was already signalling for one from the rank alongside the entrance.

Once they were installed in the back, curiosity had Tory resuming their earlier conversation. 'Did she ask you for money, then? The woman in the bar.'

'Not up front,' he told her. 'She'd be thrown out of the hotel if she went around doing that.'

'Then how did you know?' she pursued.

He smiled a little as he asked, 'Do you think I'm irresistible?'

'No!'

'Well, neither do I. So, when some stunning-looking dame comes up to me in a bar, sits down, uninvited, and asks me if I'm in need of company, I can guess everything's not quite on the level.'

'She *might* just have fancied you,' Tory argued. 'You're not that bad-looking.'

'Gee, thanks,' he said at this grudging admission, 'but, no, I don't think it was love at first sight.'

'What else did she say?'

'She asked me if I was in London on business. She then said she was *doing business*, should I be interested. I told her I was waiting for a friend and she was just offering to find a friend for my friend when you came to my rescue,' he finished in wry tones.

Tory made a slight face. This man didn't need her help to get out of such a situation. He was obviously a man of the world.

'You weren't tempted,' she challenged, 'stunning as she was?'

'Not even remotely,' he echoed her earlier words. 'Paying to have a woman tell me how great I am in bed has never held appeal.'

Tory felt herself actually blushing.

And that was before he leaned closer to murmur, 'Eliciting such information for real, now, that's a different matter.'

For once there was no amusement in his low deep drawl. It was Tory who forced a laugh.

'You don't believe I can?' he added. 'Or was that an invitation to prove it?'

It hadn't been, of course, but he still lifted a hand to her cheek and, when she didn't immediately pull away, turned her face towards his.

He stared at her so long Tory assumed that was all he was going to do. Then he kissed her. Not deeply or intimately. His lips barely touched against the corner of her mouth while a hand lightly pushed back the curls framing her face.

It was over almost before it was begun. He drew away and leaned back against the taxi leather.

Tory was left confused and somewhat irrationally annoyed. If he was going to kiss her, he should do it properly or not at all.

'An ominous silence followed,' he commented as if writing a novel, 'but still he counted himself lucky—at least she hadn't slapped him.'

'Yet,' Tory warned darkly.

But too late. A quick glance confirmed that the amused smile was back in place.

'I'm not sure I want to go to dinner with you,' she added in haughty tones.

'Well, it's too late for a rain check,' he countered. 'We're here.'

Here being a splendid row of Georgian terraced houses. Rich friends, obviously.

'Do they know I'm coming too?' she asked as he selected cash from his wallet to pay the taxi.

He nodded and, paying the driver, helped her out of the taxi before answering, 'Caro does, anyway. In fact, she's looking forward to giving you the low-down on being a features editor. A trip down memory lane, she called it.'

'What does she do now?'

'Stays at home with the children.'

'How old?'

'The twins are about three, the baby is just a few months old… You like children?' he added as they walked up the steps.

'Boiled or fried?' she quipped.

He smiled at the small joke before pursuing, 'Seriously?'

'I like them well enough,' she finally replied. 'Just as long as I can hand them back.'

'I used to feel like that, too,' he agreed. 'Then one day you find yourself thinking it wouldn't be so bad, having your own.'

The admission was unexpected, so much so that Tory stared at him, testing if he was quite serious.

'With the right person, of course.' Blue eyes met hers, half intent, half amused.

Flirting, that was what he was doing. Tory knew that. Yet it seemed important to make a statement.

'I'll never have children.' She was unequivocal about it.

He smiled a little. 'How can you be so certain?'

Tory did not smile back. He obviously thought she was making a lifestyle choice.

'I just am.' She didn't feel like going into reasons.

She had told him. That was enough.

He shook his head, as if he still didn't believe her.

His problem, she decided.

It was only later she wished she'd told him it all.

CHAPTER SEVEN

LUCAS studied Tory for a moment longer, then said, 'You'll see, one day,' before turning to press on the doorbell.

It was answered by a woman wearing a frog apron on top of a smart summer dress. She was slightly older than Tory with a pretty freckled face and red hair escaping from a band at the neck. She looked a little flustered but her face was transformed at the sight of Lucas.

'Luc, lovely to see you.' She gave him a hug and a kiss on the cheek before turning to Tory. 'And you must be the features editor to be. Pleased to meet you. Come through, but mind the toys.'

She led the way down a wide hall, which was strewn with the pieces of a wooden train set, calling out, 'Boys, Uncle Luc is here.'

The effect was immediate as two identical pyjama-clad figures came hurtling out of a room to throw themselves at Lucas Ryecart's legs. Without hesitation, he stooped down and heaved one up in each arm, much to the boys' delight.

'Play trains,' demanded one.

'Build a tent,' demanded the other.

'Pillow fight!' added the first.

'Do the swingy thing,' chimed the second.

And so it went on as the twins began to list endless possibilities now opened up to them at the appearance of 'Uncle Luc'.

'Boys!' their mother eventually called over the excited gabbling. 'Uncle Luc is having dinner. *You* are going to bed.'

This elicited a joint protest of 'Aw' and crestfallen little faces.

'You heard your mother.' Lucas put them both back on the ground. 'But if you're up those stairs by the time I count five,

I may just tell you the really scary thing that happened to my friends, Al and Bill, the time they got lost in a jungle in South America.'

'A real jungle?'

'Honestly?'

The boys' eyes were round with anticipation before Lucas began, 'One…two…'

Then there was a mad scramble as the two made for the stairs and rushed up as quickly as their legs would allow.

'You don't have to,' Caro said as he reached five.

'I'd like to.' He raised a brow in Tory's direction. 'You don't mind?'

Tory shook her head. Caro seemed friendly enough.

'It'll give us a chance to have a girl talk.' Caro grinned wickedly.

'About magazine work, I hope,' Lucas added.

'Of course. What else?' Caro feigned innocence, even as the gleam in her eye suggested he would also be a topic under discussion.

Then one of the twins appeared at the top of the stairs to shout, 'Is it five yet?'

'Shh, the baby's asleep!' his mother called back.

While Lucas promised, 'I'm coming, Jack,' and took the stairs two at a time.

'I don't know how he does it—' Caro gazed after him in puzzled admiration '—but he always gets their names right. Not even their grandmothers can do that.'

Tory wouldn't have managed it either. The boys had looked like clones of each other. 'Does he see them often?'

'He tries to—' Caro pulled a forgiving face '—but he has such a busy schedule. Still, the boys always love it when Uncle Luc comes. He's their godfather.'

'Really?' Tory assumed that was why he was called 'Uncle Luc'.

'Well, one of them,' Caro continued before glancing towards the back of the house. 'Look, do you mind if we chat in the kitchen while I get on with dinner?'

Tory shook her head, offering, 'I'd be happy to help. I'm

not much of a cook but I can peel vegetables with the best of them.'

'It's all right.' Carol smiled, leading the way through. 'Most of it's done. I just have to keep watch over various pots and pans. Poached salmon—I hope you like it.'

'Sounds delicious.' Tory meant it. 'A welcome change from chicken salad or tuna pasta, the heights of my own culinary achievements.'

Caro laughed. 'Oh, you're definitely one up on me. I used to live on a diet of sandwiches and yoghurt in my single ca reer-girl days. Life always seemed too short to cook.'

'Quite.' Tory gave the other woman a complicit smile.

'Of course, it's such an irony,' Caro ran on. 'There I was, doing features for this lifestyle magazine, full of cordon bleu recipes and articles on minimalist decor, and going home to cook beans on toast in a girl-sharing flat in Clapham with enough clutter to fill a builder's skip.'

Tory laughed at the image, before casting an appreciative glance round her present surrounds. The kitchen was large and light and airy, with up to date units and flooring in polished beech-wood.

'You have a lovely place now,' complimented Tory.

'Money,' Caro replied as she stirred a simmering pot. 'My husband's family have it.'

'Right.' Tory wasn't sure how to respond to such frankness.

Caro shrugged, dismissing it as an importance, before continuing, 'Anyway, I understand from Luc that you're also about to enter the bitch-eat-bitch world of the women's glossy.'

'I've already been through the initiation ceremony.' Grimacing, Tory relayed her brief meeting with the editorial board.

Caro's expression was sympathetic but hardly surprised. It seemed Amanda Villiers, the senior editor, was notorious in the business for savaging female staff.

Tory listened while Caro went through what her job had entailed when working for a very similar magazine to *Toi*. Obviously she couldn't teach Tory how to do the job. That required years of experience as well as talent. But she gave her enough pointers on how to *seem* to be doing the job to maintain her cover for a few days.

'You'll be fine,' Caro tried to boost Tory's flagging confidence, 'but if you do need advice, I'm available, nappy-changing permitting.'

There was a certain wistfulness in her voice that made Tory ask, 'When did you stop work?'

'The boys were about two, I think…' Caro cast her mind back '…so that's…what? Over a year ago. I was one of those having-it-all-mothers who suddenly woke up to the fact they were really having-absolutely-nothing but misery and stress.'

Tory gave an understanding murmur. 'It seems to be a trend—women re-evaluating their lives. Personally, I love my work but I don't think I could manage it all—home, family and a career.'

'You can for a while,' Caro responded, 'but then your energy levels go down while theirs go up and all of a sudden the crying babies became talkative two-year-olds well able to tell you they hate it every time you leave for work and your nanny informs you she wants to see the world, starting tomorrow, and your heart is desperate for another baby even though you're barely coping with the two you have. So it's crunch time…I was luckier than most, I suppose, because we didn't need my money.'

'Still, you must miss work,' Tory said in sympathetic tones.

'At times,' Caro admitted, shaking the contents of a pan, 'when the twins' squabbling reaches an all-time high—or possibly low—and the baby won't settle because she has a cold and the au pair has failed to return from a night out clubbing.'

'And total strangers turn up for dinner?' Tory suggested, her tone apologetic.

'Oh, I didn't mind that.'

'Really?'

'Well—' Caro pulled a face '—I wasn't too ecstatic when Luc called, but that's only because I thought you might be like his usual girlfriends—'

'I'm not his girlfriend.' A frown clouded Tory's features. 'Did he say—?'

'No, not at all,' Caro was quick to disclaim. 'Quite the opposite, in fact…'

Caro trailed off and left Tory wondering what Lucas had said about her that was quite the opposite of being his girlfriend.

'I just meant,' Caro tried again, 'that, on the few occasions Lucas has brought a woman to dinner, it has been a girlfriend and they tend to be…let's say, a certain type.'

Tory told herself she wasn't interested but, in the very next breath, asked, 'What type, exactly?'

Caro hesitated. 'Perhaps I've said enough.'

'All right.' Tory wasn't going to press her.

That was probably why Caro ran on, 'Well, it could be me, but I find them all unbearably superior. Admittedly, they're usually barristers or investment bankers or run their own PR companies and they're always clever and witty, and often fairly stunning in the looks department, too. Which is probably why they feel obliged to talk down to lesser mortals, as if we're one step up from the village idiot.'

Tory rolled her eyes in agreement. 'I know the type but I can't imagine they talk to Lucas that way.'

'Oh, goodness, no!' Caro exclaimed at the very idea. 'But that only makes it worse. They positively simper in Luc's presence, and gaze at him, all adoring eyes, like politicians' wives.'

Tory laughed as intended, before venturing, 'He probably loves it.'

Caro looked uncertain. 'Luc's never struck me as being that big an egotist,' she replied, 'although I suppose most men that gorgeous *do* have egos the size of a planet.'

'Too true,' Tory said with feeling.

Caro came back with, 'So you think he is, then?'

'What?'

'Gorgeous.'

Caro's grin made a joke of it.

Tory pulled a slight face, too. 'I didn't say that, exactly.'

'No, but he is,' Caro insisted as if it were a fact that couldn't be disputed.

Tory didn't try; she was acquainted with the phrase 'the lady doth protest too much'.

'I have wondered if it's a kind of protection,' the other woman continued in musing tones.

'Protection?' Tory had lost the thread. 'What is?'

'Going out with that kind of woman,' Caro volunteered. 'I mean, even allowing for other people's taste, no one, but no one, could have found his last girlfriend lovable. Smart, witty, classy, yes! Lovable, absolutely not.'

'What happened to her?'

'His relocation to Norwich, but I can't see that being an insurmountable problem. How far is it from London? Two hours?'

Having made the journey that day, Tory said, 'A little over.'

'No huge distance,' commented Caro, 'but that's the excuse he gave for the relationship petering out. I wondered if he'd met someone else. Any super-intelligent, arrogant, super-model types at Eastwich?'

'Not that I can think of.' Tory certainly didn't come into that category. At five-foot six, she was hardly a super-model type, was far from super-intelligent, and didn't see herself as arrogant in personality. That left her questioning whether Lucas Ryecart was stringing along some other woman besides herself.

'At any rate,' Caro resumed her original theme, 'I have this theory he dates women with whom he's in no danger of falling in love. As in, it's better *not* to love and *not* to lose, than ever love at all.'

'I always thought it was the other way round,' countered Tory.

'It is,' replied Caro, 'but, in Luc's case, he *has* loved and lost so maybe he doesn't want to go through it again.'

'I see.' Tory did see, too; she just wasn't entirely convinced.

Sensing her doubts, Caro confided in more sober tones, 'He was married once and she died.'

'Yes, I know.'

'Did he tell you?'

Tory nodded, recalling he had told her at one point.

Caro looked surprised. 'He doesn't usually talk about it—even among the family.'

The family? Tory didn't quite follow. Which family did she mean?

'Is Lucas related to you?' she finally asked Caro.

'Sort of. His wife was my sister-in-law. Or would have been, had she…' The other woman tailed off at Tory's expression and switched to asking, 'Is something wrong?'

Tory struggled to keep her emotions in check as the truth dawned. Lucas was an only child, while his late wife had one brother. There was no other link.

How could she have been so stupid? *Uncle Luc* really was Uncle Luc. She was in Charlie's, her ex-fiancé's, house. She was talking to Charlie's wife, the girl who had so rapidly replaced her.

'You really don't look well.' Caro watched Tory's face become drawn with alarm.

'I… It's a bug,' Tory lied desperately. 'I thought I was better, but it seems not. I'll have to go back to the hotel.'

Tory picked up the pashmina she'd draped over a chair and her handbag, and started making for the door.

Caro followed. 'Yes, of course, I'll go and fetch Luc. He'll—'

'No!' Tory refused rather abruptly, then softened it with, 'Honestly, I don't want to drag him away. I can hail a taxi. I'm sorry to throw out your plans. It was lovely to meet you…'

Tory garbled on until she was in the front hall, poised for escape.

Caro obviously didn't feel she should be allowed to go on her own and looked relieved at the sound of a key in the front door.

'That'll be Charlie now. I could get him to run you back instead.'

Tory said nothing, did nothing. She felt trapped, caught like a rabbit in headlights. She watched the door push open. Her eyes went to the dark-suited man entering.

For a moment she almost thought she'd got it wrong and this wasn't Charlie. He wasn't as she remembered. Five years older, he had lost some of his boyish good looks and his hair. Her heart was beating hard out of panic but it didn't kick up any extra gears, even when she realised it was most definitely Charlie.

His glance first went to his wife, who'd launched into explanations of their guest's indisposition, before it encompassed Tory. Then any hopes that she'd also changed out of recognition faded rapidly.

Charlie was clearly shocked, opening and shutting his mouth as no words came, struggling to come to terms with her presence.

When Caro sought to introduce them, 'This is Tory, by the way,' he was already mouthing the name he'd known her by: Vicki.

Quickly, she shook her head at him, the slightest movement, but he picked it up.

When she said, 'Pleased to meet you,' he followed suit.

'Yes, hello,' he murmured, and let her continue.

'I'm sorry, but I have to go. I'm not feeling too great and I've left my medicine back at the hotel.'

She waited for him to play his part, say some farewell words, encourage her to leave, perhaps open the door, but he just stood stock-still staring at her.

It was Caro who insisted, 'Charlie will run you back. Won't you, Charlie?'

She seemed oblivious of undercurrents.

Tory anticipated Charlie making an excuse and was thrown by his acquiescent, 'Yes, of course. My car's outside.'

'See.' Caro was finally satisfied with the arrangements.

She escorted Tory down the steps while Charlie went ahead to unlock the car, then opened the passenger door and waited for Tory to be installed inside.

She said, warm as ever, 'You must come again for dinner. Let me know how you get on at *Toi*.'

'Yes, thanks.' Tory smiled at the other woman whom she

had really liked—still did like—knowing she would never meet her again if she could help it.

'I'll explain to Luc,' Caro called out as they drew away from the kerb.

Tory managed a weak wave and felt a measure of relief once they were out of sight.

But Charlie drove only as far as the end of the crescent, before parking in the first available space and turning in his seat to stare at her, as if he still couldn't believe his eyes.

'I'm sorry.' Tory felt she owed him an apology. 'I had no idea. He never said.'

'He?'

'Lucas.'

'You came with him?' Charlie caught up with events. 'Oh, you're the production assistant from Eastwich.'

She gave a nod.

'My wife called you by some other name.' He frowned, trying to remember.

'Tory,' she supplied. 'It was my mother's name for me when I was little. I went back to using it after…'

She left it hanging. What to say otherwise? *After you dumped me?*

It was true enough. She'd reverted to Tory in a desire to reinvent the person she was, but he'd been more catalyst than cause. She looked at him now and felt not a single ounce of passion. How strange.

'And you didn't realise who Luc was?' Charlie concluded.

'No, I did,' she admitted. 'I realised when he took over Eastwich. It was just that he offered to introduce me to someone who'd worked on a woman's magazine—Eastwich is doing this documentary—and it wasn't until five minutes ago that the penny dropped who Caro actually was.'

'Right.' Charlie absorbed this information while still gazing at her intently. '*You* haven't changed. Not at all.'

Tory pulled a face, trying to lighten things up. 'I'm not sure that's good.'

Charlie remained serious. 'You're just the same, just the way I imagine you.'

Tory felt no satisfaction at the wistful note of regret in Charlie's voice. The past was dead for her.

'Your wife's lovely,' she said quite genuinely.

'Thanks,' he replied but it was as if she'd complimented him on a new car, and he added with more feeling, 'She's not you.'

Tory couldn't misunderstand his meaning, not when it went along with the soulful look in his eyes. It was the look he'd worn during their long-ago courtship, when she'd imagined herself in love with him, and he with her. But now, from a distance, she could see it had all been illusion.

'No, she's not,' she agreed at length. 'She's the woman who gave you the children you always wanted.'

It was a pointed remark that hit its target as he winced. 'That was cruel.'

'Was it?' Tory didn't care as she stated, 'It's a cruel world.'

'You've grown harder, Vicki.' He looked troubled by the idea.

Tory wondered what he expected. 'Life does that to people.'

'Yes… Yes, it does. You have no idea how much I wish—'

She cut across him. 'Don't.'

'But you don't know what I'm going to say.' He reached for her hand.

She pulled it from his grasp. 'I don't want to know, Charlie. I think I'll get out here.'

'Please, Vicki,' he appealed, but she already had the door open and didn't stop even when he called out, 'You have to forgive me.'

She kept walking, wrapping her pashmina round her as the cool night air touched her bare shoulders. She didn't look back.

She didn't run. Charlie Wainwright didn't frighten her. In fact, he didn't do anything to her any more, except make her sorry for his wife.

It was a revelation. For years she had wondered if it was Charlie who had stopped her forming any other serious relationship. Always, at the back of her mind, had been the idea she might just still love him. And now? Nothing.

She couldn't even stay angry with him. As she walked the

Kensington streets, heading back towards the hotel, her anger switched to another man. A tall, blue-eyed, dark-haired American with a rather nasty sense of humour.

How else to explain what he'd done? It couldn't have been coincidence. It was too far a stretch.

So what had it been? A social experiment to check how she'd react when face to face with her former fiancé?

Well, tough luck, he'd missed it, playing favourite uncle to Charlie's kids.

It was Caro she felt sorry for. Married to a husband who, at best, was a wimp, and deceived by a man whom she imagined loyal enough to make him her sons' godfather.

No one could be a real friend and engineer such a situation. Even if the plan had been to stir up things for Tory, there had always been a danger of hurting Caro along the way. He must have known that. He was no fool.

But that was what really got to Tory. She'd spent almost the whole day with Lucas Ryecart, her barriers against him slipping away. It was only now she acknowledged that she'd dressed for him this evening. Only now she admitted how jealous she'd been, seeing him with that other woman at the bar. And, in watching him with his godsons, listening to Caro talking about him with such fondness, she had been seduced into seeing him in a different light.

She supposed she should be grateful for the wake-up call, otherwise she might have been in real danger of falling for the bastard. Now anger was uppermost and kept her buoyant until she finally reached her hotel.

She hadn't eaten since lunch and the walk had given her an appetite, but it had also given her sore feet—her shoes had been new and high-heeled—and she decided to order room service. An elaborate variety of courses was on offer and she considered running up a huge bill, courtesy of Eastwich and Lucas Ryecart, but she eventually settled for a salad, omelette and a chilled bottle of white wine to calm her down. She took her meal, watching a documentary on cheating husbands. It seemed an appropriate choice of viewing for that evening.

She was getting ready for bed, mellowed somewhat by the

wine, when there was a knock on the hotel room door. She assumed it was room service although they'd already cleared her dinner. She tied the hotel's fluffy bathrobe tighter round the waist and checked she was decent before opening the door.

One glance and, registering the figure standing on the threshold, she shut it immediately before Lucas could even think to get a foot in the door.

She ignored his next knock and the several after it, and the repetitions of her name, 'Tory!' and the appeals to, 'Open up,' and 'We have to talk.'

Tory didn't see they had to talk at all. In fact, she'd already decided a resignation letter would do for their next communication. She'd been mentally composing it all through supper and preparing for bed. But she had no desire to deliver it in person.

'*Tory*—' his tone changed to barely restrained anger '—I don't want to have to do this, but you're leaving me no choice.'

Do what? Tory scowled at the door. It was thick and made of real wood. Did he imagine he could run at it and break it down? She almost wished he'd try.

'Tory!' Her name was called once more, followed by a determined, 'Right.'

She waited in anticipation for his next move. She didn't really expect him to do anything as crude as batter on the door and she was right. She heard the click of the electronic locking system and then he was in the room before she had a chance to react.

He shut the door behind him, but didn't come further into the room as he drawled, 'Don't look so panic-stricken. I'm not going to jump on you.'

'How did you get that?' She indicated the card key in his hand.

'I told them I'd lost mine,' he relayed. 'They handed another over once I'd proved I was the registered occupant of the room.'

'How low can you get?' She didn't hide her contempt.

'Lower than that,' he rejoined without apology.

'Well…?' She waited for him to state his business.

He seemed in no hurry. 'You could offer me a drink,' he said as if he were an invited guest.

'I could call Security,' she countered with a hard edge.

'You could,' he agreed. 'Go ahead, if you want.'

He leaned against the door and folded his arms. It didn't seem to bother him.

'You're so sure I won't.' Tory tried to sound threatening.

He was unimpressed. 'Not sure, no, but I don't think you like scenes. Otherwise you might have hung around at the Wainwrights.'

'I'm sorry if you feel cheated.' Her tone was derisive.

His brows drew together. 'You think I'd have liked to watch the grand reunion?'

'Why else did you stage it?' she rallied.

'Hold on a minute.' He abandoned his relaxed pose. 'I had no idea you had any connection with the Wainwrights until I came downstairs to find you gone and an agitated Charlie in your place.'

Tory wasn't convinced. 'You expect me to believe that?'

'I've pretty much given up expecting anything of you,' he said, 'but, yes, I'm telling you straight—I was as much in the dark as you.'

'All right.' It rang true. On his part, anyway. She, of course, hadn't totally been in the dark.

She must have looked guilty as the blue eyes were already studying her, narrowed.

'Or maybe even more so?' he asked astutely.

Tory suddenly found herself on the defensive. 'I did not realise who we were visiting until about a minute before Charlie came home.'

A statement of fact; he still saw behind her carefully chosen words. 'But you knew of my connection to the Wainwrights. You must have.'

Tory considered denying it. After all, he'd never actually mentioned his wife by name or his in-laws. But what would be the point?

'I did realise, yes,' she admitted, 'the first day we met.'

'No wonder you seemed familiar.' His eyes hardened with distrust. 'I must have seen a photograph or something, though I guess you've changed in…what? Five years, would it be?'

She nodded. 'My hair was longer and I wore glasses before I had contacts fitted.'

'Why didn't you say anything?' he added.

'What, exactly?' countered Tory. ' I was once engaged to your late wife's brother? Not quite the easiest of introductions to a new boss.'

'You had plenty of chances later… Do you honestly think I would have taken you to their house, if I'd been clued up?' His tone clearly told her he wouldn't.

It seemed she'd misjudged him, yet again, but rather than apologise she gave an uninterested shrug.

It was a gesture designed to annoy, and annoy it did as his mouth went into a tight line and he finally stepped away from the door to cross the room.

Misunderstanding his purpose, Tory retreated to the far corner. She felt a little foolish when he veered off towards the mini-bar.

He noted her jumpiness with a humourless smile. 'Relax. Right at the moment a drink is all I want.'

If it was meant to reassure, it didn't. His eyes lingered long enough to suggest that later he might want something else.

Tory took a deep, steadying breath and told herself to keep calm. He was playing games, that was all.

'Can I fix you one?' He bent to do a quick inventory of, 'Whisky, gin, vodka, beer…'

'No…thank you.' Tory had already had several glasses of wine earlier.

She watched as he took a couple of miniature whiskies from the cabinet and poured both in a glass, then eased his length onto the only chair.

As hotel bedrooms went, it had seemed quite spacious, but, with him in it, it suddenly felt overcrowded.

'So what happened between you and Charlie?' he asked, as if his interest was merely casual.

'Tonight?'

'No, we'll come to that. I meant before.'

Tory supposed she could have told him to mind his own business, but wasn't that making it a big deal? And it wasn't. Not really. Not any more.

'We met at college on the same media course,' she relayed, 'we went out, then became briefly engaged before having second thoughts.'

'Which one of you?'

'Which one of you what?'

'Had second thoughts?'

Both of them, Tory supposed was the truth.

She'd had second thoughts from the moment Charlie had proposed and pressed her for an immediate answer at the New Year's party they'd been attending. But she'd tried hard to ignore her doubts and let herself be caught up in Charlie's impulsiveness and sheer certainty about everything.

'Charlie,' she answered at length.

'That's not what I heard,' he drawled back at her.

Tory wasn't altogether surprised. It was Charlie who'd decided to call off the engagement but she'd left it up to him as to what story he gave people.

'I heard,' he continued at her silence, 'that all of a sudden the engagement was off and Charlie was devastated. Doesn't quite tally with the notion he was the one to back out, now, does it?'

'Who did you hear it from?' she retorted. 'His mother?'

'As I recall, yes.' He nodded. 'Charlie wasn't making much sense at the time. He just said he'd discovered something that made it impossible for you to go on together.'

That was true enough and she supposed she was glad that Charlie had been discreet, although it was questionable whether his intention had been to save her face or his own.

'I bet his mother couldn't contain her delight.' Tory knew she'd never been good enough for Diana Wainwright.

He raised a brow at her slightly acerbic tone before admitting, 'She did think you were unsuited, yes.'

'Not her sort at all.' Tory mimicked the other woman's posh way of talking.

'Yeah, okay, Diana can be a bit of a snob,' he conceded, 'but she was more concerned for Charlie and whether he'd ever get over you.'

There was a note of accusation in his voice. It seemed he'd cast her in the role of heartbreaker.

Tory resented the unfairness of it. 'Well, she was wrong, wasn't she? How long before he was married? A year, maybe?'

'And you'd prefer him to do what?' he grated back. 'Stay crying into his beer? Carry a torch for ever? Or maybe go crawling back to you?'

'I didn't want that,' Tory denied angrily.

'No?' He clearly didn't believe her.

'No!' she repeated, gritting her teeth.

He still didn't look satisfied as he muttered, 'Let's hope not.'

'Does it matter?' Tory wasn't enjoying this trip down memory lane. 'It's past, over, history.'

'Is it?'

Why was he looking at her like that?

'Yes, of course,' she declared adamantly. ' I haven't seen Charlie for five years.'

'But you saw him tonight,' he reminded her, 'and he saw you.'

What was he getting at? Obviously something, but she'd lost the plot.

'Yes,' she answered slowly.

'And?' He waited.

She still didn't know what he wanted her to say.

'And nothing,' she replied.

'He gave you a ride, you shook hands like nice polite English people do and said goodbye?' The mocking drawl in his voice was shot through with disbelief.

Colour seeped into Tory's cheeks even as she told herself he couldn't possibly know otherwise. He'd not been in the car with them and surely Charlie hadn't rushed off home to confess all.

'Something along those lines,' she finally murmured.

It was the wrong answer, evidently, as his lips curled with

contempt for her. Then he drained his whisky and set the glass down on a table with a cracking noise, before rising to his feet.

She watched him cross to the door, seemingly with the intention of leaving.

She should have been relieved but instead she found herself coming round the end of the bed, pursuing him as she claimed, 'Nothing happened between us, if that's what you're trying to imply.'

He paused mid-flight, hand on the lock, back rigid, then turned round to face her.

'Nothing happened?' he echoed, but there was a dangerous edge to his voice, and when she took a step backwards he reached out to catch her arm.

Unable to retreat, Tory stood shaking her head. 'I—I... No, nothing.'

'Liar.' The word was growled at her as he drew her closer. 'I just sat through dinner with a man who looked like a ghost had come back to haunt him. I spent most of it trying to distract his wife so she wouldn't notice how sappy he was acting, then afterwards had to listen while Charlie went on like a corny Country and Western song about the love of his life and how he'd lost her.'

And he blamed it all on her. Tory saw that in the scathing look he gave her.

'I'm not interested in Charlie,' she said in her own defence.

'And that makes it better?' It was a rhetorical question as he ran on, 'So why vamp him—to see if you could? Or a little revenge?'

'Vamp him?' Tory repeated, her own temper rising. 'Is that what Charlie said?'

'He didn't need to,' Lucas replied. 'It was obvious from the way he was behaving. Doesn't it mean anything to you, the fact he's married, has kids?'

She shook her head, denying that she'd done anything, but he chose to misunderstand, to believe the worst of her.

'Evidently not,' he concluded for himself. 'Well, I'm warning you now, go near Charlie again and I'll make sure you regret it.'

'Really?' The threat didn't scare Tory, it just made her madder. 'So how are you going to do that, Mr Ryecart? Let me guess? My P45 in the post.'

'P45?' The term didn't translate.

'P45, it's a tax form you get when you stop working for a company—' Tory switched to saying, 'Never mind. It doesn't matter. You can't sack me because I quit. As of now, this moment.'

It clearly took him by surprise as his brows arched together. Perhaps he'd imagined he was the only one who could call the shots.

'You can't quit!' he barked back.

'Oh, can't I?' Tory taunted, and tried to jerk her hands free.

He held them fast, long fingers circling her slender wrists. 'You're on contract and in the middle of an assignment. I thought you were the one who could keep work and their personal life separate?'

Tory recognised the claim she'd made that afternoon but didn't appreciate having it flung back at her.

'And this business with you and Charlie,' he continued heavily, 'has absolutely nothing to do with work, and everything to do with Caro and those three kids back there. You honestly want to wreck their lives just because Charlie was too spineless to marry you in the first place?'

Of course Tory didn't. No thought could be further from her mind, but his lecturing tone incensed her all the same.

'Why not?' she found herself saying. 'You don't expect anything better of me, do you? You imagine I'll sleep with anyone, after all… Well, anyone but you, that is,' she added with reckless intent.

She didn't regret it. Not then, anyway. She enjoyed wiping that superior look from his face.

It was replaced with a cloud of dark anger. 'You think I'd want to sleep with you now?'

His tone said he'd not touch her, but his eyes said something else, and Tory scoffed at him, 'Yes, actually, I do.'

She felt his hands tighten like bands round her arms, and waited for him to push her away.

But she had seriously miscalculated.

'Let's see, shall we?' he ground back, pulling her towards him.

At the last moment she tried to turn but it was too late. His hand was in her hair, holding her head steady. She saw his mouth curve into a humourless smile a second before it lowered on hers.

She meant to resist but she had forgotten how it felt to be kissed by this man. His lips moved against hers, warm and hard and persuasive, tongue tasting teeth until she opened to him, then thrusting inside to explore the warm, sweet intimacy of her mouth, making her breathing as ragged as his.

'You're right,' he murmured against her mouth. 'I still want you.'

It was the last they spoke, the last conscious thought formed as desire overwhelmed reason.

Afterwards Tory would try to tell herself it was down to the drink they'd both had. Afterwards she'd try to call it seduction but then she'd remember how it really had been. Too quick to be seduction. Too sweet to be force.

It was more compulsion as he began to touch her, a hand moving round, slipping inside her robe, pushing aside, seeking flesh, breasts swollen and heavy, fingering until she cried out for the mouth closing, sucking on her aching nipples. It was need and desperation as she fell with him on the bed and guided him down to the part of her that was already warm and wet and let him stroke her, deep and intimate, until desire kicked in her belly and she drew his hips to hers.

She was naked, he still clothed. Together they fumbled for his zip. Then they coupled in mutual need.

The first thrust and he filled her too completely. She moaned a little until his mouth covered hers in a sweet, drugging kiss. Then slowly he moved inside her and her body opened up as if it had always known his, and she rose and fell with him, grasping his shoulders, digging in at each shaft, panting and gasping, almost one being as they came together with wild, unrestrained pleasure.

They lay back on the bed, for a while suspended in time,

their bodies experiencing intense physical satisfaction—then gradually reality impinged and the mind took back control.

Tory remained paralysed in those first conscious moments, wondering what she had done. She'd never made love like that, with almost primitive urgency. She'd never felt like this, possessed to the core. She'd never wanted to let a man this close to her.

Every instinct told her to run. She'd nowhere to go but inside her head. So she retreated there as she slid off the bed and picked up the robe she'd been wearing and turned her back to him as she put it on.

Somehow Luc wasn't surprised by this reaction. He was more surprised by what had gone before.

He followed her up off the bed, straightening his clothes as he did so. He considered an apology but it would have been hypocrisy. He wasn't sorry for what he'd done. In fact, when he recalled her response, so warm and passionate, he wanted to do it all over again.

Her rigid stance, however, told him the cold war had resumed.

He restrained a desire to cross the room and take her back in his arms.

'You want me to go?' he surmised instead.

'Yes.' Tory didn't risk saying more.

He was equally laconic. 'Okay.'

But still Tory didn't imagine he would leave without another word, didn't believe it when she heard the door behind her open and shut.

She turned and found herself in an empty room. He was gone. Just like that.

But he couldn't be forgotten the same way. How could he be when he'd left his mark on her body, left a jagged tear on her heart?

She showered and tried to wash the smell of him, the taste of him, the touch of him from her body. She leaned against cool white tiles while hot tears of shame and rejection ran down her cheeks. She towelled her skin dry till it hurt and climbed into the crumpled bed and shut her eyes tight and prayed for sleep to come.

But it made no difference. When finally she slipped away, she found him chasing through her dreams.

It seemed as if she had opened a door that she couldn't close.

CHAPTER EIGHT

TORY woke, hoping it really had been a dream, but her eyes were drawn to the whisky glass on the table. This trace of Lucas's presence prompted vivid recall of what had happened last night.

She felt a measure of shame. She'd never indulged before in casual sex but what Lucas and she had done together could scarcely be described as anything else. And the worst part was the way he'd left her, as if he hadn't been able to wait to be gone.

She wondered how she could ever face him again. The easy option was not to. She could follow through her threat to quit her job. In the cool light of day, however, she knew such an action would damage her career as well as her finances.

And what else had she but work? It was the thing she did best, the thing that gave her life meaning and form. If she walked away from Eastwich now, how long might it be before she secured another post?

There was also a reasonable possibility that Lucas would no longer be a problem. Yes, he'd pursued her from the moment they'd met, but now he'd had her and used her and seemingly lost interest at once. Perhaps she was already history.

Tory visualised their next meeting. She'd be churned up inside while he would be his usual laid-back self. He might or might not allude to their one-night stand. If he did, it would be as a joke or a shrugged aside. No big deal. Couldn't she act the same way, regardless of how she felt inside?

Tory decided she could and would, and, driven by a mixture of pride and pragmatism, she got herself out of bed, showered and dressed and ready for her first day as an employee of *Toi*.

While she'd been nervous yesterday, she approached today very differently. She sailed into the offices with an almost reckless disregard as to whether she was found out or not, and straight away set up a meeting with her three assistants, listening as they explained the work in progress before making appropriate comments and suggesting approaches that might be taken for this or that article. She made it clear that they would have a fair degree of autonomy, and two of the young women seemed happy to accept her as their new boss. The third was Sam Hollier who'd been Acting Features Editor, and, not surprisingly, she was more hostile, although she stopped short of outright rebellion, and Tory decided she could probably handle her.

It was Amanda Villiers of whom she was most wary, but, to her relief, the lady in question failed to appear. Either she was too busy to bother or didn't really care whether Tory settled to the job or not.

Thus Tory survived the day with her credibility intact and actually stayed late, wading through some unsolicited articles sent by freelance writers. Most she earmarked for polite rejections, a couple were worth considering and one stood out as eminently printable. Unsure if she had the authority to commission the latter, she decided to play safe and placed a copy on Amanda's desk, requesting her opinion of it.

She returned to the hotel with some reluctance. Occupied throughout the day, she'd avoided thinking of Lucas Ryecart, but once back in her room she was unable to keep her mind off the events of last night. She felt she would have welcomed any distraction until Reception rang up to her room, informing her she had a visitor downstairs: Caro Wainwright.

Tory assumed it was a social call—perhaps Caro offering further work advice. Much as she'd liked her, Tory felt pursuing even the most tenuous relationship with her was inadvisable. But refusing to see her at all might prompt some suspicions in Caro's mind.

Tory resolved to go down and do her best to act normally. She greeted Caro with a polite smile and hid her surprise at the other woman's attire—an orange and black track suit over a running top.

'It's one of my gym nights,' explained Caro, 'but I decided at the last moment to come here…see how you were.'

'Much better,' Tory volunteered.

'That's good,' Caro murmured back.

Silence followed these pleasantries until Tory felt almost obliged to add, 'We could go for a drink in the lounge bar.'

Caro nodded even as she looked uncertain. 'Perhaps there's a dress code.'

Tory glanced towards a group of young men exiting the bar in question. They wore an array of scruffy denim jackets and tie-less shirts flapping loosely over jeans.

'Not from the look of that lot, there isn't,' she remarked on their dress.

Caro followed her gaze. 'Aren't they some pop group or other?'

'Possibly,' agreed Tory, before leading the way through the glass doors.

They gravitated towards a booth at the back. Tory insisted on buying the drinks and escaped to the bar. It gave her some precious minutes to compose herself.

When she returned, Caro took a good swig of the gin and tonic she'd requested.

It was Dutch courage, as she resumed, 'I'm not really sure what I want to say. I got myself riled up to come here but didn't think much further than that.'

Tory felt her stomach drop. It didn't take a genius to conclude from Caro's words, 'You know who I am, don't you?'

Caro nodded slowly.

'Lucas told you?' added Tory, a note of accusation creeping into her voice.

'When I asked him, he did,' relayed Caro, 'but not last night.'

Tory frowned, trying to sort out exactly what this meant.

Caro ran on, 'I knew there was something wrong at dinner. Charlie was acting really oddly but I thought it had something to do with work. Then, while I was making coffee, Luc changed his mind about staying and Charlie got very agitated at the idea that Luc had gone off to spend the night with you.'

'He didn't.' Tory could deny that at least.

'No, I know,' Caro stated. 'Luc told me he stayed with Chuck, his stepfather.'

So that was where he'd gone. Tory imagined the two men together, discussing Luc's latest acquisition—her! She just hoped she was being unduly paranoid.

'Anyway, Charlie thought otherwise,' Caro continued. 'In fact, to be honest, so did I. I made some joke about it—something about Luc meeting his match—and Charlie went ballistic. He made out he was upset because of his sister's memory, although he usually admired Luc for his success with women. It took me a while to figure out he minded for himself, not his sister…' Caro tailed off and her face reflected the pain she felt.

Tory wanted to say something. She just wasn't sure what. She was scared of making the situation worse.

Eventually she murmured, 'Charlie told you who I was.'

Caro shook her head. 'I guessed later, lying in bed, waiting for him to come up. I remembered your reaction to Charlie's name—your sudden bout of illness. It was obvious then that you knew him. I was just too stupid to realise it.'

'It's me that was stupid—' Tory sighed in response '—not realising who you were. I would never have gone to your house if I had.'

Caro's eyes rested on her, testing her sincerity, before she said, 'Well, it's too late to change things. The question is where we go from here.'

'I'm not sure I understand,' Tory replied carefully.

'Look, I know Charlie's rung you,' Caro informed her. 'I overheard him this morning, asking to speak to Victoria Lloyd. That's you, isn't it?'

Tory looked genuinely blank. 'I never received any calls.'

'He must have missed you,' Caro concluded, 'but that hardly matters. The fact that he's calling you at all is the issue.'

Tory could see that and ventured a possibility. 'Maybe he was calling to apologise. He *was* somewhat rude to me last night.'

'Rude?' Caro echoed in surprise.

'I'd say so. Claimed I'd grown very hard, ' Tory could relay quite truthfully, 'which is a bit of a cheek, coming from him. I mean, you know he dumped me, don't you?'

'Well, I…' Caro looked confused. 'I was never quite sure what had happened between you.'

'Not ready to commit.' Tory pulled a face. 'That's what he said. Rubbish, of course. I mean, he was ready enough when he met you a few months later, wasn't he?'

'I…um…yes, I suppose,' Caro agreed in apologetic tones.

'Well, you're welcome to him.' Tory gave a negligent shrug before reaching for her drink.

Over the rim she watched Caro's changing expressions. Having come here to warn Tory off or perhaps plead with her, Caro had not anticipated this outcome. She looked as if she couldn't quite believe things were going to be so easily resolved.

'God, jealousy does make fools of people. I really thought that you and him…' She trailed off and gave her a sheepish look. 'I wish now I'd listened to Luc.'

'Luc?' Tory repeated more sharply. 'What did he say?'

'I…' Caro hesitated, not wanting to commit another *faux pas*. 'Just that he didn't think you'd be interested in Charlie, that you had someone else.'

'When did he say this?'

'This morning when I phoned him on his mobile and started blubbering my suspicions.'

Tory's eyes darkened. She was beginning to form some suspicions of her own. What Luc and she had done last night, she'd put down to sexual urges and momentary impulses. She hadn't considered it a premeditated act on his part.

But what if it was? What if he'd slept with her entirely to discredit her in Charlie's eyes?

'He offered to tell Charlie as much—' Caro seemed to confirm the idea '—although he was convinced that I had the wrong end of the stick, which, of course, it appears I had… I really do feel a Class A Idiot.'

'That makes two of us.' Tory spoke her thoughts aloud.

'Two?' Caro raised a brow.

But Tory shook her head. Caro was never going to believe what a rat Lucas Ryecart had been to her.

'I've been making an idiot of myself all day,' Tory confided instead.

Caro was suitably distracted. 'The magazine, of course! How did it go?'

'You do not want to know.' Tory rolled her eyes, conveying disaster, and the two exchanged smiles.

It was a spontaneous reaction but the smiles soon faded. In other circumstances they could have been friends, but neither wished to risk it, Caro because her husband's ex-fiancée was prettier, smarter and a whole lot nicer than anyone in the family had led her to believe, and Tory, because Caro was too much like family to Lucas Ryecart.

So they finished their drinks, shook hands and parted company in the lobby.

Tory then went to the desk and, asking if there were any messages, collected several slips of paper.

There were four, three from Charlie, the last asking her to call him on his mobile. The message would have been easy to ignore but seemed safer to answer, and sooner rather than later.

Back in her bedroom, she dialled the mobile number given, and, when Charlie said his name, didn't give him much chance to say anything else. Spurred on by the sounds of children playing in the background, she told him straight. She didn't know why he'd been calling her, didn't want to know why unless it was to apologise for last night's rudeness, didn't want him to call again. If he did keep calling, then she would have to inform her rugby-playing boyfriend who would happily re-convey her message in person.

Charlie just managed to bluster out the words, 'Are you threatening me?' before Tory replied with a resounding, 'Yes,' and replaced the receiver with a decisive click.

Till that point she hadn't known she had such a ruthless streak. She rather liked it. In fact, it had felt positively liberating to say exactly what one thought.

She looked at the other message in her hand. She'd read it before her call to Charlie. It was brief enough:

'CALL ME. IT'S IMPORTANT. LUCAS.'

In fact, it couldn't be briefer. No one would have known they were lovers. Correction, *had* been lovers. Once. And that was one time too many.

Tory reached for the phone again and dialled an outside line, but that was as far as she got. Having vented her spleen on Charlie, she'd wasted precious reserves of anger and Lucas was nowhere near as easy to handle.

She returned the mouthpiece to its cradle. Silence was surely the best show of contempt. She limited herself to tearing the message into a hundred tiny pieces.

Tory realised, of course, that she couldn't avoid Luc for ever, not if he wanted to talk to her, but she gave it her best shot.

When her mobile rang the next day, displaying a number she didn't know, she switched it off rather than answer it, and when Lucas called the magazine's number directly, she was 'in conference' in the morning and 'out of the building' in the afternoon, lies happily relayed by the switchboard operator, Liz. The said Liz was a self-professed hater of men—having been recently dumped by one herself—and didn't need much persuasion to come up with varied excuses why Tory was perpetually unavailable.

Tory did, however, take a call from Alex.

He was ostensibly phoning to find out how she was doing, but, after some pretty token interest, launched into his own news. It seemed that Rita, his wife, had finally agreed to his coming up to Scotland to visit the children. Alex hoped to go that weekend, depending on whether he found a flat in the interim.

Tory saw where he was going and didn't wait for him to get there. Yes, he could stay another week. But only on condition that he did go to Scotland.

Alex assured her he would. In fact, he confided his intention to try and win back his wife's affections. Tory made encouraging noises although personally she felt he had more chance of winning the London marathon on crutches.

Then, almost as an afterthought, he said, 'By the way, you

have to phone Ryecart. There's been some new developments you should know about. I offered to pass on a message but he doesn't seem to trust me.'

'Snap.' He didn't trust Tory either.

Alex laughed briefly before advising, 'I'd do it soon,' and signing off with a, 'Good luck for the weekend.'

Tory was left wondering about the nature of these so-called new developments. Was it on the work front or the Wainwright business? If she could be sure it was the latter, then she'd ignore the royal command. But what if it were work—what if she were about to be exposed at *Toi* for the impostor she undoubtedly was?

She was still deliberating the matter at the end of the day and left the offices without calling him. She didn't feel ready to talk to Lucas, whatever the reason. She went back to the hotel for another night and ordered room service.

She'd just finished her meal when the reception desk put through a call from an Alex Simpson.

'Alex, what now?' she asked with an impatient edge to her voice.

'Is that the way you normally talk to your boss?' a voice drawled back.

'You!' She almost spat the word down the line.

'Yes, me,' Lucas agreed and pre-empted her next move with, 'Don't hang up! Otherwise I'll keep calling all night.'

'I could ask Reception to block your calls,' she countered.

'My calls—or Alex's?' he threw back.

'I...' Tory asked herself why she was even having this conversation. 'Calls from anyone with an American accent,' she added at length.

'I can do British,' he replied and proceeded to prove the point with, 'I say, old bean, could I speak to Miss Lloyd, room two three five?'

'They'll know you're a fraud,' she retaliated. 'No one says "old bean" these days.'

'Old chap?' he supplanted.

Tory breathed heavily in response and, resigned, asked, 'What do you want?'

'Well, why don't we start with an apology?'

'An apology!'

'From me to you.'

'Oh.'

Tory waited.

'I shouldn't have sounded off about you and Charlie the other night.'

Tory waited another moment before saying, 'Is that it?'

'Pretty much,' he confirmed.

Tory's silence conveyed the fact that she was unimpressed.

'Unless you want it written in blood,' he suggested in a far from repentant tone.

'That would be a start,' she muttered back.

'Look,' he conceded, 'I'd apologise for the rest, only it would be hypocrisy. I'm *not* sorry we made love. In fact, I'd like to do it again, maybe a bit slower next time.'

Tory was glad he was at the other end of a phone line, although she should be used to his directness by now. His casual attitude to sex was no surprise, either, but it hurt all the same.

'And take pictures for Charlie, perhaps?' she finally ground back.

'What?'

'That's the idea, isn't it? To discredit me?'

'What?' he echoed with total incredulity. 'You think I slept with you so I could boast of the fact to Charlie?'

Did she think that? Tory wasn't sure any more. But she wasn't about to backtrack.

'I haven't said one word to Charlie,' he resumed through gritted teeth. 'It isn't me he's been calling.'

Tory didn't have to go looking for the accusing note in his voice.

'That's hardly my fault,' she retorted, 'and, for your information, I have told Charlie exactly how things stand. Check if you don't believe me. I have also reassured Caro that I have no designs on her husband.'

'You called Caro?'

'Correction, she called on me. Here at the hotel.'

'I told her not to do that.' He sighed heavily. 'What did you say to her?'

'Why don't you ask her?' suggested Tory.

'I will,' he countered.

He clearly didn't trust her. He still saw her as home-wrecker material. Forget the fact she was good enough for *him* to sleep with. Or perhaps bad enough was nearer the mark?

'So, if that's all—' Tory assumed they had no more to say to each other.

'I have a full diary the rest of the week,' he continued regardless, 'but we should meet up on Friday.'

'You and Caro?'

'No, you and I.'

Tory considered the prospect, before reminding them both, 'I'm off to the Derbyshire Dales doing outdoor activities.'

'I know,' he claimed.

It left Tory a little mystified. If he knew, then why…?

'How's it going at *Toi*, by the way?' he added, distracting her.

She'd thought he'd never ask. 'Easier than expected and more interesting.'

'Not considering defection, are we?'

'I wasn't, but now you mention it…'

He laughed. 'Are you sure—all those bitchy women?'

'You imagine they're any worse than Simon and Alex?' she countered without thinking.

The trouble was she kept forgetting Lucas Ryecart had two personae—careless, skirt-chasing ex-journalist and serious media boss who happened to own Eastwich.

'I didn't mean that,' she added quickly.

'Yes, you did,' he drawled back, 'but I'll forget you said it. I'll form my own opinion of those two in time, anyway.'

Tory assumed he already had.

'Meanwhile,' he continued, 'I thought you should know that I won't be broadcasting what happened between us the other night, in case that's of concern to you.'

It was, of course. Tory didn't want a reputation for sleeping with her boss, a reputation which might follow her round the industry.

'Thank you,' she said simply.

'Our business,' he replied with a quiet sincerity.

It was another trait of the man. As direct as he could be, he was also discreet.

'Quite,' she murmured back.

Both fell silent for a moment, aware of a rare accord. Tory half expected him to follow it up with another request for a date. She was debating her answer when he spoke again.

'In fact, next time we meet,' he suggested, 'let's pretend we don't know each other.'

'I…' Taken aback, Tory took moments to recover before she bristled with offence. 'Good idea!'

'Believe me, it will be,' he replied, tone cryptic.

It was as if he were up to something. But what?

Tory didn't get the chance to probe further as he signed off with the words, 'I'll be thinking about you till then.'

Tory was left holding a dead line. She stared at it, confused by the mixed messages he was sending. He wanted to forget about her *and* think about her. It didn't make sense.

Or maybe it did. She, too, wanted to forget what had happened between them. She didn't want to lie in bed, night after night, reliving his kiss, his touch, their coming together. But she did.

It was like having a film running continuously in her head. Each time she saw it, remarkably it seemed more real, more beautiful. Each time it left her shot with physical longing.

She felt like a voyeur, not recognising herself in the girl who twined her body with Lucas's and licked the sweat of his skin and spread her legs wide and drew him into her and moaned in pleasure as he penetrated her.

She wanted to destroy the film yet she kept viewing it. She tried to edit it, to have the girl reluctant, to make the man weak, inept, but she couldn't sublimate the truth, couldn't wipe out the image of Lucas as lover, strong and powerful, encountering no resistance as she accommodated his flesh and moved for him and rose to him and welcomed each thrust of pleasure until he finally took her, groaning her name as he staked his claim.

No one had ever possessed her like that. And somehow she knew no one else ever would. She didn't call it love. She *wouldn't* call it love. But whatever it was, it still frightened her witless.

Forget they'd ever met? If only she could.

CHAPTER NINE

'HE MUST be joking!' cried Amanda Villiers as they drew up beside a dirt track where the group from *Vitalis* was already waiting.

The co-ordinator from the outdoor activity centre had just announced that they were to walk the rest of the way, carrying their luggage.

Tory wasn't the only one hiding a smile as Amanda's designer suitcases were unloaded from the boot. They had been told to travel light—no more than a rucksack of essentials—but Amanda had chosen to disregard this instruction.

'How far is it?' someone asked.

'Not far.' The driver smiled briefly. 'Two miles, maybe.'

'Two miles!' shrieked Amanda with unfeigned horror. 'I can't carry these two miles.'

'No,' the co-ordinator agreed, but didn't offer any other comment.

Instead he began to explain that they were to proceed in pairs with an assigned member of the other group, leaving at three-minute intervals.

So Amanda directed at Tory, 'You'll have to take one of these.'

If she'd begged or even asked politely, Tory might have given it some consideration, but Amanda had been particularly bloody to her over the last two days and, now they'd left the offices of *Toi* behind, she no longer felt any need to go along with her.

'No, I won't,' she answered simply. 'You shouldn't have packed so much.'

'What?' Amanda obviously couldn't believe her ears.

'Didn't you read the booklet?' Tory ran on, positively enjoying her rebellion.

Amanda visibly fumed but to no avail. Tory's name was called out and she departed without a backward glance, accompanied by her 'twin' from the other team.

He introduced himself as Richard Lake, the features editor for *Vitalis*. It was the same role Tory was pretending to fill for *Toi*, and as they fell in step he wasted no time in quizzing her on her experience. When she revealed she'd worked at *Toi* just one short week, he initially looked cheered by the fact, then more pensive.

'Someone must rate you,' was his eventual comment. 'At *Vitalis* we've been told to limp on with the staff we have until M day.'

'M day?'

'Merger day.'

'You've been told, then,' Tory said somewhat foolishly.

It drew a sharp glance. 'Not for definite, no, but you obviously have.'

'I...' Tory tried to backtrack. 'Not really. Just speculation, that's all.'

He looked unconvinced and, with a resentful tightening of the lips, forged ahead of her.

Tory sensed the weekend was going to be somewhat tense if everyone shared the same paranoia. She supposed it would make for a better documentary although she was already having ethical reservations about spying on these people.

Not that it was being done surreptitiously. In the literature on the weekend, it had stated in the small print that much of the trip would be videoed and, when they'd disembarked from the minibus, there had been one of the centre workers, dressed in one of their distinctive green uniforms, wielding a camera in the background.

Tory was willing to guess it had been trained on a querulous Amanda but it was debatable whether Amanda had noticed it. Surely she wouldn't have behaved so pettishly if she had?

Tory wondered how Amanda was surviving the walk. It wasn't particularly rough terrain but, to someone unused to exercise, it could prove arduous.

Richard, Tory's own companion, had started off at a cracking pace but, after the first mile, showed definite signs of flagging. Tory, on the other hand, was more prepared through weekly aerobics classes, squash-playing and windsurfing.

'Let's stop for a moment,' Richard suggested as they came to a wooden stile.

'Why not?' Tory wasn't tired but she could see he was suffering. 'New boots?'

He glanced up from loosening his laces and decided she was being sympathetic rather than gloating as he admitted, 'Brand spanking new. Had to buy them because I had nothing else... Do you go walking?'

He regarded her scuffed boots with some envy.

'I spent a holiday, two summers ago, tramping round the Lake District with a friend.'

'Strictly a city man myself.' He made to take one boot off.

'I wouldn't unless you have plasters,' advised Tory. 'You may struggle to get it back on.'

'I suppose you're right,' he conceded. 'Best get going. Perhaps you'd set the pace.'

'Sure.' Tory climbed over the stile and started trudging up the next field, keeping a wary eye on some rather loudly mooing cattle.

She was relieved for a limping Richard when they reached the centre. A collection of old stone buildings, it was positioned on top of a hill. In its driveway were the two minibuses which had brought the groups from London.

There was a reception committee of uniformed staff waiting for them at the entrance. Tory didn't expect to recognise anyone and just stopped her jaw from dropping when she did.

Fortunately she was too shocked to speak and possibly betray them both.

Lucas Ryecart was totally composed, of course, but then *he* obviously expected to see *her*.

'I'm Luc.' He introduced himself in the same fashion as the others had. 'I'll be acting as an observer this weekend.'

'Pleased to meet you,' Richard murmured in polite return.

Tory didn't manage any greeting but her heart was beating so loudly she imagined the whole world could hear it. As well as shock, she'd felt a rush of pleasure at seeing him again. It seemed she wasn't cured at all.

A smile played on Lucas's mouth as he added, 'We'll speak later.'

He directed the comment to both of them, but his eyes dwelled on Tory, passing a silent message on.

Then a woman from the centre claimed their attention, leading them to their sleeping quarters. Tory followed on automatic pilot, nodding at the whereabouts of washing facilities and dining areas as they passed by on their way to the dormitories.

Assigned a bottom bunk in a room for six, Tory slumped down on it the moment the woman departed with Richard. She made no move to unpack her gear but sat hugging her knees and trying to come to terms with Lucas's sudden materialisation.

All week she'd worked hard to get him out of her head while every night he'd chased through her dreams and fantasies. Now here he was, large as life and irrepressible as ever.

It made sense now, of course, that last telephone conversation they'd shared. They were to pretend they didn't know each other next time they met. Next time being this time. He'd been preparing her.

But why? Why not tell her straight he'd be here, masquerading as one of the staff? Weren't they meant to be on the same side, working for the same aim?

The answer seemed obvious and any pleasure at seeing him again went sour. He didn't trust her. Not even on a professional level. He'd given her his pet project and then had second thoughts about her capabilities. She felt both hurt and angry.

Her face must have reflected this as another arrival was shown into the dormitory and asked, 'Are you all right?'

'Yes, fine,' Tory lied and began finally to unpack her rucksack.

'I'm not,' the woman continued. 'Bloody forced march! I'm Mel, by the way.'

'Tory,' offered Tory.

Mel looked disconcerted. 'Not especially. Why do you want to know?'

It took Tory a moment to realise they were talking at cross purposes. 'No, sorry, you've misunderstood. My name's Tory—short for Victoria.'

'Oh, right.' The other girl laughed at her mistake. 'I thought for a mad moment you were a recruiter for the Conservative Party. Can't abide politics, myself. Or politicians. Greasy bunch, the lot of them.'

Tory thought that a rather sweeping statement but smiled all the same.

'I take it you're with *Toi*,' enquired Mel.

'Yes, Features Editor.' Tory had said this so often she almost believed it herself.

'I'm Advertising Sales for *Vitalis*,' relayed Mel, 'or I was when we left the office.'

'You've been promoted?' Tory queried.

'I wish.' Mel pulled a face. 'No, I just reckon no one can count on being who they were before this weekend.'

'You think it's some kind of test.'

'What else?'

'A bonding exercise prior to *Toi* and *Vitalis* merging.'

The suggestion drew a sceptical look from Mel. 'You believe that?'

Tory shrugged rather than express another opinion. She wasn't there to stir things up.

'No, it's survival of the fittest,' ran on Mel, 'or maybe the sanest after a whole weekend of closed confinement. Still, there might be some compensations. Some pretty *fit* instructors, did you notice?'

'Not really.' Tory had been too busy noticing Lucas.

'Don't tell me—you're engaged, married or blind?' Mel bantered back.

Tory shook her head, joking back, 'Single but choosy.'

'*Very*,' agreed Mel, 'if Mr America didn't do anything for you.'

Tory might have known it. Of all the men at the centre over whom Mel could have drooled, it had to be Lucas that had caught her eye.

'You must have seen him,' she ran on. 'Dark hair. Sexy

mouth. Come-to-bed eyes. And when he spoke, oh, God, I swear I fell in love right then and there!'

Mel was exaggerating, of course. At least Tory assumed she was. But it didn't help Tory, knowing other women were just as susceptible to him.

'Yes, the weekend is definitely looking up,' Mel observed with a wicked smile.

Tory felt a great pang of jealousy. She looked at Mel, tall, blonde and more than passingly pretty, and wondered if she were his type. Probably.

Probably they all were. Every woman silly enough to fall for amused blue eyes and a handsome face.

'You're welcome to him!' she told Mel and nearly believed it herself.

'Girl, you don't know what you're missing. Still, I'm not complaining. The less competition, the better. What are the rest of your team like?'

Tory wasn't sure what Mel was asking—for a rundown of their personalities or their appearance. 'I don't know them that well. I only joined the magazine this week.'

'I see.' Mel gave her an appraising look. 'No point in asking pointers on how you put up with your cow of an editor-in-chief, then?'

'Not really, no.' Tory had no inclination to defend Amanda.

'Because I've heard she's the front runner to be El Supremo,' confided Mel, 'of the new hag mag.'

Hag mag? That was a new one on Tory as she speculated on how Amanda would cope with Mel's outspokenness. Not a relationship that promised much mileage, she thought.

'You could try laughing at her jokes,' suggested Tory, 'while practising the words, "Yes, Amanda, no, Amanda, three bags full, Amanda".'

'God, that bad?' Mel rolled her eyes. 'How do you put up with it.'

Tory shrugged, suggesting indifference. She could hardly explain how temporary her role in *Toi* was.

Mel continued to gaze at her curiously and Tory worried a little if here was someone smart enough to blow her cover.

Further conversation, however, was curtailed by the arrival of more course members. They came limping in at intervals, and talk revolved around sore feet, uncomfortable beds and pointless exercises. Tory hoped the bunk left unoccupied longest was for someone other than Amanda, but that hope was dashed when she eventually made an entrance, complaining bitterly at the ruination of her new designer boots and jeans. She made no mention of the scruffy old backpack she was carrying but it wasn't hard to work out that it was on loan from the centre, a condensed replacement for all the suitcases she'd packed.

Fortunately she moaned to Sam Hollier, Tory's erstwhile assistant, and contented herself with shooting Tory venomous looks until the dinner bell was rung.

The meal of pasta and salad was well cooked and put people in better spirits. It was still very much a case of them and us, however, with the staff from *Toi* seated round one bench table and *Vitalis* grouped round another.

At the end of the room sat the centre staff in their distinctive green sweatshirts. Tory risked a quick glance in their direction and saw Lucas engaged in conversation with an athletic-looking girl in her mid-twenties. Tory's mouth thinned. Trust him to home in on the prettiest member of staff.

She tore her eyes away and dragged her mind back to the task in hand. She wasn't here to monitor Lucas Ryecart's charm rating but to concentrate on the documentary-making potential of their situation.

There was certainly a general air of dissension about the weekend, some already refusing to go caving or climbing if either activity was suggested. All considered the course to be pointless.

Tory had doubts, too. She could see the theory behind it. If the magazines did merge, the staff from each would have to be integrated so meeting on neutral ground might help reduce suspicion and rivalry. Currently, however, it was serving to increase paranoia.

After the meal, they were all shepherded into a communal room for what Tom Mackintosh, the head of the centre, described as fun and games. Reactions were mixed. Participants either looked tense, regarding it as the start of 'testing', or feigned indifference.

For their first task, they were forbidden to talk before being given a piece of paper with a number, from one to twelve, on it, and blindfolded. They then had to arrange themselves in a line in ascending order from the platform to the back of the hall.

It sounded simple but wasn't. The only way of conveying a number was to tap it out on people's hands and, though one could quickly find a neighbouring number, it was some time before they devised a method of stamping feet to establish a way of ordering the line. By that time the fun element had kicked in and there was much stifled laughter as they tried to adhere to the silence rule while grasping hands and swapping about and half tripping over each other.

It took longer than they would have imagined but there was a definite sense of triumph when they finally established with hand-squeezing codes that they were in line.

It certainly broke the ice and they followed this exercise by giving, in turn, a brief account of themselves.

The majority talked of themselves in terms of work but a few concentrated on their life outside. Tory decided to avoid spinning any tales she couldn't support and gave out true personal details like her age, single status and interests.

Afterwards they were divided into three groups of four and sent to corners of the room to tackle their next assignment, involving a sedentary treasure hunt of cryptic clues and intricate Ordnance Survey maps. It demanded lateral thinking as well as map-reading, but the real object was to get them to co-operate as a team in order to solve the mystery first. As an added incentive, the prize was a chilled bottle of champagne in an otherwise alcohol-free zone.

Tory was in the same group as Richard, her opposite number on *Vitalis*. He'd mellowed since their earlier walk together and she discovered he was both smart and witty. She was smiling at his jokes even before she became aware of Lucas observing them from a discreet distance. After that she smiled that little bit harder while stopping just short of giving Richard any wrong ideas. Their table didn't win but came a close second and gave each other consolation hugs.

Tory was tidying maps, guard down, when Lucas finally approached. 'I'll show you where they go.'

Tory could hardly refuse the offer and fell in step with him as they walked to a store cupboard at the far end.

'Are you trying to make me jealous, by any chance?' he murmured when they were out of earshot.

Guilty as charged, Tory nevertheless snapped, 'Of course not!'

'Well, you're managing it anyway,' he drawled back.

Tory risked a glance in his direction. He didn't look in the least bit jealous. He looked what he always looked. Too laid-back and handsome for *her* own good.

She was thinking of a suitable put-down when Mel, the sales executive from *Vitalis*, appeared behind them. Tory could guess why.

'Let me take those.' Lucas emptied Tory's hands of the maps, before observing, 'You've dropped something.'

'No, I haven't,' Tory was quick to deny and slower to catch on as he indicated a folded piece of paper on the floor.

'Well, someone has.' Mel bent to pick it up. 'A note, I'd say.'

The penny finally dropped as Tory snatched it from Mel's hand. 'It is mine, actually.'

'Okay, okay.' Mel held her hands up in mock defence. 'I wasn't going to read it. I can guess who it's from, though.'

Tory looked alarmed.

Lucas, however, kept his cool and lifted an enquiring brow. 'You can?'

'Well, I could be wrong—' Mel directed a hugely flirtatious smile at him '—but I'd lay money on it being our Features Editor, Richard. She's definitely caught his eye, haven't you, Tory?'

Under normal circumstances Tory would have objected. She didn't like her name being falsely linked with men. But she left it, relieved that Mel hadn't guessed the true source of the note.

He was still smiling, relaxed as ever, and when Mel began to engage him in conversation Tory took the chance to walk away.

She didn't open the note immediately. She suspected its contents would make her mad and she wanted to be alone when she read it. She didn't get that chance for a while as Tom Mackintosh, the head of the centre, rounded up the day with a little pep talk about the rationale behind the centre's courses before they were served a variety of night-time drinks back in the canteen. This time seating was less polarised with the winners of the champagne remaining vociferously bonded.

It was late when they all trooped off to dormitories. The washing facilities were limited and they took turns. Tory volunteered to go last and was locked in a shower cubicle when she finally unfolded his missive.

She expected it to offer an explanation for his appearance but it was frustratingly brief: 'TRY TO SLIP AWAY. NEED TO TALK. ROOM 12. L.'

While she showered, she debated her next actions. She had only a vague idea where Room Twelve might be—the male and female dormitories were on two different sides of a rectangle with staff rooms on the short side connecting the two. What if she crept along to the end, only to be witnessed going into his room?

She could hear Lucas's voice in her head, saying, So what? And, of course, he was right. According to her research, assignations were not uncommon on these management bonding weekends. Why should anyone conclude their meeting was anything other than this?

She could go now or she could wait till everyone slept and go later. She weighed the options up and decided on now, while she had the alibi of showering to account for her absence from her dormitory.

She quickly towelled herself dry, put on a pair of passion-killing winceyette pyjamas and stuffed her clothes and toilet bag in a cupboard to be retrieved later.

She padded down the corridor, ready with an excuse about looking for a drink if necessary. She discovered Room Twelve to be on the corner. She presumed he'd be expecting her and slipped inside, unannounced.

He was there, but not quite expecting her as he turned to face her, naked but for a towel tied loosely round the waist. From his wet hair it was evident he'd just come out of a shower.

She'd never seen him undressed before. Her eyes went from broad shoulders to a chest matted with dark hair tapering to towel level, and, beyond that, lean, muscular legs. She wasn't conscious of staring until he lifted a mocking brow, seeking her approval.

She should have ducked out of the room at that point. She wanted to. But behaving like an outraged virgin seemed pathetic under the circumstances.

So she stood her ground and, in chilly tones, said, 'You wanted to talk.'

Always perceptive, Lucas observed, 'You're mad with me, right?'

Hopping. But Tory opted for disdain. 'Mad? Why should I be mad? If you want to waste your time, checking up on me, not to mention putting the whole project in jeopardy, that's your business.'

'Mmm, I was afraid you'd see it that way.'

'There's another way?'

He grimaced at her sarcasm before explaining, 'Wiseman Global intended sending an observer to evaluate the course but their man dropped out at the eleventh hour. Chuck asked if I'd go instead. Nothing to do with Eastwich Productions. I apologise, however, if you feel undermined,' he added, almost verging on contrite.

Tory wondered if he really expected her to swallow such rot.

'If that's the case, why didn't you tell me on Wednesday when you phoned? You knew then, didn't you? Hence the "let's pretend we don't know each other" speech,' she recalled, lips twisting.

'Yes, well, I suppose I could have said something,' he conceded. 'To be honest, I was afraid you might not show.'

He gave her a long, steady, sincere look that had Tory questioning if she had the word 'gullible' tattooed on her forehead.

'And Mr Wiseman had no one else he could send?' she retorted smartly.

He hesitated, debating his answer. 'All right, you've got me. I throw in the towel.'

Not literally, Tory hoped, glancing involuntarily to his makeshift loincloth.

He read her mind and grinned slightly before continuing, 'Bad choice of phrase… Still, I admit it. Chuck has a band of yes-men only too happy to go fish for him. I volunteered solely so I could see you again, but, trust me, it had nothing to do with your work at Eastwich,' he ended on an intent note.

He had no need to say more. Tory raised her eyes to his and his gaze said it all. Her face suffused with warmth.

Lucas did nothing to hide his feelings. He'd had her and wanted her again. He wanted her enough to put up with a weekend of hard bunks and tepid showers.

He started to close the gap between them and Tory backed against the door.

'I've got to go,' she garbled out, alarmed by the racing of her own heart. 'They'll be wondering where I am.'

'I expect so,' he agreed with a slight smile.

He made no move to stop her, no move at all, but continued to look at her as if looking were enough.

Tory knew that her own feelings were the real danger. She had to get out of here. She felt the door handle pressing at her back. She just had to reach behind her and turn it.

But it seemed her limbs were paralysed. Even when he raised a hand to cup her cheek, she stood stock-still. Even when the hand shifted to caress her neck, she did nothing. The truth was she wanted this, needed it.

He drew her to him and she went. He began to lower his head to hers and she waited. He covered her mouth with his and finally freed her from passivity.

Still she didn't fight him but, moaning, parted her lips to

accept his kiss, to kiss him back, to taste him as he tasted her, exploring each other's mouths while hands explored each other's bodies.

This time both were stone-cold sober and the heat between them was spontaneous. Her hands slid over his bare back already slick with sweat, twined round the nape of his neck, buried into thick, wet hair while he pulled at her clothes, tugging free buttons to slip inside her pyjama top, seeking the swollen weight of her breasts. A thumb began to stroke and rub her nipple into throbbing life. She groaned aloud. He tore his mouth from hers. She fell back against the door. He pushed her top upwards, and bent to lick and suck on one pink bud of flesh until it ached. She grasped handfuls of his hair, forcing his head away, but only to offer her other peaked nipple to feed his hunger and hers.

When he started to push down the waistband of her pyjama trousers, she let him. She reached for him, too. He was already naked, the towel dislodged. She touched the hard pulse of his manhood and he exhaled deeply. She stroked along the thick shaft and drew pleasure from him as he groaned aloud. He let her touch him until his control began to slip, then he curved his hands under her hips and began to lift her upwards.

It took Tory a second or two to realise he meant to enter her, there, against the door. It took her another to accept that she wanted it, too, wanted him inside her. She put her arms round his shoulders and braced herself for that first loving thrust of sex.

It didn't happen. Wrapped round him, wrapped up in him, Tory had ceased to be aware of the outside world when a loud, ear-splitting ringing suddenly rent the air.

Dazed and uncomprehending in the first instant, she opened wide, alarmed eyes to Luc.

He was already up to speed, swearing aloud, 'Jesus, a fire drill!' as reality rudely interrupted their lovemaking.

Then everything happened in hurried reverse as Luc set her back on her feet and helped her to pull her pyjamas back on while footsteps ran up and down the corridors outside and doors, including their own, were rapped and a voice shouted with some urgency, 'Everybody out! This is not a drill! Everybody out!'

It was hard not to panic but it helped that Luc didn't. He had her dressed, with a warm jumper pulled over her head and a hurried instruction of, 'Go straight out!' in moments before he kissed her hard on the lips and pushed her out of the door.

It closed behind her. She knew she should be following the fleeing mass round her and understood that Luc would be out in the matter of seconds it took him to dress. But she just stood there, waiting for him.

It was one of the centre workers who took her arm and shouted above the uproar, 'For God's sake, get moving!'

He didn't give her any choice as he forcibly dragged her along the corridor to the fire exit at the end. He led her away from the house to join the others already marshalling on the driveway outside. She stood aloof from the group, watching the exit doors, and, when Luc failed to appear, she started walking back towards the building. Someone detained her, a hand grasping her arm. She tried to wrestle free but gave up as a familiar figure finally emerged from the fire exit.

Now dressed in jeans and sweatshirt, he strolled calmly from the building.

In that first instant of relief, Tory wanted to run and throw her arms about him. Fortunately relief was closely followed by sanity as she realised they were surrounded by witnesses. God alone knew if someone had already spotted her emerging from his room.

She turned round instead and walked away, suddenly unable to face him. She knew it was absurd. Five minutes earlier and they'd been about to have sex. She wouldn't call it making love. She couldn't. That took two. But here she now was, acting like a love-struck teenager.

She sought safety in numbers and clung to the crowd as heads were counted and explanations sought and finally given some time later by Tom Mackintosh. It seemed somebody had sneaked back to the day room to have a cigarette and, on finishing, had dropped the butt into a metal bin where it had ignited some waste paper. There had been no real danger, the fire contained within the bin, but enough smoke had been produced to trigger the alarms.

This information was greeted less than enthusiastically by the crowd, most standing shivering in night-wear, and accusing eyes scrutinised faces in the hope of identifying the guilty party.

Tory kept her eyes fixed to ground rather than risk catching Luc's eyes and was taken aback when Amanda Villiers declared, 'Well, far be it from me to go around accusing people, but you were absent for some time, Victoria, darling, weren't you?'

The 'darling' was as poisonous as Amanda's tone and Tory assumed no one would give her any credence but a glance round the others' faces told her otherwise.

At least Tory had the wit to say, 'I don't smoke.'

'So you say.' Amanda clearly didn't take her word as proof.

Tory was formulating another protest when she caught Luc's eye over Amanda's shoulder.

He raised a brow and Tory understood immediately. If she wanted, he would wade in and tell the group she'd been otherwise occupied.

She shook her head in horror. Bad enough that he'd discovered she was a sex maniac. She didn't want the rest of the world knowing it.

She was considering another line of defence when Mel spoke up, 'I saw Tory coming out of the shower room when the alarm went.'

'Mmm.' A sceptical sound from Amanda but she could hardly continue arguing and no one wanted to pursue it anyway when the all clear was given, allowing them to troop back inside.

Tory fell in step with Mel and, when she got the chance, mouthed the word, 'Thanks.'

'No problem.' Mel grinned back at her. 'I did actually see you coming out of a room, just not that one.'

She nodded towards Lucas, a few steps ahead of them.

Tory's face fell and she felt only a little better when Mel promised, 'Fast work—but don't worry, my lips are sealed.'

Of course it had been too much to hope that she hadn't been spotted, emerging from Luc's room. She supposed she should be grateful that Mel thought it a case of casual sex rather than conspiracy which had led Tory to his door.

Later, lying sleepless in her bunk, she wondered if subconsciously it *had* been her real reason to go calling on him. Yes, she'd wanted to know what he was up to. And true, she had been incensed at the idea he was checking on her. But it hadn't taken much for her to suspend hostilities and re-enact their last encounter. And if the fire bell had saved her from going the whole way, she'd surely been willing.

She cringed now when she considered *how* willing. It was as if she'd turned into a different person. With other men, she'd been in control, choosing where and when and how they made love. With Lucas, no thinking or planning went into it. It seemed he just had to touch her and she wanted him. She didn't need words or tender gestures from him. She didn't care how he took her, as long as he did. Passion overwhelmed everything else.

And there was no point in saying she wouldn't let him next time, because she knew she would. No way of her dismissing it as 'just sex', because it wasn't. Ordinary sex, even loving sex with Charlie had never been like that.

It was a need, a hunger, a desperate thing. She still wanted him now. Only pride stopped her slipping out of the dormitory and walking the few yards down to his room.

Pride told her that, for him, she was simply a minor distraction. He was a man who worked hard and consequently played hard. Sex was sport to him, one he happened to be good at, perhaps through practice. Love was something else, quite unconnected.

And she had to give it to him. He never used the word love, never pretended. Right from the beginning, it had been a matter of sex. He hadn't wasted time wining or dining her, impressing her or persuading her. From week one he'd asked her to leave Alex and move in with him. But it had always been clear that sex was the driving force.

So why not go along for the ride? She asked herself that

now as she lay on her bunk, knees drawn up, trying to ignore the ache of longing inside her.

She didn't have to think too hard for the answer. She'd never used the word either. Love. But she'd thought it.

And what if the ache didn't go away? What if it got worse each time they made love? What if it consumed her?

CHAPTER TEN

THINGS were meant to look different in the morning and, yes, when Tory woke to the sound of Amanda grumbling, the previous night took on an air of unreality. She felt tired and irritable rather than frustrated or lovesick as she yawned herself awake and joined the lengthy queue for the centre's temperamental plumbing.

By the time she'd queued for breakfast, she was testy enough to resist any overture.

Not that Luc made any. Tory only knew he was present because, *en route* to her table, she'd briefly caught his eye. He looked as he always did—amused by something, or maybe just life. He certainly showed no signs of regret for his behaviour last night.

Tory looked away quickly and deliberately sat on a bench with her back to him. That was how she planned getting through the rest of the weekend. By ignoring him totally.

That wasn't so easy, of course. He was there ostensibly to observe, and observe he did. Every time she looked round, he seemed to be in view, smiling even when she blanked him.

She was just glad that she was reasonably fit and didn't end up a gasping, sobbing heap in the middle of the centre's assault course like Angela, the sales director from *Toi*. Or be as scared of heights as Sam, and be pressured into abseiling down a cliff-face, only to go catatonic halfway down and have to be rescued by centre staff.

In fact Tory acquitted herself reasonably well in such physical challenges but that hardly endeared her to Amanda who became increasingly vituperative. Tory was careful to react minimally. She wanted no suggestion that she'd encouraged Amanda's frothing at the mouth for the camera.

In fact, Tory was surprised how outspoken most of the

course members were, considering they knew they were being filmed. Even if Tom Mackintosh hadn't announced it at the beginning, the CCTV cameras were easy to spot. But it seemed, after some initial reticence, people just forgot about them.

They were more wary of Lucas himself, watching from the sidelines.

'Who do you think the KGB is working for, then?' speculated Jackie, *Vitalis*'s art director, during team games that evening.

'KGB?' was echoed by Mel.

Jackie nodded towards Luc. 'Killingly Gorgeous Bloke.'

It raised some laughter before Mel suggested, 'Ask Tory.'

Curious eyes fixed on Tory and she actually felt herself go red as she muttered back, 'How should I know?'

Mel grinned mischievously but didn't pursue it; perhaps she remembered Tory had helped her out twice that afternoon when they'd been doing daft things in canoes.

'He keeps watching you,' another girl put in. 'I noticed that when we were abseiling.'

'That's what he's here to do,' Tory pointed out.

'No, *you* specifically,' she added.

'Lucky thing,' rejoined Jackie. 'I certainly wouldn't kick him out of bed.'

Neither would Tory. That was the problem.

Listening to other opinions confirmed what Tory already suspected. Lucas was too popular for his own good—or for hers.

She shrugged, a pretence of indifference, and was relieved when they returned to the task, making a mock-up format for a new magazine. As ideas began to flow and rivalries were set aside, it proved an enjoyable exercise and there was much jubilation in the group when their creation was declared the winner.

They were sitting together later, toasting each other with their prize of champagne, when Lucas and some other staff came to sit alongside, offering them congratulations. By studiously staring into her glass, Tory gave him no openings to address her directly. She knew it might seem childish but she was scared of betraying any emotion.

He, of course, was as relaxed as ever. When Jackie specifically asked him if he worked for the centre or Wiseman Global, he stated neither and, without telling any explicit lies, gave the impression that he was an interested outsider, considering running his own management course.

'Well, darling,' Jackie continued in her flamboyant style, 'if you omit the assault course, abseiling and cold showers, and fill it with hunky, available men like yourself, we'll definitely sign up, won't we, girls?'

This was greeted with general laughter and agreement.

Tory remained aloof but a surreptitious glance confirmed that Lucas wasn't in the least bit disconcerted at being centre of attention.

'I'm honoured by the compliment, ladies,' he drawled back, 'though, the truth is, I'm no longer available.'

A mock groan went round the table while Tory's eyes flew involuntarily to his. He caught the surprise in them and slanted her a smile.

'You're married?' Jackie concluded.

He shook his head. 'Not yet.'

'But considering it?' she added.

He made a balancing motion with his right hand, as if marriage might or might not be on the agenda.

'Who is she, then?' asked Mel.

The same question was burning its way through Tory's brain. Not once had he hinted there was someone else in the background, someone he was serious about.

He glanced towards her once more and, catching the daggers look she was sending, answered circumspectly, 'I can't really say at the moment.'

Tory understood. He meant he didn't dare say. It made her even angrier. Did he imagine she had so little dignity she'd fight over him?

Jackie and the others remained intrigued. 'Is she married?'

'Not to my knowledge,' he replied.

'Someone famous?'

'A model?'

'On TV?'

The suggestions came thick and fast and he scotched them with a brief laugh. 'No, nothing like that. She's just a very private person who wouldn't appreciate me telling the world about her. Especially when I haven't worked up courage yet to tell her how I feel.'

This news was greeted with a collective sigh as the rest obviously viewed him as that increasingly rare type of man—a romantic.

Tory was left biting her tongue in preference to making a scene by denouncing him as the faithless cheat she now knew he was.

When someone asked him, 'What's she like, then?' Tory couldn't sit through any more. Scraping back her chair, she muttered to Mel about being tired and, before she could hear anything about Lucas's other girl, she walked away.

She took refuge in her dormitory and was lying on her bunk, trying and failing to concentrate on a novel, when Mel appeared.

'You okay?' Mel asked.

'Fine,' she answered shortly.

'I just wondered—' Mel hesitated before taking the plunge '—you seemed a little upset when Luc was talking about his girl.'

'Upset?' echoed Tory as if she'd never felt such an emotion in her life. 'Why should I be upset?'

'No reason,' Mel pacified, 'except that after last night—'

'Nothing happened last night!' denied Tory, as much to herself as Mel. 'You may have seen me coming out of his room—'

'No *may* about it.'

'But it was not what you think.'

'No?' Mel raised a sceptical brow.

'No!' denied Tory in resounding tones.

'So you won't mind hearing about his other girl, then?' Mel challenged.

Tory wondered why Mel was determined to twist the knife.

'I couldn't care less,' she claimed.

It wasn't true, of course. Half of her wanted to hear, the other half wanted to scream.

Mel continued determinedly, 'Apparently she's a bit younger than him. Quiet but strong-willed and fairly bright. Sporty. Not very glamorous. More your girl-next-door type. Lovely, though, with a really good complexion and large, soulful eyes.'

The description didn't strike any chords with Tory but why should it? He was hardly going to go out of his way to introduce one girlfriend to another.

Not that *she* was a girlfriend. From recollection he'd never even asked her out—asking her to sleep with him wasn't the same.

'Sound like anyone you know?' added Mel at her silence.

'Why should it?' Tory echoed aloud. 'I mean… I've just met the man.'

Mel looked at her in wide-eyed disbelief.

Tory suddenly wondered if she and Luc had been sussed.

But, no, Mel just went on to shake her head and mutter, 'A case of self-induced blindness, if you want my opinion.'

Tory gave her a quizzical look, as Mel grabbed a towel and wash bag to beat the rush to the shower room.

Later, when she should have been asleep, Tory dwelled over the attributes of Lucas's lady love, as relayed via Mel, and became increasingly convinced that he'd been making it all up as he'd gone along. She remembered the half-smile he'd been wearing when he'd begun his 'true confessions'. She knew that smile, had seen it before. It was the smile that said life was a joke.

And that, she suspected, was what he'd been playing on the others—spinning out a yarn about a fictitious girlfriend to keep them at a distance.

Or could it be the opposite? Tory recalled the women's faces at his tale of romantic love, their wistful expressions at this rare breed of man who was not only handsome and sexy, but true and faithful in character. Was Lucas astute enough to realise just how desirable that made him seem? Even as he'd claimed to be unavailable, had he been casting a net to see if he could land another gullible idiot like herself?

Because that was what she was. She could pretend to be experienced, even convince herself that she knew the score, but leave her alone with Lucas for a minute and she was as easy to take in as a schoolgirl.

She had to face it. A few tender looks from him, a passionate kiss or two, and her heart was racing as if it were true love, when it really was just sex. She only realised afterwards, but by then it was too late.

Best thing was to keep away from him altogether and she managed it at breakfast the next morning which was then followed by a briefing on the day's main event, a ten-mile-round hike and treasure hunt for real. But he was waiting his moment, catching her as she went down to collect some supplies from the kitchen.

'Look, Tory—' he brought her to a halt '—about the other night…'

Tory didn't want to listen. 'Someone's coming,' she hissed at him, simply to get free.

They heard footfalls, making her lie the truth, but he didn't react as she'd hoped. Instead he pulled her inside the nearest room, an empty office.

Tory wrested her arm away, complaining, 'You're going to blow my cover.'

'I don't care,' he dismissed. 'Sorting out things between us is more important.'

'Well, *I* care,' she retorted angrily, 'and I'm the one about to go on a ten-mile hike with these people. If anything happens, I want to be able to trust them.'

His eyes narrowed. 'What do you mean—if anything happens?'

Tory wasn't exactly sure. She just had a bad feeling about this particular exercise.

'Nothing,' she discounted at length. 'Look, I have to go. The minibus will be waiting to take us to the start point.'

She reached for the door handle and he put a hand on her arm once more. 'Meet me when you get back, then?'

'There won't be time,' she pointed out. 'After the debriefing, we have to drive back to London.'

'I could take you,' he offered.

Tory shook her head. 'I have to go on the minibus to get feedback.'

She was still taking this project seriously even if he clearly wasn't.

'Okay,' he conceded, 'so I'll follow you down and meet you off the bus.'

He was obviously determined and Tory was tired of arguing. She settled for saying, 'Won't *she* mind?'

'She?'

'The girl you were telling Mel and the others about.'

His blank look changed to a surprised, then amused one. 'Oh, that girl.'

For a man caught out, he showed no signs of guilt.

'Unless of course you made her up,' Tory suggested tartly.

He raised a quizzical brow. 'Why should I have done that?'

'Who knows?' She no longer did.

'Well, no, she's real enough,' he confessed, grinning slightly, 'but there's no reason to be jealous—'

'Jealous?' Tory cut across him, pride surfacing. 'Me? You think I'm jealous?'

'I didn't actually say that.' He raised his hands in a pacifying gesture.

But Tory didn't wish to be pacified. Much safer to be angry, disdainful.

'Why should I be jealous?' she challenged and, before he might actually answer, ran on rashly, 'I have Alex, remember?'

The words were out before she realised quite what she was saying.

Mr Laid-back suddenly turned into Mr Uptight, grating, 'Alex?'

'Yes.' It was too late to backtrack even if she wanted to.

His eyes narrowed to slits. 'So, tell me, do you happen to know where Alex is this weekend?'

Tory frowned at the question. She did know the answer. Alex was in Edinburgh, trying to patch things up with his wife. But why had Lucas asked such a thing?

Unless he knew, too.

'Do you?' she countered.

She watched his face, the changing expressions, and guessed he did. She waited for him to throw it in her face—that her live-in lover was with someone else.

He opened his mouth to speak, then closed it, shaking his head.

Tory understood. On the brink of exposing Alex, he had decided against it. But why?

Perhaps it suited him—that she maintain some kind of relationship with Alex. It would justify him playing the field in turn.

'Forget it.' He finally opened the door, allowing her to leave.

Tory escaped but with a heavy heart. Why had she mentioned Alex? It made all her other earlier denials seem so many lies.

Pride, she supposed. She hadn't wanted him to think her jealous. Forget that she was—achingly, gnawingly, spectacularly—at the idea of him with some other girl.

She felt like a schoolgirl again, in love for the first time. Only she never had been. Not with Charlie or anybody else. She finally understood that. Because love wasn't the warm, pleasant feeling she'd imagined it was.

She caught the drift of her thoughts and brought herself up sharply. She had to stop this. What she felt for Lucas wasn't love either. It couldn't be. She wouldn't let it be. It was desire, pure and simple, or maybe more accurately lust, less pure but just as simple.

So why didn't she let it burn itself out? Good question. Why didn't she just give way to sexual longing and climb into bed with Lucas the very next opportunity and stay there until the fire was out?

She knew the answer. She was scared, that was why. But she resisted analysing her fear.

She didn't get a chance, anyway, as she collected the supplies and headed for the bus to find her team already boarded and waiting.

Her team? Well, not quite hers. Or even a team. Five of them. Should have been six but it seemed Jessica Parnell, the senior editor from *Vitalis*, had woken up that morning and decided life was too short to scramble over hillsides to hold on to a job she had loathed for at least the last two years. Having had this revealing thunderbolt, she had shared it in no uncertain terms with Tom Mackintosh before calling a minicab to take her to the nearest railway station.

Mel shared it second-hand as they were driven to their drop-off point.

Amanda almost purred with satisfaction. Her dismissal of, 'Bloody prima donna,' however, was too much for Carl, their advertising sales director.

Normally an anything-for-a-quiet-life type, he actually commented aloud, 'Takes one to know one.'

'I beg your pardon,' demanded Amanda with an imperious look.

For once Carl wasn't quelled. 'You heard.'

She'd heard but evidently she didn't believe it. Amanda really wasn't used to opposition. It left her fuming with silent indignation.

To Tory, it was probably the most interesting aspect of the weekend. At the office Amanda ruled *Toi* with an iron fist in an iron glove and had expected to do so at the centre, too. But gradually, as various tasks challenged people's perceptions of themselves—or possibly fatigue and irritability set in—fewer and fewer of *Toi*'s staff were prepared to dance to Amanda's discordant tune. Tory was almost sorry she couldn't return to the office to see if this defiance would continue.

Amanda now complained loudly to Lucy, the somewhat sheepish make-up editor from *Vitalis*, going as far as suggesting that some people were in for a rude awakening on Monday morning, while Carl started to sing loudly and Mel grinned, seemingly enjoying the internecine strife.

So, no, they were not a team, which increased Tory's niggling worry as they were dumped in the middle of nowhere with basic supplies, a compass, one map and a series of clues as to what landmarks they had to capture with the digital camera they were issued.

They had practised map-reading, of course, and each team had a so-called expert. Carl was theirs and did seem to know what he was doing, although from their first step in what was hopefully the right direction Amanda tried to undermine him.

Despite this, they managed to follow the right track, finding the 'bridge over troubled water', a tiny footbridge over a fast hill stream, 'Stonehenge' or a mini version of stone slabs and columns, and 'the last resting place' which turned out to be a couple of wooden crosses in what had been the back garden of an old shepherd's hut on a hill. The names Rover and Robbie could faintly be seen, etched out of the wood. Dogs, they assumed.

They rested there for lunch: beans and sausage cooked over a Primus stove. Amanda, needless to say, slated such food but she still ate her share.

They were well over halfway and beginning to feel good about themselves when the rain started. At first it wasn't heavy and they walked on, quickening their pace slightly, but then it began to come straight down, almost in sheets. On open moorland, with nowhere to shelter, they pressed on. No bitching or complaining now. Breath was saved to battle the elements.

Even Amanda kept going, but she was clearly suffering, with chafing boots and tired legs, and when they were walking along the edge of a slight incline she tripped and rolled. She didn't have far to fall. Tory scrambled down after her in seconds. But Amanda's groans sounded genuine enough and she shrieked as Tory touched her leg, trying to find the source of her injuries.

It seemed she'd smashed her knee against rock as she'd tumbled. How serious, it was hard to tell. No one wanted to peel off clothing in this downpour. But their first attempt to support Amanda to her feet and walk warned them it wasn't a simple sprain.

It was Tory who said, 'We'll have to use the CB to call in.'

Carl was reluctant. 'We'll lose if we do that.'

Tory stared at him in disbelief. 'For God's sake, Carl. The game is over. She's really hurt!' she almost shouted the words at him.

He looked resentful but took out the CB handset from his bag. No amount of fiddling with bands and aerials, however, produced anything more than static. Either it was malfunctioning or the storm had broken up the signal.

Various suggestions followed and were rejected. They could sit and wait for rescue but Carl admitted he'd deviated from their suggested route, opting for a shorter but steeper path, and it could be hours until they were located. Hostile glares were sent in Carl's direction but no one commented aloud. They still had to rely on him to get them back.

Another attempt was made to shoulder Amanda's weight between Carl and Tory. With no alternative, Amanda gritted her teeth and tried to bear it, but the occasional sob still escaped from her. It was hard not to jar her leg and their progress was painfully slow.

Tory wasn't sure they should even be moving Amanda and was relieved when they finally came upon potential shelter. 'Over there in the rock.'

It was more an indentation than a cave, with barely space for two, but they carefully lowered Amanda to the ground while they took stock. It was decided that someone should stay with Amanda while the rest walked back to the centre.

Before anyone volunteered, Amanda spoke up, 'Victoria…I'd like Victoria to stay.'

Tory was taken aback. She'd imagined Amanda would prefer just about anyone else.

She glanced down at Amanda and was awarded an almost pleading look.

'Well?' Carl prompted her for a decision.

'Fine,' conceded Tory with good grace and joked weakly, 'as long as we get the rest of the chocolate.'

'You deserve it.' Mel gave her a commiserating smile and dug out a foil space blanket and torch to hand over before the rest of the party moved on.

Tory tried to make Amanda more comfortable, propping her against a makeshift pillow of their rucksacks before draping the blanket over her. They were already very wet and the wind whipped some of the rain into their shelter, but Tory did her best to shield Amanda from it.

They didn't talk much at first but Tory finally gave way to curiosity. 'Why did you want me to stay? I mean, we haven't exactly hit it off.'

Amanda pulled a face, conceding the point, then said by way of explanation, 'That Mel character loathes me and, as for Lucy, she's such a wimp.'

'So I'm it by default,' Tory concluded dryly.

'Perhaps,' admitted Amanda in a similar tone.

Well, it was honest. Tory had to give her that. She was also quite surprised by how well Amanda was behaving in the circumstances. She was clearly in pain yet now she had something real to complain about she was almost stoical.

'How long do you think before we're rescued?' was all she asked.

'Hard to say.' Tory didn't want to hold out any false promises.

'They may struggle to find us,' added Amanda.

That possibility had occurred to Tory but it seemed important to stay upbeat. 'I think Carl pretty much knows our location on the map.'

Amanda nodded, then commented, 'God, Jessica will be laughing her socks off when she hears about this.'

'Jessica?'

'Jessica Parnell—*Vitalis*'s senior editor. She was right. What the hell are we doing, playing girl scouts at our age?'

'You're not that old,' Tory protested automatically.

Of course she should have known the older woman would come back with, 'How old do you imagine I am?'

Thirty-eight was Tory's guess so she took off five years and said, 'Thirty-three.'

'I wish,' responded Amanda, obviously pleased. But not pleased enough to reveal her real age. Instead she said, 'I've been in the business more than twenty years. It really is true about time, you know, it flies.'

There was more than a hint of regret in Amanda's tone, even a suggestion of vulnerability, but Tory wondered if they weren't just products of their current situation.

'One moment you're the hottest thing in town,' continued Amanda, 'the next you're abseiling down a bloody cliff, just to survive...and what do you have to show for it?'

The question might have been rhetorical but Tory couldn't resist answering, 'A wardrobe full of designer clothes, the chicest of sports coupés and probably a garden flat in Hampstead.'

'Notting Hill, actually—' Amanda smiled briefly '—and, yes, I admit there are compensations... Just don't go thinking they're enough.'

It seemed like well-intentioned advice but Tory wasn't used to that from Amanda. 'Why are you telling me all this?'

Amanda caught her suspicious glance and read it astutely, 'You mean when I'm normally acting like the editor from hell?'

'Something like that.' Tory was surprised by the other woman's self-awareness.

'I'm not sure.' Amanda thought about it before coming up with, 'Maybe I see myself in you if I roll back the film fifteen years.'

Tory managed not to look horrified, although she couldn't imagine herself turning out like Amanda under any circumstances.

'In fact, I'm willing to bet we come from similar backgrounds,' Amanda went on. 'Raised by a single mother. High rise flat in inner-city London. State school. And a burning desire for something better.'

Tory could have denied it. It wasn't an exact blueprint of her early life. But it was close enough.

'Is that so wrong?' she said at length.

'Not at all,' Amanda replied, 'but knowing what you *don't* want out of life isn't the same as knowing what you do. And by the time you work it out, it might already be too late.'

'So what do *you* want?' Tory wasn't convinced Amanda was being genuine.

'In the short term, out of this hole,' Amanda said with a grimace. 'In the long term, what all us career girls really secretly desire—man, home, family.'

For a moment Tory didn't react. She was waiting for one of Amanda's biting, sarcastic laughs to follow. But nothing.

Instead she ran on, 'You can deny that, if you want. I certainly did for years, then one day you wake up and smell the roses. Only by that time, they've all gone—the nice young men who would have married you. And the bastards, the ones you really wanted, they've started to settle down, too, but with younger models,' she finished on a note more rueful than bitter.

Tory didn't know what to say. Not in a million years would she have suspected that an unhappy woman, frustrated by childlessness and loneliness, lay under Amanda's usual diamond-hard exterior. She felt an impulse to comfort but didn't think Amanda would accept it—not even in her current state.

Still, she felt the need to give something back, something of herself, as she finally responded, 'It's hard not to envy people sometimes. I had a boyfriend once—a fiancé, actually. It didn't work out and he went on to marry someone else and have kids. I met him again recently and I suppose I felt envy, but it turned out they weren't as happy as they seemed.'

'Most couples aren't happy,' Amanda observed in return. 'Not truly, deeply, deliriously. Not all the time. But maybe it's enough not to be *un*happy.'

Tory wasn't sure she agreed. 'I think being married and having kids for the sake of it would ultimately make a person more unhappy than being on their own.'

'So speaks a twenty-something-year-old,' Amanda opined. 'See how you feel at forty, assuming you're still alone.'

Tory heard the note of self-pity in Amanda's voice and did wonder if it would be any different for her.

Chances were she'd still be alone.

Not that she saw herself pining for Lucas Ryecart for the rest of her life. There would be other men. Perhaps not quite as attractive or smart. Nor as sexually exciting. But would she want another relationship that was both so intense and so basically shallow again?

Yet there was no point wanting it all—husband, children, home, happy-ever-afters. No point in wanting what she couldn't have.

Maybe she was luckier than Amanda, knowing it wasn't possible, knowing it would be crying for the moon.

She didn't feel lucky, however.

Didn't look it either as Amanda remarked, 'Well, now I've depressed the hell out of both of us, can you think of a way of passing another four hours?'

Intended to raise a smile, Tory managed a weak one before suggesting with irony, 'I-spy?'

'Riveting,' Amanda applauded. 'Bags I start.'

It was as good a way as any to pass time. They followed it with a game of name the film, twenty questions and their choice of desert island discs.

As time dragged and the storm failed to let up, they both began to shiver from cold and gradually lost any enthusiasm for anything but waiting.

An hour became two, then three and Amanda fell into an uneasy sleep, jerking with each inadvertent movement of her bad leg. Tory watched over her, growing concerned that they might have to spend a night outdoors. The rain had ceased some time ago but the temperature was still unseasonably low and she wondered how cold did it need to be before hypothermia set in.

She tried distracting herself from that possibility by planning her documentary of the weekend. She would splice between the staff's lectures and worthy intentions, and the reality of how much "team building" and "attitude-changing" had been effected. Being lost on the moor would give it more dramatic impact, as proof of the centre's poor safety procedures and too exacting demands, but she would be reluctant to use it as a sign of retribution for Amanda, even if she had bitched her way through the weekend.

It was curious to think that underneath Amanda's tough exterior lay deep insecurities. Tory supposed it was the same for most people—a side they showed the world, and a side they kept secret.

Well, maybe not everyone. Involuntarily her thoughts went to Lucas. He seemed remarkably straightforward in his approach to life. He saw something he wanted, he went after it and made no apologies for the fact.

Tory wished in some ways she could emulate him. Be more ruthless, or at least more honest. After he'd tried—and pretty much succeeded—in seducing her on Friday, she'd cut him dead. Yet the truth was she'd loved it. She'd loved every second of those five desperate minutes with Luc. It had only been afterwards that she'd felt bad, seeing her easy surrender as weakness and resolving to resist the next time.

Now she wondered whether it would be simpler just to give in, to accept they were going to have a relationship and let it run its course. It would be brief. How could it be otherwise? Neither of them could commit. But if they both went into it with their eyes wide open, where was the harm?

Tory was still debating the issue when she heard it. A blessed sound. At first dismissed as imagination. How could she hear a car engine when there wasn't a road for miles? But that was what it was, or more precisely they were: four-by-fours, revving up and down gears as they tackled the terrain for which they were built.

Tory shook Amanda gently awake, then scrambled to her own feet, intending to go in the direction of the sound. Only hours of sheltering in one spot combined with wet clothing resulted in a debilitating cramp that had her collapsing back to the ground in agony.

They heard the engines cut and for an awful moment both women had visions of their rescuers searching in the wrong spot before abandoning them. It was with immense relief that they heard the voices drawing nearer.

Neither could now move but they could cry out, which they proceeded to do until they were hoarse from shouting and the first figure appeared through the clearing beyond them.

It was the abseiling coach from the centre, closely followed by three other men.

Tory had eyes for only one of them and he had eyes for only her as he dropped to his knees beside her. 'Are you all right?'

All right? She was absolutely marvellous. They had come. *He* had come.

'Your leg?' Lucas guessed.

Tory realised she was still massaging it. 'It's just cramp. Almost past. Amanda's hurt, though.'

'The medic's taking care of her.'

Tory glanced towards the little group round Amanda. A man she didn't recognise was already cutting off her trouser leg to examine the knee. Carl, their map-reader, had come, too, and was holding a folded stretcher.

'Can you walk?' Lucas added to her.

'I think so.' She let him put an arm round her shoulders and help her to her feet. Her calf muscle protested but she limped a couple of steps before finding herself being literally swept off her feet.

He told the others he was taking her back, then picked his way carefully over the rough terrain, easing them down a slight slope to where the two vehicles were.

He slid her into the rear bench seat. Her rucksack was on the floor. A pair of clean jeans, T-shirt and sweatshirt lay on the bench seat beside her.

'You'd better take off your wet clothes,' he instructed.

She nodded and shivered but didn't seem to have the energy.

He looked askance at her before saying, 'This isn't some clever plan to get you undressed, you know.'

'I know,' she echoed through shattering teeth. Reaction had set in and she felt cold to the bone.

'I'll get the heater on.' He went round to the driver's side to switch on the engine and heaters, before climbing into the back with her.

'Come on, trust me.' He unzipped her jacket. 'I promise I'll behave like a gentleman.'

Tory didn't need this reassurance. She didn't resist as he

slipped off her jacket, then outer layers of damp garments, before helping her into the dry clothes.

'You stay in the back—' he strapped her in '—and try to rest while I drive you home.'

Tory wasn't sure where he meant by home—the centre, the hotel in London or back to Norwich.

'Can we wait?' she asked as he slipped behind the driver's wheel. 'See if Amanda's all right.'

'Yes, okay,' he agreed with some reluctance. 'I'll just turn.'

It took several minutes to manoeuvre the vehicle to face the way he'd come and by that time the others had appeared, carrying Amanda on the stretcher.

Tory could see her knee had been bandaged and she watched as the men carefully eased her into the bench seat of the other off-roader.

'Where are they going to take her?' she asked Lucas as he waved a hand at the others and pulled away.

'Nearest hospital, I imagine. We can telephone the centre later,' he promised. 'For now, I suggest you hang on.'

Tory did just that as the vehicle bumped over the rough terrain and she was jolted to and fro.

It took them almost half an hour to reach what could be described as a road. Even then it was a minor one. Tory tried and failed to work out if they were going east to Norwich or south to London, but she didn't really care. The warmth of the car was lulling her into a state of drowsiness and she didn't fight it. She rested her head against the window and was asleep by the time they reached main roads.

London was her last waking thought but she was wrong.

When she woke, she was too disorientated to know where she was until Lucas came round to help her down to the street outside her flat in Norwich.

She was glad. She wasn't really injured but felt weak and shivery and home seemed the best place to recover.

He shouldered her rucksack, and, with a hand at her elbow, supported her up the steps to the front door. By chance she'd taken her house keys with her to Derby and he dug them out of one of the side pockets. He tried both keys before identifying the correct one, then used the other on her inner door.

Entering the flat, Tory was relieved to find the lights off, suggesting that Alex had yet to return. She could just about cope with this new solicitous Lucas but she suspected the old one was lurking somewhere, ready to emerge if Alex appeared.

As it was, Alex had left enough pointers to his presence. Tory felt tired just surveying the mess of take-away cartons, clothes and books.

'I take it you didn't leave the place like this,' Lucas concluded from her disgruntled expression. 'I'm amazed you put up with it.'

'And you're Mr Clean and Tidy, I suppose,' she snapped rather childishly, resenting the criticism.

'No, but I'm not a slob.' His gaze rested on a pair of male underpants actually lying on the sofa

Tory wrinkled her nose, wondering if they were dirty or not, and resolved to give Alex his marching orders as soon as possible.

'Well, thanks for the lift,' she said before Lucas could make any further comment.

She imagined he'd be dying to get away to his nice clean room at Abbey Lodge.

He ignored her, however, saying, 'You can't have eaten since lunch. I'll make you something.'

'It's all right—' a surprised Tory turned down the offer '—I just want to rest.'

'You have to eat a little,' he insisted. 'Slip into bed and I'll bring you tea and toast.'

'I doubt there's any bread,' she countered dryly. 'Alex doesn't shop.'

She made the comment without thinking.

It almost begged a sarcastic reply. He didn't disappoint, drawling back, 'I wonder what Alex actually does do... On seconds thoughts, don't tell me.'

It could have been a joke but his eyes said not. They narrowed to a point.

'Please don't...' Tory didn't finish the appeal.

He understood, though, switching back to brisk concern. 'Okay, go rest and I'll forage in the kitchen.'

Tory hesitated. She didn't have the energy to keep arguing with him but neither did she have the energy for another bedroom scene with this man.

'Don't worry, you'll be safe.' He read her with irritating accuracy. 'Sharing another man's bed doesn't appeal to me.'

Tory felt her face go red. It was absurd because she had nothing to feel guilty or embarrassed about.

'Ten minutes—' he gave her a gentle push in the direction of the bedroom door '—and I'll expect you tucked up in bed with your teddy and a long-sleeved nightgown buttoned to the throat.'

This time he *was* joking but Tory picked up the underlying message. She had nothing to worry about.

She switched to asking, 'Could you phone the centre about Amanda?'

'Yeah, sure,' he agreed easily. 'Now go on.'

She went through to her bedroom and, with some relief, saw no sign of Alex in the room. At least he had respected her privacy this far.

She undressed quickly, choosing a nightie that, though short, was suitably unglamorous, and climbed into bed, all the time wondering if she should tell him the truth. That Alex did nothing, was nothing. But would he believe such an admission?

She worried the thought round in her head but came to no conclusion before her eyes became too heavy to keep open and she let it all go.

Lucas put the tray he brought down on a chest of drawers and sat for a while on a wicker chair, watching over her. She seemed much younger in sleep and more vulnerable, but he supposed it was an illusion. She certainly had proved herself one of the toughest on the weekend's course.

He recalled his reaction when her party had returned. He'd been waiting for them, of course—waiting for her. They'd been hours late. He'd already insisted the centre call up a search party when they'd finally trooped in, wet and miserable, one of the women breaking down in sobs.

He'd been furious when he'd heard their story. Having abandoned Tory and Amanda, they had lost their bearings for a while and even wasted half an hour taking shelter themselves before continuing. The girl called Mel had tried to reassure him that Tory was fine but it had made no difference. All he'd been able to think of was Tory, her unruly mop of hair plastered wet against a face pinched with cold and her slight figure, drenched and huddling somewhere out there in the dark. He'd joined the rescue mission in his own off-roader, meeting the centre's opposition with a threat to sue if any harm had come to Tory.

His reaction seemed over-dramatic now. She had been in no real danger. She'd kept her head and waited for rescue—exactly as she should have done. But he hadn't been thinking straight; what had been happening to Tory had somehow got mixed up in his head with the accident in which he'd lost Jessica, his first wife.

Not quite the same. Jessica had died in a car crash. There had been nothing anyone could have done, least of all him. He'd been on the other side of the world. But it had still felt like a rerun—as if he'd been going to next see Tory lying on some cold mortuary slab.

He shook his head, a dismissive gesture. He wasn't a man given to premonitions and if this had been one it was way off base. Nevertheless he recognised the emotion involved—a fear of loss.

Not that he had Tory to lose. Not yet, anyway.

CHAPTER ELEVEN

TORY woke in the night to find Lucas asleep on her wicker bedroom chair. She watched him for a while as he had watched her. It was odd: most people looked relaxed in sleep. Lucas was different—he was tense and restless, as if bad things were happening in his dreams.

She watched until she found she couldn't bear it any longer. She didn't consider her next action as she slid out of the bed and came round to his side. She knew not to waken him too suddenly. She put a gentle hand on the nape of his neck, the other on his hand and exerted the faintest pressure.

She thought he would gradually come awake but he reacted instantly, shuddering at her touch and issuing a brief startled cry.

Tory might have retreated but he caught her hand in a hard, almost convulsive grip. Only when he jerked his head back and opened his eyes to see what had woken him did he ease his hold.

Tory wasn't scared. She saw a range of emotions, dread, relief, shame, flitting across his handsome face before the usual mask slotted back in place.

'Bad dream. Sorry.' He finally managed a lazy smile behind which to hide.

But Tory wasn't fooled. 'You get them often, don't you?'

She didn't know how she knew this. She just did.

He shrugged. 'Not really.'

Tory took that as a yes.

'Things you've seen?'

'Partly.'

It was a brief admission. Tory didn't press him further. If he wanted to tell her more, he would.

'I should be going,' was what he said now.

But he made no move. Perhaps he couldn't. She was standing too close.

And Tory didn't want to take a step back because she'd finally accepted. This man was her fate, for good or ill. She was tired of running from it.

She looked at him with solemn, unswerving eyes. She wanted him to take her, cover her body with the hard heat of his, be gentle, be rough, control her, possess her, but ultimately love her. She longed for it even as she acknowledged that loving this man might destroy her—especially if he couldn't love her back.

Lucas held her gaze and understood. Not totally. But enough to know she'd surrendered herself to an inevitability he'd recognised from the beginning. Him and her. Together.

He took her hand and drew her gently down. He put an arm round her waist. She was soft and warm and yielding. His desire for her was immediate but this time he didn't want to rush things.

He waited for her to make the first move. She did so tentatively, a finger tracing the small scar that puckered the corner of an eyelid. Then, braving rejection, she cupped his face with her hands and put her mouth to his.

It was the lightest of kisses, her dry lips on his. Chaste but somehow sexy, too. He had to stop himself kissing her back.

Tory wasn't discouraged by his lack of response. She understood, too. This time she had to make the running, do the seducing.

It wasn't going to be hard. His hands had already left her waist to curve round her hips and his lower body shifted against her in arousal.

She threaded her fingers into his thick dark hair until she could pull back his head slightly and once more put her mouth to his, only this time she slid the tip of her tongue between his lips, moistening them. She withdrew immediately, however, when he began to kiss her back and nuzzled teasingly at his neck, twining her arms round, softly licking and tasting his skin, biting his earlobe with gentle savagery until she felt him draw several deep, unsteady breaths. Then she slid her mouth back to his and stole his breath and his reason as she kissed him with unfettered passion.

Lucas's resolve to take things slowly broke like glass shattering as he thrust his tongue inside her sweet, moist mouth and she twisted in his arms, small firm breasts against the wall of his chest, nightgown riding up, soft bare bottom against the hardness of his groin.

They explored each other's mouths with desperate thirst while their bodies strained to join, be one. All thought was lost in the heat of desire. His hands were everywhere, sliding up her back, round to her breasts, down to her buttocks, between her thighs. Then, still seated, they shifted until she was kneeling, her legs straddling his as he dragged her nightgown over her head and put his mouth to her breasts and began to suckle on her nipples with a hunger matched by the yearning noises she made.

When he finally entered her, it was with gentle, skilled fingers. She was already damp with desire and her body closed round him in spasm, then opened and shut like a flower as he pleasured her to the point of orgasm.

She moaned when he suddenly stopped and pushed her away slightly. Then she opened her eyes and realised.

Lucas had unzipped himself, taking out flesh that throbbed painfully in long denial. She made to touch him, to offer him the same satisfaction, but he caught her hand. He was ready to come and wanted, needed to be inside her.

Tory wanted it, too, shifting with him as he went to the edge of the seat, uncoiling her legs, tilting her hips until he was able to touch his swollen flesh against the soft, moist lips of hers. Then he lifted her slightly to push inside.

Tory didn't expect it. Not the first exquisite pain from the intrusion of his manhood, nor the pleasure that followed. She was gasping with it as he raised her to meet his thrust, bracing herself against his legs and arching back to accommodate him, crying aloud each time he pierced her to the core until they came together in a blend of agony and ecstasy.

She collapsed against him, naked in his arms, stifling a sob of fright that she could feel like this, riven yet complete, fractured yet whole.

He tried to soothe her with gentle kisses, hugging her to him, whispering, 'I've hurt you. I'm sorry. I didn't mean to.'

She shook her head against his shoulder rather than tell him that pleasure overwhelmed her, that love for him was her undoing.

'Shh. Shh. It's okay.' He half carried her to the bed, then lay down beside her, stroking the unruly hair back from her face, brushing a tear away with the back of his fingers. 'Do you want me to go?'

Tory shook her head again and looked at him with sad, dark eyes, unable to express her true feelings.

She wanted him to love her.

He did. After they'd lain together for a while, still on the bed, then wordlessly begun to touch, he loved her the way he knew so well. This time slowly, infinitely gently, undressing to feel the glide of her soft, curving body against the slick sweat of his, learning each part of the other, tasting fingers, toes, the most intimate places until pleasure was a long drawn sigh that left them too high to talk.

Yes, he loved her—if only with his body.

They slept and woke with the sun to make love again and lie, content, in each other's arms. That was how they were discovered.

By Alex.

They had ten seconds warning at most.

Tory heard the outer door opening, thought it imagination, then heard it shutting.

They both heard the tentative knocking on her bedroom door.

'Tory, are you back?' Alex called softly and, eliciting no response, stuck his head round the door.

They weren't caught in the act, but close enough. Tory had managed to sit up, grab a sheet and clutch it to her front. Lucas merely leaned back against the headboard, naked.

Alex took in the scene, too thunderstruck in the first instant to say a word.

When he eventually did, it was a somewhat anticlimactic, 'R-right.'

Tory frowned darkly. She didn't feel anything was right. Spending the night with Lucas wasn't something she'd intended sharing with Alex.

'Boss.' Alex actually nodded in Lucas's direction, before leaving with a 'Excuse me. I think I'll go make coffee.'

'Curious,' drawled Lucas when Alex finally bowed out the door, barely able to hide a grin. 'He took it amazingly well, wouldn't you say?'

'I…yes.' Tory supposed she should explain and turned to do so.

'Perhaps he's gone off searching for a loaded shotgun. What do you think?' Lucas lifted a brow in her direction.

'I think you know,' Tory countered.

'Know what?'

'That Alex was up in Edinburgh, hoping for a reconciliation with his wife.'

'But if *you* knew—' Lucas cut across his own question and, staring hard at her, answered for himself, 'You couldn't care less, could you? Which probably means one of two things—you and Alex are finished, or you and Alex never started.'

'The latter.' Tory didn't see any point in keeping up the pretence. She'd used Alex merely as protection against ending up in bed with Lucas—pretty ineffective protection as it turned out. 'He was broke and homeless so I took him in until he could find somewhere else.'

'Like a stray dog?' Lucas commented dryly.

'Quite,' Tory agreed, 'only a dog would probably be more house-trained.'

Lucas smiled at the acerbic comment. It wasn't directed at him, after all.

'So has he found somewhere?' Lucas was still not happy at the idea of Alex's proximity, however platonic the relationship.

'No, and I can hardly kick him out now.' She sighed in

exasperation. 'Not if we're going to get any sort of promise out of him to keep quiet.'

'About?'

'You and I. In bed. Together.'

She spelled it out for him although she didn't really think it necessary.

He astounded her by replying almost casually, 'Do we have to keep it quiet?'

'Yes, of course. I can't possibly go on working at Eastwich with everyone knowing that you and I are…' She searched for the right words.

'Are?' he prompted and when she didn't come up with anything, suggested, 'Living together?'

'We're not.'

'We could be.'

Tory stared at him in surprise. He'd asked her before but that was so she'd move out on Alex. Now that was hardly necessary.

'Why not?' he added simply, and, catching her chin with one hand, tried more effective persuasion.

The kiss quickly threatened to get out of control and Tory pulled away, shuffling to the other side of the bed to drag on a T-shirt and jogging bottoms. She didn't need sex clouding the issue.

He followed suit, dressing in his clothes from last night, but all the time talking her round. 'You could come stay with me. I've bought an apartment in town. You could keep this place and sublet it to Alex. You can always get the sanitation department in when he vacates,' he finished on a wry note.

'I don't know.' Tory wasn't averse to the idea. She wanted to be with Lucas. But it seemed a giant step. She'd never lived with a man before, not even her ex-fiancé.

He came round the bed to take her in his arms and, smiling down at her, ran on, 'I have nice clean habits, always replace the top on the toothpaste and put the toilet seat back down.'

It wasn't the most romantic of propositions but it made Tory smile and she nodded, thinking she could later change her mind.

She should have know better, of course. With Lucas things tended to happen yesterday.

'You finish dressing and I'll go speak to Alex,' he announced and padded out to the living room, still in his bare feet.

When she later emerged, feeling a little shy, it was to find the two men chatting over a breakfast of beer and corn chips—all that Alex had bought in—having already settled arrangements.

Tory scarcely believed it and remained much in the same state until four days later when she moved into Lucas's trendy loft apartment sited in a warehouse by the river.

For a while it continued to seem unreal to her, eating and sleeping and rising with Lucas before each going off in their separate cars to Eastwich, careful to maintain distance. That proved easier than she could have hoped, as Alex kept a discreet silence before eventually leaving for a new job with BBC Scotland, and his impressive replacement plus a new Lucas—appointed programmes director made contact unnecessary between her department and senior management. Given an almost free hand, she was increasingly confident about her documentary on the so-called bonding weekend and had followed it up by actually interviewing some of the participants—including Amanda who had chucked in her job to fulfil a long-held ambition to write a novel.

She still worked alongside Simon but he was deeply involved in his own project and, with Alex gone, had turned into a demon workaholic with no time to be curious about Tory's private life any more.

That life was something else. At home, they laughed a lot, Lucas and she, and talked endlessly, greedy to know each other, their thoughts, dreams, fears and failures. She learned what those occasional nightmares were about—sights witnessed, the dead and dying, bombs missed, the bullet that hit, during his time as a correspondent. She reciprocated with tales of her childhood—ordinary everyday horrors of maternal abandonment followed by reconciliation, good times with her mother's boyfriends, bad times with not so nice ones. She wasn't looking for sympathy and neither was he. They were explanations of how they had come to this point, the events that had shaped them before they had met.

He cooked and she ate. They shopped together. He fixed things and she tidied. Someone else cleaned. They went out at times but mostly stayed in. They made love, often.

In time it became normal life. She stopped analysing it and worrying there was no future in it and just lived it.

And was happy—deliriously, amazingly, joyfully happy for four wonderful months—until one day the sense of unreality returned.

Lucas noticed her distraction straight away, but wasn't sure if he wanted to discover the cause. He just knew that he'd made her happy all these months and suddenly she wasn't. She continued to make love and let him hold her when it was over and fall asleep in his arms, but when the day came she was restless and anxious and evasive, and, like a coward, he didn't ask why.

A week passed before Tory finally told him. She'd considered concealing it as long as possible but that seemed dishonest.

'There's something you should know,' she announced over the dinner table, then followed it with a lengthy pause.

She'd been rehearsing the words all day but getting them out was something else. She half expected him to comment, *That sounds ominous*, but instead he sat, eyes fathomless, mouth unsmiling. He couldn't already know, could he?

No, she was being fanciful. She decided to tell him the whole story in the hope he might understand and at least forgive.

'When I was a child,' she began quietly, 'I had leukaemia. I was ten and I was treated with a combination of chemotherapy and radiotherapy which—'

'What are you saying, Tor?' Lucas's face was ashen. 'The cancer's returned?'

'No. No, nothing like that. I'm completely cured of it,' Tory assured him hastily. 'I'm sorry. I'm telling this badly…' She took a deep unsteady breath before going off on another apparent tangent. 'Do you remember outside Charlie and Caro's, when I said I'd never have children?'

He nodded, blue eyes fixed intently on her.

'The thing is—' she licked dry lips '—such treatment for cancer has the side effect of making people infertile.'

She paused, giving that fact a chance to sink in. A range of emotions passed over his face, too quickly for her to really read, before he murmured, 'The way you said it, I thought it was a lifestyle choice.'

'I probably gave that impression,' she admitted, 'but, at the time, I didn't feel obliged to go into detail.'

'And since?' he challenged.

Tory hung her head a little. She'd had several chances to tell the truth but had ducked them. 'I was afraid you'd dump me.'

'Because you couldn't have children?' An angry edge had crept into his voice. 'You don't think much of me, do you?'

'Charlie Wainwright dumped me,' she said in her defence.

'That's why you broke up?'

'Pretty much.'

He frowned darkly. 'I suppose you kept it from him, too.'

She nodded. 'At first. But then I didn't see us as a long-term thing.'

'You became engaged,' he reminded her heavily.

'We were at a New Year's party at his parents'.' Tory wanted him to understand how it had been. 'Loads of people there and, out of the blue, Charlie proposes in front of them all. I should have said no, I accept that now.'

Lucas also knew her well enough. 'Only you didn't want to embarrass him?'

She gave a nod, before conceding, 'I guess I fancied it a little, too, the whole package. Up till then Charlie's mother had been pleasant enough to me and his father was really nice and there were so many of them, Wainwright cousins and uncles and aunts. You felt it was a real family, that you'd almost be part of a dynasty… Do you know what I mean?'

'I should.' Lucas gave a dry smile. 'I was an in-law for four years, remember.'

'Yes, of course.' Tory had momentarily forgotten his first wife had been Charlie's sister.

'I was similarly seduced,' he admitted, 'being also an only child from a single parent set-up. But the Wainwright clan can be claustrophobic after a while, and too dependent.'

Tory realised he was referring to his own experience with the Wainwrights and raised a questioning brow.

'When I married Jessica,' he went on to explain, 'I was earning a relatively modest salary as a correspondent. She couldn't manage to live on it, nor did she want to, and she couldn't see why we had to when her parents were willing and able to supplement it, not to mention my wealthy stepfather… Call it male pride but I didn't like taking handouts.'

A shrug dismissed it as any big deal but his tone had said something else. Like all marriages, his and Jessica Wainwright's had been less than perfect.

'I appreciate that,' Tory said supportively.

He gave her a brief smile. 'One of life's ironies, I suppose, that I eventually did make it, but at the time money was our greatest source of conflict.'

'But you were happy, by and large?' Tory asked.

'Mostly.' It was a measured response, qualified by, 'Not the way I've been with you… You know I'm in love you, don't you, Tor?'

It was the first time he'd used the word love. Another of life's ironies. A week ago she would have wept with joy at it.

'Don't, Luc!' She knew he might take it back all too soon. 'Not till I'm finished saying what I have to say.'

'I thought we had. You can't have children,' he stated baldly. 'I can live with that.'

It wasn't what Tory wanted to hear.

'I can't,' she replied quietly.

His eyes narrowed. 'I don't follow.'

'I…let me explain it all,' she ran on. 'So Charlie and I got engaged and I tell him the truth next day. I don't know what I expected. At any rate, *he* couldn't live with it. His branch of the Wainwright family depended on him, so I let him off the hook.'

Lucas saw her eyes reflect painful memories and reached across the table to cover her hand with his. 'Well, I for one am glad you did. Who needs kids?' He made a dismissive gesture.

It cut through Tory like a knife. She hadn't finished her story but she couldn't now. It was pointless, unfair even.

'So we haven't a problem?' He raised a hand to cup her cheek.

The tenderness in the gesture almost undid her. But he was right. *We* didn't have a problem. *She* did. Not his fault at all.

'No,' she agreed.

'We can go on as we are,' he added.

Tory could have nodded. So much easier to lie. But she suddenly felt sick to her stomach.

'Excuse me.' She rose to her feet as she realised she was actually going to be sick. 'I have to…'

She couldn't think of any invention so she just took to her heels down the corridor to the bathroom of steel and glass. She didn't bother locking the door. Making it to the bowl in time seemed more important.

When Lucas tracked her down, she was still leaning over the sink, the cold tap running as she washed her mouth out. She sensed him behind her and glanced into the mirror to catch his image.

'I can't say I've ever had that effect on a woman before.' Lucas hid his true feelings behind humour.

'It's not you.' She straightened and immediately felt dizzy.

He saw her sway and, catching her arm, led her to a window-seat. 'Just the prospect of continuing to live with me.'

She shook her head. 'I do love you,' she admitted softly. 'I just…just feel trapped.'

'You're lying,' he accused. 'Trapped doesn't come into it, not when you love someone.'

There was a bitter note to his voice that Tory had never heard before. Perhaps she deserved it but she really couldn't cope with acrimony in her current state.

Tears sprung to her eyes and slowly, soundlessly, slid down

her face. She didn't look at him but she heard his exasperated sigh.

'For God's sake, don't cry on me, Tor… Here.' He handed her a tissue from a box on the shelf.

She used it to wipe her tears but more just replaced them. It wasn't the first time in the last week that she'd been a helpless weeping mess—or the first time she'd thrown up.

'Look, I'm sorry—' he bent to kneel at her side '—but I've let down enough women gently to read the signs. I need you to be straight up and honest with me. Just say the words: I don't love you, Luc. Then one of us will pack a bag—me, for now—and we'll shake hands and wish each other well.'

He tipped her chin up so he could see her face. She tried really hard to make it easy on them both. Got as far as 'I don't lo…', then couldn't go on.

He must see the truth in her eyes, anyway. She adored him. Was absolutely, irrevocably, painfully in love with this man.

'Please don't…' She appealed for him to understand.

Lucas didn't but he still put his arms round her and held her and rocked her until her crying subsided.

Tory clung to him, her resolve weakened by his show of compassion. She couldn't leave him. Not today. Tomorrow, maybe. Or some time later. When it showed.

For now she wanted to go on loving him, making love to him as, tears dried, she turned her head and sought his mouth with hers.

Lucas let her kiss him. Began to kiss her back. Lifted her up and carried her to their bed. Sought oblivion in her sweet, slender body. Found it too for a few precious moments.

Then he lay there, watching her catch her breath, rediscovering for the hundredth time how beautiful she was to him, and said words he promised himself he wouldn't.

'Stay with me, Tor—' He just stopped short of begging. 'Give it another chance. I'll—'

Tory put a hand to his mouth, unable to bear it and finally used the truth as a weapon to stop him.

'I'm pregnant.'

She didn't add to it, didn't need to. It hung between them like an exploded bombshell that left silence in its wake.

This time the emotions crossing his face were all too readable. Shock. Disbelief. Anger.

'Run that past me again,' he demanded at length.

She repeated simply, 'I'm pregnant.'

'You can't be.' Not half an hour earlier she'd told him exactly that. He sat up away from her in the bed. He couldn't look at her and think straight.

Tory sat up, too, leaning back against the pillows.

'I know I can't be, but I am.' She'd found out this week, although her body had been showing the signs for months. 'The doctors were wrong all that time ago or maybe it was a chance in a million and I got lucky.'

'Lucky?' He glanced round to challenge her choice of word.

'Yes.' It was how she felt, even now when his, 'Who needs kids?' had told her how *he* would feel. 'I've spent half my life thinking I'd never have children and now this.'

'You're keeping it?' he added.

'Yes.' She'd never considered otherwise. 'I didn't plan it but now it's happened, I'll live with it. That's the reason I'm leaving. I can't and don't expect anything from you, Luc.'

They had once briefly discussed contraception. He'd offered to be responsible and she'd claimed to have it covered. The mistake had been hers.

He twisted round fully and misread the mute apology on her face. 'It's not mine, is it?'

Tory hadn't anticipated such a question. Wishful thinking? Or did he genuinely believe she'd been unfaithful to him?

She shrugged. 'If that's what you'd prefer.'

'Of course it isn't!' His voice rose with his temper.

But Tory felt too emotionally fragile for a slanging match. She shifted to the edge of the bed and, picking up his discarded shirt as a shield, stood up.

He followed, making no attempt to hide his nakedness. In fact, he took the shirt from her nerveless fingers and threw it on the bed. Then he stared at her, down at the slight curve of her belly.

Tory trembled at his intensity then actually flinched when he put the palm of his hand above the place where their baby was growing.

'It's mine now.' He stroked her flesh.

The most intimate of acts without being remotely sexual. 'I—I don't understand.'

'You're mine,' he told her, 'so it's mine. Simple. Just like I'm yours. What happened before we were together has no significance.'

Tory finally caught up. He thought she'd come to him already pregnant. And now, here he was, lying through his teeth—she knew fine he hated the idea of her with another man—so he could keep her.

'I do so love you, Lucas Ryecart.' She wanted him to know that. 'But it's not going to work. "Who needs kids?" Remember? That's what you said less than half an hour ago.'

His brow creased, as if he couldn't recall ever thinking such a thing, far less saying it, even as he admitted, 'Okay, I said it. But what do you expect? The girl I'm planning to marry has just told me she can't have children. So I tell her I want four? I don't think so.'

'*Marry?*' Tory repeated in a slight daze.

'The sooner, the better, don't you think?' he countered.

Tory still looked at him in disbelief. 'Isn't that rather conventional?'

He grimaced. 'These days conventional is: the man runs out on the women, leaving her holding the baby. I'm assuming that's what he's done.'

'Who?'

'Whoever.'

Tory could have been really mad with him but for the facts a) he was willing to look after her and the child, regardless, and b) she loved him, also regardless.

'My last lover was a sports commentator who worked for ITV,' she began to recount.

'I don't think I want to hear this.'

'Well, tough! Just listen. We had a brief, rather tepid affair that ended amicably when he went off for a month to cover the World Cup.'

'But that was a couple of years ago?'

'Quite, and I'm three months pregnant.'

He looked confused but Tory decided to wait until the penny dropped by itself and, feeling a bit absurd arguing naked, went to pick up her clothes from the floor.

Lucas watched her dressing, then dressed too, but on automatic pilot as the true situation dawned on him.

'It's my baby.' It was a statement this time.

Tory turned and awarded him a somewhat cheeky grin. ''Fraid so, but there's always plastic surgery.'

'It's not funny.' For once Lucas wanted a serious conversation.

But Tory felt skittish. He'd asked her to marry him! He'd asked her to marry him while thinking she was having someone else's baby! What other love token did a girl need?

'So why did you let me believe otherwise?' he demanded, trying to remain angry with her.

'Not guilty, your honour,' she threw back. 'I said, "I'm pregnant." You said, "It's not mine, is it?" I rest my case… I'm starving. Fancy some supper?'

He looked ready to explode at the change of subject but Tory was too happy to care as she walked back through the living area to the kitchen beyond. All week she'd fretted over his reaction. She still wasn't sure precisely what it was but telling her he loved her was certainly an improvement on what she'd visualised.

He trailed her through, still arguing the toss. 'But why else keep it a secret? Why not tell me earlier? You knew days ago, didn't you?'

'I thought…' she paused to sort it out in her own head '…you'd imagine it was deliberate. That I'd got pregnant to trap you. I felt bad, too. You'd made it plain you weren't planning on children and I said I had it covered. I really did think it was impossible, you know?'

He nodded, accepting her word, and realised how each had

misread the other. 'In point of fact, kids were part of my five-year plan.'

'Five-year plan?'

'First year you live with me. Second year, I convince you to marry me. Third and fourth we consolidate. Fifth, we reproduce.'

He ticked each off with a finger and Tory was left wondering if he really could have thought that far ahead.

'I've wrecked that, then.' She grimaced in apology.

'So, things will happen a little quicker.' He shrugged and, coming round the side of the breakfast bar, put his arms round her waist from behind. 'And money isn't a problem so you can choose whether to take a career break or hire a good old British nanny or work part-time if the boss is amenable,' he ended on a wry note.

'And is he?'

'Very.'

It was banter but Tory added more seriously, 'Is he really? To fatherhood, I mean.'

'Hell, yes.' He grinned back. 'If I wait much longer, I'd be too old to swing a baseball bat.'

'Cricket bat, you mean,' she couldn't resist correcting. 'Anyway, it could be a girl.'

'Either one will suit,' he replied and Tory didn't have to see his face to know he was smiling.

She turned in his arms all the same and reached up to kiss him on the cheek and say, 'Thank you.'

He slanted her a quizzical look. 'What was that for?'

'Making it all right.' Tory still couldn't believe her luck.

'All right?' he echoed and laughed aloud. 'It's goddamn wonderful!'

And Tory finally trusted it was real, the life of happiness stretching before her, coloured vivid by the man at her side.

BETWEEN THE CEO'S SHEETS

CHARLENE SANDS

To my husband, Don, sole owner of my heart.
And to Jason and Nikki our wonderful children
who always make us proud.

One

It was the last place Gina Grady wanted to be.

But desperation was an unwelcome persuasion. And Gina was just that: desperate. Her pride and determination also played in the mix.

She needed this job.

She needed to stay in L.A.

Gina was ushered into an empty office. "Mr. Beaumont will be right with you," Mrs. Danner from Human Resources announced before exiting the office, leaving Gina alone with her thoughts.

She walked over to the massive floor-to-ceiling window and took in the view from the twelfth floor of the trendy Santa Monica high-rise, praying the interview would go well. She shouldn't be so worried.

Sam Beaumont had been her friend once. He'd always been kind. Yet, having to take him up on his offer of a job at the Triple B ranked with her top-ten most desperate acts of survival. The Beaumont name alone caused her insides to quake and she wondered at her own sanity in coming. However, it wasn't Sam but his younger brother, Wade, she hoped never to cross paths with again.

The Pacific Ocean loomed on the horizon, the pounding blue surf and white caps filling the view. She shuddered at the sight, and shook off her thoughts of Wade. She had enough to worry about without letting old fears get the better of her today.

She owed money to a whole lot of people and they didn't give a damn that she'd been swindled by a con man she had once trusted as her partner. GiGi Designs, the company she'd struggled to conceive hadn't been given a chance. Her lifelong dream had been destroyed in the blink of an eye. All that she'd worked so hard for had come crumbling down around her.

Now Gina was even more determined to rebuild her clothing design business—from the ground up, if need be.

But first, she needed to pay off her debts.

Gina tidied her long dark hair, making sure it hadn't fallen from the tight knot at the back of her head, straightened her black pinstriped suit and took a seat in front of the massive oak desk, setting her black knockoff Gucci handbag on her lap. She waited for Sam to enter his office.

She closed her eyes to steady her wayward nerves. Calmer, she took a deep breath before opening them again. But when she glanced down, she simply stared in disbelief at the nameplate outlined in solid brass on the desk:

Wade Beaumont, CEO.

"No!" Her heart thudding against her chest, she rose abruptly. She couldn't bear to see Wade again, much less work for him. She couldn't possibly swallow that much pride. She set her purse strap on her shoulder and turned to leave.

"Running away again, Gina?"

Stunned, Gina stopped abruptly and stared into the dark-green eyes of Wade Beaumont. His head cocked to one side, he was leaning against the door where she'd hoped to make her escape. He stared back at her, his lips curled into a mocking smile. "You do that so well."

Gina kept her head held high and tried to appear calm while her insides quivered uncontrollably. She'd foolishly hoped that Wade had nothing to do with Triple B, but now she'd seen the folly in that.

But she couldn't deny how handsome Wade was, standing there in a pair of black trousers and a crisp white shirt, the sleeves rolled up to his elbows. He looked older, more mature and those bold green eyes—she'd never forget the way they use to soften when he looked at her. Or the way his strong body felt crushed up against hers.

Or the day, nine years ago, when she'd run away from him.

"I…this is a mistake. I shouldn't have come," she said on a breath.

Wade ignored her comment. "You applied for a job."

"Yes, I, um assumed Sam would be running your father's company."

"Ah, so you didn't think you'd find me here?"

Gina bolstered her courage as she recalled Wade's onetime contempt for the company his father seemed to love more than his own two sons. Triple B was all Blake Beaumont had ever cared about. When she'd known him back in El Paso, she'd understood Wade's retreat from both the company and his father. She'd never have guessed that he would be at the helm now. Never. "No, I didn't actually. As I said, this is a mistake."

Gina watched his mouth twitch. He walked around his desk and picked up her resume, reading it over carefully.

"I run Triple B now from the West Coast. My father's dead and my brother's remarried and living in Texas. The company fell into my hands some time ago." He stared directly into her eyes. "I suppose you thought I'd work all my life on Uncle Lee's ranch or wind up with a small place of my own back in El Paso?"

"Actually, I hadn't given it much thought," Gina said truthfully. She had thought of Wade countless times in the past—dreamed of him and wondered how his life had turned out—but she never cared what he did for a living. It had never mattered to her.

She'd met Wade while living with the Buckleys in El Paso for the summer. Sarah, her college roommate, had been there for her after her parents had died in a boating accident. Gina had been on the boat, narrowly escaping death that day. Sarah had seen to the funeral, making all the arrangements. She'd held Gina tight, when the caskets were lowered into the ground. And after, when Gina had been uncertain of her future, Sarah had taken her home to El Paso.

The Buckleys' place neighbored Wade's uncle's ranch and the four of them—Sam, Wade, Sarah and Gina—had been inseparable. She came to depend on their friendship and slowly began to heal from her terrible loss, until the day when her world had come crashing down upon her once again.

And now, Wade sat down at his desk and leaned back studying her, his eyes raking her over. She felt exposed and vulnerable, yet unable to draw herself away from his intense scrutiny.

"You hadn't thought about me? Of course, why would you? My father took care of that, didn't he?" He gestured for her to sit down, not expecting an answer. "Take a seat. We'll do this interview."

"No, I—I don't think that would be a good idea, Wade."

"I thought you needed a job?" he said, narrowing his eyes on her.

"I do need a job." She directed her gaze to his without apology. "Just not this one."

He looked down at her resume. "You're more than qualified."

Gina's legs wobbled, so she decided to take a seat, at least for the moment.

"You've got a degree in business. And then you went on to the Fashion Institute. Did my father's money finance that?"

He asked that question so casually that Gina had to rewind his words in her mind to make sure she'd heard him correctly. Wade believed that she'd taken his father's bribe—dirty money that she'd never wanted—to stay away from him.

He believed it because she'd never denied it. She'd let him think that she'd been enticed by a large sum of money to leave El Paso.

But that hadn't been the case at all.

She'd run out on Wade for an entirely different reason. And to have Wade believe she'd accepted his father's bribery had guaranteed that he wouldn't come after her.

She'd hated what he'd done to her.

Hated the high and mighty Blake Beaumont even more.

But if given the choice all over again, Gina wouldn't have changed anything about that summer. Except the night that they made love. Though the sweet memories of the intense passion they shared were always with her, she wished she could take that night back.

Slinging her purse on her shoulder and holding her anger in check, she stood to leave. "I'm sorry," she said, and his dark brows lifted, lining his forehead. "For wasting your time."

Wade stood and glared at her. "You didn't. You're hired."

* * *

Wade watched Gina blink her gorgeous espresso eyes. Nine years had only added to her sultry beauty and it angered him that she could still make his heart race. All Wade had to do was look into those dark, deceitful eyes and admire that voluptuous body and he had trouble remembering the pain she'd caused him. He'd taken her virginity and it had been the highest of highs, claiming her as his own.

She'd run out on him then, leaving town, without so much as a goodbye. She'd gotten what she'd wanted—a load of money from his manipulative father. But if money had been her goal she should have waited. No longer the poor young man working on his uncle's ranch, Wade was floating in cash. But she'd been bought off long ago and had caused Wade enough steaming heartache to fill a Mississippi riverboat.

Gina straightened her pinstriped suit, her chest heaving, the structured material unable to hide the fullness of her breasts. Wade looked his fill, watching the rise and fall as she tried to hide her hot Irish-Italian temper.

Rosy-lipped, with a full flush of color on her light-olive skin, Gina was still the most beautiful woman he had ever seen. From the moment she'd shown up in Aunt Dottie's kitchen with an offering of fresh Italian bread and homemade pasta sauce, Wade had been a goner. She'd knocked him to his knees.

"No. But thank you."

She spoke the words carefully and instincts told Wade that she'd been tempted to take the job. Hell, one look at her and he knew he couldn't let her walk out of his office. Not until they finished what they'd started nine years ago.

"There's a big bonus involved," he said, catching her attention. Her brows lifted provocatively. He shrugged. "I'm in a bind. My personal assistant chose last month to get pregnant. She's down with acute morning sickness and took disability leave. The other qualified assistants are busy with their own projects."

"How big a bonus?" she asked. Wade knew he'd gotten her attention once again. Money, it seemed, spoke volumes with her. Why was he disappointed? He'd known the sort of woman she was, but he had to admit that back in his youth, she sure had him fooled. "It's a thousand dollars a week to start and once the project is settled, win or lose, you get a ten-thousand-dollar bonus. But I'll warn you, you'll be working long hours. Take it or leave it, Gina."

He could almost see her mind working, calculating, *figuring*. She must need a job badly. Wade had the upper hand and he knew it. She was tempted.

He sat down at his desk and rifled through papers, coming up with information on the Catalina project. He had figures to check and hours of work to do before making a bid on the biggest contract Triple B might hope to gain.

He felt her presence, breathed in the heady scent

of her exotic perfume. His better judgment told him to let her go. He'd be better off not complicating his life by choosing to work alongside the only woman he knew who could turn him on with just one look. He'd had to sit down to conceal an unwelcome yet healthy erection that pulsed from underneath the desk.

He must be crazy.

"I must be crazy, but I accept," she said softly.

Wade lifted his head and nodded, more satisfied than he wanted to be. "I expect a decent hard day's work from my employees. If you can manage that, you've got the job."

Her chin jutted up. "I can manage that. I always give one hundred percent."

Wade's mind drifted back to his uncle's barn that night so many years ago. She'd given one hundred percent of herself to him, generously offering up her body with passion and pleasure, but it had all been a trap.

This time, he'd have to be more careful.

"I'll pick you up later this afternoon. Oh, and dress comfortably. We'll be working at my home through the evening."

Gina recalled Wade's instructions and wondered at her sanity. She would never have taken this job if the compensation hadn't been so tempting. She had debtors knocking on her door and that big bonus Wade had offered would surely keep them happy for a while.

She'd changed her clothes three times before settling on a pair of white slacks and a soft-pink knit top. She brought the whole outfit together with a matching short sweater. Comfortable, but still a professional enough look for a woman about to embark on a new job with an old lover.

Gina shook her head. She still had trouble believing she would be working with Wade Beaumont after all these years. He resented her. She'd seen it in his eyes each time he glanced at her. No amount of Beaumont charm could conceal that look.

Gina lifted her briefcase filled with documents that Wade had asked her to review this afternoon. She glanced around the tiny guest apartment she lived in behind the large Spanish-style house in the Hollywood Hills. Once Wade saw where and how she lived, he would realize how desperate she'd been for this job. It was a tidy place with three rooms: a small cozy living space with one sofa, a kitchen that amounted to one wall of the living room with a range, a refrigerator and a café table for two, and a bedroom beyond that.

Her apartment suited her needs. She'd had to downsize everything in her life since Mike Bailey had betrayed her. They'd dreamed the same dreams, or so she had thought, and had gone into partnership together. The day GiGi Designs was born was the happiest day in Gina's life. The day she found out he'd absconded with all of her money and designs only compared with the day she'd had to leave El Paso and Wade Beaumont forever. She'd been heartbroken on both accounts.

Gina sighed and walked out the door, deciding to meet Wade out front. Not a minute later, he drove up in a shining black Lexus convertible. She watched him get out and approach her, his eyes focused on her clothes and she wondered if he approved of her choice of attire. Though not one of her original designs, she always chose her outfits carefully. When the door of the main house slammed, Gina turned her head to find the owner locking up.

"Hey there, Gina. Are you going out?" Marcus's eyes narrowed on Wade and she couldn't help but laugh. Her handsome fifty-something landlord was always watching out for her.

"Yes, but it's business. I have a new job."

"Ah. Well then, good luck." He headed for his car in the driveway.

"Ciao, Marcus. See you tomorrow."

When Gina turned back around, Wade's intense-green eyes burned into hers. "Do you live with him?"

Gina blinked away her anger. Wade had no right to ask her personal questions. She wondered why it mattered, anyway. He had nothing but contempt for her. "No. I don't live with him. I live in the guest-house in the back."

Wade's mouth twitched. "How convenient." He put his hand to her lower back and ushered her inside his car. She took her seat and adjusted the seatbelt as Wade started the ignition. He took one last look at the house and gunned the engine. They drove in silence for a while, until he asked, "Is that guy married?"

Gina leaned her head back against the seat and smiled inwardly. Marcus and Delia had the kind of marriage her parent's had had. That kind of love and commitment was rare and it saddened Gina to think that her parents' love had been cut short by a freakish accident. "Yes, happily."

"He's your landlord?"

"My landlord and a very dear friend."

Wade shot her another glance, this time with a dubious look in his eyes. Gina let the subject drop and stared out the window, her eyes focused on the mountain on one side of the road rather than the blue ocean waters on the other. As Wade drove down Pacific Coast Highway, the wind blew her long hair out of its tight knot.

Ten minutes later and completely wind-blown, Gina was pinning her hair back up, noting Wade's eyes on her as he killed the engine. She marveled at the impressive two-story house that sat on a strip of beach in the Malibu Colony. Wade hopped out of the car and came around to open her door. She stood and looked around for a moment, her gaze traveling past the house to the surging surf and then beyond to the stunning western horizon. "All of this is yours?"

Wade grabbed her briefcase from the car then nodded, staring directly into her eyes. "It's mine." She shivered from the cold assessing look he cast her; a look that said, "It could have been yours, too."

Or maybe Gina had imagined that. It had been nine long years and surely Wade hadn't brooded over her too long. Handsome and successful, Wade wouldn't have to look far for female companionship. He had all the markings of a man used to getting his way with women and with life in general.

Gina followed Wade through the front door and into a large vestibule. From there it seemed that she could almost touch the pounding surf as the shore came into view with brilliant clarity through enormous windows. "Take a look around," he said without ceremony. "I'm going up to take a quick shower."

Gina watched him toss both of their briefcases down onto a soft moss-green L-shaped sofa before disappearing up a winding staircase. She felt safest standing there waiting in the safety of the living room, but curiosity forced her to walk through the French doors that led onto a sweeping veranda overlooking the ocean. Wade seemed to have all things necessary for the life of a single man; a hot tub surrounded by a cocktail bar sat in one corner of the deck while a fire pit took up the other corner. In the middle of the deck, patio tables and chairs were arranged to enjoy the view of waves crashing into the sand.

Gina walked to the wooden railing and closed her eyes. Taking a deep breath she tried to calm her jittery nerves, but the combination of deep waters and Wade was too much for her.

Wade approached with two glasses of white wine. He handed her one. "To unwind."

Gina accepted the glass, grateful for the fortitude, and both of them stood leaning on the railing, gazing out. "It looks peaceful here."

Wade sipped his wine. "Looks can be deceiving."

That's exactly what Gina thought, but she was thinking of the deceptive calm of the uncompromising sea. She was certain Wade meant something altogether different.

Rather than stare at the ocean, she shifted slightly so that she could consider Wade Beaumont. His dark hair, still damp from the shower, was slicked back and tiny drops of water glistened on his neck. Late afternoon sunlight revealed a gleam in his eyes and highlighted high cheekbones leading to a beautiful mouth and the masculine line of his jaw. He had changed into a pair of tight-fitting jeans and a black polo shirt. Tan and trim with broad shoulders, his shirt couldn't hide the strength of his powerfully built chest.

Now, as in the past, Gina had trouble keeping her eyes off of Wade. He affected her like no other man ever had. Her heart pumped twice as hard when he looked at her and an unwelcome tremble stirred her body when he came near. In those clothes, he reminded her of the man she'd once known during a time in her life when she could enjoy carefree days and hot summer nights.

Gina took small sips of her wine. She wasn't much of a drinker and needed to remain in control. She couldn't afford any more slipups.

"Only one more sip," she said, "or my head won't be clear for business." Gina set the glass down on the table. Turning to Wade, she hoped that he would take the hint and lead her back inside so that they could begin their work together. She needed to prove herself on this job and, more importantly, she needed to keep her mind on business and not the glowing attributes of her new boss.

Wade didn't move from his stance by the railing. He shook his head, his eyes fixed on hers. "Sorry, Gina," he said, looking anything but sorry. "I can't work with you."

I can't work with you.

Gina blinked as Wade's words sunk in. A rapid shot of dread coursed through her system. She'd begun to think of this job as a means to an end. And she'd resigned herself to working with Wade, whether she liked it or not. Now, just like that, he dropped a bomb on her plans. What kind of game was he playing? She couldn't control the anger in her voice, "I thought you hired me today?"

Wade slammed his glass down on the top rail and turned the full force of his words on her. "Yes, I hired you. Did you think I'd let you walk out of my office without an explanation? Did you think I'd let you go again? You ran away from me nine years ago and I need to know why."

Two

Shocked, Gina stared into Wade's stormy eyes. When she finally spoke, it was softly and devoid of emotion. "We were young."

She had died that night. Leaving Wade had destroyed her and it had been a long hard road getting her life back. She didn't want to dwell on the past or how her friend Sarah had duped her into leaving Wade. The truth had come out a few years later, and she'd long since forgiven Sarah. But the fact remained: Gina had left Wade in El Paso after one secret, glorious night with him.

"Not that young, Gina. You'd graduated from college. We weren't exactly kids."

"My parents died that year. I didn't know what to do or how…or how I would survive."

"My father solved that problem for you, didn't he? He paid you off. And you took the money and ran, for all you were worth."

Yes, Gina had taken Blake Beaumont's money. It had given her a way out of a very serious dilemma. She'd fallen in love with Wade and the night she'd given him her virginity had been wonderful. She'd hoped for a future with Wade, but thinking back on it now, she wondered if she'd been too clouded by grief to see the truth. Later that night all of her hopes had come crashing down around her.

Sarah was pregnant and she'd named Wade as the father.

Gina went to bed that night, tears falling uncontrollably and her heart aching at how she'd been betrayed by the one man who had given her a measure of comfort and happiness after the death of her parents.

Blake Beaumont's offer had come at exactly the right moment. She'd wanted to hurt Wade for his calculated cruelty. She'd wanted to make him pay for his betrayal. She'd hated him.

She remembered so vividly standing there, face to face with the older man who had abandoned his two sons in favor of building his company. Triple B had been Blake's passion, not the two sweet young boys he'd pawned off on his sister and her husband to raise.

Blake Beaumont slid an envelope her way. "Take the money and this airline ticket and leave El Paso. You're a distraction Wade can't afford right now. I sacrificed his childhood so that he would one day stand beside me and run the company and that time has almost come. Sam, Wade and I, we'll build an enormous empire together. There's no room in it for you, dear."

Gina's first instinct was to rip the check up and toss it into Blake Beaumont's smug face. The selfish man wanted his son's full attention. He wanted to dictate his life—a life that didn't include love. Blake Beaumont had made it clear that he fully intended for Wade to immerse himself in Triple B. The only relationship he wanted for Wade was one of dedicated service to the company.

If her heart hadn't been broken, Gina would have laughed at the irony. Blake wanted her out of the picture but how would he feel knowing that it was really Sarah and her unborn child that would disrupt his plans? Gina had wished she could have stayed around long enough to see the look on Blake Beaumont's face when he realized his troubles were just beginning.

Gina accepted the check and ticket out of town. She knew Blake was too ruthless not to tell Wade about the bribe. And that's what she'd counted on.

Wade had a baby on the way with Sarah and that had been all that mattered. Sarah hadn't known about Gina's feelings for Wade and she'd kept it that way. By accepting his father's bribe, Gina guaranteed that Wade would stay in El Paso with his family. She'd hoped that he would realize his responsibilities to Sarah, too.

Gina lost contact with Sarah then, deciding to deal with her pain in her own way. She moved to Los Angeles and dug her heels in, determined to make a good life for herself. It wasn't until a few years later that Sarah had come looking for Gina with the whole truth.

"Answer me, Gina. Why did you run away?"

"I had good reason, Wade. It's not important now. But you have to believe that leaving El Paso when I did broke my heart."

"It broke your heart?" he said, coming to stand right in front of her, his anger almost tangible. "Funny, but I remember it differently. I remember you letting me strip you naked and take you in my uncle's barn. I remember every little moan, every whimper, every time you cried out my name. I never once heard you say your heart was broken and that you were leaving town the next day."

Tears welled in Gina's eyes and her body trembled with unspoken grief. She had loved Wade then and had felt the cold slap of his betrayal. She shed tears all the way to Los Angeles, but had made up her mind not to look back.

"Wade, when I came to see you that night I didn't know I would be leaving so soon. I…wanted you."

Wade let out a derisive laugh. "And Gina always gets what she wants, right?"

Gina hadn't gotten what she wanted. She'd lost her best friend that summer and the man she'd loved.

Wade had been so sweet, so caring. Once he kissed her and touched her skin, she'd reacted with primal, desperate need. She'd wanted Wade, thought maybe they could have a future together. His every touch and caress excited her, warmed her, told her that she'd been smart to wait to give up her virginity to the right man. They'd spoken of love and the future in vague terms, the relationship too new to know for sure. But Gina fully believed that Wade Beaumont had been the right man for her.

"It wasn't like that," she said in a calm voice, one that she almost didn't recognize.

But Wade didn't really want her explanation. He wanted to lash out. "You were a virgin, Gina. Don't think that didn't weigh on me. I wasn't a boy. I was a twenty-one-year-old man. I didn't know if I'd hurt you physically or emotionally. I didn't know what to think. I was half out of my mind when I learned that you had left El Paso the next day, catching the soonest flight out of town.

"I made the mistake of telling dear old Dad that I'd found the right girl for me during a phone conversation days earlier. Even before we made love, I knew I wanted you in my life. Next thing I know my father makes a rare visit to El Paso. He couldn't wait to tell me that you'd taken a hefty bribe from him. The man was so damn cocky. He didn't realize that I'd hate him for his part in it. He thought I'd appreciate knowing that I'd been wrong about you. But it didn't matter anymore. I pretty much wrote you off as the biggest mistake of my life."

His harsh words cut like a knife. He didn't know the agony she had gone through that night, her emotions running hot and cold, thrilled to have finally given herself to him only to find out later that he had been deceitful. She managed to bolster her courage and hoist her chin. "If that's the case, why did you bother seeing me today? Why did you *hire* me?"

"Because Sam asked me to. I did it as a favor to him, Gina. And now we're stuck with each other."

She gasped silently from the immediate shock to her system. She'd seen Sam a few months ago, crossing paths with him at the airport, his new family in tow. They'd exchanged pleasantries and when he'd found out that she was living in Los Angeles he'd offered her a job if she ever needed one.

With her pride deeply injured, Gina shot back. "Consider yourself, unstuck. I won't ask you to work with the *biggest mistake of your life.*"

Gina turned her back on Wade and walked toward the French doors. She wanted out, away from Wade for good. But just as she stepped inside the house, Wade grabbed her from behind, his hands holding her gently just under her breasts, the zipper of his jeans grinding into her derriere. She felt the pins being pulled from her hair, freeing the tresses from their knotted prison. Wade wove his hand in her hair and brought his lips to her throat, his voice a gruff whisper. "Don't run away again."

Gina's traitorous body reacted to Wade and, angry as she was, she couldn't deny the overwhelming heat pulsing through her. "You don't want me here."

"That may be true." And then he added softly, "But I need you."

Gina slammed her eyes shut. She felt herself softening to Wade and when she turned in his arms to face him, she witnessed the depth of his sincerity. "You need me?"

She glanced at his mouth just as his lips came down onto hers. He cupped her face and deepened the kiss, slanting his mouth over hers again and again. Gina reacted with a little whimper, urging her body closer. His heat was a fire that burned her. And when she sighed, he took the opportunity to drive his tongue into her mouth, mating them together. Soon, Gina's body swayed in rhythm and Wade wrapped his hands around her waist, his fingers pressing into the curve of her buttocks, drawing her closer.

She felt his erection, the hot pulsing need rubbing into her. Heart pounding out of control, she felt dizzy and wanted Wade with undeniable urgency.

"Yoo-hoo, Wa-ade? Are you home? I brought you chili, honey. Just the way you like it, hot and spicy," the low throaty rasp of a woman's voice startled Gina. She pulled away from Wade in time to see a young redhead coming up the deck steps from the beach. In a flowery bikini covered only by a hip-riding sarong, the woman held a hot bowl in her pot-holder-clad hands. She stopped up short when she reached the deck, finding Wade and Gina together. "Oh, sorry, Wade. I guess I had the wrong night. I thought we were on for the hot tub. My mistake," she said casually. "I'll just leave this here for you." She set the chili on the deck table.

"Shoot, Veronica. Sorry. I forgot." He winked at her and smiled. "I'm working tonight."

"I can see that," she said, taking a quick glance at Gina, before backing down the stairs. "Don't work too hard, honey." Gina heard her chuckle as she disappeared onto the beach.

Gina stared at Wade and abruptly everything became clear. For a moment she thought that she was back in El Paso with the young, sweet man she had given herself to unconditionally. Suddenly, she felt foolish. And stupid for thinking that nothing had changed, when, actually, everything had.

She tried to brush past him to get away, but he was like a block of granite, too strong to move without his willing surrender. He reached for her arms and held her without budging. When she glared into his eyes, he shrugged and said calmly, "She's a friend."

Gina wasn't a fool. She doubted Wade had female "friends" who came over just for a quick meal and a splash in the hot tub. She shook her head adamantly. "I think not. I'd better go. Will you drive me home or shall I take a taxi?"

"Neither. We have work to do. When I said I needed you, I meant it. I need a personal assistant for this project and we have to catch you up on the details."

"You mean you'd give up your hot-tub date?" Her voice was deliberately rich with sarcasm.

"I just did, didn't I?" Wade shot back.

Gina bristled. "Yes, you did. You dismissed her quite easily. But what about what just happened between us? Can you dismiss *that* just as easily?" His kiss had stole Gina's breath, but she had regained normal breathing.

Wade pursed his lips. He stared at hers, well-ripened and swollen from his powerful assault. "I never could dismiss you, Gina. You're hardly the kind of woman a man can forget."

"That does not answer my question."

"Listen, maybe I was out of line a minute ago. But I'm not kidding when I say I need you. As my assistant. We're setting sail first thing tomorrow so—"

Gina snapped her head up. "Setting sail? For where?"

"For Catalina island. You should have been briefed during the first interview with Helen in Personnel. It was a stipulation of the job."

Wade seemed full of surprises. First he stunned her with that incredible kiss and now this unexpected announcement of an island trip. "I wasn't informed about a trip."

"You knew about the latest project the company plans to bid on. It could be the biggest contract in Triple B's history and I intend to get it. It's right there in the file I gave you to review."

"Yes, but I didn't think—"

"It's the reason for the big bonus, Gina," he interrupted to clarify.

"But that's what I don't understand. That's a great

deal of money for a trip to Catalina. It's only a few hours away. Surely, one day isn't worth such a large sum of money."

"One day? Gina, we'll be on that island for a minimum of one week and I guarantee you'll be working long hours."

Gina slumped her shoulders. "One week?"

He nodded. "Seven days, including the weekend. So are you in or am I going it alone tomorrow?"

Gina slammed her eyes shut. She hated her own cowardice. She hadn't been on the water in any capacity since the boat accident that claimed her parents' lives. She'd dealt with the guilt at being the sole survivor, but she hadn't been forced to face her fear—until now. And she was ready. She'd been praying to find a way to conquer her anxiety and now she had the opportunity. If she didn't face her fears, she'd not only lose the revenue to rebuild her future, she'd lose part of herself all over again.

Gina made a split-second decision. She needed this job for more than one reason. But she would accept the position under one condition, and one condition only. "I'm in. Under one condition."

Wade narrowed his eyes. "I don't usually—"

"We keep it strictly business." Gina had allowed personal feelings to get the better of her in business once before and that had landed her with a pile of bills, slimy pawnshop receipts and creditors pounding on her door. She couldn't let that happen again to her pocketbook or her heart. "Agreed?"

Wade's lips thinned.

She stood her ground and kept her focus on his unflinching face.

Finally Wade nodded. "I won't do anything you don't want me to do. Now, let's go over those files. I don't want to get you home late. We'll be setting sail at eight sharp."

Gina drew in a deep breath wondering how she would fare spending her days and *nights* with the only man who could anger her, confuse her and make her ache desperately for his touch.

I won't do anything you don't want me to do.

Great, she thought ruefully. She'd just realized that Wade hadn't agreed to her terms at all, but instead, issued her a challenge.

She felt herself slowly sinking and she had to paddle fast to keep from going under. Which was saying something for a woman who had a dire fear of water.

Three

The next morning, Wade watched Gina make her way down the ramp that led to his docking slip at Marina del Rey. He'd told her to dress comfortably for the trip over to the island but as he watched her descend the steps he was almost sorry he'd given her that instruction. Her flowery sundress hugged her body perfectly and the tight white jacket she wore only accentuated her full breasts and slender waistline. July breezes lifted the hem enough to show her shapely legs as she strolled toward him. She'd pinned her hair in that knot again, but the breezy weather wouldn't allow it and those chestnut tresses fanned out in tempting disarray. The vision she created of simple elegance and unquestionable beauty turned heads at the marina. Wade winced as he caught men stop what they were doing on their boats to watch her walk by.

Wade muttered a curse and told himself this was a business trip where he needed to keep his focus. He'd never let a woman get in the way of what was important to the company. Yet, when Gina approached his yacht he had a hard time remembering that. He peered up from the stern of the boat to greet her. "Morning," he said, none too pleasantly.

"Good morning," she said, but her eyes weren't on him, or his yacht. They focused off in the distance, to the ocean that lay beyond the calm marina.

"You're right on time."

She took her eyes off the ocean long enough to answer, "Thanks to the driver you sent to pick me up." She bit down on her lip and stood there looking quite businesslike, her chin at an unapproachable tilt and her stance slightly rigid. But that dress…that dress could make a man forget his own name.

"Come aboard," he said, putting a hand out to help her.

She scanned the length of the boat and drew a deep breath as if steadying her nerves.

"You haven't changed your mind, have you?" he asked.

She gazed once more at the ocean beyond the marina and shook her head, but her soft tentative answer left room for doubt. "No."

Wade gestured with his outstretched hand. "Come on, Gina. We have to set sail soon."

From the minute he'd seen it, Wade had known he had to own this fifty-two-foot Jeanneau sloop. It hadn't mattered that he didn't know how to sail. He'd made it a hobby and a far-reaching goal to master the craft when he'd first arrived in California. And he'd never been sorry.

Gina's gaze scanned the deck and the steps leading to the quarters below. "I don't see the crew? Are they late?"

"You're looking at the crew."

Gina's dark almond-shaped eyes opened wide. "You?"

"Sam's the pilot in the family and I'm the sailor."

He stepped from the boat onto the ramp and grabbed the suitcase from her hand. "Come aboard and I'll show you around."

After a moment's hesitation, Gina accepted his help and he guided her down onto his boat, releasing her the moment her feet hit the deck.

"I had no idea this was how we would arrive in Catalina."

Wade had purposely left that detail out. He didn't know how she would've reacted to his sailing them across to the island. Some people got jittery when they realized only one man had full charge of the boat. But that was what appealed to him most about sailing—the solitude and the challenge of being at the helm. And since he'd had a hard enough time convincing Gina to take the job last night, he'd thought it best to leave their travel arrangements out of the conversation.

His old man once told him that timing was everything. Wade believed him. He knew that after that kiss last night and then the untimely appearance from Veronica, he was on shaky enough ground with Gina. She'd been ready to walk out of his life again.

But that kiss had him tied up in knots all night long. Gina had melted in his arms. That much hadn't changed. She'd tasted like wine, her lips soft and full and ripe. Her body molded to his, they fit each other like two puzzle pieces. He couldn't hide his reaction to her any more than she could to him. Wade had lost himself in that kiss and he realized that he couldn't let her go until they'd cleared up all of their unfinished business. Then and only then, would he say farewell to Gina for good.

"Can't say that I ever imagined I'd get you on Total Command."

Gina arched her brow. "Excuse me?"

"*Total Command.* The name of the boat. And the only way I operate these days.

Gina cast him a disapproving look.

"Listen, I'll get us both to the island safe and sound. There's no need to worry." Wade picked up her travel bag and stepped down into the living quarters of the boat first and reached for her hand. She advanced carefully down the steps. But when the boat rocked slightly, she lurched forward. Wade grabbed her and their eyes met as their bodies collided. Intense heat sizzled between them. She was soft where she needed to be soft, and firm in all the right places. Wade held her for only a second before stepping aside.

He showed her the open space that would serve as a living room and then they walked through the galley where he had fixed them a mid-morning snack of fresh fruit, cheese and coffee.

Next he explained about the VHF radio and the SSB, the Single Sideband system used for a wider perimeter of communication. He'd even explained to her how she should call for help in case of an emergency. "But don't worry about that. The weather is clear, the wind perfect, I'm in good health and we'll be in Catalina before lunchtime."

Gina nodded, but he didn't miss her wide-eyed expression when he described to her how she could reach the coast guard if necessary.

"And what's in there?" she asked gesturing toward a doorway.

"The master bedroom and bath. There's two more bedrooms on the opposite end of the boat."

"You don't expect, uh, you don't expect me to sleep down here."

Wade wouldn't get a lick of work done if she did. "That's not in your job description. You'll have a room in the finest inn on the island."

"And you?" she asked. "Where will you be?"

"Right here. I stay on the boat when we moor. I don't get as much time as I'd like on the boat. So I've set up an office in one of the spare bedrooms."

He guided her back to the stairs, catching a whiff of her perfume, some exotic fragrance that reminded him of sultry tropical nights. As she climbed up the steps to the top deck he admired the wiggle of her bottom and those long tanned legs as he followed her up.

"Ready?" he asked.

She drew another deep breath into her lungs then put on dark sunglasses. She looked mysterious in them, a superstar trying to conceal her identity. And in a way Gina was a mystery to him. He didn't know her mind, how it worked, what made her tick. He'd known her body and, hopefully, would try his best to know it again, but he would never believe he knew what she was thinking. He refused to make that mistake again.

Wade prepared the yacht for their departure, untying the ropes and setting the sails. Soon they were moving through the marina, past the rocks that harbored the bay, picking up wind that would take them into the Pacific Ocean.

Gina shook with fear the moment the boat began its journey out of the calm marina waters. She took a seat in the cockpit area as salty sea spray lightly drizzled her. With slight desperation she tried to block out images of the last time she'd been on the water, the last time she'd seen her parents alive.

She prayed for enough courage to sustain her through this trip and placed her faith in Wade and his sailing abilities. She watched him move along the sheets and sails, making adjustments and setting the course.

In faded blue jeans and a white tank, Wade might have looked like a typical sailor except his muscles strained harder, his body held more steadfastly, the concentration on his face appeared deeper than on any man she had ever known. Studying his fluid movements along the rigging, Gina could only admire him.

His kiss last night had been *something.*

But it had meant nothing to him.

I need you.

Yes, she understood that he needed her as his personal assistant, a right-hand man and a secretary all rolled up in one. He didn't need her in any other capacity. Not in the way she had needed him nine years ago.

Wade took his place behind the wheel and they sailed in silence for a short time. The boat rocked and waves smashed up against the hull as they sailed along. Gina shuddered, unable to suppress the trembling of her body.

Wade turned at that very instant, catching her in a moment of fear. Their eyes held for a moment before he angled around again and Gina hugged her middle, tamping down the tremors that passed through her.

A few minutes later, Wade left the wheel and handed her a life jacket. "Put this on. You'll feel better."

Gina didn't bother to protest. He was right. But though wearing a life vest might help with her fear, it wouldn't erase the memories she had locked away that were surfacing. She put her arms through the armholes and closed the jacket taut.

Wade helped her fasten the snaps and tied it for her. And when she thought he would return to the wheel, he surprised her by taking a seat by her side. "Feeling seasick?"

She shook her head. Her queasiness had nothing to do with the motion of the sea. "No."

"You're trembling and pale, Gina."

"I'm not—"

"You are."

"No, I meant to say, I'm not seasick, but this is the first time I've been on the water since…the accident."

Wade's dark brows rose. He appeared genuinely surprised.

"I realize that this is the ocean and the accident happened on a lake, but—"

"You haven't been on the water since?" he asked.

Gina closed her eyes. Memories flooded in of the ski boat, the laughter, her mother's smiling face and then…the collision. Gina went flying into the water, out of danger. Her parents hadn't been so lucky.

She shook her head and stared at the hands she'd placed in her lap. "No. I haven't had the courage. It's been almost ten years."

"So, why now?" Wade asked softly.

But she sensed he was really asking her, "Why me?" Why would she take her first boat trip with him? She'd been desperate for work she'd wanted to tell him. She needed the money and was determined to start her business again, without anyone's help this time. She'd been betrayed, but not destroyed. She wouldn't give up, and if that meant facing her fears, then so be it. She peered into a face filled with concern, an expression reminiscent of the sweet, caring Wade Beaumont she'd once known. "It's time, Wade. That's all."

Wade leaned back in the seat and put his arm around her. "That's not all. Tell me about the accident."

"I—I don't talk about it." She'd never really spoken about that day except with a support group that had really helped and understood what she'd been through. Losing both parents had been devastating enough, but to be the sole survivor of the crash that had taken four lives had been equally difficult. The result was major survivor guilt.

"Maybe you should. Maybe it'll help you overcome your fear of water."

She shook her head and gazed out upon the open sea. "I doubt that."

Wade took her hands in his and the look on his face, serious but earnest, urged her on. "Try, Gina. We're going to spend a week on an island surrounded by water. There'll be times we'll have to come back to the boat." He cast her a slight hint of a smile. "I can't have you fainting on me."

Gina peered into his eyes. They were warm with concern. But she wondered if that look was about keeping his personal assistant calm or if it was truly for her benefit.

He squeezed her hands gently, coaxing the words that she hadn't spoken to anyone but her support group. "It was Memorial Day weekend," she began, "and we never once thought to worry about drunk drivers on the water…"

Emotions rolled in the pit of Gina's stomach. She'd purged herself of her burden, sharing the events of that horrible day with Wade. He'd listened to her as she tried to communicate without tears, but at times her voice broke and she choked up. Wade sat there with a soothing arm around her shoulders, listening. And when the last words were out of her mouth, he thanked her for telling him.

"Are you feeling better?" he asked.

Gina nodded feeling a small sense of relief. "A little."

He stood and peered down at her. "You need to eat something."

"No," she said, placing a hand to her stomach. "No, I couldn't."

"If you don't want to eat, there's coffee down below." He glanced at the blue skies overhead then looked into her eyes as if deciding what was best for her. Then he took hold of her hand, guiding her up. "You look tired, Gina. Take a little rest. Get away from the water for a little while."

He spoke softly and his tone comforted. She thought she could fall for him again—if she hadn't sworn off men completely and if he would always look at her like he was now, without contempt and regret in his eyes. "Maybe I will go down below."

He walked her to the steps and turned, tugging

her close. She nearly bumped into his chest when the boat swayed. He steadied her with both hands on her shoulders then, with a slant of his head, brought his lips to hers. The kiss was brief and chaste and when it was over she gazed deeply into his eyes and smiled.

Wade looked off toward the horizon a moment then returned his focus to her face with narrowed eyes. His soft expression turned hard once again.

"Don't think I gained any satisfaction seeing fear in your eyes or hearing pain in your voice, Gina. I'm not that big a bast—"

Gina pressed her fingers to his mouth. "I know, Wade. You're not—"

He pulled her fingers from his lips. "I am. Make no mistake. But I draw the line at preying on another's weakness. Take that as fair warning."

Gina shuddered at Wade's harsh tone. He'd let her glimpse the man he'd once been, but only for a moment. The young man she'd fallen in love with was gone, she feared, forever. And she'd had everything to do with his demise. "Consider me fairly warned." She turned to walk down the stairs, feeling Wade's penetrating gaze following her every step of the way.

Wade guided the boat toward the mooring can in Avalon harbor on Catalina island and set about tying the lines to secure the boat from bow to stern. The trip had been uneventful, the weather calm, the sailing smooth. But his passenger had yet to return to the deck.

With the dinghy ready to take them ashore, Wade made his way to the cabin below. The galley was empty, the food he'd set out was untouched and there was no sign that Gina had even been there.

With a curious brow raised he walked to his master bedroom and bath, finding that room empty as well. He'd have guessed as much and smiled to himself, but his smile faded quickly when he finally found Gina, sprawled out on the bed in the guestroom.

"Gina," he said quietly.

When she didn't rouse, he entered the room and gazed down at her, lying across the bed, her hair in a tangle, the dark tresses half covering her beautiful face. The dress she wore rode up her thigh, the material exposing thoroughly tanned, shapely legs. She'd kicked off her shoes and made herself comfortable on the dark-russet bedspread. She looked peaceful and more tempting than a woman had a right to look. Hell, even her polished scarlet-red toenails turned him on.

Her eyes opened slowly, as though she'd sensed him watching her. With a sleep-hazy sigh, she stretched her limbs, reminding him of a cat uncurling after a long sleep.

"Mmmm...Wade," she purred and continued that long slow sensual stretch while keeping those lazy half-lidded eyes on him.

God, she was sexy.

But deceitful, too, he reminded himself. He could scarcely believe he'd hired her. She was his employee now and one he wasn't sure he could trust. But his brother Sam had vouched unconditionally for her. "Give her a chance, Wade," he'd said. And Wade had because of Sam's request. But the truth was that if she'd walked into his office without the benefit of his brother's recommendation, he would have hired her anyway. They had unfinished business. Period.

"I'd love to join you, Gina," he said softly, meaning every word, "but we've got a full day ahead of us."

"Oh!"

Gina bounced up from the bed, realizing where she was and with whom. Wade enjoyed every second of that bounce and struggled to keep his lust from becoming visible. Wouldn't take much to throw all rational thought out the porthole and spread his body over hers.

"Sorry, Wade." She untangled the hair that had fallen into her face. "I guess I fell asleep. The rocking of the boat..."

She bent to put her shoes on and treated him to a luscious view. From his position, the dress barely contained her full breasts when she leaned over.

"This is embarrassing," she said. "I've never fallen asleep on the job."

"I won't hold it against you. Anytime you want to slip into one of my beds, feel free."

Gina rose then and looked into his eyes. "Too bad we have a full day ahead of us," she bantered back, repeating his words.

Wade hid his amusement.

"Are we on the island?" she asked.

Wade shook his head. "Not yet. There's a little matter of a dinghy ride to the dock."

The sleep-induced rosy color drained from Gina's cheeks. "How far?"

"Not far," he said. "We'll be ashore in less than five minutes."

Gina groaned and Wade almost felt sorry for her.

"That's five minutes too long."

"Gina, you're gonna have to trust me. I'll keep you safe."

She angled her chin and probed him with those dark sensual eyes. "Trust goes both ways, Wade. Do you trust me?"

Wade held her gaze for a moment then refused her an answer and walked out the door.

Trusting Gina had never been an option.

Four

Gina held her breath through most of the dinghy ride to the mainland. Wade glanced at her from time to time, but his primary focus was on getting the small boat to shore and mooring at the dock. Once there, he secured the dinghy and stepped off the boat with her suitcase, then reached for her hand. "You okay?"

Gina nodded. "I will be as soon as my legs stop trembling."

Wade glanced down and raised a brow. "They look fine to me," he said, with a gleam in his eyes. "Come on, let's get you settled into your room."

Gina got control of her legs once she'd reached solid ground. The sun shined in the clear-blue sky and children's laughter rang out from the nearby beach. Catalina island was a nest for summer travelers wishing to get away from the daily grind of the big city. The mainland, visible on a clear day, was just twenty-two miles away. As they walked along the sidewalk, Spanish influences surrounded them, marking some of the history of the island. She noted a lovely tiled fountain bubbling up with a cool spray in the middle of a circular paved drive. Wade stopped for a minute in front of the fountain.

"Santa Catalina was originally named after Saint Catherine, the patron saint of spinsters," he said. "Lucky for my company, the island is now a resort for lovers."

"So the developer wants the resort to be known as an elite honeymoon destination?" she asked.

Wade nodded. "Can't think of a better place locally. Most of the hotels have no phones and televisions in the rooms. People get real creative to entertain themselves. This whole island spells romance."

Gina nodded as they walked past a row of swaying palms, the gentle sea breeze blowing by, the scent of sand and surf filling her nostrils. She supposed for most people that potent scent meant fun and sun and time away from the hassles of everyday life, but a resort surrounded by water only reminded her of things she'd rather forget.

Within a minute they were at the quaint town of Avalon and Gina looked down a long avenue, which she deemed to be the main street of town. The shops and cafés faced the water and swimsuit-clad vacationers swarmed them as others biked their way down the street. The only other vehicles on the busy thoroughfare were canopied golf carts. Wade continued to lead the way but soon stopped again, this time at a hotel. Villa Portofino. "Here we are," he said. She looked up to see a hotel with all the trademarks of Italy.

Gina nodded. "Nice."

"None better, unless you take a trip to Tuscany."

Gina eyed him carefully, wondering why he'd picked such an expensive place for her to stay. This was just business and she would remind him of that again, if she had to. "So your hotel will have competition."

"Not at all. We plan to build a lavish honeymoon resort with pools, tennis courts and a golf course. The Portofino is a great little beachfront hotel. It won't give us any competition at all. This is where our employees stay when in town working on the project. You won't be disappointed."

Disappointment was the furthest thing from her mind when she entered the Bella Vista suite. True to its name, the suite's wraparound balcony had a grand view of the lush hillside as well as the Catalina harbor. A king-size bed in the center of the room faced a large built-in fireplace and a table for two adorned by a vase filled with tropical flowers. The bath was full-size and encased with fine Italian marble. The whole suite was larger than her tiny guesthouse in Hollywood.

Wade set her bag down and walked to the window

to stare out at the harbor. He'd waved off the bellboy, insisting on bringing her up here himself. "It's a far cry from El Paso."

Gina sucked in her breath. What could she say to that? Wade had made something of himself, despite his father's meddling. He was his own man and he'd made the West Coast Triple B a success. Gina couldn't argue with that. "I liked El Paso, Wade. It was the best summer of my life."

He whipped around to stare into her eyes. "I thought so, too…once." His eyes hardened on that last word.

Gina remembered her final week in El Paso. Sarah had been gone during that time, traveling from Dallas to Austin with her mother to interview for teaching positions. Mr. Buckley had been busy at work and Gina had been left pretty much on her own.

After their work was done on their uncle's ranch, Gina would meet Wade and Sam for ice cream or a movie or just to talk. But before long, it was only Wade coming around. They'd gotten close that last week, closer than she might have imagined, spending all of their time together. And they'd fallen in love over hot-fudge sundaes, hot summer walks and hot sizzling kisses.

No one had really known that their friendship had escalated. It hadn't been a secret, but they hadn't made any announcements either. Certainly Sarah hadn't known. Gina hadn't the time to confide in her and when she'd returned from those interviews,

Sarah had been edgy, anxious and unhappy, until she finally revealed her pregnancy to Gina and her parents.

Gina bit back her need to tell Wade the entire truth about Sarah. But destroying his friendship with Sarah wouldn't make up for what Gina had done. She hadn't trusted Wade and she *had* taken his father's money and left El Paso. Her reasons wouldn't matter to him, because Wade was a man who expected total loyalty. She had loved him back then, very much. But he wasn't the same man she'd fallen in love with. And she wasn't the same woman. The years had taught her hard lessons.

"What now?" she asked.

Wade became all business again. "Now? We have a late lunch meeting with James Robinique from the Santa Catalina Island Company. It'll take a few hours." He glanced around the room. "Enjoy yourself. Because after that, we'll be working our tails off."

Gina nodded. At least now they would get down to business. She never minded hard work. "How should I dress?"

Wade toured her body with a possessive eye. "Robinique is a lusty Frenchman with an eye for beauty. It won't matter if you wear a burlap sack, he'll still want to get you into bed."

Gina's mouth gapped open as Wade strolled out the door. Had that been a warning? Or had Wade coaxed her into coming here for an entirely different reason? She knew how important this project was to him, but enticing an island dignitary wasn't in her job description.

Gina couldn't believe it of Wade.

But the thought niggled at her far too much.

She grabbed a down pillow and flung it at the door Wade had just closed. The pillow smacked almost silently before falling to the floor, but it was enough to satisfy Gina's frustration.

"There, now I feel better," she muttered, wishing she had a burlap sack in her wardrobe. Because if she had one, she would surely have worn it just to spite Wade Beaumont.

A little later, Gina unpacked her bag, making sure to hang all of her clothes up carefully. She'd only brought one suitcase, packing enough clothes for the week, but she could make her wardrobe last two, if need be. She knew how to accessorize, how to mix and match and stretch out her clothes for maximum versatility. She prided herself on that. She loved design. She loved to create and one day, she vowed, her creativity would pay off.

A cooling breeze lifted her hair and she strolled to the wide French door Wade had opened, but instead of closing the door, she stepped outside. On a breath, she leaned against the balcony railing and gazed out at the ocean, tamping down shivers of fear, realizing that she'd crossed this ocean today with Wade by her side. She'd spent the better part of the trip below deck, but regardless of that, it was a first step to overcoming her fear.

Here she was on a small stretch of land, completely surrounded by water, working for Wade Beaumont. "Who would have guessed," she whispered into the breeze. She was living through the two scenarios she dreaded most. And the one man she hoped to never see again had orchestrated both.

Gina decided on taking a leisurely shower, luxuriating in the scented soaps, oils and body washes provided. Feeling rejuvenated, she sat down at the dressing table and brushed her long hair, deciding on another upswept do, this time leaving strands of hair down to frame her face. She used a little mascara on her eyes, highlighted the lids and put on a light shade of lipstick.

She decided on a conservative black pencil skirt and white-linen cuffed blouse to wear for the lunch meeting. Gazing in the mirror, she nodded in approval. This was business and, despite Wade's cutting remark, she wanted to appear every bit the professional.

An hour later when Wade knocked on her door, she was more than ready. "I'm all set," she said, opening the door.

Holding a briefcase in one hand and wearing equally professional dark trousers and a white shirt, he had a no-nonsense appearance: tall, dark, imposing. *Handsome.*

He made a quick sweep of her attire and she bit back a comment about burlap as he glanced down at her black-heeled sandals. "We have some walking to do."

Gina lifted one leg and twirled her foot. "These are the most comfortable shoes I own."

Wade arched a brow, taking time to stare at her toes. "Tell me that once we're back and I might believe you. Let's go."

She grabbed her purse, locked up her suite and Wade guided her downstairs with a hand to her back. "We'll go over the details once again about the Santa Catalina Island Company," he said as they walked along the streets.

Gina had read much about it in the reports, but Wade insisted on going over all pertinent information, more to reaffirm his knowledge, she believed, than to clue her in. He would do all the talking. Gina was there to take notes and provide any assistance Wade needed.

Wade explained once again how important this lunch was. The island company had been granted more than forty-thousand acres dedicated to conservation. Rarely did they agree to any building on the island. Anything proposed had to be in tune with the land and provide sanctuary for the wildlife and flora. The developer had sealed the deal, but Mr. Robinique needed to hear the plans directly from each contractor—whoever convinced him that the land would be best protected would gain the upper hand and have the best chance at winning the contract. Robinique's influence over the final proposal couldn't be discounted. Wade had three competitors, he reminded her, but only John Wheatley of Creekside Construction could truly compete with Triple B.

They climbed a hilly street to reach the snug

Harbor Inn and, once inside, Mr. James Robinique rose from his table to greet them. He shook hands with Wade and then smiled at Gina.

"This is my assistant, Miss Grady," Wade said.

Gina offered her hand and Robinique took it, clasping both of his over hers. "It's a pleasure," he said, his blue eyes never wavering.

Gina smiled at the good-looking Frenchman, taken aback by how young he appeared. From Wade's accounting, she'd expected a more mature man. But James Robinique appeared no older than her. He clasped her hand a little longer than she deemed necessary and slowly removed it from his. When she took her seat, the two men also sat down.

Once the meals had been ordered and served, the two men enjoyed healthy portions of halibut sautéed in wine sauce and conversed while Gina nibbled on her chicken salad. Wade drank beer on tap and Mr. Robinique sipped on pinot grigio. Gina opted for iced tea. She was on the clock and taking copious notes.

"Let me assure you that we have every intention of preserving the environment on the island. As you can see from the architectural layouts, there's a bird sanctuary on the grounds, not one tree will be downed and we have enhanced the outer perimeters with ponds and streams that will add to the island's beauty and invite the natural inhabitants."

With the layouts spread across the table, Robinique looked over the designs, making mental notes, nodding his head as Wade continued to make his case.

Gina jotted down his comments and questions, something Wade had asked her to do. Wade was nothing if not thorough and he wanted no stone left unturned.

Gina had to admire Wade's tenacity. He went after what he wanted without compromise. To hear him talk, you'd never guess that the resort—which would house seventy-five rooms, forty deluxe suites, six eloquent cottages, a horse-filled stable, three pools, tennis courts and a golf course—would disrupt the land in any way.

Yet, Mr. Robinique wasn't a pushover. He didn't appear completely convinced. He had specific, detailed concerns pertaining to the ninety acres in question. Wade admitted that he must do one more survey of the land before he could satisfy those questions.

Robinique agreed to meet with him later in the week, suggesting that Wade make use of the nearby stables to go over the entire acreage.

When Wade nodded in agreement, Robinique glanced at Gina. She had stopped writing and he spoke directly to her with just a hint of a French accent. "What do you think of all this, Miss Grady?" With a wave of his hands, he gestured to the plans.

"I think Mr. Beaumont and the staff at Triple B have worked diligently to try to satisfy both the developer and your company."

He kept his focus on her and smiled. "And I think Mr. Beaumont has a loyal employee."

Gina lifted her lips.

Wade kept his gaze tightly fastened to Robinique. "Tell me, Miss Grady, are you through now, taking all those notes?"

Gina glanced at Wade. He nodded and she slipped the notepad into the briefcase. "Yes, I think so."

"Then your work is done for the day?"

"I'm not sure." She looked at Wade.

"If you are satisfied with the presentation, then I would say that our work is done for now," Wade offered. "But we will meet again later in the week."

"Then, we are finished," Robinique said, "unless you would care for coffee and dessert?"

Wade shook his head and looked at Gina. She too, shook her head. "No, thank you."

When Robinique stood, Wade took his cue and the two men shook hands. "I'll call you soon," Wade said, lifting his briefcase.

"I will expect your call," James Robinique replied, then turned to Gina. "Excuse me, Miss Grady" he began, his eyes a striking blue when focused solely on her, "but I cannot let you go without offering you our island hospitality. Would you care to join me for a drink later this evening?"

Gina felt Wade's eyes on her. He had a way of doing that, blatantly watching her with those intense-green eyes. But it was the charming blue eyes on a man with impeccable manners that had caught her off guard. Wade's words from earlier today flitted through her mind.

Lusty Frenchman.

Burlap sack.

Get you into bed.

James Robinique was certainly charming, but Gina wasn't interested in him. At one time in her life, she might have agreed to spend some time with the handsome man. Now all she wanted was to do a good job. She was here on business and she needed to keep her head in the game. She opened her mouth to answer, but Wade beat her to it.

"I plan to keep Gi-Miss Grady busy most of the night...*working.*" One side of Wade's mouth quirked up.

James Robinique blinked his eyes, then darted a glance her way before looking at Wade with a hint of envy. "I see. You are very dedicated then."

Wade nodded. "This project is important to my company."

Robinique gazed at Gina again, this time with more discerning eyes. "Yes, I can see that."

Gina's face flamed but, lucky for her, she'd always been able to hide her embarrassment under her olive complexion. Inside, she fumed. Wade had practically announced that they were lovers and all three of them knew it.

Nothing was further from the truth. Despite her need for job security, she couldn't let Wade get away with this. "I'm sorry, Mr. Beaumont, but I must take some personal time today. I've suddenly developed a terrible headache."

Blinding anger offered up the courage she needed to march out the front door of the restaurant and never look back.

* * *

Gina walked along the main streets of town until her feet ached, her anger ebbed and her heart had stopped racing like she'd just run a marathon. She peeked into shops but had no urge to stop. When tourists smiled at her she didn't smile back. She felt trapped on this island. Trapped in a job she shouldn't have taken—one she couldn't afford to lose.

She'd been out for two hours, enough time to simmer her hot Irish-Italian temper. She headed back to the hotel, contemplating a quiet night with a good book. As soon as she entered her suite, she kicked off her shoes. One flipped up and back hitting the wall behind her, the other slid across the floor to meet with another pair of shoes—a pair of *man's* shoes.

She looked up.

"Where the hell have you been?" Wade's angry voice startled her. He glared at her, arms folded, his face as firm and set as his tone.

"What are you doing in here?" she asked, none too pleased to find her boss invading her private space. "How dare you show up in my room like this!"

"You're on company time, Miss Grady. And this is a company suite."

"Oh, no. No way, Wade. This is my room and while I'm on this island, you have no right entering it without my permission. You're not paying me enough to…to—"

Wade stepped closer, until he was nearly in her

face, his green eyes, holding hers, his voice menacing. "Sue me."

Gina blinked. Anger she'd ebbed earlier rose up again with striking force. She turned her back on him, opened the front door and spoke with a quiet calm she didn't know she possessed. "Get out."

Wade strode to the door and, staring into her eyes, shoved it shut. "No one walks out on me, Gina. And no one dismisses me."

"You're so wrong. Maybe I can't throw you out of here, but I've already dismissed you." On shaky legs, she moved away from the door, away from him.

"What's got you so riled up anyway?"

Gina twirled around. Was he serious? Didn't he know how he had portrayed their relationship? "You deliberately let Robinique believe we were lovers, Wade. You staked your claim, though nothing's further from the truth. But more than that, you had no right to make that decision for me."

"Sleeping with Robinique would compromise the company."

He *was* serious. He'd actually thought she would— Furious, Gina calmed herself and took a different approach. "Quite the contrary, Wade," she began with a slow easy smile, "if I slept with him, the company would only benefit."

Wade couldn't really argue with that, though it galled him just thinking about Gina with James Robinique. Visions of making love to Gina, her soft pliant body meshed with his as they laid down on a soft cushion of hay, were never far from his mind. He remembered her, every inch of her, all too well. That night in El Paso had been magical. Though not experienced, Gina had pleased and pleasured him like no other woman had. "So, you're willing to take one for the team, so to speak?"

Her dark espresso eyes turned black as ink. She stood barefooted, hands on hips, looking at him with defiance. Only the king bed separated them and Wade's thoughts turned to it and how making love to her here would be on a soft mattress and silky sheets.

Gina's voice was deceptively calm, but the fury in her eyes gave her away. "I came here to work with you. Whether you believe me or not, I can be trusted. And if you'd given me the chance, you'd have seen me refuse Mr. Robinique's offer. I have no intention of sleeping with him or any other man. So no, I wouldn't have taken one for the team, Wade. Not like that. Now, please, it's been a long day. If there's nothing else you need from me, I'd like you to leave."

Wade stood his ground. He'd never trust Gina again, but he felt great satisfaction knowing that she would have refused Robinique. Though she'd been wrong on one account. She would sleep with one man while on this island. "Sorry, sweetheart, but you're forgetting who's the boss. And there is something else I need from you. I wasn't lying to Robinique when I said we'd be working into the night."

Gina's ire seemed to vanish. "Oh?"

Wade headed for the door. "We have a dinner meeting in exactly two hours. Be ready when I pick you up."

Gina stood there with a confused look on her face, her eyes softening, her rigid body relaxing. He glanced down at her red toenails and had never wanted a woman more.

Wade whipped the door open and exited.

Before he told her what he really needed from her.

The dinner meeting, held at a small eatery on Avalon's main street boasting buffalo milk, ended after ten o'clock. Gina had eaten quickly and immediately returned to taking notes. Wade had set up this dinner with local shop owners and proprietors to gain their support and trust, to get to know them, to assure them that if Triple B won the bid, their workers would add to the economy and not cause any trouble. Gina learned from day one that Catalina island thrived on the tourist trade. It was essential that there be no unsavory incidents and no bad press on the island. Wade was smart enough to know that, to understand their concerns.

When all was said and done, Wade escorted her outside and, as they headed toward her hotel suite, he asked. "How do you think that went?"

"By their own admission, not one of the other builders had approached them. Your assurances went a long way. I'd say you scored points."

Wade nodded. "I want to be on friendly terms when we win the bid. Our crews are the best, but get a bunch of men working in a confined area for too long and that might spell trouble. They needed to know I'd do everything in my power to keep things running smoothly."

"I think you convinced them." Wade wasn't just blowing smoke. Gina really believed he meant what he said. Nine years ago, she would never have believed that the roughriding rancher with the sweet nature would become such an astute businessman. She never pictured him in that role. Yet here he was, talking the talk, making the deals. Gina shook her head.

Wade caught the slight movement. "What?"

"Nothing, really. It's nothing."

Wade was silent for a while, then before they reached her hotel, he stopped. "I could use a drink. There's a nightclub up the street known for their tropical drinks. Care to join me?"

Gina hesitated. A nightcap sounded wonderful. She'd had a tumultuous day. She was physically exhausted but the idea of relaxing with a pina colada and some good music sounded great. "I bet the music's real loud."

"Probably," Wade replied honestly.

Gina nibbled on her lower lip. "It's probably crowded."

"Without a doubt."

"Am I on the clock?" she asked. Looking into Wade's beautiful green eyes what she really wanted to know was if his request had been a demand of the job or a simple invitation.

Wade shook his head. "Not at all. I don't like to drink alone, but if it's not what you—"

"I could use a drink, too."

"Great. Let's go," he said, with a pleased look on his face. They strolled up a slightly inclined street and, somewhere along the way, Wade twined his fingers with hers and they entered the nightclub hand in hand.

For Gina, it felt as natural as breathing.

Five

"I want to make love to you," Wade whispered in her ear, his warm breath combined with those softly spoken words caused havoc to her nerves and brought tingles to her toes.

With her arms wrapped around his neck, their bodies brushing, swaying to the jazz band's bluesy sensual ballad, Gina rested her head on his shoulder. After two piña coladas, her brain was fuzzy, but not fuzzy enough to disregard what was happening between them. She was fully aware of what Wade wanted. "It's not in my job description," she whispered back softly.

She felt Wade's smile. It was difficult not to feel the same arousing sensations, not to succumb to his body heat or the pressing evidence of that desire. Gina wanted him, too.

"I told you before, you're not on the clock, Gina."

Wade dropped his hands down lower on her back, his fingers splaying across her derriere. He made soft caressing circles as he drew her closer. "Remember how it was between us, Gina? It can be that way again."

She shouldn't allow him such liberties. The fact remained that he was still her boss. They had a job to do here on the island. But the sensations swept through her with blinding force. His touch heated her, his words enticed her and his hard body stirred her softer one. She raised her head from his shoulder to look into his eyes.

It was a mistake.

Wade's intense gaze blazed into hers, before his lips came down in a soul-searing kiss, right there on the crowded, smoky dance floor. They kissed. And kissed.

Gina's body ignited, but dire warnings fanned the flames quickly. She couldn't allow Wade in. Not again.

She shoved at his chest and pulled away from him, her body swamped with heat, defying her reasoning. "I didn't come here for this," she breathed out. "It's not a good idea."

Wade reacted immediately. "I can't think of a better one."

Rather than make a scene right there in the nightclub, Gina moved off the dance floor. She walked outside, letting the cool sea breezes clear her head. Wade was beside her instantly. "You're still a liar, Gina."

Gina scoffed and began walking down the street. "Your bedside manner needs improving, Wade."

Wade kept pace, his hand placed possessively on her back. "There's not a damn thing wrong with my bedside manner. And you'll find that out as soon as you stop lying to yourself and admit what you really want."

Gina heaved a big sigh, her head in as much turmoil as her quaking body. "What I *want* is to go to bed. Alone."

Wade curled a hand around her neck, bringing her face close, as he came around to block her from walking past him. She was forced to look into those smoldering green eyes.

They stood under the moonlit night sky with twinkling stars overhead, right outside the entrance of her hotel. "Sorry, sweetheart, but what you want is for me to crawl up inside your sheets, strip you naked and rock your world."

Gina's mouth opened. Then closed.

"It's going to happen, Gina. Bank on it."

He left her standing on the front steps of the hotel, captivated by the steamy image swirling around in her head, more angry than she ever remembered being and wishing that, more than anything, Wade Beaumont had been wrong.

Wade dressed in a pair of Wranglers, faded not by the manufacturer, but by hard work and long wear, a plaid shirt and his Stetson. He put on his boots and left *Total Command* to pick up Gina this morning.

Although clothes didn't make the man, Wade was comfortable in these, the old standbys, the worn leather of his boots and the soft cotton of his shirt reminding him of his time at Uncle Lee's ranch in El Paso. He wasn't that young man anymore. Time, with all the hardships, heartaches and headaches, had a way of changing a man.

His heart had hardened. And he knew it. He was relentless when he wanted something. Maybe that much of his old man had rubbed off on him. Wade wanted two things. He wanted to win the bid on the Catalina project and he wanted Gina.

Neither one would escape him. He would see to that.

He knocked on her door at precisely 8:00 a.m.

When she didn't answer, he knocked again, harder.

"Are you looking for me?"

Wade whipped around in the hallway and caught Gina's unfettered expression. She hadn't recognized him, that much was obvious. And once she had that genuine look vanished.

"Oh," she said, standing there, her breaths coming quickly, with sweat on her forehead, dressed in killer shorts and a white spandex top. "Wade, I didn't—"

"Do you run?"

A quick smile curled her lips. "I try."

They stood silent for a moment, gazing at each other, but Wade couldn't miss Gina's probing eyes and those few rapid blinks as she took in his appearance, as if trying to figure out which man he really was: the fast, hard businessman or the easy, kind cowboy she'd once known.

The confusion in her eyes bothered him, so he ignored her expression and swept his gaze instead to her long legs, and tanned smooth skin. More leg than she'd allowed him lately. And as his gaze traveled upward, he noted her breaths coming fast and the spandex top unable to confine the swell of her breasts and the damned enticing tips of her erect nipples.

Her hair was pulled back in a ponytail. She looked sweaty and hot and sexy enough to have for breakfast.

"I thought I had an hour before going to the stables," she said, opening the door to her suite and entering.

Wade followed her inside. "You do, but we need to eat something first. I ordered room service. Breakfast will be here soon."

In a single fluid move, Gina pulled the elastic band from her hair and chestnut strands flowed onto her shoulders, framing her face. "Let me guess, last night you didn't want to drink alone and today you don't want to eat alone."

Wade shrugged off her comment as he tossed his hat onto her bed. "Doesn't figure for me to eat alone when I have a beautiful assistant at my disposal."

"I may be at your disposal in business, Wade, but that's the extent of it."

Again, he ignored her. "You look *hot.*"

Gina frowned. "I know. I'm hot and sweaty. I must look a mess." She ran her hand through her hair in an unconscious move that had Wade approaching her.

"Not a mess." He strode the rest of the distance separating them, facing her toe to toe. *"Sexy as hell."*

Gina blinked then captured his gaze as well as his meaning. She backed up a step, her tone filled with warning as she shook her head slightly. "Wade."

Wade reached for her waist, encircling his arms around her and pulled her close. A combination of female and salty scents drifted up as she looked at him with hesitation in her eyes.

"Don't fight it, honey." Wade swooped his mouth down and took her in a long, slow, deliberate kiss that had her molding her body to his. A little moan escaped her throat when Wade cupped her buttocks, pressing her to the juncture of his thighs.

She fit him perfectly. She always had. Immediate heat swamped him and his groin tightened envisioning her on the bed with him, just a few feet away. He'd wanted her, wanted *that* ever since she'd walked into his office a few days ago.

A knock at the door broke the moment.

Wade winced at the bad timing. And, as he tugged his mouth from hers, he whispered, "Room service." Wade had a notion to send the waiter packing and finish this. Just as he began to utter those commands, Gina backed away.

"I—I need a shower."

Wade glanced at her chest, the tempting swell of her breasts straining against her spandex top with her breathes coming hard again, only this time, he knew her fast breathing had nothing to do with the run she'd just taken. "So do I—a cold one."

Gina's gaze slipped down to his jeans, her eyes riveted below his waist.

Wade ground out a warning. "Don't tempt me, Gina."

"I never mean to."

That was the problem. Gina, just being Gina, was enough of a temptation. Didn't matter what she wore, how she looked, Wade found himself wanting her, no matter what. She was beautiful to him. That much hadn't changed. From the moment he'd set eyes on her almost ten years ago, he'd wanted her. Had to have her.

The only difference between now and then was that now he knew he'd have her but he'd never keep her.

The knock came louder this time, announcing, "Room service!"

Wade let out a deep sigh, restraining his desire. "I'll get the door. You get your shower."

Gina nodded and, without a word, entered the bathroom. After a second, he heard the decided click of the bathroom door's lock.

Gina mounted a bay mare, fitting herself as comfortably as she could on the saddle. It had been almost ten years since she'd ridden a horse. She'd been taught by the best; Mr. Buckley, Sarah and

Wade all had a hand in teaching her how to ride. But she was rusty and uncertain.

"Don't let her know you're nervous," Wade said, gripping the reins, holding the mare steady from the ground. Gina took a deep breath and nodded.

"You'd think a girl born and bred in Texas would know more about horses than how to hang onto the saddle horn."

Wade grinned. "You were from Austin. That doesn't count."

"Austin was full of horses." Gina tipped her chin up in defiance.

"Right. And you rode how many?"

Wade didn't wait for an answer. He handed her the reins, then swung his long legs up and over his saddle, mounting a tall dappled-gray mare. "Follow my lead. Loosen up on the reins and use only slight motions to guide the mare. You'll do fine."

"I can't take notes and ride. Why do you need me?"

"I need another pair of eyes."

Gina doubted that. She knew for certain that scores of Triple B's finest—from architects to financial accountants—had surveyed the property already.

"Ready?"

Gina squirmed once more in her saddle and adjusted the straw hat Wade had purchased in town for her. "Ready."

Wade made a soft sound to his mare and with just the slightest click of his boot heels, the horse took off. Gina's mare followed and they rode off the stable grounds and away from the road, heading further into the interior of the canyon.

Ten minutes later, Wade reined his horse to a stop. Saddle leather creaked when he turned around in his seat. "Take a look," he said.

Gina's gaze flowed in the direction he was pointing. They had steadily climbed and had come to a low rise that overlooked the entire town of Avalon and the crescent-shaped bay below. From this distance and under clear-blue skies, the ocean seemed less threatening with a throng of boats harbored in the stunning turquoise bay. "It's remarkable."

Wade agreed with a low grumble. "It's hard to believe this place once was home to pirates and trappers."

"Yes, but I can picture it, can't you? The wildness here, the untouched land and those men coming here, some for honest work, others to do harm or hide out."

Wade cast her a long thoughtful look, his eyes narrowing as if picturing it. "Yeah, I can see that," he said, his lips quirking in a distant smile, before turning back around.

Once again he *looked* like the Wade she'd known in El Paso, only more mature, stronger, more capable, if that were even possible.

"Not much longer now," Wade said, as they passed oaks and sage and tall limber stalks of sun-yellow and white poppies.

They met up with a road again and Gina saw the gates that led to a clearing. No Trespassing signs cordoned off the area.

Wade dismounted and used a key to unlock the chains on the gate before mounting his mare again. Gina followed him inside.

The clearing where the resort was to be built was anything but clear. Tall cottonwoods blocked the sun, natural formations jutted up from the earth and canyon walls provided the backdrop.

"The architects have done a great job in preserving most of what you see. We won't down these trees. They'll be a natural part of the landscape. Out there in the distance, a wildflower meadow allows just enough land to build the main hotel and facilities. About half a mile down the road there's a secluded cove that we'll utilize for special occasions and weddings. You name it. This is the first project I've been involved with where the land dictates the building, instead of the other way around. I think Robinique understands that."

Wade spurred his mare on. "Come on. I need to see it all one more time and get your opinion."

"I've seen the plans on paper, Wade. But it's hard for me to picture it. Seems like this place needs to stay untouched."

"*Nothing* stays untouched, Gina." He cast her a narrow-eyed look from under the brim of his Stetson. "I learned that lesson a long time ago."

"So as long as it's going to be *touched,* you might as well be the one doing the touching?"

Wade stared deeply into her eyes, capturing her and making her flinch from his intensity. "That's right."

Heat crept up Gina's neck. She wanted out of this conversation, knew she should let the comment go, but she couldn't. Wade had twisted her words and suddenly they weren't speaking about the land any longer. She fought her rising anger. "When did you become so ruthless?"

Wade's voice held contempt. "You know the answer to that."

Gina slumped in the saddle. Telling him the truth now wouldn't do any good. Wade had changed. He was a man walking in the shadow of his father. He was just as driven, just as bitter. Getting involved with him again would be a big mistake. She'd already had a bad relationship with one unscrupulous man and she feared Wade Beaumont, too, would only use her then toss her aside.

Gina kept Sarah's secret close to her heart. It wasn't her secret to divulge anyway. If Sarah wanted Wade to know the truth, then she would tell him in her own time. Long-standing friendships were at stake here and Gina wanted no part in destroying Sarah's relationship with Wade. Gina was the outsider and she would always remain so. "We'd be better off just sticking to business, Wade."

Wade cocked his head and sent her a crooked smile. "That's all I was talking about. Business."

Gina's temper rose with lightning speed. There was no stopping the rage within her. She silently cursed Wade and his infuriating hold on her. She needed to get away from him. She kicked her mare's flanks just as a wild hawk swooped down from a cottonwood. The horse reared up in fright—nearly tossing Gina from the saddle—then her front hooves landed hard onto the ground and the mare took off running.

Startled, the reins dropped from Gina's hands. She grabbed for the saddlehorn, bouncing on the seat as the mare raced across the meadowland. Her hat flew from her head as she hung on.

She heard Wade's commands from behind, knew he was racing behind her, trying to catch up. Gina held on for dear life. Her shoes came out of the stirrups from the turbulent ride. She lost her balance in the saddle and her grip on the horn. Within seconds, she was tossed off the horse.

She hit the ground hard.

Dazed from the fall, she heard Wade's footsteps fast approaching. And then he was leaning down beside her with fear in his eyes and a voice filled with gentle condemnation. "Damn it, Gina. You're always running away."

Six

With her head pounding, her body twisted and the air knocked out of her, Gina squinted into the morning sun. Wade moved to obstruct the light, his tone fierce but his hands gentle as he touched and surveyed her body for injuries. "Did you hit your head?"

She gazed into his eyes as his fingers searched for a bump. "I have a hard head."

"Tell me about it," he muttered, yet the softness in his eyes belied his tone. When he didn't find a bump on her head, his hands traveled to her face, gently turning her right to left, searching for injury. "Can you untwist your body?"

Gina did exactly that. She straightened her form

then winced. "I'm sore, but at least everything's moving."

He frowned and spoke quietly, "The fall won't really hit you until tomorrow."

Gina looked up into his eyes. She liked what she saw there. In an unguarded moment, Wade let down his defenses and she witnessed the depth of his compassion. "You mean I have aches and pains to look forward to?"

"Remember when I tried to break Rocket? That horse wouldn't give in. He must have thrown me a dozen times."

Gina nodded, recalling Wade's determination to break the wild stallion his uncle Lee had captured in the mountains. After several bronc-busters had tried, his uncle Lee had just about given up and had been ready to turn the stallion loose. But Wade had been more stubborn than the stallion and had finally tamed the beast. "I remember that you had trouble walking the next day." Then it dawned on her. Slightly panicked, she tried to rise up. "You're not saying I'm going to feel like that?"

Wade placed a calming hand to her shoulder. "Hold still, honey."

In one grand sweeping movement, Gina was lifted up into Wade's arms. She automatically roped her arms around his neck. He carried her to the shade of an ancient oak.

He felt solid and warm and, when he peered down at her, she couldn't miss the concern in his beautiful green eyes.

"You're not as tough as you let on," she whispered near his ear. "Sometimes, I see the man you were in El Paso, Wade."

"I don't think he exists anymore, Gina." Wade pitched his Stetson and Gina watched the hat land near her mare's hooves. It was so telling, so obvious what that toss of the hat meant. Wade didn't want to go back. He'd moved into the role of a high-powered executive and was comfortable there.

She let out a quiet sigh. "A girl can hope, can't she?"

Wade stared into her eyes for a long moment and nodded then lowered down to sit against the base of the oak, keeping Gina firmly in his arms and on his lap. "Are you hurt? Do you feel dizzy?"

She shook her head, "I'm not hurt at all. My head's fine. You can let me up now."

"I can't," he said.

Her brows lifted. "Can't?"

"Don't want to, won't."

He smiled, right before his lips touched hers. The brush of his mouth over hers sent warm comforting shivers throughout her body.

She wound her arms tighter about his neck and he deepened the sweet kiss, coaxing her mouth open. From there, Wade took complete control, mating their tongues in a slow fiery seduction while his hand stroked her face then her throat. Gentle fingers traveled lower, unfastening the top buttons of her blouse.

Wade had her in his arms, at his mercy. Gina

couldn't fight her desire any longer. She was where she wanted to be. The Wade she'd known was still there, inside, somewhere in the soft caress of his eyes, in the caring way he held her and in the coaxing brush of his lips. She wanted Wade Beaumont to return. She wanted the man she'd once loved. She'd do anything to bring him back to her.

He slipped his hand inside her blouse. She moaned when he touched her breasts, remembering those fingers, gentle yet rough against her skin. She strained against him. He took more, easing her bra down, cupping her, flicking her nipple until she moaned louder, feeling the pulse of his erection against her thigh.

When he broke off the kiss, they looked deeply into each other's eyes. "Definitely feeling dizzy now," she whispered softly.

Wade smiled again and spoke in a low, raspy voice. "You want me."

It wasn't a question but a statement of fact. One she couldn't deny. "Yes."

Wade kissed her again and palmed her breast until spiraling heat curled up from her belly.

"This is a long time coming, Gina."

He pressed her down lower on his lap and, leaning over her, he slipped his hand under the waistband of her jeans, his fingers trekking slowly, teasing, tempting, until finally he reached her.

Gina welcomed him. His touch, the stroking of his fingers as they kissed, brought damp moist heat and an ecstasy she'd only known in his arms.

Suddenly, Wade froze, his head shooting up and he muttered a foul curse.

"What is it?" Gina asked, stunned by his quick abandonment.

"Security jeep. Coming from down the road. They must have seen the gate unlocked."

He lifted her off him and together they stood facing each other, Gina's clothes as disheveled as her mind.

"Get dressed," he said. "I'll go meet them. Explain who we are."

No words came. She could only nod.

Wade plucked his hat from the ground, yanked it onto his head and strode over to his horse. Before mounting, he turned to her with deep regret in his eyes, as he watched her button her blouse. "One of these days I'm going to make love to you in a damn bed."

Wade escorted Gina back to town, leaving her in front of the hotel. She'd been quiet on the ride back to the stables and then, as they walked back to the hotel, she hadn't said more than a few sentences. Wade wasn't in the mood for talking either. He'd had a few choice words for the security guards who needed convincing that he wasn't a trespasser. Their interruption had cost him. His desire for Gina had gone unsatisfied and that made him want her all the more.

It irritated the hell out of him how much he wanted her. She couldn't be trusted and he'd never forgive her for her betrayal, so why wasn't he satisfied with all the other women he'd had in his life?

"Take a few hours to rest. We have a late lunch meeting. I'll go to the boat and do some work. I'll be back later to pick you up."

Gina nodded, but kept her eyes from meeting his. "Okay."

Wade cupped her chin and forced her to look at him. "Are you up for it?"

She shot him a look of defiance. "I came here to work, Wade." She backed away, releasing his hold on her. "So yes, I'm up for it. But back there, that was a mistake. We've both changed. We're not the same people we were when we knew each other in El Paso. You're paying me to be your personal assistant. I don't believe sleeping with the boss is in my job description."

Wade tamped down rising anger. "*That* had nothing to do with business or the fact that I'm your boss. As I recall, you said yes and couldn't wait for me to get into your pants."

Gina's dark eyes went wide. She lifted her hand and Wade warned her with a searing glance not to even try it. When she lowered her hand, she spoke with quiet calm, her words more potent than any slap to the face. "I thought I saw an inkling of the man you once were, Wade. The man I wanted above all else, the man who was kind and generous and caring. But I was mistaken, you're *nothing* like him."

Wade jammed his hands in the back pockets of his jeans, watching her spin around and walk into the hotel lobby. Her words stung but he wouldn't be played for a fool ever again.

No matter how much he wanted her.

* * *

Wade poured himself a whiskey on the rocks, something that always soothed his bad temper, and took a seat at his desk. He let the mellow rocking of the boat and the fresh sea breeze calm him for several minutes before opening his e-mail account. He punched in his password and viewed more than a dozen messages forwarded to him from Triple B.

As he went through half of them, all having to do with the Catalina project, Wade came upon one message he hadn't expected, from Sarah Buckley.

He hadn't spoken with Sarah in over six months. They'd always remained friends, but ever since that episode with Gina years ago, their relationship hadn't been quite the same. He'd left El Paso shortly after that tumultuous summer to work at Triple B with his father. Maybe his imagination was in overdrive, but whenever he had visited his uncle and aunt in El Paso, he'd also made a stop in to see the Buckleys and, oddly, they'd been slightly distant, polite but not as friendly as he remembered. And Sarah, too, had seemed more cautious with him.

He punched in and opened the e-mail.

Wade, I know you're out of town, but it's important that you call me when you return. We need to talk.
Always,
Your friend,
Sarah

Wade sipped his drink, staring at the message for a moment, making a mental note to call Sarah once he returned to Los Angeles. Right now, he had enough to deal with, Gina being right up there on his list.

He realized his approach with Gina had been completely wrong. She wasn't an easy female to figure out but he did know that when she was backed into a corner, she came out fighting. Though she was as headstrong and volatile as she was beautiful, Wade wouldn't let her get away this time around. She had become nearly as important as the Catalina Project and both were challenges he fully intended to win. He finished his drink, took a quick shower and changed into different clothes. Before meeting Gina at the hotel, he had one important errand to run.

Gina glanced at the digital clock on the bed stand. It was ten minutes after two and Wade was late. It wasn't like him to be late for a meeting.

She glanced at her reflection in the framed beveled mirror, straightening out her tan skirt and cream knit shell top. She tossed the short tailored jacket she'd donned minutes ago onto the bed and headed to the wraparound balcony for a breath of fresh air.

Her nerves had been wrought ever since she'd come to this island. The trip over here in Wade's yacht had nearly done her in and she hadn't thought things could've gotten any worse. But they had.

She didn't know where she stood with Wade. He was her boss, that was a given. He wanted to be her lover. That's where it all got confusing. She knew enough not to get involved with him romantically, yet when he kissed her and touched her tenderly, memories flooded in, sweet hot wonderful memories of the times they had shared in the past. Gina had succumbed to him earlier today and the heat of his touch still sizzled on her lips and other highly sensitive parts of her anatomy. Wade had left his mark on her body.

A light-hearted tap on the door surprised her. She strode the distance wondering who it could be. Certainly Wade's knock had always been more commanding. When she opened the door to her suite, she stood in awe, looking at a smiling Wade, dressed in khaki shorts and a tan polo shirt, black beach sandals on his feet.

"Our meeting was cancelled," he said, walking in holding a shopping bag. "I figured we both could use some down time."

"Down time?" Gina asked, confused by Wade's uncharacteristic light mood.

"Yeah, you know…relax, soak up some sun, enjoy the beach."

Gina stared at Wade. "That sounds nice," she fibbed. The last place she could relax was staring out at the fathomless ocean. "But I'm afraid I didn't bring 'down time' clothes with me. Sorry, you'll have to go it alone." She sent him a small smile.

Wade lifted up the bag. "That's why I brought this."

Gina watched him set the bag on her king-size bed. "Oh, I was hoping that was lunch."

Wade shot her a sweeping glance, his eyes raking in her body from top to bottom. "Depends on how you look at it."

"What? What did you bring me?" Gina walked over to the white bag and tossed the contents onto the bed. Swimsuits, sarongs and fancy rhinestone flip-flops scattered. Gina lifted up a pure-white dazzling bikini. "A thong?" She turned to face him. "Not on your life."

Wade laughed. "I had to try." He gestured to the others. "What about the black one?"

Gina eyed him cautiously, before picking it up and scanning it over. The bikini had a tad more material than the thong, she noted. She shook her head. "You don't know my size."

Wade stepped closer to her and looked into her eyes. He spoke softly, with confidence. "I know your body, Gina. They'll fit."

Heat rushed up, warming her throat and blistering her face. Once again she thanked the Almighty for her olive complexion. At least she could hide her blush from Wade, if nothing else. She set the suit down. "I'd really rather stay in."

Wade folded his arms across his middle. "Okay, we'll stay in." He glanced at her then the bed. "What do you suppose we can do in here all afternoon?"

Gina flinched. "I wasn't inviting you."

Wade took a seat on the sofa, his arm spread along the top cushion. "Gina, what are you afraid of? We'll go down, have lunch at a café, then relax on the beach for a few hours."

"You know I don't like the water."

"You traveled twenty-two miles over that water to get here."

"I know. I'm dreading the trip back." Just the thought brought shivers.

Wade pointed to the clothes on the bed. "Try the red one, Gina. It's a one-piece."

Gina glanced at it and frowned. "With more cutouts than Swiss cheese."

"You noticed that, too?"

Wade didn't even try to hide his amusement. "Come on, Gina. You must be starving by now."

Gina's stomach rumbled quietly. Thankfully, Wade didn't seem to hear. She was hungry and it seemed the only way to get Wade out of her hotel room was to leave with him. "Okay, fine. I'll wear the red one."

Gina grabbed the swimsuit, a multicolored sarong and sparkling rhinestone flip-flops and stomped into the bathroom, ignoring Wade's satisfied chuckle from the sitting area.

She knew he'd be right. Everything he bought would fit her.

Perfectly.

Gina sipped her piña colada, the coconut-and-rum tropical drink sliding cold and smooth down her throat. Wearing the cherry-red swimsuit underneath the sarong cover-up, she faced Wade from her seat at the beachfront café, surprised at his casual demeanor. He'd dominated the conversation, opening up to her about his time at Triple B working with his father, learning the business, then taking over after his father died and Sam remarried and started a new life at Belle Star Stables. He'd filled her in on his life from the time he left El Paso to the present. Of course, she was certain that he'd left out choice bits about his love life and he'd skirted the issue about their onetime hot and steamy relationship.

If he'd wanted her to relax, he'd succeeded. The two empty piña colada glasses in front of her might have had something do with it as well, but Gina wouldn't look a gift horse in the mouth.

"So what about you? What did you do once you landed in Los Angeles?" he asked, his tone light, his eyes holding nothing but curiosity.

Gina had always wanted Wade to understand what her life had been like before and after she met him. There had been so many things left unsaid. Perhaps now was the time, after all this time, to come clean, at least partly. She'd always wanted Wade's trust and maybe this was the first step in gaining it back.

"I'd always liked Los Angeles. Sarah and I roomed at UCLA for four years together. We were girls from two different worlds. Though I was raised in Austin, my parents were city folks. They owned a small Italian restaurant. My mother was a terrific cook."

"As I recall, so were you."

"Thank you. It was a family-run operation. I worked there until I left for college."

"And after college, when you left El Paso, what did you do?"

Gina peered at Wade. He'd just polished off a sandwich and was working on the fries and his second beer. Because she didn't find any sign of resentment, any hint of a trap, she continued. "I looked for work and did some odd jobs here and there. Nothing too stimulating, but all the while I'd been working on clothing designs. That's when I realized I'd probably wasted four years of my life in college. I should have been following my heart. I entered the Fashion Institute and loved every minute of it. When I got out, I ventured into my own business. Or at least, I tried."

"What do you mean, you tried?" Wade asked. "What happened?" He plucked another fry up and shoved it into his mouth.

Gina took a deep breath and surged on. "I didn't have any money, so I took on a partner. A man. He seemed to have more business sense than me, some really good ideas. We took out loan after loan to fund our venture. I…trusted him."

Wade took a pull from his beer. "Mistake?"

"Big, big—huge—mistake."

Wade set his beer down and leaned in, his elbows braced on the table now. "I'm listening."

"He stole my designs and every bit of money we'd borrowed. I have no idea where he is or what happened to him."

Wade studied her a moment as if sorting something out in his mind. "Were you involved with him?"

Gina paused, hating to admit this to Wade. She'd been such a fool. "Yes. He was charming and so easy to be with…a charming con man."

Wade sat back in his seat, looking at her. "I get it now. Why you took the job working for me."

"I'm in debt, Wade. I owe a lot of people a lot of money."

"You shouldn't have to pay it all back."

Gina bit her lip, and swallowed. "Some of the loans were in my name only—a good many of them."

Wade nodded and had her gratitude for not telling her what a gullible fool she'd been.

"I plan to repay every loan. There isn't anything I won't do to clear my name. I still want my dream. I still have the designs in my head. I know I can do it, but first I need to clean up my debts."

He eyed her now, holding her gaze. He was a wealthy affluent man and her debts might seem trivial to him, but to her, the thousands she owed were monumental. "How much are we talking about here?"

Gina shrugged and smiled. "You don't want to know. It doesn't matter. Like I said, I'll do whatever it takes to get out from under all my debt. Then I plan to start GiGi Designs on my own. I'm determined."

Wade shot her a look of admiration and she wondered where that had come from. Nervous and uncomfortable from his perusal, Gina changed the subject. "Are you through with lunch?"

He smiled. "Do you see anything left on my plate?"

"Then I guess we should get the relaxing on the beach and soaking up the sun over with."

Wade stood, tossed some cash onto the table and took her hand in his. "It's hardly cruel and unusual punishment."

Gina only smiled at the comment, but for her that's exactly how it seemed. She doubted she'd ever be comfortable sitting on the beach just steps from the ocean.

Ten minutes later, they were lying against rented sand chairs, lathered in sunscreen, watching children play in the water. Wade's eyes were closed under his dark sunglasses, his chest bare and his long lean legs stretched out along a beach towel. He looked magnificent.

When one little girl slipped and went under a wave, Gina rose up and gasped. "Oh no."

Wade glanced up, noting Gina's distress. They both watched the child lift up from the water, dripping wet, her face animated and her joyous laughter ringing through the noisy beach.

Relieved, Gina sank back down, trying hard to control her irrational fear. It was enough that she couldn't stand the water, but she should be able to see others enjoying themselves without thinking the very worst. Without those terrifying flashes of memory hitting her.

"Come on, Gina. We're going for a walk."

Gina hadn't noticed Wade rise up from his chair to stand over her. He blocked the sun, peering down at her through those dark shades. "Where?"

"Along the beach."

Gina shook her head fiercely. "No, thank you."

"It'll do you good."

"I...can't, Wade." Didn't he understand her fear? She explained to him that she hadn't stepped foot in a swimming pool—or any body of water—since the accident. Her bathtub days were over as well—she was unable to sit in a tub full of water for any length of time. Sitting just feet from the bay did enough to jangle her nerves.

He reached for her hand. "I think you can. Trust me, on this." He removed his sunglasses to peer deeply into her eyes. "Come on. You'd be doing me a favor."

"A favor?" she asked incredulously. "How so?"

He swept his gaze over her, then zeroed in on her breasts, which were nearly popping out from his most conservative choice of swimsuit. Conservative for a showgirl, that is. "It's torture sitting next to you wearing that thing. Making out on a public beach isn't my style. So do me a favor and take a walk with me. I need the distraction."

Gina laughed, despite her fear. "You're such a liar, Wade. I know what you're trying to do."

"Don't be so sure that I'm lying." Then he leaned down to within a breath of her. Her gaze flowed over his strong, muscled chest, then up to his face, the hot gleam in his green eyes. "And don't tempt me. I'd rather be on a private beach with you, but this just might have to do."

Gina didn't believe him for a second, yet his

powers of persuasion couldn't be denied. "Okay, let's go for a short walk."

Wade nodded, slipped his sunglasses on and took her hand. "Let's go."

The short five-minute walk Gina had hoped for ended up being a thirty-minute stroll along the beach with Wade doing all the talking, *all the distracting.* He held her hand and she knew this time it was to lend moral support rather than any need he had for intimacy. Once they reached a secluded cove, far away from the loud boisterous beach crowd, Wade stopped by the water's edge and turned her by the shoulder to look into his eyes.

"Just stand here." He took both of her hands now and held on. They faced each other, her back to the ocean. "Keep looking at me."

Gina held her breath, her bare feet digging into the hot sand. "If you're trying to torture me, you're doing a fine job."

"I'm trying to help. The surf's coming up."

Gina flinched.

Wade held her firm. "I've got you. Don't move. Just let it wash over your toes. Gina, look at me!"

She did. She looked into his eyes. This was his best revenge. If he meant her harm, wanted to hurt her, this was the way. But for once, Gina gave him the benefit of the doubt. She believed he was sincere, wanting to help. And the only reason she came up with was that Wade couldn't stand to see weakness in others. He couldn't relate. He had no clue how hard it was for her to stand on this beach and give him her full trust.

Water lapped over her feet.

She closed her eyes and fought from running onto dry land. The chill hit her first, then the moisture as her feet dug in again, this time into cool wet sand. It lasted only seconds and once the water ebbed she opened her eyes.

Wade was there, watching her, still holding her hands tight.

"You did it." There was admiration in his voice. "I know it wasn't easy."

"Can I go back to the hotel now?"

Wade smiled. "Once isn't enough. It never is with you."

And then he brought her closer, crushing his lips to hers, lifting her onto the tips of her feet.

She barely felt the next wave as it curled around her toes.

Seven

The next few days flew by and Gina felt she'd earned every dollar Wade was paying her. She attended meeting after meeting and spent a good deal of time on the boat working on the proposal, double- and triple-checking everything. Wade was tenacious in his approach and meticulous with details. He worked with total concentration. It was only once they were done for the night that he would look at her as if he could devour her.

But they were both drained physically and mentally and Gina was grateful he kept his distance. Three days had gone by since that first episode on the beach where Wade had taken her to the water's edge. And every morning since, he'd persuaded her to take a barefoot stroll along the beach for only a minute or two with him. He'd roll his pants up, remove his shoes and urge her to do the same.

Gina had gotten accustomed to the feel of water lapping over her feet. She'd even gotten used to being below on the yacht, working in Wade's small office or at the navigation station. It was the dinghy rides back and forth to the boat that still frightened her. The small tubular boat that Wade made sure to power slowly to the dock and back, brought her close to the surface of the water and even closer to facing her fears.

And now as she sat in the dinghy, ready to head back to the hotel, Wade made the same request he'd made for the past three days. "Put your hand in the water, Gina."

And Gina gave him the same answer she'd given him for the past three days. "Not today, Wade."

But this time, Wade frowned and shot her a determined look, one she'd readily recognized from days of working alongside him. "We're almost through with our work here. It's now or never."

Gina crossed her arms over her middle. "*Never* sounds good to me."

"Then we may *never* get to shore." Wade steered the dinghy away from the shore, slowly heading the boat out of the bay.

Gina froze. Every muscle in her body tensed. Wade couldn't be serious. He wouldn't do that to her. "Wade, don't."

When he looked at her panicked expression, he

killed the engine and softened his tone. "You've got your life jacket on, we're not in deep water and, Gina, I'm here. I won't let anything happen to you. Trust me."

That wasn't the first time he'd asked for her trust. For anyone else, leaning over to put their hand in the ocean might seem easy as pie, but they hadn't witnessed the water swallowing up their parents.

But Gina also knew it was time to face her fear and not let it dictate her life anymore. On a deeply held breath, Gina, seeking his encouragement fastened her gaze on Wade then leaned over and put her hand in the water. She managed to splash it around, tamping down shivers rising up.

"I'll get back at you for this," she told Wade, without the least bit of sincerity.

"I don't doubt it," he said, with a crooked smile, watching her scoop and sift water around for a few seconds. When she pulled her hand out, he seemed satisfied. And again, he didn't pass it off and remark how easy that was for her. No, she appreciated the fact that Wade knew how hard that simple act was for her.

"Now sit back. We're heading in." He started up the motor again.

And once they docked, Wade helped Gina out of the dinghy, placing a chaste kiss on her lips. "You did good back there."

Gina felt like a child who'd won the spelling bee, a stirring of pride, relief and accomplishment. No one knew the terror she'd felt that day and, finally, with

Wade's help she was learning to accept what happened and overcome her fear. "You gave me no choice."

Wade smiled again. "I know. It's how I operate. But it worked. I think you're slowly coming around. Still want to get back at me?"

Gina looked into his beautiful deep green eyes. "I haven't decided yet."

"You can decide over dinner tonight. No work. Just play. We'll have a quiet meal at the Portofino and celebrate."

"Celebrate?"

"Our work is nearly complete here. The bid is ready and we both deserve some time to relax and enjoy."

Gina closed her eyes, imagining dim lights, soft music and a good meal. "Mmm. That sounds good."

"It will be. Come on, I'll walk you back to the hotel so you can get ready."

When he placed his hand on the small of her back, Gina stopped him. "No. I want to walk along the beach. By myself this time."

Wade looked into her eyes, studying her, then nodded. "Okay. I'll meet you downstairs in the Portofino in three hours."

Gina reached up and kissed Wade on the cheek, remarkably grateful for his heavy-handed tactics. With his help, she was finally regaining the part of herself she'd lost nine years ago.

Wade was early. He'd dressed in a casual light-silk suit and paced the floorboards of *Total Command* wishing the time would move faster. He'd shut off the computer, snapped shut his briefcase with a click and shut down his mind from work. He was ready to play.

With Gina.

He decided he'd be better off waiting at the Portofino having a drink instead of pacing the interior of the boat. So he motored into Avalon and walked the distance to the hotel as the early evening sun set on the horizon.

He was immediately greeted at the restaurant door by Peter, the maître d'. "Good evening, Mr. Beaumont. May I see you to a table?"

"Yes, thank you, Peter. There'll be just two. And I'd like a corner table.'"

"Of course," he said, "right this way."

The maître d' led him to a table in the far corner of the dimly lit room and showed him a seat. "This is fine."

"Are you enjoying your stay here on the island, Mr. Beaumont?"

Wade engaged in light conversation with Peter for the next few minutes. When Peter handed him a wine list, Wade immediately shook his head. "No need. I'll take a whiskey on the rocks. And when the lady arrives, a bottle of your finest champagne."

"Of course. I'll have your drink sent to your table right away."

Once Peter walked away, Wade scanned the restaurant in hope of finding Gina here early as well. No such luck. Then the door opened and Gina strode in, looking stunning in a delicately fitted white halter dress with enough folds and billowy flair to turn every head in the place. She wore her hair down, flowing just past her shoulders in soft waves. Wade rose immediately and took a step forward.

Gina strode directly to the bar and sidled up to a man who had his back to him. Wade stopped his approach, retreated and leaned against the back wall, sipping his drink, watching.

The man bought Gina a drink. They stood talking for a while and then they both turned slightly, so that their profiles were visible.

Blood boiled in Wade's veins the instant he recognized the mysterious man. It was John Wheatley, president and CEO of Creekside Construction, his only real competitor on the island.

What the hell was Gina doing sharing a drink and sweet smiles with him? They seemed deep in thought, with shared whispers and heads close. Obviously, she had no knowledge that he was here. Wade had arrived early on purpose and so had she. She probably didn't suspect he'd be here this early.

A myriad of thoughts ran through Wade's mind, trying to fathom why Gina would be speaking with his competitor.

And then everything became crystal clear.

Wheatley dipped into his jacket and took out a checkbook. He wrote the check, ripped it off and placed it directly into Gina's hand. She didn't bother glancing at the amount; she simply opened her purse and dropped it in. She closed the purse again without hesitation. As though she knew the amount. As though this had all been prearranged.

Wheatley and Gina exchanged a few more words, then he kissed her cheek, giving her one soulful lingering look before exiting.

Wade polished off the remaining whiskey in his glass as Gina's words struck him with full force.

There isn't anything I won't do to clear my name.

I'll do whatever it takes to get out from under all my debt.

Gina had done it again. She'd played him for a fool. To think he'd actually admired her gumption and determination. He'd liked her win-at-any-cost attitude. But he'd been blindsided. He honestly hadn't seen this coming. Yet the woman had practically spelled it out in big bold red letters. She couldn't be trusted. She had a ruthless streak in her that ran down her spineless back.

She'd conspired with the enemy. She had access to all Triple B files, all his ideas and the actual bid on the project. Wade couldn't see past his fury. But he was angrier with himself for letting down his guard. For actually beginning to believe Gina had changed. For nearly falling in love with her again.

She'd shown her true colors tonight. She was a liar and a cheat and Wade planned on making her pay. She wouldn't get away with this. As he slipped out the back door only to enter through the front again, he planned his revenge. He knew exactly what he needed to do.

Gina had put him off far too long.

* * *

Gina finished her chardonnay and was setting the wineglass on the bar just as strong arms wrapped around her waist and pressed her close from behind. Warm breath caressed her throat. "You look gorgeous tonight."

She leaned into him, closing her eyes.

Wade.

His scent alone brought shivers and Gina indulged, drinking in the feel and smell of him, man and musk. Her well-honed defenses were crumbling. She was too happy today to fight it. Things were going well, in all aspects of her life, so why not enjoy the evening with an incredibly appealing man?

"You're early," she said quietly.

Wade turned her in his arms, the flow of her soft white dress brushing his thighs. "I couldn't wait to see you again."

There was intensity on his face and in his green eyes as he cupped her chin and lifted her mouth to his. He kissed her soundly, fully, ending the kiss all too soon. She opened her eyes to find him watching her. "Let's have dinner."

He took her hand and she followed him to a table set for two in the far corner of the restaurant. He seated her and took his own seat. A waiter immediately rushed over with an ice bucket and a bottle of very expensive champagne. He set it down and Wade thanked him before turning to her. "The Portofino is known for outstanding service."

Wade wasted no time pouring from the bottle.

He filled two flutes. Bubbles sparkled to the top as he handed her a tapered glass, his smile warm and charming. "To you, Gina. I've finally come to know the woman you are."

This was a new Wade, one she hadn't seen before. Gina touched her flute to his, pleased with his toast. Had he forgiven her? Had he finally realized that she was a woman to be trusted? Could they really put the past behind them?

Slowly, step by baby step Gina was overcoming her fear of water. She had Wade to thank for that and she was grateful for his dogged persistence. He was a never-say-die kind of man and his relentless efforts had worked. That wouldn't have happened if she hadn't taken this job and come to this island.

The glasses clinked. She stared into Wade's beautiful eyes. "Don't forget Triple B. We should toast to a job well done, Wade."

Wade blinked and she thought she lost him for a moment, but then he smiled and nodded. "Right, Triple B. Let's drink to my company and your role in its success."

Gina lifted her lips to the glass. "It's a team effort."

Wade gazed at her from over the top of the glass then sipped champagne. "And you always like to be on the winning team, right?"

He spoke to her softly, but with intensity in his eyes. Gina knew how important winning this bid was for him. She agreed. "I'm hoping to be."

They finished off the bottle of champagne, dined

on Italian bread, Caesar salad, scampi and a light raspberry mocha tart for dessert as the sound of Sinatra serenaded the softly lit room. By the time the meal ended, Gina's head spun from gourmet food, expensive champagne and Wade's complete and charming attention.

She stood and sighed heavily. "Thank you for the meal. It's been a wonderful night. But I think I'm ready for bed."

Wade was by her side, taking hold of her hand. "I've been thinking that all evening, sweetheart."

Before his comment had a chance to register, Wade wrapped an arm around her waist and guided her out of the dining room, changing the subject as they made their way up to her suite.

He was close. So close. And warm. So warm by her side. Her defenses down, when he took the key-card from her hand to open the door she rested her head on his shoulder as the arm embracing her waist, tightened.

"Th-thank you," she said, "I can manage from here."

Wade shook his head. "I think you need more help," he whispered into her ear, then turned her to face him right before his lips came down on hers. He kissed her long and deep and when he was through, Gina's body quaked with raw emotion.

She didn't know which Wade he really was, the charming sexy man she'd been with tonight or the ruthless, powerful never-say-die man she'd seen this week. It didn't seem to matter. Her heart was melting, along with the rest of her body.

His breath flowed over her lips. "Let me tuck you in."

He folded her into his embrace, meshing their bodies together. His heat became her heat, his desire became her desire. She sighed, realizing she was helpless to stop the flow of passion between them. "I can tuck myself in," she said without a drop of conviction.

Wade reached up to play with the straps of her halter, brushing his fingers along the nape of her neck. "But it's more fun when I do it."

"Is it?" she breathed out.

"Try me."

She had tried him once before and she'd never forgotten. She'd given herself to him wholly and without hesitation and the night had been magical. Later when she believed he'd betrayed her, she'd run far away.

At the time, her friend Sarah didn't know what her lies had cost them. But it was too late for regrets. Maybe now, finally, they could move on.

Wade ushered her into the suite and closed the door behind them, but he didn't let her get far. He grabbed her shoulders with both hands, turned her and crushed her against him, stepping back until the door braced his body. She fell into his embrace, his strong arms circling around her.

A buzzing thrill coursed up and down her body. Her legs went weak. Wade had taken control and this time she gave in to him without resistance. "This is going to happen tonight," he said, his voice a husky whisper.

In the back of Gina's mind, she related him to his yacht, the power and sleek smooth ride that was guaranteed.

Total Command.

"Yes," she sighed, her reply unnecessary as Wade wasted no time. He lifted his hands to the back of her neck and untied the straps of her halter. His gaze left her face to watch the tapered ties loosen then fall to her shoulders. His fingers slid over the material, inching it down, further and further, until the air, warm and sultry, hit her breasts.

Wade looked at them and his breath quickened.

She wanted him to touch her, to put his mouth on her. The look in his eyes was far too tempting.

He struggled out of his jacket, then out of his shirt with Gina frantically helping as they tossed his clothes away.

Wade cupped her from behind, his hands splaying across her cheeks, tugging her closer. She meshed against him, her breasts flattened against his chest, her thighs teased by the strength of his erection.

She felt him. Wanted him. His breaths wafted over her neck, his lips nestled against her throat. He unzipped her dress, then maneuvered it down, catching her white lacy panties along the way until she was buck naked, standing before him in her two-inch heeled sandals.

"Better than I remembered," he rasped out, before spinning her around, so that they'd traded places. Gina's back was now pinned against the door. Her heart hammered hard. Wade gave her no time to think. He was on bended knee before her, stroking her calves, his hands climbing higher now, over her knees to slide smoothly up her thighs.

Sensations roared in her head, her body ached. Her mind shut down. "Open for me, baby," he said, and she did. She spread her legs and his fingers found her core. She jolted when he touched the nub that sparked flaming heat and raw, hot desire. She moaned quietly, the erotic sound reverberating in the stillness of the room.

Wade stroked her for only a second, before his mouth replaced his fingers. Gina cried out, the torturous pleasure, so long in coming, would have buckled her if not for Wade's hold on her waist, firm and unrelenting.

His mouth found her folds and parted them. Then his tongue found it's mark and Gina's temperature soared. He stroked her unmercifully while she moaned and moved, up and down, her body finding a pace and a rotation to meet his fiery demand.

He stood abruptly, grabbed a packet from his trousers before removing the rest of his clothes and in seconds, he was lifting her, fitting her to him. "Lock your legs around me, baby," he commanded, and she did. She watched him watch her, the passion in his eyes a heady elixir.

He entered her slowly, the feel of him inside her only matching the look of pure unmasked undeniable lust on his face. She closed her eyes and threw her head back, taking from him what he offered her. Slowly, as if drawing out the pleasure, he filled her.

And when he moved, she clasped him tight, squeezing out her own pleasure.

She heard him grunt then, a carnal sound of deep gratification and, from then on, he moved with quick powerful thrusts, penetrating her to her depths. He pumped harder, faster almost violently and Gina matched him, fulfilling her deepest yearnings.

He wasn't kissing her or caressing her fondly as he had in the past and Gina recognized a difference in him and the way he made love to her. But her mind and body couldn't quite sort it out. She was beyond that now anyway and she clasped her legs tighter around him, sinking into him, fully immersed in his strength and power.

She knew the exact moment when he towered over the edge. She followed him and panted with each potent deliberate thrust, until both were fully sated and spent.

Wade lowered her until her heels found the floor.

He brought her close and whispered in her ear. "Don't even think about getting dressed. I want you naked and in that bed, all night long."

They were hardly the words of love and adoration she expected. Gina pulled back and away to gaze up at him. For a moment, there was a cold bleak look in his eyes, before he blinked it away. She tried to make sense of it all, but then Wade softened his expression, his eyes turning warm and tender on her right before he kissed her. His lips were gentle and sweet and he cradled her, comforted her, gently caressing her shoulders and then her breasts finally making her feel like a woman who had just been loved.

"You want that, too, don't you, honey?" he asked, a charming smile on his face.

She didn't have to think. She was totally, one-hundred percent in love with Wade Beaumont. She reached up to kiss him soundly on the lips. "There's no place else I'd rather be, Wade."

Wade nodded, then picked her up and carried her to the bed.

The night was just beginning.

Eight

Wade made love to Gina slowly this time, enjoying the full expanse of the king-size bed. Gina relished his hands on her, leisurely seeking, exploring and caressing every part of her body. She lay back against the lush cool sheets, savoring his thorough assault and the kisses that caused a tremor to rumble through her. His mouth knew other tricks as well and she welcomed lips that bestowed pleasure at the base of her throat, her shoulders, her breasts. She offered her body and he took it all without hesitation until she felt as though they were at last truly connected.

Though Wade said little, she felt his desire, the fiery look in his eyes, the heat and passion that he couldn't conceal. She witnessed it all and wished for a future filled with that same lust and craving.

Wade reached up to place her arms above her head. He clasped her hands in one of his and held her there, her fingers scraping the headboard. He thrust into her once, holding firm, absorbing her, his eyes closing. "I wanted this…wanted you since the moment I saw you walk into Aunt Dottie's kitchen."

Opening his eyes to stare into hers, he pumped into her, again slowly. "You were the most beautiful girl I'd ever seen."

"Oh, Wade. I wanted you, too."

But Wade didn't respond to her. He continued. "I wanted a future with you, Gina, but then you ran away."

"Wade," she breathed out softly, "let's not talk about the past. Let's just think about tonight." She didn't want anything to spoil this special time with him.

He stared down into her eyes for a long moment. Then nodded. "Tonight, then," he whispered with a kiss.

Gina sighed happily and hoped this night would finally change their relationship from one of betrayal and doubt to one filled with promise and trust.

She moved her body with his, until the final culmination, collapsing him onto her chest, his breath labored and strong. She held him against her, his powerful body still hot and pulsing. When he rolled onto his back, he took her with him. He wrapped his arms around her and nestled her head under his chin.

She felt safe there and protected and she dozed peacefully for a while, tucked in Wade's strong embrace.

Gina woke up to a cool empty bed. Lazily, she glanced at the digital clock. It was one o'clock in the morning. She lifted up from the bed, searching for Wade. She found him partly dressed, wearing his trousers standing outside with arms braced on the balcony railing, looking out at the sea. A tick in his jaw beat out a rhythm as clear night stars twinkled overhead.

Quietly, Gina rose and threw on Wade's shirt. She tiptoed to the balcony and stood behind him, her heart beating fast. She was so much in love with him that she could barely stand it. But he hadn't spoken of his feelings for her and she knew that for Wade, it would take time. "Can't sleep?"

Wade spun around. The pensive look on his face vanished, but she'd seen it, just for an instant. "I'm just waiting for you."

She pointed to the middle of her chest. "Me?"

His gaze riveted to that place on her chest, then flowed over the rest of her. "I said I wanted you naked all night, but damn. You look hot in that."

A sense of relief swamped her. For a second, she'd seen a look in Wade's eyes that frightened her and threatened this newfound beginning they shared tonight. "Hot?"

He took her into his arms. She relished the feel

of him again, needing his touch. "Sexy, Gina. Gorgeous. You're a man killer, honey."

"Hardly that, Wade." Then she bit down on her lip and tilted her head to ask, "Am I killing you?"

He took her hand and led her back into the suite. "Yeah, I'm a dead man."

Wade plopped onto the bed and coaxed her to straddle him. She crawled over his thighs and looked at him with dewy, half-lidded desire, her heart and body in sync.

He reached for the shirt she wore and lowered it down to bare her shoulders. The shirt pulled open and Wade brought his hands up to rub her erect nipples with his thumbs. A low moan of ecstasy erupted from Gina's throat from the tortured explicit pleasure.

"Kill me again, honey."

Gina pulled his unzipped pants down and off and then fastened the condom before lifting over him, eager to please him, to take him inside her. Once she did, Wade's face tightened, his need and desire fully unmasked now. She moved on him, his erection tight and hard, filling her, fulfilling her and making her complete.

He coaxed her with gentle commands and she rode the waves up and down, his fingers teasing her taut nipples, then his hands lowering to guide her at the waist to set a rapid pace. Passion flowed. She took so much from his eyes, always on her: his desire, need and complete wild abandon.

The ride was crazy hot. Soul-filled and earth-shattering. She climaxed first, shuddering out of control.

"That's it, baby," he rushed out, "give me everything."

And once she did, he rolled her onto her back, taking control and thrusting into her until neither one could move another muscle.

Wade lay back on the bed, breathing hard. "You can bury me, now."

Gina snuggled up close and his arms automatically wound around her. "I'm too tired," she whispered. "Tomorrow."

Wade made a low grunt of a sound. Exhausted, he said quietly, "I don't want to think about tomorrow."

Sunshine made its way through the suite and light rays targeted Wade, hitting his face, waking him from a soundless slumber. Sleep-hazy, he nuzzled Gina's neck, her long flowing hair tickling his throat as they lay together in spoon-like fashion, with his arms wrapped snugly around her. He stroked her soft skin with gentle fingers. The scent of her and of their lovemaking during the night stirred his body once again.

She was the perfect woman for him.

He cupped her breasts, teasing the ripened orbs, then slid one hand along her torso and lower along her thigh. He could go on touching her like this, feeling her smooth sleek perfect skin and he'd never tire of it.

She stirred awake. "Mmm."

Wade nibbled on her throat and with languid movements, Gina turned in his arms. Her beautiful dark-almond eyes opened on him and she sent him a sexy smile. "Morning."

He blinked. And blinked again.

Then he remembered.

The appalling truth struck him like a bludgeoning hammer to his head.

The deceit.

The betrayal.

The check Gina had so willingly taken from his competitor.

I'll do whatever it takes to get out from under all my debt.

Her damning pronouncement slammed into him with rock-hard force. He'd almost forgotten. He'd almost been snared into her trap. He'd shared the best night of his life with a woman he had to write off—a woman who had badly burned him.

For his revenge to be complete, he had to cut her out of his life for good.

Wade winced. He hated her for making him seek revenge, for putting him in this position, for turning his life upside down again.

He'd cut her out, but the knife would slice him up just as badly. He had no choice. He had to protect himself and his company.

He had no use for a woman he couldn't trust.

Wade shoved the covers off abruptly.

Gina's eyes went wide with surprise.

He rose from the bed and looked his fill, drinking in the sight of her lying there, beautifully naked, her inky tresses falling over soft shoulders. Wade knew it would be the last time he'd see her this way.

"Wade?"

Wade pulled his trousers on and zipped them up. "Get dressed," he said harshly.

"Why? Are we late for—"

"Pack your bags. You're fired."

Gina laughed, her eyes dancing with amusement. "What kind of joke is—"

Wade loomed over her, his lips tight, his eyes hard. "It's no joke, Gina. You no longer work for Triple B."

Gina's smile faded fast. She clutched the sheet and covered herself. "You're serious, aren't you?"

Wade grabbed his shirt—the one Gina had tortured him with last night, shoving his arms through the sleeves. Damn, it smelled of her. He didn't bother with buttoning it. "Dead serious."

Gina rose and they faced each other from opposite sides of the bed, her expression not one of guilt but of puzzlement. "I don't understand."

Furious now, thinking about how she'd almost duped him again Wade spoke with deceptive calm. "I saw you last night, Gina. Accepting another bribe. This time from my biggest competitor. Don't deny it, *sweetheart*. You were at the bar last night with John Wheatley. The two of you looked awfully cozy. So don't even try to lie your way out of this one."

But Gina did begin to deny it, by continually shaking her head. “No, no.”

“Yes, yes. What kind of woman are you? Hurting me last time wasn’t enough?” Thinking of her multiple betrayals only fueled his anger more. “This time you weren’t satisfied with destroying my heart. No, that wasn’t enough. You set out to destroy my company as well. But you damn well failed. I found out and now I want you out of here.”

Gina’s face flamed. Her eyes turned black as coal. She took a step toward him, fixing her glare on him. “Are you saying that because you thought I screwed you over, you decided to do the same to me?”

Wade lifted his lips in a smug smile. “I guess the screwing went both ways last night.”

“Bastard!”

“Bitch.”

Gina closed her eyes as if trying to tamp down her fiery temper. Then she walked over to her purse and dug out the check. “Is this the check you’re referring to?”

Out of curiosity, Wade strode over to her to see how much money, was enough for her to sell him out. “Yeah, that’s it.”

She shoved it up into his face. “Read it, Wade.” Then she spoke slowly, and with unyielding determination. “Read it and know that I’ll never…ever… forgive you for this.”

Wade grabbed the check and looked at it, his mind going numb for a second, as impending dread crept in. “The Survive Foundation?”

Gina snatched the check from his hand and returned it to her purse. Her voice broke with unbridled anger. "When I left El Paso, I thought about ripping up your father's check. Maybe I shouldn't have taken it in the first place, but you see, I thought you had betrayed me. I thought—never mind."

"Tell me, Gina." He softened his voice, realizing that he might have just made a huge mistake, one that would cost him more than this project. "Why would you think I betrayed you?"

Gina immediately backed away from him, as if being near him disgusted her. Her voice elevated. There was fire in her eyes. "That's Sarah's secret to tell, but I will tell you this. I came to Los Angeles, brokenhearted, grieving from the loss of my parents and over losing you. But I had your father's money and I decided to put it to good use. I helped start The Survive Foundation, a nonprofit organization to aid and support survivors of accidents and those who are grieving."

Wade made a move toward her, but she put up her hand and shook her head. "Don't."

It wasn't so much her stance, but the depth of hatred in her eyes, that left him immobile.

She spoke with a rough bitter edge, one Wade had never heard before. "I only know John Wheatley and his wife because they lost a child to leukemia two years ago. The foundation helped them through their loss. I saw them both on the beach yesterday and he wanted to thank me. The check is a donation."

Wade sucked in oxygen as he took this all in.

He'd been wrong about her, misjudging her loyalty and—

"Get out, Wade."

Gina's command startled him. "What?"

"Get out of my room. Get out of my life. I never want to see you again!"

Wade shook his head. "No, I can't leave now. I'll admit that—"

Gina picked up a shoe and threw it at him. He ducked and the sandal missed his head but grazed his shoulder. "Get out!"

"Gina," Wade mustered warning in his tone, though in truth, he'd been poleaxed by her revelations.

"Don't *Gina,* me, Wade. I want you out of this room. Now! I never want to set eyes on you again. You're just like your father…coldhearted and ruthless and I'm tired of your accusations!"

Her voice wobbled and she held back tears. Wade saw the destruction on her face and the hurt. Damn it. Why in hell hadn't she told him all of this before?

Next, she picked up the flower vase from the sofa table, threatening to toss it. "I mean it."

Wade knew her hot temper. And he knew she wouldn't hesitate. He backed out of the room. "I'm going," he said, and exited.

He heard the crash, glass splintering against the door the instant he'd closed it and loud profane curses coming from inside the suite.

He braced his body against the wall, trying to absorb all that had happened already today. He'd been so wrong. And Gina wasn't about to forgive him easily.

Wade winced and massaged his temples. The only thing he could do was give her time to cool off. She wasn't about to speak to him now. And he needed time to sort this all out.

Somehow, he'd make it up to her.

And then he'd talk to Sarah.

Tears streamed down Gina's face, the unbelievable hurt going deep. Wade wasn't worth her tears. She never wanted to see him again. She'd loved him once, and up until this morning had hoped he was still the Wade she'd once known. The man she could trust who'd been caring and kind. But she couldn't love him anymore. And she'd fight it until her last breath not to feel anything for him ever again. He'd shown her his heartless, diabolical, calculating side. She'd been right in accusing him of being just like his father. He was and that spoke volumes for his character.

Gina shoved her clothes into her suitcase. More tears slid down her cheeks. "Bastard, jerk, idiot," she continued on until she couldn't think of any more ways to describe him, while she packed everything up and stormed out, leaving everything Wade had ever given her behind.

She made immediate arrangements with Catalina Express for transportation back to Los Angeles. She was too angry to acknowledge her fear of traveling over the water for ninety minutes on a three-tiered boat, by herself. She'd manage. With suitcase in hand, she ran along Crescent Avenue to the boat landing, rushing to make the earliest departure from the island. Once she handed in her ticket and stepped aboard, she felt not fear, but an uncanny sense of relief to be completely rid of Wade Beaumont and this island.

She braced herself, holding onto the railing. Once a few more passengers boarded, the boat motored up and took off. Gina faced her fear, forcing herself to look out over the ocean. She had more than an hour to endure on the Pacific and, once she reached the San Pedro dock, she'd have to face her future as well as her fears. One that did not include Wade Beaumont or Triple B.

And though the trip had been a test of her will, keeping herself composed while the Express glided over waves and headed home was far easier than forgetting the hurtful image of Wade as he loomed over the bed they'd just made love in. He'd coldly dismissed and fired her, demanding that she pack her bags.

He hadn't even given her the benefit of the doubt.

Or asked her up front about John Wheatley and the check she'd been given.

He'd deliberately seduced her, not out of love or compassion, but for revenge—to teach her a lesson.

And he'd gotten his revenge—a job well done. Gina had made it easy for him. She'd laid it all out on the line for him and he'd crushed her in one sweeping blow.

But just a few hours later, as Gina sat on her tiny sofa, opening the week's mail, her hand shook at the wedding invitation staring back at her. Another blow, this one not as shocking. But the timing and irony was almost too much to bear.

Mr. and Mrs. Charles Buckley request the
honour of your presence
at the marriage of their daughter
Sarah Nicole Buckley
To
Roy Zachary Winston

The rest of the words blurred as Gina's eyes misted up. After nine years, Sarah had finally gotten the man of her dreams. She'd hung in there and worked it all out.

If only Sarah hadn't told those lies nine years ago.

Then maybe Gina's whole life might have turned out differently and she, too, would have gotten the man of her dreams.

Too bad that man didn't exist anymore.

Nine

Wade slammed the phone down for the tenth time in three days. He glanced at the work piling up on his desk, the contracts he needed to go over, the payroll checks he needed to sign, but he couldn't concentrate on any of it.

Gina refused his calls. She wouldn't pick up. He got her answering machine each and every time. "Damn you, Gina."

He lifted the wedding invitation on his desk, staring at it with unblinking eyes. And the note attached. Sarah had been trying to reach him all week.

They'd finally spoken.

Wade spun around in his leather swivel chair and

stared out the big bay window. Summer gloom had set in, but even through the afternoon haze he could see the ocean, blue waters now appearing gray and dingy from the low-lying cloud cover.

Gina had crossed that Pacific. Without him. She'd faced her fears alone. He'd driven her to that. And now she refused to speak with him.

He recalled his surprise when he went back to the Villa Portofino just hours later, ready with a dozen red roses, a heartfelt apology and willing to do whatever it took to make it up to her, only to find her gone.

The hotel clerk refused to divulge any information. Wade used his influence and status, calling over the manager to extract the information. That's when he found out she'd checked out and booked a ticket on the next boat back to the mainland.

Wade hadn't seen it coming. He'd been shocked. He knew she'd been furious with him, but to actually take it upon herself to leave the island alone and fight her fear of the water, told him one very key thing—getting her back wasn't going to be easy.

"To hell with it," he muttered, standing up and jamming his hands in his jacket sleeves. He fished through the papers on his desk, until he came up with what he was looking for. Shoving the envelope in his inside pocket, he strode to the door.

One way or another, Gina was going to speak to him.

And it was going to happen tonight.

* * *

Gina brought her dinner dish to the kitchen sink and thanked her landlord and friend, Delia, once again. "The meal was delicious, Dee. Thank you. I needed this."

"I know you did. And I'm glad you finally agreed to our invitation. Marcus and I have been worried about you."

Gina tightened the elastic band on her ponytail and shrugged with a heavy sigh. Her landlords had been such wonderful moral support lately. Once she'd returned from Catalina, they'd spotted her sullen demeanor immediately and tried to cheer her up with home-baked cookies, hand delivered mango margaritas and invitations to dine out with them. She hadn't been in the mood for any of it. But, finally, tonight she'd accepted their dinner invitation and told them the whole story, from El Paso to Catalina and everything in between. "I'll be fine…soon."

Delia took the plates and rinsed them then handed them one at a time to Gina, who was arranging them in the dishwasher.

"You know, it's okay for you not to be…fine. I mean, don't knock yourself out convincing yourself everything is wonderful when it's not. Allow yourself time."

Gina wiped her damp hands on her jeans. She'd been slumming it lately, dressing down and laying low while searching the classifieds for the past few days. The job hunt was not going well. Gina's heart wasn't in it. "Time for what?"

Delia only smiled, her eyes insightful. "Just time, honey."

Gina wished she had the luxury of time. But she needed to move on with her life and the sooner the better.

"Oh and don't you worry about the rent this month. Marcus and I don't want you stressing about it."

"I have rent money, Dee. I'm not broke." Her heart had broken, but fortunately her tiny bank account hadn't, not just yet.

"No, but you have that wedding this month, don't you? It'd do you good to see the Buckleys again. Don't you think so?"

Gina had forgiven Sarah for her unwitting crimes years ago and she was happy for her, but attending anyone's wedding right now was the last thing she wanted to do. Yet she wanted to be there for Sarah and the Buckleys. "Yes, they've always been kind to me. I wouldn't miss seeing them. Sarah and I, well, we've had some drama in our lives, but we're still good friends. She's asked me to be in the wedding party."

"The change of scenery will do you good."

Marcus popped his head in the kitchen doorway. "Care for coffee outside, ladies? Stars are out tonight."

"That sounds nice, sweetheart," Dee said to him, then turned to Gina. "Coffee?"

Gina smiled and shook her head. "No thanks. Not tonight."

Marcus strode into the room to place his arm

around her shoulder. "I can't coax you into decaf? It won't keep you awake, I promise."

Gina chuckled. She wished caffeine were all that was keeping her from sleep these past few nights. "I really should be going. I'd like to do some reading."

Marcus squeezed her shoulders tight. "You hang in there, Gina." He kissed her forehead and Dee gave her a big hug.

"I'll bring over that book I was telling you about," Dee said, slanting her husband a look. "Marcus misplaced it, but I know it's somewhere in the house. I'll look for it again."

"Thanks, I'd like that. Dinner was great."

"We'll do it again soon."

"Ciao, my friends," Gina said to both of them as she walked out the back door and across the lawn to her humble but homey little guesthouse.

Once inside, she settled in, propping her feet up on the sofa with a glass of iced water and a handed down copy of *Vogue*. She glanced at her answering machine, relieved to see no new messages. She'd hoped Wade had given up calling her. Having her nerves go raw each time the phone rang was an added strain she could do without.

Gina opened the magazine and glanced at the pages. She liked to keep up on fashion, comparing the newest creations on the shelves to those in her head and finding that she always liked hers better.

One day, she'd have her own company. She hadn't given up on that dream.

When the knock came, Gina bounced up and opened the door wearing a smile. "Dee, you found the book already!"

But it wasn't Dee standing there holding a copy of *The Devil Wears Prada.* No, it was another *devil* entirely, one with bold green eyes and a solid steadfast stance. Her first thought was that she'd missed him. But she killed that thought instantly, her second thought being that she hated him. Still.

And her third thought was that he looked so darn handsome, standing there, wearing tailored Armani and a sincere expression that he took her breath away. "Whatever book you need, I'll get it for you."

"What I *need* is for you to leave," she managed quite elegantly and began to close the door.

Wade's arm jutted out, preventing that from happening. His expression fierce now, his eyes raging, he said. "We need to talk. Now. I'm tired of you refusing my calls."

Gina played innocent, just to annoy him. "Oh? Did you call? I don't recollect."

He pushed the door wide open and moved past her, letting himself in. Gina looked out at Marcus and Delia having coffee across the lawn in the patio. Marcus immediately stood, his gaze pensive as he was about to approach. Gina shook her head and gestured that all was okay.

She had to deal with Wade sometime. She knew he wasn't the kind of man to let things drop. No, he always had to have the last word.

"No more games, Gina."

"Spoken from the expert," she blurted as she took her seat on the sofa and opened the magazine again, flipping through pages she really didn't see.

He looked around. "This is nice."

"Hardly a beachside resort," she answered casually.

Wade sat down next to her and took the magazine from her hand. He set it down on the small table next to the sofa. "You're forgetting I came from humble beginnings, too."

Gina rubbed her hands up and down her jeans and then fidgeted with her ponytail. She knew her appearance wouldn't win awards, yet the look in his eyes told her it didn't matter. He caressed her with that look and made her nervous. "What do you want, Wade?"

He smiled and stared at her for a long moment. "I know the truth. I spoke with Sarah."

"And?"

Wade leaned back against the sofa cushion, making himself comfortable. "And I'm pissed. Royally pissed."

"That makes two of us." Gina sent him a wry smile.

Wade shook his head. "I had no idea. All this time, I had no idea that Sarah used me as a shield for Roy Winston."

"She was in love with Roy and she knew her parents would go ballistic if they found out. They'd warned her not to get involved with Roy. He was bad news."

Wade agreed. "He *was* bad news. He'd been suspended from high school, what, three or four times. His parents were the town drunks."

"After college, when we came back to El Paso, I remember the Buckleys telling Sarah that nothing had changed with the Winstons and Roy had gotten arrested for a barroom brawl."

Wade nodded solemnly, "Yeah, I remember that. I was there. Roy got a bad rap. Five of us were there, but the sheriff chose to arrest only Roy. He was known as a troublemaker in town, so naturally they blamed him, but all of us were just as guilty."

Gina went on, "So when Sarah thought she was pregnant, she panicked. She loved Roy, but knew her parents would never accept him. Mr. Buckley had just been diagnosed with a heart condition. Sarah feared it would send her father over the edge. She named you as the father of her baby. She knew her parents liked you, at least. They would accept it. But she didn't know that we had gotten close. If you remember, Sarah had been gone that week with her mother. I never had the chance to tell Sarah my feelings for you.

"She was only trying to protect her family. And Roy. When she told me you had fathered her baby, I was in shock. We'd just been together and I thought…"

Wade pursed his lips and leaned forward, bracing his elbows on his knees. "You thought the worst of me. The very worst."

Gina bounded up abruptly and lashed out. "What

else could I think? My best friend confided in me that you, the man I'd fallen in lo—the man I'd just had sex with for the very first time in my life, was going to be her baby's father."

"Sit down, Gina. And calm down."

"No! You don't know the hell I went through. I was so lost…so vulnerable. I couldn't tell my best friend. I'd begun to hate you and then your father showed up with the bribe. It was a way out. I couldn't stick around El Paso anymore. Not thinking you and Sarah were going to have a child together. So I took the money."

"I hated you for that."

"I know. I wanted you to. It was the only way I could think of to make sure you stayed in El Paso with Sarah. But I used your father's money for a good cause. I'm not sorry I took it. But I am sorry about the circumstances."

"And the irony of all this is that Sarah is marrying Roy," Wade said.

Gina took in a breath, amazed at how things had worked out. "He left El Paso right after that barroom brawl incident and turned his life around. He's successful now, owns his own body shop and is doing well. He came back for Sarah. He'd always loved her."

Wade stood and paced the confines of her room. "Sarah was never pregnant."

"No, she wasn't. It was a false alarm, but I only found that out later on. I'd lost contact with her. Deliberately. But she tracked me down and told me the truth a few years later. And I told her the truth about us. She was mortified, so sorry about all of it. She'd been so wrapped up with hiding her secret about Roy that she hadn't a clue about how we felt about each other. She wanted to find you and tell you the truth too, but I stopped her. What good would it do? By then, you were working in Houston with your father and I was involved with—"

"Another man."

"Yes. That's right." Gina hoisted her chin. "I'd moved on."

"So did I. But I never forgot you."

Gina let out a rueful nervous chuckle. "Right, plotting a way to hurt me. Well, it worked. Congratulations. You got your revenge, didn't you, Wade?"

Wade's voice elevated slightly, "I thought you were out to ruin my company."

Gina faced him now, coming to stand toe to toe with him. She looked at his face and condemned him with the truth. "You used me, used my body. You took something precious and made it ugly. How little you must think of me to believe that I'd sleep with you right after accepting a bribe to ruin you and your company. I don't know why you're here, but I'd like you to leave." She strode past him to open the front door. "There's nothing more to say."

Wade's green eyes flashed with indignation. She'd angered him and she was glad. It was about time someone put Wade Beaumont in his place.

Wade stood still for a moment, staring at her, then removed an envelope from his coat pocket. He set it down on the table. "We won the bid on the Catalina project. Your bonus is in there, along with your paycheck."

Gina nodded, glancing at the envelope, but said nothing. She'd earned that money—the hard way.

Wade strode to the door quickly and stopped to look deeply into her eyes. "You should have told me the truth, right from the beginning."

With that, Wade walked straight out of her life, without so much as a glance back.

Wade stared out as night fell on the Pacific Ocean. He leaned against his deck railing watching the tide creep in then recede back into the darkness of the sea. Only a few stars illuminated the sky, the night as black as his mood.

"You haven't touched your champagne, little brother," Sam said, coming up to stand beside him. He sipped from his glass and leaned against the railing. "Or would you rather have a cold beer?"

Wade shook his head. "No."

"I flew all the way out here from Texas to help you celebrate. Hell, it isn't every day a company wins the biggest bid in its history. You did it, Wade. You should be proud. Instead, I find you here looking like death warmed over."

Wade let out a self-deprecating laugh. "That's one way to describe me. Others might say you're being too kind."

"Others? Or only one other, as in Gina Grady?

"That's the only *other* that matters," Wade admitted.

"Ah," Sam said, sipping his Dom Pérignon. "So how is my old friend?"

"Intelligent, sweet, dedicated and gorgeous."

"Sounds like the Gina I remember."

Wade finally succumbed. He gulped his drink, emptying the glass in five seconds flat. "She's not a fan."

Sam chuckled. "So she's got more brains than most women. She didn't throw herself at your feet?"

Wade muttered a curse, directing it right at Sam.

He chuckled again. "Kidding. Hey, what's really up? I come here expecting a party, and you look like—"

"Death warmed over?" Wade finished for him.

"I was about to say, like you lost your best friend."

Wade grabbed the bottle and poured another drink. "Maybe I did. I made some mistakes with Gina. Now she doesn't want to have anything to do with me."

Sam's smile faded. "You're serious about her?"

Wade nodded.

Sam reflected, this time on a serious note. "I thought you two were a perfect match, even back in El Paso. That's why I recommended her for the job here in L.A., little brother. I thought, you two would pick up where you left off. I take it there's problems?"

"You don't want to know," Wade said, sipping his drink again, this time slowly and savoring the taste, letting it glide down his throat.

"I do want to know. I'm here. Lay it on me."

Wade turned to Sam. "It's a long story."

Sam smiled and put his hand on Wade's shoulder. "I'm not going anywhere."

They sat in the deck chairs for the next thirty minutes, polishing off the Dom, while Wade explained to Sam his situation, leaving out some of the more intimate details.

And after hearing him out, Sam leaned back in his chair, staring up at the stars. "Well, the easiest thing to do is forget her. Move on. Concentrate on the project."

He eyed Wade then, with an arched brow.

Wade scoffed, "Not possible. She's hard to forget. If I couldn't do it in nine years, I certainly can't do it now."

Sam smiled. "Okay, that was the first test. You passed, by the way."

Wade didn't smile back. "So I get an A. Any other bright ideas?"

Sam leaned in, and spoke directly at him, in all seriousness. "You going to Sarah's wedding?"

Wade inhaled sharply. "I haven't decided yet."

"Can't forgive her?"

"Hell, she wants me to be in the wedding party. She apologized up, down and sideways. I can't really blame her. I understand about Roy. What happened, well, it happened. It was nine years ago. I told her I'd think about it."

"If I were you, I wouldn't think too long. Gina's going and she's in the wedding."

"How do you know that?"

"Because Caroline called Sarah to say we can't go to the wedding and Sarah told her all about the wedding plans. We promised to visit soon; it would be good to see Uncle Lee and Aunt Dottie again. Besides, we have news of our own."

Wade's head snapped up. "What news?"

Sam's mouth stretched into a big grin. "We're going to have a baby. Caroline's pregnant."

Wade bounded up from his seat and Sam rose, too. He hugged his brother and myriad emotions streamed in. Happiness for his brother and the second chance he'd gotten with Caroline and her little daughter Annabelle, but then a shot of envy filtered in as well. For the first time in his life, Wade wanted what Sam had. A wife and family. And he wanted Gina to fill that role. "Geez, why didn't you say so sooner?"

Sam laughed. "She'll be pregnant eight more months. There's no rush. I wanted to tell you in person. And we're going to visit her folks in Florida to tell them the news firsthand, too. That's why we can't make Sarah's wedding."

Then Sam took his shoulder, his smile fading some. "Remember when you came out to Hope Wells and saw me with Caroline at her stables? Then later, when I left her, unable to face losing my own child, you made me see that I had a second chance in life. You made me take that chance. And now, not only did I adopt little Annabelle, I'm going to be a father again. I've got a wonderful wife and family and this time I'm doing it right. We all make mistakes, Wade. Go after what you want."

Wade hesitated, scrubbing his jaw. "I've already had a second chance with Gina. Seems the stars aren't aligned with the two of us. She's accused me of being like our father—ruthless, cold, hard-hearted. And you know, I'm beginning to believe it myself."

"That's crap, little brother. You're not your father's son. You never have been."

"She walked out on me so easily the first time. Seems that the people I care about most, don't give a sh—"

"Gina does. I guarantee it. She cares for you. From what you said, she didn't so much run away from you as the situation. Okay, so you blew it the second time. Call it even. Take another chance. The third time's the charm, they say. Go to that wedding. Make her see the real you and not some replica of Blake Beaumont."

Wade scratched his chin, pondering.

Sam prodded, "If you don't, you'll regret it the rest of your life."

Wade knew that Sam was right. He had to go to that wedding. He'd never been one to back down from a challenge. And Gina posed the biggest challenge of his life. He'd falsely accused her and hurt her deeply. Turning her feelings around would take nothing short of a miracle. "She can't stand the sight of me."

Sam chuckled, seemingly sure that Wade could pull this off. "That's the best way to start. You can only improve from there."

Wade had to smile at his brother's optimism. "I'll call Sarah. Let her know I'll be coming to her wedding after all."

Ten

Gina packed her bags, telling herself she needed this time away. Sarah had been thrilled that she'd accepted not only the invitation, but a place by her side up at the altar as a bridesmaid. She'd put this wedding together in a matter of weeks, wanting to marry Roy as soon as possible. She'd wasted enough of her life and she was ready to finally begin her future with the man she loved. Gina understood that all too well.

She'd wasted time on Wade, but her future was destined to play out much differently.

On a sigh, she snapped close her suitcase, took one look around, making sure she hadn't forgotten anything, then picked up her traveling case. She slung it over her shoulder and wheeled her luggage to the front door.

Sarah had her bridesmaid dress waiting for her in El Paso and had coaxed her into coming a week early to be a part of the pre-wedding arrangements, seeing to the decorations, favors, music and of course, to attend the rehearsal and dinner afterward.

Sarah's happiness was contagious and Gina couldn't say no. Besides, Sarah insisted that her dress would need an alteration or two. How could she argue with that? So she locked up her house and walked outside to meet Delia who had quite generously offered to take her to the airport.

When she got halfway down the long drive, Delia stepped into view, her usual jovial face, looking tentative.

"Hi, Dee. Anything wrong?"

Dee took the handle of Gina's luggage and began walking along the path towards the front of the house. "I hope not, honey.

"I hope not, too. What's up?" Gina asked, her curiosity escalating. Dee was the most laid-back, honest person she knew. Usually, she didn't skirt around issues or appear apprehensive. Right now, she was doing both.

"I hope I made the right decision."

Again, Gina hadn't a clue what she meant.

Dee opened the large swinging gates beside the front of the house that led to the street and both walked out.

Then Gina stopped.

And couldn't believe her eyes.

Wade stood at attention beside a stretch limousine, wearing jeans and boots and enough cowboy charm to set her heart racing.

She turned to Dee. "What is he doing here?"

"Apparently, taking you to El Paso."

"What?" Gina's temper flared. She glanced at Wade, who was about to approach when Dee halted him with a stopping hand.

Dee halted him with a stopping hand?

"What's going on, Dee?"

"He called about a week ago. We met him for dinner and he explained what he wanted to do."

"We? You and Marcus? He's got you on his side now?"

Dee shook her head. "No, we're on your side. We always have been. But he's sincere. And he cares for you. Marcus and I, we talked about this and think this is the right thing to do. You two need time to talk, to clear the air. You both need another chance. He wants to take you to El Paso."

Gina's eyes nearly bugged out. "He's kidnapping me?"

Dee grinned. "Romantic, isn't it?"

This time Gina rolled her eyes.

Dee turned so that her back was to Wade who stood twenty feet away. She spoke softly, "He's in love with you, honey."

Gina didn't believe it for one second. No one could convince her of that. "He didn't say that to you."

"No. He didn't have to."

Gina glanced at Wade who was wearing dark sunglasses. She couldn't make out his expression.

"God, Dee. He could have just asked me. See, this is what I mean about him. He's so calculating. He even got you involved in this."

"Gina," Dee began with all seriousness, "any guy who would go to this much trouble for you can't be all bad. He talked to us for hours and we both came away knowing that this guy really cares about you. And besides, we both know that if he had asked you, you would have turned him down flat."

"That's right. He could have respected my wishes. Well, I'm not going to El Paso with him."

"I'm afraid you are," the deep voice resonated from just behind Dee. Both women looked up at Wade. He wasn't smiling. "We both have to get there today. We might as well travel together."

Gina shot back. "I have my own ticket, thank you very much."

"Do you?" he asked, turning to look at Dee.

Dee appeared as though she wanted to slink into the sidewalk. "Honestly, Gina, I didn't think you'd fight this so hard. I thought you wouldn't mind if I cancelled the reservation I made for you."

"What?" Gina couldn't believe this. Dee, the traitor, had fully succumbed to Wade's charm. He could pour it on when he had to. "You cancelled my reservation?"

"Sorry," she said, "but I wanted to save you the money."

Wade took hold of her luggage handle and grabbed

the traveling bag from Gina's shoulder. She'd been too floored to stop him. "I've got a chartered plane waiting for us. I'd like you come with me, Gina."

"Why, Wade? Why do you want me to come with you?"

Wade removed his sunglasses and peered into her eyes. "I miss you."

It was such a clear, honest, simple statement that she couldn't quite stop her heart from accelerating. She'd missed him, too, the Wade she'd fallen in love with. She glanced at Dee, who smiled with hope in her eyes. Gina felt somewhat defeated. She could fold her arms across her middle and declare that she wasn't going. But that would seem childish. And even though she fumed at Wade's tactics, she couldn't deny that he *had* gone to some trouble for her. Riding to the airport in a limousine and flying on a chartered plane to El Paso might not be so bad after all. Besides, his latest admission nearly knocked her to her knees.

He missed her.

"I have a fitting at three o'clock at the bridal salon, so we might as well get going."

Dee smiled in relief.

For a second Wade's mouth crooked up before he took her luggage and handed it to a chauffeur who seemed to have appeared out of nowhere.

The same way Wade had.

Gina tried to relax in the plush leather seat on the Falcon 50, Wade's chartered plane. She had to admit that traveling this way sure beat the lines, the crowds and the coach seat that had been waiting for her at LAX.

Wade sat in the seat facing her, a small polished teak table between them set with a vase filled with white lilies.

Classy.

Gina glanced out the window, peering down at the tiny dotting of houses below, fully aware that Wade's eyes were on her. She felt his perusal and it heated her and made her think of the night they'd spent together in Catalina. She wondered if he was thinking the same thing.

Finally, she faced him. "You're staring at me."

Wade smiled. "I like what I see."

His voice mellow, his eyes warm on her, Gina couldn't help but be affected. "I wish you wouldn't."

Wade leaned way back in his seat. "Why?"

He was making her uncomfortable but she wouldn't admit it. "Don't you have something to do?"

"We could eat something. Coffee? Or breakfast? What would you like?"

Gina's stomach was in knots. "I couldn't eat a thing. Thank you."

He nodded and watched her. She blinked and blinked again, only to see him smiling again.

She'd been with him for six days on that island and she hadn't seen the man crack more than an occasional grudging smile, yet here he was looking at her, smiling like a schoolboy just given an *A* on his report card.

"Do I make you nervous, Gina?"

Oh, yes. "No. Of course not."

He nodded again. "Want to talk?"

She shook her head. "Not particularly."

He nodded once again and continued staring at her.

"There must be something you could do," she said, keeping the irritation out of her voice.

"Yeah, work. But that wouldn't be polite, would it?"

But staring at her with those gorgeous green eyes *was* polite? "Oh, I wouldn't mind. Go right ahead, Wade. Really, you must have a ton of work to do, now that you've won the Catalina project."

Wade reached over the seat and brought his briefcase into view. He set it down on the seat next to him and pulled out a stack of papers. "I'd rather look at you," he muttered.

Inwardly, Gina smiled, but she reminded herself not to fall victim to his charm. "You'd get further with those papers."

He glanced up. "That so?"

She didn't hesitate. "Yes."

Wade's eyes flickered, but he seemed to hold back a comment then he spread the papers out, sorting through them. "You know, you and I made a good team. Technically, you're still on the payroll. I could use help here."

Gina clamped her mouth shut, to keep it from falling open. She was still on the payroll? "You fired me, remember?"

Wade stopped sorting through the paperwork, to look deep into her eyes. "That was a mistake."

"Doesn't matter. I would have quit, anyway," she shot back quickly.

"But you didn't quit and your next check is in the mail."

Surprised, Gina's nerves teetered on end. She'd thought she was through with Triple B for good. But apparently Wade had had second thoughts. She glanced at the Catalina papers—projections, finance reports, estimates—and admitted, for what it was worth, that she had enjoyed the work. "You mean you don't think I'd try to foil your project, in some dastardly way?"

Wade cast her a look of disgust. "No, I know you wouldn't. Can you give me a break?"

"Why, did you give me one?" Oh, that came out more harshly than she intended, but the sentiment remained.

"No. I didn't. But you wanted me to believe the worst about you the first time."

"And the second time? In Catalina?"

"That was a mistake on my part. And I apologize."

Humbled now, Gina realized she had never heard Wade Beaumont apologize for anything, to anyone. "Still, I can't work with you. You don't trust me."

"Yes I do. I'd trust you with my life."

The sincerity of his words filled her head and warmed her heart. But how could she learn to trust him again?

Instead of dealing with it, she grabbed a stack of papers and bent her head, looking them over. "What do you need me to do?"

* * *

When the plane landed at El Paso International Airport, Wade escorted her off, carrying their luggage. A taxi stood waiting for them and soon Gina was back on the streets of El Paso as all sorts of memories rushed in.

"Have you ever been back?" Wade asked.

She shook her head. "No. Sarah and I have met a few times over the years, but always on the West Coast. I haven't seen Chuck and Kay Buckley since I left nine years ago."

Wade sighed. "I'd only seen them a few times, myself. Now, I understand why they'd been distant to me those times I did see them. But Sarah has owned up to the truth to everyone now. Her conscience is clear."

"And what about your aunt and uncle? Do you see them?"

"I would like to see them more. Starting up the company on the West Coast prevented that. But I've gone back for a few quick holidays trips and I've flown them out a few times to visit me."

Gina gazed through the window as they headed out of town and the city landscape rolled into a more rural one. Large fallow fields came into view alongside the fields that grew Egyptian cotton. Roadside poppies dotted the highway and, off in the distance, Gina noted the reddish hilltops of Franklin Mountain where she'd gone hiking with Wade, Sarah and Sam once. Fifteen minutes later, the cab pulled up to the Buckleys' small ranch house.

"Looks like they've painted the house, but everything else seems pretty much as I remembered."

"Things don't change much in small towns," Wade said, helping her out of the taxi and grabbing her luggage.

"Oh, I'll get that," she said, but before she had a chance to retrieve her things, Sarah raced down the steps, her shoulder-length blond hair bouncing as she approached with a big smile.

"Oh, you two came together," she said, hugging Gina immediately, "that makes me happy."

Sarah turned to Wade, her smile more tentative and a look of complete remorse on her face. "I'm forgiven, right?"

Wade looked at Sarah for a moment and Gina's heart ached for her. Gina knew firsthand his heartless wrath and she hoped for Sarah's sake Wade still considered her a friend. She didn't want Sarah's joy being marred one tiny bit, not when she'd finally made peace with everyone and was marrying the man she'd always loved.

When Wade put out his arms, Sarah climbed in and the two hugged for a long moment. "I wouldn't have agreed to be in your wedding otherwise."

Sarah pulled back and looked at both of them. "Thank you for your forgiveness and for agreeing to be in my wedding. It means a lot to me. And to Roy. You'll have to get to know him again, Wade. He's great."

"Obviously he is if you're marrying him."

Sarah's blue eyes lit. "I can hardly believe it after all this time."

"It's always been Roy, and you were smart enough to realize it," Gina said.

"Thanks." Sarah squeezed Gina's hand. "I'm so glad you're here. Mom and Dad can't wait to see you again."

"How are your parents?" Gina asked.

"They're fine. They've finally come around and have accepted Roy. Come inside, both of you."

Wade shook his head. "I'm anxious to see Uncle Lee and Aunt Dottie, but I'll come by tonight after supper. Besides, I hear you're all going to the bridal salon soon."

Sarah darted a quick glance at Gina. "That's right. We have a fitting in a few hours! Oh, this is wonderful having you both here."

Wade took Gina's suitcases to the front door. "I'll see you later," he said then strode past them, toward the taxi. Before getting inside, he stopped and looked at Gina. "I'm glad you decided to join me on the trip."

Gina nodded, biting her lip, and Sarah waved farewell but as soon as the taxi drove off, Gina muttered, "You didn't really give me a choice."

Sarah looked at her then laced an arm through hers as they walked to the front door. "Gina, you are definitely going to have to fill me in on what's really happening with the two of you. As soon as you say hello to my folks, you're spilling the beans."

Gina had to smile.

She didn't know why exactly, but it felt good to be back in El Paso.

"I've missed your pot roast, Aunt Dottie," Wade said, filling his plate a second time. "No one makes it better."

"It's your favorite," she said, passing him the mashed potatoes. He scooped another clump onto his plate and dug in. "I didn't forget."

Wade finished his next bite. "You're still set on fattening me up."

She laughed, the simple, sweet sound, reminding him of good times sitting around this table, with Sam by his side. Aunt Dottie always had a smile and a kind word.

Uncle Lee tapped his flat belly. "See this? The woman's put me on a diet. I only get pot roast when you or Sam come to visit."

"You look great," Wade said, looking over at his father's brother and seeing no resemblance. Uncle Lee had a kindly face and a loyal nature. He loved his wife, his home and his family above all else. "Aunt Dottie takes good care of you, so no complaining."

"You tell him, Wade," his aunt jested.

"I'm not complaining," he said grudgingly, looking over at Wade's plate of food, "but I wouldn't mind a second helping myself."

"Go on, Lee," Dottie said, "I'm not stopping you."

Uncle Lee reached over and forked another piece of pot roast onto his plate. "There's nothing better than the love of a good woman."

Lee winked at his wife and Dottie grinned before setting her gaze on Wade. "Speaking of a good woman, you said that you brought Gina with you. How is that girl?"

Uncle Lee chimed in, "Still pretty as sunshine? Giving you heart palpitations?"

Wade chuckled, then sipped his iced tea. "She's fine. Gorgeous as ever and won't have a thing to do with me."

Aunt Dottie put her hand over his in a consoling manner. "Now, dear. Don't let that stop you. Weddings have a way with people and she might just come around while she's here."

Wade finished his meal, tossed his napkin and pulled back from his chair. "I'm not only banking on that, I'm going to make it happen."

"So Gina's the one?" she asked, darting a quick glance at her husband.

Wade nodded while taking his plate to the sink. "Now it's time to convince her of that. Mind if I saddle up Rio? I'm going over to the Buckleys tonight."

"Not at all, that boy needs the exercise. And say hello to Kay and Chuck for us," his uncle said.

"Will do." Wade bent to kiss his aunt's cheek. "Thanks for supper."

Uncle Lee smiled up at him. "It's good to have you home, son."

Wade no longer flinched when his uncle called him "son." For years, he resented it, but as he grew older, he realized that it felt natural. He wasn't his father's son, but Lee Beaumont's son and he was out to prove that to Gina and the rest of the world if he had to.

Fifteen minutes later, after greeting the Buckleys, Wade stood in their modest living room with Stetson in hand, completely captivated by Gina from the moment she entered the room wearing a pale-pink flowing bridesmaid dress. Her face bright, her deep-brown eyes dancing, she twirled around, unaware that he watched her.

"See, the dress only needed a tiny alteration," Sarah said. "I won't say where, but Gina's bustier than the rest of us girls!"

"Sarah!" Gina playfully admonished her friend but her smile remained.

Wade's gaze riveted to that particular part of her anatomy and memories washed over him, of touching her there, putting his lips to her breasts and tasting her, loving her and making their world spin out of control.

When finally, he looked up she met his eyes…and knew what he'd been thinking.

"You look pretty, Gina," he said.

She took a swallow. "Thank you."

The mood was broken when Roy Winston entered the house and everyone was re-introduced. Wade had to admit that Roy had changed. He, too, had been a product of his parents' discord while growing up, but he'd worked himself out of that fathomless hole and came back to El Paso a new man, one who knew what he wanted. Wade had never seen Sarah or Roy so happy.

Gina went into the bedroom to change out of her dress, while the rest of the group retired to the back porch. She returned wearing blue jean shorts and a red-and-white polka-dotted midriff-exposing blouse, looking every bit an exotic version of Daisy Duke. As the evening pressed on, Wade couldn't help glancing at her every chance he got and when the evening was about to end, he took his shot, blocking the doorway as she started to head inside the house.

"It's a nice night. Take a walk with me."

She began shaking her head. "That's not a good idea."

"Come on, Gina. I'll have you back here in twenty minutes."

"I'm a little tired, Wade. It's been a long day. And tomorrow I'm spending the day working on wedding favors with Sarah and her mother."

"All the more reason to take a walk with me. I won't be seeing you tomorrow."

Gina sighed. "Wade."

"I've got something to show you."

"I bet you do," she rushed out, with a hint of playful teasing in her tone. Wade was encouraged.

"We can take Rio, if you're not up to walking."

"*Rio?*" Gina's face lit at the mention of the gelding's name. He'd once been her favorite. "I'm glad to hear he's still around."

"He isn't as feisty as he once was, but he's healthy. Come on, Gina. What do you say?"

Gina debated for several seconds, keeping him waiting. Wade wasn't a patient man, but he was learning and Gina was worth the time. "I want to be in bed in twenty minutes."

Wade stifled a witty reply. Nothing would make him happier, but he knew Gina wasn't including him in her bedtime plans.

He took her hand. "Let's go."

Eleven

"Tell me about your designs," Wade said, as they walked along a path leading to the Beaumont ranch, Rio clip-clopping along beside them.

"They're unique." Gina never minded speaking about her passion. She still had her old designs in her head and loved thinking up new ones. She had begun a new file, recreating the designs she'd lost and adding sketches of the new ones she created. "Most are still in my head, thank goodness."

"What makes them unique?" Wade asked, his attention directed solely on her. She couldn't look at him now, not when he seemed to bank on her every word. In those western clothes and tan Stetson, he looked very much like the old Wade Beaumont. But she'd been fooled once before, this time she would protect her heart. She kept her focus straight ahead as the sun made a hasty retreat, cooling the warm evening air.

"My designs were all made with gemstones. A piece of jade or turquoise held the garment together in distinct ways, either at the front or the back, sometimes on the straps. In the beginning, I worked up several pieces, sewing them by hand and adding whatever stones I had or could buy inexpensively. But I wanted higher-quality gems like amber and topaz. I learned a lot about stones, hoping to work with a larger variety one day.

"Because the gems were all different colors and all of different quality, each piece of clothing was one-of-a-kind. I sold a few to high-end boutiques and soon I was getting requests. But the gems were costly and I began formulating a plan to start my own company."

"GiGi Designs, right?"

Gina nodded and she couldn't help but smile. "Everyone thought the name stood for my initials, Gina Grady, but actually, I had designed a logo and the tag that I fastened to the clothes read, Gina's Gems."

Gina glanced at Wade and caught him smiling. "Catchy."

"I think so, too," she said, diverting her gaze from Wade's beautiful smile and tantalizing mouth, while trying to block out the look of admiration on his face.

Rio snorted and Gina laid her hand along his long neck, stroking him absently as they continued walking along.

Wade looked straight ahead. “We’re almost there.”

There was a cropping of tall mesquite trees bordering the Buckley and Beaumont spreads, a long row of them appeared to be the dividing line. Wade led her to that area, dropping the lead rope from Rio. Apparently the horse knew the terrain. He wandered off only a few feet away. “You should have your company, Gina. Sounds like it was what you were meant to do.”

“I will one day. I’m sure of that.”

Wade took hold of her hand. “Come here,” he said, guiding her to an area just beyond the trees. She viewed a large open crate and peered inside to find a mama border collie with five pups lying by her side on a quilt; two of the small pups were nuzzling on their mother voraciously, the others were fast asleep. “Oh, my. They are so sweet!” She turned to Wade, but his eyes were on the pups. “Is that your Lily?”

Wade shook his head. “No, Lily’s gone now. Sugar is her daughter and now she’s got pups of her own. I brought them out here for some peace and quiet today. I think Sugar likes it here. I’ll bring them back to the barn later tonight.”

Lily had been Wade’s dog growing up. She’d been so gentle and sweet and a great herder. Wade had loved her.

She watched him bend to pet Sugar and the mama

looked up at him with adoring eyes. "That's a good girl," Wade said, stroking her coat lovingly. "You're a good mama, aren't you?"

Gina bent, too, and together they watched the little pups. "How old are they?"

"My uncle said she gave birth three weeks ago."

Gina watched the black-and-white little bundles as they woke, one right after the other, some scrambling for a spot by their mother, ready to suckle, others climbing over each other in the crate. One looked scrawnier than the rest and, instead of the common black-and-white coloring, had a coat of red and brown and white. Gina couldn't help picking that one up.

"Is that the one you like?"

Gina nodded. "I'm a sucker for the underdog."

Wade looked into her eyes for a moment then patted the little pup's head. "I'm thinking of taking one."

Surprised, Gina kept her expression even, hugging the pup a little tighter. "Really? I wouldn't think you'd have time for a dog."

"I'd make time. I'm ready for a commitment. So, you like this one the best?"

"They're all adorable, Wade. The choice is yours. Doesn't matter which one I'd pick."

Wade cocked her half a smile. "Oh, but it does matter."

I'm ready for a commitment.

An unexpected thrill coursed through her body and Gina shoved aside the heartwarming thoughts that accompanied that feeling. She wouldn't let her mind wander down that path.

She reminded herself of Wade's ruthless, calculating behavior towards her. She didn't trust him.

Puppies or not, Gina couldn't fall victim to him again. She put the tiny puppy back into the crate. Immediately, he nudged aside one of his siblings, to get to the mother. "He's a fighter."

"You're a good judge of character," Wade said, watching her with those intent penetrating eyes.

"Am I? Seems to me I messed up a few times in my life."

Wade nodded, a serious expression crossing his features. He spoke softly. "I've done the same, Gina. But I plan to remedy that."

Gina closed her eyes briefly, blocking out the sincere tone in his voice. Then she rose. "I think I'd better get going now."

Wade didn't hesitate. "Let's ride back." With a protest ready on her lips, Wade added quickly, "I promised to get you home in twenty minutes. It's faster this way."

She watched him mount Rio, those long legs lifting up and over the saddle, before he settled himself on and reached down for her hand.

She could either take the long walk back with Wade, with thoughts of commitments and puppies plaguing her every step, or she could be home in a few minutes, the downside being she'd have to share a saddle and the close proximity with him.

"Don't be afraid, Gina," Wade said, leaning down,

coaxing her with those deep-green eyes and an open expression on his face.

But Gina was afraid. She didn't want to lose her grip on the anger and resentment she held. She opted for the fast ride. She took his hand and he lifted her up, placing her in front of him on the saddle.

He wrapped his arms around her waist and handed her the reins. His breath was warm and rousing as he whispered in her ear, "You're in control now, honey."

Gina laced her fingers through the reins, nudged Rio forward, her heart beginning to melt like butter on a hot griddle.

"Glad you realized that, Wade."

His soft caressing chuckle from behind sent shivers.

She felt anything but in control, in truth, she thought she was *losing* all control.

Fast.

Gina spent the next two days with Sarah, working on wedding favors, seating arrangements and going over the plans for the ceremony. She hadn't seen Wade, but heard from both Roy and Mr. Buckley that the men had had their tuxedo fittings and then had gone out for drinks afterward.

Roy wanted no part of a bachelor party, but secretly Gina had joined troops with the two other bridesmaids to throw Sarah a quick bridal-shower luncheon. And Dottie Beaumont had offered up her home.

Gina sat beside Sarah with Kay Buckley and Dottie in the parlor along with several of Sarah's friends from the high school where she was now employed as a college counselor. Both Roy and Sarah had settled for a life in El Paso, working in jobs they loved.

After they'd finished a lunch catered by one of El Paso's finest eateries, cake was served and the gifts were opened.

"Let's see," Gina began, looking at the list she'd marked down, keeping track of which guests gave which gift. "You have three sets of sexy lingerie, apple nectar body oils and lotions, a bottle of French perfume to go along with a full case of French wine generously given to you by principal Carol Donaldson and a half dozen Waterford wine goblets donated by the rest of the staff. I say forget the wedding and skip straight to the honeymoon!"

The ladies laughed and Sarah smiled. "I don't think so. I've been wanting this wedding for a long time, but Roy would surely take you up on it, Gina."

"Sounds good to me," Roy said, coming in the front door, his eyes only on Sarah. "I can't wait to get to the honeymoon part."

Wade came in next, looking handsome in a crisp pair of jeans and a forest-green shirt, the color highlighting the deep hue of his eyes. He searched and found Gina instantly, his gaze focused solely on her face.

Gina's breath caught. Her throat tightened. She didn't like the effect Wade had on her, but she couldn't deny that she'd missed him. Just seeing him now, with all the other single females in the room, gazing at him as if he were a sweet creamy dessert they'd like to devour, put her nerves on edge. Wade, the wealthy, handsome prodigal son, returning to his childhood home, made a great catch for a local girl.

"You boys crashing the party?" Dottie asked, her gaze flowing from Roy to Wade. Gina saw the love and admiration she had for her nephew in that one solitary look. Wade may not have had a mother or a real father, but Lee and Dottie Beaumont had loved him like their own son. He'd been fortunate to have them in his life, *all* of his life. Gina had missed that. She'd missed that unconditional love and the looks of admiration she'd once received from her parents.

Wade glanced her way again and she blinked, uncomfortable with the warmth in his eyes, the softness in his face.

"This is a shower, so I'm here to shower my bride with a gift of my own. Thanks to Wade and his help the past few days, I was able to finish it on time. Come on outside. Your wedding present is waiting."

"Roy, what did you do?" Sarah asked quietly, but with a note of pleasant surprise in her voice.

"Come outside, sweetheart. I can't bring it in."

"Well, for heaven's sake, I'm going outside," Kay Buckley said to the women, "I just love surprises!"

The rest of the women followed.

Gina was the last to rise, making a final note on

her gift list. When she reached the door, Wade was waiting for her.

"Hi," he said, his eyes set on her.

Gina took a swallow and stood rigidly. She spoke with formality, "Hello, Wade."

He chuckled and drew her into his arms, his hands wrapping around her waist, tugging her close. Before she could protest, his lips met hers in a quick, almost chaste, kiss.

Gina backed up and stared at him. "Why did you do that?"

Wade's mouth quirked up quickly. "Couldn't help myself. Haven't seen you in two days."

Another chink in her armor fell away. She pulled in a deep breath. "Wade, you shouldn't…I mean, we can't…I don't think it's—"

He put a halting finger to her lips. "Shh. You think too much. Come on," he said, taking her hand and leading her outside to the front driveway. "You have to see what Roy's done for Sarah."

And as soon as she spotted the car, gift-wrapped with a giant wedding-white bow, memories flooded in of that summer, driving around in Sarah's old, but very classic 1966 Ford Mustang. This car wasn't the original, but Roy had outdone himself renovating a replica of the model.

By far, the cherry-red convertible with tufted leather seats had been Sarah's favorite possession and she'd driven it until the darn car had no more drive left.

"And my thanks go to Wade here," Roy was

telling the bridal-shower ladies, "for donating and flying in the finishing parts, not to mention helping me work on it these past two days to get the renovation done before the wedding."

Those female eyes again shifted to Wade, then moved down to their joined hands, each one of the women giving Gina a look of envy. For once, Gina was glad she hadn't broken the connection. She glanced up at Wade. "You did that for Roy and Sarah?" she asked, her voice elevated. She couldn't conceal her surprise.

Wade gave her a quick nod.

"It was very kind of you."

Wade drew his brows up. "That *almost* sounded like a compliment."

Gina shook her head. "Sorry, but you confuse me."

Wade let go a heavy sigh. "I'm making it my mission in life to unconfuse you."

With that, he leaned in and kissed the side of her head, brushing his lips into her hair.

Which only confused Gina all the more.

"Sarah, don't pair me up with Wade, okay?"

Sarah's soft-blue eyes went wide with surprise. "Why not?" They stood in the church vestibule and were only minutes away from the wedding rehearsal. Gina knew this was asking a lot of her friend.

"Because I don't want to walk down the aisle with him. Can't you send me down with Paul?"

Sarah shook her head. "I'm sorry. You know

Paul's the best man. He's been Roy's good friend forever. And, well, I *had* to ask Joanie to be my matron of honor," Sarah explained. "I was maid of honor in her wedding just last year. It's only right. Otherwise it would have been you, Gina."

"Of course she should be your matron of honor. I know you two have worked together for years at the school and Joanie has been a good friend." Gina didn't want to make the bride feel guilty, yet she suspected something else was going on here. "What about Tim?"

"You mean, break up Tim and Tanya? They'd kill me. Those two are inseparable and their wedding is coming up in six months. Wouldn't want to cause any trouble in paradise."

Gina narrowed her eyes at Sarah. "You're matchmaking, aren't you?"

Sarah twirled a finger around one long blond strand of hair. A definite sign of guilt, as Gina recalled from their early days at UCLA when Sarah had tried setting her up on blind dates. This time, Sarah didn't try to conceal her plans. She shrugged. "Why not? I have a lot to make up for. If it weren't for me…you and Wade—"

"Wade and I wouldn't have ended up together, Sarah. So, you don't have to feel guilty. Sooner or later, I would have seen him for the kind of man he truly is."

"Oh, you mean, sweet, good-natured, gorgeous and *sexy as sin?*"

Gina's eyes popped open wide. "How would you know that?"

Sarah grinned. "He is, isn't he? God, Gina. The way he looks at you, can't you give him a break?"

Gina let go a deep sigh. "We tried, twice. Both times ended in disaster. And don't say the third time's the charm. That's just a cliché and it's not true."

Sarah lowered her lashes and shook her head. "Sorry, but I disagree. And there's nothing I can do about the wedding party. It's all set. You and Wade are a couple, at least for my wedding." But when Sarah looked up, there wasn't regret in her eyes, but sheer, unabashed hope.

Gina peered down the corridor and found Wade with Roy and the other wedding ushers waiting for the minister to begin the rehearsal. He glanced her way and their gazes locked for a long moment. Gina wondered if she was looking into the face of the sweet, caring, honorable man she had once loved. Was Sarah right? Everything inside screamed at her to be careful, to watch her step, to keep her guard up, while the power of those keen green eyes told her to do just the opposite.

When the organist began to play the traditional wedding march, Sarah's excitement bubbled over. "Here we go," she said, taking Gina's hand. "I'm so happy right now, I can barely stand it. I want the same for you, Gina. Every girl should get the man of her dreams." With that, Wade approached taking long confident strides. "Looks like yours is coming for you now."

Gina closed her eyes briefly, wishing she didn't feel

exactly the same way. Only she wasn't bubbling over with joy like Sarah at the thought. No, she gazed at the handsome, appealing man standing before her now with trepidation, wondering about her unknown future.

"Are you ready to walk down the aisle with me, honey?"

It was a loaded question and one to which Gina could only grunt an unintelligible reply.

Wade laced her arm through his, an unmistakable twinkle in his eyes and a rare but striking smile on his face.

Gina turned to face the long narrow aisle leading to the altar. She imagined what it would be like tomorrow in the tiny romantic chapel in the canyon with family and friends filling the pews, bouquets of pink lilies with streaming large white satin bows lining each aisle, the minister welcoming the wedding guests and Sarah speaking vows of love and devotion.

Sarah and Roy had had a bumpy journey to the altar, but they'd found their way. Gina didn't think it was possible for her and Wade.

Before they took their first steps down the aisle, Wade leaned over, whispering in her ear, "Trust me, baby. We'll be good together."

The warmth and power of those words seeped into her, knocking loose even more chinks in her quickly crumbling armor. But Gina was a survivor, someone who had learned how to protect herself through the most difficult of times. She wouldn't make it easy for him. After the wedding, Gina didn't doubt that they would go their separate ways. "Trust you, Wade? If only I could."

But instead of putting him off, her statement only brought his lips up in another deep and stunning smile.

Twelve

"Wade, let me straighten that tie," Aunt Dottie said, standing close behind and catching his reflection from the bedroom mirror. She'd kept the room he had shared with Sam pretty much intact, complete with baseball trophies, school pennants and family pictures on the wall. Wade was glad she hadn't changed anything. He'd always thought of this place as home, even after he'd moved to Houston with his father and later relocated out west to California.

When she was through with the tie, she faced him and patted his shoulders like she had when he was a small boy. "You're a handsome devil, Wade Beaumont, all grown up now, running your own business." Her eyes were soft on him. "In that tuxedo, you'll turn every female head."

"Thanks for the help. And I only want to turn one female head today."

"That little gal giving you trouble?" Uncle Lee asked, stepping into the bedroom, looking as uncomfortable as a man could get wearing a three-piece suit.

Wade faced the mirror to run a comb through his hair. "She's stubborn."

Aunt Dottie said, "I like to say she's strong in character."

"Hardheaded," Wade rebutted, setting down the comb.

"A woman who knows her own mind," Aunt Dottie reasoned.

Wade nearly snorted, "Driving me out of mine."

"But worth every minute of it." Aunt Dottie tipped her chin for all the independent women in the world.

"I wouldn't be going through this if she wasn't."

Uncle Lee sighed, coming to stand beside him. "You know I felt the same way about your aunt a few decades ago. I had to wear her down."

"Hmph." His aunt smoothed out the wrinkles in her soft floral dress.

"Charmed her." His uncle's eyes lit with amusement.

"And tell Wade what you did when that didn't work," she said, fussing with her updo.

"I swept her off her feet," he said, with a decided puff of the chest.

Aunt Dottie walked over to lace her arm through her husband's. She looked at him lovingly. "More like you kidnapped me, Lee. Drove me over the state line and—"

"You went willingly, Dot, as I recall."

Wade had heard this story countless times in the past, but he didn't mind hearing it once more. Seeds of inspiration were beginning to grow in his mind. Wade wasn't going to let Gina get away this time.

"I did go willingly, Lee. Haven't regretted it a day in my life."

Lee squeezed her hand, then brought his gaze up to look into Wade's eyes. "Son, if you've got your sights set on a strong-minded woman, then you've got to outthink her."

"It's in the works, Uncle Lee."

Wade grabbed his wallet and the keys to his rental car, one he'd picked solely for tonight. "You look pretty Aunt Dottie." He kissed her cheek and smiled. "I'll see you both at the wedding."

"You're sure you don't want to drive with us into town?" his uncle asked.

Wade grinned. "I need my own car if I'm going to do any kidnapping tonight."

With that, Wade left the two of them standing there speechless, their mouths ready to fall open.

"Sarah looks breathtaking," Gina said, watching her friend greet the wedding guests at the reception in the Canyon Ballroom, a lovely intimate room adjacent to the church. She'd managed to get through the ceremony with Wade by her side every second, before, during and afterward. The only time they separated was at the altar, when the ladies stood up for the bride and the men positioned themselves next to a very eager groom.

Wade wrapped his arm around Gina's waist and leaned in close. "*You* look breathtaking," he whispered. "You're the most beautiful woman here."

Gina's toes curled. His nearness, his demeanor today, the caressing way his eyes traveled over her body, warmed her in ways she didn't think possible. She cast him a quick glance. Wade had never looked more appealing, wearing that black tuxedo like a second skin, confidant, sure and so handsome that he stole her breath.

The bride and groom had their opening dance, then Sarah danced with her father and Gina couldn't help but envy her. With Gina's future so unsure, she wondered if ever she married, who would walk her down the aisle? Who would take her into his arms lovingly and sweep her away in that father/daughter dance. It was times like these when Gina missed her parents the most.

Wade's uncle Lee came to stand beside her. He wrapped an arm around her waist. "You and Wade make a fine couple," he said, with a wink. "Walking down that aisle together, gave me notions, girl."

Gina had a protest on her lips to say she and Wade were not a couple, but Uncle Lee's eyes shone just too bright, his face was too sincere and Gina found she didn't want to disappoint the man. "Thank you," she said, and when she met Wade's eyes, she found his approval.

They danced once, the obligatory wedding party invited up to share the dance floor with the bride and groom, as pictures were snapped and then they retired to their seats for dinner.

The round table seated the entire wedding party and when the meal was through, Wade took Gina's hand, placing it on his thigh. Every time he smiled at her with those green eyes, Gina felt herself losing her grip.

"I won't be coming back to work at Triple B, Wade," she began. "Even though you said I still have a job there, it's not what I want."

"I know and I agree."

That surprised her. "You do?"

He nodded, his eyes still soft on her. She'd thought her announcement might have angered him. "You should pursue your own dreams. You should start your own company."

Gina felt somewhat validated. "Thank you for that."

"For what? Realizing that you're a capable woman with a lot to offer. That you have talent and drive and that you deserve a chance, a real chance at doing what you love to do."

Gina smiled, unsure of his intentions. "Are you trying to charm me?"

"God I hope so. Is it working?"

Gina chuckled. She'd never seen Wade so forthright, so open. And while it frightened her, she couldn't help but enjoy his company this evening. "I'm not sure how I feel right now."

When the band began a slow country ballad, Wade rose. "Dance with me?" he asked, offering up his hand.

Gina thought better of it, she knew she wasn't immune to Wade, but as she glanced around the joy-filled room, she couldn't help but want to share in the festivities a little. She took a leap of faith and placed her hand in his.

"Why not? I love this song," she said as Wade guided her to the edge of the dance floor.

"And I love any excuse to hold you in my arms," he said, bringing her in close enough to smell his familiar musky scent. He wrapped his arms around her tight and between the musk and intimate proximity, the reminder of that one blissful night they spent in Catalina rushed into her thoughts.

She closed her eyes and absorbed the music, the heat of the night and the thrill of being in Wade's arms again. Wade's lips teased her temples as he kissed her gently there, whispering in her ear. "I've named the pup, GiGi. I want her to be ours."

Gina popped her eyes open. "Ours?"

Wade smiled. "Yours and mine. That's what ours means."

"But how? It isn't possible. We can't—"

Wade put a stopping finger to her lips. "We can. Anything's possible."

Gina opened her mouth to debate the issue, but Wade's lips met hers in a soul-searing kiss that nearly wiped all rational thought from her head. When she finally opened her eyes, completely breathless, she stared up at him.

"Let's get out of here. I want to be alone with you."

"We can't leave," she said through tight lips. "We're in the wedding party."

"We've taken more pictures than they'll ever need and have done everything we were here to do.

"They haven't cut the cake yet."

"They won't miss us, sweetheart. And once they have cake, the guests will start leaving. We've done our part. Come away with me."

Gina resisted benignly, "Where?"

But Wade had already begun tugging her toward the door. "You'll see."

"You've got to be kidding," Gina said, standing beside Wade's rented convertible Porsche in front of a small lake that bordered the Beaumont ranch, holding a white thong swimsuit that looked suspiciously like the one she'd discarded on Catalina island.

They'd taken a wind-blown drive, letting the breeze and soft rock music steal them away. Now, Wade stood by the car, unfastening his tie. "It's hot, honey. I'm going in for a dip."

"And you expect me to go in with you?" Gina's voice elevated to the incredulous level.

Wade came forward and lifted her bottom onto the hood of the expensive silver sports car. He trapped her between his large hands. He leaned forward, his eyes intense, but his voice a simple soft caress. "I love you, Gina. Get used to hearing me say that. I love you. But I know you can't love me back until you truly trust me."

Stunned, Gina couldn't respond.

I love you, Gina.

"I've never said those words to another woman. And I've been trying so damn hard to get you back. I want you in my life. But first—"

"I have to trust you," she said softly, finally finding her voice.

"That's right. I'm hoping this helps," he said, removing something from his tuxedo jacket. He placed it into her hand and closed her palm with his. "This was my mother's. It's all I have left of her and I want you to have it."

Gina opened her hand slowly, then gasped when she saw the brooch, a sea of tiny flawless diamonds and in the center the most perfect gem she'd ever seen. Jade.

"To start up your gem collection for your company."

"I can't take this," she said, genuinely touched. "Really, Wade. This is…this is so sweet, so kind, but I can't." And as she glanced once again at the exquisite stone, she noted, "It's the perfect match to your eyes."

"I have my mother's eyes. My father gave it to her just months before he lost her."

"He must have loved her a lot. Maybe that's why he was so—"

"Shh. I don't want to talk about him. I want you to keep it."

"But it's yours."

"That's right. And you're going to be mine."

With that, Wade smiled and began undressing one bit at a time, leaving a trail of clothes all he way down to the moonlit lake waters. She watched him dive in and come up from the water, his eyes piercing and passionate. "Trust me, Gina."

It was a request.

A plea.

And an invitation she couldn't ignore.

He loved her.

She felt the clarity of that truth, deep down in her heart. She believed him and as astonishing as that seemed, she felt the rightness of it all, finally, simply.

It was that easy.

Gina scrambled out of her clothes and slipped on the thong while Wade was busy underwater. She approached the lake now, meeting her fear, understanding it for what it was and finally being able to overcome the dread that had always plagued her.

Wade came up from the water and stood, half in, half out, a mythical god with the lake dripping from his skin, beckoning her with his eyes and one outstretched hand.

She stepped in and reached him, taking his hand. "I trust you, Wade," she said, knowing in her heart, he would never do anything to misplace that trust again.

Wade kissed her then, his mouth cold from the swim, but she felt his heat reaching out, touching her.

And together, they moved through the water.

* * *

Later, dripping wet and cold, their clothes thrown on haphazardly, they ran hand in hand into the Beaumont barn, their laughter rousing the sleeping pups.

Gina glanced at the precious litter, too happy to worry about their ruined sleep.

Breathless and burning with desire, she stared into Wade's hungry eyes.

"This is where it all began," he said.

Gina glanced at the wool blanket hanging up along a stall and the stack of hay that had once been their bed. She'd given Wade everything that night. "I've never stopped loving you, Wade. You were always there. I couldn't get rid of you, though I tried. You were my first."

Wade took her into his arms. "I plan on being your last. Until the day I die."

Gina nodded, swallowing the lump in her throat. "Okay."

Wade smiled. "Okay?"

Gina smiled back.

"We already have a family. You, me and GiGi. Wonder how she'll like my house on the beach."

"She'll love it," Gina said, peering down at the pup with the unusual colors.

"Will you?" he asked, reaching around to unzip her ruined bridesmaid gown.

"I think so," she said softly, staring into his eyes.

"And will you let me be your partner, in business and in life?"

He slipped the zipper down, notch by notch, then reached up to expose her shoulders. He kissed her there, making her head swim with delicious thoughts.

"I will, but you won't boss me around."

Wade kissed her lips. "You won't let me."

Gina smiled then and wrapped her arms around his neck, tugging him in to mate their mouths. She kissed him soundly, freely, giving him her trust, her love and her heart. "I'm glad we've got that straight."

Wade slipped her dress off, letting it puddle at her feet. She stepped over it, standing fully unclothed before him.

"I wanted you for my wife the minute I laid eyes on you," he said, quietly, reverently, his gaze gently scanning her body.

Gina removed his shirt, unzipped his pants. "You're a fast worker, sweetheart. Only took you nine years."

They stood naked before one another.

Then together they lowered down onto the hay.

They joined their bodies, bonding themselves for the future, in the barn, on a soft patch of straw, where they'd first found each other.

"Some things are just worth the wait."

* * * * *

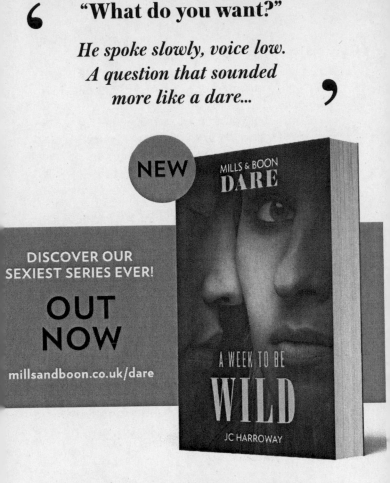

Printed by RR Donnelley at Glasgow, UK